Émile Zola

The Soil

(La terre)

Émile Zola

The Soil
(La terre)

ISBN/EAN: 9783743444300

Printed in Europe, USA, Canada, Australia, Japan

Cover: Foto ©Andreas Hilbeck / pixelio.de

More available books at **www.hansebooks.com**

THE SOIL.

ZOLA'S POWERFUL REALISTIC NOVELS.

Illustrated with Page Engravings from Designs by French Artists.

THE SOIL. (LA TERRE.)
EMILE ZOLA'S LATEST NOVEL.

FAT AND THIN. (LE VENTRE DE PARIS.)
FROM THE 24TH FRENCH EDITION.

MADELEINE FÉRAT.
FROM THE LATEST FRENCH EDITION.

A SOLDIER'S HONOUR: AND OTHER STORIES.
FROM THE LATEST FRENCH EDITION.

A LOVE EPISODE.
FROM THE 52ND FRENCH EDITION.

THE CONQUEST OF PLASSANS.
FROM THE 23RD FRENCH EDITION.

HIS EXCELLENCY EUGÈNE ROUGON.
FROM THE 22ND FRENCH EDITION.

HOW JOLLY LIFE IS!
FROM THE 44TH FRENCH EDITION.

THE FORTUNE OF THE ROUGONS.
FROM THE 24TH FRENCH EDITION.

ABBÉ MOURET'S TRANSGRESSION.
FROM THE 34TH FRENCH EDITION.

HIS MASTERPIECE? (L'ŒUVRE.)
With a Portrait of the Author, etched by Bocourt.

THE LADIES' PARADISE. (Sequel to "PIPING HOT!")
FROM THE 50TH FRENCH EDITION.

THÉRÈSE RAQUIN.
FROM THE LATEST FRENCH EDITION.

THE RUSH FOR THE SPOIL. (LA CURÉE.)
FROM THE 35TH FRENCH EDITION.

PIPING HOT! (POT BOUILLE.)
FROM THE 63RD FRENCH EDITION.

GERMINAL; OR, MASTER AND MAN
FROM THE 47TH FRENCH EDITION.

NANA.
FROM THE 127TH FRENCH EDITION.

THE "ASSOMMOIR." (The Prelude to "NANA.")
FROM THE 97TH FRENCH EDITION.

Hold your tongue or I strike Am I not the master?

THE SOIL.

(LA TERRE.)

A REALISTIC NOVEL.

BY

ÉMILE ZOLA.

WITH A FRONTISPIECE DESIGNED BY H. GRAY.

LONDON:

VIZETELLY & CO., 16 *HENRIETTA STREET,*

COVENT GARDEN.

1888.

THE SOIL.

PART I

THAT morning Jean, with a seed-bag of blue linen tied round his waist, held its mouth open with his left hand, while with his right, at every three steps, he drew forth a handful of corn, and flung it broadcast. The rich soil clung to his heavy shoes, which left holes in the ground, as his body lurched regularly from side to side; and each time he threw you saw, amid the ever-flying yellow seed, the gleam of two red stripes on the sleeve of the old regimental jacket he was wearing out. He strode forward in solitary state; and behind him, to bury the grain, there slowly came a harrow, to which were harnessed two horses, driven by a waggoner, who cracked his whip over their ears in long, regular sweeps.

The patch of ground, scarcely an acre and a quarter in extent, was of such little importance that Monsieur Hourdequin, the master of La Borderie, had not cared to send the drill-plough, which was in use elsewhere. Jean, then journeying due north over the field, had the farm-buildings exactly in front of him, a mile and a quarter off. On reaching the end of the furrow, he raised his eyes with a vacant look as he paused for a moment to take breath.

Before him were the low farm walls, and a patch of old slate, isolated on the outskirts of the plain of La Beauce, which stretched towards Chartres. Under a dull, late October sky lay ten leagues of arable land, where, at that time of year, great ploughed squares of bare, rich, yellow soil alternated with green expanses of lucern and clover; there was here not a slope, not a tree; the plain extended into the dim distance, curving down beyond the horizon, which was level as at sea. Westward, a small wood just edged the sky with a band of russet. In the centre a road—the road from Châteaudun to Orleans—of chalk-like whiteness, stretched four leagues straight ahead, displaying **as it went a** geometrical row **of telegraph-posts.** Nothing else **but three or four** wooden mills on **log** foundations, with **their sails at rest;** some villages **forming islets of** stone; and **a** distant steeple emerging from **a** depression in **the** landscape, the church itself being hidden among the **gentle** undulations of the wheat-fields.

Jean turned **and** lurched back again **due south, his left hand holding the seed-bag, and** his right **slashing the air with an unbroken sheet** of grain. He **now** had **in front of him, quite near, and cutting** trench-like through the plain, **the narrow valley of the** Aigre, **beyond** which **the district** of La Beauce resumed its unconfined course **on to Orleans.** Meadows and shady places could only be inferred **from a range of tall poplars, the yellowish** tops of which rose **out of the dell, looking, as they** just cleared **the** edge, like **short bushes. Of the little village of** Rognes, built upon the declivity, a few roofs **only were in** view, near the church, which raised on high its grey **stone** steeple, the dwelling-place of ancient families of ravens. **And** eastward, beyond the valley of the Loir,—where Cloyes, the chief town of the *canton,** nestled at two leagues' distance,— the far-off hills of Le Perche were visible, tinged with violet in the slate-grey light. There the old Dunois, now become **the** *arrondissement* of Châteaudun, lay between Le Perche **and La** Beauce, on the very frontier of the latter, at a spot which has obtained the name of Beauce the " Lousy," the soil there being less fertile. When Jean got to the end of **the** field, he stopped again, and glanced down along the stream of the Aigre, rippling bright and clear through the meadows, side by side with the road to Cloyes, which on that Saturday was furrowed by the carts of peasants going to market; then **he** turned up again.

And still, with the same step, with the same gesture, he set out north and returned south, wrapped in a living dust-cloud **of seed**; while, behind him the whip **cracked** and the **harrow buried** the germs, **at the same** quiet, contemplative rate. Heavy rains had retarded the autumn sowing; the season's manuring had been done in August, and the deep-lying fallows, duly cleared of weeds, had long been ready for a fresh yield of corn, after the clover and oats of the triennial rotation. **Now** the farmers were urged on by **fear of** coming frost, **which** threatened after the storms. The weather had suddenly turned cold and gloomy: there was no breath of wind, and

---

* The *canton* is a subdivision of the *arrondissement*, which is again a subdivision of the *département*, which is much the same as our county.

but a dull light was distributed over all this ocean of land. Seed was being sown on all sides; there was a sower to the left, three hundred yards away ; another farther off to the right; others, and yet others, lost to sight in the receding vista of the level fields. They formed little black silhouettes, mere strokes which became slimmer and slimmer, till they vanished in the **distance.** All made the same gesture, as they strewed **the** seed, which the mind's eye still saw encircling them, as with **a wave** of life. It was like a quiver passing over the plain, even into the dim distance, where the scattered sowers could no longer be seen.

Jean was coming down **for the last** time when he perceived, approaching from Rognes, a large red and white cow, the **halter** of which was held by a young girl, almost a child. The little peasant-girl and the animal were coming along the path which skirted the valley at the top of the plateau ; and, with his back turned to them, he had gone up and finished the field, when a sound of running, mingled with stifled cries, made him look round, just as he was untying his seed-bag to depart. It was the cow running away, galloping over a field of lucern, and followed by the girl, who was exhausting her strength in trying to keep it back. Fearing an accident, he shouted :

" Leave go ; why don't thee ? "

But she did nothing of the kind, only panting and abusing her cow in angry, frightened tones.

"Coliche ! Would you, then, Coliche? **Ah,** you foul brute ! **Ah,** you cursed beast ! "

So far, running and leaping to the full extent of her little legs, she had managed to follow. But she stumbled, fell once, then rose only to fall again farther on ; and from that point, the animal growing frantic, she was dragged along. Then she began to shriek, while her body left a furrow in the lucern.

" Leave go, **in** God's **name** ! " Jean continued shouting. " Leave go, why don't thee ? "

He shouted thus mechanically, out of fright ; for he also **had** started running, grasping, at length, the situation. The **rope** had evidently got entangled round her waist, and was **being** more closely twined at each fresh effort. Fortunately he **took a short** cut across a ploughed field, and made for the cow with **such** speed **that** the frightened and perplexed animal stopped dead. Jean was already undoing the rope, and seating the girl upon the grass.

" Thou hast broken nothing ? " he asked.

No ; she had not so much as swooned. She stood up, felt

herself all over, and coolly lifted her petticoats up to her thighs, to look at her knees, which smarted Meanwhile, she was still so breathless that she could not speak.

"See, it's there it hurts me," she said at last. "All the same, I'm alive and kicking; there's nothing the matter. Oh! I was frightened. Over on the road there I was a regular jelly!"

And, examining the circle of red on her strained wrist, she moistened it with spittle and applied her lips to it; then, comforted and restored, she added with a deep sigh:

"She's not vicious, Coliche. Only since yesterday she has plagued us to death, because she's in heat. I'm taking her to the bull at La Borderie."

"At La Borderie?" repeated Jean. "That's capital; I'm going back there; I'll go with thee."

He still used the second person singular, treating her as a little urchin, so slight was she for her fourteen years of age. She, raising her chin, looked seriously at the big, ruddy, crop-haired, full-faced, regular-featured young fellow, whose twenty-nine years made him in her eyes an old man.

"Hullo! I know you. You are Corporal, the carpenter who stopped as farm-hand with Monsieur Hourdequin."

Hearing the nickname, which the peasants had given him, the young fellow smiled; and he contemplated her in turn, surprised to find her almost a woman so soon, with her little bust firm and taking shape, her oval face, her deep, black eyes; and full lips, fresh and rosy as ripening fruit. She was clad in a grey skirt and black woollen bodice; on her head there was a round cap; and she had a very dark skin, scorched and burnished by the sun.

"Why, thou'rt old Mouche's youngest!" cried he. "I didn't call thee to mind. Isn't that so? Thy sister was keeping company with Buteau last spring, when he worked with me at La Borderie?"

She replied simply:

"Yes, I'm Françoise. My sister Lise went with cousin Buteau, and is now six months with child. He's bolted; he's down Orgères way, at the farm of La Chamade."

"That's it," concluded Jean; "I have seen them together."

And they remained an instant mute, face to face; he smiling at having one evening surprised the two lovers behind a mill, she still sucking her bruised wrist, as if the moisture of her lips allayed its smarting; whilst, in an adjoining field, the cow quietly plucked tufts of lucern. The waggoner and the harrow had gone off by a roundabout way, to reach the road,

Two ravens, which kept wheeling round and round the steeple, were heard to caw. **The three** notes of the angelus rang through the still air.

"Hullo ! **Twelve o'clock** already !" cried Jean. **" Let's** make haste ! "

Then, noticing La Coliche in the field : " Eh, but thy cow is doing damage ! Suppose any one saw her ! Wait a bit, **I'll** make it lively **for** her ! "

" Nay, let be," said Françoise, stopping him. **" The plot is** ours. Our folk own the whole bank as far as Rognes. We **reach** from here up to yonder ; the next **to** that is uncle **Fouan's** ; then comes aunt Grande's."

While indicating the patches **she had led the cow back** into **the** path. And not till then, **when she** again held her, fearlessly, by the rope, did she think of thanking **the young** fellow.

" Anyhow, I **owe you a pretty** debt of gratitude ! **Thanks,** you know, thanks, very much ! "

They had started walking along the narrow road which skirted **the** valley before cutting through the fields. The final peal **of** the angelus had just died away, the ravens alone kept on cawing. They trudged on behind the cow tugging at her rope, neither of the two conversing, for they had relapsed into the silence of rustics who travel for leagues, side by **side,** without exchanging a word. On their right their glance fell **on a** drill-plough, the horses of which turned close by them ; **the** ploughman bade them good-day, and **they answered him in the** same sober tone. Down on their left, along the road **to Cloyes,** carts continued to file by, the market not opening till one o'clock. These vehicles jolted heavily along on their **two** wheels, like jumping insects, so diminished in the distance as to leave merely the white specks of the women's caps distinguishable.

" There's uncle Fouan and **aunt** Rose over there, on their way to the notary's," said Françoise, gazing at a conveyance the size of a nutshell, which sped along nearly a mile off.

She had a sailor's eye, the long sight of those bred in the country, trained in details, and capable of identifying man or beast **even** when they were but little moving specks afar off,

" Oh, yes ; I've been told so," resumed Jean. " So it's **settled** that the old man divides his property among his daughter and two sons ? "

" It's settled. They've **all agreed to** meet to-day at Monsieur Baillehache's."

She again watched the **cart** in its course, and then resumed :

" We don't care one way or the other; it won't make us
any fatter or thinner. Only, on account of Buteau, sister thinks
he'll marry her, perhaps, when he gets his **share. He says one**
can't start housekeeping on nothing."

Jean laughed.

" Me and Buteau were pals, hang him! Oh, he don't think
twice about telling girls lies! And he must have 'em, by hook
or **by crook; he** gets **at 'em by** foul means, if they won't by
fair."

" He's a pig, that's flat!" declared Françoise, peremptorily.
" People have no business to play dirty tricks like that, putting
their **cousins in the** family-way and then **leaving 'em in the**
lurch."

But suddenly, **in a fit of** rage, **she** exclaimed:

" **You wait,** Coliche! I'll make you dance! There she is
at it again; **she's** mad, **the** brute, when she **gets that** way."

She had violently jerked the cow back. At that spot the
road left **the** edge of the plateau, and the cart disappeared **from**
view, while they both continued their walk on the level, now having in front of them, and on either side, only the endless expanse
of arable land. **Between the** fallows and the artificial meadows
the path ran flat and bushless, terminating at the farm, which
you might have thought within reach of the **hand,** but which
kept receding under the ashen-grey sky. They had relapsed
into silence again, no longer opening their mouths, as if impressed by the contemplative gloominess of La Beauce, so sad
and yet so fruitful.

When they arrived, the large square yard of La Borderie,
shut in on three sides by cow-sheds, sheep-cots, and barns,
was deserted. **But there** immediately appeared upon the
kitchen door-step a short, bold, pretty-looking young woman.

" How's this, Jean, you're not eating this morning?"

" I'm just going to, Madame Jacqueline."

Since the daughter of Cognet, the Rognes road-labourer,
—*La Coquette,* as they called her when she washed up the farm
dishes **at** twelve years of age—had been raised to the **honours**
of servant-mistress, she despotically required **that every one**
should treat her as a lady.

" Oh, **it** is you, Françoise," she resumed. " You've come for
the bull. Well, you must wait. The neatherd is at Cloyes
with **Monsieur** Hourdequin. **But** he'll be back; he ought to
be here now."

And as **Jean was** making **for the** kitchen, she took him
round the **waist and** fondled **him** smilingly, regardless of

spectators, hungering, as it were, for love, and not satisfied with having the master.

Françoise, left alone, waited patiently, sitting on a stone bench in front of the manure-pit, which took up a third of the yard. She was listlessly watching a group of fowls, pecking and warming their feet in the broad low layer of manure, which in the cold air began to steam with a slight bluish vapour. At the end of half-an-hour, when Jean reappeared, finishing a slice of bread and butter, she had not stirred. He sat down near her, and as the cow fidgeted, lashed its tail and lowed, he finally said:

" It's tiresome he doesn't come back."

The girl shrugged her shoulders, as though to say that she was in no hurry. Then, after a fresh silence :

" So, Corporal, they call you Jean, and nothing else ? "

" Why, no ; Jean Macquart."

" And you don't belong to our part of the country ? "

" No, I'm a Provençal, from Plassans, a town over yonder."

She had raised her eyes to examine him, surprised that any one could come from so far off.

" After Solferino," continued he, " eighteen months since, I came back from Italy with my discharge, and a fellow-soldier brought me here. Then, d'ye see, my old trade of carpenter no longer suited me, and, what with one thing and another, I stopped at the farm."

" Ah ! " said she, simply, without taking her big, black eyes off him, " it's curious, all the same."

At that moment, as La Coliche gave a prolonged, despairing low of desire, a hoarse murmur came from the cow-house, the door of which was shut.

" Hullo ! " cried Jean, " that brute of a Cæsar has heard her. Hark ! he's talking inside there. Oh, he knows his business. You can't bring one of 'em into the yard but he smells her out, and knows what he's wanted for."

Then, breaking off :

" I say, the neatherd must have stopped with Monsieur Hourdequin. If thee liked, I would bring thee the bull, and thee needn't come back again. We could manage it all right by ourselves."

" Not half a bad idea," said Françoise, getting up.

As he opened the door of the cow-house, he paused to ask :

" Must thy animal be tied up ? "

" Tied up ? No, no ! not worth while. She is quite ready ; she won't so much as stir."

When the door was opened you saw, in two rows on either side of **the** central path, the thirty farm cows, some lying in the litter, others crunching the beets in their manger; and, from the corner where he stood, one of the bulls, a black Dutch, spotted with white, stretched out his head in anticipation of his task.

As soon as he was untied, he slowly emerged. Then stopping short, as though surprised by the fresh air and sunlight, he remained motionless for a minute, bracing himself up, his sinewy **tail** swinging, his neck inflated, his muzzle outstretched to **sniff.** La Coliche, without stirring, turned towards him her large, fixed eyes, and lowed more softly. Then he advanced, pressed against her, **and laid his head on her** hind-quarters, abruptly and roughly; **with his** tongue, which was hanging out, he put her tail aside, **and** licked her as **far** as the thighs; she letting him do **as** he pleased, and keeping quite still, save for a slight quivering **of** her skin. Jean and Françoise waited gravely, their arms hanging beside them.

When Cæsar was ready, he got upon La Coliche with a jerk, **and** with such weighty force as to shake the ground. She had **not** given way, and he compressed her flanks with his two feet. But **she,** a strapping animal from the Cotentin, was so tall, so **broad** for him, who **was of** a smaller **breed, that he could not reach.** He was conscious of it, and made a **vain effort to raise** himself **and to** bring her nearer.

"He is **too** small," said Françoise.

"Yes, **a little,**" said Jean. "But that don't matter; **he'll** do it all the same.

She shook her head **in** doubt; and, as Cæsar still fumbled about, **and seemed to be** getting exhausted, she came to a resolution.

"**No,** he must be helped," she said. "If he goes wrong, it'll **be waste of** time."

Calmly **and** carefully, as if bent on a serious piece of work, **she had** drawn near. Her intentness made the pupils of her eyes retreat, left her **red** lips half open, **and** kept her **features** motionless. Raising **her** arm with a sweep she aided the animal in his efforts, and he, gathering up his strength, speedily accomplished **his** purpose. It was done. Firmly, with the impassive fertility of land which is sown with **seed the cow** had unflinchingly received the fruitful stream of the male. Indeed, she had not **even** trembled at the shock; and he had already dropped again to **the ground,** shaking the earth once more.

Françoise having withdrawn her hand, remained with her arm in the air. Finally she lowered it, saying :

" That's all right."

" Yes, and neatly done," replied Jean, with an air of conviction, mingled with a good workman's satisfaction at seeing work well and expeditiously performed.

It did not occur to him to indulge in any of the spicy remarks with which **the** farm-servants used to chaff the girls who brought their cows for this purpose. The child seemed to consider it all so simple and necessary that there was, indeed, nothing to laugh at fairly. It was Nature.

However, Jacqueline had been standing **at** the door again for an instant or so, and with a chuckle which **was** habitual to her, she cried jestingly :

" Eh ! poke your nose everywhere ! **So you** hold the candle now ! "

Jean having burst into a horse-laugh, Françoise suddenly flushed all over, quite confused; and to hide her embarrassment —while Cæsar returned of his own accord into the cow-house, and La Coliche **munched** a stalk of oats which had grown in the manure-pit—she dived into her pockets, fumbled about, eventually produced her handkerchief, untied the corner of it, in which she had wrapped up the two-franc fee, and said :

" Here ! There's the money ! And good day to you ! "

She set out with her cow, and Jean took his bag again and followed her, telling Jacqueline that he was going **to** the Poteau field, according to the instructions issued by Monsieur Hourdequin, for the day.

" Good ! " she replied. " The harrow ought to be there."

Then as the young man came up with the girl, and they went off in single file down the narrow path, she called out to them again, in her coarse, bantering voice :

" No danger, eh ? If you lose yourselves together the chit knows her way about."

Behind them the farmyard was again deserted. Neither **had** laughed **this** time. They walked on slowly, and the only sound was that of their shoes striking against the stones. All that Jean noticed of Françoise was the nape of her childlike **neck, over which** curled some short black hair **under** her round cap. At last, after going some fifty paces :

" She **does** wrong to chaff others about the men," said Françoise, sedately. " I might have answered her——"

And turning towards **the** young fellow with a mischievous upward glance :

" It's true, isn't it, that she is false to Monsieur Hourdequin,
just as **if she were** already his wife? You know as much
about **that,** maybe, as most people."

His eyes fell, and he looked sheepish. " Lord! she does **as**
she likes ; it's her affair," he answered.

Françoise had turned her back and was pursuing her road.

" That's true enough. I was only in fun, because you're old
enough to be my father, and because it's of no consequence
one way or the other. But there's one **thing, since** Buteau
played that dirty trick on my sister, I've taken an oath that I'd
rather be cut in two than have a lover."

Jean bent his head, and they spoke no more. The little
Poteau field lay at the bottom of the path, half way to Rognes.
When the young **fellow got there** he stopped. The harrow
was waiting for him, **and a sack of seed** had been emptied out
into a furrow. He filled his bag, saying :

" Good-bye, then ! "

" Good-bye," replied Françoise. " Thanks again ! "

But, **in** sudden apprehension, he drew himself **up and**
called out :

" I say ! suppose La Coliche began again ; shall I go with
you all the way ? "

She was already some distance off, but she turned round, and
through the deep stillness of the country air came **the sound of**
her calm, steady voice :

" No, no ! There's no need, it's all right ! She's **got quite**
as much as she can carry ! "

Jean, with **his** seed-bag **at his** waist, had started down the
piece of plough land, with his ceaseless gesture of throwing the
grain ; he raised his eyes and looked at Françoise diminishing
in height among the fields, looking quite small behind her lazy
cow, which was swinging heavily from **side** to side. When he
turned up again, he ceased to see her ; but, as he came back,
there she was again, **but smaller** still, so slim as to seem **like**
some new kind of dandelion, with her slight figure **and her**
white cap. Thrice she dwindled thus ; then, when he once more
looked for her, she had apparently turned down by the church.

Two **o'clock struck.** The sky remained grey, **dull, and**
cold, **as if the sun were buried under** spadefuls of ashes for
weary months, **till** the spring-time returned. The dreariness
of the clouds **was** relieved by one lighter patch towards
Orleans, as if **the sun** were shining somewhere in that
direction, leagues away; and against that glimmering patch
the steeple of Rognes stood out, the village itself sloping down

from view into the fold made by the valley of the Aigre. But
on the north, towards Chartres, the level line of the horizon
clearly separated the leaden uniformity of the waste sky
from the endless vista of La Beauce, like an ink-stroke across a
monochrome sketch. Since the mid-day meal, the number of
sowers seemed to have increased. Now each patch of the
little farm-lands had one to itself; they multiplied and teemed
like black laborious ants roused to activity by some heavy
piece of work, and straining every nerve over a mighty task,
giant-like in size as compared with their littleness. And still
you might descry, even in the most remote, the one persistent
never-varying gesture; still did the pertinacious insect-like
sowers wrestle with the vast earth, and become eventually the
victors over space and life.

Till nightfall Jean sowed. After the Poteau field there
were the Rigoles and the Quatre-Chemins. To and fro, to and
fro, he paced the fields, with long, rhythmical steps, till the
corn in his bag came to an end; while, in his wake, the seed
strewed all the soil.

CHAPTER II.

THE house of Maitre Baillehache, notary at Cloyes, was situated in the Rue Grouaise, on the left hand going to Château-dun. A little white, one-storey house it was, at the corner of which a bracket was riveted for the rope of the single lantern which lighted this broad, paved street, deserted during the week, but on Saturday nights crowded with a living tide of peasants coming to market. From afar might be seen the gleam of the two professional escutcheons against the chalk-like wall of the low buildings; and, behind, a narrow garden stretched down to the Loir.

On that Saturday, in the room which served as an office, and which looked out upon the street to the right of the entrance hall, the youngest clerk, a pale, wizened boy of fifteen, had drawn up one of the muslin curtains to see the people pass. The other two clerks—one old, corpulent, and very dirty; one younger, scraggy, and a hopeless victim to liver complaint—were writing at a double desk of ebonised deal, there being no other furniture except seven or eight chairs and a cast-iron stove, which was never lit till December, even if it snowed a month before. Rows of pigeon-holes decorated the walls, with greenish pasteboard boxes, broken at the corners and full to repletion with bundles of yellow papers, and the room was pervaded with an unwholesome smell of ink gone bad and dust-eaten documents.

However, seated side by side, two peasants, man and wife, were waiting in deep respect, like statues of Patience. So many papers, and, more than all, the gentlemen who wrote so fast, with their pens all scratching away at once, sobered them by evoking vague visions of law-suits and money. The woman, aged thirty-four, very dark, with a countenance which would have been pleasant but for a large nose, had her horny, toil-worn hands crossed over her black cloth, velvet-edged body, and was scanning every corner with her keen eyes, evidently musing on the many title-deeds which reposed here. In the meanwhile the man, five years older, red-haired and stolid, in black trousers and a long, bran-new blue linen blouse, held his round felt hat on his knees, with not a spark of intelligence illuminating his broad, clean-shaven, terra-cotta-like face, which was perforated with two large eyes of porcelain blue, having a fixed stare that reminded one of a somnolent ox.

A door opened, and Maître Baillehache, who had just breakfasted with his brother-in-law, farmer Hourdequin, made his appearance; ruddy and fresh-complexioned despite his fifty-five years, with thick lips and crow's feet, which gave him a perpetually amused expression. He carried a double eye-glass, and had a lunatic habit of always pulling at his long, grizzled whiskers.

"Ah! it's you, Delhomme," said he. "So, old Fouan has consented to divide the property?"

The reply came from the woman.

"Yes, sure, Monsieur Baillehache. We have all made an appointment, so that we may come to an agreement, and that you may tell us how we are to proceed."

"Good, good, Fanny; we'll see about it. It's hardly more than one o'clock, we must wait for the others."

The notary stopped an instant to chat, asking about the price of corn, which had fallen during the last two months, and showing Delhomme the friendly consideration due to a farmer who owned fifty acres of land, and kept a servant and three cows. Then he returned to his inner room.

The clerks had not raised their heads, but were scratching away with their pens more vigorously than ever; and, once more, the Delhommes waited motionless. Fanny had been a lucky girl to marry a respectable, rich lover without even getting into the family-way beforehand, she whose only expectations had been some seven or eight acres of land from old Fouan. Her husband, however, had not repented of his bargain, for he could not anywhere have found a more active or intelligent housekeeper. Hence he followed her lead in everything, being of a narrow mind, but so steady and straightforward as to be frequently selected as an umpire by the Rognes people.

At that moment the little clerk, who was looking out into the street, stifled a laugh behind his hand, and murmured to his old, corpulent, and very dirty neighbour: "Here's Hyacinthe the saint coming!"

Fanny bent down quickly to whisper to her husband: "Now, leave everything to me. I am fond enough of papa and mamma, but I won't have them rob us; and keep a sharp eye on Buteau and that rascal Hyacinthe."

She referred to her two brothers, having seen one of them

approach as she **looked out of the window**: Hyacinthe, the elder, whom the **whole neighbourhood knew as** an idler and a drunkard, and who, **at the close of his military service, after going** through **the Algerian campaigns, had taken to a vagabond life,** refusing **all regular work, and subsisting by poaching and** pillage, **as if he were still extortioner-in-ordinary among a** terrified people **of Bedouins.**

A tall, strapping **fellow came in, rejoicing in the brawny** strength of his forty years; **he had curly hair, and a pointed, long,** unkempt beard, with the face of a saint **laid waste, a saint sodden with strong drink, addicted to forcing girls, and to robbing folks on the highway. He had already got tipsy at Cloyes since the morning, and wore muddy trousers, a filthily-stained blouse, and** a **ragged cap stuck on the back of his neck. He was** smoking **a damp, black, pestilential halfpenny cigar. Yet, in** the depths of **his fine liquid eyes lurked a spirit of fun free from** ill-feeling, **the open-heartedness of good-natured blackguardism.**

" So father **and mother haven't turned up yet?" he asked.**

When **the thin, jaundiced clerk responded testily by a shake** of the **head, he stared for an instant at the wall, while his cigar smouldered in his hand. He had not so much as glanced at his sister and his brother-in-law, who,** themselves, did not appear **to have seen him enter. Then, without a word, he** left the room, and **went to hang about on the pavement.**

" Hyacinthe! Hyacinthe!" **droned the little clerk, turning** streetwards, and **seeming to find infinite amusement in this** name, **which brought many a funny tale back to his memory.**

Hardly five **minutes had passed before the** Fouans made **their** tardy appearance, **two old folk of slow,** prudential gait. **The** father, once **very robust, now** seventy years of age, had shrivelled **and dwindled down** under such hard work, such **a keen land-hunger, that his** form was bowed as if in **a wild impulse to return to that earth** which he had coveted and possessed. **Nevertheless, in all save** the legs, he was still hale and well-**knit, with spruce little** white mutton-chop whiskers, and the long **family nose, which lent an air of** keenness to his thin, leathery, **deeply-wrinkled face. In his wake,** following **him as** closely **as his shadow, came his wife;** shorter and stouter, **swollen** as **if by an incipient dropsy, with a** drab-coloured face perforated **with round eyes,** and a **round** mouth pursed up into **an** infinity of avaricious wrinkles. **A** household drudge, endowed with **the docile,** hard-working stupidity of a beast of burden, she **had always stood in** awe of the despotic authority ·of her husband.

"Ah, so it's you!" cried Fanny, getting up. Delhomme, also, had risen from his chair. Behind the old people, Hyacinthe had just lounged in again without a word. Compressing the cigar end to put it out, he thrust the pestiferous stump into a pocket of his blouse.

"So **we're here**," said Fouan. "There's only Buteau **missing**. Never in time, never like other people, the beast!"

"**I saw him** in the market," asserted Hyacinthe in a husky voice due to drink. "He's coming."

Buteau, the younger son, owed **his nickname** to his pig-headedness, being always **up in** arms in obstinate defence of his own ideas, which were never those of anybody else. Even when an urchin, **he** had not **been able to get** on with his **parents;** and, later on, having drawn a lucky number in the conscription, he **had run away from home** to go into service, first **at** La Borderie, subsequently at La Chamade.

While his father was still grumbling, he skipped cheerfully into the room. In him, the large Fouan nose was flattened out, while the lower part of his face, the maxillaries, projected like the powerful jaws of a carnivorous beast. His temples retreated, all the upper part of his head was contracted, and, behind the boon-companion twinkle of his grey eyes, there lurked deceit and violence. He had inherited the brutish desires and tenacious grip of his father, aggravated by the narrow meanness of his mother. In every quarrel, whenever the **two** old people **heaped** reproaches **upon his** head, **he replied:** "**You** shouldn't have made me so!"

"Look here, it's five leagues from La Chamade to Cloyes," replied he to their complaints; "and besides, hang it all, I'm here at the same time as you. Oh, at me again, are you?"

They all disputed, shouted in shrill, high-pitched voices, and argued over their private matters exactly as if they had been at **home.** The clerks, disturbed, looked at them askance, till the **tumult** brought in the **notary,** who re-opened the door of his private office.

"**You are all** assembled? Then come in!"

This private office looked on to the garden, a narrow strip of ground running down to the Loir, the leafless poplars along which were visible in the distance. On the mantelpiece, between **some packets** of papers, there was a black marble clock; the furniture simply comprised the mahogany writing-table, a set of pasteboard boxes, and some chairs. Monsieur Baillehache at once installed himself at his writing-table, like a judge on the bench, while the peasants who had entered in a file hesitated

and squinted at the **chairs,** feeling embarrassed **as to where and**
how they were to **sit down.**

" Come, seat **yourselves !** " said the notary.

Then **Fouan and Rose** were pushed forward by the rest on **to**
the **two front chairs ;** Fanny and Delhomme got behind, also side
by **side ; Buteau** established himself in **an** isolated corner
against the wall ; while Hyacinthe alone remained standing, **in**
front of **the window,** blocking **out the light with his broad**
shoulders. The notary, out of patience, addressed him
familiarly.

"**Sit down, do, Hyacinthe !**"

He had to broach the subject himself.

"**So, Fouan, you have made up your mind to divide**
your property **before your death, between your two sons and**
your daughter ? "

The old **man made no reply.** The rest were as if frozen to
stone ; there **was deep silence.**

On his part, **the notary, accustomed to such** sluggishness,
did not hurry himself. **His office had been in** his family **two**
hundred and fifty years. Baillehache, son, had succeeded Baillehache, father, at Cloyes, the line being of ancient Beauceron
extraction, and they had contracted from their rustic connection
that ponderous reflectiveness, that artful circumspection, which
protract **the most** trivial debates with long pauses and irrelevant
talk. **Having taken up a penknife the** notary began paring **his**
nails.

" Haven't **you ?** It would appear that you have made up
your mind," he repeated **at length, looking hard at the old man.**

The latter turned, looked **round at everybody, and then**
said, hesitatingly :

" Yes ; that may **be** so, Monsieur Baillehache. I spoke **to**
you about it at harvest-time. You told me **to** think it over **;**
and I have thought it over, and **I can see that it will have to**
come to that."

He **explained the why and** wherefore, in faltering phrases,
interspersed with constant digressions. But there was one thing
which he said nothing about, but which was obvious from the
repressed emotion which choked his utterance—and that was
the infinite **distress, the smothered rancour,** the rending asunder,
as it were, of his whole frame, which he felt in parting **with**
the property so eagerly coveted before his father's death, cultivated later on with the violent avidity of lust, and then added
to, bit by bit, at the cost of the most sordid avarice. **Such-**
and-such a plot represented months of bread and cheese, fireless

winters, summers of scorching toil, with **no** other sustenance than a **few gulps of water.** He had loved the soil as it were a woman **who kills, and for** whose sake men are slain. No spouse, nor child, nor any human being; but the soil! However, being now stricken in years, he must hand his mistress over to his sons, as *his* father, maddened by his own impotence, had handed **her over to him.**

"You see, **Monsieur** Baillehache, one has to look at things **as they are.** My legs are not what they used to be; my arms are hardly better; **and,** of course, the land suffers accordingly. Things might still **have gone on** if one could have come to an understanding with **one's children.**"

He glanced at **Buteau and** Hyacinthe, **who made no** sign, however; their eyes were looking into vacancy, as though they were a hundred miles away from him and his words.

" Well, am I to be expected to take strange people under our **roof,** to pick and steal? No, servants now-a-days **cost too much;** they eat one out of house and home. As for me, **I am used up.** This year, look you, I have hardly had the strength **to cultivate a quarter** of the nineteen *setiers** I possess; just enough **to provide** corn for ourselves and fodder for the two cows. So, you understand, it's breaking my heart to see good land spoiled by lying idle. I had rather let everything go than look on at such sinful waste."

His voice faltered; his gestures were those **of** resigned anguish. Near him listened his submissive wife, crushed by more than half a century of obedience and toil.

" The other day," he continued, "Rose, while making **her** cheeses, fell into them head first. It wears me out only to jog **to market.** And then, we can't take the land away with us when we **go. It** must be given up—given up. After all, we have done enough work, and **we want to die in peace.** Don't we, Rose ? "

" **That's true enough;** true **as we sit** here," said the old woman.

There **fell** a new and prolonged silence. The notary finished trimming his nails, and at last he put the knife back on **his** desk, saying :

" **Yes,** those are very good reasons; one is frequently forced to resolve on a deed of gift. I should add that it saves expense, for the legacy duties are heavier than those on the transference of property."

---

* A *setier* is about an acre and a quarter.

Buteau, despite his affectation of indifference, could not help exclaiming:

"Then it's true, Monsieur Baillehache?"

"Most certainly. You will save some hundreds of francs."

There was a flutter among the others; even Delhomme's countenance brightened, while the parents also shared in the general satisfaction. The moment they knew it was cheaper, the thing was as good as done.

"It remains for me to make the usual observations," continued the notary. "Many thoughtful persons condemn such transfers of property, and regard them as immoral, in that they tend to sever family ties. Deplorable instances might, in fact, be mentioned, children having sometimes behaved very badly, when their parents had stripped themselves of all."

The two sons and the daughter listened to him, openmouthed, with trembling eyelids and quivering cheeks.

"Let papa keep everything himself, if those are his ideas," brusquely interrupted the very susceptible Fanny.

"We have always been dutiful," said Buteau.

"And we're not afraid of work," added Hyacinthe.

With a wave of his hand Maître Baillehache restored calm.

"Pray, let me finish! I know you are good children, and honest workers; and, in your case, there is not the slightest danger of your parents ever repenting of their resolution."

He spoke without a tinge of irony, repeating the conciliatory phrases which five-and-twenty years of professional practice had made smooth upon his tongue. However, the mother, although seeming not to understand, glanced with her small eyes from her daughter to her two sons. She had brought them up, without any show of fondness, amid the chill parsimony which reproaches the little ones with diminishing the household savings. She had a grudge against the younger son for having run away from home just when he was capable of earning wages; the daughter she had never been able to get on with, encountering in her a strain too like her own, a robust activity made haughty and unyielding by the intermingled intelligence of the father; and her gaze only softened as it rested upon the elder son, the ruffian who took neither after her nor after her husband—the ill weed sprung none knew whence, and, perhaps, excused and favoured on that account.

Fouan also had looked at his children, one after the other, with an uneasy mistrust of the uses they might make of his property. The laziness of the drunkard was not so keen an anguish to him as the covetous yearning of the two others for possession. However, he bent his trembling head. What was the good of kicking against the pricks?

"The partition being thus resolved upon," resumed tho notary, "the question becomes one of terms. Are you agreed upon the allowance which is to be paid?"

Everybody suddenly relapsed into mute rigidity. Their sun-burnt faces assumed a stony look, an air of impenetrable gravity, like that of diplomatists entering on the appraisement of an empire. Then they threw out tentative glances one to another, but nobody spoke. At last the father once more explained matters.

"No, Monsieur Baillehache, we have not entered on the subject; we were waiting till we met all together, here. But it's quite simple, isn't it? I have nineteen setiers, or, as people now say, nine hectares and a half (about twenty-three acres). So that, if I rented them out, it would come to nine hundred and fifty francs, at a hundred francs per hectare (two and a half acres)."

Buteau, the least patient, leapt from his chair.

"What! A hundred francs per hectare! Do you take us for fools, papa?"

And a preliminary discussion began on the question of figures. There was a setier of vineyard; that, certainly, would let for fifty francs. But would that price ever be got for the twelve setiers of plough-land, still less for the six setiers of natural meadow-land, the fields along the Aigre, the hay of which was worth nothing? The plough-land itself was hardly of good quality, especially at the end which edged the plateau, for the arable layer got thinner and thinner as it neared the valley.

"Come, come, papa," said Fanny, reproachfully, "you musn't take an unfair advantage of us."

"It's worth a hundred francs a hectare," repeated the old man stubbornly, slapping his thigh. "I could let it out to-morrow at a hundred francs if I wanted to. And what's it worth to you, now? Just let's hear what it's worth to you?"

"It's worth sixty francs," said Buteau, but Fouan, greatly put out, sustained his price, and launched into fervent eulogy of his land—such fine land as it was, yielding wheat of itself—when Delhomme, silent till then, declared in his blunt, honest way: "It's worth eighty francs, not a copper more, and not a copper less."

The old man immediately calmed down.

"All right, say eighty. I don't mind making a sacrifice for my children."

Rose, twitching at a corner of his blouse, expressed in one word the outraged instincts of her mean nature—"No!"

Hyacinthe held himself aloof. Land had been no object to him since the five years he had spent in Algeria. He had but one aim: to get his share at once, whatever it might be, and to turn it into money. Accordingly, he went on swinging to and fro with an air of amused superiority.

"I said eighty," cried Fouan, "and eighty it is. I have always been a man of my word; I swear it. Nine hectares and a half, look you, come to seven hundred and sixty francs, or, in round numbers, eight hundred. Well, the allowance shall be eight hundred francs, that's fair enough?"

Buteau burst into a violent fit of laughter, while Fanny protested by a shake of the head, as if dumbfounded. Monsieur Baillehache, who, since the discussion began, had been looking vacantly into the garden, again turned to his clients and seemed to listen, tugging in his lunatic way at his whiskers, and dreamily digesting the excellent meal he had just made.

This time the old man was right, it was fair. But the children, heated and possessed by the one idea of concluding the bargain on the lowest possible terms, grew absolutely ferocious, and haggled and cursed with the bad faith of yokels buying a pig.

"Eight hundred francs!" sneered Buteau. "Seems you want to live like gentle folks—— Oh, indeed! Eight hundred francs, when you might live on four! Why not say at once that you want to gorge till you burst?"

Fouan had not yet lost his temper, considering the higgling natural, and simply facing the expected storm, himself excited, but making straight for the goal he had in view.

"Stop a bit! that's not all. Till the day of our death we keep the house and garden, of course. Then, as we shall no longer get anything from the crops, or have our two cows, we want every year a cask of wine and a hundred faggots; and every week eight quarts of milk, a dozen eggs, and three cheeses."

"Oh, papa!" groaned Fanny in piteous consternation. "Oh, papa!"

As for Buteau, he had done with discussion. He had sprung to his feet, and was striding brusquely to and fro; he had even jammed his cap on his head as if he were about to go. Hyacinthe also had likewise got up from his chair, disquieted by the idea that this fuss might prevent the partition after all. Delhomme alone remained impassive, with his finger laid against his nose, in an attitude of deep thought and extreme boredom.

At **this** point Maître Baillehache felt it necessary to help matters forward a little. Rousing himself up, and fidgeting more energetically with his whiskers :

" You know, my friends," said he, "that wine, **faggots, cheese,** and eggs are customary."

But he was cut short by a volley of bitter phrases.

" Eggs with chickens inside, perhaps ! "

" We don't drink our wine, do we ? **We sell it ! "**

" **It's jolly** convenient **not to** do a blasted thing and be made **warm** and comfortable, while your children are **toiling** and moiling ! "

The notary, who had heard the same **thing often enough** before, continued unmoved :

" All that is no argument. **Come,** come, Hyacinthe, sit down, will you ? You're keeping out the light; **you're a perfect** nuisance ! So that's settled, isn't **it, all of you ? You will** pay the **dues** in kind, because otherwise you would **become a** by-word. **We** have, therefore, only to discuss the amount of the allowance."

Delhomme at length indicated that he had something to say. Everybody having resumed his place, he began slowly, amid general attention :

" Excuse me ; what the father asks seems fair : he might be allowed eight hundred francs on the ground that he could let the property for eight hundred francs—only we don't reckon like that on our side. He is not letting us the land, but giving it to us, and what we have to calculate is : how much do he **and his** wife require to live on ? That **is all. How** much do **they** require to live on ? "

" That is, certainly," chimed **in the** notary, " the usual basis of calculation."

Another endless dispute set in. **The two old folks' lives** were dissected, exposed, and discussed, need by need. Bread, **vegetables, and meat** were weighed out ; clothing appraised, **linen and** woollen, **to** the utmost farthing ; even such trivial **luxuries as** the father's tobacco—cut down, after **interminable** recriminations, **from** two sous a day to one—were not **beneath** notice. When people were beyond work, they ought to reduce their expenditure. The mother, again; could she not do without her black coffee ? It was like their twelve-year-old dog, who ate, **and** ate, and made no return ; he ought to have had a **bullet put through** his head long ago ! The calculation was

no sooner finished **than it** was begun all over again, **on the**
chance of finding some **other** item to suppress: two shirts or
six handkerchiefs **in the year.** And thus, by cutting closer and
closer, by pinching and scraping in the paltriest matters, they got
down **to** five hundred and fifty odd francs, which left the children
in a state of uncontrollable agitation, for they **had set** their
hearts **upon not** giving more than five hundred.

Fanny, however, was growing tired. She **was not a bad**
sort, **having** more of the milk of human kindness than **the**
men, and not yet having had her heart or her skin hardened **by**
rough life in the open air. Accordingly she spoke of making
an end of it, and resigned herself to some concessions. **Hya-**
cinthe, for **his part,** shrugged his shoulders, **in** a **most liberal,**
not to say maudlin mood; ready to offer, out of his own share,
any **little balance which, be it** remarked, he would **never have**
paid.

"Come," asked the daughter, "shall we let it go at five
hundred and **fifty?"**

"Right you **are!"** answered he. "The old 'uns must have
a little pleasant time!"

The **mother turned to her elder son with a** smiling and **yet**
almost tearful look of affection, while the father continued **his**
contention with the younger. **He had only given way step by**
step, disputing every **reduction, and** making **a stubborn stand**
on certain items. But, beneath his ostensibly cool **pertinacity,**
his wrath **rose high** within him as he confronted **the mad desire**
of his own flesh and blood to fatten on his flesh, and **to drain**
his blood dry while **he** was yet alive. He forgot **that he had**
thus **fed upon his own** father. **His** hands had **begun to**
tremble; and he growled out:

"Ah, the rascals! To think **that** one has brought **'em up,**
and then they turn round and take the bread **out of one's**
mouth! On my word, I'm sick of it. I'd rather be already
rotting under ground. So there's no getting you to behave
decently; you won't give more than five hundred and fifty?"

He was **about to accept the sum, when** his **wife again**
twitched his **blouse and whispered:**

"No, no!"

"And that's not all," resumed Buteau, after a little hesitation.
"How about the money you **have saved up?** If you've any
money of your own you don't want ours, do you?"

He looked steadily at his father, having reserved this shot
for the last. The old man had grown very pale.

"What money?" he asked.

"Why, the money invested; the money you hold **bonds** for."

Buteau, **who** only suspected the hoard, wanted to make sure. One evening, he had thought he saw his father take a little roll of papers from behind a looking-glass. The next day and the days following he had been on the watch, but nothing had turned up; the empty cavity alone remained.

Fouan's pallor now suddenly changed to a deep red as his **torrent of** wrath at length burst forth. **He** rose up, and **shouted with a** furious gesture:

"Great heaven! You go rummaging in my pockets now. I haven't a sou, a copper invested; you've cost too much for that, you brute. But, in any case, is it any business of **yours?** Am I not the master, the father?"

He seemed to grow taller in the re-assertion of his authority. For years everybody, wife and children alike, had quailed before him, under his rude despotism as chief of the family. **If** they fancied all that at **an** end, they made a mistake.

"**Oh, papa!**" began Buteau, with an attempt at a snigger.

"**Hold** your tongue, in God's name!" resumed the old **man, with** his hand still uplifted. "Hold your tongue, or I **strike!**"

The younger son stammered, and shrank into himself on his **chair. He had** felt the **blow** approaching and had raised his elbow **to** ward it off, seized once more with the terrors of infancy.

"And you, Hyacinthe, leave off smirking! And you, Fanny, look me in the face, if you dare! **True** as the sun's shining, I'll make it lively for some of **you**; see if I don't!"

He stood, threateningly, over **them all.** The **mother** shivered, as if apprehensive of stray buffets. The children neither stirred nor breathed, they were conquered and submissive.

"Understand, the allowance shall be six hundred francs; or **else** I shall sell my **land** and invest in an annuity. Yes, an annuity! All shall be spent, and you sha'n't come into a copper. Will you give the six hundred francs?"

"Why, **papa**," murmured Fanny, "**we** will give whatever **you ask.**"

"Six hundred francs. Right!" said Delhomme.

"**What suits the rest, suits** me," declared Hyacinthe.

Buteau, **setting his teeth** viciously, gave the consent of silence. **Fouan still** held them in check, with the stern look of one accustomed to obedience. Finally, **he sat** down again, saying: "Good! Then we are agreed."

Maître Baillehache had begun to doze again, unconcernedly awaiting the issue of the quarrel. Now, opening his eyes, he brought the interview to a peaceful close.

"Well, then, as you're agreed, that's enough! Now I know the terms, I will draw up the deed. For your part, get the surveying done, portion out the lots, and tell the surveyor to forward me a note containing the description of the lots. Then, when you've drawn your numbers, all we shall have to do will be to write the number drawn against each name, and sign."

He had risen from his arm-chair to see them out. But they, hesitating, and reflecting, would not stir. Was it really over? Was nothing forgotten? Had they not made a bad bargain, which there was yet time, perhaps, to cancel?

Four o'clock struck; they had been there nearly three hours.

"Aren't you going?" said the notary to them at last. "There are others waiting."

He precipitated their decision by hustling them into the next room, where, indeed, a number of patient rustics were sitting still and rigid upon their chairs, while the small clerk watched a dog-fight out of the window, and the two others still drove their pens, sulkily and scratchily, over stamped paper.

Once outside, the family stood for a moment stock-still in the middle of the street.

"If you like," declared the father, "the measuring shall take place on the day after to-morrow—Monday."

They nodded assent, and went down the Rue Grouaise in scattered file.

Then, old Fouan and Rose, having turned down the Rue du Temple, towards the church, Fanny and Delhomme went off through the Rue Grande. Buteau had stopped on the Place Saint-Lubin, wondering if his father had a hidden hoard or not; and Hyacinthe, left by himself, relighted his cigar-end, and went into the Jolly Ploughman café.

CHAPTER III.

THE Fouans' house was the first in Rognes, on the high-road from Cloyes to Bazoches-le-Doyen, which passes through the village. On Monday, the old man was going out at seven o'clock in the morning to keep the appointment in front of the church, when, in the next doorway, he perceived his sister, "La Grande," who was already astir, despite her eighty years.

These Fouans had propagated and grown there for centuries, like some sturdy luxuriant vegetation. Serfs in the old times of the Rognes-Bouquevals—of whom not a trace survived save the few half-buried stones of a ruined château—they had been emancipated, it appeared, under Philip the Fair; becoming thenceforward landowners of an acre or so, which they had bought from the lord of the manor when in difficulties, and paid for with tears and blood at ten times the value. Then had set in the long struggle of four hundred years to defend and enlarge the property, in a frenzy of passion transmitted from father to son: odd corners were lost and bought back, the ownership was unremittingly called into question, the inheritances were subject to such a list of dues that they almost ate their own heads off; but in spite of all, both arable and plough-lands grew, bit by bit, in the ever-prevailing, stubborn craving for possession. Generations passed away, the lives of many men enriched the soil; but when the Revolution of '89 set its seal upon his rights, the Fouan of the time, Joseph Casimir, possessed about twenty-six acres, wrested in the course of four centuries from the old seignorial manor.

In '93, this Joseph Casimir was twenty-seven years of age, and on the day when what remained of the manor was declared national property and sold in lots by auction, he yearned to acquire a few acres of it. The Rognes-Bouquevals, ruined and in debt, after letting the last tower of the château crumble into dust, had long since given up to their creditors the right of receiving the revenues of La Borderie, three quarters of which property lay fallow. In particular, adjacent to one of Fouan's bits of land there was a large field, on which he looked with the fierce covetousness of his race. But the harvest had

been poor, and in the old pipkin behind his oven he had
barely a hundred crowns saved up. Moreover, although it
had momentarily occurred to him to borrow off a Cloyes money-
lender, a distrustful prudence had stood in the way: he was
afraid to touch these lands of the nobility; who knew whether
they would not be claimed again later on? So it happened that,
divided between desire and apprehension, he had the agony of
seeing La Borderie bought at auction, field by field, and for a
tenth of its value, by Isidore Hourdequin, a townsman of
Châteaudun, formerly employed in the collection of excise duties.

Joseph Casimir Fouan, in his old age, had divided his
twenty-six acres equally among his eldest child, Marianne,
and his two sons, Louis and Michel; a younger daughter
Laure, brought up to dressmaking and employed at Châteaudun, being indemnified in hard cash. But marriage destroyed
this equality. While Marianne Fouan, surnamed "La
Grande," wedded a neighbour, Antoine Péchard, with about
twenty-two acres; Michael Fouan, surnamed "Mouche," encumbered himself with a sweetheart who only expected from
her father two and a half acres of vineyard. On the other hand,
Louis Fouan, joined in matrimony to Rose Maliverne, the heiress
to fifteen acres, had acquired that total of twenty-three acres
or so, which, in his turn, he was about to divide among his
three children.

La Grande was respected and dreaded in the family, not for
her advanced age, but for her fortune. Still very upright, tall,
thin, wiry, and large-boned, she had the fleshless head of a
bird of prey set on a long, shrivelled, blood-coloured neck. In
her, the family nose curved into a formidable beak; she had
round fixed eyes, with not a trace of hair under the yellow
silk handkerchief she always wore, though she possessed her
full complement of teeth, and jaws that might have masticated
flints. She never went out without her thornwood stick, which
she held on high as she walked, only making use of it to strike
animals and human beings. Left a widow at an early age, she
had turned her one daughter out of doors, because the wretch
had insisted, against her mother's will, on marrying a poor youth,
Vincent Bouteroue; and even when this daughter and her husband
had died of want, leaving behind them a grand-daughter and a
grandson, Palmyre and Hilarion, aged respectively thirty-two
and twenty-four, she had refused her forgiveness and let them
starve to death, allowing no one so much as to remind her of
their existence. Since her goodman's death she presided in
person over the cultivation of her land; she had three cows, a pig,

and a farm-hand, **all** fed out of a common trough; and she was obeyed by those about her with the most abject submission.

Fouan, seeing her on her threshold, had drawn **near out of** respect. She was ten years older than he, and **he** regarded her sternness, her avarice, her obstinate resolution to possess **and to live,** with an admiring deference, shared by the **whole village.**

"I was just wanting to tell you about it, **La** Grande," said he. " I have made **up my** mind, and am going up yonder **to** see about the division."

She made **no** reply, **but** tightened **her grasp** upon the stick which she was flourishing.

" **The** other night I **wanted to ask your advice again, but I** knocked and no one **answered."**

Then she broke out in **shrill tones :**

" Idiot ! Advice, indeed ! **I gave** you advice. **The fool, the** poltroon you must be to give your property **up** as long as you can get about. They might have bled *me* to death, but, under the knife, I would still have refused. To see what belongs to one in the hands of others, to turn one's self out of doors for the benefit of rascally children.—No ! No ! No !"

" **But,**" put in Fouan, " if you're incapable of farming, and the land suffers accordingly."

" Well, let **it suffer.** Rather than lose half an acre of it, **I** would go and watch the thistles grow every morning."

She drew herself up grimly, in her featherless, old vulture-like way, and, drumming on his shoulder with her stick, as if to impress her words upon him more deeply, she resumed :

" Listen, and mark me. When you have nothing and they have everything, your children will refuse you a mouthful of bread. You'll end with a beggar's wallet, like a road-tramp. And when that happens, don't come **knocking at my** door, for I give **you** fair warning, it'll **be the worse for you.** Would you like to know what I shall do, eh ? Would you ?"

He waited submissively, as behoved a younger brother; **and** she returned indoors, banging the door behind her and screaming :

" **I** shall do that ! **Die in a ditch !"**

Fouan stood for **an** instant motionless before the closed door. Then, with a gesture of resigned decision, he went up the path leading to the Place de l'Église. On that very spot stood the old family residence of the Fouans, which, in the division of property, had fallen to his brother Michel, called Mouche; his own house, lower down along the road, had come to

him from his wife Rose. Mouche, who had long been a
widower, lived alone with his two daughters, Lise and
Françoise, embittered by disappointments, still humiliated by
his lowly marriage, and accusing his brother and sister, after
forty years, of having cheated him when the allotments were
drawn for. He was for ever telling the tale how the worst lot had
been left for him at the bottom of the hat; and, in the course
of time, this seemed to have become true, for he proved so
excellent at excuses and such a sluggard at work that his
share lost half its value in his hands. " The man makes the
land," as folks say in La Beauce.

That morning Mouche also was on the watch at his door
when his brother came round the corner of the square. The
division roused his spleen, reviving old grudges, although he
had nothing to expect from it. However, to demonstate his utter
indifference, he, too, turned his back and shut the door with a
slam.

Fouan had suddenly caught sight of Delhomme and Hyacinthe, who were waiting twenty yards apart from each other.
He made for the former, while the latter made for him. The
three, without speaking, scanned the path which skirted the
edge of the plateau.

" There he is," said Hyacinthe, at last. " He " was Grosbois,
the local surveyor, a peasant from Magnolles, a little village
near Cloyes. His knowledge of reading and writing had
ruined him. When summoned from Orgères to Beaugency, on
surveying business, he used to leave to his wife the management of his property, and he had contracted during his constant
pilgrimages such drunken habits that he was now never sober.
Very stout, very sturdy for his sixty years, he had a broad red
face budding all over into purple pimples; and, despite the early
hour, he was, on the day in question, in a state of abominable
intoxication, the result of a merry-making held the night before
by some Montigny vine-growers in honour of a divided inheritance. But that mattered nothing: the tipsier he was, the
clearer his brain. He never measured incorrectly, and never
added up incorrectly. He was held in deference and honour,
advisedly, for he had the reputation of being extremely spiteful.

" All here, eh?" said he. " Then come along."

A dirty, bedraggled urchin of twelve was in attendance,
carrying the chain under his arm and the stand and the staves
over his shoulder, while with his free hand he swung the square,
which was in an old burst cardboard case.

They all set out without waiting for Buteau, whom they

had just descried in the distance, standing still before the largest field of the holding. That field, some five acres in extent, was immediately adjacent to the one along which La Coliche had dragged Françoise a few days before. Buteau, thinking it useless to proceed further, had stopped there in a brown study. When the others arrived, they saw him stoop down, take up a handful of earth, and gradually filter it through his fingers, as though to estimate its weight and flavour.

"There," resumed Grosbois, taking a greasy memorandum-book from his pocket: "I have already drawn up an accurate little plan of each lot, as you asked me to do, Fouan. It now devolves upon us to divide the whole into three portions; and that, my children, we will do together, eh? Just tell me how you intend it to be done."

The day had worn on. A ripping wind was driving continuous masses of thick clouds across the pale sky; and La Beauce lay sullen and gloomy, lashed by the keen air. Yet not one of them seemed conscious of that breeze from the offing, which inflated their blouses and threatened to carry off their hats. Not one of the five, in holiday attire, as befitted the gravity of the occasion, spoke a word. As they stood on the confines of the field, amid the boundless expanse, their lineaments had a dreamy, frozen fixedness, the musing expression of mariners who live alone in large open spaces. La Beauce, flat and fertile, easily tilled but demanding continuous effort, has made the Beauceron calm and reflective, without passion save for the land itself.

"It'll all have to be divided into three," said Buteau at length.

Grosbois shook his head, and a discussion set in. An apostle of progress, by virtue of his connection with large farms, he occasionally went so far as to set himself up against his smaller clients, by condemning extreme subdivision. Would not the labour and cost of transport from place to place become a ruinous thing, when there were only odds and ends of land left that might be covered by a handkerchief? Was it farming at all, with paltry garden-plots on which it was impossible either to improve the system of crops or to introduce machinery? No: the only sensible thing to do was to make a mutual arrangement, not to adopt the murderous course of chopping a field up like so much pastry. If one of them would be content with the plough-land, another might manage with the meadows; the portions could eventually be equalised, and the distribution decided by lot.

C

Buteau, with the natural liveliness of youth, adopted a
jocose tone. " And, with only some meadow-land, what shall I
have to eat? Grass, I suppose? No, no; I want some of
everything, hay for cow and horse, corn and grape for myself."

Fouan, who was listening, nodded assent. For generations, such had been the mode of partition; and fresh acquisi-
tions, by marriage or otherwise, had subsequently swollen the
plots anew.

Delhomme, passing rich with his fifty acres or so, had
broader views; but he was in a conciliatory mood, and had
indeed only come, in his wife's interest, to see that she was
not cheated in the measurements. As for Hyacinthe, he had
gone off in pursuit of a flight of larks, with his hands crammed
full of pebbles. Whenever one of the birds, distressed by the
wind, stopped still a couple of seconds in mid-air with quivering wings, he felled it to the ground with the skill of a savage.
Three fell, and he thrust them bleeding into his pocket.

" Come, stop your talk, and let's have it cut up into three ! "
said the lively Buteau, addressing the surveyor familiarly;
" and not into six, mind, for you seem to me this morning to
have both Chartres and Orleans in your eye at once."

Grosbois, feeling hurt, drew himself up with much dignity.

" When you've had as much to drink as I have, young
shaver, see whether you can keep your eyes open at all.
Which of you clever people would like to take the square
instead of me ? "

As no one ventured to take up the challenge, he called out
harshly and triumphantly to the boy, who was rapt with admiration of Hyacinthe's pebble-shooting. The square duly installed
on its stand, the stakes were being set up, when a new dispute
arose over the method of dividing the field. The surveyor,
supported by Fouan and Delhomme, wanted to divide the five
acres into three strips parallel with the Aigre valley; while
Buteau insisted on the strips being taken perpendicular to the
valley, on the plea that the arable layer got thinner and thinner
as it neared the slope. In this way every one would have his
share of the worse end; whereas, in the other case, the third
lot would be altogether of inferior quality.

But Fouan grew heated; swore that the depth was the same
everywhere, and reminded them that the former partition
between himself, Mouche, and La Grande had been made in the
direction he indicated; in proof of which, Mouche's five
acres lay adjacent to the third of the proposed lots. Delhomme,
on his side, made a decisive remark: even admitting that the

one lot was inferior, the owner would be benefited as soon
as the authorities decided to open the road that was to skirt the
field at that point.

"Oh, yes; I daresay!" cried Buteau. "The celebrated
road from Rognes to Châteaudun, by way of La Borderie!
And a jolly long time you'll have to wait for it!"

His importunity being, nevertheless, disregarded, he entered
a protest from between his clenched teeth.

Hyacinthe **himself** had drawn near, and they were all
absorbed in watching Grosbois trace out the lines of division.
They kept a sharp eye on him, as if they suspected him of
trying by unfair means to make one share half-an-inch bigger
than the others. Three times did Delhomme put his **eye to**
the slit in the square, to make quite sure that the line fairly
intersected the stave. Hyacinthe swore at the "d——d
youngster" because he did not hold the chain right. But Buteau,
in particular, followed the process step by step, counting
the feet, and going over the calculations again in his own
way with trembling lips. With this consuming desire to
possess, with the joy he felt at getting at last a grip of the
land, **his** bitterness and sullen rage at not being able to keep
the **whole grew** and grew. Those five acres, all of one
piece, **made such a** fine field. He **had** insisted on the
division, so that no one might have what he couldn't get; and
yet the wholesale destruction drove him distracted. He again
tried to find frivolous causes of quarrel.

Fouan, standing in a listless attitude, had **been looking**
on at the dismemberment of his property without a word.

"It's finished!" said Grosbois. "And look at it how you
will, you won't find a pound difference between the lots."

There **were** still, **on** the plateau, **ten acres** of plough-
land divided into a dozen plots, none of which were much more
than an acre in size. Indeed, one was only about a rood, and
the surveyor having inquired, with a sneer, whether that also
was to be sub-divided, a fresh dispute arose.

Buteau, with **his instinctive** gesture, had stooped down and
taken up a handful **of** earth, which he raised to his face as if
to try its **flavour.** A complacent wrinkling of his nose seemed
to **pronounce it** better than all **the rest;** and, after gently
filtering **it through** his fingers, he **said** that if they left the lot
to him it **was all right,** otherwise he insisted on a division.
Delhomme **and Hyacinthe** angrily refused, and likewise
wanted their **share. Yes, yes!** A third of a rood each; that
was the **only fair way. By** sub-dividing every plot, they were

sure that none of the three could have anything which the other two lacked.

"Come on to the vineyard," said Fouan, and as they turned towards the church, he threw a last glance over the vast plain, pausing for an instant to look at the distant buildings of La Borderie. Then, with a cry of inconsolable regret, alluding to the old lost opportunity of buying up the national property:

"Ah!" said he, "if father had only chosen, Grosbois, you would now be measuring all that!"

The two sons and the son-in-law turned sharply round, and there was a new halt and a lingering look at the seven hundred and fifty acres of the farm spread out before them.

"Ugh!" grunted Buteau, as he set off again: "Much good it does us, that story! It's always our fate to be the prey of the townsfolk."

Ten o'clock struck. The main part of the work was over. But they hastened their steps, for the wind had fallen, and a heavy dark cloud had just discharged itself of a premonitory shower. The various Rognes vineyards were situated beyond the church, on the hill-side which sloped down to the Aigre. In former times, the château had stood there with its grounds; and it was barely more than a century since the peasantry, encouraged by the success of the Montigny vineyards, near Cloyes, had decided to plant vines on this declivity, though it was specially adapted for the purpose by its Southern aspect and the steepness of its slope. The wine it yielded was thin but of a pleasantly acid taste, and resembled the minor Orleanais vintages. Each owner only secured a few casks, Delhomme, the wealthiest, possessing some seven acres of vineland; the rest of the country-side was entirely given up to cereals and plants for fodder.

They turned down behind the church, skirted the old ruined presbytery which had been turned into a lodging for the rural constable, and gained the narrow chequered patches. As they crossed a piece of stony ground, covered with shrubs, a shrill voice cried through a gap:

"Father, it's raining! and I've brought out my geese."

It was the voice of "La Trouille,"* Hyacinthe's daughter, a girl of twelve, thin and wiry like a holly branch, with fair towzled hair. Her large mouth had a twist to the left, her green eyes stared so boldly that she might have been taken for a boy, and her dress consisted of an old blouse of her

---

* Shameless slattern; troll.

father's, tied round her waist with some string. The reason
everybody called her La Trouille—although she bore, by
right, the fair name of Olympe—was that Hyacinthe, who
used to yell at her from morning till night, could never say a
word to her without adding :

" Just wait, you dirty troll, and I'll make it hot for you ! "

He had begotten this wilding of a drab, whom he had picked
up in a ditch after a fair, and whom he had installed in his
den, to the great scandal of all Rognes. For nearly three years
the household had been at sixes-and-sevens, and one harvest
evening the baggage went off the way she came, in company
with another man. The child, then scarcely weaned, had
grown apace after the manner of ill weeds; and, as soon as she
could walk, she got the meals ready for her father, whom she
both dreaded and worshipped. Her chief passion, however,
was for geese. At first she had only had two, male and female,
stolen when quite young from behind a farm hedge. Then,
thanks to her maternal care, the flock had increased, and she
now possessed twenty birds, which she fed by pillage.

When La Trouille made her appearance, with her brazen,
goat-like look, driving the geese before her with a stick,
Hyacinthe flew into a temper.

" Be sure you're back for dinner, or else you'll catch it !
And mind you keep the house carefully locked up, you dirty
troll, for fear of robbers ! "

Buteau sniggered, and even Delhomme and the others could
not help laughing, they were so tickled at the idea of Hyacinthe
being robbed. His house was a sight; an old cellar con-
sisting of three walls crumbled to their original clay, a
regular fox-hole, amid heaps of fallen stones and under a cluster
of old lime-trees. It was all that remained of the château;
and when our poaching friend, falling out with his father, had
ensconced himself in this stony corner belonging to the
village, he had had to close up the cellar by building a
fourth wall of rough stones, in which he left two openings for
window and door. The place was overgrown with brambles,
and a large sweet briar hid the window. The country folk
called it the Château.

A new deluge poured down. Luckily the acre or so of
vineyard was close by, and the division into three was effected
straightforwardly, without any new ground for a quarrel
arising. There now only remained seven or eight acres of
meadow down by the river side ; but at this moment the rain
became so heavy, and fell in such torrents, that the surveyor,

passing the gate of a residence, suggested that they should go in.

"What if we took shelter for a minute at Monsieur Charles's?"

Fouan had come to a standstill, wavering, full of respect for his brother-in-law and sister, who had made their fortune, and lived in a retired way in this middle-class residence.

"No, no," he muttered; "they breakfast at twelve. It would disturb their arrangements."

But Monsieur Charles put in an appearance on his stone steps under the verandah, taking an interest in the fall of rain, and, on recognising them, he called out:

"Come in, come in, do!"

Then, as they were all dripping wet, he bade them go round and enter by the kitchen, where he joined them. He was a fine man of sixty-five summers, close-shaven, with heavy eyelids over his lack-lustre eyes, and the solemn, sallow face of a retired magistrate. He was clad in deep-blue swan-skin flannel, with furred shoes, and an ecclesiastical skull-cap, which he wore with the dignified air of one whose life had been spent in duties of delicacy and authority.

When, at the age of twenty-five, Laure Fouan, then a dressmaker in a shop at Châteaudun, married Charles Badeuil, the latter kept a little café in the Rue d'Angoulême. The young pair, ambitious, and eager to make a rapid fortune, soon left there for Chartres. But, at first, nothing succeeded with them; all they put their hands to came to grief. They vainly tried another eating-house, a restaurant, even a salt-fish shop; and they despaired of ever having a copper to call their own, when Monsieur Charles, being of an enterprising nature, had the idea of buying one of the "licensed houses" in the Rue aux Juifs, which had greatly declined, owing to an unsatisfactory staff and notorious uncleanliness. He took in the situation at a glance: the requirements of Chartres, and the void to be supplied in a large town which lacked a respectable establishment, abreast of modern progress as regards safety and comfort. Indeed, before two years had passed, Number 19, re-decorated, fitted with curtains and mirrors, and provided with a highly select staff, became so very favourably known that the number of women had to be increased to six. All the officers, all the public functionaries—in short, society in general—went nowhere else. This success was kept up, thanks to the strong right arm of Monsieur Charles and his unflagging paternal administration; while Madame Charles proved herself

extraordinarily active, keeping her eye on everything, letting
nothing go to waste, and yet shrewd enough to overlook,
when necessary, the petty larcenies of rich customers.

In less than twenty-five **years** the Badeuils saved three hundred thousand francs, and they then thought of fulfilling the
dream of their lives: an idyllic old age, face to face with
nature, amid trees, flowers, and birds. But they were kept
two years longer by their inability to **find a** purchaser for
Number **19 at the** high price they valued it. And what **a**
heartrending thing it was! An establishment furnished **by**
themselves on the best scale, bringing in a larger income
than a farm, and yet about to pass, perforce, into strange hands,
in which, possibly, it would degenerate. On his settling **in**
Chartres a daughter had been born to Monsieur Charles, **by**
name Estelle, whom he sent to the nuns of the Visitation, at
Châteaudun, when he moved into the Rue aux Juifs. In this
devout, rigidly moral boarding school, he left the young girl
till the age of twenty, to further purify her purity; sending her
some distance off for her holidays, and keeping her in ignorance
of the business in which he made his money. He only took
her away on the **day he** wedded her to Hector Vaucogne, a
young fellow employed on the local excise staff, whose excellent natural gifts were marred by extraordinary laziness.
Estelle was close on thirty, and had a daughter, Elodie, aged
seven, when, being **at** length acquainted **with the** facts by
hearing that her father's business was in the market, **she**
went to **him of** her own accord and **asked him** to give **her**
the preference. Why should so safe and flourishing **a**
business go **out** of the family? All was duly arranged.
The Vaucognes took **the** place **over,** and the Badeuils, before
a month had elapsed, **had** the fond satisfaction of ascertaining
that their daughter, although brought up to other ideas,
had turned out a first-rate manageress, which, happily, com-
pensated for their son-in-law's supineness and lack of ad-
ministrative power. They had lived in retirement at Rognes
for five years, and had the supervision of their grand-daughter,
Elodie, who, in her turn, had been sent to the nuns of the
Visitation at Châteaudun, **there to** be religiously trained in
principles of the strictest morality.

When Monsieur Charles came into the kitchen, where a maid
was whipping some eggs, while she kept her eye upon a pan
of larks fizzing in butter, they all of them, even old Fouan and
Delhomme, uncovered their heads, and seemed extremely
flattered at shaking hands with him.

"Bless me!" said Grosbois, to make himself agreeable, "What a charming property this is of **yours**! And to think that you picked it **up for a mere song**. Oh, you artful **dog**, you!"

The other **puffed** himself out like a turkey-cock.

"**A bargain, a** windfall. We took a fancy **to it, and, besides, Madame** Charles had set her heart on ending her days **in her** own part **of the country**. As for me, **where the heart is** engaged I **have** always **been indulgent**."

Roseblanche, as the property **had been christened, was the** "**folly**" of a townsman of Cloyes, **who had** just laid out upon **it nearly** fifty **thousand francs, when a fit of** apoplexy struck **him down** before the paint **was dry on the walls**. The house, very trim, and situated **on the slope of** the plateau, stood in a garden **of some seven acres, which reached** down to the Aigre. In that out-of-the-way **spot, on the confines of sombre** Beauce, no purchaser could **be found, and Monsieur Charles** had got the place **for twenty** thousand francs. **There** he blissfully satisfied all **his** tastes, fishing **the stream for** superb trout and eels, making beloved collections of rose-trees and carnations, **and** keeping **a large aviary full of** wood warblers, which **no one but** himself **tended**. **There the fond old pair ran through** an income of twelve thousand francs, in a state of perfect happiness, which **they looked** upon as the rightful recompense of their thirty years **of toil**.

"Eh?" added Monsieur **Charles**. "**At least people know** who we are, here."

"Undoubtedly **you are known**," replied **the surveyor**. "Your **money is sufficient recommendation**."

All **the rest assented**.

"True; **quite true**."

Then Monsieur Charles bade the servant bring some glasses, **he himself going into** the cellar to fetch up two bottles of wine. With their noses turned towards the frying-pan, in which the larks were browning, they all sniffed the savoury smell, and solemnly drank, rolling the wine round in their mouths.

"Gracious! It don't **come** from this part of **the country**, I know! **Capital!**"

"Another **drop. Your health!**"

"Yours!"

As they laid down their glasses, Madame Charles, an estimable-looking matron of sixty-two, with snowy frontlets, made her appearance. In her the thick, large-nosed visage of the Fouans **was** of **a pale**, pink hue; hers **was** the calm, sweet,

monastic complexion of an aged nun who had led a sequestered
life. Clinging to her with awkward shyness followed Elodie,
who was spending a two days' holiday at Rognes. Preyed
upon by chlorosis, and over-tall for a girl of twelve, her flabby
ugliness, and her thin, blanched hair bespoke an impoverished
system; and **she** had been, moreover, kept in such restraint
during her course of training for spotless maidenhood that she
was half **an imbecile.**

"**Ha!** you here!" said Madame Charles, shaking hands
with her brother and nephew, slowly and impressively, in token
of the distance between them. Then, turning round, and giving
no further heed to such fellows, she added:

"Come in, come in, Monsieur Patoir; the animal is **here.**"

Patoir was the Cloyes veterinary—short, stout, full-blooded,
and purple; with the aspect of a trooper, and wearing heavy
moustaches. He had just driven up in a mud-splashed **gig**
through the pelting rain.

"This poor darling," she went on, taking out of a warm
oven a basket **in** which an old cat lay in the throes of death;
"this poor darling was seized yesterday with a shivering fit,
and it was **then** I wrote **to** you. Ah! he's not young; he is
nearly fifteen. We had him **ten years** at Chartres, but last
year **my daughter had** to get rid of him, and I brought him
here **because he** misbehaved himself in every corner of the
shop."

"Shop" was for Elodie's benefit, she being told that her
parents kept a confectionery business, amid **such a** press of
work, that they could not receive her there. The country-folk,
however, did not even smile, for the expression was current in
Rognes, where people said that "even Hourdequin's farm **was**
not so profitable as Monsieur Charles's shop." The men stared at
the shrivelled, old, yellow, mangy, miserable cat; the old cat who
had purred in all the beds in the Rue aux Juifs, the cat stroked
and fondled **by the** plump hands of five or six generations of
women. Long had he been pampered and petted, the spoiled
darling of the saloon and retiring-rooms, licking up unconsidered
trifles of pomade, drinking the water in the toilet-glasses, a mute,
abstracted spectator of what went on, seeing everything with
his slender pupils **set in gold.**

"Monsieur Patoir, pray cure him," concluded Madame
Charles.

The veterinary **distended** his eyelids, and screwed up his
nose and mouth, all his bluff, coarse, bull-dog physiognomy
being set in motion. And he cried:

" What? You've brought me all this way for *that!* I'll cure him for you! Tie a **stone round** his neck and chuck **him** into the **water!**"

Elodie burst into tears, and Madame Charles became purple in the face with indignation.

" Why, **he** stinks, this pet of yours! Keeping a **horrid thing like** that, to give the house cholera! Chuck the beast into the **water!**"

Nevertheless, the old lady being really angry, he eventually **sat** down at the table and grumblingly wrote out a prescription.

"**Oh! all** right, if you enjoy being plague-stricken. So long as I'm paid, **what** on earth **can it matter** to me? Look here; get this down his throat, a spoonful at a time, **every** hour; and here's another mixture for two baths, one **this** evening, the **other to-morrow.**"

For the **last instant or so Monsieur Charles** had been restless feeling disconsolate at seeing **the larks** burn, while the maid, tired of beating up the omelette, stood idly by. So he briskly gave Patoir his six francs 'consulting fee, and urged the others to **empty** their glasses.

" Anyhow, the breakfast's **got to be eaten. Ah! see you again soon.** The rain has given over."

They **left reluctantly,** and the veterinary, **getting into his rickety old trap, said once more:**

" A **cat that isn't worth the cord to chuck him into the** water with! **Well, that's just how it is, when people are well** off!"

But all of them, even **Buteau, who had grown pale with** sullen envy, shook their **heads in protest; and Delhomme** the wise declared:

" Say what you will, people who have managed to put by **an** income of twelve thousand francs can't be either idlers **or** fools."

The **veterinary had** whipped **up** his **horse, and the others** made **for the** Aigre, through **pathways now converted into** torrents. They had got **to** the seven or eight acres of meadow that were to be divided, **when the rain came down again in a** perfect deluge. **But** this **time they stuck** obstinately to the task, being desperately hungry, **and anxious to** get it over. Only one dispute delayed them, with **reference to** the third lot, which was treeless, whereas a copse happened to be distributed between the other two. However, all now seemed settled and sanctioned. The surveyor promised them he would forward

the memoranda to **the** notary, **to** enable him **to draw** up **the**
deed ; and it was agreed to defer the drawing **of the** lots **till**
the following Sunday, **when it** should take place at ten o'clock,
at the father's house.

As they returned **into Rognes, Hyacinthe** jerked **out an
oath :**

" **Wait, wait,** you dirty troll, and I'll **make** it pretty hot for
you ! "

By the grassy wayside, La Trouille was leisurely driving
her geese under the muttering downpour. At the head of the
dripping, delighted flock, walked the gander, and **when he**
turned his big yellow beak **to** the right, all the other big yellow
beaks went to the right too. The child, taking fright at her
father's words, sped home to see to the dinner, followed by a
file of long-necks, which **were all stretched out** in the rear of
the outstretched neck of the gander.

CHAPTER IV.

THE following Sunday happened to fall just on All Saints' Day, the first of November ; and, on the stroke of nine, the Abbé Godard, who was priest of Bazoches-le-Doyen, with subordinate charge of the ancient parish of Rognes, reached the top of the slope which led down to the little bridge over the Aigre. Rognes, more important in days of yore, but now reduced to a population of barely three hundred souls, had had no priest of its own for years, and seemed completely indifferent to the fact, insomuch that the municipal council had lodged the rural constable in the half-ruined parsonage.

So, every Sunday, the Abbé Godard walked the two miles between Bazoches-le-Doyen and Rognes. Being stout and dumpy, with a neck red at the nape and so swollen at the throat as to tilt his head backward, he compelled himself to this exercise for the sake of his health. On this particular Sunday, finding himself late, he was puffing terribly, with his mouth wide open in his apoplectic face, the fat of which half smothered his small snub nose and tiny grey eyes; and, despite the livid, snow-laden sky, and the premature frost which had followed the storms of the week, he was swinging his hat in his hand, having bared the thick tangles of his grizzled, carroty hair.

The road made an abrupt descent, and on the left bank of the Aigre, before reaching the stone bridge, there were only a few houses, a sort of suburb, through which the Abbé rushed tempestuously. He did not even cast a glance, either up or down stream, on the slow, limpid river winding through the meadows amid clumps of willows and poplars. On the right bank began the village proper, a double row of frontages edging the high road, while others climbed at random up the slope; and just past the bridge one found the municipal offices and the school, an old barn raised a floor higher and white-washed. For an instant the Abbé hesitated, and then craned his neck into the empty entrance-hall of the school. When he turned round, he cast a searching glance into two taverns facing him : the one having a neat shop-front, filled with flasks,

and surmounted by a little yellow wooden sign bearing
the inscription : *Macqueron, grocer*, in green letters; the other
merely having its door decorated with a holly-branch, and displaying in black upon a roughly-whitened wall the words :
Lengaigne. Tobacco. The priest was making up his mind to
enter a steep lane between these two houses, a short ascent
leading straight to the front of the church, when he caught
sight of an old peasant and stopped.

"Aha! so it's you, Fouan. I'm in a hurry, but I wanted
to see you. Tell me, what's doing? It's out of the question
for your son, Buteau, to leave Lise in the plight she's in, with
her figure unmistakably on the increase. She is one of the
'Handmaidens of the Virgin.' It's a disgrace, a disgrace!"

The old man listened, with an air of deferential politeness.

"Why, your reverence, what do you expect me to do, if
Buteau holds out? And, besides, the lad's right, so far as that
goes; he can't marry at his age on nothing."

"But there's a baby!"

"To be sure there is. Only the baby's not yet born, and
one can never tell. That's just where it is: a baby's not an
encouraging thing when you can't afford a shift for its back."

He made these remarks sagely, as became an old man
who knew life. Then he added, in the same measured tone :

"Besides, an arrangement may, perhaps, be made. I am
dividing my property. The lots will be drawn for presently,
after mass. Then, when Buteau gets his share, he will, I
hope, see about marrying his cousin."

"Good!" said the priest. "That's enough. Fouan, I
rely upon you."

The pealing of a bell curtailed his speech, and he asked,
apprehensively :

"That's the second bell, isn't it?"

"No, your reverence, the third."

"Good gracious! that brute of a Bécu at it again! Ringing
without waiting for me!"

He cursed, and ran violently up the pathway. At the top
he all but had a fit; he was puffing away like a blacksmith's bellows.

The bell rang on, while the ravens it had disturbed flew
cawing round the steeple, a fifteenth-century spire, which bore
witness to the ancient importance of Rognes. In front of the
wide, open door a group of peasants were waiting, among
whom the innkeeper, Lengaigne, a freethinker, was smoking
his pipe. Farther on, against the churchyard wall, farmer

Hourdequin, the mayor—a well-built man, with strongly-marked features—chatted with his assessor, the grocer Macqueron. When the priest had passed by with a salute, they all followed him, excepting Lengaigne, who ostentatiously turned his back, pulling at his pipe.

Inside the church, to the right of the porch, there was a man hanging on to a rope, which he still went on pulling.

" That'll do, Bécu!" said the Abbé Godard, beside himself. " I've told you twenty times to wait for me before you ring the third time."

The rural constable, who was also the bell-ringer, fell to his feet, aghast at his own disobedience. He was a little man of fifty, with the square, bronzed physiognomy of an old soldier, grey moustache and goatee, and a rigid neck, seeming as if he were continually choked by a tight collar. Already very tipsy, he stood to attention, without venturing to excuse himself.

Moreover, the priest had already made off, and was crossing the nave, with a glance at the seats. There was a scanty attendance. On the left, he as yet saw only Delhomme, present in his capacity of municipal councillor. On the right, the women's side, there were at the most a dozen. He recognised Cœlina Macqueron, shrivelled, sinewy, and over-bearing ; Flore Lengaigne, buxom, mild, and good-humoured ; and Bécu's good woman, a lanky, very dirty, dark brunette. But what put the finishing touch to his wrath was the behaviour of the " Handmaidens of the Virgin " in the front row. Françoise was there between two of her friends — the Macquerons' daughter, Berthe, a handsome brunette, brought up as a lady at Cloyes, and the Lengaignes' daughter, Suzanne, a fair, plain, bold-faced hussy, whom her parents were about to apprentice to a dressmaker at Châteaudun. All the three were indulging in unseemly laughter. And, beside them, poor Lise, plump and cheerful, faced the altar, exposing her scandalous condition to public comment.

Finally, the Abbé Godard was going into the sacristy, when he came across Delphin and Nénesse pushing each other about in play, whereas they were supposed to be getting the wine vases ready for mass. The first-named, Bécu's son, aged eleven, was a sun-burnt youngster, already well-knit, and just leaving school to become a ploughman ; while Ernest, Delhomme's eldest, of the same age, fair, slim, and given to loafing, always carried a looking-glass in his pocket.

" Now, then, you mischievous imps," cried the priest, " do you think you're in a cow-shed ? "

And turning towards a tall, thin, young man, whose sallow face bristled with a few light hairs, and who was arranging some books on the shelf of a cupboard, he added:

"Really, Monsieur Lequeu, you might keep them quiet when I am out of the way!"

This was the schoolmaster, a peasant's son, whose education had taught him to hate those of his own station. He resorted to violence with his boys, treating them like brute beasts, and cloaked Republican ideas under a scrupulously formal demeanour towards the priest and the mayor. He sang well in the choir, and even looked after the sacred books; but he had refused point-blank to ring the **bell, in spite of** custom, such a task being unworthy of a free man.

"**I am** not entrusted with maintaining order in church," he responded, dryly. "At my **place,** though, wouldn't I **just** box their ears!"

And as the Abbé, **without** answering, hastily shuffled **into** his alb and stole, he went on:

"Low mass, isn't it?"

"Yes, **to** be sure, **and** be **quick**! I've got to **be** at Bazoches by half-past ten for high mass."

M. Lequeu, who had taken an old missal from the cupboard, closed the latter and went out to place the book on the altar.

"Make haste, make haste," repeated the priest, hurrying Delphin and Nénesse.

And, still perspiring, still panting, with the chalice in **his** hand, he went back into the church and began the mass, **at** which the two urchins officiated with sly, quizzical side-looks. The church had but one aisle, with a vaulted, oak-panelled roof, falling to pieces through the obstinate refusal of the municipal council to allow any funds. The rain dripped through **the broken slates of** the roofing, deep stains marked the ad-**vanced state of decay** of the woodwork, and beyond the choir, shut off by a railing, a greenish leakage aloft disfigured the fresco of the apsis, cutting the figure of an Eternal Father, wor-shipped by angels, atwain.

When the priest turned, open armed, towards the congrega-tion, he calmed down a bit on observing that some people had come in—the mayor, his assessor, some municipal councillors, old Fouan, and Clou the farrier, who played the trombone when there was a musical service. Lequeu had remained, with a stately air, in the front row. Bécu, although drunk, stood bolt upright in the background. On the women's side, especially, the seats had filled up, Fanny, Rose, La Grande, and others had

come, so that the " Handmaidens of the Virgin," now **poring**
over their books in an exemplary way, had had to **crowd closer**
together. What particularly flattered the priest was to perceive
Monsieur **and** Madame Charles, with their grand-daughter
Elodie; **he in a black frock-coat,** she in a green silk dress, both
of them solemn and splendiferous, setting a good example.

Nevertheless, he hurried over his mass, mangling the
Latin and maiming the rites. In his address, not going into
the pulpit, but sitting on a chair in the middle of the choir, he
made a miserable exhibition of himself, lost the thread of his
discourse, and **gave up as hopeless the task of ever finding it
again.** Eloquence was not his strong point; he stumbled over
his words, **and hum'd and ha'd without ever being able to
finish his sentences,** which explained why his lordship the Bishop
had overlooked him for twenty-five years in his little cure
of Bazoches-le-Doyen. The rest of the service was vamped;
the bell-ringing, during the **elevation of the Host,** sounded
like electric signals **gone mad,** and the priest **dismissed** the
congregation **with an** "*Ite missa est*," **as** smart **as the crack**
of a whip.

The church was barely empty when the Abbé Godard re-
appeared, with his hat hasily put on wrong side foremost.
Before the door stood a **group of women—Cœlina, Flore, and**
old mother Bécu—all **much annoyed at having been raced along**
at that pace. **It was making very light of them to give them**
no more **on a high holiday.**

" I say, **your reverence,"** asked Cœlina, in her shrill **voice,**
as she stopped him : " **You've got a spite against us, packing**
us **off** just like a **bundle of rags."**

" Why, **it's** like this," he replied; " **my own** people are
waiting for me. **I can't be** both at Bazoches and at Rognes.
Get a priest of your own **if** you want high masses."

This was always a sore point between Rognes and **the Abbé,**
the villagers insisting on special attention, and he **strictly**
confining himself to what he was obliged to do for **a village**
which **refused to** repair its church, and where, **moreover,**
constant scandals discouraged **him.** Indicating the " Handmaidens of the Virgin," who were leaving together, he resumed :

" **And, besides,** is it decent to go through ceremonies with
young folks who **have no** respect whatever for God's com-
mandments ? "

" You don't mean that for my girl, I hope ? " asked Cœlina,
between her teeth.

" Nor for mine, *I'm* sure ? " added Flore.

Then he lost all patience and burst out :

" I mean it for those it concerns. It's as plain as a pike-staff. White dresses, indeed. A pretty thing! I never have a procession here without one of them being in the family way. No, no ; you'd tire out God Almighty himself."

He left them ; and Bécu's wife, who had remained silent, had to make peace between the two mothers, who, in consider-able excitement, were heaping reproaches on each other on their daughters' account. But her peace-making was of such a bitterly insinuating character that the quarrel rose higher.

Oh yes! They would see how Berthe would turn out, with her velvet bodices and her piano! And Suzanne, what a first-rate idea to send her to the milliner's at Châteaudun, so that she might go the pace with the best of them!

The Abbé Godard was rushing off, when he came full upon Monsieur and Madame Charles. A broad, beaming smile over-spread his face, and his hat performed a sweeping obeisance. Monsieur bowed majestically. Madame made her best curtsey. It was fated that the priest should never get off, for no sooner had he cleared the square than he was brought up by another chance encounter. This was with a tall woman of thirty, who looked quite fifty, with thin hair and a flat, flabby, bran-yellow face. Broken down and worn out by excessive exertion, she was staggering under the weight of a faggot of brushwood.

" Palmyre," he asked, " why didn't you come to mass on All Saints' Day? It's disgraceful."

" No doubt, your reverence," she groaned, " but what's to be done? My brother is cold, and we are freezing at home. So I've been picking up these along the hedges."

" La Grande is still as hard as ever, then?"

" Rather! She'd die before she'd chuck us a crust or a log."

In a dolorous voice she repeated her own and her brother's story : how their grandmother had turned them out of doors, how she had had to take refuge with her brother in an old deserted stable. Poor Hilarion, bandy and hare-lipped, lacked intelligence ; indeed, despite his twenty years of age, he was so idiotic that no one would give him employment. And so she was bringing herself to death's door in working for him, tending him with the impassioned care and untiring tenderness of a mother.

As the Abbé Godard listened to her, his coarse, perspiring face assumed a look of the purest kindness, his little angry eyes grew beautiful with charity, his large mouth took a sweetly sad expression. This formidable scold, always being whirled

D

to and fro **by** gusts of **wrath,** was passionately **devoted to the**
wretched, and gave them everything—his **money, linen, and**
clothes. To such **a** point that in all La Beauce **you would not**
find a priest with a rustier or **a more extensively darned cassock.**

He fumbled anxiously in his pockets, and slipped a five-franc
piece into **Palmyre's hand.**

" Here ! Put it away; I've none for anybody else. I
shall have to talk again to La Grande, since she's so
wicked."

This time he got clear off. Luckily, as **he was puffing and**
blowing up the slope on the other side of the Aigre, **the Bazoches**
butcher, on his way back, gave him **a lift in** his cart **; and he**
all but vanished as he gained **the level of the plain,** jolting **along**
with **the** dancing silhouette **of his three-cornered** hat **alone**
standing out against the leaden **sky.**

Meantime the **church square had emptied, and Fouan and**
Rose had **just gone down home, where they found Grosbois**
already **waiting. A little before ten, Delhomme and Hyacinthe**
arrived **in their turn ; but Buteau was waited for in vain till**
twelve.

The eccentric rascal never could be punctual. Doubtless
he had stopped on the road somewhere to breakfast. It was
proposed to go on without him; then, a vague fear inspired
by his hot-headedness led to the decision that the lots
should not be drawn for till two o'clock, after breakfast.
Grosbois, **accepting a bit of bacon and a glass of wine** from the
Fouans, finished up **one** bottle, started **on another,** and relapsed into his usual state of intoxication.

Two o'clock, and still no Buteau **appeared. So Hyacinthe,**
languishing for debauch, **like the rest of the village, that Sunday**
feast-day, **went lounging** past **Macqueron's. This succeeded:**
the door was flung open, and **Bécu appeared shouting :**

" Come along, you rascally baggage, **and let me treat you**
to a glass."

Bécu had got **stiffer still, assuming more and more dignity as**
his intoxication increased. **A drunken, old-soldierly fellowship,**
a secret affection, drew **him towards the poacher ; but he**
avoided recognising him when **he** was on duty with his **badge on**
his arm, being always on the point of catching him *flagrante*
delicto, **and** struggling between **duty** and inclination. In the
tavern, however, when he **was tipsy, he stood him treat** like a
brother.

" Take a hand **at** piquet, eh **?" said he ; "** and, by God, if the
Bedouins bore us, we'll slit their **ears for 'em !"**

They installed themselves at a table, and **played cards** boisterously, while quart after quart of wine was **served them.**

Macqueron, with his fat, moustachioed face, **sat huddled up** in a corner, twiddling his thumbs. Since he had **been gaining** money by speculating in the light **wines** of Montigny, **he had** fallen into idle ways—hunting, fishing, and playing the **gentleman;** though he remained filthy and ragged, while his daughter Berthe flounced **to** and fro in silk. If **his wife** had heeded him they would have shut up shop, giving up both the grocery and the refreshment business; for he was growing conceited, and had dim ambitions, as yet unrecognised by himself. But she was ferociously eager for gain, and he, although concerning himself personally about nothing, was content to let her go on serving tipple, just to annoy his neighbour Lengaigne, who kept the tobacco shop, and also dealt in drink. 'Twas a long-standing rivalry, ever smouldering, and ever ready to burst into a blaze.

Yet sometimes they were at peace for weeks together; and, as it happened, Lengaigne then came in with his son Victor, a tall, awkward youth, who was to draw for the conscription the next year. Lengaigne himself, a lanky, frozen-looking man, with a little owl's head set upon broad, brawny shoulders, had remained a peasant and tilled the soil, while his wife weighed out the tobacco and drew the wine. He derived a special importance from the fact that he was barber and hair-cutter to the whole village, an avocation which he had brought back from his regiment, and which he plied either at his shop, amid the eaters and drinkers, or else, if his customers preferred it, at their own homes.

" Well, this beard of yours, is it to be done to-day, my boy ? " he asked, from the door.

" Bless me! Right you are, I told you to come," cried Macqueron. " This very moment, if you like."

He reached an old shaving-dish from its hook, and took some soap and warm water, while the other drew from his pocket a razor the size of a cutlass, which he set about sharpening on a strop fixed to the case. A squeaky voice now issued from the adjacent grocery department :

" I say," cried Cœlina, " are you going to mess the tables which people drink at ? Well, then, you sha'n't! I won't have hair found in the glasses at *my* house."

This was an attack on the cleanliness of the rival tavern, where customers ate more hair than they drank genuine wine, she said.

"Sell your salt and pepper, and hold your row!" replied Macqueron, annoyed by this public curtain-lecture.

Hyacinthe and Bécu tittered.

"An extinguisher for the good lady that!" They ordered of her a fresh quart of wine, which she brought in speechless fury. Then they shuffled the cards, and dashed them violently on to the table, as if to exasperate each other. Trump, trump, and trump!

Lengaigne had already lathered his customer, and was holding him by the nose, when Lequeu, the schoolmaster, pushed the door open.

"Good-day, everybody!"

He stood silently in front of the stove, warming his loins, while young Victor, stationed behind the players, became absorbed in watching their game.

"By the by," resumed Macqueron, taking advantage of a moment when Lengaigne was wiping the lather off the razor on to his shoulder, "just now, before mass, Monsieur Hourdequin spoke to me again about the road. Things must be settled some way or another."

The road in question was the famous one direct from Rognes to Châteaudun, which was to shorten the distance by about two leagues, for vehicles were now forced to pass through Cloyes. Of course, the farm was much interested in this new route, and to carry the point the mayor relied greatly on his assessor—himself interested in a speedy settlement. There was a question of facilitating the approach of vehicles to the church, which could now only be reached by goat-paths, and the projected line of route followed the steep lane that wound its narrow way between the two taverns. Only broaden that, and level down the ascent a bit, and the grocer's grounds—which would be by the road-side, and of easy access—would increase tenfold in value.

"Yes," he continued, "it would seem that the Government, before giving us any help, is waiting for us to vote something. That's so, isn't it? You are in it."

Lengaigne, who was a municipal councillor, but who had not as much as a square inch of garden behind his house, replied:

"I don't care a curse! What the deuce has your road to do with me?"

Then, making an attack on the other cheek, which he rasped as with a nutmeg-grater, he fell foul of the farm. These latter-day gentle folks were even worse than the nobles of old.

Why, they had kept everything to themselves in the distribution of the land, made laws merely for their own advantage, and they lived only on the distress of poor folks. The others listened, constrained, yet inwardly pleased by his temerity, for they had the peasant's immemorial, unconquerable hatred of the landowner.

"It's a good thing we are among ourselves," muttered Macqueron, glancing uneasily at the schoolmaster. "I am on the Government side. So is our deputy, Monsieur de Chédeville, who is, they say, a friend of the Emperor's."

Lengaigne began furiously shaking his razor.

"And that's another pretty rogue of a fellow! Oughtn't a rich man like him, possessing more than two thousand acres of land over there towards Orgères, oughtn't he to make you a present of your road, instead of trying to wring coppers out of the village? The low beast!"

The grocer, alarmed this time, protested. "No, no. He's very straightforward, and not proud. But for him you wouldn't have had your tobacco-counter. What would you say if he took it away from you again?"

Abruptly calming down, Lengaigne went on scraping the other's chin. He had lost his temper and gone too far; his wife was right in saying that his ideas would play him false. At that moment a quarrel was heard to threaten between Bécu and Hyacinthe. The former was in an ill-tempered, pugnacious state of drunkenness, while the other, on the contrary, grim and overbearing though he was when sober, grew more and more maudlin with every glass of wine, subsiding into the genial meekness of a tipsy apostle. Add to this their radical difference of opinion: the poacher being a Republican—a Red, as people said—who boasted of having made the gentlefolks dance the rigadoon at Cloyes in '48; and the rural constable being a wild Bonapartist and worshipping the Emperor, with whom he pretended to be acquainted.

"I swear it! We had partaken of a red herring salad together, when he said to me: 'Not a word. I am the Emperor.' I knew him at a glance, because of his likeness on the five-franc pieces."

"Maybe! Anyhow, he's a low fellow, who beats his wife and never loved his mother!"

"Hold your tongue, in God's name! or I'll break your jaw for you!"

The quart bottle which Bécu was brandishing had to be taken from him; whilst Hyacinthe, with tearful eyes, sat

awaiting **the blow in** cheerful resignation. Then they resumed
their game, **like brothers.** Trump, **trump,** and trump!

Macqueron, **rendered** uneasy by **the** assumed indifference
of the schoolmaster, **finished** by asking **him** :

"And you, Monsieur Lequeu, what do *you* say ? "

Lequeu, who was warming his slender, sallow hands **against**
the stove-pipe, smiled the bitter smile of a superior person
who is compelled by his position to remain silent.

" I say nothing," he answered. " It's none of my business."

Macqueron soused his face in a basin of water, and while
spluttering and wiping himself dry, replied :

"Well, mark my words! I mean to do something. If the
road's voted, by God, I'll let 'em have my ground for nothing."

This declaration stupefied the audience. Even Hyacinthe
and Bécu looked up, despite their intoxication. There was a
pause. They gazed at Macqueron as if he had suddenly gone
mad ; and he, spurred on by the effect produced, yet with his
hands trembling at the engagement he was taking, added:

" There'll be something like half an acre. The man who
goes back on his word is a scoundrel ! I've sworn it!"

Lengaigne departed with his son Victor, exasperated and
disgusted by his neighbour's munificence. Land didn't cost
him much, the way he robbed people.

Macqueron, despite the cold, now took his gun, and went out
to see if he could come across a rabbit he had noticed in his
vineyard the day before. In the tavern there only remained
Lequeu—who spent his Sundays there without taking **anything**
to drink—and **the two gamblers, who were** poring over **their**
cards. Hours elapsed, while other peasants came and went.

Towards five o'clock the door was roughly pushed open,
and Buteau appeared, followed by Jean. Immediately he saw
Hyacinthe, he cried:

"I'd have wagered **five francs. Don't you care a damn**
for **anybody ?** We're waiting for you."

The drunkard, **slobbering** and merry, **replied** :

"That's a **good 'un!** I'm waiting for *you.* You've kept
us hanging **about since morning,** and I think **it cool of you to**
complain."

Buteau **had** stopped **at La Borderie, where** Jacqueline,
whom, at the age of fifteen, he had knocked head over heels in
the hay, had kept him to eat some hot buttered toast with Jean.
Farmer Hourdequin having gone to breakfast at Cloyes after
mass, the two sparks had kept it up pretty late, and had only
just reached the village in each other's company.

Meantime, Bécu yelled out that he would pay for the five quarts, but that the game was to stand over ; while Hyacinthe, reluctantly unfixing himself from his chair, followed his brother, chuckling to himself, with his eyes swimming in mildness.

" Wait there," said Buteau to Jean, " and in half an hour come and pick me up. You know you dine with me at father's."

When the two brothers had entered the sitting-room of the Fouans' house, they found the company assembled in full. The father was standing up with bent head. The mother, seated near the table in the middle, was mechanically knitting. Opposite her was Grosbois, who had eaten and drunk so much as to be in a state of doze, with his eyes half-open ; while, farther off, Fanny and Delhomme were waiting patiently on two low chairs. There were some unwonted articles in the smoky room, with its shabby old furniture and its utensils worn by scrubbing : a blank sheet of paper, an ink-bottle, and a pen stood on the table beside the surveyor's hat—a monumental, rusty-black hat with which he had trudged through rain and sunshine for ten years past. Night was falling, and through the narrow window came an expiring, murky glimmer, in which the flat brim and urn-like body of the hat loomed strangely.

Grosbois, always ready for business in spite of his intoxication, woke up and stammered out :

" Now we're right. I told you the deed was ready. I called yesterday at Monsieur Baillehache's, and he showed it me. Only the numbers of the lots are left blank after your names. So we will draw, and the notary need then only write in the lots and you can sign on Saturday at his place."

He roused himself and raised his voice : " Come, I will get the tickets ready."

Fouan's children abruptly approached, making no secret of their distrust. They watched Grosbois, and kept a sharp eye on his slightest movements, as on those of a conjuror capable of juggling away the shares. First he had cut the sheet of paper into three with his drink-sodden, shaking fingers ; now he was writing the figures 1, 2, 3, and enormous, strongly-marked figures they were. The others watched his pen over his shoulders, the parents themselves nodding their satisfaction on seeing the impossibility of deception. The tickets were slowly folded up and thrown into the hat. A solemn stillness reigned.

At the expiration of two long minutes Grosbois exclaimed :

" Well, you must make up your minds. Who begins ? "

No one stirred. The night deepened, and the hat seemed to grow larger in the gloom.

"By order of seniority, eh?" proposed the surveyor. "You begin, Hyacinthe, you're the eldest."

Hyacinthe, the amiable, came forward, but he lost his balance, and all but fell sprawling. He had violently shoved his fist into the hat as though with the purpose of extracting a mass of rock from it. When he had secured one of the tickets, he had to go to the window to see.

"Two!" cried he, evidently finding something exceedingly humorous in the figure, for he choked with laughter.

"Your turn, Fanny," now called Grosbois.

When Fanny had got her hand to the bottom, she did not hurry. She fumbled about, stirred the papers round, and seemed to weigh them one after the other.

"Picking and choosing's not allowed," said Buteau, savagely. He was suffocating with passion, and had turned pale on ascertaining the number drawn by his brother.

"Eh? Why not?" replied Fanny. "I'm not looking; surely I may feel."

"Get on," murmured the father; "there's nothing to choose between 'em; one's as heavy as the other."

At last she made up her mind, and ran to the window. "One!"

"Well, then, Buteau has number three," resumed Fouan. "Draw it, my boy."

In the growing darkness they had not seen how the face of the young man changed. He burst out in wrath:

"Never, never!"

"What?"

"If you think I'm going to assent to this, you're wrong! The third lot, eh? The bad one! I told you over and over again that I wanted a different division. But you pooh-pooh'd me! Besides, can't I see through your trickery? Oughtn't the youngest to have drawn first? No, I won't draw, since there's been cheating!"

The parents gazed at his wild movements as he gesticulated and stamped about.

"My poor boy, you're going crazy," said Rose.

"Oh, yes, mamma, I know well enough you never liked me. You'd strip the skin off my back to give it to my brother. You'd all of you eat me alive."

Fouan sternly interrupted him. "Enough of this folly! Will you draw?"

"It'll have to be done all over again."

At this there was a general protest. Hyacinthe and Fanny

clutched their papers as if a forcible attempt were being **made** upon them. Delhomme declared that the drawing had been **fair,** and Grosbois, much aggrieved, threatened **to leave if his** honesty were called in question.

" Then papa shall add a thousand francs **to my** share out **of** his hoard," said Buteau.

The old **man,** taken aback **for an instant,** stammered. Then he drew himself up **and** advanced **threateningly.**

" What's that you **say ?** So you're anxious to get me assassinated, you brute ? **Raze the house to the** ground and you won't find **a** copper. **Take that paper, or, by** God, you shall have nothing at all ! "

Buteau, with a hardened and **obstinate brow, did not quail** before **his father's raised fist.**

" No ! "

An awkward silence again fell. The huge hat was now an encumbrance and obstruction, with this solitary scrap of paper, which nobody would touch, inside it. The surveyor, to cut things short, advised the old man to draw it out himself. He did **so,** gravely, and went to the light to read it, as if the number were still unknown.

" Three ! You've the third lot, d'ye hear ? The deed **is** ready, and it's quite certain that Monsieur Baillehache **won't** alter it, for once done can't be undone. As you're sleeping here, I give you the night to think it over in. So that's done with. Let's say no more about it."

Buteau, wrapped in shadow, made no reply. The others noisily assented, **while** the mother at **last made up her mind to** light a candle so as to lay the cloth.

At that moment Jean, who was **coming to meet his** com**rade,** espied two **intertwined** shadows **watching, from** the dark deserted road, **the progress of events at the** Fouans. Feathery snow-flakes **were beginning to** flutter across the slate-grey sky.

" Oh, Monsieur Jean," said a **soft** voice, **" how** you frightened us ! "

Then he recognised Françoise's long face and thick **lips.** She was nestling against **her** sister Lise, **and had one arm** round **her waist,** while she **leant** her head on her shoulder. The two **sisters** adored **each other,** and were always seen about like this, hanging **on each other's neck.** Lise taller, and of pleasant aspect, despite **her large features** and **the** incipient development of **her whole plump person, bore** her misfortune with equanimity.

" You were spying, eh ? " Jean inquired gaily.

" Why, what's going on in there has an interest for me,"
replied Lise, freely and openly. " It's a point whether it will
make Buteau come to a decision."

Françoise, with her other arm, had now caressingly encircled
her sister's swollen figure.

" What a shame, the brute! When he's got some land,
p'raps he'll be looking out for some one better off."

But Jean gave them hope. The drawing of the lots must
have come to an end, and the rest was matter of arrangement.
When he told them he was to sup at the old folks' house,
Françoise added, as she turned away : " Well, we shall see you
presently ; we're going to the evening meeting."

He watched them disappear in the darkness. The snow
was thickening and embroidering their mingled dresses with fine
white down.

CHAPTER V.

AT seven o'clock, after dinner, the Fouans, Buteau, and Jean went to share the cow-house with the two cows which Rose had decided to sell. The animals, fastened up at the farther end, near the trough, kept the closed shed warm with the powerful exhalation from their bodies and their litter; whereas the kitchen, containing only three meagre, smouldering logs, left there after the cooking, was already chilled by the early November frost. So, in the winter, the evening meeting was held in the cow-house, on the trampled earth, snugly and warmly, with no other preparation than carrying in a small round table and a dozen old chairs. Each neighbour brought a candle in rotation. Tall shadows flickered over the bare, dust-begrimed walls, reaching up to the cobwebs on the beams; and from the rear came the warm breath of the cattle, that lay and chewed the cud.

La Grande was the first to arrive, with a piece of knitting. She never brought a candle, presuming on her great age, and she was held in such awe that her brother dared not remind her of the custom. She forthwith took the best place, drew the candlestick towards her, and kept it to herself, on the score of her failing eyes. She had rested the stick, which never left her, against her chair. Glittering flakes of snow were melting on the bristles which stuck up over her fleshless, bird-like head.

" It's coming down? " asked Rose.

" It is," she replied in her curt tones. And setting straightway to work with her knitting, she compressed her thin lips, never prodigal of speech, and cast a searching glance at Jean and Buteau.

The others made their appearance behind her. First Fanny, her son, Nénesse—Delhomme never came to the meetings—then, almost immediately, Lise and Françoise, who laughingly shook off the snow which covered them. The sight of Buteau made the former faintly blush. He looked at her unmoved.

" Been all right, Lise, since we last met ? "

" Pretty well, thanks."

" Glad to hear it."

Palmyre, meanwhile, had stolen in through the half-open door, and she was shrinkingly placing herself as far as possible from her grandmother, the redoubtable La Grande, when a tumult outside made her start up. Furious stammerings, tears, laughter, and yells were heard.

" Those rascally children are at him again!" cried she.

She had made a spring forward, and opened the door again. With a bold rush, and growling like a lioness, she rescued her brother Hilarion from the mischievous clutches of La Trouille, Delphin, and Nénesse. The last-named had just joined the other two, who were hanging round the cripple and yelling. Hilarion, breathless and scared, shambled in on his twisted legs. His hare's lip made him dribble at the mouth. He stuttered unintelligibly, was decrepit-looking for his age, and brutishly hideous like the cretin that he was.

He was in a very spiteful mood, quite furious at not being able to catch and clout the urchins who were teasing him. Once more he complained that he had been pelted with a volley of snow-balls.

"Oh! what a story!" said La Trouille, with an air of surpassing innocence. "He's bitten my thumb; look!"

At this Hilarion all but choked in his struggle to get his words out; while Palmyre soothed him, and, wiping his face with her handkerchief, called him her darling boy.

" There, that'll do," said Fouan at length. " You ought to be pretty well able to prevent his catching you. Sit him down, anyhow, and let him keep quiet. Silence, you brute, or you'll be sent back home with a flea in your ear."

As the cripple continued to stutter, with the intention of putting himself in the right, La Grande, with her eyes flashing fire, seized her stick and brought it down on the table so sharply as to make every one jump. Palmyre and Hilarion collapsed in affright and stirred no more.

Then the evening began. The women, gathered round the single candle, knitted, spun, or did needlework, that they never so much as looked at. The men, stolid and taciturn, smoked in the rear, while the children pushed and pinched each other in a corner, amid suppressed giggling.

Sometimes they told stories: that of the Black Pig which guarded a treasure with a red key in its mouth; or that of the Orleans beast, which had a man's face and bat's wings, with hair down to the ground, two horns, and two tails (one to lay hold with and the other to kill with), which monster had devoured a Rouen traveller, of whom nothing remained but his hat and boots.

At other times they told tales about the wolves which, for centuries, had devastated La Beauce. In days of old, when La Beauce, now stripped and bare, had a few clumps of trees left out of its primeval forests, countless packs of wolves, urged by hunger, issued forth in winter time to prey upon the flocks. Women and children were devoured, and the old country-folk remembered how, in heavy falls of snow, the wolves would enter the towns. At Cloyes, they would be heard howling in the Place Saint-Georges; at Rognes, they would sniff round the imperfectly closed doors of the cow-houses and sheep-pens. Then came a succession of hackneyed anecdotes: of the miller surprised by five large wolves, and putting them to flight by lighting a match; of the little girl chased for two leagues by a she-wolf, and eaten up just at her own door, where she tripped and fell; legends upon legends of wer-wolves, men changed to animals, who leaped upon the necks of belated travellers, and ran them to death.

But what froze the blood of the girls gathered round the slim candle, what made them take wildly to flight and scan the darkness apprehensively as they left the house, was the villany of the *Chauffeurs*,* the notorious Orgères band of sixty years ago, at the thought of which the whole country-side still trembled.

There were hundreds of them, tramps, beggars, deserters, spurious pedlars—men, women, and children, all living by robbery, murder, and debauchery. They were the descendants of the old armed and disciplined troops of brigands, and, taking advantage of the revolutionary disturbances, they laid formal siege to lonely houses, into which they burst like bombshells, breaking the doors in with battering-rams. When night came on, they issued forth like wolves from the forest of Dourdan and the copses of La Conie, the wooded lairs wherein they lurked; and, with the darkening shadows, terror fell upon the farmers of La Beauce, from Étampes to Châteaudun, and from Chartres to Orleans.

Of their many legendary atrocities, the one which was most popular at Rognes was the pillage of the Millouard farm, only a few leagues distant, in the Canton of Orgères. Beau-François, their noted chief, the successor of Fleur d'Epine, had with him that night his lieutenant, Rouge d'Auneau, Grand-

---

* Miscreants who scorched the feet of their prisoners till the latter revealed the whereabouts of their possessions.

Dragon, Breton-le-cul-sec, Lonjumeau, Sans-Pouce, and fifty others, all with blackened faces. First, they bayonetted into the cellar the farm people, the servants, the waggoners, and the shepherd. Then they " warmed " old Fousset, the farmer, whom they had kept by himself. Having stretched his feet over the glowing coals of the fireplace, they set his beard and all the hair on his body on fire with burning straw. Then they reverted to his feet, which they notched with the point of a knife for the flames to penetrate the better. At length the old man, having decided to reveal where his money was, they let him go and carried off considerable booty. Fousset, who had strength enough to drag himself to a neighbouring house, did not die till later on. The tale invariably concluded with the trial and execution of the Chauffeurs at Chartres, after they had been betrayed by Borgne-le-Jouy. Eighteen long months were devoted to preparing the case against the prisoners, and in the meanwhile sixty-four of the latter died in prison of a plague brought on by their filthy habits. Still the trial before the Assize Court dealt with a hundred and fifteen accused, thirty-three of whom were contumacious; seven thousand eight hundred questions were submitted to the jury, and finally there were twenty-three condemnations to death. On the night after the execution, the headsmen of Chartres and Dreux had a fight over the criminals' clothes, beneath the scaffold still red with blood.

Fouan, in alluding to a murder Janville way, thus once more recounted the abominations done at the Millouard farm ; and he had got as far as the song of complaint composed in prison by Rouge d'Auneau, when the women were alarmed by strange noises in the road—footsteps, struggles, and oaths. They grew pale, and listened in terrified expectation of seeing a gang of blackened men come in like bomb-shells. Buteau, however, bravely went and opened the door.

" Who goes there ? "

He at last perceived Bécu and Hyacinthe, who, at the conclusion of a quarrel with Macqueron, had just left the tavern, carrying with them the cards and a candle to finish their game elsewhere. They were so tipsy, and the company had been so frightened, that every one began to laugh.

" Come in, anyhow, and mind you behave yourself," said Rose, smiling at her tall vagabond son. " Your children are here, you can take them back with you."

Hyacinthe and Bécu sat down on the ground near the cows, placed the candle between them, and went on with their game. "Trump, trump, and trump!" The conversation had changed; the others were now talking of the youths in the neighbourhood who had to draw in February for the conscription—Victor Lengaigne and two others. The women had grown grave, and spoke slowly and sadly.

"It's no joke," resumed Rose: "no joke for any one."

"War, war!" murmured Fouan. "Oh, the harm it does! It's simply destruction to culture. When the youths leave us, our best hands go, as is easily seen when work-time comes. And when they come back, why, they're altered, and their heart is no longer with the plough. Cholera even is better than war!"

Fanny left off knitting.

"I won't have Nénesse go," she declared. "Monsieur Baillehache explained a sort of lottery dodge to us. Several people club together, each of them lodging in his hands a sum of money, and those who have unlucky numbers are bought off."

"People must be well off to do that," said La Grande, drily.

Bécu had caught a stray word or so between two tricks.

"War! Heart alive!" said he. "There's nothing like it for making men! When you've not been in it, you can't know. There's nothing like taking shot and steel as they come! How about yonder, among the blackamoors?"

He winked his left eye, while Hyacinthe simpered knowingly. They had both served in Algeria, the rural constable in the early days of the conquest, the other more recently, at the time of the late revolts. Accordingly, in spite of the difference in period, they had some reminiscences in common; of Bedouins' ears cut off and strung into chaplets; of oily-skinned Bedouin women seized behind hedges and corked up in every orifice. Hyacinthe, in particular, had a tale, which set the bellies of the peasants shaking with tempestuous laughter, a tale of a big lemon-coloured cow of a woman whom they had set a-running quite naked, with a pipe stuck in her.

"Zounds!" resumed Bécu, addressing Fanny: "You want Nénesse to grow up a girl, then? However, Delphin shall wear regimentals in no time, I promise you!"

The children had left off playing, and Delphin raised his hard bullet-like head, already even redolent of the soil.

"Sha'n't!" he said, bluntly and stubbornly.

"Hallo!" rejoined his father, "what's that? I shall have to teach you what bravery is, my traitor Frenchman."

"I won't go away; I'll stop at home."

The rural constable raised his hand, but was checked by Buteau.

"Let the child alone! He's right. Is he wanted? There are others. Why on earth should we be supposed to come into this world just to leave home and go and get our heads broken, on account of a lot of nonsense we don't care a copper about? I've never left the neighbourhood, and I'm none the worse for it."

He had, in fact, drawn a lucky number, and was a regular stay-at-home, attached to the land, and only acquainted with Orleans and Chartres, never having seen an inch beyond the flat horizon of La Beauce. He seemed to plume himself on having thus grown in his own soil, with the limited, lush energy of a tree. He had risen to his feet and the women were gazing at him.

"When they come back from serving their term, they're all so thin!" ventured Lise, in an undertone.

"And you, did you go far, corporal?" asked old Rose.

Jean was smoking in silence, like a contemplative young man who preferred listening. He slowly took his pipe out of his mouth.

"Yes, pretty far, one might say. But not to the Crimea. I was about to start when Sebastopol was taken. Later on, though, I was in Italy."

"And what's Italy like?"

The question seemed to perplex him. He hesitated, and ransacked his memory.

"Why, Italy's like home. There's farming there, and woods with rivers. It's the same everywhere."

"Then you fought?"

"Fought? Rather."

He had again begun to pull at his pipe, and did not hurry himself. Françoise, who had looked up, remained with her mouth half open, expecting a story. And, indeed, all of them were interested; La Grande herself thumped the table afresh to silence Hilarion, who was grunting, La Trouille having devised a little diversion by slyly sticking a pin into his arm.

"At Solferino 'twas warm work; yet, gracious! how it rained! I hadn't a dry thread on me; the water was running down my back and trickling into my shoes. Wet through we were, and no mistake!"

Everybody still waited, but he said no more about the battle. That was all he had seen of it. After a minute's silence, however, he resumed in his matter-of-course way:

"Goodness me! War isn't so bad as people think. **The** lot falls upon one, doesn't it? and one must do one's duty. I left the service because I liked other things better. But **it** may have its advantages for those who are sick of their trade, and who feel furious when the foe comes and tramples **on us** in France."

"It's a beastly thing, all **the same,**" **wound** up old Fouan. "**Each** man ought to defend **his own homestead,** and nothing more."

A fresh silence **fell. It** was **very warm, with a** damp animal **warmth, accentuated by** the strong **smell of the** litter. **One of the two cows got** up **and** relieved herself, and the dung splashed down softly and rhythmically. **From** the gloom of the rafters came the melancholy chirp of a cricket, and along the walls the lissom fingers of the **women,** plying their knitting-needles, played in shadow **to and fro,** looking **amid** the darkness like gigantic spiders.

Palmyre, taking the snuffers to trim the candle with, snuffed it so low as to extinguish it. A tumult followed. The girls laughed, **the children** stuck their pin into poor Hilarion's buttocks; **and** the meeting would have been quite upset if the candle brought by Hyacinthe and Bécu, who were nodding over their cards, had **not served** to re-kindle the other one, despite **its** long wick, **which had** swollen at the top into a kind of red mushroom. **Conscience-stricken at her** awkwardness, Palmyre quaked like **a** naughty child in **terror of** the lash.

"Come," said Fouan, "who will read **us a bit of** this, **to** finish the evening? Corporal, *you* ought **to read print very** well, now!"

He had been to **fetch** a greasy little book, **one** of **the** books of Bonapartist propaganda with which the Empire had flooded **the** country-side. It had come **out of a** pedlar's pack, and was a violent onslaught upon the old monarchy: a dramatised history **of the** peasant before and since the Revolution, with the lament-like **title of "** The Misfortune and Triumph of **Jacques** Bonhomme."

Jean had taken the book, and **instantly,** without waiting **to** be pressed, he **began to** read in a colourless, stumbling, school-boy tone, heedless of punctuation. They listened to him devoutly.

He started with **the** free **Gaul** reduced **to** slavery by the Romans, and **then** vanquished by the Franks, who transformed slaves into serfs, by establishing the feudal **system.** Then began the protracted martyrdom of Jacques Bonhomme, tiller **of** the soil, slave-driven and worked to death, century after century. Many towns-people revolted, founding corporations and acquiring the right of citizenship, but the enthralled peasantry, isolated and dispossessed of everything, only managed to free themselves at a later period, buying their manhood and their liberty for money. And what a delusive liberty it was! They were overwhelmed by exorbitant and ruinous taxes; their rights of ownership were ceaselessly called iuto question, and the soil was burdened with so many charges as to leave one merely flints to feed upon! Next began the terrible enumeration of the impositions that lay so heavy on the poor peasant No one could-draw up a full and accurate list, the taxes poured in so abundantly from king, bishop, and baron all at once. Three beasts of prey tore at the same carcase. The king had the poll-tax and tallage, the bishop the tithes, the baron laid a tax on everything, and turned everything into gold. The peasant had nothing left him to call his own — neither earth, water, fire, nor even the air he breathed. He paid for this, and he paid for that; paid to live, paid to die; paid for his contracts, flocks, business, and pleasure. Paid for having the rain-water from the ditches diverted on to his grounds; paid for the highway dust kicked up by his shee p in the drought of summer. Who ever could not pay was obliged to give his body and his time, tax-able and taskable without limit; forced to till the soil, to garner and reap, to trim the vines, clean out the château moat, make and repair the roads. Then there were the dues in kind; and the manor mill, oven, and wine-press, where he was forced to leave a quarter of his crop; and the imposition of watch and ward, which survived in money even after the demolition of the feudal keeps ; and the imposition of shelter and purveyance, which, whenever the king or baron passed by, sacked the cot-tages, dragged mattresses and coverlets from beds, and drove the owner out of his house—lucky not to have his doors and windows torn from their fastenings if he were at all dilatory in turning out. But the most execrated imposition, the re-membrance of which still rankled in the hamlets, was the salt-tax; with public store-houses for salt, and every family rated at a certain quantity, which they were, willy-nilly, com-pelled to purchase of the king; and the system of collec-tion was so iniquitous and despotic that it roused France to rebellion and drowned her in blood.

"My father," interrupted Fouan, "saw the time when salt was ninepence a pound. Truly, times were hard."

Hyacinthe sniggered in his sleeve, and endeavoured to lay

stress upon **those** indelicate rights to which the little book merely made a modest allusion.

" And how about **the** bridal rights, eh? **My word! The** baron popped his **legs into the** bride's bed **on the** wedding **night; and——**"

They silenced him. The girls, **even** Lise, notwithstanding her rotundity of form, had reddened deeply; while La Trouille and the two brats, with **their eyes turned** downwards, were stuffing **their fists into** their **mouths to restrain** their laughter. Hilarion drank in **every** word open-mouthed, **as if** he understood it all.

Jean went on. He had now got to the **administration of justice, the** three-fold justice of **king, bishop, and lord, which racked** the poor folk toiling **on the glebe. There was common law,** there was statute law, and, above all, there **was the arbitrary** right of might. No safeguard, no appeal against **the** all-powerful sword. Even **in** the ages which followed, when equity put in a protest, judgeships were bought, and justice was sold. **Worse** still was the recruiting system: a blood-tax which, **for a long time,** was only levied upon the inferior rural classes. **They fled into** the woods, but were driven thence in chains, with **musket-stocks, and** enrolled like galley-slaves. Promotion was denied **them. A** younger son, nobly born, **dealt in regiments as in goods** he had paid for; sold the smaller posts **to the highest bidder, and drove the rest of his** human cattle **to the shambles. Lastly came the** hunting rights, rights **of** dove-cot and **warren, which even** now, although abolished, have left a fierce resentment **in** the peasant's heart. The chase was an hereditary madness: an old feudal prerogative authorising **the** lord to hunt here and everywhere, and punishing with death **the vassal** audacious enough to hunt over his own ground. It was **the caging** under the open sky **of the** free beast and bird for **the pleasure of one** man. It was **the** grouping of fields into hunting-captaincies ravaged by game, without it being **lawful** for the peasant **to** bring down so much as a sparrow.

"That's intelligible," **muttered** Bécu, who would have fired at a poacher as soon as at a rabbit.

Hyacinthe had pricked up his ears, now that the hunting **question was dealt with, and he slily** whistled, as if **to say** that game belonged **to those who knew how to** kill it.

" Ah! dear me!" said Rose, simply, fetching a deep sigh.

They all felt the need of similar relief. The reading was gradually bearing heavy upon **them,** with the oppressive weight of a ghost story. Nor did **they always** understand, which doubled their uneasiness. Things having gone on like that in olden times, might easily become the same again.

"Go on, poor Jacques Bonhomme," read Jean in his drawling, schoolboy way: "shedding your sweat and blood; you are not yet through your troubles."

And the peasant's Calvary was set forth. Everything was a source of suffering to him: mankind, the elements, his own self. Under the feudal system, when the nobles sallied forth to seek their prey, it was he who was hunted, tracked down, and made booty of. Every private war between lord and lord ruined if it did not slay him; his hut was burnt, his field laid waste. Later on came the "great companies,"—the worst of all the scourges that ever made our country districts desolate, —bands of adventurers at the beck and call of any one who would pay them; now for France, now against her, marking their passage with fire and sword, and leaving only bare earth behind them. The towns, thanks to their walls, might hold out, but the villages were swept away in that murderous madness which pervaded the centuries from end to end. There were centuries steeped in blood—centuries during which our unfortified districts never ceased to moan with pain: women were violated, children crushed to death, men hanged. Then, when war gave over, the king's tax collectors made provision for the continued torture of the poor; for the number and the magnitude of the taxes were nothing in comparison to the wonderful and fearful method of their collection. Villain-tax and salt-tax were farmed out; injustice presided over the distribution of all the impositions; armed troops extorted payment of treasury-dues in the same way as one might raise a contribution of war. Insomuch that scarcely any of the money ever reached the State coffers, being appropriated on its way, and dwindling more and more at every fresh pair of pilfering hands it passed through. Then famine interposed. The tyrannical folly of the law, causing the stagnation of commerce and preventing the free sale of grain, produced terrible dearths every ten years or so, whenever the season was too hot or the rains were too prolonged,—dearths which seemed chastisements of Heaven. A storm flushing the rivers, a dry spring, the smallest cloud, the slightest sunbeam that marred the crops laid thousands of human beings low, involving agonies of starvation, a sudden and general rise of prices, and periods of awful anguish, during which men browsed like brute beasts on the grass of the ditches. After war and famine, fatal epidemics set in, and killed those whom the sword and hunger had spared. Corruption ever sprang forth anew from ignorance and uncleanliness: there was the great Black Death, whose gigantic spectre looms above the old time, mowing down with its sickle the wan, melancholy dwellers in the country districts.

Then **his burden** being greater than he could bear, Jacques **Bonhomme revolted.** Behind **him** lay centuries of terrified **submission, his shoulders inured to the last,** his spirit so **crushed that he felt not** his own degradation. It was possible **to beat and** beat him; to famish him, and rob him of all he had, **without** rousing him from the timid **stupor** into which he had **sunk,** pondering confused thoughts that signified nothing even to himself. But some last injustice, some last anguish, made him suddenly spring at his master's throat like a maddened, over-beaten domestic animal. So for ever, from century to century, **the same** exasperation bursts forth, and the Jacquerie **arms the tillers** of the soil with pitchfork and bill-hook, as soon as **they** have nothing left them but to die. There were the Chris-**tian "** Bagandes " of Gaul, **the** " Pastoureaux " of the Crusades, **and in** later times **the " Croquants " and "** Nu-pieds " who fell **upon the nobles and royal** soldiers. After four hundred years the **cry of the Jacques, in their** pain and wrath, was again to sweep **over the desolate** fields, and make the masters quake in their **castle strongholds.** What if they once more became angry, they **who had numbers on** their **side ?** What if they claimed their share **of** worldly joy **? And the** vision of old sweeps by: sturdy, half-clad, tattered hordes, mad with brutality and lust, spreading ruin and destruction, as they too had been ruined and destroyed, and violating in their turn **the wives of others.**

" Calm thyself, dweller in the fields," pursued Jean, in his placid, sedulous style, **" for** thy **hour** of triumph will soon **strike** from the clock of history."

Buteau had brusquely shrugged **his** shoulders. A pretty **piece of** work, revolting. **To** be **laid hold** of by gendarmes. **Oh, yes !** All the **others, moreover, since** the little book had **begun to relate their forefathers' risings, had listened** with **downcast eyes, not** venturing **on the least** gesture, but full of mistrust **although at home.** These were things no one ought to talk about **openly ; no one need know** what they thought **on** the subject. **Hyacinthe, having tried** to interrupt, announcing that he would shortly **be at the** throats of more than one, Bécu violently declared **that all** Republicans were pigs, and Fouan had to silence **them,** solemnly, with the subdued gravity of an old man who knows a thing or two but won't **speak.** La Grande, while the other women seemed to become more interested than **ever** in their knitting, observed : " What one has one keeps "—a remark which did not appear to have any connection with what was being read. Françoise alone, her work dropping on her lap, gazed at Corporal, amazed at **his** reading so long without making a mistake.

" Ah, dear me ! **Dear** me ! " repeated **Rose, sighing more deeply.**

The style of the book **changed. It became lyrical, and** magniloquently celebrated the Revolution. **'Twas then, in the** apotheosis of '89, that Jacques Bonhomme triumphed. **After** the taking of the Bastille, **while** the **peasants** burned **the** châteaux, the night of the 4th **of August** legalised **the con-quests of centuries by recognising the freedom of man and the** equality of civil rights. " In one **night, the ploughman had be-**come the equal of the **lord** who, by virtue **of his parchments, had** drunk the peasant's sweat and devoured the **fruits of his toilsome** nights." **Abolition of** serfdom, **of all the privileges of the** nobles, of the ecclesiastical **and manorial courts of justice ; the** re-purchase of vested rights, **the equalisation of taxation, the** admission of every citizen to all **civil or military** offices—so **the list went on. The evils of the old life seemed to vanish one by one.** It was the **hosanna of a new golden age dawning for the** ploughman, who was made the **subject of a whole pageful of** eulogy, and hailed as king and **foster-father of the world. He** only was of importance : **down on your knees before his** holy plough ! The horrors of '93 **were stigmatised in burning** words, and the book **wound up with a high-flown panegyric** on Napoleon, the child **of the Revolution, who had succeeded** in " extricating it from **the grooves of License, to ensure the** happiness of the rural **districts."**

" That's **true** ! " from **Bécu, as Jean turned to the last page.**

" **Yes,** that's true," **said old Fouan. " We had** fine **times of it,** I can tell **you, when I was young. I** saw Napoleon once, **at** Chartres. **I was twenty. We** were free ; we had land ; **it was first-rate ! I** mind **how my** father once said that he sowed coppers **and** reaped crowns. Then we had Louis XVIII., Charles X., **and** Louis Philippe. Things still went on ; we had **enough to eat, and** couldn't complain. And **now** we've got Napoleon **III., and things weren't so bad, either, up** to last year. **Only——"**

He meant **to break off, but the words forced** their **way.**

" Only, what **the odds does it make** to Rose **and me,** their liberty and **their equality ? Are we** any the fatter **for it,** **after** toiling and **moiling for fifty years ? "**

Then, in a few slow and hesitating words, he unwittingly
summed up the whole of this tale. The soil so long tilled for
the lord's benefit by the cudgelled and naked slave, whose skin
was not even his own—the soil, fertilised by his efforts, passionately loved and desired during close constant intimacy, like
another man's wife, whom one tends, embraces, but must not
possess—the soil, after centuries of such longing torment, at
length taken full possession of, becoming one's own, a love-
dalliance and life-spring. This desire of ages, this hope constantly delayed, explained the peasant's love for his field, his
passion for land, for the utmost quantity possible, for the loamy
soil, palpable to the touch, and poiseable in the palm of the
hand. And yet the indifference and ingratitude of this earth!
Worship it as you would, it never warmed **nor** produced **one**
grain the more. Too much rain rotted the seeds, hail **ravaged**
the green wheat, a thunderstorm laid the stalks low, **two months'**
drought shrivelled the ears : and what with **devouring insects,**
nipping frosts, cattle plagues, and leprosies **of** noxious **weeds,**
everything conspired to bring ruin ; the struggle was a daily
one, every mistake a danger, one's faculties were **ever** at full
stretch. Surely he had never hung back ; had worked body
and soul, and **had** maddened to find his toil insufficient. He
had withered his sinews, had withheld nothing of himself from
this soil that, after having barely fed him, left him wretched,
unsated, ashamed of his senile impotence, to seek the **arms**
of another, without so much **as a** pitying thought for **those**
poor **bones of** his that would soon **be** earth.

"And that's where it is!" went on the old **fellow.** "In
youth we're always hard at it ; and, having contrived **with**
great difficulty to make both ends meet, **we** find ourselves **old,**
and have to quit. Isn't it so, Rose?"

The mother bent her trembling **head. Great** heaven, yes!
She, too, had worked harder than **a man, for** certain. Rising
before the rest of the household, getting the meals, sweeping,
scouring, wearing herself out over a thousand duties—the
cows, the pigs, the baking—and always the last in bed. She
must **have** had a strong constitution not to have broken **down**
altogether, and her only reward **was** to have lived her **life.**
One got nothing but wrinkles, and one was lucky if, after pinching and screwing, **after going** to bed in the dark and putting up
with bread and **water, one saved just enough to** keep the wolf
from the door in **one's old age.**

"All the same," resumed Fouan, "we mustn't complain.
I've heard tell there **are** districts where the land gives a deal

more trouble. Thus, in **Le** Perche, there's nought but flintstones. In La Beauce, the **ground is** still soft, and only wants good, steady work. **But it's** spoiling. It's certainly less fertile than formerly, **and fields that once gave crops of seven quarters now** yield **little more than five. And for a** year **past the prices** have **been** going **down. They** say that **corn is coming in from** savage **parts. There's** some mischief **brewing—a crisis, as** they say. **Is misfortune ever at an end?** This **universal** suffrage, now, **it don't bring meat to the pot, does it? The land tax** weighs **us down, they keep on taking our children away to** fight. **It's not a bit of use having revolutions, it's six of one and half a dozen of the other, and a peasant always remains a peasant.**"

The methodical Jean had been waiting to finish his reading. Silence being re-established, he went on softly :

" Happy husbandman, forsake not the village for the town, where **everything—milk, meat,** vegetables—must **be** bought, **and where you would** always spend more **than** necessary, because of **the opportunities** offered. Have you not fresh air and sunshine, **healthy toil, and honest** joys in the village ? Rural life is **peerless; far from** gilded pomp, you enjoy true happiness; **in proof thereof, do not the town artisans** go for jaunts into **the** country, **just as the tradesman's one dream** is to seek **retirement** near **you,** culling flowers, eating **fruit off the tree, and** gambolling **on** the sward. **Be sure,** Jacques Bonhomme, **that** money **is** but a **chimera. If your bosom be at peace, your** fortune is made.**"

Jean's voice faltered. **He was fain to repress his emotion,** this big, tender-hearted, **town-bred fellow, whose soul** was touched by **these** pictures **of rustic bliss.** The others remained **gloomy;** the women bending **over their** needles, **the** men stolid **and moody.** Was the book making **game** of them ? Money was the only desirable thing, **and** they were starving in penury. **As the young** fellow found this silence—heavy with suffering **and spleen—rather** oppressive, he ventured on a sage reflection :

" Anyhow, things would, perhaps, be better with education. People **were wretched in** former times because they **knew** nothing. **Now-a-days we know a** little, and times are certainly easier. So the **thing is to be** taught thoroughly, and have schools of agriculture.**"

Fouan, an old **fogey averse to** new-fangled ways, interrupted him violently :

" Come, hang you and your science ! The more a man knows the worse he gets on. I tell you the land gave a better

yield fifty years ago? **It** gets angry at being **worried so, and**
never gives more than it chooses, the beggar! Hasn't **Mon-**
sieur Hourdequin run through his own weight **in silver,**
pottering about **with new** inventions? No, no; a peasant **is**
bound to remain **a peasant,** that's flat!"

Ten **o'clock was** striking, **and** after this conclusive remark,
as weighty **as the** chop of an **axe,** Rose got up to fetch a pot of
chestnuts, **which** she had left **in** the hot ashes in the kitchen.
This was the usual treat on All Hallow E'en. She even brought
two quarts of white wine **to** make the **festival** complete. Thenceforward **stories** were forgotten, **the fun grew** fast and furious,
and nails and teeth alike were **busy extracting the** steaming
boiled chestnuts from their husks.

La Grande at once pocketed her share, as she **was slower at**
eating than the others. Bécu and Hyacinthe gulped theirs
down, **skin** and all, **pitching them into** their **mouths from a**
distance; while Palmyre, grown bold, cleaned **hers** with extreme
care, and stuffed Hilarion with them, as if he were a fowl. **As** for
the children, **they** " made pudding." La Trouille dug one tooth
into the **chestnut, and** then squeezed it so as to cause a thin
stream **to spurt out,** which Delphin and Nénesse licked up.
This being **very nice,** Lise and Françoise decided to do the same.
Then the **candle** was snuffed **for** the last time, and glasses **were**
clinked **to the** good fellowship of all **present.** The heat **had**
increased; **a** ruddy vapour rose from the liquid manure; **the**
cricket chirped **more** loudly in **the** great shifting shadows **of**
the rafters; and, so that the cows might join **in** the festivities,
they were given some husks, which they munched with **a** subdued and measured noise.

Finally, at half-past ten, the **party broke** up. First of **all**
Fanny led Nénesse away. Then **Hyacinthe** and Bécu went out
quarrelling, the outer cold **bringing on** a relapse of intoxication; and La Trouille **and Delphin** were soon heard sus-
taining their respective **parents,** prodding them and restoring
them **to** the right **path, as if they** were restive animals forgetful
of the **way to** the **stables. Every** time **the** door swung to, **an**
icy gust **blew in from the snow-white** road. La Grande **did**
not hurry **at all, as she twisted her** handkerchief round her **neck**
and pulled **on her mittens. Not a** glance did she vouchsafe towards **Palmyre** and Hilarion, who slunk timidly away, shivering in their **rags;** but, eventually betaking herself back to her
home, which was adjacent, she slammed the door violently
after her. There only remained Françoise and Lise.

" I say, Corporal," asked Fouan, " you'll see them on their

way as you go back to **the farm, won't you?** It's on your way."

Jean nodded **assent, while the two girls were wrapping their** shawls round **their heads.**

Buteau **had** got **up** and was pacing to **and fro in the cow-house, grim,** restless, and preoccupied. Since **the reading he** had been silent, **as** if **engrossed** by **the** book's **tales about the** laboriously acquired land. **Why** not have the whole? **A division** had become intolerable to **him.** And there **were other things besides** confusedly jostling each other **within his thick skull: wrath,** pride, a dogged resolve **to keep to his word, the** exasperated craving of the man **who would like, and yet will** not, for fear **of being taken advantage of. However, he abruptly** came to a decision.

"I am going up to bed. Good-bye!" he said.

"How good-bye?"

"I shall start for La Chamade before daybreak. Good-bye, in case **I don't see** you again."

His **father and** mother, shoulder to shoulder, had **planted** themselves in **front of** him.

"Well, **and your share?" said Fouan.** "Do you accept it?"

Buteau **walked as far as the door, then, turning round:**

"No!" **he replied.**

The old peasant **trembled in every limb.** He drew himself up to his full height, **and his ancient authority flashed forth for the** last time.

"Very good. **You are a** wicked son. **I shall give your** brother and sister **their shares,** and shall let **them farm** yours; and when I die, **I shall arrange for** them to **keep it. You** shall have nothing. **Be off with you!"**

Buteau did not flinch **from his rigid attitude.** Then Rose, in her turn, tried **to soothe him.**

"Why, you **are just as much cared** for as **the** others, silly! You're only **quarrelling with your** bread and **butter.** Accept!"

"No!" **And** then **off he** went, going up **to** bed.

Outside, **Lise** and Françoise, aghast at the scene, walked **a few** steps **in** silence. They had again taken one another's **waist,** and their figures mingled, looking quite black against the **snow** which glimmered through the night. **Jean, who** followed **them,** also in silence, presently heard **them crying.** He then tried to cheer them up.

"Come, come, he'll **think** better **of it; he'll say yes to-morrow."**

" Ah, you don't **know him !** " cried Lise. " **He'd be cut to** pieces sooner than give **way.** No, no, it's **all over !** "

Then, despairingly, **she added :**

" What *shall* I do **with his child ? "**

" Well, it'll have to come any way," murmured Françoise. This made them laugh. But their spirits were too low, and they began to **cry again.**

When **Jean had seen** them to their door he **made the** best of his **way across the plain.** It had left off snowing ; the sky **was** once **more** clear **and** bright ; a wide, star-spangled, frosty sky it was, shedding **a** crystalline blue light ; and La Beauce extended **afar,** quite white, **and level** and still **like a sea** of ice. Not **a** breath came **from** the **distant horizon ; he heard** nothing but **the tramp of** his **own thick shoes on the hard soil.** 'Twas a **deep calm, the** peacefulness **of the cold. All that Jean had** read was whirling in his brain. **He took off his cap to cool himself,** feeling **an** oppression **behind his ears, and wishing to** escape **from** thought. The **idea of that girl with child and her** sister annoyed him **too. The tramp of his thick shoes still** rang out. Then **a shooting-star started down the sky, furrowing** it with **fire in its silent flight.**

Over **there, the farm of La Borderie was** vanishing from sight, hardly **forming as much as a bump on the** white expanse of snow ; and **as soon as Jean had entered the** cross-path, he remembered **the field he had sown in the** vicinity some days before. **Looking to the left, he recognised it** under the winding-sheet that covered it. **The layer of snow,** of the lightness and purity of ermine, **was a thin** one, leaving **the** crests of the furrows apparent, **and but** imperfectly veiling the earth's benumbed limbs. **How** soundly must the seeds be sleeping ! How deep **a** rest **in those** icy flanks until the warm morn, when **the** Spring sun **would** again **awaken** them to life !

PART II.

CHAPTER I.

IT was four o'clock; the dawn was barely breaking: the pink dawn of early May. Under the glimmering sky the buildings of La Borderie still slept, half in gloom: three long buildings on three sides of the vast square yard, the sheep-cot at the end, the barns on the right, the cow-house, stable, and dwelling-house on the left. Closing the fourth side, the cart-entrance was shut, and secured by an iron bar. On the manure-pit a big solitary yellow cock sounded the reveille in brilliant, clarion tones. A second cock made answer, then a third, and thus the call was caught up and passed on from farm to farm throughout the length and breadth of La Beauce.

On that night, as on most other nights, Hourdequin had joined Jacqueline in her bed-room, a little servant's room that he had allowed her to embellish with flowered wall-paper, chintz curtains, and mahogany furniture. Despite her growing power, she had encountered violent opposition whenever she had made an attempt to share with him the room formerly occupied by his deceased wife, the conjugal chamber which he protected out of some remnant of respect. She was much hurt at this, understanding that she would never be the real mistress until she slept in the old oak bedstead with red cotton hangings.

Jacqueline awoke at early dawn and lay on her back, with her eyelids wide open, while the farmer was still snoring beside her. Amid the exciting warmth of the bed, her black eyes were still dreamy, and her nude, slim, girlish form was throbbing. Nevertheless, she hesitated; then, making up her mind, she lightly stepped across her master—moving so lightly and so deftly that he did not feel her—and noiselessly slipped on a petti-coat with hands feverish with her sudden desire. However, as she happened to knock against a chair, he, in his turn, opened his eyes.

"Why, you're dressing! Where are you going?"

"I'm anxious about the bread, and am going to look at it."

Hourdequin dozed off again, mumbling, astonished at the

excuse and with his brain at work amid his drowsiness. What an odd notion. The bread didn't need her at that time in the morning. And, goaded by a sharp suspicion, he **all at once** became wide awake. Amazed at seeing her no longer there, he **gazed** wanderingly round this servant's room, at his slippers, his pipe, and his razor. What! another freak of passion of that baggage for some farm hand? During the couple of minutes he needed to recover himself, he took a retrospect of the past.

His father, Isidore Hourdequin, was the descendant of an old **peasant** family of Cloyes, refined **and raised** to the middle **classes in the** sixteenth century. All of them had held posts in the salt-revenue: one had been granary-keeper **at** Chartres; another, controller at Châteaudun; and Isidore possessed **some** sixty thousand francs when, at twenty-six years of age, on being deprived of his office by the Revolution, he conceived the **idea** of making a fortune out of the thefts of those scoundrelly republicans who offered the national property for sale. He had an admirable knowledge of the district, he sniffed round, made calculations, and at last paid thirty thousand francs—a bare fifth **of the** true value—for the three hundred and seventy acres of La Borderie, which was all that remained of the ancient demesne of the Rognes-Bouquevals. Not a single peasant had dared **to** risk his crowns; only townsfolk, pettifoggers, and financiers derived profit from the Revolutionary proceedings. Besides, it was purely a speculation, for Isidore had no intention of encumbering himself with a farm. He reckoned confidently on selling it at its full value when the disturbances were **over,** and thus getting his money **back five-fold.** But the Directory came on, and the depreciation of property continued; so that he **could** not sell to the expected advantage. His land held him in its grasp, and he became its prisoner; insomuch that, obstinately unwilling to let any of **it go, he resolved to farm** it himself, **in the** hope of thus at **last** realising his dreams of fortune. **About** this time he **married** the daughter of a neighbouring **farmer who brought him a** hundred and twenty acres, so that **he now owned some five** hundred; and it was thus that this townsman, **sprung** three centuries previously from a peasant stock, **returned to** tillage. To tillage on a large scale, however; **to** the landed aristocracy that had replaced the old all-powerful feudalism.

Alexander Hourdequin, his only son, was **born in** 1804. He had commenced his studies, discreditably enough, at the college **of** Châteaudun. He had a passion for land, and decided to return

home and help his father, disappointing another dream of the
latter, who, finding his fortune advance but slowly, would
have liked to **sell** everything off and start his son in some
liberal **profession.** The young man was twenty-seven, when,
on the **death of his** father, he became master of **La** Borderie.
He was **a** champion of new methods; his first care, in marrying,
was to look out, not for property but for money, for, according
to him, if the farm stagnated, the fault lay in lack of capital.
The **dower** he **desired,** amounting **to fifty** thousand **francs, was**
brought him by a sister of the notary, Baillehache, **a ripe**
damsel, his senior by five years, extremely ugly, but **good-**
tempered. Then began a long struggle between the **farmer**
and his property; at first **a** prudent **one, but gradually**
made feverish by **mistakes:** a struggle **renewed every**
season, every **day,** which, without making **him** rich, enabled him **to lead the broad life of a big** full-blooded man,
resolved **to deny himself no gratification.** For several years
things went from bad **to worse.** His **wife had presented**
him with two children: a boy who had enlisted **out of distaste**
for farming, and who had been made a captain after Sol-
ferino; and a delicate, charming girl, the apple of his eye, **and**
the heiress of La Borderie, now that his ungrateful son had
become a soldier of fortune. But he lost his wife, and, **two**
months later, his daughter. This was a terrible shock. **The**
captain had left off coming to La Borderie save once a **year, and**
the father all at once found himself alone in the world, **without a**
future, without the stimulus of working for his progeny. **But**
bleed as the wound might internally, he remained outwardly
erect, violent, and overbearing. Before **the peasantry, who**
sneered at his machines, and longed **for the fall of this middle-**
class man that presumed to dabble **in** their occupation, he stood
firm. Besides, what could **he do?** He was ever the closer
prisoner of his land. The accumulated labour, and the capital
sunk, shut him in more tightly **every day,** and left him no
possible outlet **but** through disaster.

Hourdequin, square shouldered, broad and florid in face,
retaining no other token of middle-class refinement than his
small hands, had always been despotically virile towards his
female servants. Even in his wife's time he had ravished them
all, as a mere matter-of-course, a thing of no further importance.
If those daughters of poor peasants that take to dressmaking
occasionally avoid a fall, not one of those that take service in
farms escape man: servant or master. Madame Hourdequin was
still alive when Jacqueline was engaged, out of charity, at La

Borderie. Cognet, an old drunkard, used to beat her black and
blue; and she was so weazened and scraggy that the bones of
her body showed through her rags. Moreover, she was of such
reputed ugliness that children used to hoot at her. She would
have been taken for under twelve, though in reality she was
then nearly eighteen. She helped the servant, and **was** employed in menial work—in washing up, sweeping the yard, and
keeping the live-stock clean—and she **became** more and more
grimy, as if dirt were a delight **to her.** **After the** death of the
mistress, however, she seemed **to get a bit cleaner.** All the
servants used to turn her up in **the straw : not a** man came to the
farm without doing what he chose with her ; and one day, as she
went down with her **master** into the cellar, he also, though
previously disdainful, tried to see what the ill-favoured slattern
was like. But she resisted furiously, and scratched and **bit**
him so effectually that he was obliged to let her go.

From that moment her fortune was made. She resisted for
six months, and then yielded herself up, a little bit at a time.
From the yard she rose **to the** kitchen as servant proper ; **next**
she engaged a **girl as** help; then, grown quite the lady, she
had a maid of **her own.** Now the little scullion had become
a stylish, pretty-looking girl, extremely dark, with a firm breast
and strong supple limbs, such **as** develop in those previously
made unduly thin by **hardship.** She became coquettish and
extravagant, smothering **herself with all** sorts of scents,
but retaining withal a leaven **of uncleanliness. The** people
of Rognes, the neighbouring farmers, **were** none the less
amazed at the intrigue. Was it actually possible that a man
of substance should take a fancy to a wench like that, neither
beautiful nor plump—in short, " La **Cognette,**" the daughter of
that drunkard Cognet, who might have **been seen for** the last
twenty years breaking stones on the **public** highway ! A
fine papa-in-law ! And **a pretty piece of** goods she was !
The peasants did not **even comprehend** that this " piece of
goods " was their vengeance, the revenge of the village upon
the farm, of the wretched tiller of the soil upon the enriched
townsman who had become a large landholder. Hourdequin, at
his critical age of fifty-five, gradually became the slave of
his fleshly desires, feeling physical need of Jacqueline, **as one**
has the physical needs of hunger and thirst. When she chose
to be especially agreeable, she would twine round him cat-like,
and satiate him with unscrupulous, brazen shamelessness, such
as courtezans do not venture upon ; and for one of those hours
he humbled himself and begged of her still to stay after quarrels

and terrible spasms of resolution, in which he threatened to kick
her out of doors.

Only the evening before he had all but struck her, at the
close of a stormy attempt she had made to sleep in the bed where
his wife had died; and she had refused his embraces all night,
beating him away each time he approached; for, though she
constantly indulged herself with the farm servants, she kept
him on short commons, whetting his passion by abstinence so as
to augment her power over him. And thus that morning, in that
moist room, in that tumbled bed where her presence still
breathed, anger and desire again seized hold of him. He had
long had scent of her many infidelities, and now he leapt out of
bed, crying aloud: "The strumpet! If I only catch her!"

He dressed rapidly and went down stairs.

Jacqueline had flitted through the silent house in the first
faint glimmer of dawn. As she crossed the yard she gave a
start on seeing the old shepherd, Soulas, already up. But her
desire was so strong that she paid no heed. So much the
worse! She slipped past the stable, accommodating fifteen
horses, where four of the farm waggoners slept, and made for
the garret at the end where Jean had his bed—some straw and
a coverlet, but no sheets. Embracing him in his sleep, closing
his mouth with a kiss to stifle his cry of surprise, palpitating
and out of breath, she whispered:

"It's me, you big stupid! Don't be alarmed. Quick,
quick; let's make haste!"

But he took fright. He wouldn't, there, in his own bed, for
fear of a surprise. The ladder of the loft was near there,
however, so they climbed up, leaving the trap-door open, and
fell amid the hay.

"Oh, you big stupid! you big stupid!" repeated Jacqueline
in ecstacy, with her coo in the throat, which seemed to rise
from her loins.

It was near upon two years since Jean Macquart had come
to the farm. On leaving the army he had fallen in, at Bazoches-
le-Doyen, with a fellow-soldier—a cabinetmaker like himself—
at the house of whose father, a small village contractor and
builder employing two or three hands, he had resumed his
calling. But his heart was no longer in his work. Seven years
of service had put his hand out of practice, and had so set him
against the saw and plane that he seemed a different being.
Formerly, at Plassans, he stayed hard at work on his wood,
without aptitude for book-learning, just knowing the three R's,
but yet very reflective and very painstaking, resolved on making

himself independent of his horrible family. Old Macquart **kept**
him in leading-strings, appropriated his mistresses under his very
eyes, and went every Saturday to the door of his workshop to
rob him of his wages. Accordingly, when ill-usage and over-
work had killed his mother, **he** followed the example of **his**
sister Gervaise—who **had just run off to Paris** with a lover—
and decamped, so **as not to have to** keep his vagabond
father. Now he hardly **knew himself again**; not that he had
grown lazy **in** his turn, **but life in the army** had enlarged his
mind. Politics, for instance, **which had once** bored him, now
absorbed him and led him to reason upon equality and fraternity;
so that, what with habits of mouching, troublesome and indolent
sentinel work, a sleepy life in barracks, **and** the wild rough-
and-tumble **of war, he had** so changed that the tools dropped
from his hands; he **dreamt of** his campaign in **Italy;** and **a**
yearning for rest, a **longing to** stretch himself **on the grass**
and forget everything, benumbed his efforts.

One morning his master installed him at La Borderie, to
make some repairs. There was a good month's work, rooms to
floor, doors **and** windows to be set right almost everywhere.
Jean blissfully dragged the work on for six weeks. Meanwhile
his master died, and the son, a married man, went off to set
up shop in his wife's part of the country. Left at La Borderie,
where rotting wood **was** always coming to light and needing
attention, the cabinetmaker did several jobs on his own
account; then, as the harvest was beginning, he lent a hand
and stayed six weeks longer; so that, noting his zeal, and how
kindly he took to agriculture, the farmer ended by **keeping**
him altogether. In less than a year, the ex-artisan became **a**
capital farm servant, carting, ploughing, sowing, reaping,
and seeming to satisfy his desire for peace in **the restfulness** of
agriculture. Away with **saw** and plane! **His interest** was
somewhere else! He seemed born for a **field** life, with his
sober, deliberate way, his love of systematic work, his ox-like
temperament inherited **from his mother.** He started on his new
career delightedly with a relish for the country that peasants
never know, a relish due to odds and ends of sentimental reading,
and to **notions of** simplicity, virtue, and perfect bliss, **such as**
are found in moral tales for children.

To tell the **truth,** another **cause had** kept him, and **made** him
happy at the **farm.** While **he was** mending the doors, La
Cognette had made **a** display of **her** charms amid his shavings.
The temptation had, indeed, come from her, for she was attracted
by the big fellow's sturdy limbs, and judged him, by his regular

massive features, to be a man of virility. He yielded; and then continued as he had begun, dreading that he might be deemed a fool, and tormented, moreover, by a craving for the licentious hussy, who knew so well how to raise men's passions. At heart his native honesty made protest. It was dishonourable to dally with the sweetheart of M. Hourdequin, to whom he owed a debt of gratitude. Of course he adduced justifications: she wasn't the master's wife, but only his Poll, and as she played him false here, there, and everywhere, he might as well profit by it as let others do so. However, such excuses did not prevent his uneasiness from increasing in proportion as he saw the farmer grow more and more fascinated. No doubt it would not end well.

Among the hay Jean and Jacqueline were restraining their breath, when the former, whose ears were on the alert, heard the frame of the ladder creak. He leapt up, and, at the risk of his life, dropped down the opening that was used for throwing fodder down. Hourdequin's head just then appeared on the other side, on a level with the trap-door. He saw at the same glance the shadow of the retreating man, and the woman, still supine, with her legs in the air. Such a fury seized hold of him, that it never occurred to him to descend in pursuit of the gallant; but, with a buffet that would have felled an ox, he overturned Jacqueline, who was now getting up on to her knees again.

"Strumpet!" he shouted.

With a shriek of rage, she denied the evidence.

"It's false!"

He had to exercise all his powers of self-restraint to refrain from kicking her into a jelly.

"I saw it! Confess it's true, or I'll kill you."

"No, no, no! It's not true."

Then, when at length she had got upon her feet again, she grew insolent and irritating, resolved to bring her power into full play.

"Besides, what's it got to do with you?" she asked. "Am I your wife? As you don't choose that I should sleep in your bed, I'm free to lie where I like."

She spoke with her dove-like coo, as if in lascivious raillery.

"Come, move out of the way! Let me go down. I'll leave this evening."

"This instant!"

"No, this evening. Wait and think it over."

He was left quivering and beyond himself, not knowing on

whom to vent his wrath. Though he no longer had the courage
to turn her into the street forthwith, how gladly would he
have kicked her gallant out of doors. But how was he to
catch him now? He had gone straight up into the loft,
guided by the open doors, without examining the beds; and
when he got down again the four waggoners from the
stable were dressing, as was Jean, in his garret. Which of the
five had it been? One as likely as the other, and, perhaps, the
whole lot, one after the other. Nevertheless, he hoped the man
would betray himself. Then he gave his morning orders, sent
nobody into the fields, and did not go out himself, but rambled
about the farm with clenched fists, scowling and hankering
after somebody to knock down.

After the seven o'clock breakfast, this exasperated review of
the master's set the whole household in a tremble. At La
Borderie there were five hands for the five ploughs, three
threshers, two cow-herds or yard-men, a shepherd, and a little
swine-herd; in all, twelve servants, without counting the house-
maid. Hourdequin began in the kitchen by abusing the latter,
because she hadn't put the baking-shovels back in their places
on the ceiling. Then he prowled into the two barns, one for
oats, the other for wheat, the latter being of immense size, as
large as a church, with doors five yards high; and he picked
a quarrel with the threshers, whose flails, he said, cut up the
straw too much. Then he went through the cow-house, and
became furious at finding the thirty cows in good order, the
central passage scoured, and the troughs clean. He did not
know on what ground to fall foul of the cow-herds, till,
glancing outside at the cisterns, which were also under their
charge, he noticed that a discharge-pipe was stopped up by
some sparrows' nests. As in all the Beauce farms, the rain-water
from the slate roofs was here sedulously collected and conducted
off by a complicated system of gutters. So he asked, roughly, if
they meant to let him die of thirst for the benefit of the
sparrows. But the storm finally burst on the waggoners.
Although the litters of the fifteen horses in the stable were
clean, he began by bawling out that it was disgusting to leave
them in such filth. Then, ashamed of his own injustice, and the
more exasperated, while paying a visit to the four sheds at the
four corners of the farm buildings, where the implements were
kept, he was delighted to find a plough with its handles
broken. Then he regularly stormed. Did the five beggars
amuse themselves by breaking his stock on purpose? He'd
send the whole five of them about their business; yes, the

whole five of them! He'd have no invidious distinctions!
While he swore at them, his flashing eyes looked them through,
expecting some paleness or quiver that would reveal the traitor.
Nobody flinched, however, and he left them with a wild
gesture of despair.

On ending his inspection at the sheep-fold, it occurred to
Hourdequin to cross-question the shepherd Soulas. This old
fellow of sixty-five had been half-a-century at the farm, and
had saved nothing by it, having been preyed upon by his wife, a
drunkard and a drab, whom he had just had the happiness of
laying beneath the sod. He was in dread lest his old age should
presently entail his dismissal, and was hurriedly saving up the few
coppers requisite to rescue him from want. Possibly the master
might help him; but, then, there was no saying which might
die first. And did they give money for tobacco and a
nip? Besides, he had made an enemy of Jacqueline, whom
he loathed with the jealous hatred of an old servant disgusted
by the rapid advancement of such an upstart. Whenever she
gave him orders, he was beside himself with rage, remembering
how he had seen her in rags and filth. She would assuredly
have dismissed him, if she had felt herself strong enough to do
so; and this made him prudent. He wanted to keep his place,
and shunned all conflict, no matter how sure he might be of
his master's support.

The sheep-fold occupied the entire building at the end of the
yard, a gallery eighty yards long, in which the eight hundred
sheep of the farm were only separated by hurdles. On one
side, the ewes, in various groups; on the other, the lambs; and
farther on, the rams. Every two months the males, reared for
sale, were castrated; while the females were kept to renew
the flock of mothers, the oldest of which were sold off every
year. The younger were served, at fixed times, by the rams,
dishleys crossed with merinos, of superb strain, and stupid gentle
aspect, with the heavy head and large rounded nose seen in
men addicted to vice. Those entering the sheep-fold were
choked by a strong smell, the ammoniacal exhalation from
the litter: stale straw on which fresh straw was laid for three
months running, the racks being fitted with hangers, so as to
raise them as the manure-heap ascended. There was ventilation:
the windows being wide, and the floor of the loft above being
formed of moveable oaken beams, which were taken away as
the fodder got less. It was said, however, that this living
heat, this soft, warm, fermenting heap, was necessary to the
proper growth of the sheep.

Hourdequin, pushing open one of the doors, caught sight of Jacqueline escaping by another. She, also, had thought uneasily of Soulas, feeling sure she **had** been watched with **Jean; but** the old man had remained impassive, seeming not to understand **why** she made herself so agreeable, contrary to her custom. **The** sight **of the young woman** leaving the sheep-fold, where she never went, aggravated the farmer's feverish uncertainty.

" Well, Soulas," **asked** he, " **any news** this morning ? "

The shepherd, very tall and thin, with a long face intersected **by wrinkles,** and looking as though carved with a bill-hook out **of a knot of** oak, replied slowly :

" No, **Monsieur** Hourdequin, nothing **whatever, except that** the shearers are coming and will soon be at **work."**

The master chatted for a moment, so as **not to seem to be** questioning him. **The sheep, who had been fed indoors since** the first frosts of November, were to **be let** loose again towards mid-May, when the clover would be ready for them. **As for** the cows, they were seldom pastured until after **the** harvest. Yet this land **of** La Beauce, dry and devoid **of** natural herbage as **it** was, yielded good meat; and it **was** only through **routine and laziness** that the breeding of oxen was unknown **there.** Five or six pigs, **even, were** all that each **farm fattened, for its own** consumption.

Hourdequin with his hot **hand** stroked the soft and bright-**eyed** ewes who had run up with raised heads; while the lambs, **pent** up a little way off, surged against the hurdles, bleating.

" And so, Soulas, you saw nothing **this morning ? "** he asked again, looking the shepherd full in **the** face.

The old fellow *had* seen, but what availed it **to** speak ? His deceased wife, tippler and **drab, had** familiarised him with the vices of women and the **folly of men.** Very possibly La Cognette, although betrayed, **would still hold her** own, and **then** he would be made the **scapegoat, so that** an awkward **witness** might be got out of **the way.**

" Saw nothing, nothing at all ! " **he** repeated, with dull eyes and **stolid face.**

When Hourdequin re-crossed the yard he noticed Jacqueline standing **there,** nervously straining her ears, in fear of what was being said **in** the sheep-fold. She was pretending to be busy with her poultry : six hundred head of hens, ducks, and pigeons, **who** were fluttering, chattering, **and** scratching on the manure-heap, amid a constant hurly-burly. **She** even relieved her feelings a bit by boxing the ears of the swine-herd, who had upset a bucket of water he was carrying to the pigs. But a single glance at the farmer **reassured her.** He knew nothing; the old **man** had held his tongue. **Her insolence thus grew greater.**

For instance, at the mid-day repast, she displayed a provoking gaiety. **As the heavy work** had not yet begun, they now only had four **meals :** bread-and-milk at **seven,** sopped **toast at** twelve, **bread and cheese at four, soup and bacon at eight. They** fed in the kitchen, a vast **room, in which stretched a table flanked** by two forms. Modern progress was **only represented** by a cast-iron stove, which took up **a corner of the immense** hearth. At the end the black mouth **of** the oven yawned ; **and along the smoky walls** saucepans gleamed **and** old-fashioned **utensils** stood in **neat rows. As** the maid, **a stout,** plain **girl,** had baked that **morning, a pleasant scent** of hot bread **rose from** the open **pan.**

" So your **stomach's not in working** order to-day ? " asked Jacqueline audaciously of Hourdequin, who **came in last.**

Since **the death** of his wife and daughter **he sat at** the **same** table as **his servants, as in the** good old **times,** so that he might **not have to eat alone.** He took a chair **at** one end, while the **servant-mistress** did **the same at** the other. There were four-**teen of them, and the maid did the helping.**

The farmer having sat down without replying, La Cognette talked of seeing **to the food. This** consisted of **slices of** toasted bread broken **into a** soup-tureen, moistened with wine, and sweetened **with** *ripopée,* an old Beauce **word for** treacle. She asked for a second spoonful of **this ; pretended to** spoil **the** men, and vented jests that set the table **in a roar. Each** of her phrases had a double **meaning, reminding them that** she was leaving that night. **There were** bickerings and part-ings, and those who would never **have another** chance would regret not having dipped their fingers in the gravy for the last **time.** The shepherd ate on in his chuckle-headed way, while the **master,** impassive, **also seemed not to** understand. Jean, to avoid betraying himself, was obliged to laugh with the others, despite **his uneasiness ;** for, to be **sure,** he deemed himself scarcely straightforward in all this.

After the meal, Hourdequin issued his orders for the after-noon. Out of doors, there were only a few little jobs to **finish :** the oats to be rolled, and the ploughing of the fallows to **be com-**pleted, pending the time for cutting the lucern and clover. So he kept two men, Jean and another, to clean the hay-loft. He himself, now plunged into despondency, with his ears buzzing from the reaction of his blood, and very wretched, set out on

the prowl, not knowing what occupation to try, to get rid of his
vexation. The shearers having installed themselves under one of
the sheds, in a corner of the yard, he took up his stand in
front of them and watched them.

There were five sallow spindled-shanked fellows, squatting
on the ground, with large shears of shining steel. The shepherd
passed the ewes over, ranging them on the ground like so many
skin bottles, with their four feet tied together, and only just
able to lift their heads and bleat. As soon as a shearer caught
hold of one of them she became silent, and abandoned herself,
blown out like a balloon by the thickness of her wool, which
sweat and dust had coated with a hard black crust Under
the rapid shears, the animal came out from the fleece like a
bare hand out of a dark glove, all pink and fresh, clad in the
gleaming snowy inner wool. Held between the knees of a tall
wizzened man, one mother, set on her back, with her thighs
apart, and her head erect and rigid, made exposure of her
belly, which had the hidden whiteness, the quivering skin of an
undressed person. The shearers earned three sous per head,
and a good workman could shear twenty sheep a day.

Hourdequin, absorbed, was thinking that wool had fallen to
eight sous a pound, and that he'd have to make haste and sell,
or else it would get too dry, and lose in weight. The year
before, congestion of the spleen had decimated the flocks of
La Beauce. Everything was going from bad to worse; it
meant ruin, bankruptcy, for grain had been falling more and
more heavily every month. Once more a prey to agricultural
worries, and feeling stifled in the yard, he left the farm and
went to take a glance at his fields. His quarrels with La
Cognette always ended thus. After swearing and clenching his
fists, he gave way, oppressed by suffering, which was only relieved by the contemplation of the infinite green expanses of
his wheat and oats.

Ah, how he loved that land of his! With a passion un-
tainted by the keen avarice of the peasant; a sentimental,
almost an intellectual, passion; for he felt her to be the common
mother, who had given him his life and nourishment—to whom
he would return. At first, when quite young, after being brought
up upon her, his distaste for college, his impulse to burn his books
and stop at the farm, had simply sprung from his free habits,
his gay gallops over ploughed fields, his intoxicating open-air
life amid the breezes of the plain. But later on, upon succeeding his father, he had loved the land like a lover; his love
had ripened, as if he had thenceforward taken her in lawful

wedlock to make her **fruitful.** That tenderness had grown and
grown, until **he** now **devoted to** her his time, his money, his
whole life, as **to a good and** fertile wife, whose caprices, whose
treason **even, he would** condone. Many a time he flew into a
rage **when she** proved shrewish, when, too damp or too dry,
she **consumed** the seed without yielding a **harvest. Then,** he
began to doubt, and at length accused himself as if he **were an**
impotent or unskilful bridegroom : the fault must have been **his if**
a child had not been born **to her. Since then** he had been
haunted by new methods, had **plunged into every innovation,**
regretting that **he** had been **so lazy at college, and that he**
had **not studied** at one of those agricultural **schools that he and**
his father used to make fun of. How many futile attempts ;
how many experiments ending **in failure! And the machines that**
his servants **put out of order ; the chemical manure adulterated**
by **the dealers! La Borderie had swallowed up his** whole
fortune, **it now hardly brought him in bread and** cheese,
and he **was expecting the agricultural crisis to finish** him off.
No matter ; **he would remain the prisoner of his own soil,** and
would **bury his bones within it, after having** kept it **for wife up**
to **the very last.**

On that day, as **soon as he got** out of doors, **he remembered**
his son, **the** captain. **The two of them** together **might have**
achieved something fine ! **But he** dismissed from **his thoughts**
the memory of the fool **who preferred** trailing **a sword !** He
had no child now ; **he would end his** days in solitude. **Then his**
neighbours came into **his mind, more especially the Coquarts,**
some **landowners who cultivated their farm of Saint-Juste—**
father, **mother, three sons, and two daughters ;** and **who**
succeeded scarcely better than he did. At La Chamade, the
farmer, being near the end of his lease, had left off manuring,
letting the property go to rack and ruin. So it was. There
was calamity everywhere. One had to work one's self to death,
and not complain. Little by little, a soothing calm **rose from**
the **broad green** fields he was skirting. Some light showers,
in April, **had brought on the** fodder-crops beautifully. **The**
purple **clover transported him with delight ;** he forgot everything else. **Then as he was taking a short cut across some**
ploughed land, **to have a look at** the work of his two waggoners,
the soil clung to his **feet ;** he felt that it was rich and fertile, and
it seemed to clasp and hold **him** back ; taking **him once** more
wholly to itself, while the virility, the vigour, the hey-day of his
thirty years returned to him. Was not this the only wife for a
man ? Of what consequence were the whole set of Cognettes,

plates out of which every one ate, and with which one might be well content, provided they were clean enough? This excuse, so consonant with his low **craving for the** baggage, crowned his gaiety. He walked for **three hours, and** jested with **a girl** —the servant of those **very Coquarts**—who was returning from Cloyes on a donkey, and showing **her** legs.

When Hourdequin went back **to** La Borderie, he noticed Jacqueline **saying good-bye** to the farm **cats.** There were always **a** troop **of them; but** whether **a dozen,** fifteen, or twenty, nobody precisely knew, **for** the **she-cats** used to litter in various odd nests of straw, and re-appear **with** trains of five or six kittens. Next, she went up to the kennels of Emperor and Massacre, the shepherd's two dogs; **but** they detested her, **and** growled.

The dinner, in spite of the farewells taken of the animals, **went** off just as on other days. The master ate and **con-versed** as usual. And at the close of the day nothing **more** was said about anybody's departure. **They** all **went to sleep,** and darkness enwrapped **the** silent farm.

That very **night,** too, Jacqueline slept in the room of the **late** Madame Hourdequin: the **state** chamber, with its large bed in the depths of **an alcove with** red hangings. In this **room there** stood **a wardrobe, a small** round table, and an arm-chair of the Voltaire **style; while** above a little mahogany writing-table there hung **some medals,** framed under glass, and won by the farmer at agricultural competitions. When La Cognette in **her** chemise, had mounted on to the **conjugal** couch, she stretched herself upon it, with her turtle-dove chuckle, spreading out her arms and legs as if to take posses-sion of the entire bed.

On the morrow, when she fell on Jean's neck, he repulsed **her.** Things having now taken a serious turn, it wasn't **proper,** and he wouldn't consent any more.

CHAPTER II.

ONE evening, some days later, Jean was walking back from Cloyes when, a mile or so before reaching Rognes, he was astonished by the mode of progress of a peasant's cart which was going along, ahead of him. It seemed empty. No one sat on the driver's seat, and the horse, left to its own devices, was leisurely jogging back to its stable, being evidently well acquainted with the road. Accordingly, the young man quickly caught it up. He stopped it, and raised himself on tip-toe to look into the vehicle. A man was lying at the bottom—a short, fat old man of sixty, who had fallen backwards, and whose face was so purple that it appeared black.

Such was Jean's surprise that he began to talk aloud:

"Hallo, there! Is he asleep or drunk? Why, if it isn't old Mouche, the father of those two down yonder. Heavens! I think he's kicked the bucket! Well, well, here's a start!"

But, although laid low by a fit of apoplexy, Mouche still breathed, in a short and laboured way. So Jean raised his head and straightened him out; and then sat himself down in front and whipped up the horse, driving the dying man home at a round trot, for fear that he might slip through his fingers.

Just as he turned into the church-square, he perceived Françoise standing before her door. The sight of the young fellow in their cart, driving Coco, dumbfounded her.

"What's up?" she asked.

"Your father's not well."

"Where is he?"

"There. Look!"

She climbed up on the wheel and looked. For a moment she stood there, without seeming to understand, and staring stupidly at that purple face, half of which had been, as it were, wrenched downwards. The night was falling, and a great livid cloud, which turned the sky yellow, lit up the dying man as with the glow of a conflagration.

Then all at once, she burst into sobs, and ran out of sight to prepare her sister.

" Lise! Lise! Oh, my God!"

Jean, on remaining alone, hesitated. Still the old man could not be left lying in the cart. The basement of the house was three steps below ground, on the side of the square; and to descend into that dark hole seemed to him inconvenient. Then he bethought himself that, on the roadway side, to the left, another door opened level into the yard. It was a good-sized yard, enclosed by a quickset hedge; the turbid water of a pool took up two-thirds of it, and two-thirds of an acre of kitchen and fruit garden extended in the rear. Jean left Coco to himself, and the horse, of his own accord, entered and drew up before his stable, near the shed in which were the two cows.

Françoise and Lise ran up with tears and lamentations. The latter, confined four months previously, and now taken by surprise while suckling her infant, had, in her affright, kept him in her arms; and he howled too. Françoise again got on one wheel, while Lise climbed up on the other. Their lamentations grew deafening; and meantime Mouche, at the bottom of the cart, still kept up his laboured wheezing.

" Papa, answer; won't you? Say what's the matter. Oh, dear! what is the matter? Oh, dear! oh, dear! It's in your head, then, since you can't even speak? Papa, papa, do speak; do answer!"

" Come down. He'd better be got out of the trap," said Jean, sagely.

They gave no help, but only screamed the louder. Luckily a neighbour, Madame Frimat, came upon the scene, attracted by the noise. She was a tall, withered, bony old woman, who for two years had been nursing her paralytic husband, supporting him by cultivating in person, with the doggedness of a beast of burden, the single acre or so that they possessed. She was not at all put out, seeming to think the misadventure a matter of course, and she lent a helping hand as a man would have done. Jean took Mouche by the shoulders, and pulled him up until La Frimat was able to catch hold of his legs. Then they carried him into the house.

" Where's he to be put?" asked the old woman.

The two girls, who were following, had lost their wits, and did not know.. Their father's room was a small one upstairs, partitioned off from the grain-loft, and it was almost out of the question to carry him up there. Downstairs there was the kitchen, and the large double-bedded room which he had given up to them. In the kitchen it was as dark as pitch. With their arms stiff with exertion, the young man and the old woman waited, not daring to take another step forward for fear of knocking against some piece of furniture.

"Come, something must be settled, anyhow."

Françoise at last lit a candle, and just then the wife of the rural constable, Madame Bécu came in; she had smelt disaster in the air, or had been warned by that occult agency which is wont to carry news through a village in no time.

"Why! what's amiss with the poor fellow?" said she. "Ah! I see; his blood has turned. Quick! Set him on a chair."

But Madame Frimat was of a different opinion. The idea of seating a man who could not hold himself upright! The thing to do was to stretch him on one of his daughters' beds. The discussion was growing keen, when Fanny came in with Nénesse. She had heard about it while buying some vermicelli at Macqueron's, and had come to see what there was to be seen; being at the same time somewhat affected on her cousins' account.

"Perhaps," she declared, "it's best to sit him down, so that the blood may run back."

And so Mouche was huddled on to a chair near the table, on which the candle was burning. His chin drooped upon his chest, his arms and legs hung limp. His left eye had been drawn open by the displacement of that side of his face, and one corner of his twisted mouth wheezed more than the other. Silence fell. Death was taking possession of the damp room, with its floor of trodden earth, its stained walls, and its large gloomy fire-place.

Jean still waited in perplexity, while the two girls and the three women dangled round the old fellow, looking at him.

"Hadn't I better go and fetch the doctor?" the young man ventured to ask.

Madame Bécu nodded her head, but no one else made any reply. If it were to be nothing after all, why incur the expense of a visit? And if it were really the end, what good could the doctor do?

"Vulnerary's a capital thing," said La Frimat.

"I've got some camphorated spirits," murmured Fanny.

"That's a good thing too," declared Madame Bécu.

Lise and Françoise, now in a state of stupor, listened and took no steps at all. The one was nursing her baby, Jules; the other was holding a glass full of water which her father would not drink. Fanny, however, bustled Nénesse, who was held spell-bound by the contorted visage of the dying man.

"Run home and tell them to give you the little bottle of camphorated spirits on the left in the wardrobe. D'ye hear?

In the wardrobe on the left. And call at grandfather Fouan's, and at your aunt La Grande's. Tell them that uncle Mouche is taken very bad. Run, run quick!"

The urchin having bounded out of sight, the women continued their dissertations on the case. La Bécu knew a gentleman who had been saved by having the soles of his feet tickled for three hours. La Frimat, remembering that she had some linden-flowers left out of the pennyworth bought the previous winter for her good man, went and fetched it. She was coming back with the little bag, and Lise was lighting a fire, after handing her child to Françoise, when Nénesse reappeared.

"Grandpapa Fouan had gone to bed. La Grande said that if uncle Mouche hadn't drunk so much he wouldn't have made himself so sick."

Fanny examined the bottle he handed her, and then cried:

"You fool! I told you on the left. You've brought me the Eau de Cologne."

"That's a good thing, too," said La Bécu.

They forced the old man to take a cup of linden-flower tea, by inserting the spoon between his clenched teeth. Then they rubbed his head with Eau de Cologne. And yet he didn't get any better: it was most discouraging. His face had become blacker still. They were obliged to hitch him up on the chair, for he was sinking down, and on the point of tumbling flat on the floor.

"Oh!" muttered Nénesse, who had gone to the door again, "it's going to rain like I don't know what. The sky's a funny sort of colour."

"Yes," said Jean, "I saw a villainous cloud gathering." And, as if brought back to his first idea: "It's no odds. I'll go and fetch the doctor if you like."

Lise and Françoise looked at each other, frightened and anxious. At last the second came to a resolution in the generous impulse of her youth.

"Yes, yes, Corporal. Go to Cloyes and fetch Monsieur Finet. It sha'n't be said that we didn't do our duty."

Coco, in the midst of the bustle, had not even been unharnessed, and Jean had only to jump into the cart. They heard the clink of iron, and the rumble of the wheels, Then La Frimat mentioned the priest; but the others signified by a gesture that enough trouble was already being taken in the matter. And Nénesse having proposed to walk the two miles or so to Bazoches-le-Doyen, his mother lost her temper. A likely thing that she was going to let him trot off on so threatening a night,

with that dreadful **rust-coloured sky**! Besides, as the old man
neither heard **nor** answered, **one** might **as** well **knock up the**
priest **to** minister **to a** mile-stone.

Ten o'clock struck from the **cuckoo-clock of painted wood.**
Here was **a suprise**! To think that they **had been there** more
than two hours without effecting anything. But not one of them
seemed inclined to stir, **they** were fascinated **by the sight, and**
resolved to see it out. A ten-pound loaf **lay on the bread-box,**
with a knife. First the girls, racked with hunger despite **their**
anguish, mechanically cut themselves slices of bread, **which**
they unconsciously ate, quite dry. Then the three women
followed their example. The **bread diminished, and one or the**
other of them was **always cutting and munching.** No other
candle had been lighted; **they omitted even to snuff the**
one that was burning; **and it was not** lively, sitting in **that**
poor, gloomy, **bare, peasant room, and** listening to the death-
rattle of the form huddled together near the table.

All at once, half an hour after Jean's departure Mouche
tumbled **over and fell headlong to the floor.** He no longer
breathed; **he was dead!**

"What did I **tell you?** Only **you** insisted on **sending for**
the doctor," remarked La Bécu, tartly.

Françoise **and Lise,** stupefied for a moment, burst out into
fresh tears. With an instinctive impulse they had **thrown**
themselves **into each** other's arms in **their tender, sisterly**
adoration; **and in broken phrases** they **repeated:** "Oh, dear!
We have only each **other now.** It's all over; **there are only**
the two of **us.** What *will* **become of us!** Oh, dear!"

But the **corpse could not be left on the floor.** In a trice
La Frimat **and La Bécu did everything necessary.** As they
dared not carry **the body, they went and drew a** mattress off a
bed, brought it, and **stretched Mouche out upon** it, covering
him up to the chin **with a sheet.** Meanwhile Fanny lit the
candles in two **other candlesticks, and placed** them on the
floor in lieu of wax tapers on **either side of the** head. For
the moment all was well, except that Mouche's left eye, although
closed three times by one of **the women** with her thumb, **per-**
sisted in opening **again, and seemed to** be **looking at every-**
body from out of **the distorted purple face, which contrasted**
so sharply with **the whiteness of the linen.**

Lise had determined **to put Jules to** bed, and **the wake**
began. Three **times** did **Fanny and La** Bécu say they were
going, as La Frimat had offered **to** stay the night with the
young ones; but they did not **go,** continuing to talk in low

tones, and glancing askance from time to time at the corpse,
while Nénesse, who had got possession of the bottle of Eau
de Cologne, finished it up by drenching his hands and hair
with its contents.

As twelve o'clock struck, La Bécu raised her voice.

" And how about Monsieur Finet, I should like to know!
Plenty of time he gives people to die in! More than two
hours bringing him here from Cloyes!"

The door leading to the yard was open, and just then a
great gust came in, and blew out the candles on either side of
the corpse. This terrified them all, and as they re-lit the
candles, the tempestuous blast returned with greater fury, while
a prolonged howling arose and swelled in the dark depths of the
country-side. It might have been the gallop of a devastating
army approaching, so loudly did the branches crash, so deep
was the wail of the riven fields. They had run to the doorway,
and saw a coppery cloud whirl wildly across the livid sky.
Suddenly there was a rattle, as it were, of musketry, and a
rain of bullets fell lashing and rebounding at their feet.

A cry of ruin and desolation burst from their lips.

"Hail! Hail!"

Pale and aghast at the scourge above them, they stood
there watching. It lasted barely six minutes. There were no
thunder-claps; but great bluish flashes seemed incessantly to
run along the ground in broad phosphoric furrows. The
night was not now so gloomy: the hail stones lit it up with
numberless pale streaks as if jets of glass had fallen. The
noise became deafening: like a discharge of grape shot, like a
train rushing at full speed over an endlessly thundering metal
bridge. The wind blew furiously, and the obliquely falling
stones slashed everything, accumulated and covered the soil
with a layer of white.

" Hail! Oh, dear! What a misfortune! Look, look!
Exactly like hen's eggs!"

They dared not venture into the yard to pick any up. The
violence of the hurricane continued to increase; all the
window-panes were broken; and the momentum was such that
one hailstone cracked a jug, while others rolled as far as the
dead man's mattress.

"There wouldn't be five to the pound," said Madame Bécu,
poising them in her hand.

Fanny and La Frimat made a gesture of despair.

" Everything ruined! A massacre!"

It was over. The disastrous roar was heard rapidly passing

away, and a death-like silence fell. The sky, in the rear of the
cloud, had become as black as ink. A fine close rain streamed
noiselessly down. Nothing was now distinguishable on the
ground but the thick layer of hailstones : a gleaming sheet that
had, as it were, a light of its own, the shimmer of infinite
millions of night-lights.

Nénesse having rushed out of doors, returned with a perfect
iceberg, an irregular jagged mass bigger than his fist : and La
Frimat, who could no longer keep still, was unable to resist
the temptation to go and see how things were.

"I'm going to fetch my lantern; I must know what the
damage is," she said.

Fanny controlled herself a few minutes longer, prolonging
her lamentations. Oh, what a piece of work! What destruction
among the vegetables and fruit-trees! The wheat, oats, and
barley were not high enough to have suffered much. But the
vines! Ah, the vines! And, standing at the door, she
peered into the thick, impenetrable night, and quivered in a
fever of uncertainty, trying to estimate the mischief, exagger-
ating it, and imagining that she saw the land riddled with shot
and its life oozing from the wounds.

"Hey! my pets," she said at last : "I'll borrow one of
your lanterns and run over as far as our vines."

Then she lit one of the two lanterns and disappeared with
Nénesse.

La Bécu, who had no land, didn't at heart care a fig. She
fetched sighs and apostrophised Heaven, merely out of a habit
she had of feebly moaning and melting into tears on all occasions. Nevertheless, curiosity continually took her to the door;
and a lively interest fixed her there once for all as soon as she
noticed that the village was starred all over with luminous
points. Through a gap in the yard, between the cow-house
and a shed, the eye could command the whole of Rognes.
Doubtless, the hail-storm had awoke the peasants, and they
were all seized with the same impatience to take a look at their
fields, all too anxious to wait till daylight.

And indeed the lanterns came forth one by one, multiplying
and flitting lightly to and fro, in so dense an opacity, that the
arms that held them were merely conjectural. But La Bécu,
always on the watch, knew the site of every house, and succeeded in putting a name to every lantern.

"There, now! That one's lit in La Grande's house, and
that one's coming out of the Fouans', and over yonder it's
Macqueron, and next door it's Lengaigne. Bless me, poor

souls! it's heart-breaking. Well, so much the worse! **I'm off to** join them!"

Lise and Françoise remained alone with their father's corpse. The downpour of the rain continued; little moist breezes skimmed **along the ground and** guttered **the** candles. The door ought **to have** been shut, but neither **of** them thought of it, being **themselves** absorbed and agitated by the drama outside, despite **the** mourning in the house. It wasn't enough, then, to have **Death at home?** The good God was smashing up everything; **one didn't so much** as know if there would be a bit of bread **left to eat.**

"**Poor father,**" murmured Françoise; "what **a** stew he would **have been in!** Better that he can't see it."

And, **as her sister** took up the second **lantern, she added:**

"Where are you going?"

"I'm thinking of the peas and beans. I'll be back directly."

Lise crossed the yard, through the driving rain, and went into the kitchen-garden. There was only Françoise left with the old man, and even **she was** standing at the doorway, keenly agitated **by the flitting of** the lantern to and fro. She thought she **could hear** complaints and sobs. Her heart was wrung.

"Hey! What is **it?" she cried.** "**What's** the matter?"

No **voice** replied, **but the lantern ran to** and fro **more quickly, as if** distracted.

"**Tell** me, are the beans cut down? And the peas, are they hurt? Gracious! And the fruit and salad stock?"

An exclamation of grief, which now distinctly reached her ears, decided her. She caught up her skirts and ran through **the rain** to join her sister. The dead man remained, deserted, **in the** empty kitchen, lying rigid under the sheet, between the **two** dull, smoky wicks. His left eye, still **obstinately** open, **stared** at the old joists of the ceiling.

What a ravage **had laid** that **stretch of land** desolate! What a lamentation **arose** from **the scene of** disaster, half visible in the **flickering gleam of** the lanterns. Lise and Françoise carried theirs hither and thither, though it was so wet **with rain that scarcely** any light passed through the panes; and they brought **it close to** the beds, confusedly distinguishing, **in** the narrow ring **of** light, the beans and peas cut down short, the lettuces **so** chopped and hacked **that it** was futile even **to** think of utilising the leaves. The **trees,** especially, had suffered. The smaller branches **and the fruit had** been cut off as with knives. The very trunks **were** splintered and bruised, and

G

the sap was escaping through the holes in the bark. Farther on, among the vines, matters were worse: the lanterns swarmed and leaped, as if maddened, amid groans and oaths. The stocks seemed to have been mown down, and bunches of blossom bestrewed the soil in company with shattered branches and spurs. Not only was the season's crop ruined, but the stems, stripped bare, would decay and die. No one felt the rain. A dog was howling murder, and women were bursting into tears, as on the brink of a grave. Macqueron and Lengaigne, in spite of their rivalry, were lighting each other, visiting each other's ground, and joining in ejaculations of dismay, as each new vision of ruin, wan and short-lived, met their gaze, and then faded again into shadow behind them. Although old Fouan now had no land of his own, he wanted to look on, waxing wroth. By degrees they all flew into a temper. To actually lose the fruit of a year's work in a quarter of an hour! Could it be possible? What had they done to be so punished? There was no security or justice; unreasoning scourges and caprices slew the world. La Grande, in a fury, abruptly picked up some pebbles, and flung them into the air to pierce the heaven she could not discern. And she blasphemously screamed out:

"Hey, up there! Can't you manage to leave us in peace?"

On the mattress in the kitchen, the deserted Mouche was still staring fixedly at the ceiling with his one eye, when two vehicles drew up at the door. Jean had at length brought Monsieur Finet, after waiting for him at his house during nearly three hours; and had returned in the cart, while the doctor had ordered out his gig.

The medical man, tall and thin, with a face jaundiced by stifled ambition, entered roughly. In his heart he loathed this peasant connection, which he held responsible for his mediocrity.

"What, no one here? Things have mended, then."

But perceiving the corpse: "No, too late! Didn't I tell you? I didn't want to come! It's always the same old game: they call me in when they're dead."

This useless summons in the middle of the night annoyed him; and Lise and Françoise, just then returning, put the finishing touch to his exasperation by apprising him that they had waited a couple of hours before sending for him.

"It's you that have killed him, sure enough. Eau de Cologne and linden-flower tea for a fit of apoplexy! How idiotic! And, what's more, no one keeping him company. It's pretty certain he won't see salvation."

"It's because of the hail, sir," stammered Lise, in tears.

Monsieur Finet became interested, and calmed down. Dear, dear! So there's been a hail-storm? By dint of living among the peasantry he had eventually caught their passions. Jean, also, had drawn near; and they both uttered exclamations of amazement, for, in coming from Cloyes, they had not seen a single hail-stone. Some spared, and others, half a mile or so off, turned topsy-turvy! Really, what a piece of ill luck to have one's land in the damaged part of the country! Then, as Fanny returned, bringing back the lantern, La Bécu and La Frimat following her, and all the three launching out into grievous and interminable details of the harrowing things they had seen,—the doctor gravely declared:

"It's a calamity, a great calamity. There's no greater calamity for country-folk."

A muffled sound, a kind of bubbling noise, interrupted him. It came from the corpse, lying forgotten between the two candles. They all became silent, and the women crossed themselves.

CHAPTER III.

A MONTH passed by. Old Fouan, appointed guardian to
Françoise, who was entering on her fifteenth year, induced the
two girls—his ward and Lise, who was the elder by ten years
—to let all their land, excepting a strip of meadow, to cousin
Delhomme, so that it might be properly cultivated and kept.

Now that the two girls were left alone in the house, without father or mother, they would have had to engage a servant,
which would have been ruinous, on account of the increasing
price of manual labour. Delhomme, moreover, was simply
doing them a service, as he undertook to cancel the lease as soon
as either of them married, and a division of the inheritance
became necessary.

Lise and Françoise also sold their cousin their horse, which
had now become useless, but they kept the two cows, La
Coliche and La Rousse, as well as the donkey, Gédéon. Of
course they likewise kept their patch of kitchen garden, which
it became the province of the elder girl to keep in order,
while the younger one looked after the live stock. To be sure,
that made plenty of work; but they were hale and hearty,
thank God! and would soon get through with it.

The first few weeks were very burdensome, for there was
the damage of the hail-storm to be repaired, the soil to be
tilled, the vegetables to be replanted. This it was that induced
Jean to lend a helping hand. An intimacy had sprung up between him and the girls since the day he had brought their dying
father home. The day after the burial he called and inquired
after them. Next he came and chatted, growing gradually
familiar and obliging, insomuch that one afternoon he took the
spade out of Lise's hands to finish the digging of a bed. Thence-
forth he devoted to them, in a friendly way, the time that was
not taken up by his work at the farm. He belonged to the
house, to that old patriarchal house of the Fouans, built
three centuries back by an ancestor, and honoured by the
whole family with a sort of worship. When Mouche used to
complain of having had the worst lot in the distribution
of the property, accusing his brother and sister of having

swindled him, they answered: "And how about **the house?** Hadn't he got the house?"

A **poor,** dilapidated house it was, settling **down on its foundations,** cracked and rickety, patched up everywhere with odds and ends of plank and plaster. It had obviously been originally constructed of rough stones and clay; subsequently, two walls had been rebuilt with mortar; and finally, towards the beginning of the century, the owners had reluctantly replaced the thatch with a roofing of small slates, now **rotten.** Thus it had lasted, **and** thus it still held out; sunk a yard deep in the earth, as all houses **were** built in the olden time, doubtless for the purpose **of** ensuring greater **warmth.** The inconvenience of it was that, in heavy storms, they were flooded with water; and it was of no avail to sweep the hardened soil that composed the cellar-like floor; there was always a **remnant of mud in** the corners.

The house had been planned, however, with particular artfulness, its back being turned towards the far-stretching northern plain of La Beauce, whence blew the terrible winter winds. **On** that side, in the kitchen, the only opening was a narrow window, **barricaded by a shutter, on a** level with the street; while on the southern side, **one found the** other windows and the door. The place suggested one of those fisher-huts on the sea-shore, which do not expose a single chink to the ocean waves. The winds of La **Beauce** had battered the **house aslant,** so that it bent forward like an old broken-backed hag.

Jean was soon familiar with every corner **of it.** He helped to clean up the room of the deceased; that **corner** cut off from the granary by a mere plank partition, **and** containing nothing **but** an old chest full **of** straw serving **as a** bed, with a chair and a table. Downstairs he did not go beyond the kitchen, **for he** shrank from following the two sisters into their own room, where, **as** the door was always **on** the swing, one could **see** the double-bedded alcove, the large walnut wardrobe, and **a** superbly-carved round table, doubtless a relic formerly stolen **from** the château. There existed yet another room behind **this, but it** was **so damp** that the father had preferred to sleep up-stairs. They were reluctant even to store potatoes in it, for they **began immediately** to germinate. They lived in the kitchen, **a** huge **smoky room** where, **for** three centuries, many generations of Fouans had succeeded **each** other. It was redolent of sustained toil and stinted food, **of** the constant efforts of people who, while working themselves to death, had just managed not to **starve,** never having **a** halfpenny more

in December than they **had in** January.   A door that opened
flush **into the cow-house** brought **the cattle into** companionship
with the occupants, and when that door was shut, the animals
could still be seen and watched through a pane of glass let
into the wall. Next there came the stable, where Gédéon now
remained by himself; then a shed and a wood-house; and
there was no need **to** go out of doors, for you entered **every**
place in succession. Outside, the rains replenished **the pond,**
which furnished them with water **for** the **cattle and for**
domestic use. Every morning they **had to go down to the**
Aigre to bring up drinking-water.

Jean felt happy there, without **troubling his head to inquire**
what the attraction was. Lise, **who gave him a good welcome,**
was as gay and **buxom as ever. Nevertheless, she was already**
looking older than twenty-five ; **indeed, she was growing very**
plain, **more especially since her confinement.** But she had good
stout arms, **and applied herself** to her work **with such zest —**
bustling about, shouting, and **laughing—that it was delightful**
to look at her. **Jean treated her** as a grown-up woman, **and did**
not *thee* **and** *thou* **her as he did** Françoise, whose fifteen
years made her seem to him quite a mere child. The younger
girl, whose good looks out-of-door life and hard work had not
yet had time enough to spoil, retained her pretty, long face, with
its slight, headstrong forehead, its dark, pensive eyes, **and its**
thick lips, shaded by a precocious down. Although deemed
a child, she **was a woman also;** and apt to conceive, **as her**
sister used to say, without being tickled very closely. **It was**
Lise who had brought her up, their **mother being** dead; **and**
thence came their great fondness, **active and** noisy on the
part of the elder sister, and passionate **and** restrained on that
of the younger one.

Françoise was reputed to have **a** strong **will of her own.**
Injustice exasperated her. When she had said : "**This is mine,**
and that is yours," she would have gone to the scaffold rather
than retract; and, **putting** everything else aside, she adored
Lise, from a notion **that such** adoration was Lise's due. Withal,
she was tractable and very good, free from bad thoughts, and
only tormented by her early womanhood, which **made her**
nerveless, slightly dainty, and lazy. One day she also **began to**
address Jean in the second person singular, he **being quite a**
middle-aged and kindly-natured friend, who **was wont to draw**
her out, and sometimes tease her ; telling **falsehoods of malice**
aforethought, and defending injustice for **the fun of seeing her**
choke with rage.

One Sunday afternoon in June, the heat already being intense, Lise was engaged in the kitchen garden, hoeing some peas and nipping them round. She had placed Jules under a plum-tree, where he had dozed off to sleep. The sun was beating straight down upon her, and she was puffing as she bent forward to pull up some weeds, when a voice came from behind the hedge:

" What, what! No rest even on Sunday?"

She had recognised the voice, and drew herself up, with red arms and a flushed face, but laughing through it all.

" No, indeed! The work doesn't do itself on a Sunday any more than on a week-day!"

It was Jean. He skirted the hedge, and came in through the yard.

" Let that alone ; I'll soon polish off your work!"

However, she refused. She would soon have finished. And then, if she didn't do that, she would be doing something else. There was never a chance of being idle. Although she got up at four o'clock in the morning, and sat sewing till late in the evening by candlelight, she never got to the end of it all.

So as not to oppose her, Jean sat himself in the shade of the neighbouring plum-tree, being careful not to sit upon Jules. He watched Lise, stooping double again, and every now and then pulling down her petticoat, which kept working up behind and showing her fat legs ; and then with her head close to the ground, she worked away with her arms without any fear of the rush of blood that swelled her neck.

" Lucky for you," he said, " that you're sturdily built!"

She took some pride in that, and laughed complacently without getting up. He laughed too, conscientiously admiring her, thinking her as strong and energetic as a man. No improper desire was suggested to him by her attitude, by her tense calves, by this woman on all fours, sweating and smelling like an animal in heat. He was simply thinking that with limbs like that one could get through a rare lot of work. It was quite certain that, in a household, a woman of that build would be worth as much as her husband.

No doubt some association of ideas worked in him, for he involuntarily blurted out a piece of news which he had resolved to keep to himself.

" I saw Buteau the day before yesterday."

Lise slowly rose up. But she had no time to question him, for Françoise—who had heard Jean's voice, and who,with her arms bare and white with milk, was now coming from the dairy at the further end of the cow-house—flew at once into quite a temper.

"Oh, you've seen him? The cad!"

Her antipathy had increased. She could never now hear her cousin mentioned without being stirred by one of her gusts of honest indignation, as if she had had a personal injury to avenge.

"Certainly he's a cad," declared Lise calmly; "but it don't do any good to say so at this time of day."

She had stuck her arms a-kimbo, and now in a serious voice she asked:

"And what's Buteau got to say for himself?"

"Why, nothing," replied Jean, with some embarrassment, sorry that he hadn't kept a quiet tongue in his head. "We spoke of his affairs, on account of his father giving out everywhere that he'll disinherit him. Buteau says there's no hurry about that, for the old man's hearty enough, and that, anyway, he don't care a curse."

"Does he know that Hyacinthe and Fanny have signed the deed, whether or no, and that they're both in possession of their shares?"

"Yes, he knows; and he knows, too, that old Fouan has let his son-in-law, Delhomme, the share that he, Buteau, wouldn't have. He knows, also, that Monsieur Baillehache was in such a fury that he took an oath he'd never again have the lots drawn for before seeing the papers signed. Oh, yes; he knows that it's all over."

"Ah! And he said nothing?"

"No, he said nothing."

Lise stooped down in silence, walked on a bit, pulling up some weeds and showing nothing save the full rotundity of her behind; then she turned her neck round, and added, with her head down: "It comes to this, Corporal, if you want to know, I shall have to keep Jules, and that'll be the end of it."

Jean, who had heretofore held out some hopes, nodded.

"Faith! you're perhaps right."

He glanced at Jules, whom he had forgotten. The brat still slept, swathed in his long-clothes, with his little motionless face bathed in light. That was the awkward part of it, that urchin! Otherwise, why shouldn't he have married Lise, now she was free? The idea came to him all at once, then and there, as he watched her working. Perhaps he loved her. Perhaps it was the pleasure of seeing her that brought him so much to the house. None the less was he surprised, not having desired her, not even having jested with her, as he had jested with Françoise, for instance. And, pat, as he raised his head, he saw the latter standing rigid and furious in the sunshine, with her eyes so strangely ablaze with passion that he was enlivened even in the agitation of his new discovery. Just then the sound of a trumpet, a strange topsy-turvy roll-call, rang out; and Lise, leaving her peas, exclaimed:

" Why, here comes Lambourdieu! I want to order a hood of him."

On the road, on the other side of the hedge, there appeared a dumpy little man, blowing a trumpet, and walking ahead of a long vehicle drawn by a grey horse. It was Lambourdieu, a shopkeeper from Cloyes, who had added, bit by bit, millinery, drapery, shoemaking, and even ironmongery to his novelty business. He went from village to village, within a radius of five or six leagues, with a regular bazaar. The peasants had ended by buying everything from him, from their saucepans to their wedding clothes. His vehicle was made to open out and turn back, displaying rows of drawers, and enough goods to stock a whole shop.

When Lambourdieu had taken the order for the hood, he added:

" In the meantime you don't happen to want a fine silk handkerchief?"

So saying he drew out of a box some gorgeous red gold-patterned handkerchiefs, and swished them up and down in the sunlight.

" There you are! Three francs each! It's giving them away. Five francs for the pair!"

Lise and Françoise, to whom they had been handed over the hawthorn hedge, on which Jules's napkins were drying, hankered after them. But they were sensible girls; they had no need of them, and why spend money? They were indeed handing them back, when Jean suddenly made up his mind to take Lise, baby and all. So, in order to precipitate matters, he called out to the young woman:

" No, no! Keep it. I offer it you! Oh, you wouldn't pain me by refusing: it's out of pure friendship, to be sure!"

He had said nothing to Françoise, and as she still held out her handkerchief to the dealer, he glanced at her, and felt a pang of grief as he fancied he saw her cheek pale and her lips quiver with pain.

" You, too, stupid ! **Keep** it. **Nay, I** insist. None **of**
that self-will of yours ! "

He struggled with the two sisters who laughingly defended
themselves. Lambourdieu had already held out his hand,
across **the** hedge, for his five francs. And **away** he went.
The **horse** behind him started off with the long vehicle, and
the hoarse flourishes of the trumpet died away **as the** road
wound out of sight.

Jean had all at once taken it into his head to push **matters on**
with Lise, and pop the question. **But an** accident **prevented**
this. The stable-door had **no doubt been badly fastened, for**
suddenly they saw the **donkey, Gédéon,** valiantly **chewing**
some carrot tops in the kitchen garden. This **donkey,** big,
sturdy, and russet-coloured, with **a large grey cross on** his
spine, was full of artfulness, and **quite a wag in** his way. He
was very good at lifting latches **with his mouth, was wont**
to fetch bread out of the kitchen, and by the style in which he
wagged his long ears when he was reproached with his vices, it
was obvious that he understood. As soon as he saw himself
discovered he put on an indifferent, easy air; then, on being
threatened and **waved** off, he moved away; only, instead of
going back into the yard, he trotted along the walks to **the**
bottom **of the garden.** Then **a regular** pursuit **set in ; and**
when Françoise had at length caught him, he **drew himself**
together and huddled his head and legs against **his body, as if**
to increase his weight, and make slower progress. **He was**
impervious to everything, whether in the shape **of kicks or**
blandishments. Indeed, Jean **had to** intervene, **and** hustle him
from behind with his man's strength; **for** Gédéon, since he
had been under the management of the two women, had con-
ceived the most hearty **contempt for them.** Jules had awoke at
the noise and was now howling. The opportunity for popping
the question was altogether lost, and Jean had to leave without
speaking.

A week **went by.** A great shyness had come upon the young
man, who had now lost heart. Not that the transaction seemed
to him disadvantageous; contrariwise, he had, on reflection,
become more deeply conscious of its advantages. Each
side could not do otherwise than gain. If he had nothing, she
was encumbered with her infant. That equalised matters. This
was no sordid calculation on his part. He argued as much for
her happiness as for his own. Then, again, marriage, by taking
him away from the farm, would rid him of Jacqueline, who
still worried him, and **to** whom he still yielded out of fleshly

weakness. So at last he made up his mind, and waited for **an** opportunity to declare himself, conning the words he meant to say, for **even** regimental life had left him somewhat a ninny with women.

At last, one day at about four o'clock, he slipped away from the farm and went to Rognes, resolved to speak. This was the time when Françoise led her cows to evening pasture, and he had chosen it so as to be alone with Lise. But he was dismayed, at the outset, by a great **annoyance.** La Frimat was established there in her character of obliging neighbour, helping the younger woman to scald **the** linen in the kitchen.

The sisters had scoured it on the evening before, and **since** the morning the ash liquor, scented with orris root, **had been** boiling in a cauldron hanging from the pot-hook over a clear, poplar **wood** fire. With bare arms, and her skirts tucked up, Lise, with the aid of a yellow earthen jug, was drawing the water off and wetting the linen, with which the bucking-tub **was filled—the sheets at** the bottom, then the house-cloths, then the body **linen,** and, at the top of all, some other sheets. La Frimat was not of much use; but she stopped to gossip, allowing herself **that** recreation, and contenting herself, every now and then, with removing and emptying into the cauldron the pail which stood under the tub to catch the lye, that kept draining away.

Jean waited patiently, hoping she would leave. She did not do so, however; but went on talking of her poor paralytic husband, who could now only move one hand. It was a great affliction. They had never been well off; but, when he could still work, he rented land which he turned to account, whereas now she had a world of trouble to cultivate by herself **the patch** that was their own. **She** struggled her hardest; **collecting horse dung from** the roads as manure, for they kept **no animals; tending her salad stock,** beans, and peas, plant by **plant; and watering even her** three plum and two apricot trees. The result **was that she made** an enormous profit out of the ground; **and** started every Saturday for the Cloyes market, staggering **under the** burden of two tremendous baskets, without reckoning the heavy vegetables which a neighbour conveyed for her in his cart. She rarely returned without two or three five-franc pieces, particularly in the fruit season. Her constant grievance was the lack of manure. Neither the horse dung, nor the sweepings from the few rabbits and hens she kept, made a sufficient supply. She had come at length to utilising the

excrements of her old man and herself, that human manure
so much despised, which provokes disgust even in the country.
This had got abroad, and people chaffed her about it, and dubbed
her Mother Caca—a nickname which did her a deal of harm at
the market : she had seen shopkeepers' wives turn with aversion
and disgust from her superb carrots and cabbages. Despite
her great mildness, this set her beside herself with fury.

"Come, now, tell me—you, Corporal—is it reasonable ?
Isn't it permissible to use all that the good God has put in our
way ? And then to go and say that the dung of animals is
cleaner ! No ; it's jealousy ! Folks have a spite against me
in Rognes, because the vegetables grow more vigorously on
my ground. Tell me, Corporal, does it disgust you ? "

Jean replied, in embarrassment : " Well, I don't find it
exactly appetising. One ain't used to it. I daresay though,
that it's only fancy."

This frankness threw the old woman into despair. Though
she was not habitually a tale-bearer, she could not restrain her
bitterness.

"Oh, that's it, is it ? They've already set you against me.
Ah, if you only knew how spiteful they are, if you had any
idea of what they say about you ! "

Then she let loose the gossip of Rognes about the young man.
To begin with, they had execrated him because he was an artisan,
and sawed and planed wood, instead of tilling the ground.
Then, when he had taken to the plough, they had taxed him
with taking the bread out of other people's mouths, by coming
into a district that wasn't his own. Did any one know where
he came from ? Hadn't he done some evil deed at home, that
he didn't even dare to go back there ? Then they spied upon
his intercourse with La Cognette, and asserted that some fine
night the two of them would administer a bowl of devil's
broth to Hourdequin, and rob him.

"Oh, the blackguards !" muttered Jean, who became pale
with indignation.

Lise, who was drawing a jugful of boiling lye from the
cauldron, started laughing at the mention of La Cognette, a
name she sometimes twitted him with in jest.

" And since I've begun, I'd better make an end of it,"
pursued La Frimat. " Well, there's no kind of abomination
they don't talk about, since you began visiting here. Last
week—wasn't it ?—you presented them both with silk necker-
chiefs, which they were seen wearing on Sunday at mass. The
filthy beasts say that you go to bed with the two of them ! "

This settled matters. Trembling, but resolute, Jean got up and said:

"Listen, my good woman. I will make reply in your presence, which shall not stand in my way. I will ask Lise if she will consent to my marrying her. You hear me ask, Lise? and if you say yes, you will make me very happy."

She was just then emptying her jug into the bucking-tub. She did not hurry, but finished carefully watering the linen. Then, with her arms bare and moist with steam, becoming quite grave, she looked him in the face.

"So you're in earnest?"

"Thoroughly in earnest."

She did not seem surprised. It was natural. Only she did not answer yes or no; there was evidently something on her mind which annoyed her.

"You needn't say no on account of La Cognette," resumed he, "because La Cognette——"

She cut him short with a gesture. She was well aware that all the larking at the farm was of no consequence.

"There is also the fact that I've absolutely nothing but my skin to bring you; whereas, you own this house and some land."

Again she waved her arm, as if to say that in her position, with a child, she agreed with him in thinking that things were evenly balanced.

"No, no! it's not that," she declared at length. "Only there's Buteau."

"But since he refuses?"

"That's certain. And now there's no sentiment in the matter, for he's behaved too badly. But, all the same, Buteau must be consulted."

Jean reflected for a good minute. Then, very sensibly, he replied:

"As you please. It's due to the child."

La Frimat, who was gravely emptying the pail of drainings into the cauldron, thought herself called upon to approve the step—albeit favourable to Jean, the honest fellow; he surely was neither pig-headed nor brutal—and she was delivering herself to this effect, when Françoise was heard outside, returning with the two cows.

"I say, Lise," she cried, "come and look. La Coliche has hurt her foot."

They all went out, and Lise, at the sight of the limping animal, with her left fore-foot bruised and bleeding, flew into

a sharp passion—one of those surly bursts with which she used
to sweep down upon her sister when the latter was little, and
happened to be in fault.

"Another of your pieces of neglect, eh? You, no doubt,
dropped off to sleep on the grass, the same as you did the
other day?"

"I assure you I didn't. I don't know what she can have
done. I tied her to the stake, and she must have caught her
foot in the cord."

"Hold your tongue, liar and good-for-nothing! You'll
get killing my cow some day."

Françoise's black eyes flashed fire. She was very pale, and
indignantly stammered out:

"Your cow, your cow! You might, at least, say our cow."

"Our cow, indeed? A chit like you with a cow!"

"Yes, half of all that's here is mine. I've a right to take
half and destroy it if it amuses me to do so!"

The two sisters stood facing each other, hostile and
threatening. It was the first painful quarrel in the course of
their long fondness. This question of *meum* and *tuum* left
them both smarting : the one exasperated by the rebellion of
her younger sister, the other obstinate and violent under a
sense of injustice. The elder gave way, and went back into
the kitchen, so as to restrain herself from boxing her sister's
ears. When Françoise, having housed her cows, re-appeared,
and went to the pan to cut herself a slice of bread, there was an
awkward silence.

Lise, however, had calmed down. The sight of her sister's
sullen resistance was now an annoyance to her, and she was the
first to speak, thinking to make an end of it by an unexpected
piece of news.

"Do you know," she asked, "Jean wants to marry me,
and has proposed?"

Françoise, who was standing by the window eating her
bread, remained indifferent, and did not even turn round.

"What odds does that make to me?"

"The odds it makes to you," replied Lise, "are that you'd
have him for a brother-in-law, and I want to know if you'd
like him?"

Françoise shrugged her shoulders.

"Like or dislike, him or Buteau, what's the good? So long
as I don't have to sleep with him. Only, if you want to know,
the whole thing is hardly decent."

And she went outside to finish her bread in the yard.

Jean, feeling rather uncomfortable, affected to laugh, as at the whims of a spoilt child; while La Frimat declared that in her young days a wench like that would have been whipped till the blood came. As for Lise, she remained a moment silent and serious, absorbed once more in her washing. Then she wound up by saying:

"Well, Corporal, we'll leave it like that. I don't say no, and I don't say yes. The hay-making is come: I shall see our people; I'll make inquiries, and find out how things stand. And then we'll settle something. Will that do?"

"That'll do!"

He held out his hand, and shook the one she gave him. From her whole person, steeped in warm steam, there exuded a true housewifely scent: a scent of wood-ash perfumed with orris.

CПAPTER IV.

FOR the last two days Jean had been driving the mowing-machine over the few acres of meadow belonging to La Borderie, on the banks of the Aigre. From daybreak till night the regular click of the blades had been heard, and that morning he was getting to the end. The last swaths were falling into line behind the wheels, forming a layer of fine, soft, pale-green herbage. The farm having no haymaking machine, he had been commissioned to engage two haymakers: Palmyre, who worked to the utmost of her strength and harder than a man; and Françoise, who had got herself engaged out of caprice, finding amusement in the occupation. Both of them had come with him at five o'clock, and, with their long forks, had laid out the *mulons*: little heaps of half-dried grass which had been gathered together over night, by way of protecting it from the night-dews. The sun had risen in a clear glowing sky cooled by a breeze. It was the very weather to make good hay in.

After breakfast, when Jean returned with his haymakers; the hay of the first acre mowed was finished. He felt it and found it dry and crisp.

" I say," cried he, " we'll give it just another turn, and to-night we'll begin the stacking."

Françoise, in a grey linen dress, had knotted over her head a blue handkerchief, one edge of which flapped on her neck, while two corners fluttered loosely over her cheeks, and shaded her face from the sun's brilliant rays. With a swing of her fork she took the grass and flung it up, while the wind blew out of it a kind of golden dust. As the blades fluttered, a strong subtle scent arose from them : the warm scent of cut grass and withered flowers. She had grown very hot, walking on amid the continuous fluttering, which put her in high spirits.

" Ah, my child," said Palmyre, in her doleful voice, " it's easy to see you're young. When night comes, you'll feel your arms stiff."

They were not alone, for all Rognes was mowing and making hay in the meadows around them. Delhomme had got there before daybreak, for the grass, when wet with dew, is tender to cut, like spongy bread; whereas it toughens in proportion as the sun grows hotter. At that moment, one distinctly heard its resistant whirr under the scythe, which, held by Delhomme, **swept** restlessly to and **fro.** Nearer, in fact contiguous with **the** grass of the farm, there **were two bits** of land, belonging **one** to Macqueron and the other to Lengaigne. In the first, Berthe, in a genteel dress with little flounces, and a straw hat, had come in attendance on the haymakers, by way of recreation. but she was already tired, and remained leaning **on** her fork in the shade **of a** willow. In the other field, Victor, who was mowing for his father, had just sat down, and, with his anvil between his knees, was beating at his scythe. For ten minutes nothing **had been** distinguishable, amid the deep thrilling silence of the air, save the persistent hurried taps of the hammer **on** the steel.

Just then Françoise came near to Berthe.

" You've had enough of it, eh ? " asked the former.

"**More or less.** I'm beginning to feel tired. You **see,** when one isn't used to it."

Then **they chatted,** whispering about Suzanne, Victor's sister, whom the Lengaignes had **sent** to a dressmaking establishment at Châteaudun, and who, after six months, had fled to Chartres to live " gay." It was said she had run off with a notary's clerk; and all the girls in Rognes whispered the scandal and speculated on the details. Living gay to them meant orgies of gooseberry syrup and Seltzer water, in **the** midst of **a** seething crowd of men, dozens of whom waited to court you, in Indian file, in the back shops of wine-sellers.

" Yes, my dear, that's how it is. Isn't she going it ? "

Françoise, being younger, stared in stupefaction.

" Nice kind of amusement ! " she said at last. " But unless she **comes** back the Lengaignes will be all alone, as Victor has been drawn for the conscription."

Berthe, who espoused her father's quarrel, shrugged her shoulders. **A** lot Lengaigne cared. His only regret was that the child hadn't stopped at home to be turned up, and so bring some custom to his shop. Hadn't an uncle of hers, an old man of forty, had her already, before she went to Châteaudun, one day when they were peeling carrots together. And, in a lower whisper, Berthe gave the exact words and circumstances. Françoise, bending double, was suffocated with laughter, it seemed so funny to her.

" Gracious goodness ! How stupid to do things like that ! "

Then resuming her work she withdrew, raising forkfuls of grass and shaking them in the sun. The persistent hammering on the **steel** was still heard. Some minutes later, as she came near to where the young man was sitting, she spoke to him.

" So you're going to be a soldier ? "

" **Oh,** in October. Plenty of time yet ; **there's no** hurry."

She struggled against her desire to question him about **his sister, but she** spoke of her despite herself.

" **Is it** true what they say, that Suzanne is now at Chartres?"

He, completely indifferent, made answer :

" I suppose so ! She seems to enjoy it."

Then, in the distance, seeing Lequeu, the **schoolmaster,** who was seemingly strolling down by chance, he resumed :

" Hullo ! There's somebody after **the** Macqueron girl. What did I tell **you?** He's stopping and poking his face into her **hair. Get along with you, you old** nincompoop! **You** may sniff **round her,** but **you'll never get** anything but the smell ! "

Françoise began laughing again, **and Victor** pursued **the family** vendetta by falling **foul** of Berthe. No doubt the schoolmaster wasn't worth much : a bully who cuffed children, **a sly-boots whose opinions nobody** knew, capable of **toadying the** girl to get her father's money. But, then, Berthe **was no** better than she should be, with all her fine town-bred **airs. It was** no use her wearing flounced skirts and velvet bodices, and stuffing out her behind with table-napkins ; the **underneath** was none the better. **Quite the reverse,** indeed, **for she was** up to snuff ; she'd **learnt more by being** brought up at the Châteaudun school than by stopping **at home** to mind the cows. No fear of her getting herself let in for **a child ; she** preferred **to ruin her** constitution in solitude.

" How do you mean ? " asked Françoise, **who did not** understand.

He made a gesture, **whereupon she became serious, and** said, unreservedly :

" That's how it is, then, that she's always saying dirty things, and rubbing herself up against you."

Victor had begun beating his blade again ; and, tapping between each phrase, he went on saying some very improper things about Berthe.

These set Françoise off into another fit of mirth ; and she only calmed down, and went on haymaking, on seeing her sister Lise on the road coming towards the meadow. Lise went up to Jean, and explained that she had settled to go and see her

uncle about Buteau. For the last three days that step had
been agreed upon between them, and she promised to come
back and tell him the answer. When she went off, Victor **was**
still tapping, and Françoise, Palmyre, and the other women
were still flinging the grass in the dazzling light of the **vast**
bright sky. Lequeu was very obligingly giving a lesson **to**
Berthe, thrusting, raising, and lowering her fork as stiffly **as a**
soldier **at drill.** Afar off, **the mowers** advanced unceasingly,
with a constant, steady motion, swinging **on** their loins, and
with their scythes perpetually sweeping to and fro.

For an instant Delhomme stopped and stood upright, towering above the **others.** From **the** cow-horn, full of water, **that**
hung **at his** belt, he had taken his hone, and was sharpening
his scythe with a bold, rapid gesture. Then he bent his back
again, **and the** sharpened steel was heard whizzing still more
keenly and bitingly over the meadow.

Lise had arrived at the Fouans' house. At first she **was**
afraid there was no one at home, the place seemed so dead. Rose
had parted with her two cows; the old man had just sold his
horse; there were no signs of animals, no work, nothing stirring
in the empty buildings and yard. Nevertheless the door yielded
to her touch; and on entering the common room, which was
gloomy and silent amid all the mirth out-of-doors, Lise found
old Fouan standing up and finishing a bit of bread and cheese,
while his wife was idly seated and looking at him.

"Good morning to you, aunt. Everything going **on**
satisfactorily?"

"Why, yes!" answered the old woman, brightening up **at**
the visit. "Now we are gentlefolks, we have only to take **a**
holiday **all** day long."

Lise tried to make herself agreeable **to her uncle too.**
"And the appetite's all right, it seems?" said **she.**

"Oh!" he answered, "it isn't that I'm hungry. Only it's
something to do if one eats a **bit now** and then, it helps to
pass the day."

He seemed so dull that Rose started off into an enthusiastic
account of their happiness in not having to do any work. True
enough, they had earned it well: it was not a bit too soon **to**
see others running **about** while they lived on their **income.**
Getting up late, twiddling their thumbs, not caring a **pin for**
wind and weather, not having a single care—ah! **it was a**
thorough change for **them**; it **was** perfectly heavenly. He,
roused and exhilarated, joined in and improved upon her ac-
count. And yet, under all the forced joy, under the feverish

exaggeration of **their talk,** there **was** plainly perceptible the profound tedium, **the torture** of idleness, that had racked these two old folks **ever since** their arms, suddenly becoming inert, **had begun to get out of order** by disuse, like old machinery **thrown aside as waste iron.**

At length Lise ventured on the subject of **her visit.**

" Uncle, they tell me that the other **day you had a talk** with Buteau."

"Buteau is a thorough beast!" **cried Fouan,** suddenly infuriated, and not giving her time to finish. "If he wasn't as pig-headed as a carroty-haired donkey, should I ever **have had that** bother with Fanny?"

This first disagreement with his **children he had so far** kept **to** himself, but, in his bitterness **of heart, the allusion** had now escaped him.

On entrusting **Delhomme with Buteau's share,** he had intended to **rent** it **out at** eighty francs **a hectare,** while Delhomme purposed **simply** paying a double allowance: two hundred francs for his own share, and two hundred for the other. That was fair, and the old **man was** the more angry because he had **been in the wrong.**

"What bother?" asked Lise. "Don't the Delhommes pay you?"

"Oh, yes!" replied Rose. "Every three months, at **the** stroke **of twelve, the** money is there on the table. Only there are ways and **ways** of paying, aren't **there?** And my old man, being sensitive, would like **people to behave at** least decently. Whereas, since this worry about Buteau's share, Fanny **comes** to us with the same air as she **would go to the process-server,** as if she **were** being **cheated.**"

" Yes," added the old man, "they **do pay, and that's about all.** I don't think that enough. There's a certain consideration due. Their money don't pay off everything, does it? We're mere creditors now, nothing more. **And** yet we're wrong to grumble. If they'd all of them pay."

He broke off, and an awkward silence fell. This allusion to Hyacinthe, who hadn't handed in a copper, but was mortgaging his share bit by bit, and getting drunk on the proceeds, wrung **the** heart of **his** mother, who was always impelled to defend that darling scamp of hers. **She** dreaded **lest** this other sore point should be laid **bare, and so she hastily** resumed:

" Don't go fretting yourself about trifles! What's the odds so long as we're happy? Enough's as good as a feast."

She had never opposed her husband like this before, and he looked at her fixedly.

"Your tongue runs too fast, old woman. I don't mind being happy, but I won't be worried."

She shrank into herself again, huddling lazily together on her chair while he finished his bread, rolling the last mouthful over and over to prolong the recreation. The dull room sank to sleep.

"I wanted to know," went on Lise, "what Buteau means to do with regard to me and his child? I haven't worried him much hitherto, but it's time to settle one way or the other."

The two old people uttered not a word. She then questioned the **father** pointedly.

"As you saw him, he must have mentioned **me.** What did **he** say?"

"Nothing. He never opened his lips on the subject. **And,** in fact, there's nothing to be said. The priest's pestering **me** to arrange things, as if anything could be arranged **so** long as the fellow refuses to accept his share."

Lise pondered in great perplexity.

"**You** think he'll accept some day?"

"**It's** still possible."

"**And** you think he'd **marry me?**"

"There's a chance of **it.**"

"Then you'd recommend me to wait?"

"Why, that depends on yourself. Everybody acts as they feel."

She was silent, unwilling to speak of Jean's proposal, and not knowing how to get a definite answer. Finally she made a last effort.

"You can well understand that **I'm sick of not** knowing what to expect after all this time. I want **a yes** or a no. Suppose, uncle *you* went and asked **Buteau? Do!**"

Fouan shrugged his shoulders.

"To begin with, I'll never speak to the skunk again, And **then, my** girl, how simple you are! Why make a stubborn **fool like** that say no, who'd always say no afterwards. **Leave him free to say** yes some day, if it's to his interest."

"**To** be sure!" concluded Rose, simply, **once more the echo of her husband.**

Lise could get nothing more definite out of them. She left them, shutting the door upon **the room, which** relapsed into its benumbed condition; and the house seemed empty once more.

In the meadows on the banks of the Aigre, Jean and his

two haymakers **had** begun the first stack. It was Françoise who built it **up.** **Placed on a** heap in the centre, she disposed circularly around her the forkfuls of hay which the young man and Palmyre brought her. Little by little the stack grew bigger and higher, she being always in the midst, and filling **up the hollow in** which she stood with bundles of hay as soon as the wall around her rose up to her knees. The rick **was now** beginning to **take shape.** It **was already more than** two yards high, **and** Palmyre and **Jean had to raise** their forks on high. The work did not proceed without **the** accompaniment of loud laughter, inspired **by the** exhilaration of the open air, and by the jests bandied to **and** fro amid **the** sweet-scented hay. Françoise, whose handkerchief had slipped down off **the** back of her head, which was bare to the sun, and **whose hair was** in disarray **and** entangled with grass and withered **flowers — was** in the happiest **of** moods amid that growing pile **in which she** was plunged up to her thighs. She buried her bare arms in the mass; **every** bundle tossed up from below covered **her** with a shower **of** stalks; **and** at times she **vanished** from sight and pretended to **come to** grief among the eddies.

"**Oh, good gracious!**   **There's** something pricking **me!**"

"**Whereabouts?**"

"**Under** my **petticoats; up here.**"

"**It's a** spider. **Hold hard! keep your legs together.**"

And the laughter grew louder, at **improper jests that made** them split their sides.

Delhomme, in the distance, was disturbed, and turned **his** head for an instant but without ceasing **to ply** his scythe. Oh, yes! **a** lot of **work** that little **chit** must **be doing,** playing like that! Now-a-days girls were spoiled, and only worked to amuse themselves. He went on, laying the swath low with hurried **strokes,** and leaving a clear wake behind him. **The** sun sank **in the heavens, the mowers** broadened the gaps **they had made.** Victor, although **he** had left off hammering his blade, **evinced** no particular haste; and as La Trouille went by **with her** geese, he slily slipped off, and ran to meet her under shelter **of** a thick line of willows that edged the stream.

"**Aha!**" cried **Jean;** "he prefers something else **to mowing.**"

Françoise burst into a fresh guffaw.

"He's too old for her," said she.

"Too old! Listen, and you'll hear them."

Then **he** began to coo so funnily and successfully that

Palmyre, holding her stomach as if she were griped by colic,
said :

" What's come to that fellow Jean to-day? **Isn't he**
funny? "

The forkfuls of grass were being flung up higher and higher,
and the stack was steadily growing.

They joked about Lequeu **and** Berthe, **who** had eventually
sat down. Most likely she **was** having herself tickled at a
respectful distance with a straw. But let the school-master
set the pastry **to bake as** much as he liked, **he** wouldn't have
the eating of it.

" Isn't he dirty !" repeated Palmyre, who couldn't laugh,
and was consequently suffocating.

Then Jean chaffed her.

" Don't tell me that you've got to the age of thirty-two and
never yet had to do with a young man ! "

" Me! Never ! "

" **What !** No **young man ever** caught hold of you?
You've no lovers ? "

" No, no."

She had grown **quite** pale and serious, with her long grief-
stained face, already **worn** and stupefied by labour, and retaining only the clear, shallow, faithful eyes of a hound. Perchance
she was recalling her miserable, friendless, loveless life, the
existence of a beast of burden whipped back at night, heavy-
eyed, to its stable. She had stopped short, and stood grasping
her fork, with a far-away look towards the distant country-side,
that **she** had **never** even seen.

There was a silence. Françoise was listening, motionless,
at the top of the stack; while Jean, who had also stopped to
take breath, went on with his banter, hesitating to say what
was on the tip of his tongue. At length he resolved to speak out.

" Then it's all lies what **they** say **about** you and Hilarion ? "
he asked.

Palmyre's face suddenly turned from white to crimson, the
rush of blood momentarily restoring her the aspect of her lost
youth. She stammered with surprise and vexation, at a loss
for the disclaimer she desired.

" Oh, the backbiters! Only to think of it ! "

Françoise and Jean, **with a** resumption of noisy mirth, spoke
both at once, pressed her **hard,** and flurried **her.** Why, in the
ruined cow-shed, **where Palmyre and Hilarion** lodged, there was
hardly any room **to** move about. Their mattresses lay touching
on the floor ; how easy it was to make a mistake in the dark !

"Come, it's true; confess it's true! Besides, it's well known."

Drawing herself up, Palmyre, quite bewildered, gave vent to her passion and pain:

"Well, and supposing that it were true," she exclaimed, "what the devil is it to you? The poor boy hasn't so happy a life as it is."

A couple of tears rolled down her cheeks, so wrung was she by her feeling of motherhood for the cripple. After earning him his bread, supposing she did accord him what others refused him, why it cost them nothing! With the darkened intellect of clod-like beings, these pariahs and outcasts of love would have been at a loss to relate how the thing had been brought about. An instinctive approach without deliberate consent, he stung by desire, she passively yielding to his purpose; thus it had begun. Then, too, there was the happiness of their feeling warmer, in that miserable hovel where they both shivered with the cold.

"She is right, what is it to us?" resumed Jean, in his grave, kindly way, touched to see her in such agitation. "It's their own concern and nobody else's."

Besides, another circumstance took up their attention. Hyacinthe had just come down from the Château, the old cellar in which he dwelt amid the brushwood, half-way up the hill; and from the top of the road he was calling for La Trouille with all his might, cursing and bawling out that his drab of a daughter had disappeared two hours ago, without troubling her head about their evening meal.

"Your daughter," cried Jean to him, "is under the willows with Victor."

Hyacinthe raised both his hands to heaven.

"Oh, the cursed troll! Bringing dishonour upon me! I'll go and fetch my whip."

He then ran back again to fetch the large horse-whip he kept hung up behind his door for use on these occasions.

La Trouille must have heard him, for there was a prolonged rustling under the leaves, as of some one escaping; and, two minutes later, Victor carelessly strolled back. He examined his scythe, and finally returned to his work. When Jean called over to him to ask if he had got the stomach-ache, he replied:

"Rather!"

The rick was now nearly completed, more than four yards high, solid, and rounded into bee-hive shape. Palmyre flung

up the last trusses with her long thin arms; and Françoise,
standing on the apex, seemed to grow taller against the pale
sky, lit up by the pink glow of the setting sun. She **was now**
quite out of breath, quite **tremulous** after her exertion, bathed
in perspiration, with her hair clinging to her skin. Her bodice
was open, showing her **firm** little bosom, while her
skirt had burst its fastenings **and** was slipping down from her
haunches.

"Oh, dear! **How** high **it is**! **I'm** getting giddy," she said;
and then she laughed shiveringly, and hesitated; not venturing
to descend, but merely stretching out **her foot** and instantly
drawing it back again.

"No, **it's too** high. Go and get a ladder," she added.

"Sit down, stupid, why don't you!" said Jean. "Slide
down."

"**No,** no! I'm afraid; **I can't!**"

There were shouts of encouragement, and some free jesting.

Not on her stomach; that would make it swell! On her
croup, provided she had no chilblains there! He, standing
below, was getting excited as he looked up at the legs of the
girl, gradually feeling exasperated to see her so high out of
reach, and unconsciously seized with a virile desire to get close
to her and embrace **her.**

"Don't I tell **you** you won't do yourself any damage," he
called. "Roll down; you'll fall into my arms."

"No, no!"

He had stationed himself in front of the rick, and spread out
his arms, displaying his chest that she might throw herself
upon it. When she suddenly came to a decision, and, shutting
her eyes, let herself go, her fall down the slippery side of the
stack was so smart that she knocked him over and got somehow
a-straddle round his ribs. She lay on the ground, with her petticoats up, choking with laughter and spluttering out that she
wasn't hurt. On feeling her burning and perspiring form against
his **face, he had seized** her in **his arms.** Her powerful feminine
odour, **the strong smell of the hay** and the fresh air, intoxicated
him, stiffening **all his sinews with** a sudden mad desire. Then,
too, there was something **else**; a hitherto unknown passion for
this child, **now bursting into strength; a** sentimental and
sensual fondness which **had originated long** back, increasing
with their frolicsome, **hearty laughter, and** ending in this longing to clasp her there upon **the** grass.

"Oh, Jean, don't! You're breaking my bones!"

She still laughed, thinking him in play. He, catching sight

of Palmyre's saucer-like eyes, started up shivering, with the wild
aspect of a drunkard sobered by the view of a yawning chasm.
What was this? It was not Lise he wanted, but this chit!
The thought of Lise's flesh in contact with his own had never
so much as quickened his heart; whilst all his blood rose and
suffocated him at the mere idea of kissing Françoise. Now
he knew why he was so fond of visiting and helping the two
sisters. Yet the child was so young that he was ashamed and
in despair.

Lise was just then coming back from the Fouans. On the
road she had reflected. She would have preferred Buteau,
because, after all, he was the father of her baby. The old
folks were right; why push things on? The day Buteau said
no there would still be Jean to say yes.

She accosted the latter without delay.

" No answer ; uncle knows nothing. Let us wait."

Still distraught and quivering, Jean stared at her without
comprehending. Then he remembered: the marriage, the
infant, Buteau's consent, the whole arrangement that, two
hours earlier, he had considered advantageous for her and for
himself. He hastened to reply:

" Yes, yes, let us wait. That'll be best."

Night was drawing in. One star already shone in the
violet sky. In the growing twilight, the dim round outlines of
the first stacks—protuberances on the smooth expanse of
meadow—were all that was distinguishable. But the odours
from the warm earth rose in greater strength amid the calm
air: sounds were heard more distinctly, more prolonged and more
musically limpid. Voices of men and women, faint laughter,
mingled with the snort of an animal, the clink of an implement;
while some mowers, growing pertinacious over a strip of
meadow, went on unremittingly with their task, the broad
regular whizz of the scythe still resounding, although the
work was no longer visible.

V.

Two years had passed in this active monotonous country life; and, with the fated return of the season, Rognes had lived its eternal round of the same toils, the same slumbers.

There stood on the road, down by the corner where the school was, a fountain of spring water, to which all **the** women came to get their drinking-water, the houses being furnished with nothing but pools, for the use of cattle and for watering purposes. At six o'clock in the evening the fountain was the head-quarters of the district Gazette. The least events were echoed there; and there the villagers indulged in endless commentaries upon the leg of mutton that some of their neighbours had eaten **for** dinner, and the daughter of such-a-one who had been in the family-way since Candlemas. For two years the same **gossip** had run its course with the seasons, ever renewed and **never** new; always children born too soon, men drunk, women beaten; a great deal of work resulting in a great deal of wretchedness. There had happened so many things, and yet nothing at all.

The Fouans, the distribution of whose **property** had made a sensation, were vegetating so sleepily **as** to be forgotten. Things had remained at the same pass: Buteau still stubborn, and still not married to the elder Mouche girl, who was rearing her child. It was the same with Jean, who had been accused of sleeping with Lise. Perhaps he didn't; but then, why was he always hanging about the house of the two sisters? That seemed suspicious. Then there were days when the fountain-time would have been dull, but for the rivalry of Cœlina Macqueron and Flore Lengaigne, whom La Bécu continually set at each other, while pretending **to** reconcile them. Then, amid a deep **calm**, there had just broken upon them two big events —the coming **elections, and** the celebrated question of the road from Rognes to Châteaudun. These involved **a** mighty blast of gossip. The full **pitchers** remained standing in **a** row; **the** women could never get away. One **Saturday evening, indeed,** there had almost been a fight.

Now, the very next day, M. de Chédeville, the late deputy, was breakfasting at Hourdequin's farm of La Borderie. He

was doing his canvassing, and wanted to get on the right side of
Hourdequin, who had great influence with the peasantry of the
district; albeit that, thanks to his position as official candidate,
he, Chédeville, was nearly certain to be re-elected. He had
once been to Compiègne, and the whole district spoke of him
as "the Emperor's friend." That was enough. He was chosen,
as if he had spent a night at the Tuileries. This M. de Chédeville was an ex-beau; he had been the pink of fashion under Louis
Philippe, retaining Orleanist tendencies in his heart of hearts,
and he had ruined himself on women. He now only possessed
his farm of La Chamade, near Orgères, where he never set foot
save at election time. Not only was he disgusted by the
falling value of farm property, but he had been seized late in
life with political ambition, with a vague notion of restoring
his fortunes by practical statesmanship. Tall, and still elegant,
with laced bust and dyed hair, he led a reformed life, though
his eyes still sparkled at the glimpse of a petticoat, and he was
preparing—so he gave out—some important speeches on agricultural questions.

The night before, Hourdequin had had a violent quarrel
with Jacqueline, who wanted to be present at the breakfast.

"You and your deputy, indeed! D'ye think I should eat
your deputy? So you're ashamed of me?" said she.

But he held out. Only two places were laid, and she
was sulking, despite the gallant air of M. de Chédeville, who,
perceiving her, had drawn his own conclusions, and couldn't
keep his eyes off the kitchen, whither she had retired in
injured dignity.

The breakfast was drawing to a close. An Aigre trout
after an omelette, and some roast pigeons.

"The fatal thing," said M. de Chédeville, "is that commercial freedom which the Emperor had gone crazy about.
No doubt things went on well after the treaties of 1867, and
every one marvelled. But to-day the real effects are being
felt. See how prices have fallen everywhere. I am for Protection; we must defend ourselves against the foreigner."

Hourdequin, lolling back in his chair and ceasing to eat,
spoke slowly and dreamily:

"Wheat, which is at fifty-two francs a quarter, costs forty-
six to produce. If it falls any lower it means ruin. And
every year, folks say, America is increasing her exportation of
cereals. We are threatened with a regular glut of the
market. What will become of us, then? See here! I've
always been in favour of progress, science, and liberty. Well,

I'm shaken in my creed, upon my word. Yes, indeed. We can't starve to death ; let's have Protection."

He returned to the wing of his pigeon, and went on :

" You're aware that your antagonist, Monsieur Roche-fontaine, the owner of the building works at Châteaudun, is a violent Free-trader ? "

They chatted for a moment about this candidate, who employed from a thousand to twelve hundred workmen : a tall, intelligent, energetic fellow, opulent to boot, and greatly inclined to serve the Empire, but so hurt at not having secured the prefect's support, that he insisted on standing as an independent candidate. He had no chance, however ; the country electors treating him as a public foe the moment he ceased to be on the strongest side.

" Lord ! " resumed M. de Chédeville : " there's only one thing he wants : bread to be low, so that he may pay his hands more cheaply."

The farmer who had been about to pour himself out a glass of claret set the bottle on the table again.

" That's the dreadful part of it ! " cried he. " On the one hand, there are ourselves, the peasants, who want to sell our grain at a remunerative price ; and, on the other, there's the manufacturer, who drives prices down to lessen wages. It's war to the knife ; and how's it to end ? Come ! "

In truth, here was the burning question of the hour : the antagonism that strains the framework of society. This question was far beyond the ex-beau, who contented himself with nodding his head, and making an evasive gesture.

Hourdequin, having filled his glass to the brim, emptied it at a draught.

" It can't end. If the peasant makes a profit out of his corn, the artisan starves ; if the artisan feeds well, the peasant dies. What then ? I don't know. Let's feed on one another ! "

With both his elbows on the table, fairly launched, he relieved his feelings in a violent way. His secret disdain for this absentee landlord, who knew nothing of the land he lived by, betrayed itself by a certain ironical tremor in his voice.

" You've asked me for facts for your speeches. Well, to begin with : it's your own fault if La Chamade doesn't pay. The farmer you've got there is taking things easy, because his lease is expiring, and he suspects your intention of raising the rent. You're never seen ; so people snap their fingers at you and rob you. Nothing more natural. Then there's a simpler reason **for your ruin**: we're all being ruined.   **La Beauce—** fertile **La Beauce**, our nurse and mother—is worked out!"

So he went on.   For instance, **in** his young days, **Le Perche**, on the other side **of the** Loir, was a poor ill-cultivated **country**, almost grainless, the inhabitants of **which** used **to come to** Cloyes, Châteaudun, **and** Bonneval, **and hire themselves out at harvest-time.**   Now-a-days, thanks to **the continued rise in price of** manual labour, it was Le Perche that prospered, **and would soon outstrip** La Beauce; without taking into account that it was growing rich on live **stock.**   For **the markets of** Mondoubleau, Saint-Calais, and Courtalain supplied **the open** districts with horses, oxen, and **swine.**   La Beauce only lived thanks to her sheep.   Two **years** earlier, when congestion **of the** spleen had decimated the **flocks, she** had gone through **a** terrible crisis, so much so, that if **the** plague had continued, she would **never have survived.**

Then **he entered on his own** struggles, **his** own story; his twenty years' battle with the land, which had left him poorer than before.   He had **al**ways lacked capital.   He had not been able to improve certain fields as **he** would have wished.   Marling, alone, was inexpensive, **yet no** one but him had given any attention to it.   It was the same with the manures.   **No one** used aught but farm manure, which was insufficient.   **All his** neighbours scoffed at his trying chemical **manures, the inferior** quality of which, however, often justified **the mockers.   As for** the rotation of crops, he had been **bound to conform to the** custom of the country, and use the triennial system **without** fallows, now that the plan of artificial meadows and the culture of hoed plants was extending.   **Only one** machine, the threshing-machine, was beginning **to find acceptance.**   Such was the deadly, inevitable, numbing influence of routine; and if he, progressive and intelligent, felt that influence, what must it be for the hard-headed peasantry hostile to all improvement?   A peasant would starve **sooner than take a handful** of earth from his field and **carry it for analysis** to a chemist, who could tell him what it contained in excess and in what it was deficient; the manure it required, and the crops best adapted to **it.** No; the peasant was always receiving from the soil, and never dreaming of restoring anything; acquainted with no manure but that of his two cows and his horse, of which he was very thrifty.   The rest was left to chance; the seed thrown into any kind of soil, and left to germinate at random; and heaven was blasphemed if it never germinated at all.   Whenever the peasant's eyes became opened, and he decided to devote himself to a rational and scientific system, the produce would be doubled. Till then, ignorant and headstrong, without a ha'porth of progress in him, he would go on murdering the soil. **And** thus it was that La Beauce—the ancient granary **of** France, flat and arid, with nothing but her corn—was gradually wasting away through exhaustion ; weary of being bled at every vein, and of nurturing a race of blockheads.

" Ah ! Every blasted thing is failing ! " he cried, brutally. " Our sons will see the bankruptcy of the soil. **Are** you aware **that our** peasants, **who** once used **to save** up their coppers to buy a bit of land they had hungered after for years, are now buying stocks **and** shares—Spanish, Portuguese, even Mexican ? And they wouldn't risk fifty **francs to im-** prove an acre. They have lost confidence. The parents **go** round and round in a circle **of** routine like foundered animals ; the sons and daughters think of nothing but letting **the** cows run loose, and sprucing themselves up to gad off **into** town. And the worst of it is that education—that famous education, don't you know ? that was going to put everything straight—favours this exodus, this depopulation of the country, by inspiring the children with silly vanity and false ideas of comfort. See here, now. **At** Rognes they've a schoolmaster, that Lequeu, a fellow broken loose from the plough and eaten up with spite against the land he just missed cultivating. Well, how can you expect him **to** reconcile his boys to their lot, when he treats them every day like savages, like brute beasts, and sends them back to the paternal dung-heap with a scholar's contempt. The remedy, good heavens ! The **as-** sured remedy would be to have other schools—a practical system of teaching, graduated courses of agriculture. There's a fact for you. I insist upon that. It is there, in those schools perhaps, that salvation lies, if there's yet time."

M. de Chédeville, pre-occupied, and feeling thoroughly un-comfortable under this mighty avalanche of facts, hastened to reply :

" No doubt, no doubt."

Then as the servant brought in the dessert—a cream cheese and some fruit—leaving the kitchen door wide open, he caught sight of Jacqueline's pretty profile. He bent forward, winked, and fidgeted, to attract that amiable personage's attention ; and then resumed, in the mellow tones of his old lady-killing days :

" You don't tell me anything about the small holdings."

He set forth the current notions—the small proprietorships

created in '89, favoured by the law, destined to regenerate
agriculture; in short, everybody a landowner, and each man
devoting his intellect and energies to the cultivation of his
scrap of land.

"Stuff and nonsense!" declared Hourdequin. "To begin
with, the petty landowners existed before '89, and in almost as
large a proportion. And in the next place, there's a good deal
to be said on both sides about cutting up the soil."

With his elbows again on the table, eating some cherries
and spitting out the stones, he now entered into details. In La
Beauce the petty landowners, those who inherited less than
fifty acres, were in the proportion of eighty per cent. For
some time almost all the day labourers—those who worked on
the farms—had been buying bits of land, fragments of large
demesnes, and cultivating them at odd moments. That was
certainly an excellent plan, for the labourer was thus at once
bound to the soil. It might be added in favour of the system
of petty holdings that it developed worthier, more self-reliant,
and better educated men. Finally, it conduced to a com-
paratively larger yield, the produce also being of better
quality; for the owner exerted himself to the utmost, and
tended his crop minutely. But how many inconveniences
there were on the other hand! First, this superiority in
yield and quality was due to excessive work. The parents and
children toiled to death in order to live. Indeed, it was this
exhausting, ungrateful labour that was finally depopulating the
rural districts. Next, with the subdivision of the soil there
was increased transport, which spoilt the roads and augmented
the cost of production, besides leading to waste of time. It
was impossible to employ machinery on the smaller holdings,
on which, moreover, the triennial rotation was necessary.
This was certainly unscientific, for it was unreasonable to
demand two successive crops of cereals, oats, and wheat. In
short, extreme subdivision of the soil seemed so surely to por-
tend danger, that, after having encouraged it by law just after
the Revolution—for fear of seeing the large domains formed
again—the State had now begun to facilitate transfers by
diminishing the charges thereon.

"Mark this," he continued, "a strife has set in, and is
growing in acrimony, between the larger and smaller landowners. Some, like me, favour the system of large holdings,
because they seem more in accord with science and progress,
with the increased use of machinery, and the circulation of large
sums of money. Others, on the contrary, only believe in

individual effort, and **praise** the system of small holdings;
dreaming of cultivation on **the** most minute scale; **a system in
which every one** would produce his own manure, look after **his
own quarter of** an acre, sort **out** his seeds one by one, allotting
the required soil **to each** kind, **and** then raise each plant by
itself under glass. **Which of the** two will get the upper hand?
Hang me if I've **any idea!** I am well aware, as I told you
just now, that every **year large ruined farms** are dropping to
pieces in my neighbourhood, and falling into **the** hands of gangs,
and that the system of small holdings is gaining ground. I
know, moreover, at Rognes, **a** very curious instance **of an** old
woman who derives quite a comfortable subsistence for herself
and her **husband** from less than an acre **of** land. They nickname her **Mother Caca,** because she doesn't shrink from emptying
the contents of **her** own and her husband's chamber vase **on** to
her vegetables, **as** is the **custom of the** Chinese, **so it would
seem.** But that **is** hardly **better than** gardening. I can't
picture cereals growing in beds like turnips; and **if, for a**
peasant **to** be independent, **he** produced something of everything, **what** would become **of** our Beaucerons—who have only
their wheat to **rely** upon—when our Beauce has been cut up
like a chess-board? However, **if one** lives long enough, one
will see which will **triumph in the** future—the system of large
holdings or that **of small ones."**

At this point he **broke off and shouted:** "Are we going to
have **that** coffee to-day **or to-morrow?"**

Then, lighting his pipe, he resumed: **" Unless both be killed**
at once, **and** that's what folks are **in a fair way of doing.**
Mark this, agriculture is on its last legs, **and will die** if **some**
one doesn't come to its **assistance.** Everything **is** crushing it
down—taxes, foreign competition, the **continued rise in** the
cost of manual labour, **the drain of money which goes** to
manufacturing undertakings, and **stocks and shares.** To be
sure, there are no **end** of promises abroad. **Every one** is lavish
of them—the prefects, the ministers, **the** Emperor. But the
dust rises on the roads, and nothing is seen coming. Shall I
tell you **the strict** truth? Now-a-days, a cultivator who holds
on either **wastes his own** money or other people's. It's all
right for me, **because I have a few** coppers laid **by.** But I
know people **who borrow money at** five per cent., **while their**
land does not yield **them so much** as three. The **collapse is**
fatally ahead. A peasant who borrows is a ruined man. He
will infallibly be stripped of everything—to his last shirt.

" Only last week one of my neighbours was evicted, the

parents and their four children being flung into the street, after the lawyers had robbed them of their live stock, their land, and their house. And yet for years and years people have been promising us the establishment of an agricultural loan-company which would lend money at a reasonable rate of interest. I only wish they may get it! All this disgusts even good workers, who have come to such a pass that they think twice even before getting their wives into the family way. No, thanks! What! another mouth to feed—another starveling born to wretchedness! When there isn't bread enough for all, no more children are born and the nation perishes."

Monsieur de Chédeville, who was quite disconcerted, ventured on an uneasy smile, and murmured: " You don't look on the bright side of things."

"That is true, there are times when I feel inclined to let everything go hang," replied Hourdequin gaily. "And no wonder; these troubles have been going on now for thirty years. I don't know why I have persisted. I ought to have sold everything off. and taken to something else. One reason with me, no doubt, was force of habit; and then there is the hope that things will mend, and then—why not confess it?—a passionate fondness for the occupation. When once this cursed land gets hold of you, it doesn't let go in a hurry. Look here! Look at that ornament on that table. It is foolish of me, perhaps, but when I look at it I feel consoled."

He stretched out his hand and pointed to a silver cup, protected from the flies by a piece of muslin. It was a reward of merit gained in an agricultural competition.

These competitions, in which he triumphed, were the whetstone of his vanity and one of the causes of his obstinacy.

In spite of the obvious weariness of his guest, he dallied over his coffee, and was pouring some brandy into his cup for the third time when, drawing out his watch, he suddenly started up: "Goodness! It's two o'clock, and I am due at a meeting of the Municipal Council. It's about a road. We are quite willing to pay half the money, but we should like to obtain a subsidy from the State for the other half."

Monsieur de Chédeville had risen from his chair, delighted at being set free.

" In that matter I can be of service to you," he said. " I'll get your subsidy for you. Shall I take you to Rognes in my gig since you are pressed for time?"

" Just the thing!" replied Hourdequin, and he went out to

see to the harnessing of the conveyance, which had remained in
the yard.

When he came back the deputy was no longer in the room,
but eventually he perceived him in the kitchen. No doubt he
had pushed the door open; and he was standing there smiling in
front of the radiant Jacqueline, and complimenting her at such
close quarters that their faces nearly touched. Having sniffed
each other, they had summed each other up, and told each
other so by unmistakable glances.

When Monsieur de Chédeville had got into his gig again,
La Cognette held Hourdequin back for a minute to whisper in
his ear:

"He is nicer than you are. He doesn't think that I am
only fit to be hidden away."

On the road, while the vehicle was rolling along between
the wheat fields, the farmer returned to his one pre-occupation,
the soil. He now volunteered manuscript notes and figures,
for he had kept accounts for some years. In the whole of La
Beauce there were not three people who did as much, and the
small landowners, the peasants, shrugged their shoulders at
the idea, and did not even understand it. Nevertheless, one's
situation could only be made clear by accounts, which indicated what products had proved profitable and what had
entailed a loss. Moreover, accounts gave one the cost price,
and thus indicated on what terms one ought to sell. At
Hourdequin's, every servant, every animal, every field, every
tool even, had a page to itself, with debit and credit columns,
so that he was constantly enlightened as to the success or
failure of his operations.

"At all events," said he, with his hoarse laugh, "I know
how I am ruining myself." Then he broke off to indulge in a
muttered curse. During the last few minutes, as the vehicle
rolled along, he had been trying to make out what was going
on by the roadside some distance off. Although it was Sunday, he had sent a recently-purchased hay-making machine,
on a new system, to turn a cutting of lucern, which required
immediate attention. The farm-hand, being off his guard, and
not recognising his master in this strange vehicle approaching,
was making fun of the machine in company with three peasants
whom he had stopped on the way. "There," said he, "that's a
nice old tin-pot thing. It creaks like an old pulley, breaks the
grass to bits, and poisons it. On my word, three sheep have
already died of it."

The peasants, meanwhile, sneered and examined the hay-

making machine as if it were some strange, spiteful animal.
One of them even said: "All these things are devilish
inventions to ruin poor folks. What will our wives do when
people are able to make hay without them?"

" A precious lot the masters care about that," resumed the
farm-hand, launching out a kick at the machine. " Ugh! you
beast!"

Hourdequin had heard him, and popping his head and
shoulders out of the vehicle, he shouted: "Go back to the
farm, Zéphyrin, get your wages, and take yourself off."

The farm-hand stood stupefied, while the three peasants
went off, indulging in insulting laughter and loudly audible
jests.

" There," said Hourdequin, throwing himself back on the
seat. " You saw them. That's the state in which they are.
One might imagine that improved machinery burnt their
fingers. Besides, they treat me as if I were a townsman.
They take less trouble with my land than with other people's,
saying that I can afford to pay higher prices; and they are
supported by my neighbours, who accuse me of getting the
country folk into idle ways. They even assert that if there
were many like me, the farmers would no longer be able to get
their work done as they used to."

The gig now reached the foot of the hill, and was entering
Rognes by the Bazoches-le-Doyen road, when the deputy
perceived the Abbé Godard coming out of Macqueron's shop,
where he had breakfasted that morning after mass. Monsieur
de Chédeville's election worries once more took possession of
him, and he asked: " How about the religious feeling in our
country districts?"

" Oh! there's an outward show, but nothing at the
bottom of it," carelessly replied Hourdequin, who certainly
made no outward show himself. He stopped at the tavern
kept by Macqueron, who was standing at the door with the
priest, and he introduced his assessor, who was wearing a
greasy old overcoat. Coelina, looking very neat in her print
dress, ran up, pushing forward her daughter Berthe, the
pride of the family, who was genteelly clad in a silk dress,
with narrow mauve stripes.

Meanwhile, the village, which had been in a dead-alive
state, as if every one had been made lazy by so fine a Sunday,
woke up in its surprise at this unusual visit. Peasants appeared
on the thresholds, and children peeped out from behind their
mothers' skirts. At the Lengaignes' especially there was

much hurrying to and fro, and **the** husband was craning **his head out,** with his razor in his hand, while his wife, Flore, stopped weighing **twopennyworth** of tobacco to **press her face** against the window-pane, **both of** them being **extremely vexed** at seeing the gentleman get down at their rival's door. **Little** by little people came round, **and a crowd** collected, the **whole** of Rognes being **by this time aware of the** important event.

Addressing **the deputy, Macqueron, who** was flushed and embarrassed, **exclaimed : " This** is, indeed, **an** honour, **sir."**

But Monsieur **de** Chédeville was not listening to him, being enchanted with the pretty **face of** Berthe, **who,** with her bright **eyes, surrounded by** slight bluish **rings, was** staring at him **boldly. Her mother was** saying how **old she was and where** she had been to school ; while she herself, smiling **and curtsey-** ing, invited the gentleman to condescend to walk in.

" Why, certainly, my dear child ! " he exclaimed.

Meanwhile the Abbé Godard, button-holing Hourdequin, was begging him once **more to** persuade the Municipal Council to vote some funds, **so that** Rognes might at length have a priest of its **own.** He returned **to** this subject every six months, giving his **reasons—the strain it was** upon him, and the constant quarrels he **used to have with** the village ; not to mention that the service itself suffered. " Don't say no ! " he added, quickly, seeing **the farmer** make an evasive gesture. " Speak about it, **all the same ; I** will await the reply."

Then just as Monsieur de Chédeville was on **the point of** following Berthe, **he** pushed forward and stopped **him in his** stubborn, genial way.

" Excuse me, sir," he began. " **But the** poor **church here is in** such a state ! I want to **show it to you, and you** must get it repaired for me. **No one listens to me. Come, come,** I implore you ! "

Very **much annoyed, the** ex-beau **was** resisting, when **Hourdequin, on learning** from Macqueron **that** several of the **councillors were already** at the municipal offices, where they had **been waiting half-an hour,** said unceremoniously : "That's the thing ! **Go** and **see the** church. You will kill time like that until **I** have done, **and then** you can take me back home." Monsieur de Chédeville **was** thus obliged to **follow** the priest. **The** crowd **had now** become larger, and several people started **off,** dogging his steps. They had grown **bolder,** too, and every- body was thinking of asking him for **something.**

When Hourdequin and Macqueron had gone upstairs into the room where the council met, they found three councillors

there—Delhomme and two others. The apartment, a moderately large white-washed room, had no other furniture than a
long deal table and twelve straw-bottomed chairs. Between
the two windows, from which one overlooked the road, there
was a cupboard in which the archives were kept, mingled with
sundry official documents, while on shelves round the wall there
were piles of canvas fire-buckets, the gift of a gentleman, which
they did not know where to put, and which proved a useless
encumbrance, as they had no fire-engine.

"Gentlemen," said Hourdequin, politely, "I ask your
pardon. I have had Monsieur de Chédeville breakfasting
with me."

No one moved a muscle; and it was impossible to say
whether they accepted this excuse. From the windows
they had certainly seen the deputy arrive, and they were also
interested in the coming election. But it was not politic for
them to commit themselves.

"The devil!" now cried the farmer. "There are only five
of us. We shall not be able to come to any decision."

Fortunately, Lengaigne came in. At first he had resolved
not to attend the meeting, as the question of the road did not
interest him, and he had even hoped that his absence would
hamper the voting. Later on, the arrival of Monsieur de Chédeville throwing him into a fever of curiosity, he had decided
to go upstairs to find out all about it.

"Good! There are six of us now, and we shall be able to
vote," cried the mayor.

Lequeu—who acted as secretary—having made his appearance, with a snappish, surly air, and with the minute-book under
his arm, there was no further impediment in the way of opening the meeting. Delhomme, however, had begun to whisper
to his neighbour, Clou, the farrier, a tall, withered fellow, very
dark. As the others began to listen to them, they suddenly
became silent. One name had, however, been caught—that of
the independent candidate, Monsieur Rochefontaine—and then
the rest of them, after sounding each other, fell with a word, a
sneer, or a simple grimace upon this candidate, whom nobody
even knew. They were on the side of order; in favour of
keeping things as they were, and of remaining submissive to
the authorities who ensured the sale of produce. Did that
gentleman think himself stronger than the Government? Did
he imagine that he could raise corn to eighty-eight francs a
quarter? It was bold, indeed, for a man without a vestige of
support to send out circulars and promise more butter than bread.

They ended by dubbing **him an** adventurer and **a** rogue, who went on the stump through the villages for the sake of robbing **them** of their votes, just as he would have robbed them of their coppers. Hourdequin—who might have explained to them that Monsieur Rochefontaine, **a** free-trader, really shared the Emperor's ideas—wilfully **let** Macqueron display his Bonapartist zeal, and **Delhomme** propound his opinion in his strong limited, common-sense **way**; while Lengaigne, whose official position kept his mouth shut, sat growling in a corner, in**audibly repeating his** vague Republican **views.** Although **Monsieur de Chédeville** had not once been **mentioned,** he was **alluded to in** every sentence that was **uttered;** they all **grovelled, as it** were, before his title of official **candidate.**

"Come, gentlemen," resumed the **mayor;** "**suppose we** commence."

He had seated himself at the **table** in his presidential **broad-backed arm-chair.**

The assessor was the only **one** who **sat** down by his side. **Two of** the councillors remained standing upright, and **two leaned upon a** window-sill. Lequeu had handed the mayor a **sheet of paper,** and whispered in his ear. Then he left the room in a **dignified** way. "Gentlemen," **said Hourdequin,** "here is **a** letter addressed **to us** by **the schoolmaster.**"

It **was** read aloud, and proved to be a request for an increase **of thirty francs in** the master's yearly salary, the application being **based upon the** energy he displayed. Every face had **grown dark. They were always** very close with the public **money, as if it came out of their own** pockets, especially in **the** matter of **the school. There was** not **even a** discussion; they refused **the application point-blank.**

"Good! we'll tell him to wait. The young man is in too much of a hurry. And now let's deal with this matter of the road."

"Beg pardon!" interrupted Macqueron, "I want to say a word or two about church matters."

Hourdequin, surprised, now understood why the Abbé **Godard had breakfasted with the** innkeeper. What ambition **was urging the latter to push** himself to the front like this? However, his propositions met with the same fate as the schoolmaster's request. It was in vain he argued that they were rich enough to pay for a priest of their own, and that it was scarcely respectable to have to put up with the leavings of Bazoches-le-Doyen. They all shrugged their shoulders, and asked if the Mass would be any better for it. No, no! They would have to repair the parsonage; it would cost too much to have a priest to themselves, and half an hour of the other's time each Sunday was sufficient.

The mayor, hurt by his assessor taking matters into his own hands, concluded: "There is no need for any change. The council has already decided. Now about our road. We must make an end of it. Delhomme, pray have the goodness to call in Monsieur Lequeu. Does the fellow imagine that we are going to discuss his letter all day long?"

Lequeu, who had been waiting on the stairs, came in gravely, and as they did not apprise him of the fate of his request, he remained snappish and restless, swelling with covert insult. What a contemptible set of men these peasants were! However, he had to take the map of the road out of the cupboard and spread it out on the table.

The council knew the map well. It had been hanging about for years. But none the less they all approached, elbowing one another, and deliberating once more. The mayor enumerated the advantages which Rognes would derive. The gentleness of the slope would allow vehicles to drive up to the church. Then two leagues would be gained on the road to Châteaudun, which now passed through Cloyes. And the village would only have to pay the cost of some two miles of the road, their Blangy neighbours having already voted the remaining bit, as far as the junction with the highway from Châteaudun to Orleans. They listened to him with their eyes fixed steadfastly on the paper, and never opening their mouths. What had especially prevented the plan from coming to a head was the indemnity question. Every one saw a fortune to be made out of this road, and was anxious to know if one of his fields would be required, and if he would be able to sell it to the village at the rate of a hundred francs a perch. But supposing their own fields were not encroached upon, why on earth should they vote for the enrichment of others? A deal they cared about the gentle slope or the shorter route! Their horses would have to pull a bit harder, that was all!

So Hourdequin had no need to make them talk to learn their opinions. He only desired the road so eagerly because it would run past the farm and several of his fields. In the same way Macqueron and Delhomme, whose land would border the road, were in favour of the vote. That made three; but neither Clou nor the other councillor had any interest in the question; and as for Lengaigne, he was violently opposed to the project, having in the first place nothing to gain by it, and

being also aggrieved that his rival, the assessor, should reap
any advantage by it. If Clou and the doubtful one voted on
the wrong side there would be three against three, so Hourdequin became anxious. At last the discussion began.

"What's the good? what's the good of it?" repeated
Lengaigne. "We've a road already, haven't we? It's just
the pleasure of spending money, taking it out of Jean's pocket
to put it in Pierre's. Now, there's you! You promised to give
your ground up for nothing!"

This was a slap at Macqueron, who, bitterly regretting his
fit of generosity, gave the lie direct.

"I never promised anything! Who told you that?"

"Who? Why, confound it! you did! Before people, too!
Why, Monsieur Lequeu was there, he can tell us. Wasn't it
so, Monsieur Lequeu?"

The schoolmaster, angered at not being told his fate, made
a coarse gesture of contempt. What were their beastly disputes to him?

"Oh, all right!" resumed Lengaigne. "If people can't be
open and honest, we'd better live in the woods! No, no, I'll
have nothing to do with your road! A piece of jobbery!"

Seeing that matters were taking a nasty turn, the mayor
hastened to interpose.

"That's all rubbish. We haven't to enter into private
questions. It's the public interest, the interest of all, that ought
to be our leading guide."

"Quite so," said Delhomme, "The new road will be of
great service to the whole place. Only we must be
certain of our ground. The prefect keeps on saying to us:
'Vote a sum of money, and then we will see what the
Government will do for you.' Now, if it didn't do anything
at all, what's the good of our wasting our time voting?"

Hourdequin thought this the moment to publish the great
piece of news he was holding in reserve.

"Talking of that, gentlemen, I have to tell you that
Monsieur de Chédeville engages to get a subsidy representing
half the expenses from the Government. You know he is the
Emperor's friend. He will only have to speak to him about us
at dessert."

Lengaigne himself was moved at this. All the faces had
assumed a beatifical expression, as if the Host were passing.
In any case the re-election of the deputy was secured. The
Emperor's friend was the man for them, the man who had
access to the fountain-head of office and wealth—the known,

honourable, powerful **master!** Nothing **passed, however, but**
some noddings **of the head.** These things **were self-evident.**
Why mention **them?**

Still **Hourdequin was** disquieted **by the non-committal
policy of Clou.** He got up and glanced **outside; and perceiving
the rural constable, he** bade him go for **old Loiseau and bring
him in alive or dead.** This Loiseau **was an old deaf peasant,
appointed a member of the council by way of a joke; he never
attended its meetings, because they set his head in a whirl,
so he** declared. His son **worked at La Borderie, and he was
entirely** devoted **to** the **mayor.** Accordingly, on his appearance, the latter merely shouted into one of his ears that it
was about the road. Each of them was already awkwardly
filling up his voting paper, poring over the writing with
outstretched elbows, to prevent the others from reading it.
Then they proceeded to vote the half of the outlay, placing their
papers in **a little tin receptacle like a poor-box.** The majority
was **superb.** There were six votes for, and only one against—
that of Lengaigne. That beast Clou had voted right. **The
meeting was dissolved, after** every **one had** signed the minute-
book, which the schoolmaster had previously prepared, leaving
the result of the vote blank. **Then they all went** away moodily,
without **a farewell word or the pressure of a** hand, dropping
off one by one on the stairs.

"Oh, I forgot!" **said Hourdequin, coming** back to Lequeu,
who was still **waiting.** "Your request for an increase of
salary is rejected. The council is of opinion that too **much**
money is already **spent on the school."**

"A set of beasts!" **cried the young man,** green with **fury,
when** he **was alone.** "Go and live in your pig-sties!"

The meeting had lasted two hours. In front of the
municipal offices Hourdequin picked up Monsieur de Chédeville,
who was just come back from his visits round the village.
To begin with, the priest had not spared him a single **one of
the church dilapidations—the cracked** roof, the broken **windows, the bare walls.** Then, as he was at length making his
escape from the vestry, which wanted repainting, **the** inhabitants, quite emboldened, fought for him, each one trying
to bear him away, to hear some complaint, or to grant some
favour. One had dragged him off to the village pond, which was
not cleaned out for want of money; another pointed out a spot
on the bank of the Aigre where he wanted a wash-house
built; a third pressed for the widening of the road in front of
his door, so that his cart could turn round; there was even an

old woman who, having pushed the deputy into her cottage, showed him her swollen legs, and asked him whether he didn't know of a remedy in Paris. Flustered and breathless, he smiled, made himself pleasant, and kept on promising. Oh, he was a good sort, and affable to the poor !

" Well, shall we go ? " asked Hourdequin. " They are waiting for me at the farm."

Just then Cœlina and her daughter Berthe ran out again to beg Monsieur de Chédeville to come in for a moment; and that gentleman would have gladly done so, for he had at length found breathing-space, and was gratified to renew his acquaintance with the pretty, bright, dissipated eyes of the young lady.

" No, no ! " resumed the farmer, " we haven't time. Some other occasion."

He then bundled him back into the gig; while to a question from the waiting priest he answered that the council had taken no steps in the matter of the parish service. The driver whipped forward his horse, and the vehicle spun off through the midst of the friendly and delighted village. The priest alone was furious, as he set off to walk his two miles from Rognes to Bazoches-le-Doyen.

A fortnight later Monsieur de Chédeville was elected by a large majority, and towards the end of August he had redeemed his promise—the subsidy was granted for the opening of the new road, and the work was immediately put in hand.

On the evening when the first stroke of the pickaxe was given the thin and dark Cœlina stood at the fountain listening to La Bécu, who, with her lanky arms intertwined under her apron, was talking at endless length. For the last week the meetings at the fountain had been revolutionised by this mighty question of the road. The constant topic was the money paid as an indemnity to So-and-so, and the slanderous rage of the rest. Every day La Bécu kept Cœlina posted as to what Flore Lengaigne said; not, of course, to provoke dissension, but, contrariwise, to induce them to explain themselves, that being the surest way of bringing them to an harmonious understanding. Women were standing round, forgetful and listless, with their pitchers full beside them.

" Well, so she said, just like that, that it was all arranged between the assessor and the mayor how they could best swindle in the matter of the ground. And she also said that your husband was double-tongued."

At this moment Flore came out of her house with her

pitcher in her hand. When she had got there, fat and flabby, Cœlina, with her arms a-kimbo, shrewish and virtuous, broke out into vile abuse, falling upon her in fine style, flinging in her teeth her hussy of a daughter, and taxing her with behaving improperly with her customers. The other, dragging along her slippers trodden down at heel, confined herself to repeating, in a whimpering tone:

"There's a baggage for you! There's a baggage for you!"

La Bécu then threw herself between them, and tried to make them kiss each other; which all but resulted in their tearing one another's hair out. Then she let fly a piece of news.

"I say! Talking of that, you know that the Mouche girls are going to get five hundred francs?"

"You don't say so!"

The quarrel was at once forgotten. They all crowded up amid the pitchers.

Certainly! The road up there on the plateau skirted the field belonging to the Mouche girls, and cut five hundred yards off it. At a franc the yard, that made five hundred francs; and the ground that bordered the road would be enhanced in value. It was, indeed, a piece of luck.

"In that case," said Flore, "Lise has become a capital match, child and all. That big simpleton Corporal has been wide awake, all the same, in sticking out."

"Unless," added Cœlina, spitefully, "unless Buteau comes back again. His share, too, is finely improved by the road."

At this moment La Bécu turned round and nudged them.

"'Sh! Be quiet!"

Lise was coming up, gaily swinging her pitcher. Then the procession past the fountain resumed its course.

CHAPTER VI.

HAVING got rid of La Rousse, who was too fat and no longer calved, Lise and Françoise had resolved to go that Saturday to Cloyes market to buy another cow, Jean offering to drive them there in one of the farm carts. He had kept his afternoon free, and the master had given him permission to take the vehicle, on account of the rumours which were current concerning the young fellow's betrothal to the elder girl. The marriage was, in fact, decided on; or, at least, Jean had promised to lay the question in person before Buteau during the following week. The matter needed settlement; one or the other of them must marry the girl.

So they started off at about one o'clock, he in front with Lise, and Françoise by herself on the other seat. From time to time he turned round and smiled at the younger girl, whose knees were in warm contact with his loins. 'Twas a great pity that she was fifteen years younger than he; and although, after much reflection and many deferments, he had resigned himself to his marriage with the elder girl, it was, no doubt, the idea of living as a relative near Françoise that really influenced him. And then, how many things we do out of passivity, without knowing why, except that we did once determine to do them.

As they entered Cloyes, Jean applied the brake and urged the horse down the steep declivity near the burying-ground. As he came out at the intersection of the Rue Grande and the Rue Grouaise, intending to put up at "The Jolly Ploughman" hostelry, he pointed abruptly to the back of a man who was going along the latter street.

"Hallo! That looks like Buteau," he said.

"It is Buteau," declared Lise.

"No doubt he's going to Monsieur Baillehache's. Does he mean to accept his share of the land?"

Jean smacked his whip with a laugh.

"There's no knowing," he said. "He's a deep one!"

Although Buteau had recognised them a good way off, he made no sign. He went trudging on, with his back bent; and

they both watched him out of sight, thinking to themselves
that possibly they would have an opportunity for an explanation
on reaching the courtyard of "The Jolly Ploughman." Françoise,
who had remained silent, got down first by one of the wheels.
The yard was already full of unharnessed vehicles, resting on
their shafts, and the old buildings of the inn were buzzing
with life.

"Now, are we going there?" asked Jean on his return
from the stable, whither he had been with his horse.

"Certainly, at once."

When outside, however, instead of making straight for the
cattle-market—which stood on the Place Saint-Georges—by
taking the Rue du Temple, the young man and the girls hung
about and sauntered down the Rue Grande, through the
vegetable and fruit-sellers who lined the street on either side.
He wore a silk cap, and a large blue blouse over black cloth
trousers; while the girls, likewise in holiday clothes, with
their hair done up close under their little round caps, wore
dresses to match each other—a dark-coloured woollen bodice
above an iron-grey skirt, relieved by a large cotton apron with
narrow pink stripes. They did not link arms, but walked in
Indian file, their hands swinging loosely amid the jostling of
the crowd. There was a crush of servants and ladies in front
of the squatting peasant-women, who, on arriving with one or
two baskets apiece, had set them down on the ground and
opened them. They recognised La Frimat, whose hands were
blue with having carried her load from Rognes, and who had
a little of everything in her two overflowing baskets—some
salad, beans, plums, and even three live rabbits. An old man,
alongside, had just emptied out a cart-load of potatoes, which
he was selling by the bushel. Two women, mother and
daughter—the latter a notorious street-walker, named Norine—
had exposed on a rickety table some cod, salt herrings, and
bloaters, the mere remnants of barrels, the strong brine of
which made one's throat smart. The Rue Grande, so deserted
on the other days of the week, despite its handsome shops—its
chemist's, its ironmonger's, and, above all, its emporium of
Parisian novelties, Lambourdieu's bazaar—proved too narrow
every Saturday; the shops being crammed full, the vehicles
blocked, and the roadway fairly choked by the encroachments
of the market-women.

Lise and Françoise, followed by Jean, worked their way as
far as the poultry-market, in the Rue Beaudonnière, whither
the farmers had sent vast crates, in which cocks were crowing,

and from which the necks of affrighted ducks protruded.
Chickens, dead and plucked, were ranged in deep layers inside
numerous packing-cases. Here also one saw some more peasant-
women, each of whom had brought her four or five pounds of
butter, her two dozen eggs, and her cheeses—large dry ones,
small rich ones, and others of a greyish tinge, which had been
moistened with wine, and had a pronounced pungent flavour.
Others had come with two pairs of fowls tied by their feet.
Ladies were haggling, and a large consignment of eggs had
caused a crowd to cluster in front of an inn—"The Poulterer's
Meeting House." It so happened that Palmyre was among
the men who were unloading the eggs. Indeed, on Saturdays,
when there was a dearth of work at Rognes, she hired out her
services at Cloyes, carrying burdens which made her stagger.
"There's no denying she earns her livelihood!" remarked
Jean.

The crowd was now growing denser and denser. Vehicles
still poured in by the Mondoubleau road, defiling over the bridge
at a jog trot. On either hand stretched the gentle curves of
the Loir, running flush with the meadows, and embanked on the
left with the town gardens, whose lilacs and laburnums drooped
down to the water's edge. There was a bark-mill, clicking
noisily up stream, together with a large flour-mill—a huge
building, whitened by a constant stream of meal from the
blowers on the roof.

"Well!" said Jean again, "are we going there?"

"Yes, yes."

Then they retraced their steps up the Rue Grande, stopping
once more on the Place Saint-Lubin, opposite the municipal
offices, where the corn-market was held. Lengaigne, who had
brought four sacks, was standing there with his hands in his
pockets. In the middle of a ring of silent, downcast peasants,
Hourdequin was angrily holding forth. A rise had been
looked for; but even the current price—eighteen francs—was
unsteady, and a final fall of five sous was apprehended. Macqueron went by with his daughter Berthe on his arm; he in a
badly-cleaned overcoat, and she dressed in muslin, with a bunch
of roses in her hat.

As Lise and Françoise, after turning down the Rue du
Temple, were skirting Saint-George's Church, against which the
hawkers installed themselves with haberdashery, ironmongery,
and parcels of stuffs, they ejaculated: "Oh, there's aunt Rose."

And, indeed, it was the old woman. Fanny had come instead of Delhomme to deliver some oats, and had brought her

mother in the cart, just to give her an outing. They were
both waiting in front of the movable stall of a knife-grinder,
to whom the old woman had given her scissors. For thirty
years past he had ground them.

"Hallo! It's you!" said Fanny, as she turned round; and
on perceiving Jean, she added: "So you're out for an airing?"

But when Rose and Fanny found out that the cousins were
going to buy a cow, to supply the place of La Rousse, they
grew interested and joined them, the oats having been already
delivered.

The young man, left to himself, now walked behind the four
women, who formed an open line, all abreast; and thus they
turned on to the Place Saint-Georges.

This was a huge square, more than a hundred yards each way,
stretching behind the apsis of the church, which overshadowed
it with its old and lofty clock-tower of ruddy stone. Avenues
of leafy limes enclosed the four sides, along two of which,
moreover, there extended some chains riveted to stone posts,
while on the other two sides there were long bars of wood, to
which the animals were tethered. On this side of the open space,
which fronted some gardens, the grass was growing as in
an open meadow; but the opposite side, which was flanked by
two roads and bordered by various inns—"The Saint-George,"
"The Root," and "The Jolly Reapers"—was downtrodden,
hardened, and white with dust, which the wind blew to and fro.

Lise and Françoise, followed by the others, had some difficulty
in making their way across the centre of the Place, where the
crowd was congregated. Amid the confused mass of blouses
of all shades, from the bright blue of new linen to the pale blue
of twenty washings, nothing could be seen of the women save
the round white spots of their little caps. A few ladies were
bearing glistening silk parasols hither and thither. Laughter
and sudden shouts were heard, mingling at last with the
mighty animate murmur, upon which now and then there broke
the neigh of a horse or the lowing of a cow. A donkey also
set a-braying lustily.

"This way," said Lise, turning her head. The horses were
at the far end, tethered to the bar, their coats bare and quivering, and with a cord knotted to their necks and tails. On the
left, the cows were almost all loose, and were led to and fro by
the vendors, who wished to show them off better. Groups of
people stopped and looked at them; and hereabouts there was
no laughter and but little talking, merely a few scattered
words now and then.

The four women at once fell into contemplation of a black and white Cotentine cow, which was offered for sale by a man and his wife. The latter, dark-complexioned and stubborn-looking, stood holding the animal in front; the man being in the rear, motionless and uncommunicative. The scrutiny lasted ten minutes, and was solemn and exhaustive; but not a word or a glance was exchanged. They moved on, and stationed themselves similarly in front of a second cow twenty paces off. This was a huge one, quite black, and was offered for sale by a young and pretty-looking girl, almost a child, who held a hazel-rod in her hand. Then followed seven more halts, as long and as silent as the previous ones, till the line of animals for sale was exhausted. Finally the four women went back to the first cow, and again became absorbed in contemplation.

This time, however, it was a more serious matter. Drawn up in a line, they pierced the Cotentine cow through and through with their keen, concentrated gaze. On her side, also, the woman who wished to sell it had said nothing, and her glance was elsewhere, as if she had not seen them come back and draw up in line.

At last Fanny bent down and whispered a brief remark to Lise about the animal. Old Rose and Françoise also ex-changed impressions in a whisper. Then they relapsed into silence and immobility, and the scrutiny was continued.

" How much ? " Lise suddenly asked.

" Four hundred francs," replied the peasant woman.

They affected to be driven away by this, and as they were looking for Jean they were surprised to find him behind them with Buteau, the two chatting together like old friends. Buteau had come from La Chamade to buy a porker, and was negotiating for one on the spot. The pigs, which were in a mov-able pen at the back-end of the vehicle that had brought them, were biting one another and deafening the air with their squeals.

" Will you take twenty francs ? " asked Buteau.

" No; thirty ! "

" Fiddle ! Go to bed with 'em ! "

Bluff and merry, he went up to the women; accosting his mother, his sister, and his two cousins just as radiantly as if he had only left them on the previous day. They also were undisturbed, and seemed to have forgotten the two years of bickering and ill-feeling. The mother alone, who had been apprised of the first encounter in the Rue Grouaise, watched

K

him out of her puckered eyes; trying to gather why he had been to the notary's. But of this there was no indication on his face, and neither of them said a word on the subject.

"So, cousin," he went on, "you're after buying a cow? Jean told me. Well, there's one over there, something like an animal! The sturdiest in the market!"

He then pointed to the identical black and white Cotentine cow.

"Four hundred francs!" said Françoise. "Thank you for nothing."

"Four hundred francs for *you*, my little dear!" said he, tapping her jocularly on the back.

She fired up, however, and returned his tap, angry and resentfully.

"Just you let me alone, will you? I don't play with men."

He made merrier still at this, and turned to Lise, who had remained serious and rather pale.

"And you? Will you let me have a hand in it? I wager I'll get it for three hundred. Will you bet five francs?"

"All right; if you like to have a try, you may."

Rose and Fanny nodded approval. They knew this ferocious fellow of old; a stubborn bargainer he was, an impudent liar and swindler, selling things at three times their value, and getting everything for a mere song. So the women let him go to the fore with Jean, while they hung back in the rear, so that he might not seem to belong to their party.

The crowd was growing denser around the cattle. The groups of loungers were leaving the sunny central space for the side avenues, where they strolled continually to and fro; the blue of their blouses darkened by the shadow of the lime-trees, and their ruddy countenances tinged with green by the reflection of the swaying patches of leaves. However, no one was as yet making purchases; not a sale had taken place, although the market had been open for more than an hour. The purchasers and vendors were taking time for consideration, and were warily scrutinising each other askance. In front of the cows there were now more people sauntering along and making prolonged halts. Overhead, the sound of a riot was borne past on the wings of the warm breeze. It was caused by two horses, tied side by side, who were rearing, biting each other, neighing furiously, and pawing the pavement with their hoofs. There was a fright, and some women fled, while quiet was restored by a shower of blows from a whip, crackling like a discharge of firearms, and accompanied by oaths. Then in the clearance made by the panic, a flock of pigeons alighted on the ground, and hurried along picking oats from the dung.

"Well, gammer! what's your price?" Buteau asked the peasant-woman.

The latter, who had observed the manœuvres of the party, repeated calmly : "Four hundred francs."

At first he treated the matter lightly, and joked, addressing the man, who was still standing silent and apart :

"I say, old 'un! is your good-woman thrown in at that price?"

During his banter, however, he made a close examination of the cow, and found it constituted as a good milker should be— with a wiry head, slender horns, and big eyes; the belly well-developed and streaked with large veins; the limbs inclining to slimness; the tail thin, and set very high. Stooping down, he assured himself of the length of the udders and the elasticity of the teats, which were regularly defined in position and well pierced. Then, resting one hand on the animal, he began bargaining, while he mechanically felt the bones of the crupper.

"Four hundred francs, eh? You're joking! Will you take three hundred?"

Meanwhile, with his hand he was verifying the strength and proper arrangement of the bones. Then he let his fingers slip between the thighs, to the part where the bare skin, of a fine saffron colour, bespoke an abundance of milk.

"Three hundred francs. Is it agreed?"

"No; four hundred," replied the peasant-woman.

He then turned away. When he came back, she decided to speak.

"She's a first-rate animal, indeed, in all points. She'll be two year's old come Trinity Sunday, and she'll calve in a fortnight. She'd surely be just the thing for you."

"Three hundred francs," he repeated.

Then, as he was retreating, she glanced at her husband and called out :

"Here! So that I may get back, say three hundred and fifty, and have done with it."

He had stopped short, and now he began to run the cow down. She wasn't firmly set; her loins were weak; in short, she had been an ailing animal, and would have to be kept for a couple of years at a loss. Then he asserted that she was lame, which was not true. He lied for lying's sake, with obvious bad faith, hoping to irritate the woman and make her lose her head. But she only shrugged her shoulders.

"Three hundred francs."

"No; three hundred and fifty."

This time she let him go off. He rejoined the women; told them that the bait was taking, and that they must bargain for some other animal. So the party took their stand in front of the large black cow, held by the pretty girl. For this beast, as it happened, just three hundred francs were asked, and Buteau affected not to think that dear. He began to praise the cow, and then abruptly turned back to the other one.

"It's settled, then, that I take my money elsewhere?" he asked.

"Why, if it were only possible, but it isn't! You must nerve yourself a bit."

Then, leaning down and taking a full handful of udder, the woman added:

"See how plump and pretty!"

He did not assent, however; but said again:

"Three hundred francs."

"No, three hundred and fifty."

Negotiations seemed broken off. Buteau had taken Jean's arm, in definite token that he had let the matter drop. The women rejoined them, in a state of excitement, they being of opinion that the cow was worth the three hundred and fifty francs. Françoise, in particular, who was pleased with the animal, talked of giving that price. But Buteau grew vexed; why should one be swindled like that? And for nearly an hour he held out, amid the anxiety of his cousins, who trembled whenever a purchaser stopped in front of the animal. Neither did he cease to watch it out of the corner of his eye; but it was the right game to play; it was necessary one should hold out. Nobody would certainly be so ready as that to part with his money; they would soon see if any one were fool enough to pay more than three hundred francs. And, in point of fact, the money was not forthcoming, albeit the market was drawing to its close.

Some horses were now being tried along the road. One, all white, was showing his paces, urged on by the guttural shouts of a man holding the halter and running by his side; while Patoir, the chubby and florid veterinary, stood looking on beside the purchaser in a corner of the square, with both hands in his pockets, and giving advice aloud. The inns hummed busily with a constant stream of drinkers, going in and out, away and back again, amid endless discussions and bargainings. The bustle and tumult were now at their full height, and one could not hear one's-self speak. A calf, that had lost its mother, lowed incessantly. Some black griffons and large yellow water-spaniels ran howling away from among the crowd, with crushed paws. Occasional lulls would occur, in which nothing was audible save the croaking of a flock of ravens who were wheeling round the church steeple. Penetrating through the warm smell of the cattle there came a strong stench of burnt horn, a nuisance due to a neighbouring farriery, where some peasants were availing themselves of the opportunity to have their animals shod.

"Hi! Three hundred?" repeated the unwearied Buteau, as he drew near the peasant woman again.

"No. Three hundred and fifty."

As there was another purchaser standing by, also bargaining, Buteau seized the cow by her jaws and forced them open to look at her teeth. Then he let go of them with a grimace. At that moment the cow began to relieve herself, and the dung fell soft. He followed it with his eyes, and made a worse grimace than before. The purchaser, a tall thin fellow, was influenced, and went away.

"I'll have nothing more to do with her," said Buteau. "She's got curdled blood."

This time the woman committed the mistake of losing her temper, which was what he wanted. She abused him, and he retorted with a flood of filth. People gathered round and laughed. The husband still stood motionless behind the woman. At last he slightly nudged her, and she abruptly cried:

"Will you take her at three hundred and twenty francs?"

"No, three hundred."

He was going off once more, when she called him back in a choking voice.

"Well, then, you brute, take her! But, by God! if I had to go through it all again, I'd slap your face first!"

She was beside herself, and quivering with rage. He laughed noisily, added some gallant speeches, and offered to sleep with her for the balance.

Lise had immediately come up. She took the woman aside and paid her the three hundred francs behind a tree. Françoise had already got hold of the cow, but Jean had to push the creature behind, for she refused to budge. They had been trotting backwards and forwards for a couple of hours, Rose and Fanny having silently and untiringly awaited the end. Finally, on taking their departure, and searching for Buteau,

who had vanished, they found him hail-fellow-well-met with
the pig-dealer. He had just got his porker for twenty francs;
and, in paying, he counted his money out first in his pocket,
then produced the exact sum, and counted it again in his half-
closed hand. It was quite a job to get the pig into the sack
which he had brought under his blouse. The rotten canvas
burst, and the paws of the animal came through, as well as its
snout. In this condition Buteau shouldered his burden, and
carried the beast off, kicking, grunting, and squealing with alarm.

"I say, Lise, how about those five francs I won?"

She gave them to him, for fun, not expecting that he would
take them. But he did take them, and put them out of sight
in no time. Then they all made their way slowly towards "The
Jolly Ploughman."

The market was at an end. Money was gleaming in the
sunlight and chinking on the tables of the wine-shops. At the
last moment everything was hurried to a conclusion. In the
corner of the Place Saint-Georges there only remained a few
animals unsold. Little by little, the crowd had ebbed away
towards the Rue Grande, where the vegetable and fruit-sellers
were clearing the roadway and carrying off their empty
baskets. In a similar way there was nothing left at the
poultry market save straw and feathers. The carts were
already starting off again. Vehicles were being harnessed in
the inn-yards; horses' reins, knotted to the pavement-rings,
were being untied. Along all the roads, on every side, wheels
were rolling, and blue blouses were blown about by the wind
as the vehicles jolted over the pavement.

Lengaigne went by in this fashion, trotting on his little
black pony, having turned his journey to account by buying a
scythe. Macqueron and his daughter Berthe were still lingering in the shops. As for La Frimat, she went back on foot,
laden as when she started, for she was carrying back her
basket full of horse-dung, which she had picked up on the road.
Among the gilding at the chemist's in the Rue Grande, Palmyre
had been waiting half-an-hour to have a draught made up for
her brother, who had been ill for a week past—some vile drug
it was, that took one franc out of the couple she had so laboriously
earned. But what made the Mouche girls and their party
hasten their sauntering steps was the sight of Hyacinthe,
staggering along very drunk, and taking up all the street.
They presumed that he had got another loan that day by mortgaging his last bit of land. He was chuckling to himself, and
some five-franc pieces were jingling in his capacious pockets.

On arriving at "The Jolly Ploughman," Buteau said, simply and bluffly:

"So you're off? Look here, Lise, why not stop with your sister and have something to eat?"

She was surprised, and as she turned towards Jean, he added:

"Jean can stop too. I shall be very pleased if he will."

Rose and Fanny exchanged glances. The lad had certainly some idea in his head. Had he decided on marriage after going to the notary's to accept? The expression of his face still gave no clue. No matter! They ought not to hamper the course of things.

"Very good, then. You stay here and I'll go on with mother," said Fanny. "We are expected."

Françoise, who had never let go of the cow, now drily remarked: "I am going too."

She persisted in doing so. She always felt on thorns at the inn, she said, and she wanted to take her animal away at once. They had to give way, she made herself so disagreeable; and accordingly, as soon as the horse had been put to, the cow was tied behind the cart, and the three women got up.

Not till that moment did Rose, who expected a confession from her son, venture to ask him:

"You have no message for your father?"

"No, none," replied Buteau.

She looked him full in the face and pressed him: "There's no news, then?"

"If there is, you'll know it all in good time."

. Fanny flicked the horse, which set off leisurely, while the cow behind, stretching out her neck, allowed herself to be dragged along. Lise was left between Buteau and Jean.

At six o'clock the three of them sat down at a table in a dining-room of the inn, communicating with the café. Buteau, without any one knowing whether he was standing treat or not, had gone into the kitchen and ordered an omelette and a rabbit. Meantime, Lise had urged Jean to have an explanation with him, so as to bring matters to an end, and save a journey. However, they had got through the omelette, and were eating the rabbit, without the young fellow, who was ill at ease, having as yet taken any steps. Neither did the other seem to have the thing at all on his mind. He ate heartily, laughed from ear to ear, and in a friendly way nudged his cousin and his companion with his knee under the table. Then they talked on more serious topics: of the new Rognes road; and although not a

word was spoken **about** the five hundred francs' compensation,
or the **increased value of the** land, **these** weighty considerations **underlay all that was** said. At last Buteau **returned to**
his jests, **and began** clinking glasses; **while into** his **grey eyes**
there visibly passed the **idea** of this **piece of** good **business—**
this old flame he might **marry, whose field, adjacent to his own,**
had almost doubled in **value.**

" Good Lord ! " **cried he, "aren't we to have any coffee?"**
" Three coffees ! " **ordered Jean.**

Another hour passed in **sipping, and the decanter of brandy**
was exhausted without **Buteau declaring** himself. ·He ad-
vanced and retired, and **spun matters** out, just in **the same**
way as he had haggled **for the cow.** The thing **was as good**
as settled ; **but,** all the **same, a certain amount** of **consideration**
was necessary. At last he turned abruptly to Lise and said
to her :

" Why **haven't you brought the child ? "**

She began **to laugh, understanding this time** that the affair
was clenched. **Then she gave him a slap, feeling** pleased and
indulgent, **and confined** herself to **replying:**

" Isn't **this Buteau a horrid** fellow ? "

That **was all.** He **laughed too. The** marriage **was** decided.

Jean, hitherto embarrassed, now seemed relieved, and became
gay. At last he even spoke right out.

" You **have done well, you** know, **to return ; I was about**
to step into **your shoes."**

" Yes, **so I was told. Oh, I wasn't uneasy ; you would, no**
doubt, have **given me warning ! "**

" Why, **certainly! The more so as it's better** it should be
you, on account of the child. That's what we always said,
didn't we, Lise ? "

" **Always. That's the simple** truth ! "

The faces of all three melted **into** tenderness. They
fraternised ; especially Jean, who was free from jealousy, and
felt **astonished at finding** himself helping on this marriage.
He **called for some beer,** Buteau having shouted that, **good**
Lord ! **they'd have** something more to drink. With **their**
elbows **on the table,** seated **on each** side of Lise, **they now**
chatted **about the recent rains which** had **beaten down the**
corn.

In the adjacent room, **used as a café, Hyacin**the, seated at
the same table as an old peasant, **who was drunk** like himself,
was kicking up an intolerable row. **For that** matter, nobody
there could speak without shouting. **There they** sat, in blouses,

drinking, smoking, and spitting amid the ruddy smoke of the lamps; and Hyacinthe's brazen, deafening voice was ever the loudest of all. He was playing "chouine," and a quarrel had just arisen anent the last trick between him and his companion, who stuck to his winnings with an air of calm obstinacy. He appeared, however, to be in the wrong. There was no settling it, and Hyacinthe, infuriated at last, yelled so loudly that the landlord interfered. Then he got up and went from table to table, with maudlin persistence, taking his hand with him to lay the point before the other customers. He bored everybody; and finally, beginning to shout again, he returned to the old man, who, with the imperturbability of injustice, bore the abuse like a stoic.

"Poltroon! Ne'er-do-weel! Just come outside, and see how I'll pitch into you!" shouted Hyacinthe.

Then he abruptly resumed his chair facing the other, and coolly said:

"I know a game. But you must bet. Will you?"

He had taken out a handful of fifteen or twenty five-franc pieces, and piled them up in front of him.

"That's the thing. You do the same."

The old man, feeling interested, took out his purse without a word, and set up an equal pile.

"Then I take one from your heap. Now look!"

He seized the coin, put it gravely on his tongue as if it had been a wafer, and swallowed it at a gulp.

"Now, it's your turn. Take one of mine. And the one who eats the most of the other's money, keeps it. That's the game!"

The old man, whose eyes were wide open with surprise, agreed to the suggestion, and with some difficulty he caused one coin to disappear. However, Hyacinthe, while crying out that there was no hurry, gulped down the crowns like so many plums. At the fifth one he swallowed, a rumour ran round the café, and a circle of people collected, petrified with admiration. What a throat the beggar must have, to stick money down his gizzard like that! The old man was swallowing his fourth coin, when he tumbled backwards, black in the face, choking and gurgling. For a moment they thought him dead. Hyacinthe had risen up, quite comfortable and wearing a bantering air. He, for his part, had ten of the coins in his stomach, so that there was a balance of thirty francs to his credit.

Buteau feeling anxious, and fearing he might be compromised if the old man **did** not recover, had **left the table and** given orders for the horses **to** be put to. As he stared **vaguely** at **the walls, without** saying a word about paying, **although** the **invitation had come** from him, Jean settled the bill. **This** capped **Buteau's good** spirits; and **in the** yard, where **the two** vehicles **were waiting,** he took his companion **by the shoulders,** saying:

"I **expect you to come, you know. The wedding will** take **place in three weeks' time. I've been to the notary's** and **signed the deed; all the papers will be ready."**

Then, helping Lise into his own cart: "Now then, up!" he added, **"I'll see you back. I'll drive through Rognes, it won't be much farther."**

Jean returned in his vehicle by himself. He considered this natural, and **followed the others. Cloyes had relapsed** into its death-like **lethargy and was now asleep, lighted only** by the yellow stars **of the street lamps. Of the hubbub of the** market nothing **remained save the** staggering, **belated steps of** some drunken **peasant. The road** stretched afar **in deep darkness. Jean, however, did at last** descry the **other vehicle which was conveying the affianced pair.** Better so, he thought; **all was as it should be. And he whistled** loudly, freshened up **by the night air, and feeling free and cheery.**

CHAPTER VII.

Once more had the hay-making time come round, with a blue scorching sky, cooled by occasional breezes. The marriage had been fixed for Midsummer-Day, which fell that year on a Saturday.

The Fouans had enjoined upon Buteau to begin the invitations with La Grande, who was the oldest of the family. Like a rich and dreaded queen, she required to be treated with respect. Accordingly, one evening, Buteau and Lise, rigged out in their Sunday clothes, went to beg her to attend the wedding ceremony, and afterwards the dinner, which was to take place at the bride's house.

When they arrived, La Grande was knitting in the kitchen by herself; and, without checking the play of her needles, she gazed at them fixedly, and let them explain their errand, and repeat the same phrases twice over. At last, in her shrill voice :

"The wedding? Nay, nay, certainly not!" said she. "What should I find to do at a wedding? Such things are only for those who amuse themselves."

They had seen her parchment face light up at the thought of the junketing that would cost her nothing, and they were convinced that she would accept. But it was always customary to press her a great deal.

"Oh, but, aunt! Really it couldn't go off without you," they said.

"No, no! It's not for folk like me. How am I to find the time, and get the clothes I should want. It's always an expense. People can get on very well without going to weddings."

They had to repeat the invitation a dozen times before she eventually said, sulkily :

"All right; since I can't get out of it, I'll go. But I wouldn't put myself out for anybody but you."

Then, seeing that they did not leave, she battled with herself; for, in such a case as the present one, a glass of wine was usually offered. Making up her mind, she at last went down into the cellar, although there was already an open bottle up-stairs. However, the fact was she kept for these occasions a remnant of wine which had turned, and which she could not drink, it was so sour. She called it "the gnat destroyer." Having filled two glasses, she fixed her nephew and niece with so full an eye that they were obliged to drain them without blenching, for fear of giving offence. They left her with their throats burning.

The same evening, Buteau and Lise repaired to Rose-Blanche, where Monsieur Charles lived, arriving there in the midst of a tragic occurrence.

Monsieur Charles was in his garden, in a state of great agitation. No doubt some violent emotion had come upon him just as he was trimming a climbing rose-tree, for he had his pruning scissors in his hand, and the ladder was still resting against the wall. Controlling himself, however, he showed them into the drawing-room, where Elodie was embroidering with her modest air.

"So you're marrying each other in a week's time. That's quite right, my children," he said. "But we can't be of your party, for Madame Charles is at Chartres, and won't be back for a fortnight."

So saying, he raised his heavy eyelids to glance at the young girl, and then resumed:

"At busy times, during the large fairs, Madame Charles goes over there to lend her daughter a helping hand. Business has its exigencies, you know, and there are days when they are overwhelmed with work at the shop. True, Estelle has taken over the management; but her mother is of great use to her, the more so as our son-in-law Vaucogne certainly doesn't do much. And besides, Madame Charles is glad to see the house again. No wonder! We've left thirty years of our lives there, and that counts for something!"

He was growing sentimental, and his eyes moistened as he vaguely gazed, as it were, into that past of theirs. It was true. In her dainty, snug retirement, full of flowers, birds, and sunshine, his wife was often seized with home-sickness for the little house in the Rue aux Juifs. Whenever she shut her eyes, a vision of old Chartres, sloping down from the Place de la Cathédrale to the banks of the Eure, rose up before her. She saw herself, on her arrival, threading the Rue de la Pie, and the Rue Porte-Cendreuse; then, in the Rue des Ecuyers, she took the shortest cut down the Tertre du Pied-Plat, where just at the bottom — at the corner of the Rue aux Juifs and the Rue de la Planche-aux-Carpes, Number 19 came into sight, with its white frontage and its green shutters, which were always closed. The two streets which it overlooked were wretched ones, and during thirty years she had beheld their miserable hovels and squalid inhabitants, with the gutter in the middle running with filthy water. But, then, how many weeks and months she had spent at home there, in the darkened rooms, without even crossing the threshold! She was still proud of the divans and mirrors of the drawing-room, of the bedding and the mahogany of the sleeping apartments, of all the chaste and comfortable luxury—their creation, their handiwork, to which they owed their fortune. A melancholy faintness came over her at the recollection of certain private corners, the clinging perfume of the toilet-waters, the peculiar scent of the whole house, which she had retained about her own person like a lingering regret. Thus she looked forward to all the periods of heavy work, and set out radiant and joyful, after receiving from her grand-daughter two hearty kisses, which she promised to give mamma that evening in the confectionery shop.

"How disappointing! How disappointing!" said Buteau, really vexed at the idea of Monsieur and Madame Charles not coming to the wedding. "But suppose our cousin wrote to aunt to come back?"

Elodie, who was in her fifteenth year, thin-haired, and so poor-blooded that the fresh air of the country seemed to make her more anæmical still, raised her puffy, chlorotic, virginal face:

"Oh, no!" she murmured, "grandmamma told me the sweetmeats would be sure to keep her more than a fortnight. She is to bring me back a bag of them, if I'm good."

This was a pious fraud. At each journey she was brought some sweetmeats, which, she believed, had been manufactured at her parents' place.

"Well!" proposed Lise at length, "come without her, uncle, and bring the girl."

Monsieur Charles was not listening, however, having relapsed into an agitated state. He was going to the window, seemingly on the look-out for some one, and was swallowing a rising burst of anger. Unable to contain himself any further, he dismissed the young girl with a word.

"Go away and play for a minute or two, my darling," he said.

Then, when she had left—being accustomed to be sent

away while grown-up people talked—he took his stand in the middle of the room and folded his arms, while his full, yellow-tinted, respectable face—very like that of a retired magistrate —quivered with indignation.

" Would you believe it ? Such an abominable thing ! I was trimming my rose-tree, and I had got on to the highest rung of the ladder, and was bending mechanically over the wall, when what do I see ? Honorine, my maid Honorine, with a man, at their dirty tricks ! At the foot of my wall, too, the swine, the swine ! "

He was choking, and began to pace up and down, with noble maledictory gestures.

" I'm waiting for her to pack her off, the disreputable hussy ! We can't keep one. They're always put into the family-way. Regularly, at the end of six months, they become a perfect sight, and there's no having them in a respectable family. And now this one, caught in the act ! Ah ! the end of the world is come ; there are no bounds to debauchery now-a-days ! "

Buteau and Lise, who were astounded, joined, out of deference, in his indignation.

" Certainly, it's not proper ; not at all proper—oh, no ! "

He set himself in front of them once more.

" And just fancy Elodie climbing up that ladder, and coming on a scene like that ! She, so innocent, who knows nothing at all, over whose very thoughts we watch ! On my honour, it makes one shiver ! What a shock, if Madame Charles were here ! "

At that very moment, glancing out of the window, he perceived the child, who had set her foot on the lowest rung of the ladder, out of mere curiosity. He rushed forward and called out, in an agonised voice, as if he had seen her on the brink of a precipice :

" Elodie ! Elodie ! Come down ; go away for the love of Heaven ! "

Then his legs gave way, and he sank into an arm-chair, continuing to lament over the immorality of servants. Had he not come upon one in the kitchen showing the child what the posteriors of fowls were like ? He had quite enough worry as it was to keep her clear of the grossness of the peasantry, and the cynicism of animals ; and he lost heart altogether to find a constant hot-bed of immorality in his own house.

" There she is coming in," he said, sharply. " You shall see."

He rang the bell, and having by an effort recovered his calm dignity, he received Honorine seated, and in solemn fashion.

"Mademoiselle," he said, "pack up your box and leave at once. You shall be paid a week's wages in lieu of notice."

The servant, a skinny, insignificant chit of a thing, of humble and shame-faced aspect, attempted to explain, stammering out excuses.

"It's no use. All I can do for you is not to hand you over to the authorities for indecent behaviour."

Then she turned upon him.

"Oh, so it's because I omitted to pay the fee."

He rose from his seat, tall and upright, and dismissed her with a majestic gesture, his finger pointing to the door. When she had gone he relieved his feelings coarsely.

"The idea of a strumpet like that bringing dishonour on my house."

"Ah, sure, she's one; that she is!" repeated Lise and Buteau, complaisantly.

The latter thereupon resumed:

"Then it's settled, isn't it, uncle? You'll come with the child?"

Monsieur Charles was still quivering. Feeling anxious, he had gone to look at himself in the glass, and was returning satisfied.

"Where? Oh, to be sure, to your wedding. It's the right thing to do, my children, to marry. Rely on me. I will be there; but I don't promise to bring Elodie, because, you know, people are a little free at weddings. I turned the baggage out pretty sharp, eh? I won't put up with women annoying me. Good-bye, rely on my coming."

The Delhommes, whom Buteau and Lise next invited, also accepted, after the usual refusal and insistance. Hyacinthe was the only one of the family that remained to be invited. But, in sooth, he had become unbearable, being on bad terms with everybody, and bringing all his people into discredit by playing the lowest pranks. So it was decided to put him on one side, though apprehensions were entertained that he would revenge himself in some abominable manner.

Rognes was on the tiptoe of expectation. This marriage, so long deferred, was quite an event. Hourdequin, the mayor, took the trouble to officiate in person at the civil ceremony; but when asked to attend the evening repast, he excused himself, as he was obliged to pass that very night at Chartres on account of a lawsuit. Still, he promised that Madame Jacqueline should come, as they had the politeness to invite her also. For a moment, moreover, they had thought of inviting the Abbé Godard, by way of having some superior kind of person with them ; but, as soon as the wedding was even mentioned, the priest lost his temper, because it was fixed for Midsummer-Day. He had to officiate that day at high mass, established by foundation, at Bazoches-le-Doyen, so how could he be expected to come to Rognes in the morning ? However, the women— Lise, Rose, and Fanny—became obstinate, and he finished by giving way. He came at mid-day in such a passion that he flung their mass at their heads, as it were, and left them smarting under a deep sense of injury.

After discussion, it had been resolved that the wedding should take place quietly among the family, on account of the bride's position—with a child now nearly three years old. They had been, however, to the Cloyes pastry-cook to order a pie and some dessert, on which they determined to spare no expense, so as to show people that they could make the money fly on proper occasions. As at the marriage of the eldest daughter of the Bordiers—some rich farmers at Mailleville—they were to have a regular wedding-cake, two ice creams, four sweet dishes, and some little tarts. At home, some meat soup would be provided, together with chitterlings, four stewed chickens, four rabbits, also stewed, and some roast beef and veal. And all this for fifteen or twenty people—they did not know the exact number. If there were any food left after the repast, they would finish it up on the morrow.

The sky, which had been a little dull in the morning, had cleared, and the day was drawing to its close, amid cheerful warmth and glow. The covers had been set in the middle of the spacious kitchen, right in front of the fireplace and the oven, where meats were roasting, and pots boiling over large fires. This made the room so hot that the two windows and the door were left wide open, and the sweet, penetrating scent of new-mown hay came in.

Since the day before, the Mouche girls had had the assist-ance of Rose and Fanny. There was a sensation when the pastry-cook's cart made its appearance at three o'clock, bringing all the women in the village to their doors. The dessert was at once laid out on the table to see how it looked. Just then La Grande arrived, before the time. She sat down, clasped her stick between her knees, and never once took her hard eyes off the food. She questioned whether it wasn't sinful to go to such an expense. She herself, however, had eaten **nothing all the morning, so** that she might **be able** to do full justice **to the feast.**

The men—Buteau, Jean **who** had been the former's **" best-man,"** old Fouan, Delhomme **and** his son Nénesse—all in **frock-coats,** black trousers, and **tall** silk hats, that nothing **would** induce them to part **with, were** playing **at** pitch **and toss** in the yard. Monsieur **Charles came by** himself, having **on the** day before **conducted Elodie to her** boarding school **at** Châteaudun; **and, without joining in the game,** he took **an** interest in it and made some **judicious suggestions.**

At six o'clock, **when all was ready, Jacqueline had to** be waited **for. The women now let down their skirts, which** they had pinned **up, so that** the stove might not **soil them.** Lise was in blue, Françoise **in pink;** hard-coloured, old-fashioned silks which Lambourdieu had sold **to them at** double their value, passing them off as the latest Parisian novelty. **Old** Madame Fouan had looked out the violet poplin which **she had paraded for forty** years **at all** the **country weddings, and Fanny,** dressed in green, wore all her **jewels; her** watch and chain, **a** brooch, **rings** in her ears and **on her** fingers. Every minute one of **the** women would **go** out on to the road and run as far as **the church** corner **to see whether** the lady from the farm was **not in** sight. The **sauces were** burning, and **the** soup, which **had** unfortunately been served, was getting **cold in** the **plates. At length there was a** shout:

" **There she is! There** she is! "

The gig appeared, and Jacqueline **leapt lightly out. She** looked charming, having had the **good taste to set** off **her** attractions by a simple white **cretonne dress with red** spots. **There were no** jewels about **her bare skin, save** some little **brilliants** in her ears : **a present from** Hourdequin, which had **set the** neighbouring farms in **a** ferment. They were surprised **that she** did not dismiss the farm-hand **who** had brought **her,** when **they had** helped him to stable **the** vehicle. He was a kind **of giant, named Tron,** with white skin, red hair, and a child-like look. **He came from** Le Perche, and had been **at** La Borderie for **a fortnight as** yard-helper.

" Tron **remains, you know,"** said she gaily. " He'll see **me** home."

In La Beauce, people **are not partial to** the Percherons, whom they accuse of being false **and** sly. **Glances** were exchanged. **This,** then, **was** La Cognette's **last** fancy, this big brute! However, Buteau, who had **been very** agreeable and jocular since the morning, replied :

"Certainly he **can stop**! It's **enough that he comes** with you."

Lise **having given** the word to **begin**, they sat **down** to table, **with a deal of bustle** and noisy **talk**. There were three chairs **short, so** they ran and fetched **two** stools, with their **straw seats** worn through, and laid **a** plank across **them**. Spoons **were** already briskly rattling against the plates. **The soup was** cold, and **covered** with congealed bubbles **of fat.** **They didn't mind that, however.** Old Fouan made the remark **that it** would get **warm** in their **bellies, an idea which provoked** tempestuous laughter. **From that moment the scene was one** of gluttonous massacre : **the chickens, rabbits, meats appeared** and **vanished** in **succession, amid a gruesome sound of** munching. **Although very temperate at their own homes,** they stuffed **till they almost burst when visiting.** La Grande did not speak, **in order to eat the more, and she kept at it** with never-resting **jaws; it was indeed frightful to see how much** her lean, shrivelled, **octogenarian stomach** could engulf, **without** so **much as** swelling. **It had been settled that,** for the look of the thing, Françoise and Fanny should **see to the** guests, so that the bride might **not have** to get **up; but she** could not **keep still ; she** left **her chair** every **instant, tucking up her** sleeves, and giving her best **attention to the pouring out of a** sauce, or the dishing **of a joint.** In a short time, however, **the whole** table took a **share in the** waiting, and **some** one **was** always **on** his legs, **cutting** bread or trying to get hold **of a** dish. Buteau, who had **taken** charge of the wine, **no longer** sufficed as butler, **though to save** himself **the trouble of corking** and uncorking bottles **he had simply put a cask** on tap. However he could **not** get any **time to eat, and at last** Jean had to relieve him and replenish the pitchers. Delhomme, seated at his ease, declared in **his** sagacious way **that** there must **be** plenty of liquor if **one** didn't want to be **stifled.** When **the** pie, which was as **broad as a** cart wheel, **was** served there was a thrill, **the** force-meat balls making **a** deep impression. Monsieur Charles carried his politeness so far as to swear upon his honour **that he had never** seen a finer one at Chartres. **At** this point, **old Fouan, in high** feather, sparkled once more.

" I say," **he remarked, "if a** fellow had any chaps on his buttocks, he **could cure them by** sticking that on behind."

On hearing this the table went into fits, especially Jacqueline, who laughed till she cried. She stuttered out some emendatory remarks, which were lost amid her laughter.

The bridal pair faced each other, Buteau being between his

mother and La Grande, **and** Lise between old Fouan **and** Monsieur Charles. The other guests were disposed according to **their own** fancy; **Jacqueline** beside Tron, who **watched her** with his soft, stupid eyes: Jean near Françoise, and only separated from her by little Jules, upon whom both of them had engaged to keep an eye. However, on the appearance of the pie, the child displayed such strong symptoms of indigestion that the bride had to go and put him to bed. Then Jean and Françoise **were** brought side by side. **She** was very lively, deeply flushed by **the** heat **of** the large fire **on the** hearth, and over-excited, albeit **tired to** death. He **was** attentive, and wished to get up **and help** her; but she **broke** away, having moreover to hold **her** own against **Buteau, who,** being much given to teasing when in a pleasant mood, had made a **set at** her from the beginning **of** the feast. He pinched her whenever she went by, whereupon she retorted with a furious slap; **and** then she would get up again on some pretext or other, **as if** fascinated and anxious to be pinched again and to slap him **in** return. She complained that her hips were black and blue.

" **Stop where** you are, then! " repeated Jean.

" **Oh, no!** " cried **she,** " **he** mustn't think he's my master too, simply **because he's** married Lise."

They had lighted six **tallow candles as** soon as it was dark, and the meal had been in progress for three hours, when at length, towards ten o'clock, an onslaught was made on **the** dessert. From that point, coffee was drunk; not one or **two cups,** but large bowlfuls of it, without stopping. The **fun grew** more pointed. Coffee gave one vigour, it was said, **and** was excellent for the men who took too much sleep. Every time a married guest swallowed a spoonful the others split their sides laughing.

" You've very good cause **to take** some," said Fanny to **Delhomme.** She was very merry that evening, the feast **having drawn** her out of her habitual **reserve.**

Her **husband reddened,** and to excuse himself roundly declared **that it was due to** over-work; **w**hereupon their son Nénesse laughed from ear to ear, amid the burst of shouts and the thigh-slapping provoked by this conjugal revelation. However, the lad had eaten so much that he seemed to be **bursting.** Soon he vanished, and he was not seen again till the party broke up, when he was found slumbering in company with the two cows.

La Grande was the one who held out the longest. At midnight she was hard at work on the tartlets, in mute despair at

being unable to finish them. The bowls of cream had been
cleaned out, the crumbs of the cake swept up; with the freedom
of increasing tipsiness, with bodices unhooked and trouser
buttons undone, they split up into little knots, and chatted
round the table, which was greasy with sauce, and stained with
spilt wine. Songs had been started, but had come to nothing;
except that old Rose, with a maudlin expression of countenance, went on humming some past century ribaldry, a remini-
scence of her young days, to which she kept time by nodding
her head. They were also too few to dance. Besides the
men preferred to tipple brandy and smoke their pipes, the
ashes of which they shook out over the table-cloth. In a
corner, Fanny and Delhomme, with Jean and Tron before
them, were reckoning up, within a halfpenny, the pecuniary
position and expectations of the bride and bridegroom. This
went on interminably. Every square inch was appraised.
They knew every fortune in Rognes, even to the value of the
linen possessed by each household. At the other end of the
table, Jacqueline had buttonholed Monsieur Charles, whom she
was contemplating with a winning smile, her pretty, wicked
eyes aflame with curiosity. She questioned him.

"So Chartres is a queer place, eh? There's a gay life to
be led there?"

He answered her by praising the town circuit: a line of
promenades planted with old trees, which encompass Chartres
with shade. In the lower part especially, along the banks
of the Eure, the boulevards were very cool in summer. Then
there was the cathedral. He expiated on this edifice, being a
well-informed man with great respect for religion. Yes, it
was one of the finest buildings; but it had become too vast
for the present times of weak Christianity, and was almost
always empty, in the midst of its deserted square, which the
devout alone crossed on week-days. He had realised the
desolation of the place one Sunday when he had gone in
casually while the vesper service was taking place. You
shivered with the cold inside, and you could hardly see on
account of the stained glass; so that all he could eventually
descry were two little girls' schools, lost in the space like a
handful of ants, and singing under the vaulted roof in shrill,
fife-like voices. It was truly heartrending that the churches
should be thus abandoned for the drinking-shops.

Jacqueline, who was astonished to hear him say all this,
continued to stare at him steadily, with the same smile. At
last to attain her object, she had to murmur:

" But tell me now, the Chartres women——"

He understood, and grew very grave, but he unbosomed himself, under the expansive influence of the general intoxication. She, flushed and tittering, rubbed up against him as if to penetrate that mystery of a rush of men, night after night. But it was not what she imagined. He told her about the hard work of it, for, in his cups, he was wont to be melancholy and paternal. Then he grew more animated, when she told him that she had amused herself one day by taking a look at the front of the Châteaudun night-house, at the corner of the Rue Dairgnon and the Rue Loiseau: a little dilapidated house it was, with its shutters closed and rotting. Behind, in a neglected garden, there was a large silvered globe of glass reflecting the house ; while, in front of the dormer-window of the topmost floor, turned into a pigeon-house, some pigeons were flying and cooing in the sunshine. On that day, too, some children were playing on the door-step, and she had heard the words of command resounding over the wall of the adjacent cavalry barracks. He, interrupting her, grew angry. Yes, yes! He knew the place: two disgusting used-up women, and not even any mirrors down-stairs. It was these dens that brought disgrace on the profession.

" But what can you expect in a sub-prefecture ? " he added at length, calming down, with the philosophical tolerance of a superior person.

It was now one in the morning, and it was suggested that they should go to bed. When people had had a baby, there wasn't much use (was there ?) in making a fuss about getting under the blankets together. It was the same with the old practical jokes—unpinning the bedstead, and popping scratching hair, or toys that squeaked when they were squeezed. between the sheets, and so on. All that, in this case, would have come the day after the fair. The best thing to do was to drink a parting cup, and then say good-night.

At that moment, however, Lise and Fanny shrieked. Through the open window a liberal shower of cow's dung had just been thrown, and both women's dresses were splashed from top to bottom, and ruined. What swine had done that ? They ran out and looked over the square, along the road, and behind the hedge. Nobody. However, they all agreed that this was Hyacinthe's revenge for not having been invited.

The Fouans and Delhomme set out, and Monsieur Charles too. La Grande made a tour of the table, to see whether there was anything left; and finally made up her mind to go, after observing to Jean that the Buteaus would die in a ditch. Her firm, sharp step, and the measured tap of her stick, were heard down the road in the distance; while the others, all very tipsy, went staggering over the stones.

As Tron was putting the horse to the gig for Madame Jacqueline, she, already with one foot on the step, turned round and asked:

" You're not going back with us, are you, Jean? "

The young fellow, who was preparing to get in, changed his mind, glad enough to leave her to Tron, since she seemed to wish it. He watched her cuddling up against the tall figure of her new gallant, and could not help laughing when the vehicle was out of sight. He would walk back, he thought. But first, pending the departure of the others, he went and sat down for an instant on the stone bench in the yard, near Françoise, who had installed herself there, being overcome with both the heat and fatigue. The Buteaus were already in their room, and she had promised to fasten everything up before going to bed herself.

" Ah! it's pleasant here," she sighed, after five long minutes of silence.

Then quietude fell again, calm and majestic. The cool, delicious night was spangled with stars. The scent of the hay was borne so strong from the meadows of the Aigre that its balmy fragrance seemed like the perfume of flowers.

" Ah, yes! it's pleasant," repeated Jean, at length. " It does the heart good."

She made no reply, however, and he saw that she was asleep. She slid down, resting upon his shoulder, and then he stopped there an hour longer, meditating in a confused manner. Evil thoughts came to him, but died away. She was too young. It seemed to him that, by waiting, she alone would become older and get to be nearer his age.

" I say, Françoise, we'd better go to bed! " he exclaimed at last. " We might catch something out here."

She started out of her sleep.

" Dear, yes! we shall be better abed. Till we meet again, Jean! "

" Till we meet again, Françoise! "

PART III.

CHAPTER I.

So at last Buteau had got his share, that land he had so ardently **coveted, and** yet refused during more than two years and a half, in a fury compounded of longing, rancour, and obstinacy. He himself did not know why he had been so stubborn, yearning at heart to sign the deed, fearing he might be tricked, and unable to console himself for not having secured the whole inheritance, the nineteen acres now mutilated and scattered. Since his acceptance, however, a great passion had been satisfied, **the** brutal joy of possession; and that joy was doubled by the thought that his sister and brother were now the swindled parties, that his holding was worth more since the new road **ran by his field. He never met** them without a sly chuckle, and **winks that said :**

" All the same, I've taken **them in ! "**

And **that was** not all. **He triumphed also** by **his long-**deferred marriage, by the five acres adjoining his own **field** which Lise had brought him. The thought that the sisters' property must be divided did not occur to him ; or, if it did, he looked upon it as something so far distant that he hoped in the interval to hit upon some scheme of evasion. Counting Françoise's share, he had eight acres of plough land, eight **of meadow,** and about five of vineyard, and he would stick to them. **He would part with** his skin first. Above all, he would never **let any one cut** up the piece of ground which bordered the road, **and that now** comprised nearly six acres. Neither his sister **nor his brother** had a field like it. He talked of it in inflated terms, bursting with pride. A year passed by, and this first year of possession was bliss **to** Buteau. Never when he had hired himself out to others had he ploughed so deeply into the bowels of the earth. It was his ; he wanted to penetrate and fructify its inmost parts. At night he used to come in exhausted, with his plough-share gleaming like silver. In March he harrowed his wheat ; in April his oats ; taking

minute care, and throwing himself heart and soul into the task.
When all the work in the fields was done, he returned to them
just the same; lover-like, to gaze at them. He walked round,
stooping and picking up handfuls of soil with his old gesture;
delighting to crush the rich clods, and let them filter through
his fingers; and feeling supremely happy if he found them
neither too dry nor too damp, with a fine smell suggestive of
growing bread.

Thus La Beauce spread her verdure before him, from November to July, from the moment when the green tips first emerged
to that when the lofty stalks turned yellow. Wishing to have
the country under his eye without leaving the house, he un-
barred the kitchen window—the rear one, that looked out on
the plain—and there he used to station himself and survey ten
leagues of country: an immense broad bare expanse, stretching under the vaulted skies. Not a single tree; nothing but
the telegraph posts of the Châteaudun and Orleans road,
running on unswervingly till they were lost to sight. At first
there was a greenish, scarcely perceptible shade, peeping just
above the soil of the large squares of brown earth. Then this
soft green strengthened into velvet stretches, almost uniform
in tint. Then, as the stems grew taller and thicker, each plant
developed its own tinge of colour. He distinguished from afar
the yellowish green of the wheat, the bluish green of the oats,
the greyish green of the barley; infinite expanses of ground
spread out in all directions, amid glowing patches of crimson
trifolium. It was the time when La Beauce is fair and young,
thus clothed about with spring, and smooth and cool to the eye
in her monotony. The stalks grew taller; and there was then
one deep, rolling, boundless sea of cereals. At morn, in the
fine weather, a pink mist used to rise. As the sun climbed in
the limpid atmosphere a breeze would blow in large regular
puffs, furrowing the fields with a swell that started on the
horizon, and rolled along till it died away in the opposite
direction. As the plants swayed, their colour became paler;
a moire-like effect—waterings of the shade of old gold—
rippled over the wheat; the oats took a bluish hue; while the
barley quivered with violet lights. Undulation continually
succeeded undulation; a ceaseless ebb would set in under the
winds from the offing. When evening fell, the fronts of distant
buildings, brightly lit, showed like white sails; steeples looked
like masts, uprising behind folds in the surface of the plain.
It grew cold; the gloom enhanced the damp and the mur-
muring character of the ocean-like prospect; a distant plan-

tation became indistinct, and looked like the **dim** coast-line of **some** continent.

In the bad weather, also, Buteau gazed **out over** La **Beauce,** **thus spread out at** his **feet, just** as the fisher gazes from his cliff **over the raging sea,** when **the** tempest **is** robbing him **of his livelihood.** He **saw a violent storm;** a **dark** cloud shedding a livid, **leaden light, and red flashes** glowing **over** the grass-tips amid **claps of thunder.** He **saw a waterspout** come from more than **six leagues away;** at first a thin, **tawny** cloud twisted like a **rope, then a** howling **mass galloping on like a** monster; then, as **it passed** away, the crops **could be seen** torn up, and everything **trampled upon,** broken, and **razed along a** track two miles wide. **His own** fields had **escaped, and he pitied the** disasters of others **with inward chuckles of delight. As the wheat** grew, **his** enjoyment **increased. A** grey **islet formed by** a village had disappeared on the horizon behind the rising level **of verdure.** **There** only remained the **roofs of** La Borderie **which, in their** turn, were submerged. **A mill,** with its sails, remained **alone** like a waif. On all **sides there was** corn—an encroaching, overflowing sea of **corn, covering** the earth with its immensity of verdure.

"**God a' mercy!**" **said he, every** evening, as he **sat** down to table; "**if the summer's not too dry,** we shall **never be at a loss for bread.**"

The Buteaus had established themselves **in their new home.** The married **pair had** taken the large **room downstairs, and** Françoise, above **them,** put up with a little **room, formerly** occupied by old Mouche, which had been **scoured** and furnished with **a** fold-up bedstead, an old chest of **drawers, a table and** two chairs. She still busied herself **with** her cows, and led much the same life as of old. **However,** although all was outwardly calm, there **was a dormant source of** disagreement: that question of dividing the property **between** the two sisters, which had remained in abeyance. **On** the day after the **marriage of the elder girl,** old Fouan, **as** guardian of the younger **one, had pressed for** the division of the property, so as to avoid **all unpleasantness** in the future. But Buteau **had** protested. What was the good? Françoise was too young; she didn't want **her land.** Wasn't everything just **as** before? She lived with her **sister still,** she was boarded and clothed. In short, she certainly **could** have **no cause of complaint.** At all these **reasons** the old man shook **his head.** No one knew what **might** happen, the best thing **to do was to** settle everything **in due** form; and the girl herself was anxious to know

what her share would consist of, though that point being
settled she was ready to leave it in charge of her brother-in-
law. The latter, however, had his own way, by means of his
genial, obstinate, humbugging bluffness. Nothing further was
said, and he proclaimed everywhere what a happy, charming,
domestic mode of life theirs was.

"There's nothing like having a good understanding with
one another!" said he.

In point of fact there had not been any quarrel between the
two sisters, nor any domestic disagreement during the first ten
months; but then matters gradually became unpleasant. It
started with displays of bad temper. There were fits of sulking,
and at last loud words were exchanged; and, beneath it all,
the fermenting question of "mine" and "thine" was at its
ravaging work, gradually destroying affection.

Certainly Lise and Françoise no longer loved one another
as tenderly as of old. No one now met them with their arms
round each other's waists, walking out in the gloaming wrapped
in the same shawl. A separation had come between them; a
coolness was growing up. Since there had been a man in the
house, it seemed to Françoise that her sister had been taken
from her. She who once had shared everything with Lise,
had no share in this man; and he had thus become a something
foreign, an obstacle shutting her out from the heart in which
she had lived alone. All this, moreover, had a material side.
She used to leave without kissing her elder sister when
Buteau did so, feeling as shocked as if some one had drunk out
of her glass. In matters of ownership, she kept to her childish
notions with passionate earnestness. "This is mine, that is
yours;" and, as her sister belonged thenceforward to another,
she let her go. But she wanted what was her own, one-half
of the land and of the house.

This wrath of hers was also caused by another matter which
she herself could not have explained. There had, so far, been
nothing to disturb her in the house, where love scenes had
been unknown, a chill having fallen upon the place when old
Mouche became a widower. But now it was inhabited by a
brutal man with the instincts of his sex, who had always been
in the habit of running after the girls in the fields, and whose
unrestrained dalliance with her sister, which she was obliged
to be cognisant of, made her feel alike disgusted and exasperated. During the daytime she preferred to go out, and
let them indulge in their dirty tricks unrestrained. In the
evening, if they began laughing on getting up from table, she

called to them to wait till she had finished washing up the dishes. And then she rushed madly to her room, slamming the doors and muttering insults: "The beasts! The beasts!" between her clenched teeth. In spite of all, she still fancied that she could hear what was going on below her, down-stairs. With her head buried in the pillow, and with the sheets drawn up to her eyes, she grew hot and feverish; her hearing and her sight were haunted by hallucinations, and her revolting puberty made her suffer.

The worst of it was that Buteau, seeing so much of her attention given to these matters, used to chaff her about them by way of a joke. Goodness gracious! what next? What would she say when she had to go through the same thing herself? Lise, too, used to laugh, seeing nothing whatever wrong about it; and then Buteau would explain his ideas on the subject. The pleasure cost nothing, and it was perfectly lawful to indulge in it. But no children; no, no! No more of them! There was always too much of that sort of thing before marriage; people were so stupid. Thus little Jules had made his appearance, for instance; a confounded nuisance, which had to be put up with all the same. But when folks were married, they sobered down. He'd rather be a capon than have any more children. A likely thing! Bringing another mouth into a house where there wasn't too much to eat as it was! And so he kept constantly on the alert with regard to his wife, who was so plump, the hussy! that she'd get in the family-way in a trice if he'd only let her. He'd be glad to reap as much corn as the full womb of the earth could be made to yield; but no babies! They had done with children for ever!

Amidst these constant details, this copulation that rustled audibly near her, as it were, Françoise's agitation kept increasing. Folks asserted that her temper was changing; and she did yield to inexplicable moods which abruptly changed · first merry, then sad, and then surly and spiteful. In the morning she watched Buteau with a black look, whenever he unceremoniously crossed the kitchen, half undressed. Quarrels, too, broke out between herself and her sister about the most trivial matters—a cup that she had just broken, for instance. Wasn't the cup hers as well, half of it at all events? Couldn't she break half of everything, if she liked? On these questions of ownership their disputes always became most bitter, entailing grudges that lasted days and days.

The worst of it was that Buteau himself became subject to

odious fits of temper. The land was suffering from a terrible
drought, not a drop of rain having fallen for six weeks; and
he would come in with his fists clenched, made ill by the sight
of the spoilt crops—the stunted barley, the shrivelled oats, and
the wheat, which was already scorched up before coming into
ear. He actually suffered as if he had been part of the crops
themselves; his stomach shrank, his limbs were racked with
cramps, he dwindled and pined away with anxiety and anger.
In this state he, one morning, came to loggerheads with
Françoise for the first time. It was hot, and after washing at
the well, he had left part of his shirt hanging out behind. As
he was sitting down to eat his soup, Françoise, on coming
forward to help him, observed it. Then she burst out,
reddening all over:

" Tuck your shirt in, do! It's disgusting!"

He was in a bad humour already, and now flew into a
passion.

" God's truth! Haven't you done picking me to pieces yet?
Don't look, if it offends you. One would think you had some
lewd fancy in your head from the way you jaw about it!"

She reddened still more, and began to stammer; while Lise
injudiciously added:

" He's right. You end by plaguing one. Go elsewhere if
one can't be at home in one's own house."

" Quite so; I will go elsewhere," said Françoise savagely,
banging the door after her as she went out.

But on the following day Buteau was once more pleasant,
conciliatory, and jocular. During the night the sky had
clouded over, and for twelve hours a fine, warm, penetrating
rain had fallen; one of those summer rains that freshen up the
country. He had opened the window, which looked on to the
plain, and since daybreak he had stood at it with his hands in
his pockets, radiant, and watching the stream pour down, while
he repeated:

" Now we're gentle-folks, since the blessed God is doing our
work for us. Ah! thunder and blazes! The days spent like
this, idling about, are a lot better than those when one wears
oneself out for no return."

The rain still came streaming down slowly, softly, and
endlessly. He could hear thirsting, riverless, and springless
La Beauce drinking this water. 'Twas one vast murmur, a
universal gurgling, full of comfort. Everything absorbed the
moisture, everything bloomed anew under the shower. The
wheat was regaining its youthful healthfulness; it was sturdy

and upright now, bearing on high the ears which would swell mightily and burst with meal. Buteau, like the soil, like the wheat, drank in at every pore, feeling cheerful, refreshed, and restored to health, ever returning to his post at the window, and shouting:

"Go on, go on! It's like five-franc pieces falling."

Suddenly he heard some one open the door, and on turning round he was surprised to recognise old Fouan.

"Why, father! You've been frog hunting, then?"

The old man, after a struggle with a large blue umbrella, came in, leaving his wooden shoes on the threshold.

"Something like a watering!" said he, simply. "We wanted it."

During the year that had elapsed since the partition had been finally concluded, signed, and registered, he had had but one occupation: that of visiting his old fields. He was always to be met prowling round them with a deal of interest, grave or gay, according to the state of the crops; yelling at his children if things went wrong, and declaring that it was their fault if matters were at a standstill. This rain had enlivened him also.

"And so," resumed Buteau, "you've looked in to see us as you were passing by."

Françoise, hitherto silent, now came forward and said distinctly:

"No: it was I who begged uncle to come."

Lise, who was standing by the table shelling peas, left off and waited motionless, a harsh expression suddenly coming over her face. Buteau, who had at first clenched his fists, resumed his genial air, having determined not to lose his temper.

"Yes," explained the old man, slowly, "the child spoke to me yesterday. You see now how right I was when I wanted to have matters settled at the outset. To each his own. There's nothing in that for any one to get angry about; on the contrary, it prevents quarrels. It's now high time to make an end of it. She has a right, hasn't she? to know exactly how she stands. Otherwise I should be to blame. So we'll fix a day, and go together to Monsieur Baillehache's."

Lise could hold out no longer.

"Why don't she send for the gendarmes? Good Heavens! one would suppose she was being robbed. What if I were to go about and tell everybody what a filthy beast she is, and that there's no knowing where to take hold of her?"

Françoise **was about to reply in the same** strain, when
Buteau, who **had playfully caught her up from** behind, cried
out:

" A pack of nonsense! People **may badger each other, but
they love each other all** the same, **eh? A nice thing it would
be if sisters fell out! "**

The girl **had shaken** herself free, and the quarrel was about
to continue, **when Buteau** raised a joyous shout **on** seeing **the**
door again open:

" Jean! Sopping wet! Why, he's a regular poodle! "

Jean, who had run **over from** the farm, as he often **did, had**
merely thrown a sack over **his shoulders for protection ; and**
he was wet through—dripping, **steaming, and laughing good-**
humouredly **through it** all. While **he was shaking himself,**
Buteau, returning **to his window, grew more and more expan-**
sive at the **sight** of **the steady, endless downpour.**

" Oh, **how it's coming down ! What a blessing ! My ! it's**
quite a **game to see it come down like that ! "**

Then, **turning back, he said to Jean :**

" You **come pat. These two were tearing each other's
eyes out. Françoise wants the property divided, so that she
may leave us."**

" What? That child! " **cried Jean, amazed.**

His desire had become a violent hidden passion, and the
only satisfaction **he had was to see her in this house, where he**
was received as a **friend.** He would **have proposed** for **her**
half a score of times already, if he had not so keenly felt **the**
disparity in their ages. It was in vain that he had waited ; **the**
fifteen **years'** difference had **not been spanned. In the country,**
a great difference of age is **reckoned such an obstacle, that**
nobody—not she herself, **nor her sister, nor** even her brother-
in-law—seemed to imagine **he could ever** fix his thoughts on
her. And this was why Buteau received him so cordially,
without any fear of the consequences.

" You may **well say** child! " said he, paternally shrugging
his shoulders.

But Francoise, **standing rigidly erect,** with her eyes **on the**
ground, **proved obstinate.**

" I want my share."

" It would be the wisest thing," murmured **old Fouan.**

Then Jean gently took hold of **her wrists, and** drew her
towards him. Holding her thus, **his** hands quivering at the
contact of her flesh, he addressed her in his kind voice, which
faltered as he besought her to remain. Where could she go ?

Into service with some strangers at Cloyes or Châteaudun?
Was she not better off in the house where she had grown up,
amid people who loved her? She listened to him, and she
also softened; for although she scarcely thought of him as a
lover, she was wont to obey him readily, chiefly out of regard
for him and a little from fear, thinking him a very serious person.

" I want my share," she repeated, beginning to give way,
" but I don't say that I shall go away."

" Why, stupid!" interposed Buteau, " what on earth would
you do with your share if you stay? Everything is as much
yours as it is your sister's or mine. What do you want the
half for? Pooh! it's enough to send one into fits! Harkee,
the day you marry the property shall be divided."

Jean's eyes, which were fixed on her, fell, as if his heart
had failed him.

" You hear? On your wedding day."

She felt oppressed, and made no reply.

" And now, my little Françoise, go and kiss your sister.
That'll be much better."

Lise, the buxom matron, was still good-hearted in her gay,
noisy way, and she wept when Françoise fell on her neck,
Buteau, delighted at having postponed the evil day, cried out
that, God's mercy! they would have a drink. He fetched five
glasses, uncorked one bottle, and went back to fetch another.
Old Fouan's bronzed face had flushed as he explained that he
was in favour of order and duty. They all drank, women and
men alike, to the health of every one present.

" Wine's a good thing," said Buteau, slapping down his
glass, " but, say what you like, that falling water's a deal
better. Just look at it! There it goes, and there it goes
again. Isn't it glorious?"

Crowding to the windows, with radiant faces, and in a sort
of religious ecstacy, they all watched the warm, slow, endless
rain stream down, as though beneath this beneficent water they
had seen the tall green corn visibly growing.

CHAPTER II.

ONE day that summer old Rose, who had suffered from swooning fits, and whose legs were failing her, sent for her grand-niece, Palmyre, to clean the house. Fouan had gone out to prowl round the fields, as usual; and while the wretched creature, drenched with water, was scrubbing with all her might, the other woman followed her about, step by step, both of them going over the same eternal old gossip.

They began with Palmyre's misfortunes, for her brother Hilarion had taken to beating her. The soft-witted cripple had grown malicious; and, as he did not know how strong he was with his fists, which were capable of pulverising stones, she was in terror of her life whenever he seized hold of her. Still she wouldn't have any interference; and when anybody came she sent them away, managing to appease the young fellow by dint of the infinite fondness which she entertained for him. The other week there had been a scandal, which all Rognes was still talking about: such a fight that the neighbours had run in, and had found him behaving abominably.

"Tell me, my child," asked Rose, to elicit some confidential revelation, "what was the brute doing?"

Palmyre, ceasing to scrub, and squatting in her dripping rags, flew into a passion without giving an answer.

"Is it any business of those folks I should like to know? What do they want to come spying in our house for? We don't rob any one."

"Well, well!" resumed the old woman, "all the same, if you do as people say, it's a very dreadful thing."

For an instant the poor creature remained silent; and an expression of suffering came over her features as her eyes vacantly stared afar. Then, bending down once more, she mumbled, with the to-and-fro movement of her skinny arms breaking in upon her words:

"I don't know about it being so very dreadful. The priest sent for me, to say that we both of us should go to hell. Not that poor darling, anyhow. 'A natural, your reverence,' says I to him 'a mere child with no more sense than a babe three days old, and who'd have died if I hadn't fed him—and perhaps it'd have been better for him if he had?' It's my affair alone, isn't it? The day he strangles me, in one of the fits of rage such as have lately come over him, I shall see fast enough whether the blessed God'll forgive me."

Seeing that she would not obtain any fresh particulars, Rose, who had long known the truth, sagely concluded: " Sure enough, things must be one way or the other. But put it as you like, it's not a life you're leading, my girl."

Then she lamented that everybody had their misfortunes. The miseries, now, that she and her husband had gone through, since they'd been kind enough to strip themselves for their children's benefit! Once started on this topic she never stopped. It was an eternal subject of complaint with her.

"Deary me! One can get used to disrespect. When one's children are swine, they're swine, and that's all about it. But if they'd only pay their allowance——"

Then she explained, for the twentieth time, that Delhomme alone brought his fifty francs every quarter, and punctual, too, to the tick! Buteau was always in arrears, and haggled over coppers. Thus, although the money was ten days overdue, she was still awaiting payment. He had promised to pay up that very night. As for Hyacinthe, that was a simpler matter. He didn't pay anything; they never saw the colour of his money. And he'd actually had the cheek to send La Trouille that morning to borrow five francs, to enable her to make some broth for him as he was very ill. Oh, yes! they all knew what _he_ suffered from—a spark in his inside! And so the wench had been sent to the right-about in no time, with orders to tell her father that if he didn't bring his fifty francs that night, like his brother Buteau, he should have the lawyer after him.

" Just to frighten him, you know, for the poor boy's not bad at heart, after all," added Rose, whose partiality for the elder son had already softened her.

At night-fall, Fouan having come in to his dinner, she began again at table while he bent silently over his food. Could it be possible that, out of their six hundred francs, they should only get two hundred from Delhomme, scarcely a hundred from Buteau, and nothing at all from the other? That made just half the allowance. And the scamps had signed at the notary's; it was set down in black and white, and was under the charge of the law! But a vast deal their children cared about the law!

To every complaint Palmyre, who was scouring the tiled
floor of the kitchen in the dark, made the same answer, which
sounded like a refrain of misery.

"Sure enough, we've all of us got our troubles; they bring
us to the grave!"

Rose was at length deciding to light the candle when La
Grande came in with her knitting. During the summer
there was no evening meeting; but, to avoid using even a
candle-end, she was wont to spend an hour at her brother's
before groping her way to bed in the darkness. She established
herself forthwith; and Palmyre, who had still the pots and
pans to scour, breathed not a word more, over-awed by the
sight of her grandmother.

"If you want any hot water, my girl," said Rose, "undo
a faggot."

Then she contained herself for a moment, and forced herself
to talk of other matters. In La Grande's presence the Fouans
avoided complaining, knowing how pleased she was whenever
she heard them regret having parted with their property.
But passion was too much for Rose, and finally she spoke again:

"And you may as well put on the whole faggot at once, if
they call that a faggot, indeed! Merely some dead twigs and
hedge-clippings! Fanny must certainly scrape the floor of her
wood-house to send us rotten stuff like that!"

Fouan, who had remained at table, with his glass full, then
broke the silence in which he had seemingly wished to enwrap
himself.

"God a' mercy!" he shouted. "Haven't we had enough of
your faggots? They're muck, and we know it! But what's
to be said, pray, of the beastly dregs that Delhomme gives
me for wine?"

He raised his glass to the candle and glanced at it.

"Eh? What the devil has he put into it? It's worse
even than the rinsings of casks. And he's the honest one!
The two others would let us die o' thirst, before they'd go and
fetch us even a bottle of water from the river."

At length he made up his mind to drink his wine at a gulp.
But he spat violently afterwards.

"Ugh! the poison! P'raps it's to kill me right off."

After that Fouan and Rose gave way to their rancour, and,
casting all restraint aside, relieved their aching hearts. There was
a perfect litany of recriminations, each in turn exposing his or her
wrongs. Take, for instance, the ten quarts of milk per week.
To begin with, they only got six; and then what milk it was!

Although it didn't pass through the priest's hands it must be real Christian milk, judging by the way it was baptised! The same with the eggs. They must have been specially ordered of the fowls, for such little ones could never have been found in all the Cloyes markets. They were regular curiosities, and so grudgingly given, that they had time enough to go bad on the way. As for the cheeses! Cheeses indeed! Rose was doubled up with colic every time she ate any. She ran to fetch one, insisting on Palmyre's tasting it. Well, wasn't it horrible? Didn't this demand redress? They must put flour into it, and perhaps plaster as well. Then Fouan struck in, lamenting that he was cut down to a sou's worth of tobacco per day; and Rose immediately regretted her black coffee which she had had to give up. Finally, both together, they taxed their children with the death of their decrepit old dog, which they had drowned the day before, because he cost them too much to keep.

"I gave them everything," cried the old fellow; "and the scamps don't care a damn about me. It'll kill us for certain—it makes us so wild to be left in such wretchedness!"

At length they became silent, and La Grande, who had not unclosed her lips, looked from one to the other with her round, evil, bird-of-prey-like eyes.

"Serve you right!" said she.

Just at that moment, however, Buteau came in. Palmyre, having finished her work, took advantage of the opening of the door to slip out and make her escape, with the fifteen sous which Rose had just put into her hand. Buteau stood motionless in the middle of the room, maintaining the prudent silence of the peasant, who will never be the first to speak. A couple of minutes elapsed, and then the father was forced to open the discussion.

"So you've made up your mind. That's fortunate. We've had plenty of time to wait for you during these last ten days."

The son swayed carelessly from side to side, and eventually said: "One can't do more than one can. Every one knows how his bread bakes."

"Possibly. But if things were to go on at that rate, you'd be eating your bread while we starved. You signed, and you ought to pay up on the right day."

Seeing his father's ill-humour, Buteau began to laugh.

"If I'm too late, you know, I can go back. It's not so nice to have to pay as it is. Some don't pay at all."

This allusion to Hyacinthe disquieted Rose, who, not daring

to interfere, confined herself to twitching her **husband's jacket.**
He had made **a gesture of anger, but checked himself.**

"**Good.　Hand over your fifty francs.　I've drawn out the** receipt."

Buteau leisurely **fumbled in his clothes.　He had** glanced **in a vexed** way at La Grande, and seemed **put out by** her presence.　She dropped her knitting, **and** glared **at him in expectation of** seeing the money produced.　The **parents, too, had drawn near,** and **never** took their **eyes off the young** fellow's hand.　**Under the stare of those three pairs of eyes,** he reluctantly drew out **his first five-franc piece.**

"One," said **he, laying it down on the table.　Others** followed, more and **more slowly.　He went on counting them aloud,** in faltering **tones.　After producing the** fifth he stopped, and had **to make an exhaustive search to find** another ; then he shouted loudly and emphatically :

" And **six ! "**

The **Fouans still waited, but nothing** more came.

"**What, six ? "** the father said at last.　" There ought to be **ten.　Are** you making fun of us ?　**Last quarter, forty** francs ; **and** only thirty this time."

Buteau **immediately assumed a whining tone.　Nothing** prospered.　Wheat had **fallen still lower, the oats were** wretched.　There was even **a swelling on his horse's stomach,** and he had **had to send twice for Monsieur Patoir.　In short,** he was ruined, **and he didn't know how to make both ends meet.**

" That's no **concern of mine," repeated the old man furiously.** " Hand **over the fifty francs, or I'll summons you ! "**

He grew cooler, however, as it occurred to him to accept the six coins on account ; and he spoke of making out a fresh receipt.

"**Then you** will **give me the twenty francs next week ? I'll put that on** the paper."

Buteau, however, had immediately snatched up the **money lying on** the table.

" **No, no !** None of that !　We must be quits.　**Leave the** receipt **as it is, or I'm off.** Likely thing !　It wouldn't be worth while **my pinching** and screwing if I were still **to be in** your debt."

Then there **was a** terrible **scene.　Both father and son held** out stubbornly, untiringly **repeating the same** phrases ; the one exasperated at not having **pocketed the money in** the first **instance,** the other clutching **it firmly, and** determined not to **give it** up again without having the **receipt in full.　Once more**

the mother had to twitch her husband's jacket, and once more
he gave way.

"There, you confounded thief; there's the paper! You ought
to have it smacked on your jaw! Hand over the money."

The transfer was made from fist to fist, and Buteau, having
played the comedy out, began to laugh. He went off, pleasant
and contented, wishing the company a very good evening.
Fouan, who looked exhausted, had sat down at the table; and
La Grande, before resuming her knitting, shrugged her
shoulders and shouted in his face:

"You stupid fool!"

Silence ensued. Then the door re-opened, and Hyacinthe
came in. Having been informed by La Trouille that his brother
was to pay that night, he had watched him on the road, and had
waited for him to leave before presenting himself in his turn.
His mild expression was simply due to the maudlin effects of
dissipation over-night. From the door-way, his glance fell
straight on the six five-franc pieces which Fouan had been
imprudent enough to leave on the table.

"Ah, it's Hyacinthe," exclaimed Rose, pleased to see him.

"Yes, it's me. Hope I see you all well!"

He came forward, with his eyes riveted on the white coins,
which glistened like so many moons in the candle light. His
father, who had turned his head, observed his look, and
perceived the money with a start of disquietude. He clapped
a plate over the coins to hide them, but it was too late.

"Infernal fool I was!" thought he, irritated at his own
carelessness. "La Grande is right."

Then, aloud, and coarsely: "You do well to come and pay
us, for as true as that candle's shining, I'd have sent the lawyer
to you to-morrow."

"Yes, La Trouille told me so," groaned Hyacinthe very
humbly: "and so I put myself about to come, because you
surely can't wish my death, do you? Pay, good Lord!
what's one to pay with, when one hasn't even bread enough to
live on? We've sold everything—oh! I'm not kidding; come
and see for yourself if you think I'm kidding. There are now
no sheets on the beds, no more furniture, no nothing! And on
the top of that, I'm ill."

A guffaw of incredulity interrupted him. He went on
without heeding:

"Perhaps it doesn't show much, but, all the same, there's
something wrong in my inside. I cough, I feel that I'm going.
If I could only get some broth! But when one can't even get

broth, one **kicks the bucket, eh?** That's true enough. **To be** sure **I'd pay you if I had the money. Tell me** where there is any, and **I will give you some, and boil a** bit of beef to begin with. **It's now a fortnight since I tasted** meat, indeed it is! **on my honour."**

Rose began to be affected, while Fouan got more angry.

" You've turned everything into drink, you good-for-nothing vagabond. So much the worse for you! You**'ve pledged** all that fine land that had **been in the family for years and** years! **Yes,** you've been **on the spree** for months, **you** and **your** daughter; and if **it's finished** now, **well,** go and **die."**

Hyacinthe hesitated no longer, but sobbed.

" It isn't fatherly to say that. **Only unnatural people cast off their** children. It's because I'm good-hearted **that I shall come to grief. If you hadn't any money one could make** allowances! **But when a father has the** cash, does he refuse alms to a **son? I shall go and beg at other** people's houses; and a nice thing **that'll** be—a very nice thing indeed!"

At every phrase, jerked out amid his tears, he made the old **man tremble** by casting sidelong glances at the plate. **Then,** pretending to **suffocate, he** screamed in a deafening **way as if** he were having his throat cut.

Rose, who was quite upset and vanquished **by his sobs,** clasped her hands in supplication to Fouan.

" Come, husband."

But he, struggling with himself, and **still refusing, cut her** short.

" **No, no, he's only making fools of us.** Will you hold your tongue, you brute? **Is there** any **sense** in howling **like that?** The neighbours will **come in.** You're making us ill."

This **only** made **the sot increase** his **clamour,** as he bellowed out:

" **I haven't** told you. But the lawyer **is** coming to-morrow **to put** in an execution for a bill I gave Lambourdieu. I'm **a swine; I disgrace you;** I must put an end to it. Pig that I am, and I deserve to be soused in the Aigre for good. If I only had **thirty** francs!"

Fouan, tried beyond endurance, and overcome by **the scene,** started at the **mention of thirty** francs. He removed **the plate.** What good was it, when the scamp saw the money and counted it through the china?

" **Y**ou want the whole. In God's name, **is** that reasonable? Look here! You're driving us distracted. Take half, and go; and don't let us see you again."

Hyacinthe, suddenly cured, apparently took counsel with himself. Then he declared:

"No, fifteen francs is too little; it would be of no use. Call it twenty, and I'll leave you."

Then, when he'd got the four five-franc pieces, he made them all laugh by relating what a trick he had played Bécu, with some imitation bottom lines so placed in the reserved part of the Aigre that the rural constable had tumbled into the water while trying to get them out. At last he went away, after getting himself offered a glass of the bad wine sent by Delhomme, whom he called a dirty scoundrel to dare send such stuff to a father.

"He's a pleasant fellow, anyhow!" said Rose, when the door had shut behind him.

La Grande had risen, and was folding up her knitting, prior to leaving. She stared at her sister-in-law and then at her brother; and finally in her turn she went out after screaming, in a fit of passion long suppressed:

"Not a copper, you infernal fools! Never ask me for a copper, never!"

Outside, she met Buteau, who was returning from Macqueron's, having been astonished to see Hyacinthe come in there, looking very lively, and rattling a pocketful of crowns. He had at once smelt a rat.

"Oh, yes! The rascal's making off with your money. Ah, what a night of it he'll make! and what an ass he'll think you are!"

Buteau, beside himself, knocked with both fists at the Fouans' door. If they hadn't let him in he would have broken it down. The old folks were already going to bed. The mother had taken off her cap and her dress, and was in her petticoat, with her grey hair falling over her temples. When they decided to open the door, he burst in upon them, shouting in a stifled voice:

"My money! My money!"

They recoiled in fear and bewilderment, not understanding him as yet.

"Do you suppose I half-kill myself for that scoundrel, my brother? So he's to do nothing, and I'm to provide for him! Oh, no! Oh, no!"

Fouan tried to deny it, but Buteau coarsely interrupted him.

"What's that? Oh, you're going to lie, now! I tell you he's got my money. I smelt it; I heard it rattling in the blackguard's pocket! My money, that I sweated for, and that he's going to **spend in tipple**! If it's not so, show it me! Show me the coins, **if you have** them still. **I know** them; I can tell **them. Show me the** coins!"

He stubbornly repeated this phrase **a** score of **times, as if** applying the spur to his anger. He got **to** thumping **the table** with his fist, demanding the coins on the spot, at once, swearing **that he** did not want to take them back, **but** simply **to** see them. **Then,** as **the** old folks shook **and** stammered, **he burst** out **furiously**:

" He's got them ; that's **clear**! Hell and thunder, if **I ever** bring you another copper! One might bleed one's-self **for you**; but I'd **sooner cut** off my arms than keep **that** sodden **cur**!"

At last, however, the father also got into a passion.

" Now then, haven't you **about** finished," said he. " Is it any business of yours what **we do?** The money's my own, and I can do what **I like with it.**"

" What's that you say ?" retorted Buteau, going up to him, pale and **with clenched** fists. " So you expect me to give up everything. **Well, then, I tell you it's** simply filthy—yes, filthy—to get **money out of** your **children,** when you have certainly enough **to live on.** Oh ! **it's no use your** denying it! You've got a hoard in there, I know !"

The startled old man was struggling **wildly, his voice and arms** both failing him, with nought of his **old authority left to** turn **his** son out.

" No, no; there's not a copper. **Will you go off?**"

" Suppose I look! Suppose I look!" repeated Buteau, already opening some drawers and tapping **the** walls.

Rose, terrified, and dreading **an encounter** between **father** and son, hung on the latter's shoulder, **and** faltered :

" **Y**ou unfortunate fellow, do you want to kill **us?**"

Turning sharply upon her, he seized her **by** the wrists, and **shouted in her** face, regardless of **her poor,** grey, worn, and **weary head**:

" **It's all your fault!** It was you that gave the money **to** Hyacinthe. **Y**ou never liked me, you old hag!"

With **these words he gave her** so rough a push that, uttering a faint cry, she **fell swooning** in a heap against the wall. He looked at her for an instant as she reclined there, huddled up like a bundle of **rags, and then madly rushed out,** slamming the door and swearing.

The next day Rose could **not** leave her **bed.** Doctor Finet was called in, and returned **three** times, without being able to afford her any relief. At **his** third visit, finding her in

extremity, he took Fouan aside, and asked as a favour to be
allowed to write out the burial certificate, and leave it. This
plan, which he generally adopted for distant hamlets, would
save him a journey. Nevertheless, Rose survived for thirty-six
hours longer. The doctor, when questioned, had replied that she
was dying of old age and over-work: that the end was bound
to come when the body was worn out. But in Rognes, where
the story was known, all the folks said that she had died of
"curdled blood," meaning apoplexy. There were a great many
people at the funeral, and Buteau and the rest of the family
behaved with great decorum.

When the grave had been filled up, old Fouan went back
alone to the house where the two of them had lived and suffered
for fifty years. He ate a bit of bread and cheese standing.
Then he prowled through the empty buildings and garden, not
knowing what occupation would enable him to get rid of his
grief. He had nothing more to do now, so he went up to his
old fields on the plateau to see if the wheat were growing.

CHAPTER III.

FOR a whole year Fouan lived in this fashion, **silent and alone, in the empty house.** He was ever to be found there **on** his legs, roaming hither **and thither with trembling hands and** doing nothing. He would stay **for hours in front of the mouldy** troughs in the cow-house; and then he would turn and station himself at the door of the empty **barn, as if riveted there in** profound reverie. The garden still gave him some occupation; but he was growing weaker, **and** stooped more and more, as though the soil were recalling **him** little by little to herself. Twice had he been picked up lying face downwards among his young salads.

Since those twenty francs had been given to Hyacinthe, Delhomme alone paid his share of the allowance. Buteau stubbornly refused a single copper, declaring he would rather go into a court of law than see his money pass into the pockets of his disreputable brother. The latter did, indeed, from time to time, wring some alms from his father, whom his tearful heroics prostrated.

Then it was that Delhomme, seeing the **old man's growing** distress, **his enfeeblement and** forlornness, conceived the **notion** of taking **him into his own home.** Why should not Fouan sell the house **and live at his daughter's?** He would want for nothing there ; and they would no longer have to pay him the two hundred francs' allowance. The next day Buteau, having heard of this offer, hastened to make a similar one, with an elaborate display of filial affection. Money to fling away— no, no, indeed! But if it were merely a question of caring **for** his father, why the latter could come and eat and sleep and enjoy himself. At bottom, no doubt, Buteau's **idea must have** been that his sister **was only trying to get hold of the old man** with the intention of grabbing the suppositious hoard. Yet **even** he was beginning **to doubt the existence of** that money, which he had hunted after in vain. And he was in two minds —offering his father **a shelter out of pride, expecting that** the old man would refuse, and yet **exasperated at the** notion that he might accept Delhomme's **hospitality.** Fouan, on his side,

displayed great repugance, almost dread, as regards both pro-
posals. No, no! Better dry bread in his own house than
roast meat at other people's; it was less bitter. He had lived
there and there he would die.

So things went on till mid-July—Saint Henri's day, which
was the patronal feast-day of Rognes. A travelling ball-room,
under canvas, was usually set up in the meadows of the Aigre;
and on the road, in front of the municipal offices, there were
three stalls, one kept by a cheap-jack, who sold everything
down to ribbons; a shooting-gallery, and a game of turn-about,
at which sticks of barley-sugar could be won. That day Monsieur Baillehache, who was breakfasting at La Borderie, profited
by the occasion to go and have a chat with Delhomme, who
begged him to accompany him to Fouan's, and persuade the
old man to listen to reason. Since Rose's death the notary also
had advised Fouan to take up his abode with his daughter
and sell the house, which was now uselessly large. It was
worth some three thousand francs; and he, the notary, even
offered to take care of the money and to pay Fouan the interest
on it in little sums, according to his humble wants.

They found the old fellow in his customary bewilderment,
trudging about at random in a state of stupor, in front of a
heap of wood, which he wanted to saw up without having the
strength to do so. That morning his poor hands shook even
more than usual, for on the night before he had undergone a
terrible onslaught from Hyacinthe, who, to get hold of twenty
francs, in view of the morrow's festivity, had brought all his
resources into play, bellowing maddeningly, crawling on the
ground, and threatening to kill himself with a knife which
he had purposely concealed up his sleeve. At this the old man
had given the twenty francs, as he at once confessed, with an
air of anguish, to the notary.

"Tell me, would you do otherwise? I'm dead beat, dead
beat!"

So Monsieur Baillehache took advantage of the circumstance.

"I've not come to talk about all that," said he. "You can't
keep on like this. You won't even have your own skin left
you. At your age it isn't prudent to live alone; and if you
don't want to be eaten alive, you must listen to your daughter.
Sell this place and go and live with her!"

"Ah! so that's your advice, too?" muttered Fouan.

He glanced askance at Delhomme, who affected to hold
himself aloof. However, remarking the old man's look of
distrust, he spoke out.

"You know, father," he began, "that I say nothing, because you perhaps imagine that I have some selfish object in inviting you. Good gracious, no! You'll give us extra work at home, but then it annoys me to see you so uncomfortably situated when you might be living at ease."

"Well, well," replied the old fellow, "we must think it over. As soon as I make up my mind, I'll be sure and let you know."

Neither his son-in-law nor the notary could get anything more out of him. He complained of being bustled. His authority, which had gradually died out, just lingered in this obstinacy of old age—this obstinacy which made him regardless even of his own comfort and well-being. In addition to his vague dread at the idea of no longer having a house of his own—a dread which was by no means unnatural, seeing how much he already suffered from having no land left him—he said "no," because they all wanted to make him say "yes." The brutes had something to gain by it, then? Well, he would say "yes" when he chose to do so, and not before.

On the evening before, Hyacinthe having been weak enough in his rapture to show La Trouille his four five-franc pieces, had gone to sleep clutching them in his hand, for on the last occasion the minx had stolen one from under his bolster, taking advantage of the fact that he had come home drunk to assert that he must have lost it out of doors. On awaking he had a fright, the coins having escaped from his grasp during his sleep; but he found them again, quite warm, under his buttocks, and was then thrilled with a mighty joy. His mouth was already watering at the thought of how he would spend the cash at Lengaigne's. It was the village fête, and no one with any decency would go back home at nighttime with any change left in his pocket. During the morning La Trouille vainly coaxed her father to give her one of the five-franc pieces, just a little one, she said; but he repulsed her, and was not even grateful for the stolen eggs with which she made him an omelette. No, no! It didn't suffice that she was fond of her father; money was made for men. Then in a fit of wrath she put on her blue poplin dress—a present dating from the period of plenty—saying that she, too, was going to enjoy herself. She hadn't got twenty yards from the door when she turned round and called out:

"Father, father, look!"

Her hand was raised, and she displayed between the tips of her slender fingers a five-franc piece which shone like a sun.

Hyacinthe fancied that he had been robbed, and, growing pale, he fumbled in his pockets. But the twenty francs were there all right. The hussy must have sold some of her geese, and the dodge striking him as funny, he chuckled paternally and let her go.

He was only strict on one point: morality; and it was on that account that, half-an-hour later, he fell into a violent passion. He also was going out, and was on the point of fastening the door, when a peasant, in holiday garb, passing along on the road below, hailed him.

"Hyacinthe, ahoy! Hyacinthe!"

"What is it?"

"I have just seen your daughter."

"What of it?"

"Well, there's a fellow with her."

"Whereabouts are they?"

"In the ditch over there, at the corner of Guillaume's field."

On hearing this Hyacinthe raised both hands furiously to heaven.

"All right; thanks," said he to the peasant. "I'll fetch my whip. The dirty drab! Bringing dishonour on me like this, indeed!"

Having returned into his house, he took down from behind the door, on the left, a long horse-whip which he only used on these occasions; then with the whip under his arm he set out, creeping past the bushes as if after some game, so as to come upon the guilty couple unawares.

When, however, he turned round the bend of the road, Nénesse, who was keeping watch on a heap of stones, caught sight of him. It was Delphin who was with La Trouille. The two were taking turns, the one acting as outpost while the other amused himself.

"Look out!" cried Nénesse; "here's Hyacinthe."

He had seen the whip, and he started off across country like a hare.

La Trouille and Delphin were in the grassy ditch. What a nuisance! So here was her father coming! Still she had her wits sufficiently about her to hand Delphin her five-franc piece.

"Look here," said she, "hide this somewhere. You can give it me back again. Quick, cut away, hang you!"

Hyacinthe came up like a hurricane, shaking the ground as he ran, and brandishing his whip, which smacked with a sound like that of crackling flames.

"Oh, you foul drab, you!" he shouted; "I'll rouse you!"

He was so infuriated, on recognising the rural constable's
son, that he missed the lad, as the latter scuttled off on all
fours through the brambles. La Trouille, hampered by her
petticoats, could neither escape nor plead innocence. A lash
of the whip soon set her upright, and brought her out of the
ditch. Then the sport began.

"Take that, you dirty troll! See if that won't quiet you!"

La Trouille, without saying a word, accustomed to these
races, leapt away like a goat. Her father's usual tactics
were to bring her back home like that, and then lock her up.
So she tried to make her escape towards the plain, hoping to
tire him out; and on this occasion she all but succeeded, thanks
to a chance encounter. For the last moment or so, Monsieur
Charles and Elodie, whom he was taking to the fête, had been
standing there stock-still, in the middle of the road. They had
seen everything; the young girl staring wide with innocent
stupefaction, the father red with shame and bursting with
indignation. The worst was that as that shameless hussy La
Trouille recognised him she tried to obtain his protection. He
repulsed her, but the whip was within range, and, to avoid it,
she took to dodging round her uncle and cousin; while her
father swore more loudly than ever, coarsely reproaching her
with her misbehaviour. Meantime he also dodged round
Monsieur Charles, and launched forth a volley of lashes, with all
his might. Monsieur Charles, dumbfounded and aghast at
being thus encircled, could only bury Elodie's face in his waistcoat, so that she might not see or hear anything. To such an
extent did he lose his wits, that he himself became very coarse.

"Now, then, you dirty troll, will you leave me alone? Who-
ever cursed me with such a family in this strumpets' country?"

As soon as La Trouille was dislodged she felt that she was
lost. One lash of the whip, which curled round her up to her
arm-pits, made her spin like a top; another knocked her down,
and dragged out a wisp of her hair. After that, brought back
into the right road, her only idea was to get home as sharply
as possible. She leapt over the hedges, cleared the ditches,
and cut across the vineyards, without fear of impalement on
the stakes. However, her little legs could no longer hold
out; the lashes still rained down upon her round shoulders,
upon her loins, indeed over all her precocious flesh. Not
that she cared a straw; she had got to think it rather
amusing to be tickled so hard. With a nervous laugh she
finally leapt into the house, and took refuge in a corner, where
the big whip could no longer reach her.

"Hand over your five francs," said the father, "by way of penalty."

She swore that she had lost them while running home, whereupon he sniggered incredulously, and rummaged her all over. Finding nothing, he flew into a passion again.

" What! So you've given them to your gallant! You blessed fool! You amuse them, and then you pay them! "

After that he went off in a towering rage, locking her in, and calling out that she should stay there all by herself till the next day, as he didn't mean to return.

La Trouille, when once he had gone off, made an inspection of her body, which was just striped with two or three weals. Then she put her hair straight, and tidied her dress. Finally, she calmly undid the lock—a trick at which she had grown extremely skilful—and bolted off, without even taking the trouble to refasten the door. Nicely robbed the robbers would find themselves, if any came! She knew where to find Nénesse and Delphin again: in a copse beside the Aigre. They were, indeed, waiting for her there; and now it was her cousin Nénesse's turn. He had three francs with him, the other threepence. She had got her money back, and she decided goodnaturedly that they would spend the whole lot together. They returned to the fair, and she set them a-shooting for macaroons, after buying herself a big bow of red satin, which she stuck in her hair.

Meanwhile, on arriving at Lengaigne's, Hyacinthe fell in with Bécu, who had his official badge fastened on to a new blouse. The scamp apostrophised the constable vehemently.

" Look here, you! You've a pretty way of going your rounds! D'you know where I found your swine of a boy? "

" Where? "

" Why, with my daughter! I'll write to the prefect and have you cashiered, you swine's father—swine, yourself! "

This made Bécu fire up.

" Daughter, indeed! Why, she's always flourishing her legs in the air—and so now she's led Delphin astray? Hell and thunder! I'll send the gendarmes after her! "

" Just try it on, you thief! "

Then the two snarled in each other's faces, till, all at once, the strain was relaxed, and their fury dropped.

" We must have an explanation; let's go in and liquor," said Hyacinthe.

" I haven't a copper," replied Bécu.

Then the other merrily produced his first five-franc piece, tossed it in the air, and stuck it in his eye.

" Well, shall we spend it, you gay dog? Come along, my buck ! It's my turn now ; you've paid often enough."

They went into Lengaigne's, chuckling for joy, and slapping each other affectionately on the back. Lengaigne had had an idea that year. As the owner of the strolling ball-room refused to come and pitch his tent in the village, disgusted at not having cleared his expenses the year before, the innkeeper had daringly made a ball-room of his barn, which adjoined his tavern, with its front door communicating with the road. He had even made another doorway in the party-wall, so that ball-room and tavern communicated. This idea had brought him the custom of the whole village, and his rival, Macqueron, was furious at having his house empty.

" Two quarts at once ; one for each of us !" yelled Hyacinthe.

As Flore, bewildered and radiant at sight of the throng of people, was attending to his order, he noticed that his arrival had interrupted Lengaigne, who had been reading a letter aloud, standing amid a group of peasants. On being questioned, the taverner replied, with a deal of dignity that, it was a letter sent by his son Victor from the regiment.

" Ah, indeed, the rascal !" said Bécu, becoming interested. " And what does he say? You must begin it again for us."

So Lengaigne read it over again.

" My Dear Parents,—This is to tell you that we have been here at Lille in Flanders for a month, less seven days. The country's not bad except for the dearness of the wine, for which we have to pay as much as eightpence a quart."

In all the four closely-written pages there was hardly anything else. The same detail recurred with infinite monotony, spun out into lengthened phrases. However, they all expressed surprise each time that the price of the wine was mentioned. So there were parts like that! How horrid ! In the last lines of the letter came an attempt at sponging: a request for twelve francs to replace a lost pair of shoes.

" Ah, the rascal !" repeated the rural constable. "Something like a fellow that, good God."

After the first two quarts, Hyacinthe asked for two more : bottled wine, at a franc apiece, paying as he was served so as to create astonishment, and rapping his money on the table, in a way that revolutionised the tavern. When the first five-franc piece had been expended in drink, he pulled out a second one, screwed it into his eye, as before, and cried out that there was plenty more where that one had come from. So the afternoon slipped by, amid a bustle of drinkers passing in and out, and increasing tipsiness. Dull and sedate though they were on work-days, they were now all yelling, thumping, and spitting vehemently. It occurred to one tall thin fellow to get shaved, and Lengaigne sat him down forthwith in the midst of them, and scraped his skin so roughly, that the razor was heard going over the leathery integument as if at work on a scalded pig. A second took the first one's place; 'twas fine sport. And how the tongues wagged! There was Macqueron, now, who didn't dare show himself outside. Wasn't it this fool of an assessor's own fault if the usual ball hadn't come? Arrangements might have been made. But, sure enough, he preferred voting roads, and getting three times as much money for his land as it was worth. This allusion provoked a tempest of laughter. Fat Flore, whose triumph the day was to be, kept neglecting her customers to run to the door, bursting into insolent mirth, whenever she saw Cœlina's jaundiced visage behind the opposite window-panes.

"Cigars! Madame Lengaigne," thundered Hyacinthe at last. "Expensive ones, mind! Penny each!"

As night was falling, and the petroleum lamps were being lit, Madame Bécu came in to look for her husband. But he had started on a monstrous game at cards.

"Are you coming?" she said; "it's past eight. You must have some dinner."

He stared at her with tipsy majesty.

"Go to blazes!" he replied.

Then Hyacinthe displayed intense delight. "Madame Bécu," said he, "I invite you. Eh? Yes, we'll just peck a bit, between the three of us. D'ye hear there, mistress? Give us your best: some ham, some rabbit, and dessert. And don't be anxious. Just look here. Attention!"

He then pretended to fumble himself all over. Then he suddenly produced his third coin, and held it up.

"Cuckoo! Aha, there it is!"

Everybody was doubled up with laughter, and one fat man all but suffocated. That rascal Hyacinthe was thundering funny! And some of them, by way of a joke, felt him from head to foot, as if he had had crowns all over him.

"I say, La Bécu," he repeated a dozen times over while he

was eating, " if Bécu don't mind, we'll sleep together ? **What do you say ? "**

She was very dirty, not having known, she said, that she should stop at the fête; and she laughed, did this dark pole-cat of a woman, wiry and rusty like an old needle; while Hyacinthe, without further delay, grabbed hold of her legs under the table. **Meantime** the husband, blind drunk, dribbled and chuckled, shouting out that two men would be **none too many** for the hussy.

It was ten o'clock when the ball began. **Through the communicating** doorway the four lamps, fastened **by iron wires to** the beams, could be seen blazing. Clou, the farrier, **was there with** his trombone, as **well as** the nephew of **a Bazoches-le-**Doyen rope-maker, who played the violin. **The admission was** free, but you paid two sous for **each dance you joined in.** The beaten soil underfoot had just been **watered, on account of the** dust. Whenever the instruments left off **playing,** the sharp, regular detonations of the neighbouring shooting-gallery could be heard. The **road,** usually so gloomy, was all ablaze with the reflectors of **the two other** booths ; the trinket stall glittered **with** gildings, **while the** turn-about was bedecked with mirrors **and** hung with red curtains like a chapel.

" Hallo ! Why, there's my little **daughter ! "** cried Hyacinthe, with swimming eyes.

So it was. La Trouille was just coming **into the ball, attended** by Delphin and Nénesse ; and the father **did not seem** at all surprised to see her **there,** although he had **locked her in.** She not merely had the red **bunch** of ribbons flaunting in **her** hair, **for** round **her** neck there was now a heavy imitation **coral** necklace, formed **of** beads of sealing-wax, which showed blood-red against her dark skin. All three of **them,** moreover, tired of rambling about in front of the booths, were dull and sticky with sweetmeats, of which they had eaten more than they could digest. Delphin, who was only happy when out and about **in all the** hidden nooks of the country-side, **wore a** blouse, and **his** shaggy round savage-like head was **bare.** Nénesse, **on** the other hand, already yearning after the **refine**ments of **town** life, **was** clad in a suit of dittos bought **at** Lambourdieu's, one of those scant outfits turned **out** wholesale by cheap Paris clothiers ; and he wore a round felt hat, to mark his contempt of the village, which **he** looked down upon.

" Petty ! " called Hyacinthe. **" Little daughter, come** and taste this. First-rate, ain't **it? "**

He let her drink out of his glass, while Madame Bécu asked
Delphin sternly:

" What have you done with your cap? "

" Lost it."

" Lost it?   Come here, and and I'll cuff you? "   But Bécu
interposed, chuckling complacently at the recollection of his
son's precocious gallantries.

" Let him be!   He's getting a big boy now.   And so, you
scum of the earth, you've been amusing yourselves together?
Ah! the lickerish dog."

" Go and play," concluded Hyacinthe paternally.   " And
mind you're to be good."

" They're as drunk as pigs," said Nénesse, with an air of
disgust, as he went back to the ball-room.

La Trouille laughed.

" I should just think so!   I quite expected it.   That's why
they're so amiable."

The dancing was getting lively.   The explosive blasts of
Clou's trombone, which smothered the faint music of the little
fiddle, were all that could be heard.   The ground, watered over
copiously, was turning to mud under the thick-soled boots of
the dancers; and presently, from all the shaken petticoats,
from the jackets and bodices that grew moist under the arm-
pits with broad stains of sweat, there uprose a strong goat-
like smell, accentuated by the smoky acridity of the lamps.
Between two quadrilles, a sensation was created by the arrival
of Berthe, Macqueron's daughter, arrayed in a foulard dress,
exactly like those that the tax-collector's young ladies had
worn at Cloyes, on Saint Lubin's day.   Could her parents have
given her leave to come?   Or had she slipped out behind their
backs?   It was observable that she danced all the time with
the son of a wheelwright, whom her father had forbidden her
to speak to, on account of a family quarrel.   Jests were
bandied about.   Apparently she was no longer content with
her pernicious solitary habits.

Hyacinthe, tipsy as he was, had, for the last moment or so,
noticed that beast Lequeu, stationed beside the communicating
door-way, and watching Berthe as she curvetted about in
her gallant's arms.   He could not restrain himself.

" I say, Monsieur Lequeu," he exclaimed, " you're not
leading your sweetheart out? "

" What sweetheart? " asked the schoolmaster, green with
bile.

" Why, the pretty dark-ringed eyes, over there! "

Lequeu, furious at having been detected, turned his back, and stood motionless, in one of those haughty spells of silence in which he enwrapped himself, out of prudence and disdain. Lengaigne having come forward, Hyacinthe buttonholed him. "Aha! he had given that paper-stainer over there one for his nob! Rich girls for him, indeed! Not that Berthe was such a catch, for she had a peculiar physical defect." Being now thoroughly aflame, he swore to the truth of his assertion. It was current talk from Cloyes to Châteaudun. Stupefied by this information, the others craned over to look at Berthe, making slight grimaces of repugnance whenever her white skirts came flying round that way, in the course of the dance.

"You old rogue," resumed Hyacinthe, beginning to address Lengaigne familiarly, "your girl's all right."

"Rather!" replied the taverner, complacently.

Suzanne was now in Paris, in the swell set, people said. Lengaigne, acting discreetly, used to hint at a good situation she had there. Meanwhile peasants still kept coming in, and a farmer having asked after Victor, the letter was produced again. "My dear Parents,—This is to tell you that we have been here, at Lille in Flanders. . ." They all listened anew; even people who had already heard the letter read five or six times over, gathered round again. Not really eightpence a quart? Yes, really; eightpence!

"A beastly country!" repeated Bécu. At that moment Jean made his appearance; at once going to glance into the ball-room, as if he were looking for some one. Then he returned looking disappointed and uneasy. For the last two months he had not dared to pay such frequent visits to Buteau, for he felt that the latter was cool, not to say hostile. Doubtless he, Jean, had ill-concealed his feelings for Françoise, the growing affection which now fevered him, and his comrade had noticed it. It must have displeased him, interfering with his plans.

"Good evening," said Jean, drawing near a table where Fouan and Delhomme were drinking a bottle of beer.

"Will you join us, Corporal?" said Delhomme, politely.

Jean accepted; and after clinking glasses:

"Funny thing Buteau hasn't turned up," he said.

"Here he is, pat!" said Fouan.

And, indeed, Buteau now came in, but all by himself, and Jean's face grew still darker. The other strolled round the tavern, shaking hands; then, on reaching his father and brother-in-law's table, he stood there, refusing to sit down or to take anything.

"Lise and Françoise don't dance, then?" Jean finally asked, in a faltering voice.

Buteau looked at him hard out of his little grey eyes.

"Françoise has gone to bed," he replied; "it's the best place for young folks."

An incident near them now attracted their attention, and cut the conversation short. It was Hyacinthe at loggerheads with Flore, whom he had asked for a quart of rum to make some punch, and who refused to bring it.

"No! No more! You're drunk enough."

"Hallo! what's that she's saying? Do you fancy that I sha'n't pay? Why, I'll buy up your whole shanty, if you like. I've merely to blow my nose. Here! Look at this!"

He had concealed his fourth five-franc piece in his hand; and now pinching his nose with his fingers, he blew it loudly, and apparently drew out the coin, which he then paraded round like a monstrance.

"That's what I blow from my nose, when I've got a cold!"

A round of applause shook the walls, and Flore, quite vanquished, brought the quart of rum and some sugar. Next a salad-bowl was wanted, and then the scamp took possession of the whole room, stirring the punch, with his elbows squarely set, while his red face was lighted up by the glow of the flames, which increased the heat of the atmosphere, already densely befogged by the lamps and pipes. Buteau, exasperated at sight of the money, suddenly broke out:

"You thundering swine, aren't you ashamed of tippling away like that with the money you rob our father of?"

The other adopted a low-comedy tone.

"Oh, it's you, young 'un! I suppose it's your empty stomach that makes you talk such rot!"

"I tell you, you're a dirty beast, and you'll finish at the galleys. To begin with, it was you that killed our mother with grief."

The sot rattled his spoon and stirred up a tempest of flame in the salad-bowl, while he split his sides with laughter.

"Right you are; go on. Sure enough it was me—supposing it wasn't you!"

"And I tell you further that spendthrifts of your kidney don't deserve that the corn should grow. Only to think that our property—yes, all that land that the old folks took so much trouble to leave us—has been pledged by you, and handed over to others. You dirty blackguard, what have you done with the land?"

At this Hyacinthe was **roused.** **His punch** went out, **and** he settled himself, leaning back in **his chair,** seeing that all **the** drinkers **were** silently listening, to judge between him and **his** brother.

" The land **!** " **he yelled:** " why, **what** the deuce does **the** land care for you? **Y**ou're its slave, it robs you of your enjoyments, your strength, your life! You idiot! And it doesn't **so** much as make **you** rich! While I, who fold my arms and **despise it,** confining myself to giving it a kick or **two,** why, I, **you see, am** independent and **can wet my whistle!** Oh, you confounded simpleton ! "

The peasants laughed again, **while Buteau, surprised by the** roughness of the attack, could only **mutter :**

" **A** good-for-nothing lazy **lout; who does no work and** boasts of it."

" **Land, indeed! A lot of humbug !** " resumed Hyacinthe, **now thoroughly aroused.** " Well, you *must* be an ancient, if you still **believe in humbug like that!** Does it exist, this land? It's mine, **it's yours, it's** nobody's. Wasn't it once the **old** 'uns ? **And hadn't he** to cut it up to give it to us ? And won't you cut **it up for your young** 'uns ? **Very well,** then ! It comes and goes, increases and diminishes—diminishes especially; for there you are, a fine gentleman with your seven **or** eight acres, when father had over twenty. I got disgusted with my share. It was too little, so I blued the lot. **And,** besides, I like sound investments, and, **look'ee !** young 'un, land's shaky ! I would **not put** a copper **into it.** It's **bad** business, and there's **an** ugly catastrophe at hand that'll **wipe** you all **out.** Bankruptcy! A set **of** blockheads! "

A death-like silence gradually spread through the tavern. **No one** laughed **now.** The anxious faces of the peasants were turned towards this tall ruffian, who, in **his** cups, poured out the muddled contents of **his** brain—the confused ideas that he had formed as an Algerian campaigner, **as a** hanger-about town, and tavern politician. **What** was paramount in him was the old leaven of '48, the **humanitarian** communistic views of **one** who still worshipped **at the shrine** of '89.

" Liberty, equality, **fraternity !** " **he shouted.** " We must hark back to the Revolution. We were swindled **in the** division of property; the gentlefolks have taken everything, and, by God, they shall be forced to give it back. Isn't one man as good as another ? Is it fair, for instance, such a lot of land held by that ass at La Borderie, while I've got none? I want my rights ; I want my share ; everybody shall have his share."

Bécu, who was too drunk to uphold the principle of authority, approved without understanding. Still, he had a gleam
of sense left, and imposed certain limitations.

"That's so, that's so," said he; "but the king's the king, and
what is mine isn't yours."

A murmur of approbation ran round, and Buteau took his
revenge.

"Don't listen to him; he's only fit to kill!"

There was a fresh burst of laughter, and Hyacinthe, losing
all control, stood up, wildly shaking his fists in the air.

"Just you wait a bit. I'll talk to you, you cursed coward!
You're in fine feather now, because you've got the mayor,
the assessor, and that twopenny-halfpenny deputy on your
side! You lick his boots, and you are fool enough to think
that he's a power and will help you to sell your corn. Well,
I, who have nothing to sell, I don't care a fig for you or your
mayor, assessor, deputy, or gendarmes! To-morrow, it'll be
our turn to be the stronger; and it won't be me alone, it'll be
all the poor devils who are starving to death. Ay, and it'll be
you, too; you, I say! when you've got tired of keeping the
gentlefolks, without having so much as a crust of bread to eat
yourselves. A pretty plight they'll be in, the landowners.
They'll have their jaws broken, and the land'll be free for any
one to take. D'ye hear, young 'un? I'll take that land of
yours and —— on it!"

"You just try it on, and I'll shoot you down like a dog!"
shouted Buteau, so wild with rage that he went out, slamming
the door after him.

Lequeu, having listened with a reserved air, had already
left, unwilling, as an official, to compromise himself any further.
Fouan and Delhomme, with their faces over their liquor,
breathed not a word; feeling ashamed, and knowing that if they
interposed the sot would only shout the louder. The peasants
at the surrounding tables were eventually getting angry.
What! Their property wasn't their own? It would be taken
from them? And, growling, they were about to pummel the
communist soundly and turn him out, when Jean rose up. He
had not taken his eyes off the speaker, or missed one of his
words, as he sat there listening with a serious face, as if seeking what justice might underlie these things that shocked him.

"Hyacinthe," said he quietly, "you'd better hold your
tongue. It's not the sort of thing to say; and if by any
chance you are right, you're not very clever to put yourself
so in the wrong."

So wise a remark from so cool a speaker calmed Hyacinthe instantaneously. He fell back in his chair, declaring that, after all, he didn't care a fig. He then began larking again; kissed Madame Bécu, whose husband was asleep with his head on the table, and finished up the punch, drinking out of the salad-bowl. The laughter had recommenced, amid the dense smoke, and he was voted a funny fellow, all the same.

At the far end of the barn, the dancing was still going on. Clou was still smothering the squeaky notes of the little fiddle with his thunderous blasts of trombone accompaniment. Sweat drained off the bodies of the dancers, and exhaled amid the ruddy smoke of the lamps. La Trouille, whirling about in turn in the arms of Nénesse and Delphin, was conspicuous by her red bow. Berthe, too, was still there, faithful to her gallant and dancing with no one else. In a corner, some young men whom she had cast off were tittering together. Oh, well; if that great gawky was willing, she did right to stick to him; there were plenty of others who, for all her money, would have certainly thought twice before marrying her.

" Let's go home to bed," said Fouan at last to Jean and Delhomme.

Outside, when Jean had left them, the old man walked on in silence, apparently pondering over all he had just heard. Then, abruptly, as if that had decided him, he turned to his son-in-law.

" I'll sell the shanty and come and live with you. That's settled. Good-bye!"

He went slowly home. His heart was heavy; as his boots stumbled over the dark road, a terrible sadness made him stagger like a drunken man. As it was, he had no land, and he would soon have no house. It seemed to him that people were already sawing down the old rafters and pulling off the slates from over his head. He now had not the shelter of a single stone left him; he was like a beggar wandering along the roads, by day and night, unceasingly; and when it rained, the chill, never-ending down-pour would fall upon his head.

CHAPTER IV.

THE bright August sun had been climbing the horizon since five o'clock, and La Beauce displayed its ripe grain under the glowing sky. Since the last summer showers, the green, ever-growing expanse had little by little turned yellow. It was now a tawny sea of fire, that seemed to reflect the flaming atmosphere: a sea that gleamed and swelled at the least breath of wind. Nothing but corn; corn to infinity, without a glimpse of house or tree! Now and then in the heat of the day, a leaden calm enwrapped the ears, while a fruitful odour rose smoking from the soil. The period of gestation was finishing; it could be realised that the swelling seed was bursting from the womb in warm, heavy grain. At sight of this mighty plain, this giant harvest, one felt uneasy as to whether man, with his insect-like form, so small amid such immensity, would ever be able to get through it.

During the last week, at La Borderie, Hourdequin, having finished his barley, had been engaged upon his wheat. During the previous year his reaping-machine had got out of order; and, discouraged by his servants' hostility, and having himself grown doubtful as to the efficacy of machinery, he had had to provide himself with a staff of reapers since Ascension Day. According to custom, he had hired them at Mondoubleau, in Le Perche. There was the foreman, a tall, lean fellow, five other reapers, and six pickers-up, four of them women and two of them girls. A cart had brought them to Cloyes, where a conveyance from the farm had gone to fetch them. Everybody slept in the sheep-cot—empty at that time of year—the girls, women, and men being all huddled together pell-mell in the straw, half-undressed on account of the great heat.

This was the season when Jacqueline had the most trouble. The sunrise and sunset decided the work of the day or the morrow. They shook off their fleas at three in the morning, and returned to their straw at about ten at night. She always had to be up the first, for the four o'clock soup; just as she went to bed the last, after serving the heavy nine o'clock meal of bacon, beef, and cabbage. Between these two meals there

were three others; bread and cheese at eight, soup again at
twelve, a sop of milk by way of a snack in the afternoon. In
all, five meals, copiously washed down with cider and wine,
for the harvesters, who work hard, are exacting as regards
their food. However, she merely laughed, as if stimulated by
her duties. She was lithe like a cat, with sinews of iron, and
her resistance to fatigue was all the more surprising, on
account of her amours with that big lubber Tron, whose soft
flesh whetted her appetites. She had made him her creature,
and she took him into the barns, the hay-loft, and even the
sheep-cot, now that the shepherd, whose espionage she feared,
passed the night out-of-doors with his sheep. And withal she
became more supple and active. Hourdequin neither saw nor
heard anything. He was in his harvest fever, something out
of the common, the great annual crisis of his passion for the
soil. His brain became on fire, his heart beat fast, and his flesh
quivered at sight of the ripe, falling grain.

The nights were so sultry that year, that sometimes Jean
could not stay in the loft, where he slept, near the stable.
He preferred to stretch himself, with all his clothes on, on the
pavement of the yard. It was not merely the intolerable
living heat of the horses, and the exhalations from their litter,
that drove him outside; but sleeplessness, the ever-present
image of Françoise, the constant idea of her coming, of his
seizing her, and devouring her with his embraces. Now that
Jacqueline, being busy elsewhere, left him to himself, his affection for the young girl turned into a madness of longing.
Scores of times, while he suffered at night-time, in a state of
semi-somnolence, he swore that he would go the next day and
win her; but, on rising up, as soon as he had dipped his head
into a bucket of cold water, he thought it disgusting: he was
too old for her. And then the next night the torture began
again. When the harvesters arrived, he recognised among
them a woman, now married to one of the reapers, with whom
he had been familiar two years before, while she was yet a
girl. One evening he slipped into the sheep-cot, and pulled
her by the feet as she lay between her husband and her brother,
who were both snoring open-mouthed. She got up and came
to him, and they lay silently together in the sultry darkness on
the trodden soil which, although it had been raked over, still
retained, from the winter sojourn of the sheep, so keen an
ammoniacal odour as to bring tears into one's eyes. During
the three weeks that the reapers were there, he came back to
the sheep-cot every night.

After the second week in August, the work made progress. The reapers had started with the northern fields, and were working down towards those which bordered the valley of the Aigre. The immense stretch of corn fell sheaf by sheaf. Every cut of the scythe told, leaving a circular incision. The puny insects, seemingly lost amid their gigantic task, came forth from it in triumph. Behind them, as they slowly marched onward in line, the razed ground re-appeared, bristling with stubble, over which trampled the pickers-up, bending down It was the season when there was the most gaiety about the vast sad solitude of La Beauce, now full of people and animated by the constant motion of labourers, carts, and horses. As far as the eye could reach, there were parties advancing with the same slant progress, with the same swinging of their arms; some so near that the swish of the steel was audible, others extending in black streaks, like ants, as far as the edge of the sky. On all sides gaps were appearing, as though the plain were a piece of cloth wearing into holes all over. Shred by shred, amid the ant-like activity, La Beauce was stripped of her court mantle formed of cloth-of-gold, her sole summer adornment, the loss of which left her desolate and naked. During the last days of the harvest, the heat was overpowering, especially one day when Jean near the Buteaus' land, and, with his cart and pair, was removing some sheaves to a field of the farm where a large stack, six and twenty feet high, was to be built with some three thousand trusses. The stubble was splitting atwain with the drought, and the heat scorched the motionless wheat which was still standing. The latter seemed as if it were itself flaming with visible fire, in the quivering of the sun-rays. Not the shelter of a leaf; no shadow on the ground save the scanty ones of the toilers. Perspiring since the morning under this blazing sky, Jean had been loading and unloading his cart, without saying a word, simply glancing at each journey towards the field where Françoise, bending double, was slowly gathering behind the reaping Buteau.

Buteau had had to take Palmyre to help him; for Françoise did not suffice, and he could not rely on Lise, who had been in the family way for the last eight months. This had exasperated him. After all the precautions he had taken, how could it possibly have happened? He used to jostle his wife about, accusing her of having done it on purpose, and complaining lugubriously for hours together, as if some destitute wretch or stray animal were coming to eat him out of house and home. Although eight months had gone by, he never noticed Lise's

condition without abusing it.   Curse the thing !   A goose was
not so stupid !   It was the ruin of the household !

That morning she had come to help in the gathering ; but
he had sent her back, furious with her heavy, clumsy movements.
She was to return, however, with the four o'clock snack.

" Good God ! " said Buteau, who was bent on finishing a bit
of ground ; " My back's baked, and my tongue's a perfect chip."

Then he straightened himself ; his sockless feet were thrust
into thick shoes, and he wore nothing but a shirt and canvas
smock, the former hanging half out of the open smock and
showing the hair of his sweating chest down to the navel.

" I must have another drink ! " said he.

Then he took from under his jacket on the ground a quart
bottle of cider, which he had sheltered there.   At last, having
swallowed two mouthfuls of the tepid drink, he thought of
the girl.

" Aren't you thirsty ? "

" Yes."

Françoise took a deep draught from the bottle without
repugnance.   While she bent backward, with her loins curved,
and her rounded bust straining the thin material of her dress,
he looked at her askance.   She also was dripping with
moisture, in a print dress half undone, the body being unhooked at the top and showing her white flesh.   Under the
blue handkerchief with which she had covered her head and
neck, her eyes seemed very large in her quiet face, glowing
with the heat.

Without another word Buteau, with his hips swinging, resumed his work, felling a swath with every stroke of his scythe,
the swish of which kept time to his tread.   Stooping down again,
she followed him, carrying in her right hand her sickle, which
she made use of to gather up each armful of corn from among
the thistles.   At every three steps she laid the wheat regularly
in bundles.   Whenever he straightened himself, just long
enough to pass the back of his hand over his brow, and saw
Françoise too far in the rear, stooping, with her head quite
close to the ground, in the position of an expectant animal, he
called out to her in a husky voice, his tongue seemingly getting
drier than ever :

" Now, then, lazybones !   You ought to know better than
to fool away your time like that ! "

In the adjacent field, where for three days the straw of the
bundles had been drying, Palmyre was engaged in binding
the sheaves.   He did not watch her ; for, contrary to the usual

practice, he had arranged to pay her per hundred sheaves, on
the pretext that she was old and worn out, and had lost her
strength, so that he should lose if he paid her by time—at the
rate of a franc and a-half per day, which was what the younger
women earned. Even to secure this piecework she had had to
implore him; and he had taken advantage of her position,
assuming the resigned air of a Christian performing a work of
charity. The poor creature collected three or four bundles—
as many as her shrivelled arms could hold—and then tightly
tied the sheaf with a band she had prepared. This work, so
fatiguing that it is usually reserved for the men, was exhausting her. Her breast was crushed by the constant loads it had
to sustain; her arms were strained by dint of embracing such
massive bundles, and tugging at the bands of straw. She had
brought with her in the morning a bottle, which she went and
filled every hour or so at a neighbouring stagnant, poisonous
pool; and she drank greedily of the water, in spite of the
diarrhœa, which had torn her to pieces since the beginning of
the hot weather, her health being already ruined by over-work.

The azure of the sky had grown pale, as if it were whitened
by the heat; and burning coals seemed to fall from the sun,
now glowing more fiercely than ever. It was the oppressive
noontide hour of the siesta. Delhomme and his party, who had
been stacking some sheaves near by—four below, and one to roof
the others in with—had already disappeared, and were all lying
down in some hollow. For an instant longer old Fouan could
be seen, still standing up. He had sold his house a fortnight
previously, since when he had been living with his son-in-law,
following the harvest-work with all the feverishness of yore.
In his turn, he soon felt obliged to lie down, and also disappeared from view. There was nothing remaining against the
blank horizon, or the blazing background of the stubble, save
the withered figure of La Grande, who was examining a tall
stack which her people had begun to erect among a little tribe
of smaller ones already partially pulled to pieces. She seemed
like a tree hardened by age, with nothing to fear from the sun,
as, without a drop of perspiration on her, she stood there bolt
upright, feeling sternly indignant with the sleepers.

" Pish! My skin's absolutely crackling," said Buteau at
last.

And, turning to Françoise:

" Let's sleep a bit! "

He looked round him for a little shade, but found none. The
sun was beating down perpendicularly, and there was not so

much as a bush to shelter them. At last he noticed that at **the**
end of the field, **in a** sort of little ditch, some wheat which **was**
still **standing** threw a brown **streak of shadow.**

"Hullo there, Palmyre!" cried he. "Don't you follow
our example?"

She was fifty **paces off, and replied in a stifled voice,** which
reached them like a whisper:

"No, no! I haven't time."

She was now the only worker left in **all the** glowing **plain.**
If she didn't take her franc-and-a-half home with **her** at **night-**
time, Hilarion would beat her; for he **no longer confined**
himself to his accustomed ill-usage, **but robbed her as well,**
that he might have money to buy brandy with. However, **her**
strength was now forsaking **her.** Her flat figure, planed
straight like **a plank by** sheer **hard** work, creaked **as if**
it were about to snap at every **fresh sheaf she picked up and**
bound. With ashen face, **worn like some old copper coin,**
seemingly sixty years of age though actually **but thirty-five,**
she let the burning sun drink **up her** life-blood **in the despairing**
efforts **she made,** like **a beast of burden about to fall and**
perish.

Buteau **and Françoise** had stretched **themselves side by**
side. They were steaming with sweat, **now that they had**
ceased to move about, and they lay in silence **with closed**
eyes. A leaden slumber instantly weighed **them down; they**
slept for an hour; and the perspiration **poured unceasingly**
from their limbs in the motionless, **heavy, furnace-like atmo-**
sphere. When **Françoise opened her eyes** again, she saw
Buteau lying on his side, **watching her with** the jaundiced
look that had disturbed her **for some time past.** She re-closed
her eye-lids, and pretended to go to **sleep** again. Without
his having yet spoken to her, she **knew well** enough **that** he
desired her, **now** that she had grown **up, and** was quite a
woman. The idea maddened her. Would **he dare, the swine!**
he whom she heard rioting with her sister every **night? Never**
before had his lustful manner so exasperated her. **Would he**
dare? And she awaited his addresses, unconsciously **wishing**
for them, but resolved, if he touched her, **to** strangle him.

As she closed her eyes Buteau suddenly seized hold of her.

"You swine! **you** swine!" she stammered, repulsing **him.**

He chuckled **with a wild look,** and **whispered:**

"Stupid! **Keep still! I tell** you **they're asleep; no one is**
looking."

At that moment, Palmyre's wan and agonised face appeared

above the corn. She had turned round at the noise. But she didn't count, any more than if **a** cow had lifted up its muzzle. **And,** indeed, she returned, with indifference, to her sheaves. **The** cracking of her loins was again heard at each effort she **made.**

"Stupid," said Buteau. **"Lise** won't know."

At the mention of her sister, Françoise, **who was** on the eve of giving way, nerved herself for renewed resistance. From that moment she remained firm, beating **him** with her fists and **kicking him** with her bare legs. Was he hers, this fellow? **Did** he think she wanted some one else's leavings?

"Go and find my sister, you pig!" **she exclaimed.** And then she gave him **such** a kick in a tender part that he was forced to let her go, pushing her away so brutally that **she** had to stifle a cry of pain.

It was high time that the scene should finish, for Buteau, **when** he got up, perceived Lise returning with the snack. He **walked** on to meet her, and engaged her in talk, so as to allow Françoise **the time to** tidy her dress. The idea that she was going to tell everything made him regret not having stunned her with a kick. However, she said nothing, but sat down amid the bundles of wheat with a stubborn and insolent air. He **had resumed his reaping,** but she still stayed there idly, like a princess.

"What is it?" asked Lise, tired **with her journey, and** sitting down as **well:** "you're not working?"

"No, it bores me," replied Françoise, savagely.

Then Buteau, afraid to storm at her, fell foul of his wife. What was she up to, stretched out there like a sow, warming her belly in the sun? And a sweet thing, indeed, it was. A fine pumpkin to set out to ripen. At that phrase she began to laugh with all her old buxom gaiety. Maybe it was true that the warmth ripened the little one and brought it on; and so, under the flaming heavens, she rounded her huge figure, which seemed like **the** protuberance of some germ rising from the fruitful soil. But he did not laugh. He brutally made her get up, and insisted on her helping him. Inconvenienced by her condition, she was fain to kneel down, picking up the **ears of corn with a side long** movement, and panting as she **laboured on.**

"As you're doing nothing," she said to her sister, "you might at least go back home and make the soup."

Françoise went off without a word. Although the heat

was still stifling La Beauce had again assumed an aspect of
activity. The little black specks of harvesters re-appeared,
swarming to infinity. Delhomme was once more reaping with
his two men, while La Grande, watching the growth of her
stack, was leaning on her stick, quite prepared to bring it
across the face of any idler. Fouan also went to have a
look at the stack; next he again became absorbed in his son-
in-law's work; and then he wandered retrospectively and re-
gretfully to and fro, with heavy gait. Françoise, with her
head still dizzy from the shock she had experienced, was going
along the new road, when a voice called to her :

" Come along. This way ! "

It was Jean, half hidden behind the sheaves which he had
been carting from the neighbouring fields since the morning.
He had just unloaded his waggon once more; and the two
horses were waiting motionless in the sunshine. The erection
of the large stack would not be begun till the morrow, and he
had merely piled up some heaps, three walls which enclosed, as
it were, a room ; a deep snug nest of straw.

" Come along ! " he said. " It's me ! "

Françoise mechanically complied with the request. She did
not even think of glancing back. Had she turned round, she
would have noticed Buteau craning forward, surprised to see
her leaving the road

Jean now began jestingly :

" It's proud you're getting, to go by without giving a
good-day to your friends ! "

" Why, you're so hidden," she replied, " that you can't be
seen."

Then he complained of the cold shoulder that the Buteaus
now always turned upon him. But she was not composed
enough to talk of that; she remained silent, or only let a brief
word fall now and then. She had spontaneously dropped upon
the straw, at the far end of the nook, as though she were
thoroughly tired out. Her head was full of one thing, the
attack of that man over yonder at the edge of the field; his
hot hands, of which she still felt the powerful grip ; his masculine approach, that she still seemed to expect, breathing short,
in an anguish of desire, against which she struggled. She
closed her eyes, choking.

Then Jean spoke no more. Seeing her thus, supine and
yielding, the blood pulsed strongly through his veins. He had
not calculated on this encounter, and he still held back, thinking that it would be a shame to take advantage of such a child.

But the loud beating of his heart upset him. He had so long
desired her! A vision of possession drove him frantic, as
during his feverish nights. He lay down near her, contenting
himself first with one of her hands, and then with both hands;
which he crushed between his own, without so much as
venturing to raise them to his lips. She did not draw them
away, but re-opened her dreamy, heavy-lidded eyes, and looked
at him without a smile, without any sign of shame, her face
nervously strained. It was this mute, almost painful look of
hers that all at once urged him to brutality. He made a dash,
and seized her like the other.

"No, no," she faltered; "I entreat you."

But she made no defence. She only gave a cry of pain.
It seemed as if the ground were giving way beneath her, and
in her dizziness consciousness failed her.

When she re-opened her eyes, without saying a word,
without making a movement, after remaining for a moment in a
state of stupor, the thought of the other one came back to her.
Jean, on his side, was displeased. Why had she yielded? She
could not love a veteran like him! And he also remained
motionless, aghast. Finally, with a discontented gesture, he
tried to think of something to say, and failed. Embarrassed
still further, he resolved to kiss her; but she at once recoiled,
unwilling that he should touch her again.

"I must go," he muttered "You stay here."

She made no answer, but stared vaguely up at the sky.

"Won't you? Come, wait five minutes, so that you mayn't
be seen coming away at the same time as me."

Then she decided to open her lips.

"All right, be off!"

That was all. He smacked his whip, swore at his horses,
and with his head bent trudged away by the side of his cart.

Meanwhile, Buteau's astonishment at Françoise's disappearance behind the sheaves continued; and when he saw Jean
make off, he had a suspicion of the truth. Without confiding
in Lise, he crept off like a wary hunter, and finally leapt full
into the midst of the nook of straw. Françoise had not stirred,
in the torpor that benumbed her; she was still gazing vaguely
upwards.

"Oh, you strumpet! So that vagabond's your lover, and
I'm only good to be kicked! Great God! We'll soon see
about that."

He had already got hold of her; and she plainly realised by
his heated look that he intended to take advantage of the oppor-

O

tunity. As soon as she again felt his burning hands, she once more resisted. Now that he was there, she no longer regretted or wanted him. Her whole nature revolted rancorously and jealously against him, albeit she was herself unconscious of the freaks of her will.

" Will you let me go, you swine !" she said. " I'll bite you!"

For the second time he had to leave go of her. He spluttered with fury, enraged at the thought that she yielded to another.

" Oh, I had a notion that there was something between you two," he said. " I ought to have kicked him out a long time ago, you hussy ! "

Then he gave vent to a flood of filth. She, although maddened on her own side, remained stiff and pale, affecting perfect calmness, and replying curtly to all his dirty speeches:

" What's it got to do with you ? Can't I do what I like ? "

" Very well. Then I shall turn you out of the house immediately we get back ! I shall tell Lise how I found you, and you may go and do as you like elsewhere."

He was now pushing her in front of him towards the field where his wife was waiting.

" Tell Lise ! " said Françoise. " What do I care ? I shall go away if I choose."

" If you choose ! Oh, indeed ! We shall see about that. You'll be kicked out, neck and crop ! "

By way of taking a short cut, he was driving her across the field which had hitherto belonged in common to her sister and herself, and the partition of which he had always postponed. Suddenly he was seized with consternation. A new idea had just flashed like lightning through his mind. It had occurred to him that if he turned her away this field would be cut in two, and that she would take half of it, and perhaps give it to her gallant. The thought froze him, and both nipped his lust and wrath. No; that would be folly. He must not let everything go because a girl had baulked him for once. There was plenty of sport to be had any day; but if a fellow once got hold of some land, the thing was to stick to it.

He said nothing more, but slackened his pace, feeling puzzled as to how he might recall his violent words before he reached his wife. At length he made up his mind.

" Well, I'm not fond of making mischief," he said ; " it's your seeming disgust of me that annoys me so. Otherwise, I hardly care to vex Lise, situated as she is."

She fancied that he, too, was afraid of being exposed.

"You may be sure of one thing," she answered; "if you speak, I shall do the same."

"Oh, I'm not afraid of that," he resumed, coolly and quietly. "I shall say you are lying, in revenge, because I caught you." Then, as they were getting near, he concluded, quickly: "So it shan't go any further. We must both of us talk it over some other time."

Lise, however, was beginning to feel surprised, unable to understand why Françoise was coming back with Buteau like that. He was explaining that the lazy thing had been sulking behind a hay-stack, down yonder, when suddenly a harsh cry interrupted him, and the matter was forgotten.

"What's that? Who screamed?"

It was a weird cry, a long screaming sigh, like the death-gasp of an animal having its throat cut. It rose up and died away amid the pitiless glare of the sun.

"Eh? What is it? A horse surely, with its bones broken!"

They turned round, and saw Palmyre still standing in the next field, amid the bundles of wheat. With her failing arms, she was pressing against her shrivelled bosom one last sheaf, which she was striving to bind. But, raising a fresh cry of agony, and letting the whole lot fall, she spun round and fell prone among the corn, struck down by the sun that had been scorching her for the last twelve hours.

Lise and Françoise ran up, Buteau following at a more careless pace; while everybody from the surrounding fields came forward: the Delhommes, Fouan, who was strolling about there, and La Grande, who was scattering the stones with the ferule of her stick.

"What's the matter?"

"Palmyre in a fit."

"I saw her fall from over there."

"Good Heavens!"

All of them stood round and watched her, not venturing too near, however, for they were struck with that mysterious awe which disease always inspires in the peasantry. She was stretched, face upwards, on the ground, with her arms extended as if she had been crucified on that earth, which, by the hard toil it exacted, had worn her out so soon, and was now killing her. Some vessel must have broken, for a stream-let of blood flowed from her mouth. Still, she was dying more from exhaustion, brought on by toil such as would have over-tasked a beast. A withered, shrunken thing she looked among the stubble, a mere fleshless, sexless bit of frippery, exhaling a last faint gasp amid the rich, fertile harvest.

La Grande, the grandmother who had renounced her and never spoke to her, at last came forward, saying:

"I really think she's dead." Then she prodded her with her stick. The body, with its eyes glaring vacantly in the brilliant light, and its mouth gaping as if to inhale boundless breezes, did not stir. On the chin the thread of blood was clotting. Then the grandmother added:

"Sure enough she's dead; better so, than to live at the expense of others."

They all stood motionless and aghast. Could anybody venture to touch her, without summoning the mayor? At first they spoke in whispers; then they began to shout again, to make themselves heard.

"I'll go and fetch my ladder from over yonder against the stack," said Delhomme eventually. "It'll serve as a stretcher. It's a bad thing to leave a corpse on the ground."

When he came back with the ladder, and they wanted to take some sheaves to make a bed for the body, Buteau grumbled.

"You shall have your corn back," they said.

"I should just hope so, indeed!" he answered.

Lise, a little ashamed of this meanness, added two bundles as a pillow, and Palmyre was laid upon the ladder, while Françoise, in a sort of dream, bewildered by this death, which had occurred so soon after her own adventure, could not take her eyes off the corpse. At sight of it she felt saddened, and, above all, she was astonished that that thing could ever have been a woman. She remained on guard with Fouan, pending the removal; and the old man said nothing either, though he seemed to think that those who died were very fortunate.

At sunset, when they all went home, two men came and took the stretcher away. The burden was not a heavy one, and there was hardly need of a relay. However, some others were in attendance, and quite a procession was formed. They cut across the field, to avoid a bend in the road. The corpse was stiffening on the sheaves, and some ears fell down behind the head, and swayed to and fro at each jolt of the bearers' measured tread.

In the sky above there now only remained the heat that had accumulated during the day, a ruddy heat that weighed heavily in the blue air. On the horizon, on the other side of the Loir valley, the sun, steeped in vapour, now cast over La

Beauce a sheet of yellow rays on a level with the ground. Everything seemed tinged with the fine golden glow of the fair harvest evening. Such corn as was still standing displayed egrets of rosy flame, the stubble ends bristled with a ruddy gleam, and afar, projecting in all directions above the level, tawny sea, the stacks rose up one behind the other, apparently growing preposterously large. On the one side they seemed to be in flames, while on the other they were already black, casting shadows that stretched from end to end of the vast plain.

A solemn stillness fell, broken only by the song of a lark far aloft. None of the worn-out toilers spoke; they followed the corpse with bent heads, as resignedly as a flock of sheep. And there was no sound save a slight creaking of the ladder as the dead woman rocked to and fro on the way back through the ripe corn.

That night, Hourdequin paid off his harvesters, who had finished the work they had bargained to do. The men went away with a hundred and twenty francs a-piece, the women with sixty, for their month's work. It had been a good season; not too much corn blown down, to jag the scythe, nor a single storm during the cutting. Accordingly, it was amid loud acclamations that the foreman, at the head of his party of men, presented the harvest-home sheaf, with its ears woven crosswise, to Jacqueline, who was looked upon as mistress of the household. The " Ripane," the traditional farewell meal, was very merry. Three legs of mutton and five rabbits were eaten, and the liquor circulated till so late into the night that they all went to bed more or less tipsy. Jacqueline, herself intoxicated, all but let herself be caught by Hourdequin while she was hanging round Tron's neck. Jean, quite dazed, had flung himself on the straw in his garret. Despite his fatigue, he could not sleep, for the image of Françoise had returned and tormented him. This surprised—in fact, it almost angered—him. He had had such little pleasure with the girl, after spending so many nights longing for her! He had subsequently felt so forlorn, that he had been inclined to vow that he would have nothing more to do with her. And yet now, scarcely was he lying down, when, evoked by carnal lust, she again uprose before his mind, and he again yearned for her as before. What had transpired bad only whetted his fleshly appetite. How could he manage to see her again? Where could he clasp her on the morrow, during the following days, for ever? Suddenly a rustling made him start. A woman was nestling near him; it was the picker-up from Le Perche, who was astonished that he had not joined her on this last night. At first he repulsed her; but, finally, he stifled her with his embraces; and it seemed to him that she was that other one whom he would have crushed likewise, clinging, clinging, till they swooned.

At the same moment, Françoise, starting from her slumber, got up, and, longing for air, opened the dormer-window of her room. She had just dreamed of fellows fighting, and of dogs tearing down the door below. When the air had cooled her a little, her mind again ran upon the two men—the one who wanted her, and the other who had taken her. This was the limit of her reflections: the thought simply revolved in her mind, without her giving it any consideration or coming to any decision. Something at last caught her ear. It had not been a dream, then? A dog was howling, afar off, on the banks of the Aigre. Then she remembered: it was Hilarion, who, since night-fall, had been howling over Palmyre's corpse. They had tried to drive him away, but he had clung and bitten, refusing to leave the remains of his sister, his wife, his all in all; and he howled endlessly, with a howling that filled the night.

For a long time Françoise listened, shuddering.

215

CHAPTER V.

" I ONLY hope La Coliche won't calve at the same time as me!" repeated Lise every morning.

Lost in thought she stood in the cow-house, gazing at the cow, whose belly was distended beyond measure. Never had any animal swollen to such an extent. She looked round as a barrel on her shrunken shanks. The nine months fell exactly on Saint-Fiacre's Day, for Françoise had been careful to note the date on which she had taken her to the bull. Lise, on her side, was unfortunately by no means certain, that is within a few days. Still the child would certainly be born somewhere about Saint-Fiacre's Day, perhaps on the day before, perhaps on the day after. So she repeated, forlornly:

" I only hope La Coliche won't calve at the same time as me! A pretty job that'd be! Yes, good gracious! We should be in a nice pickle!"

La Coliche, who had been ten years in the house, was greatly spoilt. She had come to be considered as one of the family. The Buteaus nestled near her in winter time, having no other firing than the warm exhalation from her flanks. She, in return, displayed great affection, particularly towards Françoise, whom she could never see without a tender feeling moistening her large eyes. She would lick her with her rough tongue till the blood came ; or seizing her skirt between her teeth she would pull her near, so as to have her all to herself. Accordingly she was taken great care of, now that her calving time drew near : warm mashes, excursions out at the best times of the day,—in fact, she met with hourly attention. All this was not merely due to their fondness for her ; they remembered the five hundred francs she represented, as well as the milk, butter, and cheese she gave ; quite a fortune, which would be lost in losing her.

A fortnight had elapsed since the harvest. Françoise had resumed her every-day life in the household, as though nothing had occurred between her and Buteau. He seemed to have forgotten ; and she herself was glad to avoid thinking of these

matters, which disturbed her.   Jean, whom she had met and
warned, had not called again.   He used to watch for her beside
the hedges, and implore her to slip out and meet him in the
evening in ditches which he particularised.   But she refused,
in alarm, concealing her coldness under an assumption of great
prudence.   Later on, she said, when she wouldn't be so much
wanted at home.   One evening when he surprised her going
down to Macqueron's to buy some sugar, she obstinately refused to accompany him behind the church ; and talked to him
the whole time about La Coliche, about her bones which were
giving way, and her hind-quarters which were opening : sure
signs, which made him remark that the time could not now be
far off.

And now, just on Saint-Fiacre's Eve, Lise was seized with
severe pains, as she went into the cow-house after dinner with
her sister to look at the cow, who, with her thighs drawn apart
by the swelling of her womb, was also in pain, lowing softly.

" What did I say ? " cried Lise, furiously.   " A nice mess
we're in now."

Towards ten o'clock, Buteau, annoyed at nothing having
happened, decided to go to bed, leaving Lise and Françoise
obstinately remaining in the cow-house beside La Coliche,
whose pains seemed to be increasing.   They both began to feel
uneasy.   No progress was made, although, as far as the bones
were concerned, the labour seemed at an end.   There was the
passage, so why did not the calf come out?   They stroked the
animal, encouraged her, and brought her dainties—sugar,
which she refused, with her head bent and her croup pro-
foundly agitated.   At midnight, Lise, who had hitherto been
writhing and groaning, found herself suddenly relieved.   In
her case it had only been a false alarm ; some wandering
pains.   But she was convinced that she had driven it back, just as
she would have repressed a need of nature.   The whole night
through she and her sister sat up with La Coliche, nursing her
carefully, and even applying fomentations of hot rags ; while
Rougette, the other cow, the one last bought at Cloyes
market, astonished by the lighted candles, watched their
movements with her large, bluish, drowsy eyes.

At dawn of day, Françoise, seeing that nothing had yet
come off, decided to run over and fetch their neighbour La
Frimat, who was renowned for her knowledge, having assisted
so many cows that people readily had recourse to her in
ticklish cases, so as to avoid sending for the veterinary.   On
her arrival she made a grimace.

"She don't look well," she muttered. "How long has it been like this?"

"Why, for twelve hours."

She kept on walking round the animal, poking her nose everywhere, and alarming the other two with her dissatisfied grimaces and the way she jerked her chin.

When Buteau came in from the fields to breakfast, he also took fright, and talked of sending for Patoir, albeit shuddering at the idea of the expense.

"A veterinary!" said La Frimat tartly, "to kill her, hey? Old Saucisse's animal died before his very eyes. No! See here. I'll open the bladder, and I'll look after your calf for you!"

"Why," remarked Françoise, "Monsieur Patoir says the bladder shouldn't be opened. He says that the water inside is a help."

La Frimat shrugged her shoulders in exasperation. Patoir was an ass! Then she slit open the pocket with a pair of scissors. For a moment La Coliche breathed more easily, and the old woman triumphed. Lise and Françoise watched her with anxiously quivering eyelids, as she tried to ascertain the posture of the calf. Buteau himself, who had not gone back into the fields, waited breathless and still.

"I can feel the feet," she muttered, "but not the head. It's a bad sign when you can't feel the head."

"Better not bustle her," said La Frimat, sagely; "it'll come all right by-and-bye."

It was now three o'clock. They waited till seven. Nothing happened, however, and the house was a perfect hell. On the one hand, Lise, obstinately remaining on an old chair, was writhing and groaning; on the other, La Coliche was lowing incessantly amid shiverings and sweatings, which grew more and more serious. Rougette, the second cow, also began to low with fright. Françoise was at her wits' end, and Buteau kept swearing and bawling alternately. At last La Coliche, her strength failing her, fell on to her side, and lay stretched out upon the straw panting pitiably.

"We sha'n't get the brute!" declared Buteau; "and the mother will die as well!"

Françoise clasped her hands entreatingly.

"Do go and fetch Monsieur Patoir! Cost what it may, go and fetch Monsieur Patoir!"

Buteau had grown gloomy. Then, after a final struggle with himself, he got out the cart without saying a word.

La Frimat, who affected to pay no **further** heed to the **cow** since the veterinary **had** again **been** mentioned, was **now** getting anxious **about Lise.** The old woman was also good at accouchements; all the neighbourhood **had passed** through her hands. **She** seemed uneasy, and did not conceal her apprehensions **from La** Bécu, who called **Buteau back as he** was putting the horse **to.**

"Look here! **Your** wife's not well. **Suppose you bring back a** doctor **at** the same time?"

He stood mute and staring. What? **Another of 'em to be** coddled! Not **likely** that he **was going to pay for everybody!**

"No, **no!**" cried Lise, in an interval between two throes. "I shall **be all** right. **We can't be throwing money into the** gutter like **that!**"

Buteau hastily whipped up his horse, **and the cart on its way** to Cloyes vanished amid the falling shades of night.

When Patoir at last arrived, two hours later, everything was in the same state: La Coliche lay groaning on her side, and Lise, writhing like **a** worm, was half falling off her chair. Things had lasted thus for twenty-four hours.

"Which **is** my patient, hey?" asked the **veterinary, who was of a** jovial disposition.

And addressing Lise familiarly:

"**Then, if** it's not you, my fat beauty, **please put yourself to** bed. **You want** it badly."

She made **no answer, nor did she go.** He was already examining the cow.

"Heavens! **she's in** a wretched state, this beast of yours. You always come for me too late, you clumsy wretches!"

They all listened to him with a respectful, despondent, hang-dog look; that is, all of them excepting La Frimat, who screwed **up** her lips in high disdain. Patoir, taking off his **coat and** turning up his shirt sleeves, proceeded to make an **elaborate** examination.

"**Of course,**" he resumed, after an instant's pause, "**it's** exactly **as I thought.** Let me tell you, my children, it's all up with this **calf of yours.** I've no wish to cut my fingers against his teeth, **in turning him** round. Besides, I shouldn't get him out any the **more if I did** so, and I should certainly damage the mother."

Françoise burst into **sobs.**

"Monsieur Patoir," said she, " I implore you, save **our** cow. Poor Coliche! she's so fond of me!"

Both Lise, sallow with a fit of griping, and Buteau, in **rude** health, so unfeeling as they were regarding the woes **of** others, now lamented and softened, making the **same** supplication.

"Save our cow, our old cow that has given us such good milk for years and years," they begged in chorus. "Pray save her, Monsieur Patoir."

"Well, one thing must be clearly understood : I shall be forced to **cut** up the **calf."**

"Who cares **a curse for the calf ? Save our** cow, Monsieur Patoir, **save her ! "**

Then the veterinary, who had brought a large blue apron with him, borrowed a pair of canvas trousers. Stripping himself quite naked in a corner, behind Rougette, he slipped on the trousers, and then tied the apron round his loins. When he reappeared in this scanty costume, with his genial bull-dog face and **his** fat and dumpy figure, La Coliche lifted her head **and, no** doubt from astonishment, ceased to complain. However, no one even smiled, so wrung with anxiety was every heart.

"Light some candles ! " said Patoir.

He set four on the ground, and then lay down flat on his **stomach** in the straw, behind the cow, who was now unable to get up. For a moment he remained flat, examining her. Near by he had placed a little box, and, having raised himself on his elbow, he was taking a bistoury out of it, when a husky groan startled him, and he at once assumed a sitting posture.

"What, still there, my stout matron ? Well, I thought that couldn't be the cow ! "

It was Lise, seized with the final pangs.

"**For** goodness sake go and get your business over in your own room, and leave me to do mine here ! It disturbs me ; it acts on my nerves, 'pon my honour it does, to hear you straining behind me. Come, come ! It's not common sense ! Take her away, **the rest** of you ! "

La Frimat and La Bécu decided to take her each by an arm and lead her to **her room.** She surrendered herself, no longer having the strength to resist. But on crossing the kitchen, where a solitary candle was burning, she asked to have all the **doors** left open, with **the** idea that she would **thus** not be **so far off. La** Frimat had **already** prepared the bed of anguish according to rural custom—a simple sheet spread out in the middle of the room over a truss of straw, and three chairs turned down. Lise squatted down and stretched herself, with her back against one chair and one leg against each of the others. She was not even undressed.

Buteau and Françoise had remained in the cow-house to light Patoir; they squatted on their heels, each holding a candle, while the veterinary, again stretched out on his stomach, cut a section round the left ham with his bistoury. He loosened the skin, and then pulled at the calf's shoulder, which came away. Françoise, pale and faint, dropped her candle and fled with a shriek.

"My poor old Coliche," she exclaimed; "I won't see it! I won't see it!"

Thereupon Patoir lost his temper, the more so as he had to rise up and extinguish an incipient conflagration, caused by the fall of Françoise's candle among the straw.

"Drat the wench! She might be a princess, with her nerves. She'd smoke us like so many hams," he remarked in a peevish tone.

Françoise had run and flung herself on a chair in the room where her sister was being confined. The latter's exposure did not disturb her. It seemed a mere matter of course, after what she had just seen. She waved from her memory that vision of living severed flesh, and gave a stammering account of what was being done to the cow.

"It's sure to go wrong; I must go back," said Lise suddenly; and despite her sufferings, she made an effort to get up from among the three chairs. But La Frimat and La Bécu grew angry, and held her down.

"Good heavens! will you keep still! What on earth possesses you?" exclaimed La Frimat.

"So as to keep you quiet," said La Bécu, "I'll go myself and bring you the news."

From that moment La Bécu did nothing but run to and fro between the room and the cow-house. To save continually making the journey, she at last shouted out her report from the kitchen. The veterinary was still busily occupied with his nasty, troublesome job, and he emerged from it disgustingly filthy from head to foot.

"It's all right, Lise," exclaimed La Bécu; "don't be uneasy. We've got the other shoulder, and it will soon be all over now."

Lise saluted each phase of the operation with a heartrending sigh; and no one knew whether the lament was for herself or for the calf. There was not the slightest cessation of her travail, and she seemed to be seized with inconsolable despair.

"Oh, dear, how unlucky! Oh, dear, how unlucky to lose such a fine calf!"

Françoise likewise lamented, and the regrets they **all ex**-pressed grew so aggressive, so full of implied hostility, that Patoir felt hurt. He hurried to them, stopping, however, outside the door, for decency's sake.

"I say! I give you warning. Just remember that you implored me to save your cow. **I know you** so well, you beggars. Now, don't you go about telling everybody that I killed **your calf.**"

"**That's** right enough, right enough," muttered Buteau, going back with him into the cow-house. "All the same, it was you **that cut it** up."

As Lise lay prostrate among the three chairs, **a kind of** billow passed over her. Françoise, who in her desolation **had** so far seen nothing, **became** quite thunderstruck.

"**A** little more **patience,**" said La **Frimat.** "**It'll soon be all** right."

Françoise, on her part, shook herself free from the fascination of the sight, and feeling embarrassed, went and took her sister's hand.

"**My** poor **Lise,**" she said affectionately, "**what** great trouble you're in!"

"Oh, yes, yes! And no one pities me. **If I** only had some pity! Oh, dear! It's beginning **again.** Won't it **ever** be born?"

This **kind of** talk might have gone on for a considerable time, but **some** exclamations were heard **in** the cow-house. They came from Patoir, who, astonished to **find La** Coliche still quivering and moaning, had suspected the presence of a second **calf.** And, indeed, there was one. Buteau ran into his wife's room carrying the little animal, which hung its astonished head **in a** tipsy-like way.

Amid **the** general acclamations at the sight, Lise broke into an endless, irresistible peal of mad laughter, stuttering:

"Oh, how funny it looks! Oh! it's too bad to make me laugh like **this!** Oh, **dear!** Oh! oh! how I am suffering! No, no! don't make me laugh any more: I've had enough!"

The climax was at length reached.

"It's a girl," declared La Frimat.

"No, no!" said Lise, **who** felt disappointed, "I don't want **one: I** want a boy."

Patoir went away, after two quarts of sweetened wine had

been given to La **Coliche.** **La Frimat undressed** Lise and put
her to bed, **while La Bécu, assisted by** Françoise, cleared away
the **straw and** swept **up the** room. **In** ten minutes' time all
was **in order.** No one would have **had any** idea that a confinement had just taken place, except for **the** constant mewling
of the baby, who was being washed in warm water. **However,** after being swathed, the infant gradually became quiet ;
while the mother, now utterly prostrate, fell into **a** leaden sleep,
and lay with her face congested, almost black, **between** the thick
brownish sheets.

Towards midnight, **when** the **two neighbours had left,**
Françoise told Buteau **that he had better go up into the**
hay-loft **to** sleep.   She **had laid a mattress on the floor,**
and meant to stay there **for the night, so as not to leave**
her sister **alone.**   He **made no answer, but finished his** pipe
in silence.   **All was quiet, save for the heavy breathing of**
the sleeping Lise,

As Françoise **was kneeling on her mattress, at the very foot**
of the bed, in a darkened corner, Buteau, **still silent, suddenly**
came up behind her and laid her flat.   **She turned her head,**
and **instantly** grasped the situation, **from** the **look of his drawn,**
flushed face.   He was at it again ; he had **not relinquished his**
purpose, and, presumably, the longing was a **violent one, since**
he attacked her thus beside his wife, and just **after occurrences**
which were scarcely of an engaging kind.   **Françoise repulsed**
and overturned him, however, and then there **was a suppressed,**
panting struggle.

With a snigger, **and in a choking voice, he said :**
"Come, **come !** Why **should you mind ?** I'm **equal to**
taking on the two of you."
He knew her well, and **felt sure she would** not scream. Nor
did she. She resisted without a word, too **proud to** call to her
sister, unwilling to acquaint **any one, even Lise,** with her business.   He was stifling her, however, and seemed on the point
of succeeding.
"It'll be so convenient, as we're living together, and **shall**
be always with each other," he said.
But suddenly he gave a cry of pain. She had silently dug **her**
nails into his neck. Then he grew mad, and spoke of Jean,
saying :
"Don't think you'll marry him, that blackguard fellow of
yours. Never, so long **as you're under age."**
As he was now doing her brutal violence, she kicked him so
vigorously that he howled aloud. Then he bounded up in alarm,

looking anxiously towards the bed. His wife was sleeping so soundly, however, that she had not stirred. Nevertheless, he went off, with a terrible threatening gesture.

When Françoise had stretched herself on the mattress, amid the deep stillness of the room, she lay there with her eyes open. She would never let him have his way, that she wouldn't, even although she herself were perchance desirous. And she felt astonished at it all ; for the idea that she might marry Jean had never yet occurred to her.

CHAPTER VI.

JEAN had been engaged for a couple of days in some fields
which Hourdequin owned near Rognes, and where he had set up
a steam threshing-machine, hired from a Châteaudun engine-
builder, who sent it about from Bonneval to Cloyes. With his
cart and his two horses, the young man brought the sheaves
from the surrounding ricks, and then took the grain to the
farm; while the machine, puffing away from morning till night,
scattered golden dust in the sunlight, and filled the country-
side with a terrific, incessant snorting.

Jean was not well, and was ransacking his brains as to how
he might best recover possession of Françoise. A month had
already gone by since he had clasped her, on that very spot,
among the wheat which they were now threshing; and since
then she had always escaped from him, apprehensively. He
began to despair of renewing the intercourse; and yet his
desire was increasing, becoming an all-absorbing, maddening
passion. As he drove his horses, he wondered why he should
not go to the Buteaus and roundly ask for Françoise's hand.
There had been no open definitive rupture between them. He
still bade them good-day as he passed, and, if he did not call on
them, it was solely because he was influenced by the disquietude of guilt. As soon as this idea of marriage occurred
to him, as the only means of getting the girl back, he persuaded
himself that it was the path of duty, and that he should be
acting dishonourably if he did not marry her. The next morning, however, when he returned to the machine, he was
seized with fear; and he would never have dared to risk the
step had he not seen Buteau and Françoise set off together for
the fields. He then bethought himself that Lise had always
been favourable to him, and that, with her, he would possess
more confidence. So he slipped away for a few moments,
leaving his horses in charge of a fellow-servant.

" Why, Jean ! " cried Lise, sturdily up and about again after
her confinement; " no one ever sees you now. What's up ? "

He made some excuses, and then, with the brusqueness of
shy people, he hurriedly broached the subject, in such an awk-

ward way, however, that at first it was open for her to think
that he was making her a declaration. For he reminded her
that he had loved her, and that he would willingly have taken
her to wife. However, he at once added :

"And that's why I'd **all** the same marry Françoise if she
were given me."

Lise stared at him **in such** astonishment that he began to
stammer :

"Oh, I'm well aware that it can't be settled straight off. I
only wanted to talk to you about it ! "

"Well, **it** takes me by surprise," **she** replied at length,
"because I hardly expected such a thing, on account **of** your
ages. First of all, we must know what Françoise thinks."

He had come formally resolved to tell the whole tale, thus
hoping to make the marriage inevitable. But at the last
moment a scruple restrained him. If Françoise had not confessed to her sister, if no one knew anything about it, had **ho**
the right to speak ? He was discouraged, and felt ridiculous,
on account of his thirty-three years of age.

"Most certainly," he muttered, "she should be consulted.
Nobody would force her."

Lise, however, having **once** got **over her** astonishment,
looked at him as genially as ever. Evidently **the** idea did not
displease her. She was even quite gracious.

"It shall be as she chooses, Jean. I'm not like Buteau,
who thinks her too young. She's getting on for eighteen, and
she has the build for two men, let **alone one. And,** besides,
love is all very well between sister and sister, of course ; but
now that she's a woman, I'd rather have a servant under orders
in her place. If she says yes, take her ! You're a good sort,
and the old cocks are often the best."

She had been unable to restrain these words of complaint
anent the gradual estrangement which was irresistibly increasing between herself and her younger sister : that hostility,
aggravated by little daily jars, a secret leaven of jealousy and
hatred which had been doing its stealthy work ever since a
man had come into the house with his will and his lust.

Jean, in his delight, kissed Lise warmly on both cheeks.

"It happens that we're just christening the baby," she
added, "and we shall have the family to dinner this evening.
I invite you, and you shall make your proposal to old Fouan,
who's the guardian, that is if Françoise will have you."

"Agreed ! " cried he. "I'll see you to-night ! "

He rapidly strode back to his horses, and drove them all

day long, making his whip resound with clacks which rang out
like gun-shots on the morning of a fête.

The Buteaus were, indeed, having their child baptised after
a deal of delay.   First of all, Lise had **insisted on waiting** till
she was quite strong and well again, wishing to join in the
feast. Next—on ambitious thoughts intent—she had obstinately
resolved to have Monsieur and Madame Charles for godfather
and godmother, **and** they having condescendingly **consented, it**
had been necessary to wait for Madame Charles, who **had just**
started for Chartres to lend **a** helping hand in her daughter's
establishment, for as it was now the time of the September
fair, the house in the Rue aux Juifs was always full.   However,
as Lise had told Jean, the christening was to be simply a
family gathering, with Fouan, La Grande, the Delhommes, and
the godparents.

At the last moment there had been serious difficulties with
the Abbé Godard, who was now incessantly at loggerheads
with Rognes.   So long as he had cherished the hope that the
Municipal Council would indulge in the luxury of a priest of
its own, he had been content to bear his troubles patiently:
such as the four miles **or so** which he had to walk for each
mass, and the **vexatious** demands which this irreligious village
made upon him.   But he could now no longer deceive himself
with false hopes.   Every year the council regularly refused
to repair the parsonage.   Hourdequin, the mayor, declared
that the expenses were already too heavy ; and Macqueron, the
assessor, alone paid court to the priesthood, in furtherance of
certain hidden ambitious designs.   So the Abbé Godard, no
longer having any reason to keep on good terms with Rognes,
became severe in his treatment of the village, and only vouchsafed it the strictest minimum of **worship.**   He did not treat
the inhabitants to any extra prayers, or any display of tapers
and incense for amusement's sake.   He was always quarrelling
with the women of the village.   In June there had been quite
a pitched battle on the subject of the first communion.   Five
children—two little girls and three boys—had'been attending
his catechism class on Sundays after mass, and to avoid having
to return to confess them, he insisted on their coming to him at
Bazoches-le-Doyen.   Thereupon a first sedition arose among
the women.   A pretty thing, indeed !   Three-quarters of a
league to go there, and the same distance back !   Who was to
know what might happen, with boys and girls running about
together ?   Next, there was a terrible storm when he refused
point-blank to celebrate the full ceremony at Rognes: high

mass, with singing, and so forth. He intended to hold this celebration in his own parish, whither the five children were free to repair, if they wished to do so. For a whole fortnight the women raved with fury round the fountain. What! He christened them, married them, and buried them in their own village, and now he wouldn't give them a decent communion! He was obstinate, however, and merely officiated at low mass, dismissing the five communicants without even a blossom or an oremus by way of consolation. When the women, vexed even to tears at seeing such a paltry ceremony, entreated him to have vespers sung in the afternoon, he flew into a passion! Nothing of the kind! He gave them their due. They would have had high mass, vespers, and everything else at Bazoches if their obstinacy had not made them rebel even against the blessed God Himself! After this quarrel a rupture seemed imminent between the Abbé Godard and Rognes, and the least jar would certainly bring about a catastrophe.

When Lise went to see the priest about the christening of her baby, he talked of fixing it for the Sunday, after mass. But she begged of him to return on the Tuesday at two o'clock, for the godmother would not return from Chartres till the morning of that day; and he eventually consented, recommending the party to be punctual, for he was determined, he cried, that he would not wait a second.

On the Tuesday, at two o'clock precisely, the Abbé Godard reached the church, panting from his journey, and damp owing to a sudden shower. No one had yet arrived. There was only Hilarion, who, at the entrance of the nave, was engaged in clearing up a corner of the baptistery, encumbered with fragments of old flag-stones, which had always been seen there. Since the death of his sister, the cripple had lived on public charity, and it had occurred to the priest, who used to slip odd francs into the poor fellow's hand from time to time, to employ him on this work of clearance, which had been resolved upon scores of times but always deferred. For a few moments he interested himself in watching Hilarion's task. Then he was taken with a first fit of anger.

"Good gracious! are they making a fool of me? It's already ten minutes past two," he exclaimed.

Then, as he looked at the Buteaus' silent, sleepy-looking house across the square, he noticed the rural constable waiting under the porch, and smoking his pipe.

"Ring the bell, Bécu!" he cried; "that'll bring the sluggards along."

So Bécu, who **was very** drunk, as usual, hung on to the bell-rope, while the priest went to put on **his surplice.** He had **drawn** up the entry in the register on **the previous** Sunday, and he intended to perform the ceremony by himself, without the **help of** the choir-children, who brought him to the verge of distraction. When all was ready, he again became impatient. Ten minutes more had **elapsed, and the bell** still rang out, with exasperating persistence, amid **the deep silence** of the deserted village.

" What on earth are they about? They **ought to have** some one at their backs with a stick ! " said the **priest.**

At last he saw **La Grande come forth from the Buteaus'** house, walking along in her spiteful, old-queen-like **way, dry and** upright, like a thistle, despite her eighty-five years.

A great worry was distracting **the** family. All **the** guests **were there, excepting the godmother, who had been** vainly **awaited since the morning. Monsieur** Charles, quite dumb-**founded, declared over and** over again that it **was** most surprising, that he had received a letter only the night before, and that Madame **Charles,** who **was** detained perhaps at Cloyes, **would certainly** arrive in **a minute or** two. Lise, **anxious, and** knowing that the priest **was not** over-fond **of** waiting, finally took it into her head **to despatch** La Grande to him, so as **to** keep him patient.

" What's the meaning of this? " **he asked her, from a dis-**tance. " Are we going to begin to-day or to-morrow? **Per-**haps you think that God Almighty **is at** your beck and call? "

" In a moment, your reverence ; in a moment." replied the old woman, with her impassive calmness.

Hilarion was **just then bringing out the last** fragments of the flag-stones, and **he went by carrying** an immense block against **his** stomach. He swayed from side to side **on his** crooked shanks, but he did not bend, being as firmly set as **a rock,** with muscles strong enough to have carried an ox. His hare-**lip was** dribbling, **but not a drop of** sweat moistened **his hardened skin.**

The **Abbé Godard,** provoked by La Grande's equanimity, fell upon her **at once.**

" Look here, La Grande," said he, " now that **I've** got hold of you, is it charitable of you, who are **so well** off, to let your only grandson beg his bread along the roads ? "

" **The** mother disobeyed **me ;** the child is nothing to me," she answered harshly.

" Well, I've given **you** fair warning, **and I** tell you again that if you're so hard-hearted as that you'll go to Hell. He would have starved to death the other day but for what I gave him, and now I'm obliged to invent a job for him."

On hearing the word "Hell" La Grande slightly smiled. As she herself said, she knew too much about it: the poor folks' Hell was on this earth. The sight of Hilarion carrying paving-stones set her thinking, however, far more than the priest's threats did. She was surprised; she would never have imagined that he was so strong, with his jacket-sleeve shanks.

"If it's work he wants," she replied at last, "I daresay he can be found some."

"His proper place is with you. Take him, La Grande," said the priest.

"We'll see. Let him come to-morrow."

Hilarion, who had understood, began to tremble to such a degree that he all but crushed his feet as he dropped his last slab. As he went off he cast a furtive glance on his grandmother, like a whipped, terrified, submissive animal.

Another half-hour went by. Bécu, tired of ringing, was smoking his pipe once more in the sunshine. La Grande remained there, silent and imperturbable, as if her mere presence sufficed as a mark of respect to the priest; while the latter, whose exasperation was on the increase, kept running every instant to the church door to cast a fiery look across the empty square towards the Buteaus' house.

"Ring, Bécu, why don't you!" he shouted all at once. "If they're not here in three minutes' time, I'm off!"

Then as the bell pealed out madly once more, and set the aged ravens a-fluttering and a-cawing, the Buteaus and their party were seen to leave the house one by one and cross the square. Lise was in consternation; the godmother had still not arrived, and so they settled to stroll quietly over to the church, in hopes that perhaps that would bring her a little quicker. But they were only a hundred yards away, and the Abbé Godard at once began to hurry them up.

"I say, you know, are you trying to make a fool of me?" he called. "I consult your convenience, and in return I'm kept waiting an hour! Make haste! Make haste!"

Then he pushed them all towards the baptistery: the mother carrying her newly-born child, the father, grandfather Fouan, uncle Delhomme, aunt Fanny, and even Monsieur Charles, who, in his black frock-coat, looked very dignified as a god-parent.

"Your reverence," said Buteau, with an exaggerated air

of humility, in which **a** sniggering slyness lurked, "if you would only be so good as to wait a tiny bit longer——"

" **Wait !** What for ? "

" Why, for the godmother, your reverence ! "

The Abbé Godard became so red that apoplexy seemed imminent. Half suffocating, he stuttered out :

" Get somebody else ! "

They **all looked at** each other. Delhomme **and** Fanny **shook** their heads ; and Fouan declared :

" Impossible. It would be bad breeding."

" **A** thousand pardons, **your** reverence," said Monsieur Charles, who thought that it devolved **upon him as a person** of good breeding **to explain matters ;** " it's partly our **fault,** but not quite. My **wife had** expressly written **me that she** would be back this morning. She's at Chartres."

The Abbé Godard started, **and, losing all control,** breaking all bounds, **he** shouted :

" At *Chartres !* At Chartres, indeed ! I regret for your sake that you **have a** finger **in** this pie, Monsieur Charles. But the thing **sha'n't go on. No, no !** I won't put **up** with it **any longer !** "

Then he burst forth :

" **No** one here cares what outrage he **offers God in my person ;** I get a **fresh** buffet every time I come **to** Rognes. **I've** threatened long enough, and now I'll do it. I leave to-day, and I will never return. Tell **your** mayor that, **and** find a **priest** and pay him, if you want **one.** I'll speak to **the** bishop, and tell him who you are ; I'm sure he will approve of my course. We'll soon see who'll get the worst of it. You shall live priestless, like brute beasts."

They were all staring **at him curiously, with the** inward indifference of practical folk who no longer feared the God of **wrath** and chastisement. **What** was the use of quaking and **prostrating themselves,** and purchasing forgiveness, when the very **idea of the devil now** made them smile, and when they had ceased to **believe** that the wind, the hail, and the thunder were **controlled by an avenging** Master ? It was **certainly** waste **of time. It was better for** them to keep **their** respect for the Government gendarmes, who held the reins **of** power.

Despite their assumed air of deferential gravity, the Abbé Godard saw that Buteau was sniggering, that La Grande was disdainful, and that even Delhomme and Fouan were perfectly **unmoved ; and** this loss of influence completed the rupture.

" I'm perfectly aware that your cows have more religion

than you have," said he. " Well, good-bye! Dip your bar-
barian child into the pond, and christen it like that!"

Then he ran away and tore off his surplice, crossed the
church again, and bolted in such a whirl of wrath that the
christening party, thus left in the lurch, could not even get in
a word, but stood open-mouthed and open-eyed.

The worst of it was that at that very moment, as the Abbé
Godard was going down Macqueron's new street, they saw a
covered cart coming up the high-road—a cart containing
Madame Charles and Elodie. The former explained that she
had stopped at Châteaudun to kiss the child, who had been
granted a two days' holiday. She seemed extremely sorry
for the delay, and declared that she had not even gone on
to Rose-Blanche with her trunk.

" Some one must run after the priest," said Lise; "it's only
dogs that are left unchristened."

Buteau ran off, and was heard trotting down Macqueron's
street. But the Abbé Godard had got a good start; and
Buteau crossed the bridge and mounted the slope, only catching sight of the priest when he reached the crest of it, just
where the road turned.

" Your reverence, your reverence!"

At last the priest turned round and waited.

" What is it?" he asked.

"The godmother's there. Christening isn't a thing to refuse
one."

For an instant the Abbé stood motionless. Then he came
back down the hill behind the peasant, at the same furious
pace; and thus they re-entered the church without exchanging
another word. The ceremony was hurried through. The
priest mangled the godparents' *Credo*, anointed the child,
applied the salt, and poured out the water, all with the same
violence. He had soon got to the signing of the register.

" Your reverence," now said Madame Charles, " I've a box
of sweetmeats for you, but it's in my trunk."

He thanked her in dumb-show and went off, after turning
to them all once more and repeating:

" Good-bye, again!"

The Buteaus and their party, breathless at having been
carried along at such a pace, watched him as he disappeared
at the corner of the square, with his black cassock flying
behind him. All the villagers were in the fields; there were
merely a few urchins about, on the chance of obtaining some
plaster-of-Paris sweetmeats. Amid the deep silence one only

heard the distant snorting of the steam thrasher, which never rested.

On re-entering the Buteaus' house, at the door of which the cart with the trunk was waiting, they all agreed to have a little something to drink, and then to separate until dinner in the evening. It was now only four o'clock, so what would they have done in each other's company till seven? Then, when the glasses and the two quarts of wine were set out on the kitchen table, Madame Charles absolutely insisted on having her trunk got down, so as to make her presents there and then. Opening the trunk, she first took out the baby's dress and cap—which came somewhat behind time—and next six boxes of sweetmeats, which she gave to the mother.

" Do these come from mamma's confectionary shop? " asked Elodie, who was looking at them.

For a second Madame Charles felt embarrassed. Then she calmly replied :

" No, my darling ; your mother does not keep this kind."

And, turning towards Lise, she added : " I thought of you, too, in the matter of linen. There is nothing so useful in a house as old linen; so I asked my daughter for some, and ransacked all her drawers."

Hearing linen mentioned, everybody had drawn near— La Grande, the Delhommes, and Fouan himself. Gathering in a ring round the trunk, they watched the old lady unpack a whole lot of rags, all clean and white, and exhaling, despite the washing, a persistent odour of musk. First came some fine linen sheets, in tatters; then a quantity of chemises, all slit down, with the lace palpably torn off.

Madame Charles unfolded the things, shook them out, and explained :

" The sheets are not new. They've been quite five years in use ; and in time, what with friction and so on, they wear out. You see that they've all a large hole in the middle, but the edges are still good, and a host of things may be cut out of them."

They all stuck their noses into the sheets, and felt them, with approving nods, particularly the women — La Grande and Fanny, whose pinched-up lips were expressive of suppressed envy. Buteau was indulging in silent laughter, tickled by certain jocular ideas which he kept to himself, for propriety's sake ; while Fouan and Delhomme testified by their extreme gravity to the respect they felt for linen, which was the only wealth, worth calling so, next to land.

"As for the chemises," resumed Madame Charles, unfolding them in their turn, "see for yourselves. They're not worn at all. Lots of slits in them, no doubt! They're torn to ruination! And as they can't always be sewn up again, because that would make thick seams, and look a little paltry, why, they're thrown away for old linen. But they'll come in handy for you, Lise——"

"Why, I'll wear them," cried the peasant woman. "It makes no odds to me to wear a mended chemise."

"As for me," declared Buteau, with a sly wink, "I shall be glad enough if you'll make me some handkerchiefs out of them."

This set them laughing undisguisedly. Little Elodie, who had not taken her eyes off a single sheet or chemise, now cried out:

"Oh, what a funny smell! How strong! Was all that linen mamma's?"

Madame Charles did not hesitate a moment.

"Why, certainly, darling. That is, it's the linen of her shop-girls. A lot of girls are wanted in business, I can tell you!"

As soon as Lise had put the whole lot away in her wardrobe, with Françoise's help, they clinked glasses and drank the health of the baby, whom the godmother had christened Laure, after herself. Then they tarried for a moment, lost in conversation; and Monsieur Charles, sitting on the trunk, was heard questioning Madame Charles, without waiting to get her alone, so great, indeed, was his impatience to hear how things were going on over yonder. It was still a passion with him; his head was always running upon the house so energetically established in days gone by, and so deeply regretted since! The news was not good. True enough, their daughter Estelle had a hand and a head; but their son-in-law Vaucogne, that milksop Achilles, did not give her proper support. He spent the whole day smoking his pipe, and let everything go to rack and ruin. The curtains of No. 3 were stained, the mirror in the small red drawing-room was cracked, the water-jugs and basins were chipped all over the house; and he never so much as raised a finger. And a man's arm was so necessary to ensure due respect for one's goods and chattels! At every fresh piece of damage thus brought under his notice, Monsieur Charles fetched a sigh, and became paler. One last grievance, communicated in a whisper, finished him off.

"Lastly, he himself goes upstairs with that stout woman of No. 5——"

" What's that you say ? "

" Oh, I'm sure of it ; I've seen them."

Monsieur Charles, who was quivering, clenched his fists
in a burst of exasperated indignation.

" The wretch ! Disgracing himself in that way ! That
beats everything ! "

With a gesture, Madame Charles silenced him, for Elodie
was coming back from the yard, where she had been to see
the hens. Another quart bottle was drained, and the trunk
was again placed in the cart, which Monsieur and Madame
Charles followed on foot as far as their house. All the others
also went off to give a glance indoors while awaiting the
feast.

As soon as Buteau was alone, feeling dissatisfied with this
waste of an afternoon, he took off his jacket and set to work
threshing in the paved corner of the yard ; he wanted a sack
of corn for the morrow. However, he soon got tired of threshing alone. To warm him to his work he needed the cadence
of two flails, keeping time together. So he called to Françoise,
who frequently helped him in this work, as her loins were
strong, and her arms as hard-set as a young man's. In spite
of the slowness and the fatigue of this primitive method of
threshing, Buteau had always refused to buy a machine, saying, like all petty landowners, that he preferred to thresh at a
time just the quantity he needed.

" Hallo, Françoise ! Are you coming ? " he called.

Lise, who was leaning over some veal stewing with carrots,
after commissioning her sister to look after a loin of roast-
pork, wanted to prevent the girl obeying. But Buteau, who
was not in the best of temper, threatened them both with a
hiding.

" You cursed females ! I'll smack your saucepans across
your heads for you ! One may well sweat for one's bread
when you'd go and fry the whole house, to gobble it down
with other people ! "

Françoise, who had already slipped on a working dress for
fear of getting her best clothes stained, was obliged to follow
him. She took a flail with handle and flap of cornel wood,
secured together with leather buckles. It was her own,
polished by friction, and closely bound with string to prevent
its slipping. Swinging it round over her head with both hands
she brought it down on the wheat, striking the latter smartly
with the whole length of the flap. She went on without stopping, raising the flail very high, turning it as upon a hinge,

and then banging it down again with the mechanical, rhythmical movement of a blacksmith; while Buteau, opposite her, swung his flail in alternation. They soon became hot. The rhythm was accelerated, and nothing could now be seen but the flying flaps, rebounding every time and whirling behind their necks like birds tied by the feet.

After ten minutes or so, Buteau gave a slight cry. The flails stopped, and he turned the sheaf round, whereupon the flails started again. At the end of another ten minutes he ordered a new pause, and laid the sheaf open. It had to pass thus six times under the flaps before the grain was fully separated from the ears, and the straw could be tied up. Sheaf succeeded sheaf, and for two hours the regular noise of the flails pervaded the house, though above it, in the distance, there arose the prolonged snorting of the steam-thresher.

Françoise's cheeks were now flushed and her wrists swollen, and from all her glowing skin there emanated a kind of flame that quivered visibly in the air. Her open lips were panting. Bits of straw had become entangled in the loose locks of her hair. At every stroke, as she raised the flail, her right knee stretched her petticoat, her hip and bosom expanded, straining her dress, while the contour of her well-set frame showed roughly through the fabric. A button flew off her bodice, and Buteau saw her white skin beneath the sunburnt line of her neck—an eminence of flesh that kept rising with the swing of her arms in the powerful play of the shoulder-muscles. This seemed to excite him still more; and the flails still fell, while the grain leapt and fell like hail under the panting strokes of the coupled threshers.

At a quarter to seven, at close of day, Fouan and the Delhommes presented themselves.

"We must finish this," shouted Buteau to them, without stopping. "Keep it up, Françoise!"

She stuck to it, striking still harder in the enthusiasm prompted by the labour and noise. And thus it was that Jean found them when he in his turn arrived. He felt a spasm of jealousy, and looked at them as if he had surprised them together. Busy with this warm work, each striking true in turn, both perspiring, so heated and so disarranged, they seemed to be engaged in some other more private business than that of threshing wheat. Perhaps Françoise, who was going at it so zealously, had the same idea, for she suddenly stopped short in embarrassment. Then Buteau, turning round, remained motionless for an instant, with surprise and wrath.

" What do *you* want here ? " he cried.

Lise was just then coming out to meet Fouan and the Delhommes. She drew near in their company, and cried in her sprightly way :

" Ah, yes ! I forgot to tell you. I saw Jean this morning and asked him to come in to-night."

Her husband's face was so terribly inflamed that she added, by way of apology :

" I've a notion, Fouan, that he has a request to make of you."

" What about ? " said the old man. Jean flushed and stammered, feeling very vexed that the matter should be broached so abruptly and publicly. However, Buteau violently cut him short, the smiling look which his wife cast upon Françoise having sufficed to enlighten him.

" Do you come here to make a laughing-stock of us ? She's not for the likes of you, you ugly bird ! "

This brutal reception gave Jean back his courage. He turned his back and addressed the old man.

" This is the matter, Fouan. It's a very simple thing. As you are Françoise's guardian, I ought to apply to you for her, oughtn't I ? Well, if she will have me, I'll have her. I ask her in marriage."

Françoise, who was still holding her flail, dropped it in amazement. She ought to have expected this; but she had not imagined that Jean would venture to propose for her in such a fashion all at once. Why had he not spoken to her about it first ? It flurried her; she could not have told whether she was trembling with hope or fear. Vibrating from her recent toil, her bosom heaving under her unfastened bodice, she remained there between the two men, glowing with such a rush of blood that they felt the heat radiate even to where they stood.

Buteau did not allow Fouan time to answer. He went on in growing fury :

" What ? You dare ask that. An old man of thirty-three marry a child of eighteen. Merely fifteen years difference ! Isn't it monstrous ? Fancy giving young chickens to a fellow with a dirty hide like yours ! "

Jean was beginning to lose his temper.

" What's it got to do with you," he replied, " if she likes me and I like her ? "

And he turned towards Françoise for her to pronounce. But she stood there startled and rigid, without seeming to

understand. She could not say no, but she did not say yes.
Buteau, moreover, was glaring at her so murderously as to
make the yes stick in her throat. If she married, he would
lose her and the land as well. The sudden thought of this
result put a finishing touch to his wrath.

"Come, papa ; come, Delhomme. Doesn't it revolt you ;
this child to that old brute, who doesn't even belong to our
part of the country, and who comes from God knows where,
after traipsing about here, there, and everywhere? A
carpenter who failed in his calling and turned peasant,
because he had some disgraceful affair to keep secret, of
course."

All his hatred of the town artizan burst forth.

"And what then? If I like her and she likes me !" repeated
Jean, restraining himself, and resolving, out of courtesy, to let
her be the first to relate their story. "Come, Françoise, say
something."

"Why, that's true !" cried Lise, carried away by the desire
to see her sister married, and thus get rid of her: "what have you
to do with it, Bateau, if they agree ? She doesn't need your
consent, and it's very good of her not to send you about your
business. You're getting a perfect nuisance !"

Buteau clearly realised that the matter would be arranged,
if the girl were to speak. He especially dreaded that the
marriage would be considered reasonable if the past connection
were made public. Just then La Grande came into the yard,
followed by Monsieur and Madame Charles, who were returning with Elodie. Buteau beckoned them to approach without
yet knowing what he would say. Then an idea struck him,
and with his face swollen and shaking his fist at his wife and
sister-in-law, he yelled out :

"You cursed cows ! Yes, cows, trolls, both of you ! If
you want to know the truth, I sleep with the pair of them !
and that's why they think they can make a fool of me ! With
the pair of them, I tell you ! Strumpets that they are ! "

These words came in a volley full in the faces of Monsieur
and Madame Charles, who both stood there open-mouthed.
Madame Charles made a rush as if to shield the listening
Elodie. Then, pushing her towards the kitchen garden, she
cried in a very loud voice :

"Come and see the salads, come and see the cabbages !
Oh, such fine cabbages ! "

Buteau invented fresh details as he went on, relating that
when one had had her share it was the other one's turn ; using

the coarsest terms, and venting a flood of sewerage in un-
utterably beastly words. Lise, in sheer astonishment at this
sudden fit, simply shrugged her shoulders, repeating :

" He's mad ! It isn't possible otherwise. He's mad ! "

" **Tell him** he **lies !** " cried Jean to Françoise.

" Most certainly he lies ! " said the girl, composedly.

" Oh, I lie ? " resumed Buteau. " Oh ! And it isn't true
what happened between us at harvest-time ? **I'll** pretty **soon**
bring you under, the two of you, strumpets that you **are !** "

This rabid audacity paralysed **and** astounded Jean. **Could
he** now explain what had happened **between himself and
Françoise ?** It seemed to **him** that **it would be foul to do so,**
particularly as she did not give him any assistance. **The others**
—the Delhommes, Fouan, and La Grande—remained reserved.
They had not seemed **surprised ; and they** evidently thought
that, if the fellow did **sleep with the two of** them, he could
dispose **of** them **as he chose.** When a man has his rights, he
asserts them.

From that moment, Buteau felt himself victorious in the
might of his undisputed possession. He turned towards Jean
and cried :

" **And** you, just you come here again worrying **me in my**
household. To begin with, you'll be off pretty sharp. Eh ?
you won't ? Wait, wait a bit."

He picked up his flail, and whirled the flap round. **Jean**
only just had time to catch up the other one—Françoise's—to
defend himself with. There were shrieks, and some attempt
to interpose ; but the antagonists were so terrible, that every-
one recoiled. With the long handles of the flails, blows could
be dealt at several yards ; so that the yard was soon left clear.
Jean and **Buteau** remained alone **in** the middle, at a distance
from one another, enlarging the circle of their twirls. **They**
no longer spoke but kept their teeth clenched. **No** sound was
heard but the sharp smack of the pieces of wood at each
exchange of blows.

Buteau had launched the first one, and Jean, still stooping,
would have had his head split open, had he not leapt backwards.
By a quick contraction of his muscles, he at once raised his
flail, and brought it down in the same style as a thresher
crushing grain. But the other was also striking ; and the two
flaps met, and swung back upon their straps like wounded
birds swooping wildly. Thrice there was the same shock.
Each time the flaps whirled and whizzed through the air, and
they all but fell and split the skulls they threatened. The con-

test could not be of long duration, for the first blow must be a mortal one.

Delhomme and Fouan, however, were rushing forward, when the women shrieked. Jean had rolled over in the straw, Buteau having treacherously aimed a whip-like blow, which swept along the ground, and, although fortunately deadened, reached his opponent's legs. Jean got up again without letting go of his flail, which he brandished with a fury increased tenfold by pain. The flap made a wide sweep and fell on the right, while the other was expecting it on the left. A fraction of an inch nearer and Buteau's brains would have been dashed out. As it was, his ear was grazed, and the blow coming down obliquely fell full on his arm, which was sharply broken atwain. The bone was heard to snap as if it had been breaking glass. Buteau's hand fell limply down, dropping the flail it was holding.

" The murderer ! " yelled Buteau, " he's killed me! "

Jean, with a haggard face and blood-shot eyes, also dropped his weapon. He glanced round at them all for a moment, as if stupefied by the sudden turn that things had taken, and then limped away with a wild gesture of despair.

When he had turned the corner of the house, going towards the plain, he espied La Trouille, who had witnessed the fight over the garden hedge. She was still chuckling over it, having come there to prowl around the christening party, to which neither she nor her father had been invited. What fun it would all be for Hyacinthe—this little family fête and his brother's broken arm ! She was wriggling as if she were being tickled, and nearly fell over backwards, so highly was she amused.

"Oh, Corporal, what a whack ! " she cried. " The bone gave such a crack ! It *was* fun ! "

He made no answer, but slackened his pace with a dejected air. She followed him, whistling to her geese, which she had taken with her, so as to have a pretext for eavesdropping behind the walls. Jean returned mechanically to the threshing-machine, which was still in action, though the day was waning. He thought to himself that it was all over ; that he could never go back to the Buteaus, that they would never give him Françoise. What folly it was ! Ten minutes had sufficed : an unsought quarrel, and so unlucky a blow, just when everything was in such trim ! And now, never, never more ! The snorting of the machine amid the twilight was prolonged like a great cry of distress.

Another encounter just then occurred. **At the corner of a
cross** road La Trouille's geese, which **she was taking back**
home, found themselves face to face with old Saucisse's geese
on their way down to the village, unaccompanied. **The** two
ganders, in the van, pulled up short, **resting on one leg,** with
their large yellow beaks turned towards each **other.** All **the**
beaks of each flock turned simultaneously in **the same direction**
as the leaders', and the geese's bodies were inclined to **the same**
side. For an instant perfect immobility was preserved. **It**
was like **an** armed reconnaissance ; two patrols exchanging
watch-words. Then one of the ganders, with round, contented
eyes, went straight on, while the other bore **to the** left ; and
each troop filed off behind its own leader, going about its business with the **same uniform** waddling gait.

PART IV.

CHAPTER I.

AFTER the shearing and the sale of the lambs in May, Soulas, the shepherd, had removed the sheep from La Borderie. Nearly four hundred head there were, which he led away without any other assistance than that of the little swine-herd Firmin, and his two formidable dogs, Emperor and Massacre. Until August the flocks grazed in the fallows amongst the clover and lucern, or in the waste-lands along the roads; and barely three weeks had now elapsed since he had turned them out into the stubble, immediately after the harvest, in the last blazing days of September.

This was the terrible season of the year. The fields of La Beauce lay stripped and desolate and bare, without a single fleck of green about them. The torrid summer, and the complete absence of all moisture, had dried up the splitting soil, and almost all signs of vegetation had disappeared. There was nothing left save a tangle of dead grass, and the hard bristles of the stubble-fields, which stretched out their mournful, bare nudity as far as the eye could reach, making all the plain look as though some giant conflagration had swept from horizon to horizon. The soil still seemed to be giving out a yellowish glow, a weird, threatening light, livid like that of a storm. Everything looked yellow, a frightfully mournful yellow; the baked earth, the stubble, and the high-roads and by-paths, rutted and torn up by passing wheels. The slightest breeze set clouds of dust flying, and covering the banks and hedges as with cinders. The blue sky and the blazing sun only seemed to render the scene of desolation still more mournful.

Upon that particular day there was a high wind, blowing in quick, warm puffs, which brought along heavy, scudding clouds; and when the sun shone fully out, his rays seemed to burn the skin like red-hot iron. Ever since early morning, Soulas had been expecting a supply of water for himself and his flock—water which was to be brought to him from the

farm—for the stubble lands where he found himself lay to the
north of Rognes, far away from any pond. In the grazing
ground, between the light, movable hurdles secured with
staves the sheep were lying on their bellies, panting and
breathing only with difficulty ; while the two dogs, stretched
at full length outside the hurdles, were also panting, with their
tongues lolling out of their mouths. The shepherd, to protect
himself from the wind and to procure a little shade, was seated,
leaning against a little hut raised on two wheels—a narrow
box which served him for bed, and wardrobe, and pantry—and
which he pushed along at every change of the grazing ground.

At noon, however, when the sun shone down perpendicularly, Soulas rose to his feet again, and scanned the distance
to ascertain if he could see Firmin returning from the farm,
where he had sent him to find out why the water did not come.

At last the little swine-herd made his appearance.

" They'll be here soon," he cried. " They had no horses
this morning."

" You silly little fool, haven't you brought a bottle of
water for us to drink ourselves ? "

" Oh, dear, I never thought about it."

Soulas struck out a swinging blow with his closed fist,
which the lad avoided by jumping aside. Then the shepherd
began to swear, but he decided that he would eat without
drinking, although he was almost choked with thirst. By his
orders, Firmin warily took out of the hut some bread a week
old, some shrivelled walnuts, and some dry cheese. Then they
both sat down to eat, intently watched by the two dogs, who
came and sat down in front of them, getting a crust tossed to
them now and then, so hard that it cracked between their teeth
as if it had been a bone. In spite of his seventy years, the old
man got as quickly through his food with his gums as the
youngster did with his teeth. Soulas was still straight and upright, flexible and tough like a thornwood stick. Time seemed
merely to have scored furrows in his face, which was gnarled
like a tree trunk beneath a tangle of faded hair, now the colour
of earth.

The little swine-herd did not manage to escape his cuffing,
for just as he was about to stow the remains of the bread and
cheese inside the hut, and was no longer suspecting an attack,
Soulas gave him a thumping whack which sent him rolling
into the shelter-place.

" There, you silly little fool," cried the old man ; " take and
drink that, till the water comes ! "

Two o'clock arrived without there being a sign of anybody coming. The heat had gone on increasing, and was well-nigh intolerable amid the complete calms which suddenly set in. Then, every now and again the breeze would rise and sweep up the powdery soil in little wheeling whirlwinds which seemed composed of blinding, suffocating smoke, and terribly enhanced the pangs of thirst.

At last **the shepherd, who bore his** sufferings with stoical, uncomplaining patience, **gave a grunt of satisfaction.**

"Thank heaven!" he exclaimed; "they've come none too soon."

Two carts, which in the distance **looked scarcely bigger** than a **man's** fist, had now at length made **their appearance on** the line where the plain intersected the horizon. **In the first** one, **which** was driven by Jean, Soulas had distinctly recognised the barrel of water. The second one, which Tron was in charge of, was loaded with sacks of corn, which were being **taken to the mill,** whose lofty wooden carcass could be seen **some** five hundred yards away. This second cart came to a **stand**-still **on the road, and** Tron accompanied Jean through the stubble-fields **up to the** sheep-fold, under pretence of lending him a hand **with the** water, but really for the sake of idling and indulging in **a few** minutes' gossip.

"Do they want us **all to** die of thirst?" cried the shepherd.

The sheep, also **having** sniffed the water, had sprung up in eager tumult, and **were now** pressing **against the** hurdles, craning out their heads, **and** bleating plain**tively.**

"Patience! patience!" replied Jean; "**there's** something here to make you tipsy."

The men now quickly put the trough into position, and filled it by the aid of a wooden spout. Some of the water **ran** over, and the two dogs lapped it up eagerly, while the **shepherd and** the little swine-herd, too thirsty to wait any longer, **drank** greedily out of the trough. Then the whole flock swarmed up to it, and the air was filled with the flowing murmur of refreshing water, and the gurgling sound of animals and **men** swallowing it, and splashing and drenching themselves **with** it **in delight.**

"Now," said Soulas, who **had** become quite cheery again, "you would be doing me a kindness if you would help me to move the pens."

Jean and Tron both helped him. The hurdles were constantly moved over the surface of the far-spreading stubble, never being kept for more than two or three days in the same position, just sufficient time to enable the sheep to crop down the stray vegetation. This system, moreover, had the advantage of gradually manuring the land, patch by patch. While the shepherd, assisted by his dogs, looked after the sheep, the two men and the little swine-herd pulled up the stakes and carried the hurdles some fifty yards further on. Then they again fixed them so as to enclose a vast square, into which the animals rushed of their own accord before it was quite completed.

Despite his great age, Soulas was already propelling his wheeled-hut towards the fold.

" What's the matter with Jean ? " he presently asked. " One would say he was burying God Almighty ! "

Jean only shook his head sadly. He had been very gloomy ever since he believed that he had lost Françoise.

" Ah ! there's some woman in the matter, I expect," continued the old man. " The confounded hussies, they ought all to have their necks wrung ! "

Thereupon the giant-limbed Tron began to laugh with an innocent air.

" Ah ! " he said, " it's only those who are past everything that say that."

" Do you mean to say that I am past everything ? " exclaimed the shepherd, contemptuously. " When did you find that out ? But there's one wench, my lad, whom it's best for you not to touch, or you may be sure that matters will have a bad ending."

This allusion to Tron's connection with Madame Jacqueline made the farm-hand blush up to his ears. Soulas had caught them together one morning in the barn behind some sacks of oats ; and in his detestation of the ex-scullerymaid, who was now so stern and harsh towards her old pals, he had, after much deliberation, determined to open his master's eyes as to her conduct. However, at his first word, the farmer had looked at him with so angry an expression that he had said no more, resolving to remain silent, unless La Cognette forced him to extreme measures by bringing about his dismissal. The consequence was that they were now living together in a state of hostility: Soulas dreading that he might be turned away like a broken-down old beast of burden, and Jacqueline biding her time till her influence became sufficiently consolidated to induce Hourdequin, who was attached to his shepherd, to dismiss him. Throughout La Beauce nobody understood the art of sheep-grazing better than Soulas did. His flocks were well-fed and there was neither loss nor waste, the fields being clean shaved from one end to the other, without a blade of grass being left behind.

The old man, possessed by the propensity for talking which often leads those who live solitary lives to take any opportunity of unbosoming themselves, now continued:

"Ah, if my jade of a wife, before she managed to kill herself, hadn't put all my brass down her throat as fast as I earned it, I'd have taken myself off the farm of my own accord before now, so as to get away from the sight of so much beastliness. That Cognette has made a lot more money by her face than with her hands, and it's her looks, not her deserts, that have gained her her present position! Just to think of the master letting her lie in his dead wife's bed, and being so infatuated with her that he has ended by taking his meals alone with her, just as though she were his lawful wife! She'll turn us all out of the place, neck and crop, at the first opportunity, and the master himself into the bargain. A filthy sow who has wallowed with every dirty hog!"

At every sentence spoken by the old man, Tron clenched his fists more tightly. He was brimming over with suppressed rage, which was rendered the more terrible by his giant-like strength.

"There that will do!" he cried; "you'd better just shut up. If you hadn't got into your dotage, I'd have knocked you down before now. There's more decency in her little finger than there is in the whole of your old carcass."

Soulas, however, only shrugged his shoulders jeeringly at the other's threat; and, though he scarcely ever laughed, he now broke out into a sharp grating giggle, which seemed to come from some mechanism rusted by disuse.

"You great simpleton, you! You're as foolish and gullible as she's cunning! Oh, yes, she'll swear hard enough to her virginity! Why, I tell you that all the country-side has had to deal with her! She was scarcely fourteen when she and old Mathias, a hunch-back who's dead now, came together in the stable; then later on, as she was kneading the dough, she had to do with that little scamp Guillaume, the swine-herd, who's in the army now, and who found her alone in the kitchen; and she's been with every farm-labourer that's ever come into the neighbourhood, in every sort of place imaginable, in every hole and corner, as is very well known all over the place. Oh! you haven't far to seek, if you want to tax her with it. I myself saw a fellow

belonging to **these** parts with **her in the** hay-loft one morning
not long ago."

He broke **out into a fresh** giggle, **and** the sidelong glance
which **he** cast at Jean seemed to make the latter very uneasy.
IIc had been fidgetting about in silence ever since the con-
versation had turned upon Jacqueline.

" **It'll** be bad for any one whom I **find touching her now,"**
growled Tron, as angry as a dog who has **had its bone snatched**
from it. " **I'll** spoil his **appetite for** him ! "

Soulas gazed at the **fellow for a moment, surprised by this
show** of brutish jealousy.

" Well, that's your own **affair, my lad,"** he drily **said in**
conclusion, **and** then **he relapsed into one of his fits of con-**
templative silence.

Tron finally **returned to the cart which** he was driving to the
mill, while **Jean remained** for a few minutes longer with the
shepherd to **help him to** hammer **down** some of the hurdle
stakes. **The old man, noticing his** silence and gloomy appearance, began to question him.

" **I trust it isn't La Cognette that's upsetting your heart ? "**
he said.

The young fellow shook his head energetically **in sign of
denial.**

" Is it some other wench, then ? **Who is it, for I don't**
remember having seen you with any **one ? "**

Jean glanced at old Soulas, and bethought **himself that the**
counsel of old men was often valuable **in** matters of this sort.
He also felt a longing to unbosom himself, and so he told him
the whole **story,** how he had possessed Françoise, and how **he**
was hopeless **of** ever seeing her again since the fight with
Buteau. IIe had even been afraid for a time, **he** said, that the
latter would prosecute him on account of his broken arm, which
still prevented his doing any work, though it was now half-
way well again. Buteau, however, had probably thought **it**
more prudent **to** keep the law from spying into his concerns.

" You have had to do with Françoise, then ? " said the **old**
shepherd.

" Yes, once."

The old man reflected with a grave **look, and** finally continued :

" You had better tell old Fouan all about **it ;** perhaps he will
give her to you."

Jean heard this with astonishment. IIe had never thought
of such a simple plan. The fold was now complete, and he

went away, saying that he would go and see old Fouan that very evening. As he plodded along behind his empty cart, Soulas **resumed** his everlasting watch, his thin, erect figure standing out like a greyish bar against the flat expanse of the plain. The little swine-herd was lying down between the two dogs **in** the shadow of the movable hut. The wind had suddenly dropped, and the **storm** clouds **had** rolled away towards the east. It was as hot as ever, and the sun was blazing in a sky of unflecked blue.

That evening Jean left his work an hour earlier than usual, and went to the Delhommes' to see old Fouan before dinner. As he was going down the hill-side, he caught sight of the Delhommes amongst their vines, where they were stripping off the leaves, so as to expose the fruit to **the** sun. There had been some heavy rains during the closing quarter of **the** moon, and the grapes were ripening badly, so that it was necessary to take every advantage of the late sunshine. As the old man was not there with his children, Jean quickened **his** steps, in the **hope of being** able to speak to him alone—a course which he much preferred. The Delhommes' house was at the other end of Rognes, across the bridge; it was a little farm, which had recently received various additions in the shape of barns and out-houses, and the buildings now formed three irregular blocks, enclosing a fairly large yard. The latter was swept every morning, and even the dunghills were kept in a state of the greatest neatness.

"Good day, Father Fouan!" Jean shouted to **the old man** from the road, in a somewhat tremulous voice.

Fouan was sitting in the yard with his stick between **his legs.** His head was bent down, and he was so absorbed in his thoughts that he did not hear Jean's greeting. A second shout, however, made him raise his eyes, and presently he recognised **who was** addressing him.

"Ah, **is it you,** Corporal?" said he. "Are you coming to see us?"

His greeting was so pleasant and so destitute of spite that the young man went into the yard. He did not, however, dare to speak immediately on the subject which had brought **him** there. His courage failed him at the thought of openly confessing his intercourse with Françoise. They talked together of the fine weather, and the good it would do the grapes. If they only had another week of sunshine the wine would be excellent.

"What a happy man you must be!" said Jean, wishing to

make himself agreeable. "There isn't **such** another **fortunate** fellow in the whole country side."

" Yes, indeed."

" **And such** children, too, as you've got! You'd have a long **way to go** before you found better ! "

" **Yes,** yes, indeed ; **but** every **one has his troubles, you know."**

The old man seemed to have grown gloomy. Since he had taken up his abode with the Delhommes, Buteau had no longer paid him his share of the allowance, saying that he did not want his sister to profit by his **money.** Hyacinthe had never given him a copper from the **outset, and** Delhomme, now that he boarded and lodged with him, **had** discontinued all payments. It was not, however, the want **of pocket-money** that troubled the old **man, for he received from** Monsieur Baillehache a hundred **and** fifty **francs a year, just twelve francs and a-half** per month, the interest **on the sum realised by the sale of his** house. With this he **was quite able to pay for all his little luxuries, his** daily allowance of **tobacco, his drop of brandy at** Lengaigne's, and his cup of coffee at the Macquerons'. **Fanny, who was a very** careful house-wife, never **took any coffee or brandy out of her** cupboard unless **some one were** ill. **However, despite the** fact that he had the means of taking **his** pleasure away from home, and **wanted for** nothing in his daughter's house, the old man felt aggrieved **and seemed to** live in a constant state of discontent.

" Ah, yes, indeed," said **Jean,** unwittingly putting his finger on Fouan's **sore** place, " when one lives with other folks, it isn't quite the same as being in **one's own house."**

" You're quite right there. **Quite right !"** replied the old man in a grumpy voice.

Then he rose from his **seat, as though he felt a yearning** impulse to assert his independence.

" **Let us go and have a glass** together," he **said.** " **I dare say that I may offer that much** to a friend ! "

As he was entering **the house, however, his courage** began to ebb.

" Wipe your **feet,** Corporal," he **said,** " **for they** prate so much, you know, **about their** cleanliness and tidiness."

Jean went inside with an awkward gait, intending to make a clean breast of what he had to say before **the** others came back. He was surprised by the trim **order of** the kitchen. The pans were gleaming brightly, and there was not a speck of dust on the furniture, while the flooring was quite worn

with the amount of scrubbing it had received. Some cabbage-
soup of **the day** before stood warming by the side of a cinder-
piled **fire.**

" Here's your good health ! " said the old man, who **had**
taken a couple of glasses and a partially emptied bottle **from**
the side-board.

His hand trembled slightly **as he drained his glass,** as if he
felt an uneasy alarm about what **he was** doing. As he put the
glass down with **the air** of a man who has risked everything,
he abruptly exclaimed :

" Would you believe, now, **that Fanny has never once**
spoken to me since the day before yesterday, just because I
spat? Spat, indeed, just as though every one didn't spit ! I
spit, of course, when I feel so inclined ! One had better have
done with it altogether than **be** worried in this way ! "

Then filling his glass a second time, and delighted **at**
having found some one to whom he could pour out his complaints, he eased his mind, never giving Jean an opportunity **to**
get in a word. His troubles, however, did not appear to **be**
very grievous ones, and were born chiefly of the angry indignation of an old man, to whose feelings and faults but little
toleration was accorded, and upon whom his children were
trying to force a mode of life different from **what** he had been
accustomed to. However, he was as much affected by his
grievances, slight though they were, as he could have been by
actual cruelty and harsh treatment. A remark repeated in too
loud a tone was as hard for him to **bear as a blow** would have
been ; and his daughter made **matters** still worse by her **ex-**
cessive touchiness, which seemed to find an offence **and in-**
sulting intention in every little sentence which **she could twist**
into an equivocal meaning. The result of all this was that the
relations between father and daughter were becoming more
and more strained and embittered every day. **She** who formerly, prior **to** the division of the property, had certainly been
the kindlier hearted **of** the children, was now degenerating
into a cross-grained **shrew,** subjecting the old man to perfect
persecution, **constantly** following **him** about with her broom
and duster, and finding fault with him both for what he did
and for what he omittted to do. Without being subjected to
actual cruelty, Fouan was **kept** in moral **torture, over** which
he silently moaned in any quiet corner he **could find.**

" You must try to take it easily," **repeated** Jean, at each of
the old man's complaints. " An understanding can always be
arrived at with a little patience."

Fouan, however, who had just lighted a candle, now became angrily excited.

"No, no, I've had quite enough of it!" he cried. "Ah, if I'd only known what was in store for me here! It would have been better for me if I had died when I sold my house! But they are very much mistaken if they think they're going to keep me here! I'd rather go and break stones on the road."

He was almost choking with emotion, and he was obliged to sit down. Jean profited by the opportunity to speak out:

"I say, I wanted to see you," he began, "about what took place the other day. I have regretted it very much, but I was obliged to defend myself—wasn't I?—since an attack was made upon me. All the same, it was agreed between me and Françoise. But at present you are the only person who can put things straight. If you would go to Buteau's, you could explain matters to them."

The old man became very grave, He wagged his chin, and seemed embarrassed as to what he should say; however, the return of Fanny and her husband spared him the necessity of replying. The Delhommes showed no surprise at finding Jean in their house; they gave him their customary cordial welcome. Fanny, however, had immediately caught sight of the bottle and the two glasses on the table. She removed them, and went to get a duster. Then she spoke to her father for the first time for forty-eight hours.

"Father," she said, "you know that I won't have that kind of thing."

Fouan rose up, trembling with indignation at this public rebuke.

"At me again! Am I not even at liberty to offer a glass of wine to a friend? Go and lock your precious wine up! I'll drink water for the future!"

Fanny was now dreadfully put out by being thus charged with avarice.

"You can drink the house dry and burst yourself, if it gives you any pleasure to do so," she exclaimed, quite pale with anger; "but I won't have my table marked with your sticky glasses, just as though the place were a tavern."

The tears sprang to the old man's eyes.

"A little less anxiety about appearances, and a little more affection, would become you better, my daughter," he said.

Then, while Fanny was vigorously wiping the table, he went and stood in front of the window, and painfully overcome by his bitter thoughts, looked out into the dark night, which had now fallen.

Delhomme had avoided openly taking any part in the incident, but he had, by his silence, supported his wife's firm attitude. He would not allow Jean to go away before he had finished the bottle of wine with him, pouring the remaining contents into some glasses which Fanny brought to them on plates. She now began, in low tones, to defend her conduct.

"You've no idea of the trouble that old folks are. They're full of all sorts of whims and bad habits, and would rather die than be corrected. There's nothing really bad about my father; he's not strong enough for anything of that kind now; but I'd rather have to look after four cows than one old man."

Jean and Delhomme nodded their heads in acquiescence. However, Fanny's further remarks were interrupted by the sudden entrance of Nénesse, dressed in town-fashion in a fancy-patterned coat and trousers, bought ready-made at Lambourdieu's, and with a little hard-felt hat on his head. His long hairless neck, his blue eyes, and his pretty soft face, gave him a rather girlish look, as he stood there swaying from side to side. He had always had a horror of the soil, and he was leaving the next morning for Chartres, where he was going to take service in a restaurant where public balls were given. His parents had for a long time offered a strenuous opposition to his desertion of agriculture, but at last the mother on being coaxed had persuaded the father to consent. Since the morning Nénesse had been larking with his friends in the village, by way of bidding them good-bye.

He seemed surprised for a moment at finding a stranger in the room; but throwing off his hesitation, he exclaimed:

"I say, mother, I'm going to stand them a dinner at Macqueron's. I shall want some money."

Fanny looked at him keenly, and opened her lips to refuse his request. But she was so vain that Jean's presence checked her words. Their son might surely spend a score of francs without ruining them! And thereupon she left the room, stiffly and silently.

"Have you got any one with you?" Nénesse's father asked.

He had caught sight of a shadow by the door; and on taking a step forward, he recognised the young man who had remained outside.

"Oh! it's Delphin. Come in, my lad."

Delphin ventured into the room, excusing himself as he made his greetings. He was wearing a blue blouse and heavy field-boots. He had no tie round his neck, and his face was brown from exposure to the hot sun.

"Well," continued Delhomme, who had a high opinion of the lad, "will you be setting off for Chartres one of these days?"

Delphin opened his eyes widely, and then energetically exclaimed :

"Oh ! Curse it all ! No, I should be suffocated in the place."

The father cast a side-long glance at his son, and then Delphin, coming to the rescue of his friend, continued :

" It's all very well for Nénesse to go there, as he looks so well when he's dressed up, and can play the cornet."

Delhomme smiled, for he was very proud of his son's skill with the cornet. Fanny now returned with a handful of two-franc pieces. She slowly counted out ten of them into Nénesse's palm. All the coins were quite white from having been kept beneath a heap of corn. She never trusted her money to her wardrobe, but hid it away in small sums in odd corners all over the house, underneath the corn, or the coals, or the sand ; the consequence being that when she paid the coins away they were sometimes one colour, and sometimes another, white, black, or yellow.

" It will do, all the same," said Nénesse, by way of thanks. " Now, Delphin, are you coming ? "

Then the two young fellows went off together, and their merry laughter could be heard dying away in the distance.

Jean now emptied his glass, seeing that old Fouan, who had kept aloof during the whole of the last scene, had left the window to go out into the yard. Then he said good-bye to the Delhommes, and went out in his turn, finding the old man standing alone in the black night.

" Now, Fouan," said Jean, " will you go to Buteau's and arrange about my having Françoise ? You are the master, and you have only got to say the word."

" I cannot, I cannot," replied the old man in the darkness, with a jerky voice.

Then he broke out excitedly, and unbosomed himself of his brooding wrath. He had done with the Delhommes, he declared, and in the morning he would go to live with Buteau, who had offered to give him a home. Even if his son beat him, he would prefer that to being gradually tortured to death by his daughter's pin-thrusts.

This new obstacle exasperated Jean, and he spoke out bluntly :

" I must tell you, Monsieur Fouan, that Françoise and I have been together."

The old peasant uttered a simple exclamation: "Ah!" Then, after a moment's reflection, he added: "We had better wait. By-and-bye we'll see what can be done."

Fanny now appeared at the door, and called to her father to come in, as the soup was ready.

"Stick your soup behind!" shouted the old man, turning round to her. "I'm going to bed."

And, indeed, he went upstairs to bed, with an empty stomach, and boiling over with anger.

Jean walked slowly away from the farm, so absorbed in his vexation that he found himself in the level plain again without being conscious of the road he was taking. The blue-black sky gleamed with stars, and the night was close and hot. The immobility of the atmosphere told of the approach of a storm now passing afar, and the reflection of lightning could be seen towards the east. As Jean raised his head he caught sight on his left hand of hundreds of phosphorescent eyes gleaming like candles, and turning towards him at the sound of his steps. It was the sheep in the pen, alongside of which he was now passing. Then he heard Soulas ask in his drawling voice: "Well, my lad?"

The dogs, who were lying on the ground, had not stirred, for they had scented that Jean belonged to the farm. The little swineherd, driven from the wheeled hut by the excessive heat, was sleeping in a furrow; the shepherd standing quite alone on the cropped plain, which was now enveloped in night.

"Well, my lad, have you settled it?"

"He says," replied Jean, without even stopping, "that if she's in the family-way he'll see."

He had already stridden past the pen, when old Soulas's response reached him, sounding solemnly in the deep silence.

"That's true. You must wait."

Jean continued on his way. La Beauce lay stretched around him, buried in a leaden sleep; and there was an overwhelming sense of the silent desolation of the scorched stubble and the baked, parched soil in the burnt smell that floated in the air, and in the chirrup of the crickets which sounded like the cracking of embers among ashes. Nothing but the dim forms of the ricks rose above the melancholy nakedness of the plain; but every twenty seconds or so, low on the horizon, the lightning flashed in violet streaks of mournful aspect, which swiftly disappeared.

CHAPTER II.

THE next morning Fouan took up his abode with **the Buteaus.**
The removal of his belongings did not give him **any**
trouble, as they merely consisted of **a** couple **of** bundles **of**
clothes, which he carried himself in two journeys. **It was in**
vain that the Delhommes tried **to bring** about an **explanation;**
he went off without replying **to them.**
At Buteau's house he was **given the** big **room on the**
ground-floor—behind the kitchen—which **had** hitherto merely
been used for **the storage of potatoes and** beet-root for the
cows. This **room, unfortunately, was only lighted** by **a** small
window, **some six or seven feet** from **the ground,** and it was
always as dim **as a cellar.** Then, too, **the floor of** hardened
soil, the heaps **of** vegetables, and the **rubbish that had been**
tossed into the corners gave rise to **a copious moisture, which**
trickled down the bare plaster of **the walls.** The Buteaus,
besides, left everything just as **it** was, **and merely cleared out**
a corner for an iron bed, a chair, and **a deal table.** The old
man, **however,** seemed quite delighted.
Buteau now felt very triumphant. **Ever** since Fouan had
been living **with the** Delhommes he **had been mad** with jealousy,
for he knew very well **what would be said in** Rognes. It
would be reported from **mouth to mouth that it** made no
difference to the Delhommes having **to** keep **their** father; **but**
the Buteaus, poor folks, had barely sufficient for themselves.
So now, during the earlier time of Fouan's stay with him, he
plied him with **food** in the hope of fattening him, and thus
proving to the neighbourhood that **there** was no scarcity in
his house. Then, too, there were the hundred and fifty francs
a year, the proceeds of the sale of the house, which he felt sure
the old man would leave **to** the one who looked after him and
took care of him. Moreover, he reflected, **now** that Delhomme had no longer **to** support his father, **he would** doubtless
begin to pay his share **of** the allowance **again, two** hundred
francs a year, and in **this** expectation he **was not** disappointed.
Buteau **had** reckoned **upon** getting these **two** hundred francs,
he had calculated **everything,** and he flattered himself that he

would get the credit of being a good and dutiful son without
it costing him anything, besides having the prospect of reaping
a substantial reward later on ; to say nothing of the secret
hoard which, so he still suspected, the old man must possess,
though he had never been able to make certain on the point.

For Fouan the change was a perfect honeymoon. He
was feasted and **shown** to the neighbours. Didn't he look
plump and well ? the Buteaus asked. There were no signs of
wasting or decline about him, were there ? The little ones,
Laure and Jules, were always playing with him, keeping him
amused and delighted. But what, perhaps, pleased him most
was the liberty to indulge himself in his elderly whims and
ways, and to comport himself as he liked in the greater freedom
of this household. Though Lise was a good and cleanly house-
wife, she lacked Fanny's precise tendencies and susceptibilities,
and the old man was allowed to spit wherever he liked, to go
out and come in as the fancy seized him, and to eat **every**
minute if he chose, prompted by that spirit of the peasant who
cannot pass a loaf without cutting a thick slice off it. Three
months passed away in this pleasant fashion. It was now December ; and although the severe frosts froze the water in the
old man's jug at the foot of his bed, still he made no complaints. When it thawed, the moisture soaked through the
walls of his room, and ran down them in dripping streams ; but
he seemed to take all this as a matter of course ; he had been
brought up in the midst of similar discomforts. So long as he
had his tobacco and coffee, and was not badgered and worried,
he declared he needed nothing more.

Matters began to cloud **over,** however. **One** fine, **sunny**
morning, Fouan, on going back to his bedroom to get his pipe
—the others imagined that he had already left the house—
found Buteau there struggling to get the better of Françoise.
The girl, who was strenuously resisting him, without, however,
saying a word, pulled herself together and left the room, after
taking **the** beetroot which she had come to get for the cows.
The old man, on being left face to face with his son, became
angry.

" You filthy swine, to be going after that girl, with your wife
only **a** yard or two away ! " he cried. " And it wasn't she
who wanted you either ; I could see her wrestling with
you ! "

Buteau, however, who was still panting and flushed, received
the old man's remonstrances very badly.

" Why do you come poking your nose into everything ? " he

retorted. " You'd **better** shut your eyes and hold your jaw, or you'll find it the **worse for you**."

Since **Lise's** confinement, and **the** fight with Jean, Buteau had **been hotly** pursuing Françoise again. He had waited till his **arm was** strong, and now all over **the house he** systematically **made onslaughts on the girl, feeling** sure that if he could **but once overcome her** she **would belong to him in** future **as much as he wished.** Was **not this the best way of preventing the marriage, and of keeping both the girl and her land ?** His **passion for the two became intermingled, as it were ; his resolute determination to retain the land, and not to part with what was in his** possession, **being blended with his unsated sexual lust, now** exasperated **by resistance.** His **wife was becoming** enormously stout, a **perfect heap of flesh, and she** was **still suckling, with Laure constantly** hanging **at her** breasts **; whereas the other one,** the little sister-in-law, exhaled a most appetising **odour ; her bosom, moreover,** being firm and elastic **like** the **udder of a young heifer.** He didn't **turn** up his **nose at either of** them, by the way ; in fact, he wanted **to have them both, the one** soft and flabby, and the other firmly **built ; both of them were attractive in** their different styles. **He considered himself** quite a good enough cock to have two **hens, and he dreamt** of leading a pasha-like life, petted, caressed, **and** glutted with enjoyment. Why shouldn't he marry both sisters, if he could get them **to consent to his doing so ?** It seemed to him to be the best way of keeping things pleasant, and of **avoiding a division of the property,** which he dreaded as much **as though he were threatened with having one of his** limbs **wrenched off.**

Now, **whenever he and** Françoise found themselves alone for a moment, whether **in the** stable **or the** kitchen or anywhere else, it mattered **not where, there was a** sudden attack and defence ; Buteau rushing upon the girl, and the girl striking him. **It was** always the same short, sharp struggle ; the man seizing Françoise firmly **round the** waist, and the **girl, with** clenched teeth and **savage** eyes, forcing him to let go **his hold** by striking **him with full** force with her **clenched fist.** Not a word **was spoken by either** ; there was no **sound** but that **of** their hot **breath, a sort** of stifled panting, the deadened **stir of** a struggle. **Then Buteau** would with difficulty restrain a cry of pain, while the girl straightened **her** clothes and limped **away,** feeling bruised and sore. These scenes took place when **Lise was in** the next room, and sometimes even when she was **in the** same room, with her back turned to them while **she** arranged some linen in the wardrobe. It was as though the wife's presence excited the husband; he being at the same time **certain** of the girl's proud and resolute silence.

Quarrels, however, had broken out since old Fouan had seen them among the potatoes. **He** had bluntly told Lise everything that he had seen, **so** that she might prevent her husband from making any further **attempt** upon his sister-in-law. Then Lise, after shouting **to her** father to **mind** his own business, angrily attacked her **younger sister.** She had only herself to blame, she **cried, for** enticing the men on, and what **had** happened **to her was only what was to be** expected; **all the** men were swine. **In the evening,** however, Lise made **such a scene** with **Buteau** that she came out of her room the next morning with her eye **bunged up** and blackened by a heavy blow which he had dealt her **with his** fist during the discussion. After that there was constant quarrelling going on. There were always two of the inmates of the house trying to bite each other's heads **off,** the husband and wife, or the husband and his sister-in-law, **or else the two** sisters, **even if they** were not all three engaged **in** devouring one another.

Then it was that **the slowly** and unconsciously-developed hatred between Lise and Françoise became truly bitter. Their whilom tender affection **for** each other gave place to a savage feeling, which kept them irritated with one another from morning till night. The real and only cause of it all was this man, Buteau, who was like some poisonous leaven. Françoise, quite upset by his perpetual onslaughts, would have succumbed long previously if her will had not shielded her against desire each time he touched her. Her obstinate notions of abstract justice, **her** resolute determination neither to give up what was her **own nor** to take what was another's, brought her no little **trouble.** She was angry with herself for feeling jealous and execrating her sister for possessing this man, rather than have shared whom she herself would have died. When he pursued her, she angrily **retaliated by** spitting upon him, and sent him back, befouled **with her** saliva, to his wife. To do this seemed in **some way to** soothe her struggling desires: it was as though she had spat in her sister's face in her envious contempt, for the pleasure in which she had no share. Lise, on the other hand, was free from jealousy, feeling quite **certain that** Buteau had merely bragged in asserting that he **enjoyed** both of them—not that she believed **him** incapable of **such a** thing, but she was convinced that her sister was too **proud** to yield. The only grudge she felt against Françoise

was that, owing to her persistent rejection of Buteau's advances, the whole house was becoming a hell upon earth. **The**
fatter she grew, the more complacent she seemed to become,
taking a lively delight in existence, **and** egotistically craving
for pleasant, easy surroundings. It seemed to her the height
of folly that her husband and sister **should go on** quarrelling
like that, marring the sweetness of life, when **they** really had
everything that was necessary for their happiness. The **girl's**
perverse disposition was the sole cause of all the **trouble.**

Every night **when she went to** bed she **exclaimed to**
Buteau:

"It's **all** my sister! **But if** she causes **me any more**
annoyance, I'll have her turned out of the house!"

This course, however, would by **no means** have **suited**
Buteau.

"A **fine notion, indeed!** Why, we should have all the
country-side crying shame **on us!** What a plague you women
are! I shall have to duck **you both** in the pond till you can
live together in harmony."

Two **months more passed away, and** Lise, who was so
upset, might have sugared her coffee twice, as she said, without
finding **it to** her palate. She divined whenever her sister had
repelled some fresh onslaught of her husband's, for she then
had a further experience of his angry ill-temper, and she now
lived in constant dread of these repeated repulses, **feeling**
anxious whenever **she caught sight of him creeping up slily**
behind Françoise's skirts, and making **sure that when he**
came back again he would be in a violent temper, breaking
everything that came in his way, and making the whole house
wretched. These were hateful days to her, and she could not
forgive the obstinate wench for not restoring tranquillity.

One day **matters reached a terrible** pitch. Buteau, who
had gone down into the cellar **with** Françoise to draw some
cider, came up again so harshly repulsed, and in a state of
such raging anger, that for the merest trifle, just because his
soup **was** too hot, he hurled his plate against the wall, and then
rushed out of the room, after knocking Lise down with a blow
that would almost have killed an ox.

Crying and bleeding, she struggled on to her feet again,
with her cheek sadly swollen, and at once fell foul of her sister.

"You dirty drab!" she cried, "go to bed with him, and
have done with it! I'm sick to death of it all; and if you
persist in being obstinate, simply to make him beat me, I'll run
away!"

Françoise listened to her, quite pale and horrified.

" **As** true as God hears me, I'd rather do that," continued Lise. " Perhaps he'd leave us in peace then ! "

She fell down on a chair, and began to sob spasmodically. Her fat body, which had now begun to shrink, bespoke her recklessness, her one desire for quiet happiness, even at the cost of sharing her husband with another. She would still keep a share of **him herself**, and would have all that was necessary. People, **she** thought, had foolish ideas on these matters. A husband was not like a loaf, that **was** consumed at each **bit one** ate. Ought they not to agree amongst themselves, **and** live together in a friendly fashion ?

" Come, now, why won't you ? " she asked.

Choked with disgust, Françoise could only cry, angrily :

" You are more disgusting than he is ! "

Then she, too, went away to sob in the cow-house, where La Coliche gazed at her with her big, sad eyes. What roused her indignation was not so much the thing itself as the complaisant part she herself was to play—to surrender herself just for the sake of securing peace and quietness in the house. If Buteau had been her own husband, she thought she would never have consented to give up the least bit of him. Her bitter feeling against her sister turned into one of scorn and **contempt**, and she **vowed to herself** that **she** would be flayed alive **rather** than give way.

Her life now became still more embittered than before. She became the general drudge of the house, the beast **of** burden that came in for everybody's kicks and buffettings. She was reduced to the level of a hired servant overburdened with work, and continually rated, and thumped, and ill-treated. Lise would **not** permit her a single hour's leisure ; but made **her** rise before daylight, and kept her up so late at night that the poor girl often fell asleep without having enough strength left her to undress herself. Buteau took a malicious pleasure in torturing her by his familiarities, slapping her on the loins, pinching her thighs, and falling upon her with all sorts of savage caresses, which left her bleeding, and with her eyes full of tears, but as obstinately silent as ever. Buteau himself laughed, and derived some little satisfaction whenever he saw the girl growing faint, and with difficulty refraining **from** crying out from sheer pain. Her body was sadly discoloured and disfigured with bruises and scratches. In her sister's presence she especially forced herself to repress every sign of suffering, and to comport herself **as** though a man's

hands were not actually fingering her **flesh.** Sometimes, however, she could not altogether **control** herself, but replied
to Buteau's **attacks by** a swinging **blow.** Then there would
be a general engagement. Buteau would belabour Françoise;
while **Lise,** under the pretence of **separating** them, would
assail them both with vigorous kicks **from her** heavy boots.
Little Laure and her big brother Jules **yelled at the** top of
their voices, and **all the** dogs about the premises began **to** bark,
arousing **the pity of the** neighbours for Françoise. " **Ah, poor
girl!** " they **used to say;** " she **must have rare pluck to remain
in** such a place ! "

IIer remaining with **the Buteaus was, indeed, the standing
wonder of** all Rognes. **Why didn't she run away ? the neigh-**
bours asked of each **other. The** knowing ones **shook their**
heads ; **the girl was not of age, she** still had **another eighteen
months to wait. To run away** would be to her own **disadvan-
tage, for she could not take her** property with her, and she
showed her **sense by remaining.** Ah ! if Fouan, her guardian,
had **only supported her** cause ? But he himself hadn't too
easy **a life with his** son-in-law ; he had his own peace and
quietness to look **after, and,** for the sake of his own comforts,
was obliged to stand **aloof.** The girl, **moreover,** with her independence and self-reliance, had forbidden **him to interfere in**
her affairs.

Every outbreak now ended in the same **way.**

" Off you go at once ! **Clear out** with **you !** "

" Oh, yes, that's just what you'd like ! **Once I** was foolish,
and wanted to go away ; **whereas now** you may kill me if you
choose, but you won't get **me to** go. I shall stop here, and
wait for what belongs to me. **I** want the land and the house,
and I mean to have them, too ; every inch and every stone ! "

For the first few months Buteau's great fear had been that
Françoise might prove to be with child. IIe had counted the
days since he had caught her and Jean together among the
corn, and he kept casting anxious, sidelong glances at the girl,
for the arrival of a baby would have spoilt everything by
necessitating **his** sister-in-law's marriage. The girl herself
was quite easy about the matter ; but when she noticed the
manifest interest that Buteau showed in her figure, she took a
pleasure in puffing herself out, in order to deceive him. And
whenever he seized hold **of** her, she always imagined that he
was measuring her **with** his big fingers, **the** consequence of
which was that she ended by saying to him, with a defiant
air :

"**Ah,** there's one coming, and growing fast enough!"

One day she even folded up some towels and wrapped them round her. But in the evening there was almost a massacre. A feeling of terror now seized her at the murderous glances **which** her brother-in-law cast at her; she felt quite sure that if she had really been with child the brutal fellow would have struck her some foul blow in the hope of killing her. So she discontinued her acting.

"Go and get yourself a baby!" said Buteau one day to her, with a leer.

"If **I** haven't **got** one, **it's because I don't** choose," she replied, angrily, turning pale.

This **was** quite true. She obstinately rejected **Jean's** advances. Buteau, however, was none the less noisily **triumphant**, and he now began to abuse the girl's lover. A fine **sort of a** man he must be! he cried. Why, he must be rotten! He might be able to break people's arms by cowardly tricks, **but** he hadn't backbone enough about him to put a girl in the family-way! After that he began to overwhelm Françoise with sarcastic allusions **to** Jean, and indulged in filthy jokes about her own person.

When **Jean** heard **of** Buteau's remarks about himself he threatened to go **and** break his jaw. He was constantly haunting Françoise, **and beseeching** her to yield again. He'd soon let them see, he said, **if he couldn't** get a child, and a big one, too! His lustful desire was now heightened by anger. But the girl was always ready with some fresh reason for putting him off. She had no great dislike for him, it is **true,** she simply had no desire for him, that was all; and, indeed, she must have been completely free from all desire whatever not to have given way and surrendered herself when she fell into his arms behind a hedge, still flushed and angered by **one** of Buteau's onslaughts. Oh, the filthy swine! She always spoke **of him as a** filthy swine, boiling over with passion and excitement; but growing suddenly cold and calm again when Jean tried to profit by the opportunity. "No, no!" she cried. She felt ashamed at the thought of it. One day, when he pressed her very closely, she told him that he must wait a little longer, till the evening of their wedding-day. This was the first time that she had said anything that could be interpreted into an engagement, for she had hitherto always avoided giving Jean **a** definite answer when he asked her to be his wife. After that it was taken for granted that he should marry her, but not until she was of age, and became entitled to her property, in

a position to demand the rendering of accounts.   This, **Jean**
now felt, was the most prudent course : he advised the girl **to**
be as patient as she could in the meantime, and he ceased to
worry her with his importunities, except at times when the idea
of a spree was strong within him.   Françoise, feeling easy and
tranquil at the thought of a promise which was not to be
redeemed for a long time, contented herself by grasping his
hands so as to make him desist, and gazing at him with her
pretty, beseeching eyes, the look of which seemed to say that
she did not wish to risk **having a** child **unless its** father was **her**
husband.

Though **Buteau had now** satisfied himself that she **was not**
in the family-way, he was seized with **a** fresh fear that **she**
might become so if she saw anything more of Jean.   He was
still greatly bothered about the latter, for folks told him on all
sides that Jean had vowed he would get Françoise with
child.   So Buteau now exercised unremitting surveillance over
his sister-in-law from morning till night, forcing her to work
every single minute of the day, keeping her near-by under
threat of a hiding, just as though she had been some beast of
burden which could not be trusted to itself for a moment.
This was a great torture for the girl.   Either her brother-in-
law or her sister was continually behind her, and she could not
so much as go to the yard without being followed by **a spying
eye.**   At night they locked her up in her bedroom ; **one**
evening, after a quarrel, she even found **the** shutter of **her**
little window secured by a padlock.   In spite of all their strict
surveillance, however, she managed now and then to make her
escape, and upon her return there were very violent scenes,
the girl having to submit to the most disgusting questions, and
sometimes even to examinations of her person, Buteau seizing
hold of her by the shoulders while his wife partially undressed
her and scrutinized her.   All this brought her upon easier
terms with Jean, and she made several appointments with him,
taking a pleasure in thwarting her tormentors.   She might
even have yielded **to** her lover, if she had known that **Buteau**
and Lise were hiding behind them watching.   At all events,
she again repeated her promise, that come what might, she
would certainly be his in time; and she swore to him in the
most solemn way that Buteau had lied when he boasted that
he slept with both the sisters.   He had said that, she continued,
from mere braggartism, and in the hope of bringing about a
state of affairs which did not exist.   Jean, who had previously
been much tormented on this score, was quite satisfied with

Françoise's explanation, and felt much easier in mind. As they parted they kissed each other affectionately; and from this time forward the girl took the young man for her confidant and adviser, trying to see him as often as possible, and doing nothing without his sanction and approbation; while he, on his side, now made no further attempts upon her, but treated her like a comrade whose interests were identical with his own.

Every time now that she ran to meet him behind a wall, the conversation was of a similar kind. The girl excitedly tore open her bodice or pulled up her sleeves.

" See!" she exclaimed; " just look where that swine has been pinching me again!"

Then Jean would look at her flesh, remaining quite calm and unimpassioned.

" He shall be made to pay for it! You must show it to the women about here. But don't try to do anything to avenge yourself just at present. By-and-bye we will have justice, when we have got the power on our side."

" And that sister of mine," continued Françoise, " stands by and watches him. Only yesterday, when he sprang upon me, instead of throwing a pail of cold water over him, she never stirred."

" Your sister will have a bad time of it yet with this scoundrel. You needn't be afraid. He can't force you, so long as you refuse to let him have you, and you can get over all the rest. If we keep united, we shall beat him."

Although old Fouan did his best to steer clear of the quarrels, he was always made to suffer from them. If he remained in the house and tried to keep silent he was straightway forced into the row; and if he went out he found himself upon his return in the midst of a scene of confusion, his mere appearance often sufficing to rekindle the flame again. So far, he had never had any real physical suffering, but there now commenced a season of privations, of scantily-doled food, and a suppression of all his little indulgences. The old man was no longer stuffed with grub, as had been the case at first; every time that he cut too thick a slice of bread he was assailed with abuse. What a bottomless pit his belly was! they cried. The less he did, the more he stuffed and swilled! Every quarter, when he went to Cloyes to receive from Monsieur Baillehache the interest on the money realised by the sale of his house, he was strictly watched, and his pockets were emptied on his return. Françoise was reduced to pilfering her sister's coppers to buy him a little tobacco, for she herself was kept equally destitute of pocket-money. The old man also felt very uncomfortable in the damp room where he slept, now that he had broken one of the panes in the window, the aperture having merely been stuffed with straw to save the expense of a new piece of glass. Oh, those beastly children! he moaned; they were all equally barbarous! He growled and grumbled from morning till night, and bitterly regretted having left the Delhommes, sick at heart at now finding himself so much worse off than before. However, he concealed his feelings as far as possible, and it was only his involuntary exclamations that testified to their existence, for he knew that Fanny had asserted that he would return and ask her on his knees to take him back again. That remark made it impossible for him to return; it would sear his heart for ever, like a bar of iron that he could never remove. He would rather die of hunger and indignation with the Buteaus, so he told himself, than return and humble himself before the Delhommes.

One day as Fouan was returning from Cloyes, where he had been to receive his dividends from the notary, he sat down to rest on the slope of a dry ditch. Hyacinthe, who happened to be prowling about the neighbourhood examining the rabbit holes, observed the old man deeply absorbed in counting a number of five-franc pieces in his handkerchief. He immediately stooped down and crawled along in silence till he got close up to his father. As he lay there, concealed from sight, he was much surprised to see Fouan carefully knotting up a considerable sum of money, as much, probably, as eighty francs. Hyacinthe's eyes glistened at the sight, and his wolfish teeth were bared in a quiet smile. The idea of a secret hoard at once returned to his mind. The old man evidently had some secret investments, the dividends of which he received every quarter, taking advantage of his visits to Monsieur Baillehache to do so without any one being the wiser.

Hyacinthe's first impulse was to put on a piteous air and beg for twenty francs. On second thoughts, however, this seemed too paltry a scheme, and, thinking of a better plan, he glided away as noiselessly as he had come, with all the sinuous suppleness of a snake. Thus Fouan, who had now set off again, did not feel the least suspicion when, a hundred yards further on, he met his son, who seemed merely to be on his way back to Rognes. They walked on together and talked. The father fell foul of the Buteaus, who were destitute of all human feeling, and whom he accused of starving him to death. Then the son, with a filial, sympathetic air, his eyes damp with emotion, offered to rescue his father from these wretches by taking him to live in his own house. Why shouldn't he come? he asked. There was no worrying or hardship there; they led a merry life from morning till night. La Trouille cooked for two now, and she could just as easily cook for three. And fine cookery hers was whenever there was any money.

Astonished by his son's offer, and overcome with a feeling of vague uneasiness, Fouan shook his head in token of refusal. No, no, indeed. At his age a man could not flit about in that sort of way from one house to another, changing his mode of life every year.

"Very well, father; but think the matter over. I am quite sincere in my offer. My place will always be open to you. When you have had enough of those filthy scamps, come and live with me."

Hyacinthe then went off, perplexed and wondering, asking himself how his father spent his income, for he unquestionably had one. A heap of money like that coming in four times a year must amount to a nice sum—at least three hundred francs. If he did not spend the cash he must be hoarding it up somewhere. It was clearly a matter to be investigated. It must be a really magnificent hoard by this time!

That day—a mild, damp October day it was—when Fouan returned home, Buteau claimed the thirty-seven francs and a-half which the old man had received, as was usual, every quarter since the sale of his house. It had been agreed that Buteau should receive this money, as well as the two hundred francs paid yearly by the Delhommes, on account of the old man's board and lodging. That day, however, a couple of five-franc pieces had got mixed up with those which the old man had secured in his handkerchief; and when, after turning out his pockets, he only produced twenty-seven francs and a-half, his son burst into a violent fit of rage, treating him as though he were a thief, and accusing him of having frittered away the missing ten francs in drink and disgraceful dissipation. The old father, in a state of great consternation, and keeping his hand upon his handkerchief, full of alarm lest it should be examined, stammered out excuses, and swore that he must have lost the money in pulling out his handkerchief to blow his nose. Again the house was topsy-turvy until night.

What had put Buteau into such a savage temper was, that while bringing his harrow back he had seen Jean and Françoise hurrying away behind a wall. The girl, who had gone out on the pretence of getting some grass for her cows, had not yet returned, for she knew what kind of reception awaited her. The night was already falling, and Buteau, in a furious rage, went out every minute into the yard, and even on to the road, to see if the hussy were coming back. He swore at the top of his voice, and poured out a torrent of filthy language, without observing old Fouan, who was sitting on the stone bench, calming himself after the row, and enjoying the warm softness of the air, which made that sunny October like a spring month.

The sound of clogs was now heard coming up the slope, and Françoise made her appearance, bending double, for her shoulders were laden with an enormous bundle of grass, which she had tied up in an old cloth. She was panting and perspiring, almost hidden beneath her burden.

"So here you are, you filthy hussy!" cried Buteau. "You'll soon find out your mistake if you imagine you can make a fool of me, and go off with your lover for a couple of hours at a stretch, when there's work to be done here!"

Then he knocked her over on to the bundle of grass, which had fallen down, and threw himself upon her, just as Lise came out of the house to rave, in her turn, at the girl.

"Ah, you dirty jade," she cried, "let me get at you and I'll kick you. Have you no shame at all?"

Buteau had already firmly seized hold of the girl by her petticoats. His outbursts of rage always turned into sharp desire. While he attacked her he growled, nearly choking, with his face empurpled and swollen by the rush of blood.

"You damned cat!" he sputtered out, "I'll have my turn now! Heaven's lightning sha'n't prevent me!"

Then there began a furious struggle. Old Fouan could not see very well in the darkness, but he was able to observe that Lise was standing there, looking on, without making any attempt to interfere, while her husband struggled and fought with Françoise, over whom he sprawled. In the end, however, the girl managed to shake him off.

"You swine! You filthy swine!" she cried, in a panting voice, "you haven't succeeded, and you never shall—no, never! never!"

Then she strode up to Lise and addressed her in taunting triumph. Her sister was just silencing her by a heavy blow on the mouth, when old Fouan, having sprung up from his seat, quite disgusted and horrified at what he had seen, rushed forward, brandishing his stick.

" You filthy brutes, both of you ! " he cried ; " can't you leave the girl alone ? There's been more than enough of this ! "

Lights were now seen in the neighbouring houses. All these goings-on were beginning **to** make people feel anxious, **so** Buteau hurriedly drove his father and Françoise into the kitchen, where the candlelight showed Laure and Jules crouching in a corner, where they had taken refuge in their terror. Lise also had come in, bewildered and silent ever since the old man had issued out of the darkness. Fouan now addressed himself **to** her again.

" It was too revolting on your part," he said. " I saw you looking on ! "

Buteau now brought down his fist on the table with all his strength.

" Silence ! " he cried ; " the matter's done with. I'll smash the next one who says another word about it ! "

" And if I choose to speak," demanded Fouan, **in a** quavering voice, " will you smash me ? "

" You as soon as another. I'm quite sick of you ! "

Françoise bravely came forward between the two men.

" I beg of **you not to** interfere, **uncle.** You have seen that I am able to take care of myself."

The old man, however, pushed her aside.

" Leave me alone. At present you are not concerned. It is my business now. Ah, you would smash me, would you, villain ? " he cried, raising his stick. " **You** had better take **care** that I don't chastise *you !* "

But Buteau quickly snatched the old man's stick from him, and tossed it under the dresser. Then, **with** a wicked look in **his** leering eyes, he planted himself straight in front of Fouan, and spoke to him cheek-by-jowl.

" Will **you** just leave me alone, eh ? Do you think I mean to tolerate your airs ? **No, no.** Just look at me if you want to know who I am."

Both the men stood silently confronting each other for a moment or two, glaring fiercely, as though they hoped to cow each other by their glance. The son, since the division of the property, had grown stouter and stood more solidly on his legs, and his jaws seemed **to** project further from his bull-dog-shaped skull, with its narrow, retreating brow ; while the father, worn out by his sixty years of toil, had shrunk still further, his stoop increasing slightly day by day. His loins seemed broken, and his body bent forward towards the ground.

His huge nose was the only feature which retained its pristine shape and **proportions.**

"Who **you are?**" retorted **Fouan.** "**I know it** only too well. **I begot you.**"

Buteau sniggered.

"**Ah,** you shouldn't have done so!" he replied. "**Everybody** his turn. There's your blood in me, you know, and I **hate to** be interfered with. So once more I tell you, **leave me** alone, or it will be worse for you!"

"**For yourself, you mean. I never** spoke to my father in **such** a way."

"Oh, come now, that's a stiff 'un! Why, **you would have** killed your father if he hadn't died before **you had time!**"

"You lie, you filthy swine! And, by the **Lord God, you** shall **unsay** that this **very minute!**"

Françoise, for the second **time, now tried to interpose;** and Lise herself, **terrified by** this fresh outbreak, made a similar effort. **But the two men thrust** the women aside, and confronted **each other,** breathing violently in each other's faces, as **they** stood there, father against son, boiling over with that spirit of overweening despotism which the one had bequeathed **to the other.**

Fouan wanted to exalt himself by attempting to regain **his old absolute** supremacy as head of the family. For **half a** century, in the days when he still retained his property **and** authority, his wife, his children, and his cattle had trembled **at** his word.

"Say that you **have lied, you** filthy swine; **say** that you have lied, or I will make **you dance, as surely** as that candle is burning there!"

Raising his hand, he threatened his son with that gesture **which** had once made all **his** family sink to the ground.

"**Say that you have lied!**"

Whenever Buteau in **his** younger days had felt a buffet coming **he had raised his** elbow to shield himself, his teeth chattering the while; but now he merely shrugged his shoulders with an air of insolent contempt.

"You are **vastly** mistaken. You imagine that you frighten me," he said. "**It was all very well when** you were the master to treat us like that!"

"I am the master—the father!"

"Nonsense, you old joker; you are **nothing at all.** Ah, so you won't leave me alone, won't you?"

Then seeing that the old man's unsteady arm was descending **to deal a** blow, he seized hold of it, and crushed it in his rough grasp.

"What a pig-headed fellow you are!" he cried. "**Can't you get** it into that old noddle of yours that no one cares a fig **about** you now? Do you suppose that **you** are good for any**thing** at all? You are so much expense, **and** that's all! When a **man** has outlived his time, and passed **his land** over to others, he ought to be content **with** chewing his grub quietly, and keep from being a nuisance to other folks."

He shook his father to emphasise what he **was saying**; and then, giving **the** old **man** a final shake, **he hurled** him backwards, trembling and quaking, upon a chair near the window. And there **the** old man remained, half choking, for a moment, conquered and humiliated by the complete loss of his old authority. It was all over with him. He counted for **nothing** at all, now that he had stripped himself of his property.

Complete silence reigned in the kitchen, and all remained **in embarrassed** inactivity. The children had scarcely dared to **breathe for fear of** receiving a cuffing. Presently, however, **work** was begun again as if nothing unusual had happened.

"**Is** that grass going **to be** left out in the yard?" asked Lise.

"I'll go and put it **in the cowhouse**," replied Françoise.

When **she** had returned, **and after** they had dined, Buteau, who was quite incorrigible, thrust his hand into her bodice, to hunt for a flea which she said was biting her. She no longer showed any signs of annoyance, and, indeed, **she** joked about it.

Fouan had never moved, but still remained stiff and silent **in his** dark corner. Two big tears were rolling down his **cheeks.** He called to mind the evening when he had broken **with the** Delhommes; and now again on this evening he ex**perienced the same** bitterness and humiliation at finding himself **no longer the** master; **the same** anger which had then made **him obstinately refuse to eat.** They had called to him three **times,** but **he** refused to join in the meal. Presently he sprang up, and went **off** to his bedroom. The next morning, as soon as it was light, he left the Buteaus, to take up his quarters with Hyacinthe.

CHAPTER III.

HYACINTHE was a very windy individual, **and he was constantly** going **off** in explosions, which kept the **house in a** lively state, for **he** never allowed one of these reports **to pass** without indulging **in** some facetious **jest.** **He** had a **contempt** for **your** timid little **reports, suppressed as** much as **possible,** and sounding **as though they were** ashamed of themselves. He himself never **let off aught but loud** detonations, crisp and crackling, **like gun shots; and every time, as** he **raised** his leg with a gesture **of self-satisfied complacency, he** summoned his daughter in **a tone of urgent command and with an air** of serious gravity.

"Come here, you troll, come here at once!"

As soon as the girl hurried forward, the explosion **was** allowed **to take** place, going off with such a sharp vibrati**ng** **report that** La Trouille quite started at the noise it **made.**

"Quick, run after it and catch it, and see if it's **come out** straight!"

At other times when she approached him, **he would give** her his hand.

"Pull hard, now, you jade! **Make it go off with** a good crack!"

Then, when the explosion took **place** with all the sputter and row of a tightly jammed charge, he exclaimed:

"Ah, that's a hard one! but I'm much obliged to you all the same."

Then at other times he would hold an imaginary gun to his shoulder and pretend to take aim carefully; and when the explosion had taken place, he would cry out:

"Run off and retrieve, you lazy bitch!"

La Trouille used to laugh till she fell down on her buttocks, almost choked. It was a continual fresh and ever increasing merriment. **Used as she was to the sport, the** final explosion, with **its** comical eruptive noisiness, never **failed to** shake **her** with laughter. Oh, **what a** funny fellow **he was, this father of hers!** Sometimes he would talk of a lodger **who had fallen** into arrears with his **rent, and** whom he **was obliged to eject;** **at** other times he would turn round with **an air of surprise, and** bow gravely, as though the table had wished him good-morning; and at others he would trumpet out a series of salutes for his reverence the priest, his worship the mayor, and the ladies. It seemed almost as though the fellow's belly was a sort of musical-box, from which he **conld** extract any sound he chose; **and** one day, when the company at **The** Jolly Ploughman **at** Cloyes wagered a glass that he could not let off six discharges one after another, he victoriously won the bet. This accomplishment of his had become a source of honour and glory. La Trouille was quite proud of him; and, as soon as ever he raised **his leg, she** began **to** wriggle. **She was** constantly admiring **him, and his** prowess inspired her with mingled **con-** sternation and affection.

On the very evening of the day **when old F**ouan took up **his** quarters at the Château, as the old burrow in which the poacher buried himself was called, at the very first meal which the girl served to her father and grandfather, standing behind them in the respectful attitude of a servant, there were loud and merry explosions. The **old** man had given his son five francs, and a pleasant odour spread about—that of the kidney-beans and **veal and** onions, which the girl knew so well how to cook. As she was bringing **in** the beans she almost broke the dish in her excitement. For, before sitting down to table, Hyacinthe let off three sharp, regular reports.

"The salute for the feast!" he exclaimed. "Now we can begin!"

Then, bracing himself up, he gave vent to a fourth single discharge, very loud and odoriferous.

"That's for those brutes, the Buteaus!" **he cried.** "Let them stuff **it** down their throats!"

Fouan, who had maintained a gloomy demeanour ever since **his arrival,** now suddenly broke out into a snigger, and **signified his** approbation by nodding his head. This seemed to have put him **at his ease. He,** too, in **his** time, had been noted as a joker, and his children had grown up quietly at home in the midst of the paternal bombardments. He rested his elbows on the table, and gave himself up to a pleasant feeling of enjoyable comfort as he sat opposite that hulking rascal Hyacinthe, who gazed at him **in** return with his damp eyes and his **air** of jovial scampishness.

"**Ah!** God Almighty, dad. We'll enjoy ourselves. You **shall see my** dodge. I'll undertake to make you merry. Will you **be any** better off when you're underground with the moles, for having denied yourself a tit-bit up here?"

Though he had been a sober man all his life, Fouan, who now felt a craving to drown his worries, replied in the same strain :

" Well, yes, indeed, it's better to eat up everything rather than **leave** any for the others. Here's your good health, my lad ! "

La Trouille now served **the veal and onions.** There was a momentary silence, and Hyacinthe, to prevent the conversation dropping, let fly a prolonged flourish, which passed through the straw seat of his chair with all the varied modulations of a human cry. **Then he** immediately **turned to his daughter with** a gravely interrogative air.

" What did you say ? " he asked her.

She **could** make **no** reply, **but was obliged to sit down and** hold her sides. She was still **more upset, however,** by some final facetiousness **between the father and son, after** the veal and **the cheese had been cleared away,** and they began to smoke **and help themselves to** the bottle of brandy which had been **placed on the table.** They sat silently for some time, **boozy with drink.**

Presently, Hyacinthe slowly raised his leg, and let off a loud explosion. Then looking towards the **door :**

" Come **in !** " he cried.

Fouan, **who felt himself** challenged, and who had for a **long** time past been regretting his loss of form, now **once more** regained the accomplishment of his youthful days, and, raising his leg, he **also** broke **out into a noisy explosion.**

" Here **I come !** " he exclaimed.

Then they both clapped their hands, slobbering and laughing. They enjoyed **it** immensel**y.** But **it** was too much for La Trouille, who had **fallen down on the** floor, and was so **shaken** with wild spasms of laughter that she, too, gave vent **to a** slight explosion, but soft and musical, like a note from a **fife in** comparison with the sonorous, organ-like sounds of the two men.

Hyacinthe sprang up with an air of indignant protest, **and stretched out** his arm with a tragical gesture of authority :

"**Out of the room** with you, you dirty sow. **Out of the** room **at** once, you stink-pot ! I'll teach you to show proper respect to your father and grandfather ! "

He had never tolerated this familiar**ty on** her part. It was only for people of a certain age. He cleared the air as it were with **his** outstretched hand, and pretended to be nearly choked by **the** little flute-like sound. His own, and his father's, he said, **only** smelt of gunpowder. Then, as the culprit, who had turned very red, and was **quite** upset by her forgetfulness **of** etiquette, hung back and showed **a** disinclination to leave, he, himself, cast her out of the room with an energetic shove.

"**Go and** shake your petticoats, you filthy sow, and **don't venture in** here again for another hour, till you've got yourself well ventilated!" said he.

That day was the **commencement of** a careless life full of jovial merriment. The **girl's bed-room was given up to the** grandfather. It was one **of the divisions of the old** cellar, cut off by **a wooden partition.** La Trouille herself, relinquishing her room with **the** greatest **willingness, now took up her quarters at** the far end of **the cellar, in** an excavation in **the rock, which** led, so the local **legends said, into some** immense subterranean **caverns which had been blocked up by** land-slips. **Unfortuu- ately this fox-hole of** a Château was getting more deeply buried **every winter by the action** of the heavy **rains, which** flowed **down the steep slope of the hill and** swept the **earth and pebbles along with them.** The old ruin, with its **ancient foundations and** rough repairs, would have disappeared alto- **gether if the aged** lime-trees that had been planted over it had **not kept the stones together by** their thick, spreading roots. However, when **the spring-time** came round it was a charmingly fresh **little spot, a kind** of grotto lying hid beneath a tangle of **briars and hawthorns.** The sweet-briar that grew iu front of the window was starred over with **pink** blossoms, and the door was wreathed with **a drapery of wild honey- suckle,** which had to be lifted like a **curtain before one could** enter the place.

It was by no means every evening that La **Trouille was called** upon to cook kidney beans and veal and **onions.** This only happened when the old man had been induced **to** part with a five-franc piece. Hyacinthe **never** attempted to obtain the money **by any** show of force or **harshness; he** worked upon his father's love **of** good **living and his paternal** feelings to despoil him of **his money.** There was always a good deal **of** feasting **at the commencement** of each month, when Fouan received **his sixteen francs'** allowance from the Delhommes; and every quarter, **when the notary** paid him his dividend of thirty-seven francs and **a-half, there** was the most uproarious junketting. At first the **old** man, clinging to his ingrained habits of parsimony, would only hand out **half a** franc at a time, expecting that amount to last for **a long** while; but, by- and-bye, he gradually surrendered himself to **his** scamp of a son, who flattered him **and** wheedled him, and sometimes so

worked upon **his feelings** by his extraordinary stories that
he was dissolved **in tears,** and easily prevailed upon to part
with two **and** three francs. He, too, **then took to** stuffing
himself with food, saying that it was **best to enjoy** one's-self
while **one** could.

In justice **to** Hyacinthe, however, it must **be said that he
fairly** divided everything with the old man ; **and, if he robbed
him,** he also kept **him** amused. The **lazy fellow, with his**
knavishness, was, **at all** events, a better **sort than** Buteau, **and**
indeed he often boasted to that effect. **At first, when his belly
was** delighted with fat living, he dropped **all thought even**
about his father's supposed hoard, and did **not make the least**
attempt to discover anything concerning it. **Old Fouan was**
quite free to do as he pleased so long as he **cheerfully provided**
the means for their festive junkettings. **It was only during**
the second fortnight of the month, when **the old man's pockets**
were **quite empty, that his son** indulged **in speculations as to**
where the money **of which he had** caught a glimpse **could be**
hidden away. He **could not** get hold **of a copper of it. He**
grumbled at **La Trouille** who served **him dish after dish of**
potatoes without **butter ; and, as** he felt **a painful void in his**
belly, **he reflected that it was really most idiotic for them
to remain** on such short commons simply for the sake of
hoarding up some money. It would certainly be necessary **to**
unearth that hoard some day and have a fling with it.

Still, **even** on the evenings when he **had fared most**
wretchedly, and when he felt utterly weary **and tired out, he**
bravely struggled **against circumstances, and was as genial**
and hilarious **as if he** had just **made an excellent dinner :**
restoring the general gaiety by a cannonade of heavy guns.

"There, that's **for** the turnips, La Trouille, and that's for
the butter ! " he cried.

Fouan, too, kept brisk and cheerful even during those painful times—the last days of the month—for the daughter and the
father then scoured the **country for** the means of keeping the
pot boiling, **and the** old man, who was gradually induced to
join them, ended by employing his time in **the same way. He**
had become angry when he first saw La Trouille come home
with a fowl which she had fished up **from** over a wall with a
piece of looped string ; but on a second occasion she made him
shake with laughter by attaching a hook baited with some
meat to the end of a string, which she concealed among the
branches of a tree, allowing the baited hook to dangle down in
front of a troop of **ducks** who were taking a walk. One of

them suddenly rushed forward, and swallowed meat, hook, and **string at** a bolt. Then **it** immediately rose in the **air**, being **sharply** pulled up by the girl, before it was able to utter a **single** quack. This was not a very honest proceeding certainly ; **but** they argued that animals which lived out-of-doors belonged **to** those who could catch them, **and that so** long as one did not steal money, one's honesty could not be impeached. From that time **the** old man took some interest in the adventures of the young marauder, **who** performed **some scarcely** credible feats, such as **stealing** a **sack of** potatoes and then getting the owner of them **to help her to** carry **them home;** milking **cows out at** pasture **into a bottle;** and sinking the laundresses' **linen to** the bottom **of the** Aigre by loading it with stones, and then going and fishing **it up** again **during** the night.

She was continually **to be** met on the roads, her geese affording her a pretext for her perpetual wanderings, and she **would** sit for hours on the slope of a ditch on the look-out for **an** opportunity, with a sleepy, innocent air, as though she had **not a** thought in the world beyond attending to her geese. She often even **made** use of these latter as watch-dogs, the gander giving her notice, by his hissing, of the inopportune approach of any **one** who might surprise her at work. She was now eighteen **years old,** but she was scarcely any taller than she had been **at twelve;** being still **as** slight and supple as a hazel-branch, with **her** kid-like head, her green eyes, and her large mouth, twisted towards the left. Her little, childish bosom had grown hard beneath her father's old blouses, without **in** any way developing. She was more like a boy than a girl, **and** seemed to care about nothing save her geese. However, although she scoffed contemptuously at men, this did not prevent **her,** when **she** got larking with some lad of her own age, from **ending** with a little amatory **amusement, almost** as a matter **of** course, **for it seemed to** her quite natural, and no consequences **ever followed. She** was lucky enough to keep clear of the tramps **and** vagrants that passed along the roads, for grown-up **men,** finding nothing tempting about her, left her alone. As **her** grandfather said, amused and won over by her quaint ways, apart **from the** fact that she was given to thieving and didn't care much about decency, she was a rum sort of girl, **more** decorous and less disreputable than might have been expected.

Fouan found especial amusement in accompanying Hyacinthe in his prowling rambles about the fields. Every peasant, even the most honest, is at heart a poacher, and the old man took

a deep interest in the setting of snares, and the laying of lines,
and in all the various other ingenious devices of this campaign
of ruses, this continual warfare carried on against gamekeepers
and gendarmes. As soon as the laced hats and yellow shoulder
belts of the latter were seen emerging from a lane and making
their way through a corn field, the father and son, lying on
some sloping bank, pretended to be asleep. Presently, however,
the son would creep on his hands and knees along the ditch,
and take up his traps; while the father, with his honest elderly
countenance, would keep a careful watch on the receding hats
and shoulder belts.

There were some splendid trout in the Aigre, which they
sold for forty and fifty sous apiece to a dealer at Châteaudun,
but the fish were so artful that it was necessary for the men to
lie flat on their stomachs on the grass watching them for hours.
They often, too, sallied out as far as the Loir, from whose
slimy bed some very fine eels were to be obtained. When his
lines brought him nothing, Hyacinthe had a very simple
plan for securing a haul. During the night he plundered the
fish-preserves of the river-side residents, Fishing, however,
he only indulged in as an occasional amusement; the pursuit
of game was his absorbing passion. He ravaged the neighbourhood for miles around, and no prey was too humble for
him. He would snare quails as well as partridges, and even
starlings as well as larks. He seldom fired a gun, for the
report of firearms carried too far over a level expanse. There
was not a single covey of partridges that ever rose from the
clover and lucern without his recognising it, and he knew perfectly well when and where he could easily lay his hands upon
the young birds, drowsy with sleep and soaked with the night-
dew. He was extremely clever in liming twigs for the capture
of larks and quails, and he hurled stones with a deadly aim at
the dense flocks of starlings which the high winds of autumn
brought into the district. For twenty years past he had been
exterminating the game of the neighbourhood, and there was
now scarcely a rabbit to be seen amongst the brushwood about
the Aigre, a fact which extremely angered the local sportsmen.
It was only the hares that escaped him. There were very
few of them, however, and what there were scampered safe
from his pursuit over the open country, where it was too risky
to follow them. He smacked his lips at the thought of the few
hares which were to be found on the La Borderie land, and
every now and then he risked being sent to gaol, by sending
one rolling over with a shot from his gun. When Fouan saw

him going out with his gun, he always refused to accompany him. It was too hazardous and foolish, he said ; he would certainly get caught one day or other.

And caught he did get, as was only natural. Farmer Hourdequin, exasperated by the destruction of his game, had given the most stringent orders to Bécu, and the latter annoyed at never being able to catch any one, had determined to pass his nights on a stack and keep watch. One morning, just at daybreak, the report of a gun, the flame of which flashed in front of his face, awoke him with a start. It was Hyacinthe, on the look-out behind the stack, who had just killed a hare at short range.

" Ah, God Almighty ! it's you, is it ? " cried the rural constable, seizing hold of the gun which the other had laid down so as to pick up the hare. " Ah ! you scamp, I ought to have guessed it was you ! "

They were boon companions at the taverns, but in the fields they could not meet without danger ; the one being constantly on the point of arresting the other, and the latter being determined to wring his neck.

" Well, yes, it's I ! " replied Hyacinthe ; " and I don't care a fig for you. Come, give me my gun back ! "

Bécu was·already regretting his capture. He generally turned to the right whenever he saw Hyacinthe on his left. What was the good of having a bother with a friend ? he used to say. But this time his duty was evident, and it was impossible for him to close his eyes. And, besides, when a man is taken red-handed, the least that can be expected of him is to be civil !

" Your gun, you scamp ! No, I'm going to keep that and take it to the mayor. Now, you be quiet, and don't try to play any of your tricks, or I'll let you have the other barrel in your guts ! "

Hyacinthe, deprived of his gun and in a great rage, thought for a moment of making a spring at the other's throat. However, when he saw him directing his steps towards the village, he followed him quietly, still holding the hare dangling from his hand. The two men walked on for nearly a mile without speaking, but casting fierce furtive glances at each other. A violent scene seemed inevitable every moment, though both of them were regretting what had happened more and more acutely every minute. How unfortunate it was that they had come across each other in that way !

As they passed behind the church, at a couple of steps from the Château, the poacher made a last effort.

" I say, old fellow, don't be stupid ; come inside, and have a glass."

" No, I must go and lay an information," replied the rural constable stiffly.

He was obstinate, like an old soldier whose orders are his only law. However, he stopped, and, as his companion took hold of his arm and tried to induce him to come with him, he ended by saying :

" Well, if you've got pen and ink, it will make no difference, I don't care where the statement is drawn up, whether in your house or elsewhere, so long as it is drawn up somewhere."

When Bécu arrived at Hyacinthe's abode, the sun was just rising. Old Fouan, who was already smoking his pipe at the door, guessed what had happened, and began to feel very uncomfortable, the more so, as matters assumed a serious aspect. Some ink and a rusty old pen were hunted up, and the constable, spreading out his elbows, and assuming an air of deep thought, began to rack his brains for suitable phrases. In the meantime, La Trouille, at a word from her father, brought a quart of wine and three glasses ; and by the time Bécu had got to his fifth line, he accepted a bumper feeling exhausted by his struggle with the complicated statement of facts. Then the situation gradually became less strained. A second quart of wine was produced, and then a third. Two hours later, the three men were talking together in loud and friendly voices. They were all very drunk, and they had quite forgotten the incident of the morning.

" You blessed cuckold ! " suddenly cried Hyacinthe to Bécu, " you know that I do as I like with your wife."

This was quite true. Since the day of the local fête he had tumbled Bécu's wife in quiet corners, looking upon her as an elderly person with whom no particular show of delicacy was necessary. Bécu, however, whose wine had made him irritable, now lost his temper. Although he was able to tolerate the poacher's relations with his wife when he was sober, the mention of them wounded his feelings when he was drunk.

" You filthy swine ! " he bellowed out, brandishing an empty bottle.

Then he hurled the bottle, which broke against the wall, just missing Hyacinthe, who went on with his maudlin chatter, smiling a weak, tipsy smile. To appease the cuckold, they settled to remain there together, and eat the hare at once. Whenever La Trouille cooked a "civet," a pleasant odour spread from one end of Rognes to the other. It was a rough

sort of **feast,** which lasted all day. They were **still at table,**
sucking **the** bones, when darkness closed in. **Then they**
lighted **a** couple of candles, and still sat on. Fouan **found**
a couple of two-franc pieces, and sent the girl off **to buy a**
quart of brandy. The **men were** still sipping their liquor
after the whole village **had** fallen asleep. As Hyacinthe's
fumbling fingers were groping about for something with which
he could light his **pipe, they came across** the unfinished report,
which was lying on **the corner of the table,** stained with **wine**
and gravy.

" Ah, it's **true, we ought to get this** finished **! " he** stammered
out, his belly shaking **with** tipsy laughter.

As he looked at the paper he tried **to** think **of some facetious**
trick by which he might show **his** deep contempt **both for the**
report **and the law. Then** he suddenly raised **his leg, and,**
slipping the paper underneath him, he let off **on the face of it**
a heavy, sonorous discharge, one of those explosions **which, he**
used to say, came from a tightly-loaded mortar.

" There, it's signed for you now ! "

They all began to laugh merrily, even Bécu himself. There
was no dulness that night at **the** Château !

It was about this time that Hyacinthe made a friend. **As**
he went to hide one evening in **a** ditch till the gendarmes **he**
had espied passed by, he found it already occupied **by** another
man, who, like himself, **was** desirous of escaping observation.
They began to talk. The stranger seemed **a** pleasant fellow.
His name, he said, was Leroi, but he **was** generally known **as**
Canon. He **was** a journeyman carpenter, **and** had **left Paris**
some two years before on account of certain little incidents **in his**
career which had had troublesome consequences, preferring **to**
live in the country, and to wander from village to village,
staying a week here and a week there, and going about to the
different farms **to** offer his services whenever patrons were
scarce. Trade, **he said,** was shocking bad just now, and he had
taken to begging **on the** high **roads as he** tramped along. He
had been living **on stolen vegetables** and fruit, hustled about
from pillar to post, and was only too happy whenever he **was**
able to get a night's lodging behind a hay-rick.

It must be said, however, that his appearance **was not** calculated to inspire any **confidence.** His clothes were all in rags,
and he was very dirty and very ugly, bearing **evi**dent marks of
a life **of** wretchedness and vice. His face, fringed with a
scanty growth of hair, was so fleshless **and** pallid that the
women shut their doors and windows at the mere sight of him.

What was worse, however, than his appearance was his conversation. He talked about cutting the throats of all the rich folks, and of having, some fine day, a glut of licentious pleasure with the wives and wine of other people. He let fall all kinds of threats in a tragic voice, clenching his fist, and launching out into wild revolutionary theories which he had picked up in the slums of Paris. He ranted, for instance, in the most virulent language about the rights of the people, and their coming enforcement, his flood of words quite frightening and dazing the peasants who heard him. During the last two years the inhabitants of the farms had been accustomed to see him make his appearance at night-fall asking for a corner and a bundle of straw for a bed. When he sat down by the fire he quite froze every one's blood by his terrible words. Then the next morning he went off, to reappear again a week later on, at the same gloomy twilight hour, and with the same prophecies of approaching ruin and death. And it was because his gloomy and uncanny appearance about the neighbourhood caused so much fear, and excited so much angry indignation, that he was now always sent about his business as soon as possible.

He and Hyacinthe, however, took to each other at once.

"Ah," cried the latter, "what a mistake I made in not cutting every throat in Cloyes in '48! Come along, old fellow, and let's have a glass together!"

He then took Canon off to the Château, where he made him sleep that night, inspired with more and more respectful admiration for the tramp the longer he listened to him. He considered him to be a man of superior mind, one who knew what he was talking about, with his plans for reorganising society at a single swoop. Two days afterwards, Canon went away. A fortnight later, however, he appeared again in the twilight, and after that he constantly dropped in at the Château —eating and sleeping there as though he were at home, and swearing each time he came that the well-to-do classes would be swept clean out of existence before another six weeks had gone by. One night when the father was out poaching, Canon made an attempt to ravish the daughter; but La Trouille, scarlet with shame and boiling over with indignation, scratched him and bit him so severely that he was obliged to let her go.

Fouan was no fonder of Canon than La Trouille was. He accused him of being an idle good-for-nothing, and of trying to bring about a state of general rapine and bloodshed; and, whenever the vagrant was in the house, the old man grew quite

gloomy and silent, and went out of doors to smoke his pipe.
There was another matter, too, which was disturbing his life
again, and causing an increased disagreement between himself
and his son, indisposing him for all his former hilarious merriment.
Hitherto Hyacinthe, in parting with his share of the land, had
never disposed of it to any one save his brother Buteau or his
brother-in-law Delhomme, to whom indeed he had sold the
greater portion, a little bit at a time. Fouan had always given
his signature, as was necessary, without saying a word in
opposition. So long as the land remained in the family, he
had no objection to its being sold. But now a troublesome
question arose about the last field, upon which the poacher had
borrowed money. The mortgagee was threatening to put it
up to auction, as he had not received a copper of the interest
that had been agreed upon. Monsieur Baillehache had been
consulted, and had declared that the field would have to be
sold, and sold at once, if they did not wish to be ruined by law
costs. Buteau and Delhomme, unfortunately, refused to buy
it, being angrily indignant with the old man for allowing himself to be preyed upon by that rascal his elder son ; indeed they
had sternly resolved to do nothing for him as long as he remained where he was. The consequence was that the field
was now to be sold by order of the authorities ; writs and
stamped paper were already flying about. It would be the
first piece of land that had gone out of the family. The old
man could get no sleep at nights for thinking of it. This
land which his father and grandfather had looked at with such
longing eyes, and had worked so hard to obtain; this land
which, when acquired, had been guarded as jealously as a wife,
was now being frittered away in law-costs, passing into the
possession of another, some neighbour, for half its value ! The
old man groaned with rage, and he was so heart-broken that
he sobbed like a child. Oh, that scamp of a poacher !

There were now several terrible scenes between the father
and son. The latter, however, never replied, but allowed his
father to exhaust himself in reproaches and lamentations. The
old man would stand there vociferating and unburdening himself of his wrathful indignation in the most tragic fashion.

" Yes, you are a murderer ! It is just as though you had
taken up a knife and sliced off a bit of my flesh ! Such a
splendid field as it is ! There isn't a finer anywhere ! A field
where anything will grow by just being planted ! What a
poor miserable creature you must be to allow it to go to
another ! Ah, good heavens, to another ! The very thought of

it going to an outsider makes my blood turn! And it's all
caused by your cursed drunkenness! You have drunk the
land away, you filthy, swilling swine!"

Then, as the old man almost choked with anger, and nearly
sank down from sheer exhaustion, his son quickly answered:

"It's really very foolish of you, dad, to worry yourself in
this way. Fly at me as much as you like, if it relieves you
in any way at all; but you really ought to take things more
philosophically. One can't eat the land, you know! You'd
pull a very wry face if any one served you with a dish of soil,
wouldn't you? I've borrowed money on it, because five-franc
pieces are the crop it best suits me to raise on it. If there's a
surplus of a few crowns, we'll drink them! That's the sensible
way to look at things. We shall have more than enough of
the soil when we're dead!"

On one point, however, father and son were perfectly in
accord, and that point was their common detestation of Vimeux
the bailiff—a shabby little fellow who was entrusted with the
discharge of such duties as his colleague of Cloyes refused to
undertake, and who had ventured one evening to come and
leave a formal notification of judgment at the Château.
Vimeux was a very dirty-looking little creature, a bundle of
yellow beard and whiskers, from the midst of which there
peered forth a red nose and a pair of bleared eyes. He was
always dressed in shabby-genteel fashion—a tall hat, black
trousers, and a frock-coat, but these garments were most
shockingly worn and stained. He was notorious in the neighbourhood on account of the terrible thrashings he had received
from the peasants every time that he had been compelled to
serve them with unpleasant documents in places distant from
all help and succour. Stories were told about sticks being
broken over his shoulders, of his being ducked in ponds, of his
being pursued for a couple of miles and kept running at full
speed by the continued application of pitch-forks; and of a
certain sound thrashing that had been administered to him by a
mother and her daughter, after his trousers had previously been
let down.

On the evening when Vimeux paid his visit to the Château,
Hyacinthe was just entering the house with his gun. Old
Fouan was sitting on the trunk of a tree smoking his pipe and
watching the bailiff's approach.

"See the disgrace you are bringing upon us, you rascal!"
the old man growled to his son.

"Just you wait a moment!" returned the poacher.

Vimeux, on catching **sight of** the gun, came to a stand-still some thirty yards away. **The** whole of his dirty, shabby, black-clothed **person** quaked **with** fear.

"Monsieur Hyacinthe," **he** began in **a** weak, quavering voice, "I have come about **the** business **you** are aware of. I leave this here. Good evening."

He then laid the official document **on a** stone, and was already hastily retiring, **when the** poacher **called** out to him:

"Do you want **me to come and** teach **you** politeness, you confounded paper-stainer? **Just be good** enough to bring that paper **to me!**"

Then, as **the wretched** man stood **speechless and rooted to** the ground **with terror,** daring neither **to** advance **nor to** retreat an **inch,** the poacher took aim at him with **his gun.**

"I'll just send you a little bit of lead," **he cried,** "if you **don't** make haste and do what I tell you. **Look sharp now, take up** your paper, and bring it here! Oh, you **must come nearer than** that; and nearer than **that.** Hurry along now, **you miserable eunuch, or** I shall fire!"

Frozen **and pale with terror,** the bailiff tottered along on his short legs. **He** cast **an imploring** glance **at** old Fouan. But **the** latter **went on quietly** smoking **his** pipe, meditating savagely **anent the** expenses **attaching to the** law, and full of bitter rancour against the **man who, in the** eyes of the peasantry, personified them.

"Come along, or I shall **fire! There, that's better now;** you have managed to get **here at** last. **Now, give me your** paper. No, not in that way, **with** the tips **of your fingers as** though you were reluctant to part with it. **Give me it politely** and cordially. There, that's very nicely done!"

Vimeux, paralysed with fright **at** the sight of the grinning **poacher,** stood blinking his eyes **and** shaking in his shoes at **thought of the** blow or cuff which **he** felt sure **was** coming.

"**Now then, turn round!**"

The poor **fellow knew only too well what** this meant, and he remained **stock-**still, nervously **twitching** his posterior.

"Turn round, **or** I'll **come** and turn you myself!"

The luckless bailiff felt **that he** could do nothing but submit to his fate; and with **a pitiably** wretched air he turned himself round, and presented to **view his** poor little fleshless posterior, **as** shrunken as that **of** a half-starved tom-cat. Then the poacher, taking a vigorous spring, brought his foot to bear full **on** the **centre** of Vimeux's buttocks, and with such energy that he sent the luckless bailiff reeling over on to his nose fully four yards away. **The** poor fellow painfully struggled on to his feet again, **and bol**ted off in a state of abject terror as he heard the **poacher yelling after him :**

" **Look out ! I'm going to fire ! "**

Hyacinthe had indeed raised his gun to his shoulder, but he then contented himself with lifting his leg and letting off such a violent explosion that Vimeux, terrified by the report, fell headlong on to the ground again. This time his black hat fell off, and rolled away amongst the stones. He ran after it, picked it up, and then bolted off faster than before, pursued by a constant cannonade from the poacher, and a jeering accompaniment of noisy laughter which drove the wretched fellow quite crazy. Careering wildly down the slope, looking like some hopping insect, he had got a hundred yards away, but the echoes still repeated the sound of the fusillade. In fact, all the country-side reverberated with it, and there was a final terrific discharge just as the bailiff, who, in the distance, now looked about the size of an ant, disappeared into Rognes. La Trouille, who had hastened out on hearing the noise, lay down on the ground, holding her sides and clucking like a hen; while old Fouan took his pipe out of his mouth so that he might laugh more at his ease.

The following week it was necessary for the old man to make up his mind to give his signature, so that the land might be sold. Monsieur Baillehache had found a purchaser, **and it** seemed most **prudent to follow** his advice. It was consequently settled **that the father and** son should go to Cloyes on the third **Saturday in September, the** eve of Saint Lubin's **Day, which was one of the two fêtes of** the town. The old man relied upon getting rid of his son **in** the midst of the holiday-makers and going to fetch the dividends of his hidden investment, as he had done since July. They were to make the journey both ways on foot.

As Fouan and Hyacinthe were standing before the closed barrier at the level-crossing just outside Cloyes, waiting for a train to pass, they were joined by Buteau and Lise, who drove up in their cart. A **violent** quarrel **immediately** broke out between **the two brothers, and** they **hurled** volleys of filthy abuse at each **other till the** gate was **opened ;** Buteau, as his horse carried him **away down** the hill **on the** other side, even turned round, his blouse puffed out by **the** wind, and hurled behind him a volley of insults which **he** would have done better to keep to himself.

" Go along with you, you worthless fellow, I am supporting

your father!" roared Hyacinthe with all his might, making a
speaking-trumpet of his two hands.

Fouan felt very unhappy **when** he reached Monsieur
Baillehache's office in the Rue **Grouaise,** and the more so as it
was full of clients, people **who were** taking advantage of
market-day to transact their business. The old man and his
son had to wait for nearly **two hours.** The scene recalled to
Fouan's mind that Saturday when he had decided upon the
division of the property. It would have been better if he had
hanged himself rather than done that. When the notary at last
received them, and the signature had to be affixed, the old man
took out his spectacles and wiped them; but his tearful eyes
fogged the glasses, and his hand trembled so much that it was
necessary **to** place his fingers on the very spot where he was
to inscribe his name, which he proceeded to do, making a lot of
blots. It tried him so much that he was now perspiring and
trembling, and glancing about him in dazed confusion, just **as
though** he had been undergoing a surgical operation, as if
he were a man who, after having a leg amputated, looks
about him for the severed limb. Monsieur Baillehache administered a severe lecture to Hyacinthe, and then dismissed
them both with a **dissertation** upon the law. The division
of property, so he declared, was immoral, and it would certainly
be one day made illegal, to prevent it from over-riding the
system of inheritance.

After leaving the notary's, Fouan contrived to give his son
the slip in the crowd in the Rue Grande, just by the door of
"The Jolly Ploughman." Hyacinthe, indeed, played into **his
father's** hands, and quietly smiled to himself, for he felt quite
sure what the old man's purpose was. Fouan at once made
his way to the Rue Beaudonnière, where, in a bright-looking
house, with a courtyard and garden, lived Monsieur Hardy,
the tax-collector, a stout, jovial person, with a florid face and
a carefully-trimmed black beard. He was greatly feared by
the peasants, who accused him of upsetting them with his
threats. **He received his visitors in** a narrow office, cut at wain
by **a balustrade, on one side of** which he himself sat, while
those who came to see him remained on the other. There **were
frequently** a dozen people there at once, standing crowded
together. At the present moment, however, Buteau, who had
just come in, happened to be the only person there.

Buteau could never make up his mind to pay his taxes
promptly and at once. **When** he received the demand-note
in March he got into **a bad** temper for a week, and stormed

angrily, and in turn, at the land-tax, the head-tax, the tax on
personal property, and that on doors and windows. His
greatest wrath, however, was poured out upon the growing
increase in the total amount, which got more and more
every year. Then he waited till he was served with a
free summons. This gave him an additional week. Then he
paid a twelfth part of the taxes every month, whenever he
went to market; and every month all the old torture of mind
began over again. He felt quite ill on the eve of paying an
instalment, and he went off with his money in as miserable a
frame of mind as though he were going to execution.
Oh, that damnable government! It robbed everybody!

"Ah, is that you?" Monsieur Hardy exclaimed, cheerily,
at sight of him. "I'm glad to see you here, for I was just
going to put you to the expense of a summons!"

"That would have capped the business!" snarled Buteau.
"But you must understand that I'm not going to pay those six
francs increase on the property-tax. It's really most unjust!"

The collector began to laugh.

"What, are you going to begin all that discussion over
again? It is always the same old story every month. I have
already explained to you that it is obvious that the planting of
your meadow by the Aigre must have increased your income.
Oh, we know very well what we are about, I can assure
you!"

Buteau, however, boiled over with angry remonstrances.
His income was increasing in a pretty sort of way, forsooth!
His meadow had once measured a couple of acres, but the river
had altered its course and robbed him of a great slice of his
land, and yet he still was forced to pay the tax on two acres!
Was that justice?

Monsieur Hardy quietly replied that he had nothing to do
with the survey, and that Buteau must get that altered if he
wanted his tax lowered. Then, under the pretence of explaining details to him, he overwhelmed him with a flood of
figures and technical terms which were completely unintelli-
gible to an outsider.

"Well, it makes no difference to me whether you pay or
not," he said in conclusion, with a bantering smile; "I shall
merely have to send the bailiff to you if you don't."

Frightened and abashed, Buteau now quickly cooled down;
recognising that, as might lay on his opponent's side, there was
no other course for him but to yield. However, the fear which
forced him to yield only increased his long-standing spite

against the vaguely understood and complicated system of rule
to which **he** was forced **to bend—the** government—its courts
and **the** staff of officials, all loafing gentle-folks, as he was
wont **to** say. Very reluctantly he drew out his purse with
trembling fingers. He had received a large number of coppers
in the market, and **he fingered every coin** before letting go his
hold of it. He counted **the sum** three times over, paying it all
in coppers; **and** the size **of** the pile gave an additional wrench
to his heart-strings. With sad and troubled eyes he was
watching the collector **put the** money away in **the** safe, when
old Fouan made his appearance.

The old **man had** not recognised his son from behind, **and**
he was **seized with** consternation when Buteau turned round.

" Ah, how do you do, Monsieur Hardy ? " he then stammered
in confusion. " I was passing by, and I **thought I'd** just **come
in and wish** you good morning. I **don't often** get a chance **of
seeing you** now."

Buteau, however, was **not** deceived. He said **good**
morning, **and went** away **as** though he were in a hurry, but
five minutes later he returned again, to ask some question
which he pretended he had forgotten before ; and he did this
just as the collector was handing Fouan his quarter's dividend,
seventy-five **francs, in** five-franc pieces. Buteau's eyes
glittered, but he pretended not to notice what was going on ;
indeed he carefully avoided looking at his father, and affected
not to have seen the old man throw his handkerchief over the
coins, and then fish for them, and thrust them down to the
bottom of his pocket. This time they both **left** together :
Fouan greatly distressed in mind and casting suspicious glances
at his son, while Buteau was in an excellent humour and mani-
fested a sudden renewal of affection for his father. He kept
close to him, and insisted upon taking him **off** with him in his
cart, in which, indeed, he drove him to " The Jolly Ploughman,"
where **they found Hyacinthe** in company of little Sabot, a vine-
dresser **from** Brinqueville, **a** well-known facetious character,
who, like **his** companion, was windy enough to keep a mill
turning. **Just** now, upon meeting, they had wagered ten
quarts of wine as to which of them could blow out the greater
number **of** candles. Several friends, laughing noisily and manifesting great enthusiasm, had accompanied them into a room at
the back of the premises. A circle had been formed, and one of
the rivals was placed on the right and the other on the left,
ready to commence operations. Each of them had his own
special candle, and just then little Sabot had succeeded in ex-

tinguishing the flame ten **times, w**hereas Hyacinthe **had** scored only **nine** times, having once failed in producing **the necessary amount of** wind. He appeared annoyed; his reputation was at stake. It would **never do** for Rognes to be beaten **by** Brinqueville! So he blew **as never blacksmith's bellows had** blown—Nine! ten! **eleven! twelve!** The drummer from Cloyes, who had **been appointed to re-light the candle, was** himself almost blown **away.** Little Sabot, **who had with** difficulty extinguished **his tenth candle, was** now quite exhausted, but his **opponent triumphantly blew out another couple,** which he bade the drummer light for a final demonstration ; and, when they were lighted, they burned with a bright yellow flame, the colour **of gold, which rose up like the sun in its glory.**

" What a wonderful chap he is !" the spectators cried. " What guts he has got ! He ought to have a medal ! "

The company shouted and laughed and cheered till they almost split their throats. They felt a good deal of real admiration and envy, for a man must be very solidly built to be able to contain so much wind, and to discharge it just as he pleased. They spent the next two hours in drinking the ten quarts of wine, and nothing else was discussed but the feat they had just witnessed.

While his brother **was** fastening **up his trousers again,** Buteau gave him **a friendly** slap across **the buttocks, and this** victory, so pleasing **to the** family pride, **seemed to have put** them on the best terms again with **each other.** Old Fouan related, in the **most** sprightly fashion, **a story of his** youthful days, of the time when the Cossacks **were in La Beauce.** One of them had gone **to sleep on the bank of the Aigre with** his mouth open, and Fouan recounted how he had so freely discharged himself thereinto that he had buried the sleeping man's face up to the hair.

The market was now drawing to a close, and the company separated, all very drunk.

Buteau took Fouan and Hyacinthe **off with him in his cart,** and Lise, to whom **her** husband had whispered **a** word or two, made herself **very pleasant** and agreeable. They all petted the father, and made a great **fuss with him ;** and there was no more quarrelling. The elder son, who was now getting sober again, was deep in **thought.** He felt **sure** that the reason why his younger brother **was** manifesting such unusual amiability was that he, also, had discovered the secret payments made by the collector. And then he sadly reflected that even if his

scamp of a brother had hitherto had the delicacy to refrain from
plundering his father's hoard, he certainly would never be
weak enough to let it fall into any one else's hands. He determined, however, that as the family were now on good terms
together once more, he would diplomatically, and without showing any signs of vexation, make a full inquiry into this important matter. When Rognes was reached, and the old man
asked to be set down, the two brothers sprang out of the gig,
and rivalled each other in their demonstrations of respect and
affection.

"Lean on me, father."

"Give me your hand, father."

They then carefully assisted him out of the trap, and the old
man remained standing between them, full of uneasy consternation, for he now felt sadly certain that they had discovered
his secret.

"What has come over you all?" he asked. "Why you seem
to have suddenly grown very fond of me?"

Their amiability, indeed, quite frightened him. He would
rather have seen them comporting themselves as usual towards
him—rough and harsh, and wanting in respect. He foresaw
a world of trouble in store for him, now that they knew
of his secret hoard; and he returned to the Château in a very
distressful state of mind.

It happened that Canon, who had not made his appearance
for the last two months, was now there, sitting on a stone
and waiting for Hyacinthe's return. As soon as he caught
sight of him, he called out:

"There's that daughter of yours in Couillard's wood, and
there's a man with her."

The father almost exploded with rage and indignation,
and the blood rushed angrily to his face.

"The lewd hussy," he said, "to disgrace me in that way!"

He took down a big carter's whip which was hanging
behind the door, and then hurried off down the stony bank to
the little wood. La Trouille's geese, however, kept guard
over her like faithful watch-dogs, when she was up to her pranks.
The gander immediately sniffed the father's approach, and
darted forward, followed by the whole flock. Raising his
wings and stretching out his neck, the male bird broke out
into a continuous, menacing hiss, while the rest of the flock,
forming into line of battle, also stretched out their necks,
and opened their great yellow beaks, ready to bite. The
poacher cracked his whip at them, and the sound of a hasty

retreat then became audible behind the bushes. La Trouille had heard the warning, and had made **her** escape.

When Hyacinthe restored the whip to its place, **he seemed** overcome by a deep philosophical sadness. It migh**t be that** his daughter's persistent lewdness filled him with **pity** for human passions, or it might merely be the natural reaction after his triumphant hilariousness at Cloyes. Shaking his rough scampish-looking head :

" Bah **!" he** cried to Canon, **"** it isn't worth that much ! "

And **then,** raising his leg **over** the valley that was now **buried in shadow,** he **let** off **a** violent and contemptuous deton- **ation, as though he wished** to overwhelm **the** neighbourhood.

CHAPTER IV.

IT **was now early** in October. The vintage was about to commence; a **week** of merry joviality, during which such families as had fallen out were in the habit of getting reconciled over pots of new wine. For a whole week Rognes stunk of grapes, such a quantity of which was eaten that the women were pulling up their petticoats and the men letting down their trousers behind every hedge ; while the lovers, with juice-stained faces, kissed each other greedily amid the vines. The evil of all this was that the men got drunk and the girls **in** the family-way.

On the morning after his return from Cloyes, Hyacinthe duly began to hunt for his father's hoard ; for in accordance with all probability the old man did not carry his money and vouchers **about** with him ; he must hide them away in some secret corner. But although La Trouille assisted her father in his search, they turned the house topsy-turvy without any result, and this despite their cunning and practice in marauding. It was not until the following week that **the poacher,** chancing to remove from a shelf a cracked earthenware pan, which was no longer used, discovered therein, beneath **some** lentils, a packet of papers very carefully enclosed in a piece **of** gum-covered canvas which had been torn out of an old **hat.** There was not a single coin, however. The cash must **be** hidden somewhere else, and there must be a pretty pile of **it,** the poacher reflected, for his father had spent nothing for **the** last five years. There was the scrip there, however, re-presenting three hundred francs a year in five per cent. Rente. As Hyacinthe was counting the bonds and examining them, a piece of stamped paper, covered with large handwriting, fell from the packet, and the perusal of this document quite stupefied the poacher. The murder was out now ! He **had discovered** where all the money had gone !

It was the most amazing story possible. A month after **the** old man **had** divided his property among his children he had fallen ill ; brooding sadly over the fact that he had now absolutely nothing of his own, not even so much as a handful

of corn.   He could not go on living in this way, he moaned to
himself; and it was then that he was guilty of a sad piece of
folly—folly as infatuated as that of those lustful old men who
spend their last coppers in secretly stealing back to some drab
who has gone into other keeping.   Despite all his earlier shrewdness, Fouan had allowed himself to be completely gulled by
that cunning old sharper, Saucisse.   That earth-hunger, that
furious desire for possession which feverishly racks the bodies of
all the old peasants who have spent their lives on the soil, had
so completely mastered him, that he had entered into a written
agreement with Saucisse to pay him fifteen sous every day as
long as he lived, on condition that he, Saucisse, left him upon
his death an acre and a quarter of land.   A pretty bargain this,
considering that Fouan was seventy-six, and that Saucisse was
ten years younger.   As some justification, however, of Fouan's
conduct, it should be said that Saucisse had been crafty enough
to take to his bed just before the bargain was struck; and he
had coughed so distressingly, seeming so near the point of
death, that Fouan, goaded on by his covetousness, and thinking himself the craftier of the two, had eagerly pressed for the
completion of the agreement.   The moral to be drawn was,
that it was preferable to take on with a wench rather than sign
an agreement; for the payment of the daily fifteen sous had
now been going on for five years, and the more Fouan paid,
the more lustful he grew, and the more passionately he yearned
for the land.   What! after cutting himself free from all the
weary bondage of the soil, when he had nothing more to do
than to spend the remainder of his days in peaceful tranquillity,
watching others wearing themselves out in tending the
ungrateful earth, he had once more returned to her, so that she
might finish him off.   No, really, wisdom was seldom to be
found among men, either young or old.

   For a moment Hyacinthe felt inclined to appropriate both
the scrip and the agreement, but his courage failed him.   Such
a deed would have necessitated flight.   Then, full of angry
disappointment, he placed the papers under the lentils again, at
the bottom of the pan.   His exasperation was so great that he
could not hold his tongue.   The next day all Rognes knew of
the agreement with old Saucisse, and the daily payment of
fifteen sous for an acre and a quarter of poor land that was not
certainly worth three thousand francs.   In five years nearly
fourteen hundred francs had been paid, and if the old rascal
lived for another five years, he would be pretty certain to keep
both the field and its value.   Old Fouan was plentifully chaffed

about his bargain, as was natural. Since he had divested himself **of all his** property, he had been unceremoniously passed by **on the roads,** but now he was again saluted and addressed deferentially since it was known that he had an invested income, and might possibly come in for some landed estate.

His own family seemed especially revolutionised by the discovery. Fanny, who had previously been on very cold terms with her father, annoyed at his having gone to live with his disreputable **elder** son instead of returning to her house, now brought him some linen—some old shirts of **her** husband's. She was actuated less **by** motives of self-interest than by an unconscious respect **for the head** of **the family, who once more** acquired some importance, as he was in the **possession of** property. Her father, however, was very hard and unbending, and he could not refrain from alluding to that cutting speech of hers as to his begging on his knees to be taken back again. **He had never forgotten it; and, on** receiving Fanny, he **exclaimed: "So it is** you, then, who are coming on your knees **to get me back?"** The young woman took this rebuff very **badly, and** when she got home again she wept with shame and anger. **She** was touchy to an extreme; a look sometimes sufficed to wound her; and honest, hard-working, and well-to-do though she was, she had fallen out with almost all the country-side. After that, Delhomme undertook **to pay** the old man's allowance, for Fanny swore that she **would never** speak a word to him again.

As for Buteau, he quite astonished everybody one day **by** making his appearance at the Château, coming, so he said, **to pay a** little visit to his father. Hyacinthe sniggered, brought **out the brandy** bottle, and they had a glass together. But his **sneering surprise** turned into absolute amazement when he saw **his brother produce** two five-franc pieces and lay them down **on the table.**

"We must settle accounts, father," said Buteau. "Here is the last quarter's allowance."

Ah! the scamp! he had never paid his father a copper for **years past, and now** to do this he must have designs upon him. He was no doubt offering him this money in the hope of getting him to return to his house. The truth is, that as Fouan reached out his hand to take up the coins, Buteau pushed it **aside and** hastily picked up the money himself.

"What I mean is, that I want you **to** know I have the cash all ready. I will take care of it, and **you** will know where to find it whenever you want it."

Hyacinthe began to scent mischief and grow annoyed.

" I say," he began, "if you want to get father away from
me——"

" What ! you're not jealous, **are** you ? " Buteau laughingly
replied. " Don't you think, now, that it would be more natural
if **father** stayed a **week** with me, and then a week with you,
and so on ? Eh ? suppose you cut yourself in two, dad ! Well,
here's your health in the meantime ! "

Before taking his leave, he invited them to **come and assist
at** the vintaging the next day, and he promised that they should
stuff their bellies full **of** grapes. **Indeed,** he made himself so pleasant and agreeable, that the other two **confessed**
that although he was a great rascal he was **nevertheless an**
agreeable fellow ; of course, providing that one **didn't let him**
take one in. Then they willingly accompanied **him part** of
his way home.

Just as they reached the bottom of the hill they met Mon-
sieur and Madame Charles, accompanied by Elodie, who were
returning **to** Roseblanche, after **a walk** along the bank of the
Aigre. They were all three of them **in** mourning **for** Madame
Estelle, as the girl's mother was called. She had died in July,
from over-exertion ; indeed, every time **that** the grandmother
had returned from Chartres she had always reported that her
poor daughter was killing herself, such **a** deal of trouble did
she take to maintain the reputation of the establishment **in the**
Rue aux Juifs, **with** which **her worthless** husband occupied
himself less and less. Keen, **indeed, had been** Monsieur
Charles's emotion at the funeral, to which he had not dared to
take the young girl, **who had** only been informed of **her**
bereavement when her mother had already lain for three **days**
in the grave. Great also **had** been Monsieur Charles's heart-
pangs when, for the first time for many years, he had again
gazed upon Number **19,** that house **at the** corner of the Rue de
la Planche-aux-Carpes, with its yellow-washed front and closed
green shutters ; **that** house which had been the work of his life,
and which he now found hung with black drapery, the little
door standing open, and the passage **barred** by the coffin,
standing between four lighted tapers.

He was deeply touched by the manner **in which** the whole
neighbourhood shared in his grief. The ceremony passed off
in the most satisfactory manner. When the coffin was brought
out of the passage into the street, all the women of the neighbourhood crossed themselves, and the funeral procession made
its **way** to the church amidst signs of general mourning. The

five women of the house were there in dark dresses, and com-
ported themselves with an air of decorum, as was generally
remarked that evening in Chartres; and one of them even shed
tears at the grave-side. In that matter, indeed, Monsieur
Charles had every reason for satisfaction, but how he had
suffered the next morning when he had a chat with his son-in-
law, Hector Vaucogne, and visited the house. It had already
lost all its brilliancy, and the many laxities which he noticed,
laxities which **would never** have been tolerated in his own
time, fully indicated **the** absence of masculine authority. He
observed, however, with pleasure that the decorous behaviour
of the five women at the funeral had created such a favourable
impression in the town that the establishment remained full
all the week. Upon leaving Number 19, full of uneasy
thoughts, he gave Hector plainly to understand that, now poor
Estelle was no longer there to look after affairs, it was his duty
to reform and settle down seriously to the business of life, if
he did not wish his daughter's fortune to be lost.

Buteau, on seeing the Charles family, at once invited them
to come to the vintage, but they declined on account of their
mourning. Their faces were very sad, and they spoke and
moved about in a weary, heart-broken fashion; they could not
be prevailed upon to promise anything further than just to go
and taste the new wine.

"**It** will be **a little** change **for this poor darling,**" said
Madame Charles; "and she has so few amusements here, since
we took her away from school. She's seventeen, you know,
now, and we couldn't keep her there always."

Elodie listened with downcast eyes, blushing shyly. She
had grown very tall and slim, as pale as a lily vegetating in the
shade.

"And what are you going to do with this tall young lady?"
Buteau asked.

The girl's blushes deepened; and her grandmother replied:

"**Ah!** that I can **scarcely** tell you. We shall leave her
perfectly free to follow her own inclinations."

Meanwhile Fouan had taken Monsieur Charles aside.

"Is he looking after the business?" he asked with an air of
interest.

Monsieur Charles **shrugged his** shoulders, **and** assumed an
aggrieved air.

"Ah, that's just **what is troubling** us **so much.** I saw a
person from Chartres this morning. It's very sad! The
house **is** done for! The supervision is so wretched that

fights go on in the **passages, and fellows actually walk away** without **paying."**

Then **he crossed his arms and drew a** long breath **to ease** himself **of a** new worry which had been stifling him, **by reason** of **its** enormity, ever since the morning. "And **would you** believe it," he resumed, "the reprobate goes to the café, **now?** Going to a café, indeed, when there is one in his own house!"

"He must be daft, **then!**" fiercely exclaimed Hyacinthe, who had been listening.

They now relapsed **into** silence, **for** Madame **Charles and** Elodie were drawing near with Buteau. They **were speaking** of the dear departed, **and the** young girl **remarked how sad it** made her **that** she had **not been able** to **kiss her poor mother.**

"But it **seems she died so suddenly,"** she added, with her innocent air, **"and they were so busy in the shop——"**

"Yes, making confectionery for **some christening parties,"** hastily interrupted Madame Charles, **with a sidelong glance,** full of meaning, at the others.

Not one of them smiled. **They all preserved a** gravely **sympathetic air.** The girl **had** bent her gaze upon a ring she was wearing, and she kissed it, with her eyes full of **tears.**

"**This** is all I have that belonged to her," she said. "**Grand**mother took it from her finger and brought it and **put it on** mine. She **wore it** for twenty years, and I shall **keep it all my life."**

It was an old wedding-ring, of **common make, that** had once been engine-turned, but it was now so **worn that nearly** all the turning had disappeared. Its **aspect seemed to tell** that **the** hand on which it had **grown so thin had** never recoiled **from** any **task** or duty, but **had been ever** active and energetic, washing glasses and pots, making beds, rubbing, cleaning, dusting, and leaving no corner untouched. This ring, indeed, seemed **to tell** so much, **and it** had left particles of **its gold** in so many scenes of the past, **that** the men gazed at **it** with **earnest** eyes in silent emotion.

"**When** you have worn it away as much as your mother did," said Monsieur Charles, choking with **a** sudden spasm of grief, "you will have really deserved a rest. If it could speak, it could tell you that money is earned by hard work and orderly habits."

Elodie burst into **tears,** and pressed **the** ring to her lips again.

"I want you, you know, to be married **with** this ring when **we find** you a husband," said Madame Charles.

The mention of marriage, however, was too much for the sorrowing girl, and she was so overcome with confusion that she threw herself wildly on her grandmother's breast, and hid her face out of sight.

"Come, now, don't be so shy and nervous, my little pet," said Madame Charles, smiling, and trying to calm the girl. "You must get accustomed to the idea: there's nothing dreadful about it. You may be quite sure that I wouldn't say anything improper before you. Your cousin Buteau asked just now what we were going to do with you. Well, we shall begin by marrying you. Come, now, dear, look up, and don't rub your face against my shawl like that. It will make your skin quite red and inflamed."

Then she added in a low tone, speaking to the others, with an air of profound satisfaction:

"What an innocent darling she is! She is guilelessness itself!"

"Ah, if we hadn't this dear angel," said Monsieur Charles, "we should be quite overcome with trouble—on account of the matter I mentioned to you. By the way, with all this worry my roses and pinks have suffered this year; and I can't tell what has gone wrong with my aviary, but all my birds are ailing. I have only found a little consolation in fishing; yesterday I caught a trout weighing three pounds. One ought to do one's best to be happy when one is in the country, don't you think so?"

Then they parted, Monsieur and Madame Charles renewing their promise to go and taste the new wine. Fouan, Buteau, and Hyacinthe walked on a few yards in silence, and then the old man gave utterance to what they were all three thinking.

"Well," he exclaimed, "the youngster who gets her with the house will be a lucky fellow!"

Bécu, who with the office of rural constable combined that of public drummer, had duly beaten his instrument by way of proclaiming the commencement of the vintage; and on the Monday morning the whole country-side was in a state of excitement, for every inhabitant had his vines, and not a single family would on any account have missed going to the slopes of the Aigre that day. The excitement of the village had, however, been brought to a climax by the fact that the new priest—for Rognes had at last allowed itself the luxury of a priest—had arrived on the previous evening at nightfall. Owing to the darkness he had only been indistinctly seen. The tongues of the villagers were consequently wagging most energetically, and the more so as the circumstances attending the priest's arrival were somewhat peculiar.

For some months after his quarrel with the inhabitants of Rognes, the Abbé Godard had persistently refused to set foot in the village. He only baptized, confessed, and married those who came to seek his services at Bazoches-le-Doyen. If any one had died at Rognes, they would doubtless have crumbled away waiting for him ; though this point was never clearly settled, for no one took it into his head to die during this great quarrel. The priest had declared to his lordship the bishop that he would rather be dismissed than carry the blessed sacrament into such a region of abomination, where he was so badly treated by an utterly reprobate population of adulterers and drunkards, who, moreover, were sure of everlasting damnation, since they worshipped only the devil ! And his lordship, apparently, agreed with the Abbé, for he allowed things to go on as they were till the rebellious flock showed signs of contrition.

Rognes was, consequently, without a priest; there was no mass, no anything, and the place was in a perfectly heathenish condition. At first some of the villagers felt a little surprise ; but, then, things went on much as usual, in spite of all this. It neither rained more nor blew more than it had done before, and the village was saving a considerable sum of money, as it had no priest to pay. Then the villagers began to ask themselves whether it would not be as well to do without a priest altogether, as one did not really seem indispensable, and experience already proved that the crops did not suffer, and that they themselves did not die any faster owing to the absence of a pastor. Many of them professed themselves of this opinion —not only the wild scamps, like Lengaigne, but some steady, practical men of sound common-sense like Delhomme. Many others, however, on the other hand, were annoyed at not having a priest. It was not that they were more religious than the others, or more inclined to believe in the Divinity, but the fact of having no priest seemed to indicate that the village was either too poor or too miserly to pay for one. The villagers of Magnolles, only two hundred and eighty in number, ten fewer than the inhabitants of Rognes, supported a priest, and threw the fact at their neighbours' heads in such a provokingly scornful fashion that it led to blows. Then, too, the women clung to their old customs, and there was not one of them who would have consented to be married or buried without the services of a priest. The men themselves had occasionally gone to church, because every one went there. In short, there had always been a priest, and there must be one now, though they reserved to themselves perfect liberty of thought and action.

The municipal council was naturally called upon to deal with the question. Hourdequin, the mayor, who although he did not observe the practices of the faith still favoured religion as an instrument of government, made a political mistake in not taking any part in the contest, from a conciliatory desire not to show any bias in the official position which he held. The village was poor, said one party, so what was the use of burdening it with the expense—a considerable one for its small resources—which would be incurred in repairing the parsonage? Moreover, it was still hoped that the Abbé Godard would be induced to return. At last it came about that Macqueron, the assessor, who had formerly been a determined enemy of the cloth, placed himself at the head of the band of malcontents, who felt humiliated at not having a priest in the village. From that moment Macqueron must have entertained a desire to overthrow the mayor in view of taking his place. It was said, too, that he had become the agent of Monsieur Rochefontaine, the manufacturer of Châteaudun, who was again going to oppose Monsieur de Chédeville at the approaching elections. Hourdequin, whose farm demanded his close attention at that moment, and who was weary of his work, showed but little interest in the meetings of the council, letting his assessor take whatever steps he pleased; and the latter quickly won over the whole council to his views, and persuaded the members to vote the necessary funds for the establishment of a parish. Since Macqueron had contrived to get paid for that piece of land which had been required for the new road, and which he had formerly promised to give up gratuitously, he had been secretly called a sharper by the councillors, but in his presence they manifested great respect for him. Lengaigne alone protested against the vote, which, so he declared, would hand the village over to the Jesuits. Bécu, too, grumbled at it, for he had been turned out of the parsonage and garden, and had been housed in a tumble-down old cottage. For a month workmen had been employed renewing the plaster, putting in fresh panes of glass, and replacing the broken slates; and thus it came about that a priest had at last been able to install himself in the little house, which had been newly whitewashed for his reception.

At early dawn the carts began to start for the vineyards, each of them carrying four or five large casks called *gueulebées*, and having one end knocked out. The girls and women sat in the carts among the baskets, while the men accompanied them on foot, whipping the horses forward. There was a perfect procession, and conversations were carried on from cart to cart amidst a general uproar of laughter and shouting.

Lengaigne's cart followed immediately behind the Macquerons', and, thanks to this, Flore and Cœlina, who had not spoken to each other for six months past, made friends again. Flore was accompanied by Bécu's wife, and Cœlina by her daughter Berthe. Their conversation immediately turned upon the subject of the new priest, and, amid the tramp of the horses, a flow of words rose up into the sharp air of the early morning.

"I caught a glimpse of him as he was getting his luggage down."

"Indeed! and what sort of a man is he?"

"Well, it was so dark I could scarcely see, but he seemed very tall and thin, and not strong; with a face as though he kept Lent perpetually. He seemed about thirty, with a very gentle expression."

"I hear that he comes from Auvergne, from the mountains where the folks are buried in snow for two-thirds of the year."

"How awful! Well, it will be a pleasant change for him to come here."

"Yes, indeed! You know, I suppose, that he is called Madeleine?"

"No. Madeline?"

"Madeline, Madeleine. Well, at all events, it isn't a man's name."

"I daresay he'll come and see us in the vineyards. Macqueron promised that he would bring him."

"Ah! Well, we must watch for him."

The carts drew up at the foot of the hill-side, along the road that skirted the Aigre. Presently in every little vineyard the women were busily at work amid the lines of stakes, bending down and cutting off the grapes with which they filled their baskets. The men had enough to do in emptying the women's baskets into their own, which they carried on their backs and emptied into the open casks. When all the casks of a cart were full, the vehicle was driven off; its load was discharged into the vat, and then the casks were brought back to be filled again.

There was such a heavy dew that morning that the dresses of the women were speedily soaked through. Fortunately, however, the weather was very fine, and the sun soon dried them **again.** There had **been no** rain for three weeks, and the grapes, about which the greatest fears had been entertained, had suddenly ripened and sweetened. Thus they **were all in** high spirits that fine morning, grinning and **bawling, and** indulging **in most indelicate** jokes which made **the girls** wriggle.

"How conceited **that Cœlina used to be** about her Berthe's delicate complexion **!" said Flore to Madame** Bécu, standing up and looking **at Madame Macqueron in the** adjoining vineyard; "why, the **girl's face is now getting** dreadfully yellow and shrunken."

"Yes," replied Madame Bécu, "that **comes of** not marrying the girl! **They were** wrong **not to give her** to the wheelwright's **son.** And they tell **me, indeed, that she has done** herself harm by bad habits."

Then bending double she went on cutting off the **bunches.**

"All that, however," she presently continued, "**does not prevent the** schoolmaster from being constantly **about the place."**

"Oh, that Lequeu," cried Flore; "he would grope with his nose in **the mud if he** thought he could pick up **a** copper or two ! See, there he **is coming to help them, the** stupid fool !"

Then they relapsed **into** silence. Victor, **who** had returned from his regiment **barely a** fortnight **before, was** taking their baskets and emptying **them into** the **one which Delphin** carried on his back. That cunning **snake, Lengaigne, had hired** Delphin for the vintage, pretending **that his own presence was** necessary at the shop. The youngster, **who had never left** Rognes, gaped with amazement at sight **of Victor, who had** assumed a swaggering, rollicking manner ; being, **moreover, wonderfully** altered in appearance, with **his** moustache and his little tuft of beard, his bumptious **ways, and his** forage-cap, which he still made a point of wearing. However, he was **sorely mistaken if he** thought that **he was an** object of envy **to his** companion ; all his **stories** of barrack-life, and his exaggerated **lying tales of** merry-making, and girls, and drinking **bouts, were quite thrown** away. The young peasant shook his **head in dazed** stupefaction, and without feeling **in** the least attracted. **To leave** his nook would be paying too high **a** price for all those fine pleasures, he thought. He had **already** twice refused to **go** and make his fortune in a restaurant **at** Chartres with Nénesse.

"But when are you **going** to be a **soldier,** you whippersnapper ?" Victor asked.

" What? I a soldier! **No, no!** I shall draw a lucky number ! "

The contemptuous Victor could not get any other answer from him. What a coward, he thought, was this big **hulking** fellow with the build of a Cossack ! As **he** talked he **went** on emptying **the** women's baskets **into the one** which Delphin carried, and the **young** peasant did not so **much as bend** under **the load.** Then **Victor** pointed to Berthe, and joked **about** her in such a way **that** Delphin burst out into a fit of laughter, the basket on his back **being almost** capsized. As he went down the hill and emptied **the** grapes **into one** of **the casks,** he could still be heard almost choking **with merriment.**

In the Macquerons' **vineyard, Berthe still** continued **to play the fine** lady, using **little scissors, instead** of a bill-hook, **to cut off the** bunches, **showing herself also** nervously afraid of **thorns and wasps, and** expressing **great** alarm **because** her thin **shoes, quite saturated with** dew, did not dry again. Although **she detested Lequeu, she** tolerated his attentions, feeling flattered **by the courtship of** the **only** educated man **present. Presently he took out his handkerchief to wipe the girl's shoes; but just then an unexpected apparition attracted their attention.**

" Good gracious ! " exclaimed Berthe, " **did** you **ever see such a** dress ? I heard that she had arrived yesterday **evening, at** the same time as the priest."

It was Suzanne, the Lengaignes' daughter, **who had unex**pectedly ventured to **visit** her native village, **after leading a** wild life **in** Paris **for** three years. She had reached **home the** previous evening, and had lingered late in bed, letting her mother **and** brother **set out** for the vineyard, and resolving to join **them there later on, and appear in** the midst of **the peasants** in **such a showy toilet as would quite overwhelm them with admiration. And she** certainly **did** create an immense **sensa**tion **; for she had** donned a **blue** silk dress of so bright **a hue** that **the blue of the** sky looked quite pale and faded. **As she** stood **in full relief** amid the dark green of the vines, **bathed in** a flood **of sunshine,** she looked a real **swell—something** wonderful. She immediately began to talk **and laugh loudly,** nibbling at the **grapes,** which she held up **in** the **air** and **then** dropped into her **mouth.** She joked with Delphin and **her** brother Victor, who seemed very proud of her, and she excited the wondering admiration of her mother and Madame Bécu, who, leaving off their **work,** gazed at her with damp, straining eyes. The vintagers **in the** more distant vineyards joined in the general admiration; work was stopped, and every eye was turned **upon** the girl, who had grown and improved out of all recognition. People had once thought her plain, but now she looked really appetising, no doubt on account of the **way** in which she brought her little **fair** locks of hair **over her** phiz. The resul**t** of this inquisitive **examina**tion was a great feeling of deferen**ce** for this plump girl attired in such costly raiment, and with such a smiling face, betokening prosperity.

Cœlina, turning quite yellow with bile, **and** biting her lips, burst out angrily before her daughter **Berthe and** Lequeu.

" My gracious, what a swell ! Flore tells every one she meets that her daughter has servants and a carriage in Paris. And **I** daresay **it's** true, too, for she must be making a deal of money **to** be able **to** deck her body out in that way ! "

" Oh, those ne'er-do-wells ! " said Lequeu, who **wanted to** make himself agreeable. " Every **one** knows ho**w they get their money ! "**

" **What** does it matter **how they** get it," retorted Cœlina bitterly, " **so** long **as** they do get it ? "

Just at this moment Suzanne, who had caught sight of Berthe, and had recognised in her one of her old companions among the Handmaidens of the Virgin, came up to her.

" Good morning. How are you ? " she said very politely.

She scanned her with a scrutinising glance, and noticed her faded complexion. Then, rejoicing in the soft richness of her own milky flesh, she suddenly exclaimed, breaking out into a laugh :

" Everything's going on all right, I hope ? "

" Quite so, thank you," replied Berthe, annoyed, and feeling **quite** crushed.

The Lengaignes were the heroes **of the** day, and the Macquerons felt that their noses **were put** out of joint. **Cœlina** angrily compared the sallow scraniness of her **daughter, whose** face was already wrinkled, with the sleek **and rosy beauty of** the other girl. Was it just that that hussy, **who gave herself** up to men from morning till night, should **look so** fresh **and** bright, **when a** virtuous maiden grew as **faded and** wan **in her** lonely bed **as** if she had had three con- **finemen**ts? No, **indeed, virtue** went unrewarded, and it wasn't **worth** while for a **girl** to remain living an honest life with her **parents !** All the vintage parties greeted Suzanne enthusias- **tically.** She kissed the children who had grown taller, and she stirred the old **folks'** hearts by reminding them of the past. What does **it matter** what one may be, as long as

one has succeeded and is independent of other people's
patronage? And Suzanne, said the peasants, showed that she
had a good heart by not despising her family, and by coming
back to see her old friends now that she had grown rich.

At the first stroke of noon they all sat down to eat their
bread and cheese. On a line with the tops of the stakes you
saw rows of women's heads covered with blue kerchiefs.
None of them had any appetite, however, for they had been
stuffing themselves with grapes ever since day-break. Their
throats were sticky with the sugary juice; their bellies, as
round and swollen as barrels, rumbled with the purgative
effects of what they had swallowed. Already at every minute
some girl or other was obliged to retire behind a hedge. The
others naturally laughed, and the men got up and guffawed
jocosely as the girls went past them. It was a scene of general
merriment, quite free from all constraint.

They were just finishing their bread and cheese when
Macqueron came in sight on the road at the foot of the hill-
side, accompanied by the Abbé Madeline. Then Suzanne was
abruptly forgotten, and all eyes were turned upon the priest,
To tell the truth, he did not create a very favourable impression. He was as lank as a pike-staff, and gloomy and
ascetic-looking. However, he bowed in front of each vineyard, and said a pleasant word or two to every one, so that
the peasants ended by finding him very polite and gentle. He
evidently hadn't got any will of his own; they meant to make
him do as they pleased. It would be easier to deal with him
than with that cross-grained, cantankerous Abbé Godard!
As he passed on, they joked and grew merry again behind his
back. Soon he reached the top of the hill, and then, a prey to
vague fear and gloomy melancholy, he stood motionless, gazing
upon the vast grey plain of La Beauce. The big bright eyes
of this mountain-born priest filled with tears as he thought of
the narrow hill-bound landscapes of the gorges of Auvergne.

Buteau's vines were close to him. Lise and Françoise were
gathering the grapes, while Hyacinthe, who had not failed to
bring his father with him, had already got tipsy with the
grape juice which he had swallowed while pretending to empty
the small baskets into the large ones. The grapes were fermenting inside him, puffing him out with such a volume of gas
that it sought escape from every aperture. The presence of
the priest, too, seemed to excite him.

"You dirty brute!" Buteau cried to him, "can't you at
least wait till his reverence has gone away?"

Hyacinthe, however, would not submit to the reprimand; assuming the air of a man who could be as refined as he chose, he replied :

"I'm not doing it on his account; I'm doing it to please myself."

Old Fouan had sat down on the ground, tired, but rejoicing in the lovely weather and the fine vintage. He was grinning maliciously at the thought that La Grande, whose vines were on the adjoining plot, had come to wish him good-day. She, like the others, had begun to treat him with respect, now that she had learnt that he still had some money of his own. However, she had turned away from him abruptly, having caught sight of her grandson, Hilarion, greedily taking advantage of her absence to stuff himself with grapes. She promptly administered a hiding to him with her stick. The gluttonous pig! he ate more than he put in the basket!

"Ah, that aunt. What a lot of people will be pleased when she's under ground," exclaimed Buteau, as he came and sat down for a moment by his father's side by way of paying court to him. "It's a crying shame that she should abuse the poor innocent in that way, for if he's as strong as a donkey, he's also quite as stupid."

Then he began to fall foul of the Delhommes, whose vines were down below, skirting the road. They had the finest vineyard in the neighbourhood, some seven acres all in one plot, and it took a good half-score hands to get in the crop. The carefully tended vines produced larger bunches than any of the neighbours' vineyards, a fact of which they were so proud that they affected to keep their own party quite distinct from the others, even disdaining to smile at the sudden colics which sent the girls in the adjoining plots scuttling behind the hedges. They were too much afraid of their legs, Buteau hinted, to care to climb up the hill to greet their old father, and so they pretended not to be aware of his presence there. Then he began to abuse Delhomme as a clumsy, cross-grained ass, who put on all sorts of airs, pretending to be industrious and just; and Fanny, too, was a shrew, losing her temper over the merest trifles, and demanding worship as though she were a saint. She remained quite unconscious of all the wrong she did to others!

"The truth is, father," Buteau continued, "that I've always been fond of you, whereas my brother and sister—Ah! I've always regretted that we parted for a mere nothing."

He then began to throw the blame of what had taken place

U

upon Françoise, whose head, he said, had been turned by Jean.
However, she **had** become steady **now,** he continued. If she
showed **any nonsense, he** would cool **her blood** by ducking her
in the **horse-pond.**

"**Come, now, father, let** bye-gones **be forgotten.** Why
shouldn't **you come back to** us? Will **you?**"

Old Fouan remained discreetly silent. **He had been** expect-
ing the offer which his younger son **now made; but he** was
unwilling to give a definite reply either one way or the other,
not feeling at all certain as to his **best course.**

Buteau assured himself **that his brother was at the other
end** of the vineyard, **and then resumed:**

"It's hardly fit for you to stay with that scamp Hyacinthe.
You'll probably be found there murdered **one** of these days.
Now, if **you'll come back to me,** I'll board **and** lodge **you, and**
pay you **the allowance as well.**"

The old **man raised his eyes** in amazement; and as he still
remained **silent, his son determined to** overwhelm him with his
lavish **offers.**

"**And I** will **take care that** you have all your little luxuries,
your coffee, and your glass, and your four sous' worth of
tobacco; everything you **wish** for, in fact."

It was too tempting, and the old man began to feel **alarmed.**
Certainly, things were getting bad at Hyacinthe's, **but what**
if there should be a repetition of the old goings-on **when he**
got back **to** the Buteaus' again?

"Well, we must see," was all he said; **and then he got up,**
anxious to bring the **conversation to** a close.

The vintaging **lasted until nightfall**; the carts incessantly
carrying off the grape-laden casks, and bringing **them** back
empty. Under the wide expanse of rosy sky, among the vines
gilded by the setting sun, the flitting of the baskets, large and
small, became brisker, **each** worker being excited by the
intoxicating effects of all **these grapes** that were carried to and
fro. Berthe now had a misfortune. She was seized with such
a sharp and **sudden attack of colic** that she was not able to run
off, and **her mother** and Lequeu were obliged **to** form a
rampart round her with their bodies, while she relieved herself
amongst the **stakes.** The vintagers in the adjoining plot
observed what **was** happening, and Victor and Delphin wanted
to take her some paper. But Flore and Madame Bécu restrained them, saying that there were limits which only ill-bred
persons would out-step.

At last they all set **off home** again. The Delhommes led the

way ; La Grande forced Hilarion to help the horse in pulling
the cart along; and the Lengaignes and the Macquerons
fraternised together in a maudlin, tipsy tenderness which
made them forget their rivalry. What attracted most attention
on the return home was the mutual politeness of the Abbé
Madeline and Suzanne. The priest, **seeing** how well the girl
was dressed, took her for a lady, **and they** walked along side
by side, **the** Abbé showing her every attention, while she put
on her sweetest manners, and inquired at what time mass was
celebrated on Sunday. Behind them came Hyacinthe, who, in
his hatred of priests, recommenced his disgusting tricks, determined **in** his tipsy obstinacy to have a spree. At every five yards
he lifted up his leg and let fly. **That hussy** Suzanne bit her
lips to keep from laughing, while the **priest pretended** not to
hear ; and gravely exchanging pious remarks **they walked on**
behind the file of vintage carts, escorted by **this disgusting**
music.

At last, as they **were** nearing Rognes, Buteau and **Fouan,**
who felt quite ashamed of Hyacinthe, made an attempt **to**
silence him. But he still persisted in continuing his tricks, **and**
protested that his reverence was quite under a mistake if **he**
felt in any way hurt.

" **Don't I tell** you **that I mean no** offence to any one, and
that I am simply doing **it for** my own amusement ? " he repeated.

The following week the Buteaus invited their friends to
come and taste the new wine. Monsieur and Madame Charles,
Fouan, Hyacinthe, and some four or five others were to meet
at seven o'clock and partake of some leg of mutton, nuts, and
cheese—a real repast, in fact. During the day Buteau had
barrelled **his wine.** There were six casks of **it,** full to the bung.
Some of his neighbours, however, were not so far advanced in
their operations. One **of** them, **who was** still vintaging, had
been **hard at work** all the morning treading his grapes in a
state of complete nudity ; another, armed with a bar, **was**
watching the fermentation, and beating down the stalks and
skins that **rose to the** surface of the bubbling must ; a third,
who had **a** press, squeezed the grape skins in it, and then threw
them into his yard in **a** reeking heap. Scenes like these **were**
going on in every house; and from the burning vats, the streaming presses, the overflowing casks, indeed from all Rognes
there arose the fumes **of the** wine, which were so strong as to
suffice to make every one intoxicated.

Just before leaving the Château that day, Fouan was seized

with a vague presentiment, which induced **him to** remove his papers from their hiding-place beneath **the lentils** in the pan. He thought **it as** well to conceal them **about his person,** for he fancied he had detected Hyacinthe and **La Trouille looking** up into **the air** with a meaning expression. **They all three** set out, **and** arrived at the Buteaus' **house at** the **same time as** Monsieur **and Madame Charles.**

The full moon was so large and bright that it gave almost as much light as the sun; and as Fouan entered the yard, where one could have seen **well** enough **to pick up a pin,** he observed that Gédéon, the donkey, was in **the outhouse, with** his head inside a bucket. Fouan was **not much surprised to** see him at liberty, for he **was a very cunning fellow, and** frequently raised the latch with his mouth. The bucket, however, excited **the** old **man's curiosity, and,** going up to it, he recognised it **as one of the buckets used in the cellar,** which had contained **some wine from the press,** left after Buteau had finished **filling the casks.** That cursed Gédéon was emptying it.

"Look sharp here, Buteau!" called the old man. "Here's this **donkey of yours up to fine tricks!**"

Buteau appeared at **the kitchen door.**

"What's the **matter?**" he asked.

"Gédéon's swilled all the **wine up!**"

Amid this shouting, the donkey quietly finished **sucking up** the liquor. He had probably been at work for the **last** quarter of an hour, for the bucket held **some four or five** gallons. Every drop of the **wine** had been drunk, and Gédéon's belly was as round as a bottle, **and** seemed on the point of bursting. When at last he **raised** his head, his **tipsy nose was** dripping with **wine,** and **there was a** red line **across it, just** under his eyes, showing how far he had **dipped his phiz into** the liquor.

"Oh, the brute!" roared Buteau, rushing up; "it's just like his tricks. There never was a creature so **full of vice.**"

Generally, when Gédéon heard himself reproached for his vices, he assumed an air of contemptuous **indifference,** and leisurely **spread out his** broad ears; but **to-day he** seemed completely intoxicated, and lost to all **sense of** respect, for he positively sniggered as **he** wagged his head about, thus shamelessly expressing the enjoyment he had **derived** from his debauchery. He stumbled when his master **gave** him a violent shove, and would have **fallen** if Fouan had **not** propped him up **with** his shoulder.

"The damned pig is **dead** drunk!" cried Buteau.

"'Drunk as an ass!' This is the moment to apply the proverb," remarked Hyacinthe, who grinned merrily as he gazed at the animal with sympathetic admiration. " A bucketful at a draught! What a magnificent swallow!"

Buteau, however, saw nothing to laugh about; neither did Lise nor Françoise, who had now hurried up, attracted by the noise. To begin with, there was the loss of the wine; and more than that, there was the confusion into which the disgraceful conduct of the donkey threw them in presence of Monsieur and Madame Charles. These latter were already biting their lips on account of Elodie. To make matters worse, chance would have it that Suzanne and Berthe, who had been taking a stroll together, had met the Abbé Madeline just by the door, and the three of them had stopped there, and were looking on waiting for the finish. A pretty business this, under the eyes of all these fine folks!

" Shove him along, father!" whispered Buteau. " We must get him back into the stable as quickly as possible! "

Fouan shoved, but Gédeón, finding himself very happy and comfortable where he was, declined to stir. He showed no malice, only a good-humoured tipsy perversity. There was a merry jocular glance in his eye, and his dripping mouth seemed twisted into a smile. He made himself as heavy as he could, and reeled about on his outstretched legs, pulling himself together again after every shove, as though he looked upon the whole business as some merry game. Buteau, however, intervened, and shoved the donkey in his turn, whereupon Gédeón turned a summersault, with his four feet in the air; rolling about on his back and braying so loudly that he seemed not to care a curse for all the people looking at him.

" Ah, you foul, good-for-nothing brute!" roared Buteau, assailing the animal with a shower of kicks. " I'll teach you to put yourself into this condition!"

Hyacinthe, full of indulgence for the intoxicated donkey, now interposed.

" Come, come," he exclaimed, " since the brute is drunk, it's no use lecturing him, for he can't understand you. You had much better help him back to his stable."

Monsieur and Madame Charles had drawn on one side, quite shocked by the shameless conduct of the donkey; while Elodie, blushing as deeply as though she had been forced to look upon some indecent spectacle, turned her head away. The group at the door, the priest, Suzanne, and Berthe assumed an **attitude** of silent protestation. Several neighbours now came **up and began to sneer noisily.** Lise and Françoise almost **wept from shame.**

Buteau, however, screwing down **his rage, endeavoured,** with **the help of** Fouan and Hyacinthe, **to get Gédéon on his** legs **again.** This **was no** easy matter, **for the tipsy brute,** with **the bucketful of wine in** his belly, **seemed to weigh as** much **as five hundred thousand** devils. **As soon as they had** raised him on one side he fell down again on the other ; and at last the three men got quite exhausted by trying to shove him up, and supporting him with their knees and elbows. Finally they had managed to get him on to his feet again, and **even succeeded in forcing him a few** steps **forward, when** he **suddenly stumbled and fell over** backwards. The whole yard **had to be crossed to reach the stable.** What was to be done ?

"Ten thousand devils take him !" cried the three men, as they examined him from every point of view, quite at a loss as to how they should next proceed.

It then occurred to Hyacinthe to prop the **animal** up against the side of the shed, and **then** push him along, keeping him **propped up against the wall** of the house, till the stable **was reached. This** plan **succeeded** very well at first, although **the animal** got sadly **scratched and** grazed by the rough wall plaster. The misfortune **was** that presently **this** scratching and grazing became more **than the** brute could **bear,** and, suddenly wrenching himself **free from** the hands that **were** holding him to the wall, he **reared up and** pranced about.

Old Fouan **was almost** knocked down.

"Stop **him ! stop him !"** yelled the two brothers.

Then in **the dazzling brightness of the moonlight** Gédéon **was to be seen gallopping about the** yard **in frantic zig-zags, with his two huge ears swaying** wildly. **The men had shaken his belly too violently, and the poor** brute **now felt very ill. A tremendous preliminary** retch brought **him** to a **standstill, and he almost toppled over.** Then he **tried** to set off again, but **his** legs **stiffened and** he stood rooted to the ground. He stretched **out his neck,** and his flanks were shaken **by** violent spasms. **Finally,** reeling about like a drunken man striving to relieve **himself,** and reaching his head forward at every effort, he vomited a perfect river of red fluid, a furious torrent that flowed on **as** far **as** the pond.

A **ringing** chorus **of** laughter resounded from the door, where **some** peasants **were** clustering together ; while the

Abbé Madeline, who had a weak stomach, turned very pale
between Suzanne and Berthe, who led him away with indignant
protestations. The offended demeanour of Monsieur and
Madame Charles plainly proclaimed that the exhibition of a
donkey in such a condition as this was a breach of all decorum,
and even of the simple politeness due to passers-by. Elodie,
in weeping consternation, threw her arms round her grandmother's neck, asking if the animal were going to die. It was
in vain that Monsieur Charles cried out: "Stop! stop!" in
the old imperious tone of a master accustomed to be obeyed,
the wretched brute went on bringing up this ruddy stream till
the whole yard was full of it. Then he slipped down and
began to wallow about in the mess, with his legs widely
separated, and in such an indecent posture that no tipsy man,
lying across a footway, could ever have presented a more disgusting sight to passing spectators. It really seemed as
though the brute were purposely doing all he could to disgrace
his master. The spectacle was really too dreadful, and Lise
and Françoise, covering their eyes with their hands, fled for
refuge into the house.

"There! there! we've had enough of this! Carry him
away!"

Indeed, nothing else could be done, for Gédéon, who had
become as limp as a wet rag, and very drowsy, was fast falling
asleep. Buteau went off to get a stretcher, and six men helped
him to lift the ass on to it. Then they carried the animal
away; his legs hanging down, his head dangling about, and
already snoring so noisily that it seemed as though he were
braying, and still jeering contemptuously at everybody.

This adventure naturally threw a cloud over the commencement of the feast; but the party quickly recovered their spirits,
and they ended by partaking so freely of the new wine that,
towards eleven o'clock, they were all in much the same condition as the donkey. Every moment or so one of them found
it necessary to retire into the yard.

Old Fouan was very merry; and he reflected that it might
really be advisable for him to come and reside again with his
younger son, for the wine promised to be excellent that year.
He was obliged to leave the room in his turn, and was thinking
the matter over, outside in the dark night, when he was startled
to hear Buteau and Lise, who had come out immediately after
him, quarrelling as they squatted down, side by side, against
the wall. The husband was reproaching his wife for not
showing herself sufficiently affectionate towards his father.

The fool she was, said he, why she ought to wheedle and coax
the old chap so as to get him back into the house again; and
then they could lay their hands on his hoard.   The old man,
suddenly sobered and quite cold, felt at his pockets to make
sure that he had not been robbed of his bonds; and when, after
the parting embraces all round he again reached the Château,
he had firmly resolved not to change his quarters.

That very night, however, he beheld a sight which froze his
blood.   He saw La Trouille in her chemise steal into his
room, which was lighted up by the bright moon, and prowl
about, carefully searching his blouse and his trousers, and
even looking under his chamber-vase.   It was evident that
Hyacinthe, having missed the papers which had been removed
from their hiding-place under the lentils, had sent his daughter
to try and find them.

After that Fouan felt unable to remain any longer in bed;
his brain was too excited.   So he got up and opened the
window.   The night was now dark, and an odour of wine
streamed up from Rognes, mingled with the stench of all the filth
beside the walls, over which folks had stridden for a week past.
What should he do?   Where should he go?   As for his bonds,
he would never again let them leave his own possession.   He
would sew them to his skin.   Then, as the wind swept the
strong odour into his face, he thought of Gédéon.   A donkey
had a splendid constitution and no mistake, he said to himself;
it could get ten times as drunk as a man without coming to
any great harm.   But what was he to do himself?   Robbed in
his younger son's house, robbed in his elder son's house;
there really seemed no choice.   The best thing seemed to be to
remain at the Château, and keep his eyes open, and wait.   Every
bone in his old body was shaking.

CHAPTER V.

THE months glided along; winter passed away, and then the spring. At Rognes matters went on in the same old way; whole years were necessary for the accomplishment of any really perceptible change in that weary, dull life of work and toil, which began afresh with every returning day. In July, amid the burning heat of the blazing sun, the approaching elections threw the village into a state of excitement. This time they were invested with a peculiar interest, and the canvassing visits of the candidates were eagerly discussed and anxiously awaited.

On the morning of the Sunday for which the arrival of Monsieur Rochefontaine, the contractor of Châteaudun, had been promised, there was a terrible scene at the Buteaus' between Lise and Françoise, showing that hostility can go on smouldering invisibly beneath an outward appearance of calmness till it breaks out with unquenchable violence. The last slender bond of union between the sisters, which had always been strained almost to breaking, though constantly knotted again, had at last become so slight, worn away by perpetual quarrelling, that this time it snapped atwain, beyond all hope of repair. And the immediate cause of this final rupture was the merest trifle in the world.

As Françoise was bringing her cows home that morning she stopped to have a moment's chat with Jean, whom she met in front of the church. It must be confessed that she did so purposely, stopping just in front of the Buteaus' house, with the express intention of irritating them.

"When you want to see your men," Lise cried angrily to her as she returned into the house, "be good enough to choose some other place than just under our windows!"

Buteau was standing by mending a bill-hook and listening.

"My men!" retorted Françoise. "I see too many men here. And there's one fellow, let me tell you, whom I could see if I wanted, not under the window, but in this very house, the swine that he is!"

This allusion to Buteau made Lise wild with anger. For a long time past she had been consumed with an absorbing

desire to **turn** her **sister out of doors, so that the** house might
become peaceful; **and this even at the risk of a** law-suit, and
having **to surrender half the land.   It was her** persistence in
this respect that led her husband **to beat her, for** he was quite
opposed to her scheme, hoping to trick **the girl out of her** land
somehow, and also to succeed in **getting possession of** her
person.   The wife was exasperated at no **longer being** mistress
in her own house, and showed **a peculiar kind of** jealousy.
While she was quite ready **to let her husband forcibly** possess
himself of the girl for the sake of making an **end of the matter,**
yet, at the same time, **it enraged** her to see him lusting so **hotly**
after this chit, whom she hated for her youth, her **firm-fleshed**
bosom, and the roundness of her **arms,** that showed so plumply
whenever her sleeves were **rolled up.** She would have liked to
stand by and see her husband **foul and** wreck all these alluring
charms, and she **would** gladly have helped him. Indeed, the
mere fact of sharing her husband with her sister would not
have caused her any trouble. Her anguish of mind arose
from **their** rivalry, which was growing even more bitter and
rancorous, and **the consciousness that** her sister was prettier
than herself, and thus capable of stimulating her husband's
hot desires.

"You drab!" she screamed, "it is you **who lead him
on**! If you weren't always leering at him he **wouldn't be for**
ever running after you. You nasty slut!"

Françoise turned quite pale. This slander was more than
she could bear. And quietly, **but with** deliberate animosity,
she replied:

"We've had quite enough **of this.** It is time there was an
end of it. Wait another fortnight, and I'll no longer annoy
you with my presence. Yes, in another fortnight I shall be
twenty-one, and then I'll take myself off."

"Ah, you're longing to be of age, are you, so that you can
worry us, eh? Well, you hussy, there's no fortnight about the
matter; off you go this very moment."

"Very well, I'm quite agreeable. Macqueron wants a
girl, and I'm sure he'll take me. Good day."

Thereupon Françoise went off without another word.
Buteau then threw down the bill-hook which he had been sharpening, and rushed forward in the hope of restoring peace
between the two women by the administration of a couple of
whacking cuffs. But he was too late, and he could only vent
his angry exasperation by dealing a blow at his wife, from
whose nose the blood began to stream. The devil take all

the women! What he had feared and struggled against so
long had come to pass. The girl had taken flight, and now
there **was** a heap of dirty troubles **in** store for him. He **saw**
in his mind's eye both the girl **and** the land scampering away
from him.

"I'll go to Macqueron's this afternoon," **he** roared. "She'll
have to come back, even if I have to kick her here all the way."

Macqueron's house was in a state of great excitement that
Sunday, for one of the candidates, Monsieur Rochefontaine, the
proprietor of the building works at Châteaudun, was expected
there. Since the last election Monsieur de Chédeville had fallen
into disfavour on account, some people said, of his ostentatious
friendship with certain members of the Orleanist party; while
others asserted that it was owing to his having offended the
Tuileries by a scandalous intrigue with the wife of one of the
ushers of the Chamber of Deputies, who was quite infatuated
about him, despite his age. However this might be, the patronage
of the prefect had certainly been withdrawn from the retiring
deputy and conferred upon Monsieur Rochefontaine, the former
candidate of the Opposition, whose establishment had just been
visited by one of the ministers. Monsieur Rochefontaine had also
written a pamphlet on Free Trade, which had been very favourably noticed by the Emperor. As for Monsieur de Chédeville,
annoyed at being discarded in this way, he persisted in his
candidature, being particularly desirous of retaining his position
as deputy, since it enabled him to dabble in financial jobbery.
The rental of La Chamade was no longer sufficient for his
needs, the place being mortgaged, and in a half-ruined condition. Thus, by a singular chance, the situation of affairs had
been reversed—the landowner had become the independent
candidate, while the contractor enjoyed the patronage of the
Government.

Although Hourdequin was mayor of Rognes he still remained faithful to Monsieur de Chédeville, and had made up
his mind not only to ignore any instructions he might receive
from official sources, but even to work openly for his candidate's cause, should that be necessary. At first he felt that it
was not a manly or honourable thing to veer round like **a**
weather-cock at the slightest breath from the prefect's lips;
and then, as this was a struggle between a Protectionist and
a Free-trader, he became convinced that, in the present crisis of
agricultural affairs, his interests would be better forwarded by
the former. The annoyance which Jacqueline caused him,
added to the cares and anxieties of his farm, had prevented him

for some time past from devoting himself to the duties of his
mayoralty. Being always engaged in watching the lascivious
wench who, with the luck that so often attaches to wrong-
doing, managed to satisfy with impunity her lustful hankering
after Tron's brawny manhood, the mayor left his assessor,
Macqueron, to attend to current affairs. Consequently, when
he again returned to preside over the council, instigated thereto
by the personal interest he took in the election, he was astonished to find it rebellious, in fact stiffly hostile.

This was the outcome of Macqueron's underhand intriguing,
which, prosecuted with all a copper-skin's craft and wiliness,
was at last approaching an issue. Ambition had come to this enriched peasant, who had relapsed into a state of complete idleness, and who dragged himself about dirty and slovenly amid all
his gentlemanly leisure, which really bored him to death. And
this ambition now formed the one pleasure of his existence.
Why should not he himself be mayor? Since that idea had
first dawned upon his mind, he had striven to undermine Hourdequin's position, working upon the ingrained, deep-rooted,
though perhaps unconscious hatred that all the natives of Rognes
in former times had entertained for their lords, and that they
now felt for the son of the townsman who to-day possessed
the land. Of course he had got it for nothing! It had been
nothing more nor less than a robbery at the time of the Revolution. Poor peasants never had such luck. It was only your
scamps and scoundrels who managed to fill their pockets in this
way. And there were pretty goings-on, too, at La Borderie
with the master's infatuation for that hussy La Cognette, in
spite of her amours with all the farm-hands.

Talk of this kind was now freely indulged in in the neighbourhood, arousing indignation even among those who would
not have hesitated to sell their own daughters to prostitution,
or even to commit incest with them themselves, if they had
seen their way to profit by so doing. The members of the
municipal council said at last that a townsman ought to exercise his thievish and wanton propensities amongst his fellows,
and that a peasant-community ought to have a peasant-mayor.

It was in a matter concerning the election that Hourdequin,
to his great surprise, first became aware of the council's
hostility towards himself. When he began to speak of Monsieur de Chédeville, all the councillors sat as expressionless as
so many wooden images. Macqueron, seeing that the mayor
meant to keep faithful to the old deputy, had realised that this
would be the best question on which he could fight the battle,

and it seemed to him to afford an excellent chance of over-
throwing his opponent. Overflowing with zeal, he had set himself on the prefect's side in favour of Monsieur Rochefontaine;
loudly asserting that he was doing his duty as became a
loyal assessor, and that all honest folks were bound to support
the Government. This profession of faith was quite sufficient,
and he was under no necessity of indoctrinating the members
of the council, for in their fear of the broom they were always
on the side of the broom-stick, resolved upon supporting the
established powers, so that things might remain unaltered and
the price of corn be kept high. These were the views of Delhomme, who had such a reputation for justice and integrity, and
he won Clou and others over to his side. It was their duty,
he said, to support the Emperor's nominee, for the Emperor
knew what he was about and studied the country's interests.
The fact that Lengaigne, exasperated to find Macqueron invested with such importance, was Hourdequin's only supporter,
ended by fully compromising the mayor. Calumnies soon
began to be bandied about, and the farmer was accused of
being a " Red," and of holding the same views as the blackguards who wanted a republic, in the hope of exterminating
the peasantry. So persistently, indeed, were these reports
circulated, that the Abbé Madeline took alarm, and, believing
that he owed his cure to the assessor, listened to his talk and
worked for Monsieur Rochefontaine, although the bishop himself still supported Monsieur de Chédeville.

A final blow now destroyed every remaining vestige of the
mayor's influence. It was reported that, when the famous
direct road between Rognes and Châteaudun was opened,
Hourdequin had put half of the subvention voted for the
highway into his own pocket. How he had been able to do
such a thing no one could explain; but this only made the
matter more mysterious and abominable. When Macqueron
was questioned on the subject, he assumed an air of confusion
and reserve, like a man who is compelled to keep silent out of
a regard for certain proprieties. The truth was that he himself
had set the story afloat, in the hope of making his own action
in the matter—the gratuitous offer of his land, followed by
its sale for three times its value—appear in a more favourable
light. The whole village was upset, and the municipal council
became divided into two parties, one comprising the assessor
and all the councillors excepting Lengaigne, while the other
was composed of Lengaigne with the mayor, who at this junc-
ture grasped the gravity of the situation for the first time.

A fortnight previously Macqueron had expressly journeyed
to Châteaudun for the purpose of prostrating himself before
Monsieur Rochefontaine. He had besought him to stay at no
other house but his own, if he should condescend to visit
Rognes. And this was the reason why the innkeeper, that
particular Sunday morning, incessantly went out on to the road
on the look-out for the arrival of the candidate. He had fore-
warned Delhomme, and Clou, and a few other members of
the municipal council, and they were emptying a bottle of
wine to get the time over. Old Fouan and Bécu were also of
the party, playing cards, as well as the schoolmaster, Lequeu,
who pretended that he never took anything to drink, and who
was deep in the perusal of a newspaper he had brought with
him. The assessor was annoyed, however, by the presence of
a couple of other customers, Hyacinthe and his friend Canon,
the vagabond working-man, who were sitting there opposite to
each other gossipping over a bottle of brandy. Macqueron
kept casting furtive glances at them, seeking for some excuse
to turn them out, but in vain, for the scamps, contrary to their
usual wont, were not shouting. They simply seemed to be
deriding every one else. Three o'clock struck, and Monsieur
Rochefontaine, who had promised to come at about two, had
not yet arrived.

"Cœlina!" suddenly cried Macqueron to his wife, "did you
bring up the Bordeaux, as I told you just now?"

Cœlina, who was looking after the customers, expressed by a
gesture her sorrow for her forgetfulness, whereupon her husband
himself rushed off to the cellar. In the next room, where the
haberdashery business was carried on, and the door of which
was always kept open, Berthe was playing the fine lady, and
showing some pink ribbons to three peasant girls; while
Françoise, who had already settled down to her new duties,
was dusting the drawers with a feather broom, despite the fact
that it was Sunday. The assessor, glad of any opportunity
that ministered to his craving for authority, had at once taken
the girl into his house, flattered by the fact of her seeking his
protection. His wife happened to be in want of an assistant,
and he undertook to board and lodge Françoise until he could
bring about a reconciliation between her and the Buteaus. The
girl swore that she would kill herself if she were taken back to
their house by force.

A landau, drawn by two superb Percheron horses, now
suddenly halted before the door, and Monsieur Rochefontaine,
who was its only occupant, alighted, surprised and hurt that

there **was no** one to receive him. He was hesitating about entering the tavern when Macqueron came up from the cellar, holding a bottle in each hand. The sight of the candidate overwhelmed him with confusion and despair. He **was at a loss** how to get rid of his bottles, and he stammered out:

" Oh, sir, how very unfortunate ! I have **been** waiting for **you** for two hours without stirring, and **then** directly I go down **into** the cellar for a moment you arrive ! And **it** was altogether on your account **that** I went, too ! Will **you have a** glass of wine, Mr. Deputy ? "

Monsieur Rochefontaine, **who** was as **yet only a** candidate, and who ought to have been touched by **the poor** devil's evident trouble, **now** seemed only the more put **out.** He was a tall fellow, barely twenty-eight **years** of age, with closely-cropped hair and squarely-cut beard, and carefully, though not elegantly dressed. His manner was cold and abrupt ; he spoke **in a** curt, imperious style, and everything about him told of one **who** was accustomed to command, and of the state of obedience **in** which **he kept the** twelve hundred workmen employed in his **works.** He seemed **determined to** drive these peasants along **as** with a whip.

Cœlina and Berthe had **darted** forward, the latter's bright eyes glistening boldly beneath **their** reddened lids.

" Please do us the honour **of coming** in, sir," she said.

The candidate, however, **surveying her** with a quick glance, had at once estimated her **at her** worth. Still he entered the house, but refused to sit down, remaining standing.

" Here are some of our friends **of** the council," **said** Macqueron, who was beginning to recover his equanimity. " They are delighted to make your acquaintance, I'm **sure.** Are you **not, gentlemen** ? "

Delhomme, Clou, and the others had risen from their seats, thunderstruck by **Monsieur** Rochefontaine's stiff demeanour. Their feeling **of** deference became **one of** the deepest respect, that awe and cringing humility which every manifestation of superior power and authority awoke in them. In the profoundest silence they listened to what the deputy had decided to tell them ; the theories which he held in common with the Emperor, and more especially his ideas about national progress, to which **he** owed the Government's favour, **in** preference to the **former deputy,** whose opinions were condemned. Then **he began to promise them** new roads, railways, and canals ; yes, a canal **which** would traverse La Beauce, and at **last** slake the thirst **which** had been parching it up for centuries. The peasants

listened to him in stupefaction. What was he talking about ?
Water through their fields ! He went on for some time longer,
and then concluded by threatening those who voted wrongly
with the severity of the Government and bad seasons. His
listeners looked at one another. Here, indeed, was a man who
could make them tremble, and whom it would be well to have
for a friend.

"Of course, of course!" Macqueron kept repeating after
each of the candidate's sentences, though, at the same time,
he felt a little uneasy at his stern manner.

Bécu, however, wagged his chin energetically in approval
of this military kind of speech ; and old Fouan, with his eyes
wide open, seemed to be declaring that here, indeed, was a
man! Lequeu, who usually preserved such an impassible
demeanour, had grown very red, though it was impossible to
guess whether he felt pleased or angered. It was only
different with those two scamps, Hyacinthe and his friend
Canon, whose faces plainly expressed contempt, and who felt
so vastly superior to their neighbours that they sniggered and
shrugged their shoulders.

As soon as Monsieur Rochefontaine had finished speaking,
he turned towards the door. The assessor was overwhelmed
with despair.

"What, sir, won't you do us the honour of taking a glass
of wine ?" he cried.

"No, thank you ; I am already very late. They are expecting me at Magnolles, at Bazoches, and at a score of other
places. Good day!"

Then he was gone. Berthe made no attempt to accompany him to the door. In fact, on returning into the haberdashery shop, she exclaimed to Françoise :

"What an impolite fellow. If I were a man I'd vote for
the other one!"

Monsieur Rochefontaine had just got into his landau again,
when the cracking of a whip caused him to look round. It
was Hourdequin coming up in his modest gig, driven by Jean.
The farmer had only heard by chance of the candidate's
visit to Rognes, one of his waggoners having met the landau
on the road ; and he had immediately hastened off to meet the
foe face to face, feeling all the more uneasy as for the last
week he had been vainly trying to persuade Monsieur de
Chédeville to put in an appearance. The old beau was doubtless tied fast to some woman's apron-strings, probably those
of the pretty wife of the usher of the Chamber.

" Ah, so it's you ? " the farmer cried cheerily to **Monsieur Rochefontaine.** " I didn't know **that** you had already commenced your campaign."

The two vehicles were **drawn** up alongside of each other. Neither of the two men got down, but, **after** bending forward and shaking hands, they **settled** themselves in their seats, and in this position conversed together **for a few** minutes. They **were** acquainted **with each** other, having occasionally met at breakfast at the **house of the** mayor of Châteaudun.

" You are opposing me, then ? " suddenly asked Monsieur Rochefontaine, **in his curt way.**

Hourdequin, who, from **his** position **as** mayor, did not care to display his opposition **to** the **Government** candidate too openly, **lost countenance for a** moment, seeing that Monsieur Rochefontaine was so well informed.

However, he was by no means deficient **in** sturdy **courage, and he replied in a** light and pleasant tone, so as **to give a** friendly appearance **to** his explanation :

" Oh, I don't **oppose any one.** I look after myself; **and** the man who will protect **me** is the man for me. Here's corn fallen to forty-six francs **the** quarter, just what it costs me to **produce it.** One **may just as** well starve without giving one's-self the trouble to work ! "

The other at once burst out excitedly :

" Oh, I understand ; it's **Protection** you want, isn't **it ?** A **tax, a** prohibitive duty **on** foreign wheat, **so** that French corn may go up to double its present price. Then you'd have France in a state of starvation, the four pound **loaf at a** franc, and all the poor folks dying from hunger ! How dare **you, a man** of progress, advocate such a monstrous state of **affairs ? "**

" **A man of progress, a man of progress,"** repeated Hourdequin in his cheery, pleasant fashion. " Yes, certainly, I'm a man of progress, but I have to pay so dearly for progress that I soon shan't be able to afford myself the luxury any longer. Machinery, **chemical** manures, and all the other new contrivances are all very **fine** things in their way, I've **no** doubt, and it's very easy to argue in their favour, but there's just this fault about them, **that,** in spite of all the logic **in the** world, they are bringing us to ruin."

" Because you are too impatient, and **because** you expect **science to** give you immediate **and** complete results, and because you grow so discouraged by the necessary preliminary experiments that you even doubt what has been formally

proved, and **finally** fall **back into a** condition of denying
everything."

"Possibly **that may be so. I may have only been** making
experiments. Well, suppose the Government decorates me for
what I have already done, and lets some other folks continue the
course ! "

Hourdequin **burst out** into a hearty laugh **at his own**
jocoseness, which he seemed to think quite conclusive.

"You **wish** the working-man to die of **hunger, then ? "**
Monsieur **Rochefontaine sharply** continued.

" Excuse **me, I wish the** peasant **to be** able to live."

" But **I, who** employ twelve **hundred hands, can't raise their
wages** without becoming bankrupt. **If corn rose to ninety**
francs, my workmen would die **off like so many flies."**

" Well, **do** you **suppose that I don't employ men ? With**
corn at forty-six **francs we have to go with empty stomachs,**
and poor fello**ws are lying starving at the bottom of every**
ditch **all over the country-side." Then he** added, laughingly :

" Well, every one argues **from** his own point of view. If I sell
you bread at a low price, it **is the soil of** France that goes into
bankruptcy ; and if I sell **you it at a high** price, I can understand very well that the cost of workmanship will **go up, and
the price of manufactured** goods **increase, such as** my
clothes, tools, **and the** hundred other things that I **require.
Ah,** it's **a** pretty mess, and we shall end **some day by ruining**
each other all round ! "

The two men, **the farmer and the manufacturer, the Pro-**
tectionist and the Free-trader, looked in **each other's** faces, the
one with a sly good**-humoured smile, the other** with an unflinchingly hostile **expression. They furnished** a complete
example of the **modern war of economics, each** taking his stand
on the struggle for existence.

" **The** peasant will certainly be compelled to supply the
workman with food," said Monsieur Rochefontaine at last.

" **To** be able to do that," retorted Hourdequin, "he himself
must first have something to eat."

Then he sprang down from his gig, and Monsieur Rochefontaine **flung** the name of some village to his coachman.
Macqueron, annoyed that his friends of the council, standing at
the door, had heard **this conversation,** now again proposed that
they should all have a glass together, but the candidate once
more refused, and without shaking hands with any one, threw
himself back in his landau, while the two **tall** Percheron horses
started off at a rattling trot.

Lengaigne, standing at his door on the other side of the road, where he had been setting a razor, had witnessed the whole scene. He now broke into a peal of jeering laughter, and, after a filthy expression, cried out to his neighbour:

"So you had all your trouble for nothing?"

Hourdequin, however, had gone into the tavern, and had accepted a glass of wine; and as soon as Jean had secured the horse to one of the shutters, he followed his master. Françoise quietly beckoned to him to come into the haberdashery shop, and then told him of her departure, and of all that had led to it. The young man was so affected by the girl's story, and so afraid of doing something before the company that might compromise her, that he at once returned into the tavern and sat down on a form, after simply saying that they must see each other again to come to some understanding.

"Well, confound it all," cried Hourdequin, putting down his glass, "you must have pretty stiff digestions if you vote for that youngster!"

His conversation with Monsieur Rochefontaine had decided him to oppose him openly at all risks. He spared him no longer, but compared him with Monsieur de Chédeville, that worthy gentleman who showed no fine airs amongst the peasantry, but was glad to be able to render them any service he could. He was a genuine and true-hearted old-fashioned French nobleman, indeed; while that tall piece of stand-offishness, that mushroom millionaire, looked down at them contemptuously from the height of his grandeur, and even refused to drink a glass of the wine of the district, fearing, no doubt, that it might poison him. It surely wasn't possible that they meant to support him; nobody changed a good sound horse for a blind one.

"What fault have you got to find with Monsieur de Chédeville?" he continued. "For years past he has been your deputy, and has always looked after your interests. And now you desert him for a man whom you looked upon as a scoundrel at the last elections, when the Government opposed him. Confound it all, what are you thinking about?"

Macqueron, who did not want to engage in a direct contest with the mayor, pretended to be busy helping his wife. All the peasants had listened to Hourdequin in stolid silence, without their faces giving the slightest clue as to their secret thoughts. It was Delhomme who answered at last:

"We didn't know him then."

"Ah, but you know him now, this fine fellow! You heard

him say that he wanted to see corn cheap, and that he would vote
for the importation of foreign corn to bring down the price of
our own. I have already explained to you that that means
complete ruin for us. After that, you surely can't be such
fools as to believe in the fine promises he makes you. When
he has once got your votes, you'll soon find him turning round
and laughing at you."

A vague smile played over Delhomme's tanned face, and all
the latent cunning of his narrow intelligence showed itself in
the few sentences which he now slowly spoke.

"He said what he said, and we believe what we believe.
He or another—does it much matter? We've only one wish,
and that is that the Government should be strong enough so
that people may do their business quietly; and the best way of
ensuring that is surely to send the Government the deputy it
asks for, isn't it? It's enough for us that this gentleman from
Châteaudun is the Emperor's friend."

On hearing this last remark Hourdequin felt bewildered.
Why, Monsieur de Chédeville himself had been the Emperor's
friend at the last election! Oh! the miserable race of serfs that
ever belonged to the master who chastised and fed it! To-day,
as ever, these fellows were still full of the hereditary humility
and egotism, seeing nothing and caring for nothing beyond
their meal that day.

"Well," he shouted, "I swear to you by all that's sacred
that on the day this Rochefontaine is elected I will send in my
resignation. Do they take me for a mere puppet, to say black
to-day and white to-morrow? Why, if those blackguards of
republicans were at the Tuileries, you'd be on their side, you
would indeed!"

Macqueron's eyes glistened brightly. The mayor had just
decreed his own fall, for the undertaking which he had given
would, in his present state of unpopularity, suffice to make all
the country-side vote against Monsieur de Chédeville.

Just at that moment Hyacinthe, who was sitting unnoticed
in his corner with his friend Canon, burst into such a loud titter
that all eyes were turned upon him. Leaning his elbows on
the table, resting his chin in his hands, and grinning contemptuously as he gazed round at the assembled peasants, he
cried out:

"A pack of poltroons! a pack of poltroons!"

Just at that moment Buteau came in. In crossing the
threshold, his quick eye caught sight of Françoise in the
haberdashery shop, and of Jean, sitting against the wall, listen-

ing and waiting for his master. Good! the girl and her lover were there, and now they'd see something!

" Ah, here comes my brother, the greatest poltroon of the lot!" exclaimed Hyacinthe.

Threatening expressions were now heard, and the peasants were about to turn their slanderer out of the tavern, when Leroi, otherwise Canon, raised his hoarse voice, which had ranted at all the Socialistic meetings in Paris.

" Hold your jaw, my fine fellow, they're not such fools as they look. Listen to me, now, you other chaps, you peasants. What would you say if a notice should be stuck up on the door of the municipal office, printed in big letters, and containing this announcement: ' Revolutionary Commune of Paris. First: All taxes are abolished. Second: Military service is abolished.' Well, what would you say to that, you earth-grubbers?"

Canon's words produced such an extraordinary effect that Delhomme, Fouan, Clou, and even Bécu himself sat gaping blankly, with widely staring eyes. Lequeu let his paper fall; Hourdequin, who was leaving the room, came back again; and Buteau, forgetting all about Françoise, sat down on a corner of the table. They all gazed at the ragged fellow, the vagabond tramp who was the terror of the districts he passed through, and who lived upon extorted alms and what he could steal. Only the previous week he had been expelled from La Borderie, where he had appeared in the gloaming like a spectre. It was owing to this that he was now staying with Hyacinthe, pending a fresh disappearance.

" Ah, I see that such an announcement would be welcome," Canon continued gaily.

" Indeed it would!" confessed Buteau. " It was only yesterday that I took a lot of money to the collector again. There's no end to those taxes! The authorities seem to want the very skin off one's body!"

" And what a blessing it would be," exclaimed Delhomme, "if one were not forced to see one's sons marched off! It's costing me a pretty penny, I can tell you, to get my Nénesse exempted."

" And then, if you don't pay," added Fouan, " they take your lads from you and have them shot!"

Canon nodded his head, and grinned in triumph.

" Well, you see that after all those earth-grubbers are not quite such fools as you thought!" he said to Hyacinthe.

Then, turning to the others, he continued:

" They are always telling us that you are Conservatives,

and that you wouldn't allow **any change**. But it's conservative of your **own** interests that you **are, isn't it?** You'll let us work, and you'll help in anything **to** your own advantage. You'**d be** prepared **to** do a good deal, **wouldn't you,** for the sake of keeping your money and your **children?** Of course you would, or you'd be a set of arrant **blockheads."**

No one was drinking now, and an **uneasy expression began to appear on** the peasants' heavy faces. **Canon continued his address, revelling** beforehand in the effect **which he was going to** produce.

"And that's why I'm at ease. **I've known all about your** feelings since you've driven **me** away **from your doors with stones.** As that stout gentleman **here said, you will all rally** to our side, to us, the Reds and **the Communists, when we are** installed **at** the Tuileries."

"No, **no! indeed no!**" cried Buteau, Delhomme, and the others, all at **once.**

Hourdequin, who **had been listening attentively, shrugged** his shoulders.

"You're **wasting your breath, my good** fellow," he said.

Canon, however, still smiled with the confident expression of a believer, and leaning back against the **wall, he rubbed first** one shoulder and then the other **with an air of quiet** satisfaction. Then he began to tell them **all about the coming** revolution, vague mysterious hints of **which had been wafted** from farm to farm, alarming both masters **and servants.** Their comrades in Paris, **he** said, **would commence by forcibly** assuming the **reins of government.** There would not be much difficulty about that, **and it would not be necessary to** shoot as many people as might, perhaps, be expected; all **the** big bazaar would topple **down at the** least **touch; it was** so thoroughly **rotten.** Then, **as soon as they had gained** supreme power, they would abolish all payment of rent and confiscate all large fortunes, **so that that** all the **money, as well as all** the machinery and **plant,** would come into **possession of the nation.** Then they **would** reorganise **society upon an entirely new basis,** making it **one vast financial,** industrial, **and commercial house** of business, **in** which each would have **his fair share of work** and comfort. In the country districts **matters would be still simpler.** They would commence by **turning** out **the land-**owners and taking possession of the soil!

"You'd better try it **on!**" interrupted Hourdequin. "You'll find yourself received **with** pitchforks! The poorest little landowner in the country wouldn't let you carry **off** a handful **of his soil!**"

"Have I said a word about touching poor folks?" replied Canon, blandly. "No, **we are** not such fools as to quarrel with the small owners. No, no, we shall not touch the land of the poor fellows who are making a starvation livelihood out of a few acres. It's only the plump gentlemen like yourself, with their four and five hundred acres, who grow rich by the sweat of their labourers, whose possessions we shall confiscate. Ah, confound it, I don't fancy you'll find **any of** your neighbours coming **to** your **defence** with their pitchforks. **They'd** be only too glad **to see you** stripped."

Macqueron **broke** out into a loud laugh, **as** though **he** looked upon **the** whole **matter as a** joke, **and** the others followed his example. **The farmer** turned somewhat pale, feeling that the old hereditary hatred still **abode in the** peasants' breasts. The scoundrel was right. Every one **of all** these peasants, even the honestest of them, would **help to** plunder him of **La Borderie.**

"**But in my case now,**" asked Buteau, gravely; "**I own** about a score **of acres, shall I be** allowed to keep them?"

"By all **means,** my friend; but later on when you see the results attained in the national **farms** around you you will certainly come of **your** own accord, without the least solicitation, and add your own land to them. We shall do everything on a large scale, with the command of great capital, and all the resources of art and science at our disposal. But that's a matter I don't know so much about. You ought **to** hear some of the people up in Paris relate how it is that agriculture is hopeless if carried on upon any other basis than this. Yes, you'll come and offer your land of **your** own accord."

Buteau's face now wore an expression of profound incredulity. He no longer understood Canon, still he felt **reassured at being** told that he would not **be** forced to give up anything. As for Hourdequin, his curiosity was excited upon hearing Canon **hazily** hold **forth on** the subject of this **great scheme of national** farming, and **he** once more lent an attentive ear. The others awaited the finish as if they had been at the theatre. Lequeu, whose pallid face kept flushing crimson, had twice opened his mouth as though he were going to interpose a remark, but each time, like a prudent man, he had withheld it.

"**And** what is my **share** to be?" suddenly exclaimed Hyacinthe. "Every one must have his share! Liberty, equality, and fraternity!"

Canon at once lost his temper, and raised his hand as though he were going to strike his friend.

"Hold your row with your liberty, and equality, and fraternity! Does any one need to be free? No, freedom's a farce. You want the gentlefolks to put us into their pockets again, eh? No, no, people must be forced into being happy, whether they will or no! And as for equality and fraternity, would you ever consent to being the equal and the brother of a bailiff? No, no; it was by believing nonsense of that kind that the Republicans of '48 made fools of themselves!"

Hyacinthe, quite at a loss, simply declared that he was in favour of the great Revolution.

"Hold your tongue; you rile me!" cried Canon. "That's your tune, eh? A nice pack of lies always being drummed into our ears! Can that ridiculous farce be compared for a single moment with what we mean to do? You'll see it all when the people are the masters; and it won't be very long coming, all's cracking, and I'll promise you that this century of ours will finish up in a very much prettier fashion than the last one did. There'll be such a sweeping clean-out as has never yet been witnessed!"

All the company shuddered, and even that sot Hyacinthe drew back, alarmed and disgusted at hearing that they were not all to be brothers. Jean, who had hitherto been interested in what was going on, also made a gesture of repulsion. Canon, however, had sprung to his feet, with his eyes glistening, while his face seemed bathed in a prophetic ecstasy.

"And it must come," he cried; "it's fated. It can no more help happening than a stone thrown up in the air can help falling down. And we shall have no more twaddling priests, and stories of another world, and right and justice, things which no one has ever seen any more than they've seen God. No, the only thing we shall concern ourselves about is being perfectly happy. Ah! my fine fellow, we shall arrange matters so that every one shall have the greatest amount of enjoyment with the least possible amount of work. We shall make machinery work for us, and four hours' daily superintendence of it will be the most that will be required. It may be that in time we shall have absolutely nothing to do, and be able to fold our arms in complete idleness. And everywhere there'll be a glut of pleasure; and all our desires will be pampered and satisfied. Yes, there will be meat, and wine, and women galore, and we shall be able to take treble the quantity of pleasure that we can take now, for we shall be stronger and healthier. There will be no more poverty, no more **invalids, no more old** folks, thanks to **our** improved organisation, our **easier life,** our perfect hospitals, and comfortable free homes. **It will be** an absolute Paradise ! **All** the science in the **world** will be called into use **for our pleasure !** And life will **then be** real enjoyment ! "

Buteau, **fairly carried away, brought his fist** down upon the table **with a bang as he shouted :**

" No **more taxes ! no more conscription ! no** more worries of any sort ! **nothing but pleasure !** Yes, I'm **quite** willing to sign that programme."

" Certainly," **observed Delhomme, sagaciously.** " A man would **be his own** enemy **not to sign it."**

Fouan also expressed **his approval, as did** Macqueron, **Clou, and the others.** Bécu, **who, with his authoritative** principles, **was quite** stupefied and overcome, stepped up to Hourdequin, **and** asked him in a whisper if **he** ought not to take this blackguard **who** attacked the Emperor to the lock-up. The farmer, however, **calmed him by** shrugging his shoulders. Happiness ! **Ah, yes,** they now dreamed of winning it through science, as they **had** previously dreamed of winning it through right and justice ! **Perhaps the new theory** might **be** the more logical, **but anyway it was not likely to bear the** expected fruit **yet awhile ! The farmer then again prepared to** leave, and called to **Jean, who** was still **absorbed in the** discussion, **but** just at that moment Lequeu **suddenly yielded to his eager** longing to join in the debate. He had **for some time past been** choking with suppressed rage.

" Take care," he burst out in his **shrill voice, "take care** that you are not all killed before this fine state of affairs comes off ; killed **by** hunger, or by the bullets of the **gendarmes, if starvation** should make you refractory——"

The others looked at him without understanding him.

" Nothing **can be more certain,"** he continued, " if corn continues to be imported **from America,** in a hundred years from now there won't be **a single peasant** left in all France. Do you think **that our land can contend with** yonder one ? **Long** before **we have had time to put these new** plans in practice, **the** foreigners **will have inundated** us with grain. I have **read a book which tells all about it. Y**ou fellows are **all doomed——"**

In his angry **excitement, he** suddenly **became** aware that **all the** scared faces were **turned** towards him ; and he did not **even** finish the sentence he **was** uttering, **but** making an angry gesture, pretended to bury himself in his newspaper again.

"The American corn will certainly do for you all," exclaimed Canon, "unless the people take possession of the large holdings."

"And I," said Hourdequin in conclusion, "I tell you again that this American corn must not be allowed to enter the country. And now go and vote for Monsieur Rochefontaine if you are tired of having me for your mayor, and want to see corn at forty-three francs."

He then mounted into his gig, followed by Jean, who exchanged a meaning glance with Françoise. As the young man whipped the horse on, he said to his master:

"It doesn't do to think too much about all those affairs, they would drive one crazy."

Hourdequin signified his approval by nodding his head.

In the tavern, Macqueron was now talking in a low but animated tone with Delhomme, while Canon, who had once more assumed an air of supercilious scorn for everybody, finished the brandy, and ridiculed the snubbed Hyacinthe, dubbing him "Miss Ninety-three." Buteau, waking up from a reverie, now suddenly noticed that Jean had gone away, and he was surprised to see Françoise still standing at the door of the room, where she and Berthe had come to listen to what was going on. He felt annoyed with himself for having wasted his time over politics, when he had serious business on hand. Those wretched politics seemed able to make a man forget everything else. He now entered into a long conversation with Cœlina, who ultimately prevented him from making an immediate scandal. It would be much preferable, she said, if Françoise returned to his house of her own accord, when they had succeeded in calming her. Then he went off, threatening, however, that he would return to fetch the girl with a rope and a stick, if the Macquerons did not prevail upon her to come back.

On the following Sunday Monsieur Rochefontaine was elected deputy; and Hourdequin having sent in his resignation to the prefect, to avoid being dismissed, Macqueron at last became mayor, and almost burst through the skin in his insolent triumph.

CHAPTER VI.

THE week passed away, and Françoise still persisted in her refusal to return to her sister's house. There was a terrible scene one day on the road. Buteau, who was dragging the girl away by the hair, was obliged to let go on having his thumb severely bitten. Macqueron then became so alarmed that he turned the girl out of his house, saying that as he was the representative of the law he could not encourage her in her rebellion.

La Grande happened to be passing at the time, and she took Françoise home with her. The old woman was now eighty-eight years of age, but she never thought about dying except as a means of bequeathing to her heirs the worry of endless litigation in reference to her fortune. She had made an extraordinarily complicated will, mixing everything up with absolute delight; and, under the pretext of wronging no one, she had left such directions as would compel the heirs to devour one another. She had done this quite deliberately, feeling a satisfaction in the thought that although she could not take her property with her to the grave, she would at any rate go off with the consolation of having done her very best to set all her relations by the ears. Nothing gave her more plea-sure than to see them quarrelling with one another, and this it was that prompted her to take her niece into her own house. Her natural stinginess made her hesitate just for a moment, but she came to a decision at the thought that she would get a large amount of work out of the girl in return for a small amount of food. That very evening, in fact, she made her wash the whole house. When Buteau made his appearance, she stood up and confronted him with her wicked-looking old nose which resembled the beak of some aged bird of prey; and he who had talked of smashing everything at the Macquerons' here began to tremble and stammer, too much paralyzed by the fear of losing his share of La Grande's property to dare to engage in a struggle with her.

" I want Françoise here," she said, "and I mean to keep her, since she is not comfortable with you. Besides, she is of

age now, and you have certain accounts to render her. We
shall have to talk about them."

Buteau went off in a furious frame of mind, alarmed at the
trouble and annoyance which he realised were in store for
him.

Just a week afterwards, indeed, about the middle of August,
Françoise at last came of age. She was now her own mistress.
By her change of residence, however, she had done little more
than change her troubles, for she, also, trembled before her
aunt, and was nearly killed by over-work in this cold, parsi-
moniously-managed house, where everything had to be made
shiny without any expenditure upon soap or brushes. Cold
water and elbow-grease had to suffice for everything. One day
the girl almost got her head cut open by a blow from her aunt's
stick, merely for forgetting herself so far as to give the fowls
some grain.

Several of the neighbours said that, in her anxiety to spare
her horse, La Grande harnessed her grandson Hilarion to the
plough; and, even if that was an exaggeration, there was no
doubt but that she did treat the lad like a beast of burden,
beating him and almost killing him with work, abusing of his
great strength to such a degree that he sank down quite worn
out with exhaustion, and feeding him so miserably, with mere
crusts and leavings, just as though he were a pig, that he was
always on the verge of starvation, as well as being stupefied
with fear. When Françoise discovered that she was meant to
make up the second horse in the pair, her one thought was of
how she might get away from the house; and then it was that
she suddenly determined to marry.

She was simply prompted by the wish to finish with it all.
With her ingrained and obstinate ideas of justice, ideas which
even in her childhood had caused her no little trouble, she would
rather have killed herself than have gone back to her sister's.
She wanted nothing but justice, she told herself, and she
despised herself for having submitted so long. She now made
no reference to the swinish Buteau; it was only of her sister
that she spoke harshly, saying that if it had not been for her
they could still have continued living all together. Now that
this rupture had taken place between them, a rupture which
could never be healed, she only lived to obtain her property,
her share in the inheritance. The thought of this worried her
from morning to night, and she went wild on account of the
endless formalities that would have to be gone through. What
was the good of them all? This is mine! that is yours! Why

couldn't the whole thing be settled in a couple of minutes? It
could only be, she declared, because every one was in league
to rob her. She suspected the whole family, and came to the
conclusion that her only means of extricating herself from this
predicament was to take a husband.

Jean, certainly, had not got an inch of land, and he was
fifteen years her senior. But then no one else had asked for her,
and perhaps no one else would have dared to take her, from
fear of Buteau, who was so generally dreaded in Rognes that
no one cared to have him for an adversary. Then, too, she and
Jean had had to do with each other once ; though this fact was
not of much importance, since it had had no consequences. On
the other hand, he was gentle, and kindly, and straightforward.
Why not take him, since there was no one else she cared about,
and as her only object in marrying was to get some one to defend her interests and to do what she could to enrage Buteau ?
Yes, she, too, would have a man of her own !

Jean still retained a great affection for her, although with
time his lustful desire to possess her had greatly quieted down.
But he still adhered to her, and looked upon himself as engaged
to her by reason of the promises they had exchanged. He had
waited patiently till she was of age, without harassing her to
depart from the waiting course she had determined upon, and
he had even restrained her from acting in any way against her
own interests while she remained at her sister's. As a result,
there was now every reason why all honourable people should
be on her side. And, although he blamed her for the tempestuous way in which she had left the Buteaus, he repeated
that she now had the game in her hands. Whenever she chose
to speak of the other matter he should be ready and willing to
hear her.   -

Their marriage was agreed upon in this wise, one evening
when he had come to meet her behind La Grande's cowhouse.
There was a rotten old gate there, opening into a court, and
they were leaning against it, he outside and she inside, with
the stream of liquid manure from the stable trickling between
their feet.

The girl was the first to refer to the subject.

" If you're still of the same mind, Corporal, I'm willing to
consent now," she said, looking him straight in the eyes.

He returned her look, and replied slowly :

" I've not said anything to you about it lately, because it
would have seemed as if I wanted your property. But you
are right all the same. Now's the time."

Then there was a pause. Jean had laid his hand upon the girl's, which was resting upon the gate. Then he resumed: "You mustn't let any of the neighbours' gossip about La Cognette trouble you. It's three years and more since I even touched her."

"And you," she exclaimed, "you mustn't worry yourself about Buteau. The swine brags everywhere that he has had to do with me. Perhaps you believe it?"

"Everybody in the neighbourhood believes it," Jean murmured, evading a direct reply.

Then, seeing that she was still looking at him, he continued: "Well, yes, I did believe it. I knew the scoundrel so well, that I didn't see how you could possibly have prevented him."

"Oh, he tried often enough, and I suffered dreadfully at his hands; but if I swear to you that he never gained his ends, will you believe me?"

"Yes, I believe you."

Then, in token of his pleasure, he closed his fingers round her hand, and kept it pressed in his own as he stood with his arm resting on the gate. Noticing that the dribbling stream from the stable was wetting his boots, he set his legs apart.

"You seemed to stick on there so persistently," he continued, "that it almost appeared as though you enjoyed his buffetings."

The girl felt ill at ease, and her frank, straightforward gaze was lowered.

"And the more so," he added, "as you wouldn't have anything more to do with me. Well, it's all the better now, isn't it? That baby I so wanted still remains to come. It's altogether more respectable, too."

He stopped to tell her that she was standing in the dirty stream.

"Take care; you are wetting your feet."

She took them out of the slush, and then observed:

"We are agreed about it, then?"

"Yes, we are agreed. Choose any time you like."

They did not even kiss each other, but just shook hands across the gate like a couple of friends. Then they went off in opposite directions.

When Françoise informed her aunt that same evening of her intention to marry Jean, explaining to her her need of a husband to assist her in recovering her property, La Grande at first made no reply. She sat stiffly in her chair with her eyes widely opened, calculating the loss and gain and pleasure

which she was likely to derive from the marriage, and it was
only the next day that she expressed her approval of it. She
had been thinking the matter over all night long as she lay on
her straw mattress, for she slept very little now, and would lie
with open eyes till day dawned, plotting how she might make
things disagreeable for the different members of her family.
This marriage seemed to her to be so pregnant with unpleasant
consequences for everybody, that she longed to see it come
off with quite a youthful feverishness. She could already
foresee even the smallest among the numerous vexations which
would arise from it, and she was scheming how she might
embitter them, and render them as fatal as possible. She was
so pleased, indeed, that she told her niece that she would take
the whole matter upon herself for affection's sake. She
emphasised the word by a terrible shake of her stick. Since
the others had cast the girl off, she would take the place of her
mother, and folks would see how she managed matters.

As a first step, La Grande summoned her brother Fouan to
talk to him about the accounts of the guardianship. The old
man, however, could not give her any information. It wasn't
his doing, he said, that he had been appointed guardian, and as
Monsieur Baillehache had managed everything, he ought to be
applied to. Moreover, when he discovered that the old woman
was bent upon annoying the Buteaus, he affected still greater
bewilderment. Age, and the consciousness of his weakness,
filled him with uneasy alarm for himself; he felt that he was
at everybody's mercy. Why should he quarrel with the
Buteaus? He had twice almost made up his mind to return to
them after nights of quaking fear, during which he had seen
Hyacinthe and La Trouille ferretting about his room, and even
thrusting their bare arms under his bolster, trying to rob him
of his papers. He felt quite convinced that he would be
murdered some night or other at the Château if he did not
escape from it.

La Grande, being unable to glean anything from him,
dismissed him in a state of great alarm, shouting out that he
should be prosecuted if he had tampered with the girl's
property. Then she attacked Delhomme, as a member of the
family council, and gave him such a fright that he went home
ill, Fanny coming at once to tell the old woman that they
would prefer paying money down to being worried with law-
suits. La Grande chuckled. The game was beginning to be
very amusing!

The question she now set herself to solve was whether the

division of the property should be pressed forward as the next step, or whether the marriage should take place first. She pondered over it for two nights, and pronounced in favour of an immediate marriage. Françoise, married to Jean and claiming her share of the property, assisted by her husband, would anger the Buteaus extremely. She then hurried things forward, seeming to regain the nimble activity of youth, and she busied herself about obtaining the necessary documents on behalf of Françoise, and made Jean give her his. Then she made all the arrangements both for the civil and religious weddings, and her eagerness even carried her so far that she advanced the necessary money, taking care, however, to obtain in exchange for it a receipt signed by both Jean and Françoise —a receipt in which the sum advanced was doubled by way of providing for the interest. The glasses of wine which she was forced to offer to the guests during the preparations wrenched her heart-strings more than anything else, but as she was provided with her vinegary liquid, her " gnat destroyer," folks were not pressing in this respect. She decided that there should be no wedding feast on account of the divided state of the family. After the mass they would merely just swallow a glass of the " gnat destroyer," by way of drinking the health of the newly-married pair.

Monsieur and Madame Charles, who were invited, excused themselves on the ground that they were greatly worried on account of their son-in-law, Vaucogne. Fouan, who was in a most uneasy state of mind, went off to bed, and sent a message saying that he was ill. The only relation present was Delhomme, who consented to act as one of Françoise's witnesses, to mark the esteem which he felt for that steady fellow, Jean. The latter, on his side, only brought his witnesses—his master, Hourdequin, and one of the farm-hands, a companion. Rognes was topsy-turvy, and at every doorway people watched for this wedding, which had been so energetically pushed forward, and which seemed likely to provoke so much quarrelling and fighting.

At the ceremony at the municipal offices Macqueron, inflated with self-importance, went through the formalities, in presence of the ex-mayor, in an exaggerated manner. At the church there was a painful incident. The Abbé Madeline fainted while he was saying mass. He was not feeling well. He regretted his native mountains since he had begun to live in flat La Beauce, and he was extremely distressed by the indifference of his new parishioners for religion, and so upset by the con-

tinued chattering and squabbling of the women, that he no
longer dared even to threaten them with hell. They had
realised that he was of a yielding disposition, and they took
advantage of this to tyrannise over him even in religious
matters. However, Cœlina, and Flore, and all the other women
present at the ceremony, **expressed** extreme sorrow **for his**
having fallen with his nose against the altar, and they declared
that it was an omen of misfortune and approaching death for
the bride and bridegroom.

It had been settled that Françoise should continue to live at
La Grande's **till she had received her share of** the property;
for, with her characteristic determination, she had quite made
up her mind **that** she would have the house. So what was the
good of taking one elsewhere just for a fortnight or so? Jean,
who was to retain his post as waggoner at the farm, would
in the meantime join her every evening. **Their** wedding night
was a very sad and stupid one, though they were glad to be at
last together. When Jean took his wife in his arms, **she**
began to sob so violently that she almost choked: not that **he**
used the least roughness towards her; **on** the contrary, **he**
treated her with **the** utmost gentleness. In reply to **his**
questions she told him, still sobbing bitterly, that she had no
complaint to make against him, but that she could not help
crying, though she did not know **why she was doing so.** Such
a wedding night as this was not calculated to make a man very
ardent. Though he embraced her and held her clasped in his
arms, a feeling of troubled constraint seemed to have come between them. Apart from that they got on very well together,
and being unable to sleep, they spent the remainder of the night
in speculating as to how their affairs would progress, when they
got hold of the **house** and land.

The next morning Françoise was anxious to demand her
share **of the** property. But La Grande **now** showed no great
hurry to have the matter settled. She wanted to make her spiteful enjoyment last as long as possible, bleeding her relations
by slow degrees with pin-thrusts; and then, again, she profited
too much by the services of Françoise and her husband, who
paid the rent of the bedroom by two hours' work every evening,
to be anxious to see them leave her and establish themselves in
a house of their own.

It was necessary, however, to ask the Buteaus how they
proposed to divide the property. La Grande, **on** behalf of her
niece, claimed the house, half the arable land, and half the
meadow, foregoing the half of the vineyard as a set-off against

Y

the house, estimating it **as** being of **the** same value.   It was
a very fair proposal, and if matters had been thus arranged
in a friendly way, a recourse to the law, which always retains a
good slice of everything it gets hold of, would have been
avoided.   Buteau, whom La Grande's arrival had revolutionised
—he was forced to be respectful with her **on** account of her
money—dared not listen any longer, but rushed out of the
room, afraid lest he might so far forget his own **interests as to
strike the** old **woman.**

Lise who **was left alone with her, and whose ears were red
with anger, stammered out :**

" **The** house, indeed !   **She wants the house, does she ? this**
heartless hussy, this good-for-nothing who **has got married**
without even coming to see me !   Well, aunt, you can **tell her**
from me that if **ever she gets this house it** will **only be because
I'm dead ! "**

La Grande remained **perfectly calm.**

" **All right, all right, my child.   There's no** occasion to **get
excited.   You also want the house.   Well, you have an equal
right to it.   We will see what is to be done."**

For the next three days the old woman **went** backwards
and forwards from one sister to the other, reporting to each
of them all the abuse which the other had indulged in, **and**
exasperating them to such a degree that both of them almost
took to their beds.   La Grande, unwearying **in her embassies,**
impressed upon them how great her affection for them **was, and**
what an amount of gratitude they **owed her for under-**
taking this unpleasant **task.   It was finally settled that**
the land should **be divided between the two sisters, but that**
the house, the **furniture, and the** live stock should be sold, since
they could **not agree about them.   Both the sisters** swore that
they would buy the house, even if they had to part with their
last chemise to do it.

So Grosbois came to survey the land and divide it into **two
lots.   There were two** and a half acres of meadow land, **about
the same amount of vineyard,** and about **five** acres of plough
land.   It was this latter that Buteau, since his marriage, had
been so **determined to retain,** for it adjoined a field of his own
which **he** had **obtained** from his father, **and** the two plots
together made up **a parcel of** between **seven** and eight acres,
such as no other peasant in all Rognes possessed.   He
was, consequently, full of bitter wrath when he saw Grosbois
setting up his square and sticking his poles into the ground.
La Grande was there superintending, but Jean had thought it

best not to be present, fearing that there might be a fight if he
came. As it was, there was an angry discussion. Buteau
wanted the line of division to be drawn parallel to the valley of
the Aigre, so that his wife's share might still adjoin **his own
field ;** while La Grande, on the other hand, insisted that **the line
should** be drawn perpendicularly, asserting that this was the
way in which the family property had always been divided for
centuries past. The old woman **won the day,** and Buteau
clenched his fists and almost choked with suppressed rage.

"**Curse it!** Why, if the first lot falls to me," he blurted
out, "**my land will be** cut up into two pieces. There will be
this piece in one place, and my own field in another."

"Well, my lad," rejoined the old woman, "you must draw
the lot that suits you best."

For a month past Buteau had been in a state of the angriest
excitement. **In the** first place, Françoise was escaping him.
He had become quite ill with longing desire, now that he was
no longer able to seize hold of the girl as he had been **wont
to do, and to** obstinately hope on that he would **succeed in
effecting his purpose** some day or other. And, now that she
was married, the thought **that** another man could do as he
pleased with **her, ended** by putting him in a perfect fever.
And then this **other man was now** trying to get his land into his
possession, **too.** He felt that he would as soon lose a limb.
The girl he might, perhaps, have, but not the land; the land
which he, Buteau, had always looked upon as his own, and with
which he **had sworn never to part !** He began to indulge in
the most bloodthirsty thoughts, and ransacked his brains **for**
some method by which he might be able to keep the land,
dreaming vaguely of murders and acts of **violence,** which only
his terror of the gendarmes prevented him **from** committing.

At last a meeting was arranged at Monsieur Baillehache's
office, at which Buteau and Lise, for the first time since the
marriage, again **found** themselves in **the** presence of Françoise
and Jean, **whom La Grande had** accompanied for the
pleasure of **the** thing, **and** under the pretext of seeing **that**
nothing wrong was done. The five of them went into the
private office in silence, comporting themselves stiffly. **The**
Buteaus seated themselves **on** the right. **On the** left, Jean remained standing behind Françoise's chair, as though to express
that **he was not** of the meeting, but had simply come to support
his wife. **The** aunt, tall and scrany, sat down in the middle,
turning her round eyes and **her** hawk-like beak first on one couple
and then on the other with **a** satisfied air. The two sisters did

not even appear **to know** each **other. They sat there with a**
hard expression **on** their faces, without **exchanging a single**
word **or look. The** men, **however,** had given **one** another a
rapid **glance, gleaming** and penetrating like a dagger thrust.

"**Now, my friends,**" said Monsieur Baillehache, **who re-**
mained calm amid all these expressions of **murderous hate,**
"we are first of all going to finish with the division **of the land,**
upon which subject we **are now** quite agreed."

He then made **them affix** their signatures **forthwith. The**
parchment was already engrossed, blanks **being left after the**
names of the parties for **the** description **of the various parcels,**
and they **all** had **to sign before** the lots were **drawn, which**
ceremony was immediately proceeded with, in **order to prevent**
any **trouble.**

Françoise, having **drawn number two, number one was,**
of course, **left for** Lise, **and** Buteau's **face turned quite purple**
from the angry surging of his blood.   **Luck was always against**
him ! **.Here was** his **land cut atwain, and this hussy and**
her man had their share between his two parcels !

"**The devil take and confound them all !**" he growled from
between his clenched teeth.

The notary requested **him to restrain his feelings till he got**
into the street again.

"This will cut up our land," remarked Lise, **without turning**
towards her **sister.** "Perhaps we might **be able to make an**
exchange. It would suit **us better,** and **be to no one's dis-**
advantage."

"No!" **said Françoise, drily.**

La Grande **nodded her approval. It would** bring bad luck
to **interfere with the ruling of chance.** The result of the
drawing made the **old woman gay. As** for Jean, who was still
standing behind his **wife, he seemed so** determined to hold
himself aloof from **the** proceedings that **he** had **not moved,** and
his face was a perfect blank.

"**Come** now, let us finish with it all," said the notary.

The two sisters had, by common consent, deputed **him to**
arrange for **the sale of the** house and furniture and live **stock.**
The **sale was advertised to** take place **in** his office on the
second Sunday **in the** month, and the conditions **of the sale**
stated that the purchaser could have the right of **entering into**
possession on the same **day.** When **the sale** was over, the
notary would at once proceed to balance accounts between the
two co-heiresses. The different parties concerned signified
their approval of all this by silently nodding their heads.

Just at this moment, however, Fouan, who had been summoned to attend the meeting as Françoise's guardian, was introduced by a clerk, who prevented Hyacinthe from coming in at the same time, on account of his intoxicated condition. Although more than a month had elapsed since Françoise had attained her majority, the accounts of the guardianship had not yet been rendered; and this fact tended to complicate matters. It was necessary for the accounts to be passed before the old man could be released from his responsibility. He looked first at one party, and then at the other, straining his little eyes, and trembling with increasing fear lest he should find himself compromised and given up to justice.

An abstract of the accounts had been prepared, and it was read by the notary. They all listened to it attentively, full of uneasy anxiety, since they could not completely understand, and fearing that if they let a word pass unheard that very word would somehow bring them into trouble.

"Have you any observations to make, any of you?" asked the notary when he had finished reading the abstract.

They all looked bewildered. What observations? Perhaps they had forgotten something, and were allowing themselves to be robbed.

"Excuse me," La Grande suddenly interposed, "but this by no means suits Françoise. My brother must be intentionally shutting his eyes if he can't see that the girl's being defrauded."

"I! what? eh?" stammered Fouan. "I haven't taken a copper of hers, so help me God!"

"I say that Françoise, since her sister's marriage, now nearly five years ago, has been employed as her servant, and that she is entitled to wages."

Buteau sprang up from his seat at this unexpected demand, and Lise almost choked with anger.

"Wages!" she cried; "wages to a sister! That is too ridiculous!"

Monsieur Baillehache hushed them, and declared that the girl was perfectly entitled to claim wages if she chose to do so.

"Yes, I do claim them," said Françoise; "I wish to have everything that is my due."

"But then you must take all her food into account!" cried Buteau, wild with excitement. "She makes short work with bread and meat! Just you feel her, and say if you think that she's got as fat as that on air!"

"And then there's her linen and dresses!" Lise added

furiously ; "and her washing ! Why, she used to sweat so
much that she'd soil a chemise in a couple of days."

"If I sweated like that," replied Françoise, with annoyance,
"it was because I worked so hard."

"Sweat dries and doesn't soil," interposed La Grande, curtly.

Monsieur Baillehache again intervened. He told them that
a debtor and creditor account would have to be drawn up, the
wages on one side and the board and lodging and other
expenses on the other. Then he took a pen, and made an
attempt to draw up a statement from the information they
gave him. It was a terrible business. Françoise, backed
up by La Grande, showed herself very exacting, setting a high
price upon her services, and detailing at length all that she had
done while she was with the Buteaus: her work in the household, and with the cows, and out in the fields, where her
brother-in-law had made her labour like a man. The exasperated
Buteaus, on the other hand, swelled out the list of expenses as
much as possible, counting up every meal, telling lies about
the girl's clothes, and claiming even the money which had been
spent in presents for her on fête-days. But, despite all
they could do, they found themselves with a balance of a
hundred and eighty-six francs against them. Their hands
trembled and their eyes blazed as they tried to think of something else that they might charge for.

The statement was about to be passed when Buteau
suddenly cried out :

"Stop a moment. There's the doctor. He came twice
when she was out of sorts ; that makes another six francs."

La Grande was by no means inclined to let the others enjoy
this victory undisturbed, and she stirred up old Fouan to make
him recollect how many days' work the girl had done on the
farm while he was living in the house. Was it five days or
six, at a franc and a half the day? Françoise cried six, and
Lise cried five, hurling the words at each other's heads as
though they had been stones. The distracted old man now
supported one and then the other, tapping his forehead with his
fists. Françoise, however, carried the day, and there was now
a balance to her credit of a hundred and eighty-nine francs.

"Well, is everything included now ?" asked the notary.

Buteau seemed quite crushed and overwhelmed with this
ever-increasing liability, and no longer struggling, he sat there
hoping that affairs had now seen their worst.

"I'll take off my shirt if they want it," he groaned in a
doleful voice.

La Grande, however, had kept a last terrible bolt in reserve. It was a very important and simple matter, which everybody seemed to have forgotten.

" And then there's the five hundred francs compensation **for the** road up yonder."

Buteau now sprang wildly **to his feet, his** eyes projecting **out** of his head, and his mouth **wide open.** He could say nothing, **however; no discussion** was **possible.** He had received the **money, and was** bound to **hand half** of it over. For a **moment** he ransacked his brains for something to say, but he **could not** think of anything at all ; and in the wild anger that was rising and making his head throb, he suddenly rushed forward at Jean.

" You filthy blackguard !" **he cried, "** it is you who killed our friendship ! If it hadn't been for you, we should still have all been living together in peace and quiet ! "

Jean, who had very sensibly preserved silence, was now forced **to** assume an attitude **of** defence.

" Keep off !" he said, " or I'll strike."

Françoise and Lise had hastily sprung up and planted themselves in front of their respective husbands, their faces swollen by their gradually accumulating hatred, and their nails outstretched and ready **to** tear each other's faces. A general engagement, which neither Fouan nor La Grande seemed inclined to prevent, would certainly have taken place, and caps and hair would soon have been flying about, if the notary had not thrown off his professional calmness.

" Confound it **all !**" he cried, " wait till you've got outside. **It's** disgusting that you can't settle your accounts without fighting ! "

Then as the quivering antagonists quieted down, he added :

" You are now agreed, I think, eh ? Well, I will have the accounts made out in proper form, and then, when they have been signed, we will proceed to the sale of the house, and get the whole matter done with. Now you can go, and mind you are careful. Folly sometimes turns out very expensive ! "

This remark finished pacifying them. As they were leaving, **however,** Hyacinthe, **who** had been waiting outside for his father, attacked the whole family, and roared out that it was a foul shame to involve a poor old man in their dirty business for the sake of robbing him, no doubt ; and then, as his drunkenness made him affectionate, he took his father away, as he had brought him, in a cart, bedded with straw, which he had borrowed from a neighbour. The Buteaus went off on one

side, while La Grande pushed Jean and Françoise towards "The
Jolly Ploughman," where she had herself treated to some black
coffee. She was radiant.

"At any rate I've had a good laugh!" she exclaimed, as
she put the remains of the sugar into her pocket.

La Grande had another idea that same day. When she got
back to Rognes, she hurried off to make an arrangement with
old Saucisse, who had once been a lover of hers, so folks
declared. The Buteaus having threatened to bid against Françoise for the house, even though it cost them all they possessed,
it had occurred to her that if Saucisse bid on Françoise's behalf
the others might not have any suspicions, but let him secure the
house; he was their neighbour and might very well wish to
enlarge his premises. In consideration of a present the old
man immediately consented to do as he was asked.

On the second Sunday of the month, when the sale came off,
matters turned out just as La Grande had foreseen. Once
more the Buteaus were seated on one side of Monsieur Baillehache's office, and Françoise and Jean and La Grande on the
other. There were also various other people there, some
peasants, who had come with a vague idea of bidding, if things
went very cheaply. After four or five bids from Lise and
Françoise, the house stood at three thousand five hundred
francs, which was just about its value. When they got to
three thousand eight hundred, Françoise stopped. Then old
Saucisse came upon the scene, pushed the bidding up to four
thousand francs, and then on to an additional five hundred.
The Buteaus looked at each other in consternation. They felt
as though they could really go no higher; the thought of such
a large sum of money quite froze their blood. Lise, however,
let herself be carried away as far as five thousand francs; but
then the old man quite crushed her by immediately bidding
five thousand two hundred. That settled the business, and the
house was knocked down to him for the five thousand two
hundred francs. The Buteaus sniggered. It would be very
pleasant to handle their share of this big sum of money, now
that Françoise and her filthy blackguard of a husband had
failed to get the house.

However, when Lise, upon her return to Rognes, once more
entered the old house where she had been born and where she
had hitherto lived, she burst into tears. Buteau, also, was
dreadfully cut up and down-hearted, and he relieved his
feelings by falling foul of his wife; swearing that if he had
had his own way he would have parted with the last hair on

his head rather than have let the house go. But your heartless women, he cried, refused to open their purses, except it were for self-indulgence. In this, however, he was lying, for it was he himself who had held Lise back. Then they got to blows. Ah! The poor old patrimonial abode of the Fouans, built by an ancestor three hundred years previously, and now crazy and cracked, mended and patched in every part, sunken and thrown forward by the sweeping winds of La Beauce! To think that the family had lived in it for three hundred years, that they had grown to love it and honour it as a holy relic, and that it was counted as a leading item in the inheritances! Buteau, at the thought of losing it, knocked his wife down with a back-hander, and when she struggled up again she kicked him so violently that she nearly broke his leg.

On the evening of the next day matters were even worse—the thunderbolt fell. Old Saucisse had gone in the morning to complete the sale, and by noon all Rognes knew that he had bought the house on behalf of Françoise, with her husband's authorisation; and not only the house, but the furniture also, and Gédéon and La Coliche. There was a howl of anguish and distress at the Buteaus', as though lightning had stricken them. Husband and wife threw themselves upon the ground, and roared and wept in their wild despair at finding themselves defeated, outwitted, by that hussy of a girl. What maddened them, perhaps, more than anything else, was the knowledge that the whole village was laughing at them for their lack of penetration. To be fooled in this way, and turned out of their own house by such a trick! No, indeed, it was too much! They would not submit to it!

When La Grande presented herself the same evening on Françoise's behalf, and politely inquired of Buteau when it would be convenient for him to give up possession, he thrust her out of the house, casting all prudence to the winds and only making use of a foul expression.

The old woman went off chuckling, simply remarking that she would send the bailiff. The next day, indeed, Vimeux, with a pale, uneasy face, and looking more pitiable than usual, came up the street and gently knocked at the door, anxiously watched by all the gossips in the neighbouring houses. No notice was taken of his knock, and he gave a louder one, and even summoned up enough courage to call out and explain that he had come to serve a notice to quit. Then the window of the garret was opened, and a voice roared out the same foul word as had been addressed to La Grande; while the contents

of a chamber utensil were flung **upon** Vimeux, who, soaked
from head to foot, had to go off without serving the notice. For
a whole **month** Rognes roared over his ad**venture**.

La **Grande, however,** now immediately **went off to** Châteaudun **with Jean,** to consult a lawyer. The latter explained to
her that at least five days would be necessary before the
Buteaus could be ejected. Complaint would have to be
formally laid ; then an order would have to be obtained from
the presiding judge ; this order would then have to be registered, and then the ejectment would take place, the bailiff being
assisted by the gendarmes, if necessary. La Grande tried hard
to get matters settled a day sooner, and when she returned
to Rognes—it was then Tuesday—she told every one that on
the Saturday evening the Buteaus would be turned into the
street at the point of the sword like thieves, if they did not
voluntarily take themselves off in the meantime.

When this was repeated to Buteau, he made a threatening
gesture and told every one he met that he would never leave
the house alive, and that the soldiers would have to **break**
down the walls before they dragged him out. His **fury**
acquired such an extravagant character that the whole
neighbourhood was at a loss to know whether he was pretending to be mad, or really was so. He passed wildly along
the roads, standing in the front of **his cart, and keeping his
horse at** the gallop, without replying **when he was spoken to**
or warning the foot passengers. He **was met at** nights, too,
now in one part of **the** neighbourhood, **now in** another, returning **from nobody knew where,** possibly **from seeing** the
fiend. **One man who had ventured up to** him **had** received a
heavy cut from his whip. He spread terror abroad, **and** the
whole village was soon constantly on the look-out. One
morning it was seen that he had barricaded the house, and terrible cries were heard from behind the closed doors, piteous
howls in which the neighbours fancied they could distinguish
the voices of Lise and her two children, Laure and Jules. The
whole **neighbourhood was** revolutionised, and **took counsel
together** as to what **should be** done ; with **the result that an**
old peasant risked **his life by** raising **a ladder to one** of the
windows, in view **of climbing** up to see **what** was going on
inside. Buteau, however, opened the window, and overturned
both the ladder and **the** old man, the latter almost having his
legs broken. Couldn't **a** chap be left alone in his own house ?
Buteau roared as he shook his fists, and he threatened to
murder everybody if they made any further attempt to inter-

fere with him. Lise also appeared with her two children, and gave utterance to a flood of virulent language, abusing her neighbours for poking their noses into what did not concern them. After that no one dared **to** make any further attempt at interference; but the general **alarm** increased at every fresh outburst, and people shuddered as they listened to the dreadful uproar. The more **cynical fellows** thought that Buteau was only acting, **but others swore that** he had gone off his **n**ut, and that some terrible result would ensue. The truth, however, was never known.

On the Friday, **the day before** the Buteaus **were to** be ejected, another **scene caused** great emotion. Buteau, having met **his father near the** church, began to cry like a calf, kneeling down on the **ground** in front of the old man, and **asking** pardon of him **for all** his previous misconduct **It was** probably owing to **that, he** said, that his present **troubles** had **come** upon him. **H**e besought his father to **return to** live **with** him, seeming to think that this alone **could put** fortune again **on** his side. Fouan, worried by all this braying, and amazed by his son's seeming repentance, promised to entertain the proposal **some** day, when all the family worries were over.

At last the Saturday **arrived.** Buteau's excitement had gone on increasing, and **from morn** to night he was ever harnessing and unharnessing his **horse again** without the slightest reason. Folks fled out of the way when they saw him driving furiously along, full of consternation at the sight of all this aimless rushing about. At about eight o'clock on the Saturday morning Buteau once more put his horse between the shafts, but did not leave his premises. He **took up** his stand at the door, calling out to every one who passed by, sniggering and sobbing and yelling out his troubles **in** coarse language. Oh, it was a nice th**ing, wasn't it**? to **be** made a fool of by a young **hussy who'd been his keep for the last** five years! Yes, she was a strumpet, and so was **his wife!** Yes, a couple of fine strumpets, who fought together as to which of them he should belong. He continued harping upon this lie, inventing all kinds of nasty details out of spite and revengeful bitterness. Lise having come to the door, there was another atrocious scene between them. Buteau thrashed her in sight of everybody, and then sent her back again, limp and subdued, while he himself felt relieved by the hiding he had given her. He still remained at the door on the look-out for the agents of the law, which he jeered at and reviled. Had the law stopped on the way to make a beast of herself? he cried. At last, no longer expecting the bailiff, he became triumphant.

It was not till four o'clock that Vimeux made his appearance, accompanied by a couple of gendarmes. Buteau turned pale, and hastily closed the yard door. Possibly he had believed that matters would never be pushed to an extremity. A death-like silence fell upon the house. Protected by armed men, Vimeux was now quite insolent, and knocked at the door with his two fists. No answer was vouchsafed. Then the gendarmes came forward and made the old door shake with the butts of their guns. A crowd of men, women, and children had followed them; all Rognes was there, waiting to see the siege. Then suddenly the door was thrown open again, and Buteau was seen, standing in the front of his cart, and lashing his horse forward. He came out at a gallop, right into the midst of the assembled crowd.

"I'm going to drown myself! I'm going to drown myself!" he bellowed out amid the cries of alarm.

It was all up, and he was going to make an end of it by hurling himself and his horse and cart into the Aigre!

"Look out, there," he shouted; "I'm going to drown myself!"

Fright dispersed the inquisitive folks, as Buteau lashed his whip and the cart rushed wildly out. However, just as he was going to dash down the slope, at the risk of smashing the wheels of the vehicle, several men ran forward to arrest his course. The obstinate fool was quite capable of making the plunge, they cried, just for the sake of annoying people! They caught him up, but there was a struggle; while some sprang to the horse's head others had to climb into the cart. When they led him back to the house again, he clenched his teeth and stiffened his whole body, but said not a single word, letting fate take its course, with no other protest save the silence of impotent anger.

La Grande now made her appearance with Françoise and Jean, whom she was bringing to take possession of the house. Buteau contented himself with staring at them with the sombre gaze with which he now watched the completion of his misfortune. Lise, however, began to cry out and struggle, as though she were mad. The gendarmes had ordered her to take what belonged to her and quit the premises. There was nothing left for her but to obey, since her husband was poltroon enough, she cried, to stand by without striking a blow in her defence. With her arms a-kimbo, she began to abuse him.

" You craven! to stand by and allow us to be turned into the street in this way! You haven't got any pluck, **eh?** Why don't you hit the swine! **Get out** of my sight, **you** coward! You're no man!"

As she went **on** yelling **all this in his face,** exasperated by **his** quiescent demeanour, he **at last gave her** such a violent **shove** that she **moaned. However, he still** persisted in his **silence,** and merely glowered at **her with his** sombre eyes.

" **Come** now, look sharp," **cried Vimeux,** triumphantly, " We shan't go **away till you have given up the keys** to the new owners."

Lise **thereupon began to** remove her goods in a wild paroxysm **of rage.** During **the** last three days she and Buteau had already **transferred a** great many things, tools and implements, and **the** larger domestic **utensils,** to the **house of** their neighbour, **La** Frimat. It was **indeed** evident **that they had** really anticipated the ejection, for they had made arrangements **with** the old woman to have the use of her house till they had time to settle down again. The place was too big for La Frimat, who **merely** retained **the** bed-room **to** which her paralysed husband **was** confined.

As the furniture and live-stock had been sold together with the house, Lise merely **had to remove her** linen, her mattresses, and a few other trifling **articles.** Everything **was** tossed out of the door and windows into the **middle** of the **yard, while** the two little ones yelled as though they thought **that their** last day had come, Laure clinging to her mother's skirts, while Jules, who had tumbled down, was wallowing **in the midst of** the ejected property. As Buteau made no attempt to assist his wife, the gendarmes, like good fellows, began to place the bundles in **the cart,** which was still standing in front of the door.

However, **the row** commenced **all** over again when Lise **caught** sight of Françoise and Jean, standing beside La Grande. **She** rushed forward and gave free flow to all her accumulated wrath and **spite.**

" **Ah, you** filthy cat, you've come to look on with your tom, have you? Yes, feast your eyes on our trouble! It's just as though you were drinking **our** blood! You thief! you thief! **you** thief!

She almost choked as she shouted this **last word,** which she hurled again at her sister every time she came out into the yard with some fresh burden. Françoise did not reply. She was very pale, her lips were closely pressed together, and her eyes seemed to be on fire. But soon she assumed an air of suspicious watchfulness, and gazed at everything that was brought out, as though she wished **to make** sure that nothing belonging to her-**self was taken away.** Presently **her** eye fell upon a kitchen-**stool which had been included in** the sale.

"That belongs **to me,"** she exclaimed in a **rough voice.**

"Belongs to you, does it?" replied **her sister;** "go and fetch it, then!" and she hurled the stool into the pond.

The house was at last evacuated. Buteau took hold **of the** horse's bridle, while Lise picked up **her** two children, **her two last bundles, Jules in** her **right** arm **and Laure in the left.** Then, as she finally left her home, she stepped up to Françoise and spat in her face.

"There! take that for **yourself!"**

Her sister immediately spat back at her.

"And **you take that!"**

After **these farewell words, the** offspring of their bitter hatred, Lise **and** Françoise slowly wiped their faces, without taking their eyes **off** one another. They **were** sundered for **ever now; there was** henceforth nothing in common between **them save their kindred** blood, which surged with such **hot hate.**

Finally, Buteau opened his mouth **again to roar out the** order to start, which he coupled with **a threatening gesture in the** direction of the house.

"It won't be long before we come back again!"

La Grande followed them to see **the end of it all;** and, indeed, now that the Buteaus were completely **overthrown, she** resolved to turn against Françoise and **Jean, who had left her** so speedily, and whom she already **found much too** happy together. For a long time the villagers continued standing about **in groups,** talking to each other in undertones. Françoise **and Jean had** entered the **empty house.**

While the Buteaus were unloading their bundles at **La** Frimat's they were amazed to see old Fouan appear. **With** a frightened look, and glancing behind him as though **he was** afraid **of being** pursued, **he** asked: "**Is there** a corner **here for** me? **I have come to** sleep here."

He **had just fled in** terror from Hyacinthe's. For a long time past whenever he awoke during the night **he** always saw that bony creature La **Trouille** prowling in **her** chemise about his room, searching for the papers, which he had now taken the precaution to conceal out-of-doors in a hole in a rock, which he had stopped up with earth. The girl was sent on this errand by her father on account of **her** light suppleness, and she glided

about with bare feet just like a snake, insinuating herself
everywhere, between the chairs and under the bed. She
evinced the greatest enthusiasm in the search, feeling certain
that the old man placed the papers somewhere about his person
when he dressed himself, and exasperated that she could not
discover where he hid them on going to bed. She had convinced
herself that he did not put them in the bed itself, for she had
felt everywhere with her slender arm, with such skilful dexterity
that Fouan had scarcely known that she had touched him. On
that particular day, however, soon after breakfast, he had had a
fainting fit, falling against the table in a state of unconsciousness; and, as he came to himself again, still so overcome
that he kept his eyes closed, he realised that he was lying on
the ground near where he had fallen, and he could feel that
Hyacinthe and La Trouille were undressing him. Instead of
doing what they could to bring him round, the wretches had
had but one idea, that of at once profiting by the fit to search
him. La Trouille manifested an angry roughness in her search,
not going about it in her wonted gentle manner, but pulling
roughly at his jacket and trousers, and even examining every
corner of his flesh to make sure that he had not concealed his
treasure there. She turned him round, and then, stretching out
his limbs, she searched him as though she were ransacking
some old bag. Nothing! Where could he have hidden the
papers? It was enough to make one cut him open and look
inside!

The old man was in such terror lest he should be murdered
if he moved that he still feigned unconsciousness, and kept his
eyes closed and his legs and arms rigid. But as soon as he
found himself free again he fled, firmly resolved never to
spend another night at the Château.

"Tell me, can you give me a corner?" he asked again.

Buteau's spirits seemed to revive at his father's unexpected
return. It was money that was coming back.

"Certainly I can, dad! We'll squeeze together to find a
corner for you. It will bring us luck, too. Ah, I should be
a rich man, if merely a good heart were needed to make one
so!"

Françoise and Jean had slowly entered the empty house.
The night was closing in, and the rooms lay silent in the
mournful, fading light. Everything there was very old. This
patrimonial roof had sheltered the toil and wretchedness of
three centuries, and there was an air of solemnity about the
place such as dwells in the gloom of an ancient village church.

The doors were still standing open. It seemed as though a
storm of wind had blown through the house; the chairs lay overturned on the ground amid the general chaos of the removal.
The place looked as though it were dead.

Françoise slowly went over it, examining every corner.
Vague recollections and confused sensations awoke in her as
she proceeded. In that spot she had played as a child. It
was in the kitchen, near that table, that her father had died.
As she stood in the bedroom, in front of the bed stripped of its
mattress, she thought of Lise and Buteau, and of the nights
when they had embraced each other so vigorously that she
could hear the sound of their panting breath through the
ceiling. Was she even now to be tormented by them? She
felt as though Buteau were still there. Here he had seized
hold of her one night, and she had bitten him. And here
again, too, and here. There was not a corner in the whole
house that did not suggest some painful recollection.

Then as Françoise turned round, she started at seeing Jean.
What was this stranger doing in the house? There was an
air of constraint about him, as though he were on a visit, and
did not like to take the liberty of touching anything. She felt
overwhelmed with a feeling of solitude, and grew sick at heart
to find that her victory had not made her more joyful. She
had fancied she would enter the house, full of happiness,
triumphant in the thought of having ejected her sister; but
now the house afforded her no pleasure, and her heart was
heavy and ill at ease. Perhaps it was the dying day that was
filling her with melancholy!

When the night had quite fallen, she and her husband were
still wandering from one room to another in the darkness, without having had the courage even to light a candle.

Presently, however, a noise brought them back into the
kitchen, and they became merry on recognising Gédéon, who
had effected an entrance after his usual custom, and had his
head inside the sideboard, which had been left open. Close by,
inside the stable, they could hear old La Coliche lowing.

Then Jean, taking Françoise in his arms, kissed her tenderly,
as though to say that, despite everything, they would be happy.

PART V.

CHAPTER I.

PRIOR to the ploughing, La Beauce, stretched beneath the grey, damp, November sky, was hidden from sight by a covering of manure. Carts were lumbering along the country roads, piled up with old straw litter, which filled the air with a smoky vapour; it was as though the vehicles were bearing a supply of heat to the soil. Little piles of litter from cattle-sheds and stables rose up over certain fields like surging waves, while on other patches the manure had already been spread out, and soiled the land with a dingy flood. In this mass of fermenting dung the rich fertility of the coming spring lay brooding; the decomposed matter was returning to the universal womb, and life would once more spring from death. From end to end of the vast plain the air reeked with the strong odour of the dung, which by-and-bye would bring forth bread for men.

One afternoon Jean was taking a heavy load of manure to his plot of land on the plateau. It was a month since he and Françoise had taken up their abode in the old house, and they had now dropped into the monotonous, though busy, routine of country life. As Jean approached his field he espied Buteau in the adjoining plot, with a pitchfork in his hand, engaged in spreading out the manure which had been placed there in heaps the previous week. The two men cast sidelong glances at each other. Being neighbouring owners, they frequently met and worked in close proximity to each other. Buteau greatly suffered, for the loss of Françoise's share, torn from his seven-acre plot, had left him with two detached parcels, one on the right and one on the left of Françoise's strip, and he constantly had to make circuits to get to one parcel from the other. The two men never said a word to each other. The chance was that some day a quarrel would break out between them, and then they would murder each other with their pitchforks.

Jean now commenced to discharge his load of manure. He had mounted on to the top of it; and, buried in it up to his hips,

he was throwing it down with his pitchfork, when Hourdequin passed by, having been engaged in a round of inspection
all the morning.   He had retained a kindly recollection of his
servant, and he stopped to speak to him.   His form seemed to
have aged, and his face was worn with the anxiety which his
farm and other matters were causing him.

" Why have you never tried phosphates, Jean? he asked.

Then, without waiting for a reply, he went on talking for a
long time, as though he were trying to drown his thoughts.
The true solution of successful agriculture, he said, was to be
looked for in these various natural and artificial manures.   He
himself had tried everything, and had just passed through that
craze for manures which sometimes seizes hold of farmers like
a fever.   He had tried all manner of things, one after another;
grass, leaves, the refuse of pressed grapes, rape and colza oil-cake,
crushed bones, flesh cooked and pounded, blood dessicated and
reduced to a powder; and it was a source of vexation to him
that the absence of any slaughterhouse in the neighbourhood
prevented him from trying the effects of blood in a liquid state.
He was now using road-scrapings, the scourings of ditches,
the cinders and ashes from stoves, and especially scraps of
waste wool, having purchased the sweepings of a woollen
manufactory at Châteaudun.   His theory was that everything
that came from the soil was a proper material to return to it.
He had great pits filled with compost at the rear of his farm,
and in them he stowed all the refuse of the whole neighbourhood, whatever he could get hold of, even offal and putrifying
carcasses picked out of stagnant ponds and elsewhere.   It was
all golden, he said.

" I have sometimes had very good results with phosphates,"
he remarked to Jean.

" But one gets so dreadfully cheated," Jean replied.

" Yes, certainly, if you buy from chance agents who are
trying to do a small business in the country.   At each market
there ought to be a chemical expert who understands these
artificial manures, which it is so difficult to get unadulterated.
The future lies in them, I'm sure, but before that future comes
I'm afraid we shall all be done up.   We must have courage,
however, and be content to suffer for the sake of others."

The stench of the dung which Jean was moving seemed to
have somewhat revived the farmer's spirits.   He revelled in it,
and inhaled it with a sense of vigorous enjoyment, as though he
smelt in it the procreative elements of the soil.

" No doubt," he resumed after a pause, " nothing has yet

been discovered which equals farm-yard manure; **but one never** can get a sufficient quantity of it. And then **the men** just toss it on to the ground. They don't know how **to prepare** it or how to manipulate it. See, now, that dung of yours has been burnt by the sun; you don't keep it covered."

Then he launched out into invectives against routine, **when** Jean confessed that he still made use of Buteau's old dung-**hole** in front of the cow-house. For some years **past he** himself, he said, had introduced layers of soil and **turf into his** pits, and had set up **a system** of pipes to **convey the slops** of the kitchen, with the urine of **the** family **and cattle, and** indeed all the drainings **of** the **farm, down to a** reservoir; and twice **a week** the dung-hill was watered with this liquid-manure. Now-a-days he even carefully saved and utilised all the **contents** of the privies.

" **It** is downright folly," he exclaimed, " to waste **the good** things that God gives us! For a long time I had **scruples of** delicacy about it, just as the peasants have. But **old Mother** Caca converted me. You know old Mother Caca, don't you? She's a neighbour of yours. Well, it was she alone who went about matters in the right way; and the cabbage **over** whose roots she used to empty her slops was the king of cabbages, both in size and flavour, and **it was** so simply on account of what the old woman did."

Jean laughed as he jumped down from his **cart,** which was now empty, then he began to divide his manure into little heaps. Hourdequin walked on after him, amid the warm reek which floated round them.

" The yearly refuse of Paris alone would be sufficient **to** fertilise some seventy thousand acres," said the farmer. " It has all been properly calculated. And yet this is all wasted! There is only just a small quantity of dried night-soil utilised. Just think of it; seventy thousand acres! Ah, if we could only have it **here, it** would cover all La Beauce, and then you would see the wheat grow !"

He embraced the whole level extent of La Beauce in a sweeping gesture; and in his enthusiasm he mentally beheld **all** Paris pouring out its fertilising flood of human manure over the spreading tract. Streamlets were trickling along in all directions, overflowing the fields as the sea of sewage **mounted** higher and higher beneath the glowing sun, sped onward by a breeze which wafted the odour far and wide. The great city was restoring to the soil the life it had received from it. The earth slowly absorbed the fertilising tide, and from the glutted and fattened soil there burst forth great teeming harvests of white bread.

"We should want boats in that case," remarked Jean, who was at once amused and disgusted by the novel idea of submerging the land beneath a sea of sewage.

Just at that moment the sound of a voice made him turn his head, and he was astonished to see Lise in her light cart, which was drawn up at the side of the road. She was shouting to Buteau at the top of her voice:

"I'm just off to Cloyes to fetch Monsieur Finet. Your father has fallen down in a fit in his bedroom. I'm afraid he's dying. You'd better go home and see to him."

Then, without waiting for a reply, she whipped her horse forward, and rattled along the straight road, disappearing out of sight in the distance.

Buteau leisurely continued spreading out his last heaps of manure, growling to himself as he did so. His father ill; here was a nuisance! Very likely it was all a sham, just to get himself coddled and pampered! Then he put on his jacket again, as the thought struck him that after all something serious must be the matter with the old man, since his wife had of her own accord decided to go to the expense of a doctor.

"Now, there's a fellow who's stingy with his manure!" observed Hourdequin, looking with interest at the dung in the adjoining field. "A niggardly peasant has niggardly land. Ah, he's a wretched scamp, and you will do well to beware of him, especially after the worries you've had with him. How can you expect things to prosper when there are so many scoundrels and lewd hussies in the land? There are far too many, far too many!"

Then, saddened once more, he went off in the direction of La Borderie, just as Buteau, with his slouching gait, had got back to Rognes. Jean, left to himself, went on with his work, piling up at every ten yards or so a fresh heap of the manure, from which an ammoniacal vapour was rising in still greater force. Other heaps were smoking in the distance, blurring the line of the horizon with a fine bluish mist. All La Beauce would lie warm and odorous until the coming frosts.

The Buteaus were still quartered at La Frimat's, occupying the whole of her house, except the back room on the ground-floor, which she reserved for herself and her paralytic husband. As for a long time past she had had neither a horse in her stable nor any cows in her cow-house, her tenants had placed their own animals there. They found themselves rather cramped for room on the whole, and they chiefly regretted the loss of their kitchen-garden and orchard; for La Frimat naturally retained her acre or so of ground for her own use, especially as by desperately hard work she managed to get out of this strip of land just sufficient to support her old husband and provide him with a few luxuries. This want of a kitchen-garden would of itself have sufficed to make the Buteaus move to other quarters, had they not perceived that their proximity was a source of much annoyance to Françoise. There was only a wall between the grounds of the two houses, and the Buteaus used to declare, in loud tones, on purpose to be overheard, that they were only just staying at La Frimat's for a time, for they would certainly return to their old home very soon. As this was a matter of certainty, what was the use of troubling themselves with another removal? They never condescended to explain by what means their return to their old home was to be effected, and it was this calm assurance, this persistent expression of certainty on their part, based upon she knew not what, that sent Françoise almost wild, and quite spoilt her pleasure at finding herself mistress of the house. Then, too, Lise occasionally reared a ladder against the shed, and mounted it, to assail her sister with coarse abuse. Ever since the accounts had been balanced between them at Monsieur Baillehache's office, she had accused her sister of robbing her, and she was never weary of hurling the most abominable accusations from one yard to the other.

When Buteau at last reached the house, he found old Fouan lying on the bed in the little closet which he occupied behind the kitchen, under the staircase leading to the loft. The two children, Jules and Laure, the former of whom was now eight years of age, while the latter was three, had been left to watch him; and they were amusing themselves with making streams of water on the floor by pouring out the contents of their grandfather's jug.

" Well, what's the matter, eh ? " asked Buteau, standing in front of the bed.

Fouan had recovered consciousness. His widely opened eyes slowly turned towards his son, and fixed their stare upon him, but his head remained quite motionless, and he looked as though he were petrified.

" Come, now, dad, none of your jokes! I'm too busy for them," said Buteau. " You mustn't go off the hooks to-day."

Then, as Jules and Laure had now managed to break the jug, he gave them a couple of cuffs which set them howling.

The old man's eyes were still staring, widely open, with the pupils enlarged and rigid. If he could not express himself more intelligibly than that, thought Buteau, there was nothing more to be done at present. They must wait and see what the doctor said. He now regretted having come away from the field, and he began to chop some wood in front of the kitchen, for the sake of doing something.

Lise returned almost immediately with Monsieur Finet, who made a lengthy examination of the ailing man, the Buteaus awaiting the result with an uneasy air. The old man's death would have been a release to them, if he had been carried off at once; but, if he were to linger on for a long time they might incur heavy expenses, and then again, if he died before they had succeeded in possessing themselves of his hoard, Fanny and Hyacinthe, as they foresaw, would give them a deal of trouble. The doctor's silence served to increase their uneasiness, and when he took a seat in the kitchen to write out a prescription, they determined to question him.

"Is it anything serious, then? Will it last a week? Dear me, what a lot you are writing down for him? What can it all be?"

Monsieur Finet made no reply. He was accustomed to be questioned in this way by the peasantry, who lost their heads in the presence of illness, and he treated them like so many animals, refraining from entering into conversation with them. He had great experience with common-place complaints, and generally saved his patients, being perhaps more successful in dealing with them than a man of greater science would have been. However, the mediocrity to which he accused the peasants of having reduced him made him harsh and stern towards them. This only served to increase their deference, despite the doubts they continually entertained as to the efficacy of his draughts. Would it be worth the money it cost? That was the question always uppermost in their minds.

"Do you think, then," asked Buteau, alarmed by the sight of the page of writing, "that all that will make him better?"

The doctor merely shrugged his shoulders. Then he again returned to the sick man's bed-side, feeling interested in the case, and surprised to notice symptoms of fever after this slight attack of cerebral congestion. Keeping his eyes fixed upon his watch, he again counted the beats of the old man's pulse, without trying to extract the slightest information from him. Meantime Fouan continued staring at him with his stupefied air.

" It will be a three weeks' business," said the doctor as he
went away. " I will come again to-morrow. Don't be surprised if he's off his nut to-night."

Three weeks! The Buteaus had had ears for those words
only, and they were full of consternation. What a pile of
money it would cost them if there would be a pageful of
medicine every night! And what made matters worse was
that Buteau now had to get into the cart and drive off to the
druggist's at Cloyes. It was a Saturday, and when La Frimat
returned from selling her vegetables she found Lise sitting
alone, and feeling so miserable that she could do nothing. The
old woman expressed the bitterest grief when she heard what
had happened. She never had any luck! she cried. If it had
happened some other day, when she had been at home, she
might at least have profited by the doctor's presence to consult
him about her husband.

The news had already spread through Rognes, for the impudent La Trouille had called at the house, which she would
not leave without touching her grandfather's hand, so that she
might return and tell Hyacinthe that the old man was not dead.
Then, after this shameless slut, La Grande made her appearance, evidently sent by Fanny. She planted herself by the
side of her brother's bed, and formed her opinion of his
condition by the appearance of his eyes, just as she judged the
eels from the Aigre; and she went away with a perk of her
nose, as though to say that he would certainly get over it this
time. The family now took matters easily. What was the
good of troubling themselves, as the old man would in all probability recover?

The house was topsy-turvy up to midnight. Buteau had
returned in an execrable temper. There were mustard-plasters
for the old man's legs, a draught to be taken every hour, and
a purgative, in case he seemed better, for the morning. La
Frimat proffered her assistance, but, at ten o'clock, growing
drowsy, and not feeling much interested in the matter, she
went to bed. Buteau, who wanted to do the same, tried to
hustle Lise off. What was the good of their staying there?
he cried. They couldn't do the old man any good by just
looking at him!

Fouan was now rambling in his talk, speaking inconse-
quentially in loud tones. He appeared to imagine that he was
out in the fields, hard at work, as in the far-off days of his
youthful vigour. Lise, whom these reminiscences of the past
affected with an uneasy disquietude, as though her uncle were

already buried and **was now** restlessly wandering **on** the earth again, was about **to follow** her husband, **who was** undressing himself, **when she stopped** to put away **the old man's** clothes which **were still lying on a** chair. She carefully shook them, after having made a lengthy examination **of the pockets, in** which she found nothing but **some string and a damaged knife.** As she next proceeded to hang them up in the cupboard, she suddenly caught sight of a little bundle of papers in the middle of a shelf, right in front of her eyes. Her heart gave a great leap. Here was the secret treasure! **the treasure which had** been so anxiously sought for during the **last month in all sorts** of extraordinary places, and which was now openly presented **to her** sight as if to **invite her to take it!** It was evident **that** the old man **had just been going to transfer it to some fresh** hiding-place when **he was seized by the fit.**

"Buteau! Buteau!" she called in so stifled a voice that her husband **at once ran to her in his shirt, imagining that his father was dying.**

For a moment he, too, remained choking with amazement. Then a **wild delight took possession of** them both, and taking hold of **each other's hands** they jumped about opposite each other like a **couple of goats,** forgetting all about the sick man, who was now lying **with** his eyes shut and his head seemingly riveted to the pillow. **He was** still rambling on, spasmodically, in his delirium. Just now he fancied that he was ploughing.

"Come, **now,** get along, **you brute!** Confound it all, **there's** a great piece of flint, and **it won't yield!** The handles are getting broken, and I **shall have to buy new ones.** Get along, you **brute, get along!**"

"Hush!" murmured Lise, turning round with a startled air.

"Stuff!" retorted Buteau. "You don't suppose he understands, do you? Can't you hear him drivelling?"

They now both seated themselves near the bed, for their sudden shock of delight left their legs quite weak and tremulous.

"**No one can ever** say that we hunted about for it," **Lise** observed, "**for,** as God is my witness, I wasn't thinking about his money at all! It tumbled into my hand. **Let us** see what there is."

Buteau had already unfolded the papers, and **was reckoning** them up aloud.

"Two hundred and thirty, and seventy; that's just three hundred altogether. That's exactly what I reckoned it at before, **when I saw** him draw fifteen five-franc pieces **for** the quarter's interest at the tax-collector's. Doesn't it seem **funny, now,** that these shabby bits of paper are just as good **as real** money?"

Lise again hushed him, alarmed by **a** sudden snigger from **the** old man, who now seemed **to** be imagining that he was engaged in reaping the famous harvest in Charles X.'s time, which was so plentiful **that there was not** room enough in which to garner it all.

"What a **lot! what a lot!** Did ever any **one** see such a harvest? **What a lot!** what a lot!"

His choking laugh sounded like **a death-rattle; and** his delight must have been altogether internal, **for not a trace of** it appeared on his rigid **face.**

"Oh, it's only some of **his** crazy thoughts that he's snigger**ing about,"** Buteau remarked, shrugging his shoulders.

There was now an interval of silence, during which **the husband** and wife looked at the papers, absorbed in thought.

"Well, what are we to do with them?" Lise murmured, presently. "Oughtn't we to put them back again?"

Buteau made an energetic gesture of refusal.

"Oh, yes, indeed, we must put them back again," his wife protested. "He will look for them, and he will make an outcry if he doesn't find them, and then we shall have a fine row with our swinish relatives."

She now checked herself **for the** third time, startled by hearing her father sobbing. He seemed to be a prey to some bitter, hopeless grief, for his sobs sounded as though they came from the very depths of his soul. It was impossible **to** guess what was troubling him, for he only moaned out in **a voice that** gradually grew more hollow:

"It's all over—all over—all over."

"And do you suppose," Buteau now exclaimed violently, "that I am going to leave these papers in **the** possession of that old chap who**'s off his** nut, for him to burn them or tear them up? No, **indeed."**

"Yes, that is perhaps true," murmured Lise.

"Come, now, we've had **quite** enough of the matter; let's go to bed. If he asks for the papers, I'll make it my business to **reply to** him; and the others had better not try to worry **me!"**

They now went off to bed, after concealing the papers under the marble top of an old chest of drawers, **w**hich seemed to them to be a safer hiding-place than one of the drawers themselves, even if they were kept locked. The old man was left alone, without a candle, for fear of fire, and he continued sobbing and talking deliriously all through the night.

On the morrow Monsieur Finet found him calmer, and altogether better than he had expected. Ah, those old plough horses had their souls well riveted to their bodies! he exclaimed. The fever which he had feared did not seem likely now. He prescribed steel, quinine, and other expensive drugs, filling the Buteaus with renewed consternation; and, as he was leaving, he had a struggle with La Frimat, who had been on the watch for him.

"My good woman," he said, "I have already told you that there is really no difference between your husband and this block of stone. I can't put life into stones, can I? You must know very well what the end will be; and the sooner the better both for him and for you."

He then whipped up his horse, and the old woman sank down on to the block of stone in a flood of tears. It was already a weary long time, a dozen years and more, that she had been burdened with the support of her husband, and her strength was failing her with advancing age. She was afraid, indeed, that ere long she would be too weak to cultivate her patch of ground: but all the same, it upset her to think that she might soon lose the infirm old man, who had become like her child, whom she lifted and dressed and undressed and pampered with dainties. Even the unparalysed arm which he had hitherto been able to use was now growing so stiff that she herself was obliged to put his pipe into his mouth.

At the end of a week Monsieur Finet was astonished to find Fouan on his legs again. He was still very feeble, but he was obstinately bent on getting about, saying that the best way to keep from dying was to be determined not to die. Buteau sniggered behind the doctor's back with a contemptuous grin, for he had tossed all the prescriptions, after the second one, aside, declaring that the best way was to let the complaint feed on itself till it was exhausted. On market-day, however, Lise had been weak enough to bring back with her from the town a draught, which had been prescribed on the previous evening; and when the doctor paid his last visit on the Monday Buteau told him that the old man had nearly had a relapse.

"I don't know what it was they put into the bottle you ordered, but it made him dreadfully sick," he said.

That day, in the evening, Fouan at last spoke on the subject nearest his heart. Ever since he had left his bed he had been prowling about the house with an air of anxiety, with his mind

quite **blank as** to where he **had** deposited his papers. **He**
ferretted and searched everywhere, and made desperate efforts
to remember where he had put them. Then, at last, a vague
recollection dawned upon him. Perhaps he had not hidden
them away anywhere, but had left them lying on the shelf.
But, then again, supposing he was mistaken in his fears, supposing no one had taken the papers, was it advisable to give the
alarm, and confess to the existence of this money, which it had
cost him such a struggle in the past to get together, and concerning which **he** had **ever since** maintained the most
determined silence? For two days he struggled **on** against
contending emotions—the despair with which **the** sudden
disappearance **of** his money filled him, and the fear of
the consequences of indiscreetly opening his mouth. Gradually,
however, a clear **recollection** of matters returned **to** him, and
he remembered having placed the packet **of** papers **on the
shelf on** the morning of his attack, pending an opportunity **to
slip them** into a chink in the rafters of the ceiling, which **he** had
just discovered as he lay on his bed gazing into the air. **Plun-**
dered and desperate, he now unbosomed himself.

They had just finished their evening meal. Lise was putting
the plates away, and Buteau, who had been watching his father
with leering eyes ever since the day he had left his bed,
expected the outbreak, **and was** swinging himself on his chair,
thinking **that the** explosion **was now** really **coming off,** for the
old fellow seemed so very **wretched** and **excited. He was
not** mistaken, for Fouan, who had been persistently tottering
about the room on his shaky legs, now suddenly halted **in** front
of his son.

" Where are the papers ? " he demanded **of him in a hoarse
voice,** and the words almost seemed to **choke him.**

Buteau opened his eyes widely, with **an expression** of pro-
found surprise, as though he failed to **understand.**

" Eh ? what ? **What do** you say ? **Papers !** what papers ? "

" My money ! " roared the **old man,** bracing himself to his
full height, and assuming **a** threatening expression.

" Your money ! What have you still got some money left ?
Why, you swore that we had cost you so much that you hadn't
a copper to call **your own.** Oh, you cunning old chap, so **you**
really have some money."

He was still swinging about on his chair, sniggering and
highly amused, triumphant **at** having had such **a** good scent,
for he had been the first to suspect the existence **of** the treasure.

Fouan trembled in every limb.

" Give it back to me ! "

" Give it back to you? I haven't got your money ! Why, I don't even know where it is! "

" You have robbed me of it. Give it back to me, or I swear that I will make you give it up by force."

And, in spite of his great age, he seized Buteau by the shoulders and shook him. The son now sprang up from his chair and seized hold of his father in turn. But it was not to shake him, but simply to roar out in his face :

" Yes, I've got it, and I mean to keep it. I'm going to take care of it for you, you crazy old stupid, with your rambling wits. It was high time, too, that I did take the papers, for you were going to tear them up. He wanted to tear them, didn't he, Lise ? "

" Oh, yes, as sure as I'm here ! He didn't know a bit what he was doing."

Fouan was overwhelmed with consternation upon hearing this. Could it really be true that he was going mad, since he could recollect nothing of what had taken place ? Supposing he had really wanted to destroy the papers, just like a child playing with pictures, in that case he could no longer be good for anything, and was only fit to be killed ! He was now quite broken down, and all his courage and strength left him ; he could merely stammer out tearfully :

" Give them back to me ! "

" No ! "

" Give them me, since I'm all right again now."

" No, no, indeed ! you'd only wipe yourself with them, or use them to light your pipe ! "

After that the Buteaus obstinately persisted in their refusal to surrender the papers. They spoke about them quite openly to their neighbours, and they gave an exciting account of how they had arrived just in time to snatch them from the old man's hands when he was about to tear them up. One evening they even showed La Frimat a rent in one of the documents. Surely no one, they protested, could blame them for preventing such a misfortune, for the money would have been destroyed and lost to everybody. The neighbours publicly expressed their approval of the Buteaus' conduct, though they privately suspected them of lying. Hyacinthe was in a terrible rage. To think that the treasure which it had been impossible for him to find in his own house should have been so speedily discovered by the others ! One day, indeed, he had actually held it in his hands, and had been fool enough not to stick to

it! **He** swore to himself that he would call his brother to
account when the old man died. Fanny, too, said that the
money would have to be divided. The Buteaus did not say
the contrary, but, of course, the old man might recover posses-
sion, or give the bonds away by deed.

As for Fouan, he poured the story of his wrongs into the
ears of everybody he came across, waylaying every one he
could, and bemoaning his piteous lot to them. In this way,
one **morning, he** went into **his niece's yard to pour** out his
troubles **to Françoise and Jean.**

Françoise **was helping** her husband to load **a cart** with
manure. While **the latter stood** in the dung-hole and threw
the manure into the vehicle with his pitchfork, Françoise, standing aloft, trampled it **down with her feet to** compress it.

The old man stood leaning **on** his stick in front **of them,**
and began bewailing his sad fate.

" I'm dreadfully harassed about **this money of** mine, **you
know, which** they **have** taken from me and won't give **me**
back. What should you do if you were in my place? "

Françoise let him repeat the question three times before
she said anything in reply. She was annoyed at his coming to
talk to her in this way, **and received him coldly,** being anxious
to avoid all cause of quarrel with the **Buteaus.**

" Well, uncle," she answered at last, " it's really no business
of **ours, you know.** We **are only too glad to** have finished
with our own troubles."

Then turning her back upon him, she **continued treading**
down the dung which rose around her up to **her** thighs. **As her**
husband went on tossing up forkful after forkful, she all
but vanished amid the steamy smoke from the disturbed
manure, and yet she felt at ease, with her heart in the right
place, amid the asphyxiating fumes.

" **I'm not mad ;** that can be seen, can't it ? " Fouan continued,
not seeming **to have heard Françoise.** " They ought to give
me back my money. **Do you and Jean,** now, think me capable
of destroying it ? "

Neither Françoise nor Jean said **a** word.

" **I** should, indeed, have to be mad to do that, and I'm not
mad — you and your husband could bear witness to that, couldn't
you ? "

Françoise now suddenly braced herself up, standing on the
top of the loaded cart. She looked very tall and sturdy and
vigorous, almost as if she had sprung into life and grown up
there where she was **standing,** and as if that scent of rich

fecundity had emanated from herself. As she stood there with
her hands resting on her hips, and her bosom swelling roundly,
she looked a real woman.

"There, there, uncle, that's enough!" she said. "I've told
you already that we don't want to have anything to do with
all that squabbling. And, while we are on the subject, perhaps
you would do as well not to come here again."

"Do you mean to cast me off, then?" asked the old man,
trembling as he spoke.

Jean now thought it time to interpose.

"No; but we don't want to be mixed up in any quarrels.
There would be a three days' row if they were to see you here.
Every one has his own peace and quietness to look after, you
know."

Fouan stood motionless, gazing at them one after the other
out of his poor dim eyes. Then he went away.

"If ever I want any help," he said, "it is clear I shall have
to look somewhere else for it."

They allowed him to go away, though they felt uneasy and
troubled. They were not yet evil-hearted. But what could
they do? They could not have helped him by interfering in
the matter, and their own peace and quietness would have been
ruined to no purpose. While Jean went off to get his whip,
Françoise carefully collected the fallen straws with a shovel and
threw them on to the cart.

The next day there was a violent scene between Fouan and
Buteau. Every day, indeed, there were bitter passages between
them about the papers, the old man doggedly repeating his
"Give me them back again!" and the son refusing to do so,
with his "Hold your row, and let me alone!" But matters
had gradually grown more serious, especially since the old man
had set about trying to discover where his son had hidden the
bonds. He now, in his turn, prowled inquisitively about the
whole house, examining drawers and closets, and tapping
against the walls to see if he could discover any hollow place.
His eyes were continually straying from one spot to another,
in the one fixed idea that had seized hold of him; and as soon
as ever he found himself free from observation, he got rid of
the children and recommenced his search, with all the eagerness
of some young scapegrace who flies off to make love to the
servant-maid as soon as his parents are out of the way. That
day, however, Buteau returned home unexpectedly, and found
Fouan stretched on the floor on his stomach, with his nose
under the chest of drawers, trying to ascertain if there were

any possible hiding-place there. The sight almost put Buteau beside himself, for his father was unpleasantly warm in his scent now. What he was seeking below was hidden away above, sealed down, as it were, by the heavy weight of the marble slab.

"You confounded old addle-pate ; so you are playing the snake now? Get up at once ! "

He dragged his father by the legs, and then set him on his feet again with a vigorous pull.

"Haven't you got tired of thrusting your eye into every little hole and cranny? I'm getting quite weary of seeing you poking about in every chink and crevice in the house."

Fouan, annoyed at having been discovered, looked his son in the eyes, and cried in a sudden burst of anger :

" Give them back to me ! "

" Hold your jaw ! " roared Buteau in his face.

" Well, I'm made too wretched here. I shall go away."

" All right ! Off you go, then, and a pleasant journey to you ! And if ever you come back here you'll show that you've got no spirit ! "

As he spoke, he seized his father by the arm, and thrust him out of the house.

CHAPTER II.

Fouan made his way down the hill. His anger speedily evaporated, and when he reached the bottom and gained the high-road he stopped short, feeling dazed and confused at finding himself in the open with nowhere to go to. The church clock struck three, and the damp wind of the grey November afternoon blew piercingly cold. The old man shivered; it had all taken place so quickly that he had not even been able to pick up his hat. Fortunately, however, he had his stick with him. For a moment or two he began to walk on towards Cloyes. Then he asked himself where he was going to in that direction, and he turned round and made his way back towards Rognes, with his usual dragging gait. As he reached the Macquerons', he felt inclined to go in and have a glass. He searched his pockets, but he could not find a copper, and he felt ashamed to show himself, fearing that they might have already heard of what had happened. He fancied that Lengaigne, who was standing at his door, was watching him with that suspicious glance which is given to some disreputable tramp; and Lequeu, who was looking out of one of the school windows, did not even nod to him. It was easily understood; he was once more an object of contempt to every one, now that he was again without any means, now that he had been stripped anew, and this time to the very skin.

When he reached the Aigre, he leant his back for a moment or two against the parapet of the bridge. The thought of the night that was now closing in filled him with uneasiness. Where could he sleep? He had not the least shelter to turn to. The Bécus' dog passed by, and the old man looked at it with envy; that dog, at anyrate, knew that its kennel and bed of straw were awaiting it. He tried to think of some refuge, but his brain was confused, and his outburst of anger had exhausted him and made him drowsy. His eyelids closed heavily, as he tried to recall some sheltered corner where he would be protected from the cold. Then his mind seemed to become the prey of a night-mare, and he saw all the country-side revolving before him, bare, and swept by the gusts of wind.

However, with sudden energy, he shook himself, and tried to
throw off his drowsiness. He must not lose heart in this way.
Folks would never let a man of his age die with cold out-of-
doors.

He now mechanically crossed the bridge, and found himself
opposite the Delhommes' little farm. Immediately he caught
sight of the house he turned aside and went round to the back, so
that no one should see him. There he halted again, leaning
against the wall of the cow-house, in which he heard his
daughter Fanny's voice. Had he had any thought of returning to her? The old man himself could not have answered
this question; his feet had mechanically carried him there.
In his mind's eye he could see the inside of the house as plainly
as if he had entered it: the kitchen on the left, and his old bedroom on the first floor, at the end of the hay-loft. His former
spite was fading away; and his legs shook so with emotion
that he would have fallen to the ground had he not had the
support of the wall. For a long time he remained there like
this, with his back resting against the house-side. Fanny
was still talking inside the cow-house, but he could not distinguish what she was saying. Perhaps it was this muffled
sound of his daughter's words that stirred up the old man's
heart. She seemed to be scolding a servant, for her voice grew
louder, and Fouan finally heard her addressing such cutting
remarks, in a harsh, stern voice, to the unfortunate servant
girl, that the latter burst out into tears. These words affected
the old man painfully; all his feelings of emotion vanished, and
he sternly braced himself up, feeling convinced that if he had
pushed open the door, his daughter would have received him
with the same harsh tones. He could again hear her saying:
" Oh, my father will return and ask us, on his knees, to take
him back again." That never-forgotten speech of hers had,
like a knife, irretrievably severed every bond between them.
No, no! Sooner die of hunger and sleep at the bottom of a
ditch than see her triumphing over him with her haughty
assumption of perfect irreproachableness! At this thought he
removed his back from the wall, and painfully went on his
way.

To avoid following the road, Fouan, who believed that
every one was watching for him, went up the right bank of the
Aigre, beyond the bridge, and soon found himself in the midst
of the vineyards. His intention was to reach the plateau without
having to go through the village. He was obliged, however,
to pass near the Château, where his legs now seemed to carry

him instinctively like those of some old horse going to the
stable where he has been accustomed to eat his oats. The
ascent up the hill made him **pant, and he** sat down to get
his breath back, and began **to think. Certainly if he** were to
go inside and say to Hyacinthe: " I am going to appeal to the
law ; help me against Buteau," the scamp would **receive him**
with an explosion of welcome, and they would spend **an eve-**
ning of jovial riot together.

From where he **was sitting he could hear the sound of**
merriment ; proceeding, no **doubt,** from some tipsy **debauch**
which would be prolonged **till** morning. **Attracted by the**
sound, and already feeling a void **in his stomach,** he approached
nearer, and recognised Canon's voice, together with the **smell**
of some stewed beans, **those beans** which La Trouille **knew so**
well how to cook whenever **her father wanted to celebrate the**
arrival of **his friend. Why shouldn't he,** Fouan, go in and join
the two scamps in their merry-making ? He could hear them
warmly disputing amid the clouds of smoke from their pipes,
and apparently so gorged with wine that he positively envied
them. A sharp explosion from Hyacinthe stirred the old man
with emotion, and he had already reached out his hand towards
the door when La Trouille's shrill laughter **paralysed him. She**
was now the object of his fear, and in his mind's eye he **could**
still see her, scrany and clad in her chemise, stealthily **approach-**
ing **him** like a snake, and warily feeling **him and making him**
her prey. What good would **it do even if** the father did assist
him to recover his money ? **The daughter would be there to**
strip him of it **again.**

Suddenly **the door of the Château was thrown open, and the**
girl appeared and **cast a glance** outside, having fancied she
could hear something. **The old man just had time to throw**
himself behind the **bushes ; and, as he made his escape, he**
could see La Trouille's green eyes glistening in the gloaming.

When Fouan gained the open plain he experienced a sort
of relief in finding himself quite alone, able to die without
interference and observation. For a long time **he** walked on
at random, now **going** straight before him, **and then turning**
aside, **without any reason** or plan **whatever. The night had**
now fully fallen, **and the icy** wind **scourged him bitterly.**
Every now and then, as some fierce gust swept past him, **he**
was obliged to turn his back to it, his breath quite failing him,
and his few white hairs bristling upright on his head. Six
o'clock struck ; all Rognes must now be at table. His stomach
and his legs began to feel **faint,** and he was obliged to slacken

his pace. At last he set off in the direction of La Borderie, and then, after making a sudden turn, he was surprised to find himself again on the edge of the valley of the Aigre.

Between a couple of squalls, a violent lashing shower poured down. The old man was soaked to the skin, but he still walked on, encountering two other downfalls, and at last he shivered with cold and weariness. Presently, without knowing how he got there, he found himself in the open square by the church, in front of the old family house of the Fouans, where Françoise and Jean now dwelt. But no, he could not seek a refuge there! They had driven him away! The rain now began to pour down again in such heavy torrents that he began to lose all heart. He stepped up to the Buteaus' door and peeped into the kitchen, whence streamed the odour of cabbage soup. All his poor trembling body was longing to submit and return : a physical craving for food and warmth was urging him to enter. But amid the noise of people eating, he could distinguish some words.

" Well, what if father doesn't come back? " Lise was asking.

" Oh, don't bother about him," replied Buteau; "he's too fond of his belly not to come back when he feels hungry."

Treading as silently as possible, Fouan now glided away, fearing lest he should be seen stealing back like a beaten dog for a bone. He was nearly choked with shame and humiliation, and fiercely resolved that he would go away and die in some corner. They should see if he was so fond of his belly! He made his way down the hill again, and then let himself sink upon the trunk of one of the felled elm-trees on the grass in front of Clou's farriery. His legs could carry him no further, and he lost all hope in the black loneliness of the road. Every one was indoors, and the houses were all so closely shuttered on account of the bad weather that it seemed as though there were not a living soul in all the neighbourhood. The heavy shower had had the effect of laying the wind, and the rain soon streamed down perpendicularly in ceaseless torrents. The old man felt too weak even to get up and look about for a shed or stack to shelter him. Utterly stupefied by misery and exhaustion he continued to sit perfectly motionless, his stick between his legs, and his bare head washed by the rain. He had resigned himself to his fate. When a man has neither children nor home nor anything, he must tighten his trouser strap and sleep out of doors. Nine o'clock struck, and then ten. The rain came down still more violently, soaking the old man's bones through and through. Then some lanterns

gleamed through **the** darkness, flitting hastily away; the
evening gatherings were breaking up. Fouan started on recognising La Grande, who was probably returning from the
Delhommes', **where she** had been spending the evening for the
sake **of** saving her own candle. Then **he** got up with a
painful effort that made his limbs crack **and** followed her; but
she had entered her house before he could overtake her. When
he stood before the closed **door,** he hesitated and his courage
fell. At last, however, he ventured to knock, impelled **by** his
utter wretchedness.

He had come at an unfortunate time, **for La** Grande **was in**
a frightfully bad temper, the result of **an unfortunate affair**
which had upset her during **the previous week. One evening,**
when she was alone with her grandson **Hilarion,** it had occurred
to her **that she might as well employ his strong arms** in chopping some **wood before he went off** to sleep; **and, as** the lad
set about the **work somewhat languidly, she remained in** the
wood-house, **abusing him. So far, this brutish, distorted fellow,**
as strong as a bull, had, in his abject fear of his grandmother,
allowed her to abuse his brawny muscles **without even a**
glance of rebellion. For some few days past, **however, he**
had been looking rather dangerous, and had begun to **quiver**
beneath the weight of his excessive tasks, flushing hotly **with**
surging blood. To excite him, La Grande unwisely **struck**
him across the back of his neck with her stick. **As she did so,**
he let the cleaver fall, and glared at her. **This seeming rebel-**
lion drove the old woman almost **wild, and** she rained a shower
of blows upon **the lad's flanks and hips.** Then Hilarion
suddenly rushed **at her, and she expected, in fear** and
trembling, that he **was going to strangle her or kick her to**
death.

But this was not his intention. **He** had, perforce, practised
too much abstinence since the death of Palmyre, and his anger
turned into sexual rage. Brute-like, **he** recognised neither
relationship nor age, nothing but her sex, in this old grandmother of eighty-nine, whose body was **as** dry as a stick,
and who had barely anything of the woman about **her.** However, she was still **strong** and vigorous, and able to defend
herself, **and she scratched** and fought, till at last managing to
lay hold of the cleaver, she split her grandson's skull open with
a heavy blow. The neighbours ran up on hearing her cries,
and she related to them all that had happened. She was all
but overcome, she said; little more, and the villain would have
succeeded in violating her. Hilarion did **not** die till the next

morning. The magistrate came to make an investigation; then there was the funeral, and all sorts of other worries, from which the old woman had now outwardly recovered, though at heart the ingratitude of the world had deeply wounded her, and she had firmly resolved never to help any member of her family.

Fouan knocked at the door timorously, and it was not till he had done so a third time that La Grande heard him. Then coming to the door, she asked:

" Who's there?"

" It's I."

" Who's that?"

" I, your brother!"

She had, doubtless, recognised his voice at once, but she delayed matters, and questioned him just for the sake of making him speak. After a pause, she asked him again:

" What do you want?"

The old man trembled, but made no reply. Then La Grande roughly threw the door open; and as the old man was about to enter, she barred the way with her scrany arms, and forced him to remain outside in the pouring rain which was still relentlessly streaming down.

" I know very well what you want," she exclaimed. " I heard all about you to-night. You have been idiot enough to let them strip you again; you haven't even had wit enough to keep the money you had hidden away! And now you want me to take you in, eh?"

Then, seeing the old man trying to excuse himself, and stammering explanations, she burst out violently:

" Didn't I warn you over and over again? Times and times I told you what a fool you were making of yourself by giving up your land! But now you are finding out the truth of my words, turned out of doors by those scamps your children, and wandering about in the night like a tramp, like a beggar that hasn't even got a stone to lay his head upon!"

Stretching out his hands he burst into tears, and tried to push La Grande's arms aside, and force his way into the house, despite her. But she firmly held her ground, and finished saying what she had upon her mind.

" No, no, indeed! Go and beg a shelter from those who have stripped you! I owe you nothing! The rest of the family would only accuse me of interfering in their affairs again. But apart from all that, you have given up your property, and I will never forgive you for it!"

Then, bracing herself up and exposing her withered neck, she glared fiercely at him with her round, hawk-like eyes, and slammed the door violently in his face.

"It serves you right—go and die on the road."

Fouan remained standing stiffly outside the pitiless door. The rain was still streaming down with monotonous persistence. Presently he turned away and stepped once more into the inky darkness which the slow, icy downpour from the heavens was flooding.

Where did he go? He could never quite recollect. His feet stumbled in the puddles, and he groped about with his hands to avoid running against the trees and walls. He no longer reflected, he no longer recognised anything : this little village, every stone of which he knew so well, seemed like some unknown and far-off terrible spot, where he was a stranger, lost, unable to find his way. He turned to the left, but, fearing lest he should fall into some hole or other, he turned round again to the right ; then he stopped alto-gether, trembling all over, finding danger at every turn. Presently he discovered a railing, and he followed it till it brought him to a little door, which opened at his touch. Then the ground seemed to slip away beneath his feet, and he rolled down into some sort of a hole. Here, at anyrate, he felt more comfortable, for he was sheltered from the rain and the place was warm. A grunt soon warned him, however, that he had a pig for a neighbour, and the disturbed animal, thinking that some food had arrived, was already poking its snout into his ribs. Fouan began to struggle with it, but he felt so weak that he made all haste to escape, for fear he might be devoured. Still he could go no further, and he let himself drop down outside the door, huddling himself up closely against it so that the projecting roof might shelter him from the rain. Heavy drops, however, still continued to soak his legs, and icy gusts of wind seemed to freeze his saturated clothes to his body. He envied the pig, and would have re-turned to it, if he had not heard it gnawing at the door be-hind his back and snorting ravenously.

In the early dawn Fouan awoke from the painful somno-lence into which he had sunk. A feeling of shame again took possession of him, as he told himself that his story must be the common talk of the neighbourhood, and that every one knew he was a pauper tramping the roads. A man stripped of everything could not hope for either justice or pity. He kept himself well under the hedges as he walked along, in the constant fear of seeing some window open and being recognised by some early-rising woman in his miserable condition as a poor old outcast. The rain was still falling, and when he reached the plain he concealed himself in a rick. He spent the whole day in gliding from one place of concealment to another, **in such a** state **of** alarm, indeed, **that,** when **he had lain in any one** hiding-place for a couple of hours, he felt sure that he **was about** to be discovered, and crept out and concealed himself **somewhere else.** The one thought that now racked his brain **was whether** it would take him a long time to die in this way. **He was now not** suffering so much from cold, but he was tortured with **hunger, and** he said to himself that it was from hunger that he would **die.** He might perhaps have **to** live through another night and another day! Still he **did not waver; he** would rather stay and perish where **he was than** return to the Buteaus.

But as the darkness again began to close in, he was seized with **an** agonising terror at the thought **of** having to spend another night out in the ceaseless deluge of rain. His bones were beginning to shiver with cold again, and an intolerable aching hunger was gnawing at his stomach. When the sky grew black and dark, he felt as though he were being drowned and swept away into the streaming gloom. His mind grew confused and blank, and his feet carried him along mechanically. A purely animal instinct was shaping **his** course, and thus it happened that, without any conscious intention of doing so, he found himself once more in the kitchen of the Buteaus' house, the **door of** which he had opened.

Buteau and Lise were just finishing the remains of the previous **day's** cabbage-soup. Upon hearing **the door open** the husband turned his head and looked at Fouan, who stood in silence, wrapped **in the steam from** his saturated **clothes.** For a long time the son **thus looked at his father** without saying anything. Then he broke **out into a** snigger:

"Ah, I knew quite well that you'd show you'd got no spirit!"

The old man, standing bolt upright, and seeming as though rooted to the ground, answered not a word.

"Well, all the same, give him some grub, wife, since it's hunger that has brought him back!"

Lise had already risen and brought a plateful of the soup. Fouan took it and sat down apart from the others on a stool, as though he declined to join his children at table. He began to swallow the soup ravenously, his whole body trembling with

the violence of his hunger.   Buteau now leisurely finished his
meal, and then began to sway about on his chair, making darts
with his knife at scraps of cheese, and then putting them into
his mouth.   He was watching the old man's ravenous appetite
with interest, and followed the movements of his spoon with a
mocking leer.

"Your walk in the fresh air seems to have given you a rare
appetite," said he.   "But you mustn't take these strolls every
day, you know ; it would come in much too expensive !"

The old man still went on gulping down the soup, with a
hoarse sound in his throat as he swallowed it; however, he did
not say a word.

"A nice old gentleman you are, to stay out all night in this
way," his son continued.   "You've been after the girls, I bet ;
and it's they who've emptied you so, eh ?"

Still there came no reply.   Fouan persisted in his dogged
silence, making no sound except such as resulted from his
greedy gulping.

"Don't you hear that I'm talking to you?" Buteau at last
shouted in irritation.   "You might at any rate have the politeness to answer me ?"

Fouan, however, still kept his blank gaze fixed on the soup.
It seemed as though he neither heard nor saw, but was miles
away in his isolation.   It was as if he wished to imply that
he had merely returned to eat, and that, although his belly
was in the kitchen, his heart was there no longer.   He now
energetically began to scrape the bottom of his plate with his
spoon, so as to lose nothing of the soup.

At last, Lise, affected by the sight of such keen hunger,
interposed.

"Let him alone," she said, "since it pleases him to play the
dummy."

"I'm not going to have him playing the fool with me
again !" retorted Buteau angrily.   "I've had quite sufficient
of that already.   Let to-day be a lesson to you, you pig-headed
old fool !   If you give me any more of your nonsense, I shall
leave you to starve out on the road !"

Fouan, having now quite finished his soup, rose painfully
from his seat, and, still maintaining his unbroken silence—a
sepulchral silence that seemed to grow ever more oppressive
—turned his back and dragged himself under the staircase to
his bed, on which he threw himself without undressing.
Somnolence seemed to descend on him like a thunderbolt.
He was sound asleep in a moment, wrapped in a leaden slumber.

Lise, who stepped up to look at **him,** came back and told **her** husband that he looked as though he were dead. Buteau, however, after going to see him, shrugged his shoulders. Dead, indeed! did fellows like him die like that? Only he must have knocked about to be in such a state. When they came to look **at** him the next morning, he did not appear to have moved, and he **slept** on throughout the day and the following night, and only awoke once more the second morning, after remaining annihilated, as it were, for thirty-six **hours.**

"Ah, there **you** are again at last!" **cried** Buteau with a snigger. "I was beginning to think **that** you meant to go on sleeping **for ever,** and would **never** want anything more to eat."

The old man neither looked at him **nor** spoke to **him, but** went out and sat down on the road to breathe the fresh air.

From this time forth Fouan isolated himself in moody silence. **He** seemed to have forgotten all about the papers **which** **Buteau** had refused to restore to him. At any rate, he **never** spoke **about** them and never attempted to discover where they were; perhaps feeling indifferent about them, but certainly resigned. His rupture with the Buteaus seemed complete, and he persisted in maintaining his dogged silence. as though he were a creature **cut off** from all others, and entombed. Nowhere, under **no circumstances,** no matter what might **be** his need, **did** he ever **speak a word to the** Buteaus. He **shared in the common existence of** the household; he slept there, ate there, saw his son and daughter-in-law, and elbowed them from morning till night, but he never gave them a look **or a** word; it was as if he had been blind and dumb, as if he were a ghost abiding amongst living beings. Buteau and Lise soon grew tired of worrying him without getting even a sigh in answer, and **they** left him alone in his obstinate silence. They both ceased to **speak to him and to look at him.** They began to consider him merely as a piece of peripatetic furniture, and at last they grew perfectly unconscious of his presence. The horse and the two cows were of more account than he **was.**

In the whole house Fouan had but one friend, little **Jules,** who was now completing his ninth year. Laure, who was four years old, looked at him with the same harsh gaze as her parents did, and wriggled out of his arms, conducting herself, indeed, as though she were full of bitter indignation against one who ate but did no work. Jules, however, delighted in being with the old man, and got on wonderfully well with him. He

was, as it were, the last link uniting Fouan to the others, and
he became his messenger and mouthpiece. Whenever a definite
yes or no became absolutely necessary Lise sent the lad to
the old man, who, for him alone, consented to break his silence.
Fouan being neglected, the lad played the part of a little servant-maid, helped him to make his bed of a morning, and
carried him his allowance of soup, which the old man ate near
the window, resting the plate upon his knees, for he had refused to resume his place at the table. Then the two played
together, and the old man, delighted when he met the lad out-
of-doors, took hold of his hand and went off with him for a long
ramble. Upon occasions like these Fouan made up for his
long silences, and poured forth so much chatter that he almost
dazed his little companion, though he could no longer speak
without difficulty. He seemed to be losing the use of his
tongue, now that he had ceased to employ it. But the aged
grandfather who stammered, and the lad who had no ideas
beyond birds' nests and blackberries, got on remarkably well
together. The old man taught his grandson how to lime twigs,
and made him a little cage to keep crickets in. The lad's frail
hand was now his only support along the roads of La Beauce,
where he no longer had either land or relatives left him; and
thanks to Jules he felt some pleasure in living a little longer.

In point of fact, however, it was as if Fouan had been
struck out of the list of the living. Buteau took his place and
acted in his name, received his money and gave receipts for
it, upon the pretext that his father no longer possessed his wits.
The interest on the money derived from the sale of the old
man's house, amounting to a hundred and fifty francs a year,
was paid by Monsieur Baillehache direct to Buteau, whose only
difficulty had been with Delhomme, the latter refusing to pay
the annuity of two hundred francs to any one excepting his
father-in-law, and insisting upon the old man's presence to
receive it. As soon, however, as Delhomme's back was turned,
Buteau took possession of the cash. He thus received three
hundred and fifty francs a year, but he used to say in a
whining voice that he had to add as much more to it, and even
more than that, to defray the expense of his father's keep. He
never referred to the scrip he had appropriated. That was
quite safe, and they could all settle about it later on. He
alleged that the dividends were exhausted in keeping up the
payments to old Saucisse, fifteen sous every day, for the purchase of the acre and a quarter of land. He protested that it
would never do to let this agreement break through, now that

so much money had been paid under it. There was a report,
however, that old Saucisse, under the pressure of some violent
threat, had consented to annul the agreement, and to hand
Buteau half the money he had received under it, a thousand
francs out of two thousand; and the fact that the old scamp
held his tongue was accounted for by his fear of letting his
neighbours know too **much** of his affairs, and by his unwillingness to confess that he, also, had been worsted in his turn.
Buteau had, indeed, realised that Fouan would die the first, for
he was now so infirm that he could scarcely **stand upright;** had
he received **a cuffing he** would probably **have fallen to** the
ground powerless **ever to rise** again.

A year passed away, and yet Fouan was still alive, although
he was growing weaker every day. He was no longer the
neat old peasant of yore, with a clean-shaven face, and dressed
in a clean new blouse and black trousers. His big bony **nose,**
which appeared to be stretching forward towards the ground,
seemed to be the only feature left in his withered, fleshless
face. His stoop had increased slightly every year, and by this
time he was almost bent double; he now only had to take the
final somersault which would land him in his grave. He
dragged himself along by the aid of two thick sticks, his face
half covered by a long, dirty white beard, his body clad in the
soiled and ragged cast-off clothes of his son; and he was in such
an unpleasantly neglected condition that he looked quite repug-
nant in the full light of day, resembling one **of** those tattered
old tramps to whom passers-by give a wide berth. In the wreck
only the animal part of his nature survived, **with the mere**
instinct of living. A feeling of ravenous hunger always made
him fall keenly on his soup, and he was never satisfied; he
stuffed himself with bread when he happened to be alone in
the house, **and he even** stole Jules's bread and butter from him,
unless the lad resisted. In consequence **of** his predatory
habits, the Buteaus reduced his quantity of food at meal-times,
and they even took advantage of the situation to under-feed
him, pretending that he stuffed himself till he nearly burst.

Buteau accused him of having ruined himself during **his**
stay at the Château with Hyacinthe, and this accusation was
well founded, for this whilom sober, self-stinting peasant, who
had once lived upon bread **and** water, had there fallen into
ways of dissipation, contracting a taste for meat and brandy,
so that he now suffered at being deprived of them. Vicious
habits quickly take hold of a man, even when it is a son who
debauches his father. The wine disappeared so rapidly that

Lise was obliged to lock it up; and, on the days when any
meat soup was being cooked, little Laure was set to mount
guard over it. Since the old man had run into debt with
Lengaigne for a cup of coffee, both Lengaigne and the
Macquerons had been warned by Buteau that he would not
pay them if they supplied his father on credit. The old man
still maintained his tragic silence, but sometimes when his
plate was not quite full, or when the wine was removed without any being given to him, he fixed his bleared eyes upon his
son in a prolonged stare, in the impotent rage of his ravenous
craving. Did they want him to die of starvation? he seemed
to be asking.

"Oh, you may stare at me as hard as you like!" Buteau
used to say, "but do you imagine I'm going to pamper brutes
that do nothing? Those who like meat ought to earn it, you
miserable old greedy-guts! You ought to be ashamed of
yourself for going in for dissipation at your time of life!"

Though Fouan's obstinate pride had prevented him returning to the Delhommes', for he brooded unforgetfully over his
daughter's stinging remark, he tolerated every indignity from
the Buteaus, their cutting speeches, and even their blows. He
no longer thought about his other children, but surrendered
himself in utter weariness, without any idea of making his
escape from it all. He would be no better off anywhere else,
so what was the good of troubling himself to move? When
Fanny met him she passed by stiffly, having sworn that she
would not be the first to speak. Hyacinthe, who was more
good-natured, though he had borne his father a grudge for
some time on account of the shabby fashion in which he had
left the Château, amused himself one evening by making the old
man abominably drunk at Macqueron's, and then leaving him
in this condition outside Buteau's door. There was a dreadful
scene; the house was upset; Lise was obliged to wash the
kitchen out, and Buteau swore that if such a thing occurred
again he would make his father sleep on the dung-heap, so that
the old man got afraid, and became so suspicious of his elder
son that he no longer dared to accept his offers of refreshments.
He often saw La Trouille with her geese while he was sitting
out of doors at the road side. The girl would stop and examine
him with her little eyes, and even talk to him for a moment or
two, while her geese waited behind her, standing on one leg
and poking out their necks. One morning, however, the old
man discovered that she had stolen his handkerchief, and from
that time forth whenever he caught sight of her in the distance

he shook his sticks at her threateningly, as if to drive her away. She made sport of him and amused herself by setting her geese at him, only going off when some passer-by threatened to cuff her if she did not leave her grandfather in peace.

So far Fouan had been able to walk, and this had been a source of much consolation to him, for he still took an interest in the soil, and constantly re-visited his old property, just as some worn-out old rakes haunt the presence of their former mistresses. He wandered slowly along the roads with his crazy old gait, and remained standing for hours at the edge of a field, supporting himself on his two sticks. Then he would drag himself to another field, and again become absorbed in motionless contemplation, looking like some gnarled old tree growing there, and withered by age. His dim eyes were no longer capable of distinguishing clearly between oats and wheat and rye. Everything seemed blurred and fogged to him, and even his recollections of the past were dim and confused. This field, he fancied, had yielded so many bushels in such a year, but he kept confounding dates and figures. He was constantly possessed by one bitter, haunting thought. The soil which he had so yearned for, and which he had won and possessed, the soil to which for sixty long years he had devoted everything—his limbs, his heart, his very life—this ungrateful soil had passed into the arms of another lover, for whom it now brought forth plentifully without reserving aught for him. A deep sadness overwhelmed him at the thought that it knew him no longer, that he retained not a particle of it, nothing even of what it had produced, neither a copper nor a mouthful of bread. And now he would soon have to die and rot away beneath it, beneath that fickle indifferent soil which would drain fresh youth from his old bones! It had really not been worth his while to wear himself out with hard toil and labour when this was the end of it all—utter penury and infirmity! Whenever he had thus made the round of his old fields, he returned home and threw himself on his bed, so overwhelmed that he could not even be heard breathing.

He was deprived of this last interest he took in life when he lost the use of his legs. It soon became so painful to him to walk about that he scarcely went beyond the village. There were three favourite spots where he was fond of sitting on fine days—the logs in front of Clou's farriery, the bridge over the Aigre, and a stone bench near the school. He tottered slowly from one to another of these halting-places, taking nearly an hour to go a couple of hundred yards, and dragging his

wooden shoes after him as though they were heavy carts, as he
shambled painfully along in the crazy wreck of his frame.
Wrapt in oblivious abstraction, he frequently sat on the end of
a log for a whole afternoon, huddled up, and feasting on the
sunshine. His eyes were open, but he remained motionless in
a kind of drowsy stupefaction. Passers-by no longer took any
notice of him, for he had ceased to be a living creature, he was
merely a thing. Even his pipe had become a burden to him,
and he had almost ceased to smoke. The pressure of the stem
upon his gums pained him, and the labour of filling and lighting
quite exhausted him. His one desire was to sit perfectly
motionless, for as soon as he stirred, even in the full warmth
of the noon-day sun, he felt frozen and began to shiver. His
power of will and his authority had already perished, and he
was now in the last stage of decrepitude, leading a mere animal
life, like some old brute suffering amid abandonment from the
fact of having once led the life of a human being. However, he
made no complaints, realising that a foundered horse, though
it may once have worked well, is sent to the knacker's as soon
as it makes no return for the oats it consumes. Old folk, in a
like way, are good for nothing, and are only a source of
expense, so the sooner they are out of the way the better. He
himself had wished for his father's death; and now if his
children, in their turn, impatiently awaited his own, it neither
surprised nor hurt him. It was natural that this should be
the case.

If ever a neighbour cried out to him: " Well, Fouan, you
still manage to keep alive ! " he would mumble out: " Ah, yes,
dying is a wearily long business, but it isn't the want of the
will that keeps me from it."

He only spoke the truth, with the stoicism of the peasant,
who accepts death without a murmur, and even desires it
when he is stripped of everything, and the soil calls him back
to her.

But there was still another grief in store for him. Jules
cast him off, instigated thereto by Laure. Whenever the girl
saw her brother with their grandfather she seemed jealous, and
with her eyes fiercely glistening she would call him angrily
away. The old man was a nuisance, she said; it was much
more amusing for them to play together. If her brother did
not at once go off with her, she hung on to his shoulder and
pulled him away. Then she made herself so agreeable that the
lad forgot the little household services which he had hitherto
rendered his grandfather. And by degrees Laure completely

won **Jules over** to her side, like a real **woman who** has set **her** mind **upon a** conquest.

One evening Fouan **had gone to** wait for **Jules in front of the school, feeling so tired that** he wished **for the** lad's **hand to help him up the** hill. Laure, however, **came out** with **her** brother, **and when** the old man's trembling **fingers** sought **the** lad's, she **burst out into a** sneering laugh.

"There he is boring you again!" said she. "Leave him to **see after** himself." Then, turning to the other children, she **added**: " Isn't he a **sawny** to let himself be plagued in this way?"

Jules blushed **at the** sound of his schoolfellows' jeers, and, wishing to **show** what a man he was, he jumped aside, repeating his sister's expression to the old companion of **his** walks :

"**You** plague me !"

Dismayed, and with tears filling his troubled eyes, Fouan stumbled as though the ground failed him, like the little hand **that** had been withdrawn. The jeering laughter increased, **and Laure** made Jules dance with her round the old man, **singing the** childish rhyme :

> " He shall **fall** on the ground, and there he shall lie,
> And whoever shall help him, shall **eat** his bread dry ! "

Fouan, **half fainting, was nearly two** hours in getting home, so feebly **did he drag his feet along.** This was the last blow. The **lad ceased bringing him his** soup and making **his bed,** the palliasse **of which was now not** turned once a **month.** Without even this **urchin to talk to,** the old man **buried** himself in absolute silence, and his isolation became complete. **Never** did he **speak a** word about anything to any one.

CHAPTER III.

THE winter ploughing had commenced, and Jean, that cold grey February afternoon, had just arrived with his plough at his big patch of ground on the plain, where he still had a good couple of hours' work before him. It was a strip at the edge of the field that he was going to plough, intending to sow it with a new variety of Scotch wheat, a course which had been recommended by his old master, Hourdequin, who had moreover promised him several bushels of seed-corn.

Jean at once set to work, beginning at the spot where he had left off on the previous day ; and, putting his plough into position and grasping hold of the arms, he started his horse, shouting in a gruff voice :

" Gee woh !   Gee woh !"

Violent rains, coming after excessive heat, had so stiffened the clayey soil that it was with great difficulty that the plough-share and coulter broke off the strips of earth through which they cut.   The heavy clods could be heard grating against the mould-board as the latter turned them over, burying the manure with which the field was covered.   Every now and then a stone or some other obstacle gave the plough a sudden shock.

" Gee woh ! Gee woh !" cried Jean, as grasping the handles with his outstretched arms he guided the plough so correctly that the furrows were as straight as if they had been traced out by rule and line.   Meanwhile his horse, keeping its head down and burying its hoofs in the soil, drew the plough forward with a steady regular motion.   Whenever the implement got clogged, Jean jerked off the earth and weeds, and then it glided on again, leaving the rich soil behind it upraised, quivering and trembling, as though alive, and with its very entrails exposed.

He reached the end of the furrow, and then turned round and commenced a new one.   Presently he became affected by a sort of intoxication due to the strong odour exhaled by the disturbed soil, an odour suggestive of damp recesses where the seed would germinate.   His slow monotonous gait and his fixed gaze completed his feeling of dazed abstraction.   He would never succeed in becoming a genuine peasant, he thought. He was not a native of the soil, and he still retained the feelings of a town-bred workman, of a trooper who had served through the campaign in Italy; and things that the peasants could not see or feel were very visible and apparent to him—the great mournful peacefulness of the plain and the deep breathing of the soil beneath the sunshine and the showers. He had always had visions of retiring into the peace of the country, but how foolish he must have been to imagine that it was only necessary to lay down the gun and the plane and to grasp hold of the plough to satisfy his taste for tranquillity! Though the soil might be peaceful and kindly to those that loved it, the villages that clung to it like nests of vermin, full of human insects that preyed upon its flesh, sufficed to dishonour and pollute it. He could remember no sufferings in his previous life equal to those which he had endured since his arrival at La Borderie, now a long time ago.

Being obliged to raise the arms a little in order to ease the plough, a slight unevenness in the furrow annoyed him, and he began to display still greater care in guiding his horse.

"Gee woh! Gee woh!"

Yes, indeed, what troubles he had gone through during these last ten years! First, there was his long period of waiting for Françoise, and then his warfare with the Buteaus. Not a day had passed without some painful event or without some angry words. And now that he had got Françoise, now that they had been married for a couple of years, could he say that he was at last happy? Though he himself still loved her, he had divined that she did not love him, and that she never would love him as he wished to be loved, unreservedly, with her whole heart and soul. They lived together in peaceful harmony, indeed, and they were prospering in their work and saving money. But that was not everything. He could feel that she was cold and reserved, and occupied by other thoughts than of himself when he held her in his arms. She was now five months gone with child, but even this fact had not brought the husband and wife into closer sympathy; and Jean felt more and more the feeling which he had first experienced on the day they had taken possession of their house, the feeling that his wife still looked upon him as a stranger, a native of another country, born no one knew where; a man whose thoughts were not those of the villagers of Rognes; who seemed to her to be even differently made, and who could never be really united with her, even though he was the father of the child she bore within her.

After her marriage, Françoise, in **her** exasperation against the Buteaus, had brought **a** piece **of** stamped paper from Cloyes, **one Saturday,** with the intention of making a will and leaving **everything** that belonged to her to her husband, for **she had been told** that the house and the land would **revert to her sister** supposing she died **without issue, and** that **her husband would not be** able **to claim anything save** the **furniture and cash. Subsequently, however, she seemed to have** thought **better of the matter, for the sheet of stamped paper** still lay **in a drawer quite white. This had been a source of much secret pain to Jean, not from any mercenary feeling, but because he looked upon his wife's remissness as implying a want of affection for himself. But, indeed, it** mattered nothing, **now that a youngster was coming into the world!** What **would be the use of making a will under those circum-** stances? **And yet despite such reflections as these, his heart** felt **very heavy whenever he opened the drawer and saw the** piece **of stamped paper which had now become useless.   .**

Jean **stopped ploughing to give his horse a little** breathing- **time, and the sharp, frosty wind enabled him to** shake off his **abstraction. He slowly let his gaze wander to the** blank **horizon,** over **the immense plain, where, far away** in **the** distance, other **ploughs were at work, looking blurred and hazy** in the dull **grey atmosphere. He was now surprised to perceive** old Fouan, **who had come from Rognes along the new** road, **in** compliance **with one of those instinctive cravings** which he still experienced **at times, to look once more at** some field **or** other. On catching **sight of him, Jean lowered** his head, and **for a moment or two concentrated his gaze upon the gap-** ing **furrow and the eviscerated soil at his feet.   It was firm** and **yellow beneath the surface, the upturned clods seemingly revealing young and healthy earth, while the** manure **was buried in a bed of rich fecundity.   As** Jean gazed downwards, **his thoughts grew confused and strangely** intermingled. **How odd it seemed that one should have to grub** up the **soil in this way to get bread!   What a source of worry it was that he was** not **loved by Françoise!   Then came more vague** reflections about other **matters, about** the growth **of the** crops, about his little **one** who would **soon** be born, and **about** all the toil which folks underwent, often without being any the happier for it.

Then he grasped **the arms** of the plough again, and shouted his deep-toned cry:

"Gee woh!   Gee **woh!**"

He **was** just finishing **his** ploughing when Delhomme, who was returning on foot from a neighbouring farm, **stopped to** call to him from the edge of **the** field.

" Hallo ! Corporal, have you heard the news ? **We're** going to have war it seems."

Jean left go of his plough and drew himself up, surprised to feel such a shock at his heart.

" War ! **How's that ? "** he **asked**

" With **the Prussians, so they say. It is all** in the newspapers."

With a fixed gaze **Jean** pictured **Italy, the battles** fought there, and all the carnage from which **he had been** fortunate enough **to** escape without **a** single wound. **Then** his most ardent wish had **been to** live a quiet life in **some** peaceful nook, but now **these few** words shouted from the roadway by **a** passer-by, this thought of war, **had** sufficed to send his blood surging hotly through his veins !

" Ah, well, if the Prussians are making **game of us,"** said he. **" we** can't let ourselves be flouted by them ! "

Delhomme, however, **looked** upon the matter differently. He shook his head gravely, and declared that it would be the ruination of the country districts if the Cossacks came back again, as in Napoleon's time. Fighting did no one any good. It would be much better to try to arrange affairs peaceably.

" I say this," he **added,** "in the interests of others, for I have just been depositing **some** money **with** Monsieur Baillehache, so that, whatever **happens,** Nénesse, who has to draw in the conscription to-morrow, won't **have to** join the ranks."

" Ah, yes, and it's the same with me," said Jean, who had now calmed down. " I've served my time, and owe them nothing further, and I'm married, too ; so, whether they go to war or not, it won't make any difference to me. Ah! so it's to be with the Prussians this time ! Well, we shall give them a good hiding, **just as** we did the Austrians, and then there'll be an end of the **matter."**

" Good **evening, Corporal ! "**

" Good evening ! "

Then Delhomme went **on** his way again. Presently he stopped to tell the news to some one else ; and then, further on, he told it a third time, and so the report of the threatened approach of war quickly flew across La Beauce, through the mournful greyish atmosphere.

Jean having finished **his** ploughing, determined to go at once to La Borderie, to get the seed-corn which had been promised to him. He took the horse out of the plough, and sprang on to its back, leaving the plough in a corner of the field. As he was riding off, he again thought of Fouan and looked round for him, but could not see him. He thereupon concluded that the old man had taken shelter from the cold behind a rick of straw which was standing in Buteau's field.

When Jean arrived at La Borderie, and had tethered his horse, he called without eliciting any response. Everybody appeared to be at work away from the house. However, he went into the kitchen and stamped on the floor with his feet, and presently heard Jacqueline's voice proceeding from the cellar where the dairy was. Access to it was obtained through a trap-door opening at the foot of the staircase, and so awkwardly placed that an accident was always being feared.

" Who's there ? " she called.

Jean had squatted down on the top step of the steep little staircase, and she recognised him from below.

" Ah ! so it's you, Corporal ? "

He, too, could now see Jacqueline in the semi-darkness of the dairy, which was lighted merely by a grating in the wall. She was busily working among the bowls and the pans, from which the whey was dripping slowly into a stone trough. Her sleeves were rolled back as far as her arm-pits, and her arms were white with cream.

" Well, why don't you come down? You're not afraid of me, are you ? "

She addressed him in the same familiar manner as of yore, and she laughed in her old enticing way. Jean, however, felt ill at ease, and did not move.

" I've come for the seed-corn," he said, " that the master promised me."

" Oh yes, I know. Wait a moment, and I'll come up."

When she emerged into the full light, Jean saw that she was looking very fresh and glowing ; and her bare, white arms exhaled a pleasant odour of milk. She looked at him with her pretty, mischievous eyes, and ended by asking, in a bantering way :

" Well, aren't you going to kiss me? There's no reason that you should get stiff and unpleasant just because you're married."

Then he kissed her, trying to make the sounding salutes which he imprinted on both her cheeks seem mere marks of friendship. But her presence disturbed him, and recollections of the past sent his blood thrilling through his veins. He had never felt like this with his wife, although he loved her so much.

"Come along," now continued Jacqueline, "and I'll show you the seed-corn. Every one is out, even the servant-girl is away at market."

She crossed the yard, and then, entering the barn, stepped behind a pile of sacks. The seed was lying there in a heap on some boards. Jean had followed her, feeling somewhat disturbed at finding himself alone with her in this dim, out-of-the-way spot. He now suddenly began to affect a deep interest in the seed-corn, which was of a fine new Scotch variety.

"How big the grains are!" said he.

Jacqueline, however, began to speak in her cooing tones, and quickly brought him to a subject which had greater interest for her.

"Your wife is in the family-way, eh? Tell me, now, does she make herself as pleasant with you as I did?"

Jean turned very red, and Jacqueline took a malicious delight in seeing him thus disturbed. Presently some sudden reflection cast a gloom over her face.

"I've had a good many troubles, you know," she continued, "but, happily, they are all over now, and they have ended to my advantage."

The fact was that Hourdequin's son, Léon, the captain, who had not been seen at La Borderie for years past, had one day suddenly arrived there. He had observed, that same night, that Jacqueline occupied his mother's bed-room, and this had led him to make inquiries, whereupon he speedily learnt exactly how matters stood. For a little while Jacqueline trembled with uneasy alarm, for she had formed the ambitious design of marrying Hourdequin, and thus securing the reversion of the farm. The captain, however, played his cards too clumsily. He wanted to extricate his father from Jacqueline's meshes by letting himself be surprised in bed with the young woman. But he showed his hand too openly, and Jacqueline affected airs of the nicest virtue, screaming, weeping, and declaring to Hourdequin that she would leave the house at once, since she was no longer treated with respect in it. Then there was a terrible scene between the two men. The son tried to open his father's eyes, but this only made matters worse; and two hours later the captain left the house again, exclaiming, as he crossed the threshold, that he would rather lose everything than acquiesce in the present state of affairs, and that if he ever returned, it would only be to kick the hussy out of doors.

Jacqueline, in her triumph, now made the mistake of imagining that she merely had to ask for her own terms. She de-

clared to Hourdequin that after such treatment, with which,
indeed, **the** whole country-side was **ringing,** she would be
compelled **to leave** him unless he made **her his wife.** She even
began **to** pack **her boxes.** The farmer, **however, upset** by his
quarrel with his son, rendered all the **more angry by a** secret
consciousness that he **was** in the wrong, **and a feeling of** sorrowing regret for all that had occurred, gave her **a couple of**
such vigorous cuffs as almost shook the life out of **her. And
then she said nothing more about** going **away, realising that
she had been** in **too great a hurry.** Still, she **was** now absolute
mistress of the **house, openly sleeping in the conjugal bedroom,** taking her **meals alone with Hourdequin, giving** orders
to the servants, regulating **the** expenses, keeping **the keys of**
the safe, and behaving so **despotically** that the farmer **always**
consulted **her** before taking **any step.** He was failing and
ageing quickly, and Jacqueline **trusted that she would be able**
to **overcome** his last scruples **and** induce **him to marry her**
when **she had quite** exhausted his remaining **manhood. In the
meantime, as he** had sworn to disinherit his son, she **used all her
wiles to induce him to make a** will in her favour; and **she
already looked upon herself as the owner of** the farm, for she
had succeeded in wringing a promise **from Hourdequin** that he
would leave it to **her.**

"If I've been knocking myself up **for years past,"** she said
to Jean, "it certainly hasn't been out **of love for his good**
looks."

Jean could not restrain a laugh. **While speaking Jacqueline**
had been plunging her **bare arms again and again into the heap**
of **corn,** covering her skin **with a soft floury** powder. **Jean**
looked at **her,** and **suddenly gave utterance to a** question **which
he speedily regretted.**

"And are you as thick as ever with Tron?"

Jacqueline **gave no sign of being offended.** She **spoke**
quite frankly, **as to an old friend.**

"Oh, I'm very **fond of** him, the great stupid **fellow; but**
he's really very unreasonable. He's so dreadfully jealous, and
we have terrible **scenes** together sometimes. The master's the
only one he'll tolerate, and I really believe that he comes
sometimes at nights and listens at the door, to find out whether
we are sleeping or not."

Jean laughed again; but Jacqueline **seemed to** consider it
no laughing matter. **She** felt a vague **fear of that** big fellow
Tron, who was cunning **and** treacherous, **like** all the men of Le
Perche, she said. He **had** threatened to strangle her if she

proved unfaithful to him ; and consequently she now consorted with him in fear and trembling, despite the charm that his huge limbs had for her. She herself was so slim that this big fellow could have crushed her between his thumb and fingers.

At last, shrugging her shoulders with a pretty air, as much as to say that she had conquered others quite as difficult to manage, she continued :

" We used to get on better with one another than that, eh, Corporal ? "

Still keeping her merry eyes fixed upon him, she began to pound the corn again ; while Jean fell a victim to her charms once more, forgetting all about his departure from La Borderie, his marriage, and the child that was soon to be born to him. He seized hold of her wrists under the corn, and then slipped his hands up her arms, all velvety with flour, till they reached her white child-like breast, to which her habits of debauchery seemed to have imparted a firmer plumpness. This was what she had been wishing to bring about ever since she had caught sight of him at the mouth of the trap-door ; and she felt an additional malicious joy in taking him from another woman, and that woman his lawful wife, and proving that it was still herself that he loved best. He had already seized her in his arms and thrown her down, panting and cooing, upon the heap of corn, when the shepherd Soulas, with his tall fleshless figure, emerged from behind the sacks, coughing loudly and spitting. Jacqueline hastily sprang to her feet, while Jean panted and stammered out :

" Oh, this is it, is it ? Well, I'll come back presently and take fifteen bushels of it. What splendid stuff it is, isn't it ? "

Jacqueline, bursting with anger, fixed her eyes on the shepherd, who showed no signs of going away.

" It is really past all bearing ! " she muttered between her clenched teeth. " Whenever I think I am alone, he always contrives to turn up and haunt me ! But I'll have him sent off about his business ! "

Jean, who had now recovered his calmness, hastily left the barn, and went to unfasten his horse, without paying any attention to the signs of Jacqueline, who would have concealed him in the conjugal bed-chamber itself rather than have foregone her desire. Anxious to make his escape, Jean said that he would return the next day, and he was setting off on foot, leading his horse by the bridle, when Soulas, who had gone outside to wait for him, intercepted him at the gate.

" So she's got even you back into her meshes again ! Well,
at any rate just tell her to keep her tongue quiet, if she
doesn't want to set mine wagging. Ah, there will be a pretty
business, by-and-by, you'll see ! "

Jean, however, passed on his way with a rough gesture,
refusing to mix himself up any further in the matter. He was
full of shame ; annoyed at the thought of what he had so
nearly done. He had believed that he really loved Françoise,
and yet he had never felt one of these impetuous thrills of
desire for her ! Could it be that he really loved Jacqueline
more than his wife ? Had a passion for the hussy been
smouldering within him all this time ? All the past
woke up within him into fresh life, and he was angered at
himself to feel that he would certainly return to Jacqueline in
spite of all his desire to the contrary. Then he excitedly
sprang on to his horse and galloped off, so as to get back to
Rognes as soon as possible.

That same afternoon it happened that Françoise had gone to
cut a bundle of lucern for her cows. It was generally her task
to do this, and she settled to do it on that particular afternoon
as she relied on finding her husband in the field, ploughing.
She did not care to trust herself there alone, for fear she might
come across the Buteaus, who, in their anger at no longer
having the whole field to themselves, were perpetually seeking
any excuse for a violent quarrel. She took a scythe with her,
and counted upon the horse for bringing back the bundle of
lucern. As she neared the field, she was surprised not to
see her husband there, though she had not warned him of
her intention to come. The plough was still there, but where
could Jean have gone ? She felt still more nervous when she
observed Buteau and Lise standing at the edge of the field,
shaking their arms with a show of anger. She fancied
that they had just stopped for a moment on their way back
from some neighbouring village, for they were wearing their
Sunday clothes, and had no appearance of being engaged in
work. For a moment she felt inclined to turn back and
make her escape. Then she felt indignant at her own alarm ;
surely she was not going to be afraid of cutting lucern on her
own land ! So she continued to walk forward at the same
pace, and carrying the scythe on her shoulder.

As a matter of fact, whenever Françoise met Buteau, and
especially when he was alone, she was always overcome with
nervous confusion. For two years she had not spoken a single
word to him, but she never could see him without her whole

body being thrilled with emotion. This emotion might be
caused by anger, or it might be the result of some very
different feeling. Several times she had seen him in front of
her on this same road when she had been going up to her plot
of lucern ; and he would turn his head round two or three times
and glance at her with his yellow-streaked grey eyes. Then
she would feel a slight thrill pass through her body, and would
quicken her steps in spite of all her efforts not to do so ; while
Buteau, on the other hand, would slacken his pace, and so she
would find herself compelled to pass him, and, as she did so,
their eyes would meet just for a second. Then she was troubled
with the disturbing but pleasant consciousness that he was just
behind her ; and she felt enervated and scarcely able to continue walking. The last time they had met in this way, she
had been so overcome that she had fallen down at full length
in an attempt to jump from the road into her patch of lucern ;
and Buteau had nearly burst with laughter at the sight.

That evening, when Buteau maliciously told his wife of her
sister's tumble, they glanced at each other with gleaming eyes in
which the same thought was expressed. If the hussy had
killed herself and her unborn child her husband would take
nothing, and the land and house would return to themselves !
They had learnt from La Grande the story of the postponed
will, which had now become unnecessary on account of Françoise's condition. But they never had any luck! There was
no chance of fortune putting both mother and child out of their
way at a single stroke ! They returned to the subject as
they went to bed, and talked about the death of Françoise and
her unborn baby merely for the sake of talking. Talking of
folks' death doesn't kill them ; still, if Françoise, now, really
died without an heir, what a stroke of luck it would be !
What a heavenly retribution ! In the bitterness of her hate,
Lise actually swore that her sister was no longer her sister, and
that she would willingly hold her head on the block if that was
all that was wanted to enable them to return to their own
house, from which the wicked drab had so treacherously
evicted them.

Buteau was not quite so vindictive, and he declared that he
would be sufficiently pleased for the present if the youngster
were to perish before it was born. Françoise's condition was
a source of much irritation to him, for the birth of a child would
destroy all his obstinately entertained hopes, and definitely
deprive him of the property. As the husband and wife got into
bed together, and Lise blew out the candle, she broke out into

a peculiar little laugh, and said that, so long as a youngster
had not actually come into the world, it could easily be prevented from making its appearance. After lying silent for some
time in the darkness, Buteau asked his wife what she meant.
Then cuddling close up to his side, and holding her mouth
to his ear, she made a very singular confession.   Last month,
she said, she had been troubled to find herself in the family way
again, and so, without saying anything about it to him, she had
gone off to consult La Sapin, an old woman living at Magnolles,
who had the reputation of being a witch.   A pretty reception
he'd have given her if she had told him how matters stood.
La Sapin, however, had quickly put everything right.   It was
a very simple affair.

Buteau listened to his wife without showing either approval
or disapproval, and his satisfaction at what had occurred could
only be gathered from the joking way in which he observed
that Lise should have brought the prescription away with her for
Françoise's advantage.   Lise, too, seemed merry, and, grasping
her husband closely in her arms, she whispered to him that La
Sapin had taught her something else, oh, such a funny trick !
What was it ? asked Buteau.   Well, a man could undo what
a man had done, replied Lise.   He had only got to make the
sign of the cross on a woman three times and say an *Ave*
backwards, and if there were a little one, it would disappear immediately.   Buteau began to laugh, and they both
affected incredulity, but they still retained so much of the
ancient superstition of their race, that they were privately inclined to believe what they pretended to disbelieve.   Indeed,
everybody knew that the old witch of Magnolles had turned a
cow into a weasel, and had brought a dead man to life again.
Surely it must be true if she said it was !   The idea made
Buteau grin.   Would it really be effectual ?   Stay, now,
why shouldn't he really try it on Françoise, suggested Lise,
he and she knew all about each other ?   Buteau, however,
now protested against this allegation, as his wife, showing
signs of jealousy, began to pinch and thump him ; and they
presently fell asleep in one another's arms.

Ever since that night they had been haunted by the thought
of the child that was coming into the world to deprive
them of the house and land for ever ; and they never met
the younger sister without immediately glancing at her condition.   Thus as they now saw her coming up the road, on
this afternoon when she wanted to cut some lucern, they
took her measure with their eyes, and were quite startled

to notice how swiftly matters were advancing, and how **little** time there was left in which to take any steps.

"The devil take him," cried Buteau, going forward to examine **the furrows;** "the blackguard **has** filched **off a** good foot of **our land!** It's **as plain** as possible; see, there's the boundary-**stone!"**

Françoise had continued to approach with leisurely, easy steps, **concealing** her feeling of uneasy alarm. She now understood **the cause of the** Buteaus' angry gestures. Jean's plough **must have sliced** off a strip of their land. Disputes were **continually arising** on this **score,** and not a month passed without **some quarrel taking place as** to the boundary-line. Blows **and litigation seemed likely to be** the inevitable result.

"**You are trespassing on our land,"** cried Buteau, raising **his voice, "and I shall** prosecute **you!"**

The young woman, however, stepped up to **her patch of lucern, without even turning her** head.

"**Don't you hear us?" now** screamed Lise, in a towering rage. "**Come and look at** the boundary-stone for yourself, if **you think we're liars! Y**ou'll have to make good the damage!"

Her **sister's persistent silence and** contemptuous air now so thoroughly **enraged her that she lost all control** over herself, and rushed **up to her, clenching her fists.**

"So **you think** you **can flout** us as you please, do you, hussy? **I** am your elder sister, and I'll teach you to treat me with proper respect; and I'll make you go down on **your** knees and beg my pardon for all your impertinence to me!"

She **was** now standing in front of Françoise, mad with hate **and anger,** hesitating whether she should kill her sister with **her fists, or whether she should kick her to death** or knock out **her brains with a stone.**

"**Down on** your **knees, hussy,** down on your knees!"

Still persisting **in her silence,** Françoise now spat in her sister's face, **just as she had done on** the evening of the ejectment. Lise **then broke out into a** roar, but Buteau immediately interposed, and thrust **her** violently aside.

"Get away!" he said; "this is my business."

Ah, yes, she would gladly get away, and leave him to settle **the matter.** He was at perfect liberty to wring her sister's **neck or** break her back; **he** might cut her up and give her flesh **to** the dogs, or he might make her his drab; and, so far from trying **to** prevent **him,** she would do all she could to help him. She now braced herself up and glanced round her, keeping watch so that no one should come **and** interfere with whatever her husband **chose to do.** The vast **grey** plain stretched out beneath **the gloomy sky, and not a single human being** was in view.

" Now's the time ! There's no one in sight ! "

Buteau then stepped up to Françoise; and, as the young woman saw him advancing with stern-set face and stiff-braced arms, she thought he was going to thrash her. She still held her scythe, but she began to tremble, and Buteau seizing hold of the implement by the handle, tore it from her and tossed it into the lucern. Her only means of escaping him was by stepping backwards. She continued doing so till she reached the adjoining field, making for the rick which stood there, as though she hoped to use it in some way as a protecting rampart. Buteau followed her up quite leisurely; and he, on his part, seemed to be wishing to drive her towards the rick. His arms were slightly extended, and his face was broadened by a silent grin which disclosed his gums. Suddenly it flashed upon Françoise that he did not mean to thrash her. No, it was something **very different that he meant;** that something which she had so long refused him. She now began to tremble still more violently, and she felt as though all her strength were failing her; she who had always so valiantly resisted and belaboured him, and sworn that he should **never gain his ends !** But she was no longer the high-spirited **girl she had been;** she had just completed **her** twenty-third **year, on Saint Martin's** Day, and she **was now a woman, with the fresh bloom already** taken off **her by hard work, though her lips were still red and** her eyes as big **as crown-pieces. She felt such a sensation of** flushed languor **that her limbs seemed quite enervated and life-** less.

Buteau, still continuing to force her backwards, at last spoke in a deep, excited voice.

" You know very well that all is not over between us. This time I mean to succeed ! "

He had now managed to bring her to a stand against the **rick; and he abruptly took her by** the shoulders and threw her upon her back. **Dazed and** enervated though she was, **for a** moment or two **she began to** struggle and fight, instinctively prompted thereto **by her** old habits **of** resistance. Buteau, however, dodged her **kicks.**

" What difference can it make to you, you silly idiot ? " said he. " You needn't be afraid ! "

Françoise now burst into **tears, and seemed** taken with a

sort of fit. Though she made no further effort to defend herself, she was so violently shaken by nervous contortions
that Buteau could not succeed in his purpose. His anger at
being thus foiled maddened him, and, turning towards his
wife, he cried out:

"You damned helpless idiot, what are you standing staring
there for. Come and help me!"

Lise had remained standing bolt upright some ten yards
away, without ever stirring ; now scanning the distance to see
if any one was coming, and now glancing at Françoise and
Buteau, without any sign of feeling on her face. When her
husband called her, she did not evince the slightest hesitation,
but strode up to him, and seizing hold of her sister, she
sat down upon her as heavily as if she wanted to crush her.
Finally Buteau proved victorious. He was just rising when
old Fouan popped out his head from behind the rick, where
he had sought shelter from the cold. The old man had seen
all, and it evidently frightened him, for he at once concealed
himself behind the straw again.

Buteau having risen to his feet, Lise looked at him keenly.
In his eagerness he had forgotten all about the three signs
of the cross, and the *Ave* repeated backwards. His wife
stood frenzied with wild indignation. It was merely for his
own pleasure that he done the deed!

Françoise, however, left him no time for explanations. For
a moment she had remained lying motionless on the ground,
as though she had fainted beneath a sensation such as
she had never before experienced. The truth had suddenly
dawned upon her. She loved Buteau! She never had, and
never would, love any other. This discovery filled her with
shame, and she was angered against herself at finding how
false she was to her own ingrained ideas of justice. A man
who did not belong to her! A man who belonged to that
sister whom she now so hated! The only man in the world
whom she could not possess without being false to her own
oath!

Springing wildly to her feet, with her hair dishevelled
and her clothes all disarranged, she spat out the anger that
was raging within her in spasmodic bursts of abuse.

"You filthy swine! Yes, both of you! you're both filthy
swine! You have ruined and destroyed me! People have
been guillotined for doing less than you've done! I will tell
Jean, you filthy swine, and he'll settle your accounts for
you!"

Buteau shrugged **his** shoulders, and smiled his leering smile. He felt immensely satisfied, now that he had at last succeeded in gaining his ends.

" Nonsense, **my** dear! You were dying **for it!** "

This bantering speech had **the** effect of **completing** Lise's exasperation, and she **vented all her rising anger against her husband upon** her **sister.**

" It's quite true, you drab; I saw **you!** " she shouted. " I always said that all **my** troubles came **from you!** Will **you** dare to say now **that you** didn't debauch **my husband,** yes, debauch **him** directly **after we** were **married, when you were** only a child whom I still whipped **? "**

She now manifested the most violent **jealousy,** a jealousy which appeared **somewhat singular** after all the complacence she had recently **shown.** If Françoise had never **been born,** she thought, she **herself would never have** had to share **either** property **or husband!** She hated her sister for being younger and fresher **and more attractive than herself.**

" You're a **liar !** " cried Françoise, wild with anger. " **You** know that **you** are **lying !** "

" A liar, am I ? **You'll tell me, I suppose, that you** didn't pursue him even into **the cellar?** "

" **I !** indeed ! I'd a deal to **do** with it, hadn't I ? **You cow ! you** helped him ! Yes, and you'd have broken my **back,** if you could ! **You must** either be a filthy pimp, or else **you** wanted to murder me, you dirty drab **!** "

Lise replied by a violent blow, **which so** maddened Françoise that she threw herself wildly upon **her sister.** Buteau stood sniggering with **his** hands in his pockets, **and** made no attempt to interfere, like a **self-satisfied cock** watching a couple of **hens** quarrelling **for** him. **The two women** continued **fighting** savagel**y,** tearing each other's caps off, their faces **clawed and** bleeding, and their **hands eagerly** seeking any **spot where they** might tear and rend. In scuffling and wrestling **they returned to** the **patch** of lucern, and Lise suddenly broke out **into a loud** roar**, for Françoise** had driven **her** nails deeply into **her neck** Then, losing **all self-control,** the idea of murdering her **sister** occurred to her. She had caught sight of the scythe lying **on** her left hand. The handle had fallen across a clump of thistles, and the blade was sticking point upwards **in** the air. Like a flash of lightning she hurled Françoise on **to the** gleaming steel with all her force. The unfortunate young woman tottered **and** fell, uttering a terrible shriek. The blade of the scythe **had** pierced **her** side.

"Good God! good God!" stammered Buteau.

It **was** all over. A single second had settled it all; **the** irreparable had been accomplished. Lise, dazed at seeing her wish so quickly realised, stood watching her sister's severed dress as it reddened with **a stream of** blood. Had the blade penetrated deeply enough **to cut the** little **one**, that the blood flowed so plentifully? she wondered.

Old Fouan's **pale** face again peeped forth from behind the **rick.** He had seen everything, and was perfectly stupefied.

Françoise lay quite still, and Buteau, who had stepped up to her, dared not touch her. A gust of wind now darted over the field, and **filled him with a** wild terror.

"She **is dead! In God's name, let us bolt!"**

He seized hold of Lise's hand, and they flew along the deserted road as though they were possessed. The low, gloomy sky seemed as though it was about to fall down upon their heads, and behind them the sound of their galloping feet raised echoes which sounded as though a crowd of people were in **hot** pursuit of them. They both ran wildly on over the cropped **and** naked plain; Buteau, **with his blouse swelling about** him **in the wind, and** Lise, with her **hair all loose and dishevelled,** carrying her **cap in** her hand. **And as they ran they both kept** repeating the same words, panting **like hunted animals:**

"She is dead! In God's **name, let us bolt!"**

Their strides grew **longer, and soon they could not articu- late** distinctly; still, **as they fled wildly on, they gave vent to** panting exclamations **which kept time, as it were, with their** bounds:

"**Dead! good God!** Dead! good God! **Dead! good God!"**

Then they disappeared from sight.

Some minutes later, when Jean trotted up on his horse, he **was** filled with terrible consternation.

"What—what has happened?" he **cried.**

Françoise had opened her eyes, but **still lay** rigidly motionless. She gazed **at Jean** for a long **time** with her great **troubled eyes, but she said nothing.** Her mind seemed to be far away, **absorbed in thought.**

"You **are wounded! You are** bleeding! Speak to me, I beseech you!"

Then he turned to **old** Fouan, who had at length ventured **to** approach.

"You were here? Tell **me** what has happened!"

Then Françoise spoke, but very slowly, **as** though she were thinking **of what she** should **say.**

"I came to cut some grass—I fell on to my scythe—it went into me here. Oh, it's all over with me!"

Her eyes sought those of Fouan, telling him, and him alone, other things—things that only her own family should know. Dazed as was the old man, he seemed to comprehend her meaning.

"Yes, that is what happened," he said; "she fell and wounded herself. I was there, and saw it."

Jean galloped off to Rognes for a stretcher to carry his wife home. She lost consciousness again on the journey, and they never expected to get her to the house alive.

CHAPTER IV.

IT happened that on the following day, Sunday, the young men of Rognes were to go to Cloyes for the conscription-ballot; and as La Grande and La Frimat, who had hurried up to the house in the dusk, were undressing Françoise and putting her to bed with the utmost care, the roll of the drum could be heard on the road below, sounding to the poor folks like a knell amid the mournful gloom.

Jean, who was quite off his head with troubled anxiety, had just set off to fetch Doctor Finet, when near the church he met Patoir, the veterinary surgeon, on his way to attend old Saucisse's cow. He forcibly dragged him into the house to see the ailing woman, in spite of his unwillingness to go. But when Patoir saw the hideous wound, he point-blank refused to interfere in the case. What good could he do? Death was plainly written there! Two hours later, when Jean came back with Monsieur Finet, the surgeon made a gesture of hopeless despair. Nothing could be done beyond administering anæsthetics for the sake of deadening the pain. The five months' pregnancy seriously complicated the case; and the unborn child could be felt moving within its mother's wounded body, dying indeed of its mother's death. Before the doctor went away, he dressed the wound as best he could, and, although he promised to return in the morning, he warned Jean that his wife would most probably pass away during the night. She lived through it, however, and she was still lingering on, when, towards nine o'clock in the morning, the drum began to beat again, summoning the young men to meet in front of the municipal offices.

All through the night the flood-gates of heaven had been open, and Jean had listened to a pouring deluge of rain as he sat watching in his wife's room, stupefied with troubled grief, and with his eyes full of big tears. The roll of the drum sounded as though it were muffled as he heard it in the close, damp air of the morning. The rain had now ceased, but the sky was still of a leaden grey.

For a long time the drum-beating continued. The drummer

was a new one, a nephew of Macqueron's, who had just left
the service, and he beat his drum as though he were leading a
regiment into action. All Rognes was in a state of anxiety,
for the rumours of approaching war, that had lately been
circulated, had greatly increased the emotion which always
attended the conscription-ballotting. The prospect of being at
once marched off to be shot by the Prussians was not an alluring one. There were nine young men of the neighbourhood to
ballot upon this occasion, probably a larger number than had
ever before been known. Among them were Nénesse and
Delphin, once so inseparable, but severed of late owing to the
former having taken a situation in a restaurant at Chartres.
On the previous evening Nénesse had gone to sleep at his father's
farm. When Delphin saw him he scarcely knew him, he was
so changed; dressed quite like a gentleman, with a cane and
a silk hat, and a blue scarf clasped by a ring. He now had
his clothes made to order by a tailor, and cracked jokes about
Lambourdieu's ready-made suits. His neck was still scrany
and long, and absolutely devoid of hair on the nape. Delphin,
on the other hand, had grown massive and sturdy; his limbs
were heavy, like his movements, and his face was tanned and
baked by the sun. He had grown up like some vigorous plant
in that beloved soil to which he was so firmly rooted. However,
he and Nénesse immediately renewed their broken chumship, and
were as good comrades as ever. After spending a part of the
night with each other, they appeared arm-in-arm the next morning in front of the municipal offices, in obedience to the persistent
summons of the drum.

A number of the relations of the nine young men were
gathered there. Delhomme and Fanny, proud of their son's
distinguished appearance, wished to be present to see him off,
though they felt no anxiety, as they had provided for his
exemption. Bécu, wearing his constabular badge of office,
threatened to cuff his wife because she began to cry. What
was she blubbering for? he asked. Wasn't Delphin fit to
serve his country with credit? The lad, however, would be
sure to escape, and draw a lucky number. When at last the
nine young fellows were all got together, a feat which it took
a good hour to accomplish, Lequeu handed them the banner.
Then they began to discuss who should carry it. The general
rule was to choose the tallest and most vigorous of the
number, and so it was agreed that Delphin should carry it.
He seemed very nervous and timid, in spite of his big fists,
shy at finding himself mixed up in matters which he did not

understand. He seemed **to** find the long pole awkward **to** manage, and then it might conduct him to misfortune, **he** reflected sorrowfully.

At the two corners of the street, Flore **and** Cœlina **were** giving a final sweep to their respective public parlours, in view of being ready for the evening. Macqueron was looking out of his **door with** a sorrowful **countenance** ; then Lengaigne appeared **at** his, with **a sniggering grin** on his face. He was in **a** very triumphant frame **of mind just** then, for the excise-officers had recently seized four casks **of** wine which they had found concealed beneath one **of** his rival's wood-stacks. Macqueron, it **was said,** would be dismissed from his mayoralty in consequence, and every one felt quite sure that the anonymous letter which had led to the wine being discovered had emanated from Lengaigne. To make matters worse, Macqueron **had** another trouble on his shoulders. His daughter Berthe **had** so compromised herself with the wheelwright's son, whom **he had** previously refused as a son-in-law, that he was now constrained to let him have her. For the last week the gossips at **the** fountain had talked of nothing save the daughter's marriage and the prosecution of the father. It was certain that the latter would at least be fined ; and **it was by** no means unlikely that he would be sent to gaol. And so the mayor, seeing his neighbour's insulting grin, **retired** again, feeling painfully conscious that every one else was also sniggering at him.

Delphin had now grasped the banner, and the drum sounded the march. Nénesse fell into position, and the other **seven took up** their places behind him. They formed quite a **little** troop as they filed along over the level road. A swarm **of** children ran forward with them, and Delhomme, Fanny, Bécu, and several other relatives accompanied them to the end of the village. **Freed** of her husband, Madame Bécu hurried away and slipped furtively into the church. Then, glancing around and finding that she was quite alone, she fell down on her knees, though, as a rule, she was by no means addicted to displays of devotion, and burst into tears, while beseeching the good God to grant her son a lucky number. She remained for more than an hour stammering out this heartfelt prayer. Far away, towards Cloyes, the banner was gradually fading from sight in the distance, and the rolling of the drum was lost **in** space.

It was nearly ten o'clock when Doctor Finet made his appearance again, and he seemed surprised to find Francoise still alive. He had quite expected that he would merely have to

give the certificate for her burial. He shook his head as he
examined the **wound**. Ever since the previous evening, not
having **an** idea **of the real facts,** he had **been** pondering over
the story **that had been told** to him in connection with the
wound. **He** now desired to have the whole narrative repeated
to him ; and he could **not yet** understand how the unfortunate
young woman had managed to fall **in such a** disastrous fashion.
He **finally took his leave,** indignant at Françoise's culpable
clumsiness, and annoyed at having to **pay** yet another visit **to
certify the death.**

Jean still remained in a state of mournful gloom, watching
intently over Françoise, who closed her eyes in persistent
muteness as soon as she ever caught her husband's questioning
glance. He divined that some lie or other had been told him,
and that his wife was hiding something from him. In the
early morning he had escaped for a little time, **and** had run up
to the lucern field to see if he could discover anything. But
he could learn nothing definite from his inspection. The foot-
marks had been nearly effaced by the heavy rain which had
fallen during the night, but he discovered a corner where the
lucern seemed to have been beaten down, and he concluded
that this was the spot where Françoise had fallen. After the
surgeon had gone away, Jean again sat down by the side of
the dying woman's bed. He was now quite alone with her, for
La Frimat had gone off to breakfast, and La Grande had been
obliged to return home for a moment to see that things were
not going wrong in her absence.

"Are you in pain?" Jean asked his wife.

Françoise closed her eyes tightly, and made no reply.

"Tell me, now, aren't you concealing something from
me?"

If it had not been for her weak and painful breathing one
might have supposed that Françoise was already dead. Ever
since the previous evening she had been lying on her back,
silent and in the same position, as though incapable of either
motion or speech. She was burning with fever, but all her
power of will seemed to offer a determined resistance to the
approach of delirium, so acute was her fear of letting anything
escape her. She had always possessed a strongly-marked
character, full of obstinate determination; doing nothing like
other people, and giving utterance to ideas which filled everybody who heard her with amazement. Loyalty to her family was
probably actuating her now, a loyalty which over-rode all feeling
of hatred and craving for vengeance. What good would ven-

geance do her, now that she was dying? There were matters
which were best buried with one's self, shut up in the spot
where they had been born; matters which must never, no never,
be disclosed for a stranger's enlightenment; and Jean was
a stranger, whom she had never been really able to love with
genuine love. It was perhaps in punishment for having given
him her hand that she was never to bring into the world the
undeveloped child quickening within her.

Ever since Jean had seen his wife brought home in a dying
condition, his thoughts had been harping on the unmade will.
All through the night he had kept thinking that, if she died
intestate, he would be entitled to nothing, save half of the
furniture and the money—a hundred and twenty-seven francs
locked up in the drawer. He loved Françoise dearly, and be
would have made any sacrifice to keep her; but the thought
that, together with his wife, he would also lose the house and
land, still further increased his grief. As yet, he had not
dared to say a word on the subject: it seemed so hard-hearted,
and then there had always been other people in the room.
But at last, seeing that he would never be able to glean any
further information as to the manner in which the accident had
happened, he determined to tackle this other matter.

"Are there any arrangements that you would like to make?"
he asked.

It did not seem as though Françoise heard him. Her eyes
were closed, and her face was quite expressionless.

"If anything happened to you, you know, your sister
would take everything. The paper is still there in the
drawer."

He brought the sheet of stamped paper to her, and then
continued, in a voice that grew more and more embarrassed:

"Would you like me to help you? Are you strong enough
to write, do you think? I'm not thinking about myself; but
I only fancied that you wouldn't like those folks who have
treated you so badly to have anything you left behind."

Françoise's eyelids trembled slightly, proving to Jean that
she had heard him. So she must still be averse to making a
will! He was quite astounded; he could not understand it at
all. Probably Françoise, herself, could not have explained
why she persisted in thus lying like a corpse, before the time
had come for her to be boxed-up within four boards. But the
land and the house did not belong to this man, who had come
athwart her life like some mere passer-by. She owed him
nothing; the child would go away with herself. By what

right should the property be taken away from the family?
Her obstinate, childish ideas of justice protested against such
a thing. This is mine, that is yours; let us each take our own
and say good-bye! However, other thoughts besides these
were vaguely floating through her mind. Her sister Lise
seemed far away from her—lost in the distance—and it **was
Buteau** alone who seemed **really present to** her; Buteau whom,
**in spite of all his ill-treatment, she pardoned and loved and
longed for.**

Jean was getting **vexed. The desire for the soil was now**
gaining hold of him, too, **and embittering his mind.** He
raised Françoise in bed, and attempted **to get her into a sitting**
position and to put a pen **between** her fingers.

"Come now," he said, "**see if you** can't manage **it. You**
can't like those scamps better **than me, and** want them to have
everything!"

Then Françoise **at** last opened **her eyes,** and the look that
she turned upon Jean quite stupefied him. **She knew** that she
was going to die, and her **big,** widely-opened eyes **were** full
of hopeless despair. Why was he torturing her like this? they
seemed to say. She could not, and she would not! Besides,
it was her own affair. A low moan of pain was the only sound
that escaped her lips. Then she fell back **again, her eyelids**
closed, and her head lay rigid and motionless **on the** pillow.

Ashamed of his unkind persistence, Jean now felt **so miser-**
able and confused that he was still standing **there with the**
sheet of stamped **paper in his hand when La Grande came**
back into the **room.** She saw **it, and knew what it** meant;
and at **once took Jean aside to** inquire if Françoise **had** made a
will. He stammered out that he had just **been** going **to
conceal the** paper to prevent **any one** bothering **his** wife about
it, a course which La **Grande** seemed to approve of, for she
was on the Buteaus' side, foreseeing all kinds of rows and
abominable scenes if they succeeded in inheriting the property.
Then, seating herself in front of the table, and recommencing
her knitting, she continued:

"Well, no one will **find** himself wronged by **me, I'm sure,**
when I'm taken away. My will has been made long ago.
Every one is remembered, and I should think I was acting
very wrongly if I showed an unfair preference for any one.
None of my children are forgotten, as they will see for themselves one of these days."

She recited this formula daily to one or another member of
her family, and she made a point of repeating it by the death-

bed of her relatives. Every time she delivered herself of it, **she** chuckled in secret at the thought of that famous will of hers which would set the whole family by the ears when she was gone. She had been careful that it should not contain a single clause that was not pregnant with a lawsuit.

" What a pity it is," she added, " that one can't take one's property **with** one! **But, since one** can't, others must needs have the enjoyment **of it.**"

La Frimat now returned, sat down at the other side of the table, **opposite to La** Grande, and also began to knit. So the afternoon glided away. The two old women sat quietly gossipping **with each** other, while Jean, who could not settle in any **one** place, kept walking up and down, perpetually leaving the room and then returning in a state of feverish restlessness. The doctor had said that there was nothing to be done, and so they did nothing.

At last, La Frimat began expressing her regret **that** Sourdeau, the bone-setter at Bazoches, who was equally expert in the treatment of wounds, had not been sent for. He just said a few words and then breathed over his patients, and then the wounds closed up at once.

"Oh, **he's a** splendid fellow!" exclaimed La Grande **in a** respectful way. " It was he who put the Lorillon's breast-bone right. Old Lorillon's breast-bone, you know, fell out of its place, and hung down and pressed so heavily on his stomach that he almost died from exhaustion. Then, to make matters worse, the old woman caught the dreadful **complaint as** well: for, as you know, it is contagious. Presently they all had it, the daughter, the son-in-law, and their three children. They would certainly all have died of it if they had not sent for Sourdeau, who put everything right again by just rubbing their bellies with a tortoise-shell comb."

The other old woman confirmed every detail of this story with **a wag of the** head. It was all well known, and there was no doubt about it. Then she herself adduced another fact in support of Sourdeau's skill.

" It was Sourdeau, too, **who** cured the Budin's little girl of fever by just cutting a live pigeon in two and applying it to her head."

Then she turned to Jean, who was standing quite dazed by the bedside.

" If I **were** you," she said, " I should send for him. It's perhaps not too late, even now."

Jean, however, answered merely with an angry gesture.

His town-breeding prevented him from believing such stories. The two women then went on gossipping together for a long time, telling **each other of** various quaint remedies, **such as** placing parsley **beneath one's bed to** cure lumbago, or keeping three acorns **in** one's pocket in the case of inflammation, or drinking a glass **of water which had** been exposed to **the moon** in view of **getting rid of wind.**

"Well, if you're **not going to send for Sourdeau,"** La Frimat abruptly **exclaimed, " at any rate you'd better send for** his reverence the priest."

Jean again **replied** by an **angry gesture, and La Grande** compressed her lips tightly,

" What good would his reverence **do ? "**

" What good would **he do?** Why, **he would bring the** blessed sacrament, and **there's some comfort in that, some-** times."

La Grande **shrugged her** shoulders, as though to express that now-a-days no one believed in such old-fashioned ideas.

" Besides," **she added, after a** pause, " the priest wouldn't **come. He is ill.** Madame Bécu told me just now that he is going **away in a carriage on** Wednesday, as the doctor says that he **will** certainly **die if he** remains in Rognes."

As a matter of fact, the Abbé Madeline's **health had** gradually been getting worse during the two **years and a-half** that he had been stationed at Rognes. **A feeling of home-** sickness, a broken-hearted longing for his native mountains **of** Auvergne had been preying upon him **with increasing** severity every day he had spent in that flat **land of La Beauce, where** the sight of the **far-spreading boundless plain** filled **his heart** with despondent **melancholy. Not a** tree nor **a rock was to be seen ; and instead of rushing** cascades of **foaming water, there were** only stagnant **pools. The** priest's eyes **lost their** brightness, and **he** grew more **fleshless** than ever, till people said that he **was** going **off in** a consumption. Yet he might still have been reconciled to remaining there if he could have de- rived any consolation from the women of his parish. But it was just the **other** way. Coming, as he did, from a pious and faithful flock, his timid soul was overwhelmed with grief and consternation at finding himself in so irreligious a parish, where only the merest outward forms of the faith were com- plied with. The women deafened and dazed him with their screaming and quarrelling, and so abused his yielding nature that they practically took the religious direction of the place **into** their own hands : **while** he, a man full of scrupulous sensitiveness, and constantly afraid of involuntarily falling into sin, stood by in silent consternation. But there was a final blow in store for him. On Christmas day, one of the hand-maidens of the Virgin had been seized with the pangs of labour while in church. Since then the priest had been getting worse and worse, and now he was going to be carried back, in a dying condition, to Auvergne.

"So, then, we're without a priest again?" exclaimed La Frimat. "I wonder if the Abbé Godard would come back to us."

"Ah, the surly fellow!" cried La Grande; "he would burst with spite if he had to come!"

The sudden arrival of Fanny made them silent. She was the only member of her family who had come to see Françoise on the previous evening, and she had now returned to ascertain how she was getting on. Jean pointed to his wife with his trembling hand. The room was hushed in sympathetic silence, and Fanny lowered her voice to inquire if the dying woman had asked for her sister. No, they said, she had never opened her mouth on the subject; it was just as if Lise had not existed. Forsooth, it was very strange, for death is death, all previous quarrelling notwithstanding; and when should peace be made if not ere the final departure?

La Grande now expressed the opinion that Françoise should be questioned on the subject. She got up from her seat, and stooped over the dying woman.

"Tell me, my dear," she said, "wouldn't you like to see Lise?"

But Françoise lay perfectly still; she gave no other sign than a scarcely perceptible quiver of her closed eyelids.

"She is perhaps expecting us to bring her. I'll go for her."

Then, still keeping her eyes closed, and turning her head on the pillow, Françoise softly said "No." Jean desired that her wishes should be respected, and the three women sat down again. They now began to feel astonished that Lise did not come of her own accord; but there was often a great amount of obstinate feeling shown in families, they reflected.

"What endless troubles one has!" Fanny now exclaimed with a sigh. "Ever since this morning, I've been nearly worried to death over this balloting; and yet really I've no cause for worry, since I know very well that Nénesse won't be taken from us."

"Ah! yes, indeed," murmured La Frimat; "but one can't help feeling anxious and excited, all the same."

Once again the dying woman was entirely forgotten, and the gossips began to talk about luck and chance, about the young men who would be marched off, and about those who would remain. It was now three o'clock, and although the party was not expected back till five o'clock at the earliest, reports of what had happened were already circulating in the village, wafted over from Cloyes, no one knew how, by that species of ærial telegraphy which flies from village to village. The Briquets' son had drawn No. 13, so there was no chance of his escaping! The Couillots' son, on the other hand, had drawn No. 106, and that was certainly a safe number! However, nothing positive seemed to be known about the others. There was only a lot of contradictory reports, which tended to increase the excitement. Nobody appeared to know how Delphin and Nénesse had fared.

"My heart is palpitating dreadfully," exclaimed Fanny. "How stupid of me!"

Then they called out to Madame Bécu, who happened to be passing. She had been to the church again, and was now wandering backwards and forwards like a disembodied spirit. Her trouble was so great that she did not even stop to talk.

"I can't contain myself any longer; I'm going to meet them!" said she.

Jean was standing in front of the window, gazing vaguely out of it, and paying no attention to the women's talk. Several times since the morning he had seen old Fouan prowling round the house with his dragging gait. He now suddenly caught sight of him again, pressing his face against one of the panes of glass, and trying to make out what was going on inside the room. Jean thereupon opened the window, and the old man, looking quite stupefied, began to ask in stammering tones how Françoise was. Very bad, Jean told him; in fact, it was all over with her. Then Fouan thrust his head in at the open window, and stood gazing at Françoise for such a long time that it almost seemed as though he were unable to go away. When Fanny and La Grande saw him, they returned to their previous idea of sending for Lise. But when they tried to get the old fellow to fetch her, he shivered with alarm and made his escape. He muttered and repeated over and over again:

"No, no; impossible, impossible!"

Jean seemed struck by the old man's appearance of terror; however, the women let the matter drop. After all, it only concerned the two sisters, and it was no business of theirs to force them to see and kiss each other. At this moment a sound was heard, feeble at first, and like the droning of a big fly; then it grew louder and louder, rolling along like a gust of wind breaking among trees.

Fanny leaped up excitedly.

"The drum!" she cried. "Here they come! Good evening!"

And thereupon she hurried away, without even giving her cousin a last kiss.

La Grande and La Frimat also left the room and went to look out at the door. Only Françoise and Jean were left: the wife still persisting in her obstinate silence and rigidity, hearing, perhaps, everything that was said, but wishing to die, like some wild animal earthed-up at the bottom of its burrow; the husband standing in front of the open window, racked by uncertainty, and overwhelmed by a troubled grief to which everything seemed to contribute. Ah, that drum! how the sound of it vibrated and echoed through his whole being. And as its roll broke ceaselessly through the air, with his grief of to-day there mingled recollections of the past, of barracks and battles, and of the dog's life led by poor wretches who had neither wife nor child to love them!

As soon as the banner came into sight, far away in the distance, on the flat level road looking grey and dingy in the fading light of the evening, a swarm of children scampered off to meet the conscripts, and a group of relatives posted themselves just at the entrance to the village. The nine young men and the drummer were already very drunk, and as they came along in the mournful evening light, decorated with tri-coloured ribbons, and the greater part of them having numbers pinned upon their hats, they bellowed out a warlike chorus. As they approached the village, they roared out the words of their song louder than ever, and by way of brag, marched forward with a swaggering air.

Delphin was still carrying the banner; but he was holding it on his shoulder, as though it were some troublesome rag of which he could not conceive the use. He came along wearily, with a gloomy expression on his face, and did not join in the singing of the others. There was no number pinned on his cap. As soon as Madame Bécu caught sight of him, she rushed forward in a tremble, at the risk of being overturned by the advancing band of conscripts.

" Well ? " she cried.

But Delphin angrily thrust her aside without slackening his pace.

" Get out of the way, and don't bother me ! "

Bécu himself had also stepped forward, as full of anxiety as his wife ; but when he heard his son's surly words, he did not dare to say anything ; and, as his wife broke out sobbing, it was all he could do to restrain his own tears, despite all his patriotic enthusiasm.

" It's of no use talking about it ! He's been drawn ! "

They now both lagged behind on the deserted road, and slowly and sadly returned to the village—the husband thinking of the hard life he had endured in the past as a soldier, and the wife swelling with wrath against the God to whom she had twice prayed, and who had not hearkened to her.

Nénesse was wearing a magnificent number " 214 " on his cap, daubed in red and blue paint. This was one of the highest numbers, and the young fellow was triumphing in his luck, brandishing his cane and keeping the time as he led the wild chorus of his comrades. When Fanny saw the number, instead of rejoicing, she broke out into a cry of deep regret. Ah ! if they could only have foreseen this they would never have invested those thousand francs in Monsieur Baillehache's lottery to ensure their son's exemption ! Still, although the young man was thus ensured against being taken from them, his mother and father both embraced him as if he had just escaped from some great peril. But he hastily exclaimed :

" Do leave me alone ! and don't worry me in this way ! "

The little troop continued on its tipsy, riotous march through the wildly excited village. The young men's relations dared not venture upon any further questions or demonstrations, as it was clear that they would only meet with an angry repulse. All the young fellows seemed to have come back in the same surly frame of mind, both those who had been taken and those who had escaped. But, anyway, they would not have been able to give a clear account of what had happened, for their eyes were projecting wildly from their heads, and they were as drunk and noisy as though they had all been at some uproarious merry-making. While one little fellow who had been taken, was facetiously trumpeting with his nose, two others who would almost certainly escape came along with pale faces and downcast eyes. Still, if the wildly excited drummer at their head had led them down into the depths of the Aigre, they would all have followed impetuously in his train.

When they at length halted in front of the municipal offices, Delphin gave up the banner.

" There, thank heaven; **I've** had enough of **that damned**
thing **which** has brought me nothing but ill-luck! " he said.

Then **he** seized hold of Nénesse's arm, and dragged him off
with him, while the rest **of the** party invaded Lengaigne's
tavern, where they **were** joined **by** their relations and friends,
who **at** last succeeded in learning **what had** happened. Macqueron meanwhile looked out from his door, heart-sore at the
brisk business his rival was doing.

" Come along," said Delphin to Nénesse in a sharp, curt
way, as though he were forming some determined resolution.
" I want to show you something."

Nénesse allowed himself to be taken off. They would have
time to come back and drink afterwards. The noisy drum had
ceased to din their ears, and they felt a sensation of pleasant
quiet and repose, as they strolled off together along the now
deserted road which was growing grey in the falling darkness.
As Delphin walked on in silence, buried in reflections which
could scarcely be pleasant ones, Nénesse began to talk to him
about a very important matter. A couple of days previously,
at Chartres, having obtained a few hours' liberty from his
employer, he had gone up to the Rue aux Juifs, and had there
learnt that Vaucogne, Monsieur Charles's son-in-law, wanted to
dispose of his business. He was too unsteady to be able to
make it pay, and he **was robbed right and left by the** women.
But what a business **it might become, and what profits** might
be reaped if it **were in the hands of an energetic, steady-**going
young fellow, **with a shrewd head and strong willing arms,**
and already with some experience **of the trade!** His idea was to
frighten Monsieur and Madame **Charles into the belief that**
Number 19 was in **great** danger **of being suppressed by the**
police in **consequence of** the **immoral proceedings that**
habitually **took place there, and thus prevail upon** them **to let**
him **have the place for a mere** song. **Ah, that would be** much
better than grubbing the soil! Why, he could be a gentleman
at once!

Delphin **was listening in a** very absent-minded fashion; in
fact, he **was busy with his** own thoughts, from which he woke
up with **a start, as his companion** gave him a sly poke in the ribs.

" Some **folks** are **born to be** lucky," he murmured. " You
were sent into the world **to be a** pride to your mother."

Then **he** relapsed into **silence** again, and Nénesse, as though
he had quite settled matters in his own mind, began to explain
the improvements he **would** make at Number 19, if his parents
would **advance him** the **necessary money.** He was perhaps a

little young, he allowed, but **he felt** a genuine vocation **for** the business.

He now caught sight **of La Trouille gliding** up towards them along the gloomy **road, on her way, probably,** to some amatory assignation or **other; and wishing to show his** easy **manner** with women, **he gave her a smart slap as she** went past. La Trouille at **once returned it, but then** recognis-ing the two young men, she exclaimed:

"Hallo, is it you? How you have grown!"

She laughed merrily, at thought, no doubt, of their sprees in earlier days. Of the three, she had changed the least; and, despite her one and twenty years, she still looked a mere chit of a girl, being as slight and supple as a poplar shoot, with a bosom as **undeveloped as a child's.** The meeting seemed to please **her, and she kissed the two young men one after** the other; **she would even have been quite willing to** proceed to further **lengths if they had suggested it, by way of** marking her **pleasure at seeing them again, just as men clink** glasses together **when they meet after a separation.**

"I've got something to tell you," said Nénesse jokingly. "I'm very likely going to take Charles's shop. Will you come and have a situation there?"

Then the girl abruptly **ceased** laughing, and was **overcome with emotion, bursting** into tears. The surrounding **darkness** seemed **to lay hold of** her, and she disappeared from **sight,** sobbing **out like a** broken-hearted child:

"Oh, how beastly! how beastly! I sha'n't love you any more!"

Delphin had remained silent, and with an abstracted air he now resumed his course.

"But where is it you are taking me?" Nénesse finally asked. "What is this strange thing you want to show me?"

"Come along, and you will see by-and-bye."

He then hastened his steps, and left **the** high-road to make **a short cut through the vines to the** house in which the rural constable **had** been lodged by the authorities since the parsonage had been **given up to** the priest! He lived there with his father; **and he at once** conducted his companion into the kitchen, where he lighted a candle, seeming pleased to find that his parents had not yet returned home.

"We'll have a **glass** together," **he** exclaimed, placing a bottle and a couple of glasses on the table.

When he had swallowed some of the wine, he smacked his **tongue, and** then continued:

" I want to tell you that if these fools think they are going
to keep me, simply because I have drawn a bad number, they
are mightily mistaken. When uncle Michel died, I was obliged
to go and stay three days at Orleans, and it nearly killed me, I
was so miserable at being away from **home.** I daresay you
think **it** very foolish of me, but I can't help it. The feeling is
stronger **than** I am ; and away from home I am like a tree torn
up by the roots. And now they **want to take me** off and send
me to the devil, to all sorts of places that I've never even heard
the name **of !** Ah, **well,** they'll find **out their** mistake presently ! "

Nénesse, who had **often** heard him prate **in this** strain before, shrugged his shoulders, and replied :

" It is very easy to talk, but you'll have to go, all the same.
The gendarmes would soon march you off, you know."

Without making any reply, Delphin turned aside, and **with
his** left hand took hold of a small hatchet hanging against **the
wall, and** used for chopping firewood. Then, without any
hesitation he calmly laid the fore-finger of his right hand upon
the edge of the table, and, with **a** smart blow of the hatchet,
completely severed it.

" There, that's what I wanted to show you ! " he said. " I
want **you** to be able **to** tell **the** others that I have done what
a coward would scarcely **do.**"

" You maniac ! " cried **Nénesse, quite** overcome with the
sight of what Delphin had **done.** " **You** have crippled yourself
for life ! "

" I scoff **at** them all ! Let the gendarmes come **as** soon
as they like ! I'm quite certain now that I sha'n't be forced
away ! "

Then he picked up the severed finger and tossed it into the
wood fire. After shaking his bleeding hand, he roughly
wrapped his handkerchief round it, fastening it tightly with a
piece of string so as to stop the flow of blood.

" **Well,** this needn't prevent **us finishing** the bottle before
we join the others," said he. " **Here's** to your health ! "

" And here's to yours ! "

By **this time** there **was so much noise and so much tobacco-**
smoke **in** Lengaigne's public-room that it was impossible to
see one another or to hear even one's-self speak. Besides the
young fellows who had just returned from balloting, there
was a crowd of idlers. Hyacinthe and his friend Canon were
there, busily engaged in making old Fouan drunk, the three
of them sitting round **a** bottle of brandy. Bécu, whom his

son's bad luck, combined with the large amount of drink he had swallowed, had quite overcome, was snoring noisily, with his head on one of the tables. Delhomme and Clou were there, too, playing a game of piquet, and also sat there Lequeu, with his nose buried in a book which he was pretending to read in spite of all the surrounding uproar.

A fight among the women had served to increase the general excitement. It had occurred in this way: Flore having gone to the fountain to fill her pitcher with water, there met Cœlina who, bursting with hatred and jealousy, threw herself upon her, clawing her furiously with her nails, and accusing her of being bribed by the excise officers to betray her neighbours. Macqueron and Lengaigne, who had rushed up, very nearly came to blows themselves; the former swearing that he would contrive to have the latter caught while he was damping his tobacco, and the latter sarcastically asking the former when they might expect to hear of his resignation. A crowd gathered, everybody mingling in the quarrel for the mere pleasure of shaking their fists and hearing themselves shout; and a general murderous engagement seemed at one time inevitable. This was averted, however, and the incident ended, but not without leaving a feeling of unsatisfied anger, and a longing to come to blows.

A passage between Victor, Lengaigne's son, and the conscripts almost brought about an explosion. The former having served his time in the army was swaggerng before all the young fellows, shouting louder than the loudest of them, and goading them on into making all sorts of idiotic wagers; such as emptying a bottle of wine by holding it in the air and pouring its contents down their throats, or sucking the contents of a glass up through their nostrils, without touching it with their mouths. Suddenly, as some reference was made to the Macquerons, and the approaching marriage of their daughter Berthe, young Couillot began to snigger and titter out the old jokes about the girl. They would be able now, he said, to ask the husband all about her, on the day after the wedding. They had heard such a deal about her, that it would really be satisfactory to get at the truth!

Victor thereupon caused intense surprise by a show of angry warmth. Hitherto he had been one of those who most persistently attacked the girl, whereas now he shouted out:

"There, we've heard quite enough about it now. She has everything that the others have. She has!"

This assertion provoked a loud clamour. Victor had seen,

then? She had been his mistress, **eh**? While vigorously denying **the** truth of this accusation, and striking his breast with his
fists, he adhered to his recent statement, whereupon young
Couillot, who **was** very drunk, violently contradicted him,
though **he** knew absolutely nothing about the matter. In
point of **fact**, he was simply actuated by pig-headed perversity.
Victor **bellowed out** that he **had once** said the same as Couillot,
and that, if he now said differently, **it certainly wasn't** for love
of the Macquerons! It was because **the truth is the** truth!
And then **he fell upon the conscript,** whose **friends were** obliged
to drag him from his grasp.

"Say as I say, damn you, or I'll **wring your neck!**"

In spite of Victor's violence, however, **several of the com-**
pany **still** retained their doubts **on** the subject. **No one could**
understand his hot outburst **of** anger, for he generally showed
himself very hard towards women, and he had publicly
repudiated his sister, whom **her** impure amours, so it was said,
had now landed in an hospital. That foul Suzanne! Ah!
she did well to keep her tainted carcase away from them!

Flore now brought up fresh supplies of wine, but glasses
were chinked in vain; the atmosphere **was** still heavy with a
brooding storm of angry **abuse** and **violence.** No one had any
idea **of** going off **to** dine. Drinking **keeps folk** from getting
hungry. The conscripts **at last began to** troll **out a** patriotic
song, accompanying it with **such heavy blows** upon the tables
that the flames of the three **petroleum lamps** flickered wildly,
and emitted puffs of acrid smoke. The atmosphere **was get-**
ting unbearable, and Delhomme and Clou opened the **window**
behind **them.** Just at that moment Buteau entered **the room**
and glided into a corner. His face did not wear its usual air
of braggart self-assertion. Indeed there was a look of uneasy
anxiety in his little eyes, and he glanced at the company one
after another, as though he were trying to read their thoughts.
He had doubtless come to listen **to the gossip,** in view of discovering **whether any of** his neighbours entertained any suspicion of him. He had felt quite **unable** to stay any longer at
home, **where he had shut himself up since** the previous evening
without stirring **out. The presence of** Hyacinthe and Canon
seemed to produce **a deep effect upon him;** so much so, indeed,
that he refained from **quarrelling with** them for making old
Fouan drunk. For a long **time he sat** gazing earnestly at Delhomme. But it was Bécu, sleeping on amid all the surrounding
uproar, who more than any one else seemed to exercise his
thoughts. Was the rural constable really asleep, or was he

only artfully pretending to be so? **Buteau** nudged him with his elbow, and **felt** somewhat relieved **on** discovering that he was slobbering all over his sleeve. He **then** concentrated his attention upon the schoolmaster, upon whose face he fancied he **could** detect a most extraordinary expression. **Why** was he looking so different from what he usually did?

As a matter **of** fact, Lequeu, although pretending **to be** **absorbed** in his book, **was** shaken **by** sudden **starts**, with **his** features contracted by a rising fit of anger. The conscripts, with their songs and idiotic merriment, seemed to be completely upsetting him.

" The infernal brutes !" he muttered, still managing to **restrain** himself.

For some months past his **position in the village had** been growing **very** uncomfortable. He had always been rough and harsh with **the** children, and **he was given to sending them** off home to the paternal dung-heap **with a box on the ears.** But latterly he had grown still **more violent, and there had been** a **nasty** business about a little **girl's ear which he had slit** with a blow from a ruler. Several of the children's parents had then **written, asking that he might be removed. Now, too,** Berthe **Macqueron's approaching** marriage destroyed **a** long-standing **hope of** his, **annihilating the** edifice he had been mentally **con-**structing for years **past. It** came upon **him** like a thunderbolt. Oh, those hateful **peasants! a** foul brood **that** denied **him** its daughters, and was **about to get** him **turned adrift merely on** account of a little hussy's **ear !**

He now suddenly **tapped the book he was holding,** just as though he **were** in **his class-room, and cried out** to the **conscripts :**

" **For** goodness' sake, let **us have** a little less noise ! You **seem** to think it would be **very amusing** to have your brains blown out **by the Prussians !** "

' **The company turned their** eyes **upon** him in amazement. Amusing? **No there was** certainly nothing amusing in that idea ! Delhomme observed, however, that every one was bound to defend **his own** homestead and soil, and that if **ever** the Prussians came **to La** Beauce they would find that the Beaucerons were **no** cowards. But as to being sent off to fight for other folks' fields! **No,** there was certainly nothing amusing about that !

Just then Delphin **now** made his appearance, accompanied by Nénesse. His face was greatly flushed, and his eyes were glistening feverishly. He had heard Delhomme's remark, and, as he seated himself at **one of the** tables with the conscripts, he shouted out :

" Yes, if the Prussians **show** their faces here, we'll make mince-meat of them pretty **sharp !** "

The handkerchief secured round his hand attracted attention, **and** inquiries **were made as** to what **was** the matter. Oh, nothing at **all ! he said ; he** had merely cut himself. Then, **bringing down his other fist** with such **violence as to make** the **table rattle, he ordered a** bottle of **wine.**

Canon and Hyacinthe were looking at **the young fellows, not with any show of anger, but** rather with **an air of condescending pity. To be so happy, the** conscripts must **certainly be very** young **and idiotic. By-and-bye, Canon,** who **was now very** drunk, grew maudlin over his **theories for the reorganisation of** future happiness. **Resting** his **chin on his hands, he spoke as** follows :

" War, confound **it ! Ah ! it's time we** became the masters ! You all know my scheme ; no more military service, **no** more taxes ; everybody's appetites and desires completely satisfied with the least possible amount of work. You approved of the plan yourselves, and declared that **a man** must be his own enemy not to approve of it. And it **will** soon **be** realised ; the day is fast approaching **when you will be** able **to** retain your money and your children, providing you **only rally** to our side."

Hyacinthe was just nodding **his approval,** when Lequeu, quite unable to restrain himself any longer, **burst out** violently :

" Shut up, you infernal buffoon, with your **earthly** paradise **and** your precious schemes of forcing **every** one **to be** happy in spite of themselves ! It's **all** a preposterous lie ! Could such a state of affairs possibly exist among us ? We **are** too rotten and polluted. Before such things could happen, some wild, savage crew—Cossacks or Chinese—would have to come and make a clean sweep of us."

This outburst on the part **of the** schoolmaster created such a feeling of amazement that every voice was hushed, and complete silence reigned in the room. What next ? This cold-blooded, sneaking fellow, who had never allowed any one to have the least inkling of his private opinions, had at last spoken out ! They all listened to him attentively, especially Buteau, who anxiously waited for **the** rest of his discourse, as though what he was going to say might have some sort of connection with the subject that was uppermost in his mind.

The smoke had cleared off, thanks to the open window, and

the soft, damp, evening air had streamed into the room, reminding one of the peacefulness of the slumbering country outside.
The schoolmaster, bursting the bonds of timid reserve which
had restrained him for ten years, no longer caring for anything,
cast all decorum of speech to the winds, smarting under the
blow that had wrecked his means of livelihood, and letting off
all the accumulated hatred which was choking him.

"Do you think that the people about here are bigger fools
than their own calves, that you come telling them that roasted
larks will fall from the sky into their mouths? Before any
such scheme as yours becomes practicable, the earth itself will
have been annihilated."

Canon, who had never yet come across his match, visibly
quailed before the schoolmaster's violent onslaught. He made
an attempt to fall back upon his stories about his friends in
Paris, repeating their theories of all the land reverting to the
State, which would organise enormous farms, conducted on
strictly scientific principles. However, Lequeu cut him short.

"Yes, I know all about that nonsense! But, long before
you get a chance of trying your fine system of agriculture, all
our French soil will have disappeared, submerged beneath a
deluge of corn from America. Listen now for a moment:
this little book that I have been reading again supplies a lot
of particulars on the subject which will entirely bear me out.
I said so, once before. Yes, indeed, our peasants may take
themselves off to bed, for the candle is burnt out."

Then, in the tone of voice in which he was wont to give a
lesson to his pupils, he proceeded to speak about the corn
supplies of America. There were mighty plains over there, he
told them, as large as kingdoms, in the midst of which La Beauce
would be quite lost, like a mere clod of earth. The soil, too,
was so fertile that, instead of having to manure it, it was
necessary to drain off its exuberant richness by a preliminary
crop; but, in spite of that, two full crops were harvested every
year. There were farms of seventy thousand acres in extent,
divided into sections, which were again cut up into sub-sections,
each section being under the supervision of a steward, and
each sub-section under the direction of a foreman. They were
provided with houses for the men, stables for the cattle, sheds
for the tools, and other buildings where all the cooking was
carried on. There were whole battalions of farm-servants,
who were hired at spring-time, and organised just like
campaigning armies—boarded, lodged, and physicked, and then
paid off in the autumn. The furrows ploughed and sown there

were miles in length, and there were spreading seas of ripening
corn, the limits of which extended far out of sight. Men were
merely employed there as supervisors, all the actual work being
done by machinery. There were double-ploughs, furnished
with deep-cutting discs; sowing-machines, weeding-machines,
reaping-machines, and locomotive threshing-machines, that also
stacked the straw. There were ploughmen who were skilful
engineers, and squads of workmen who followed every machine
on horseback, always ready to dismount and tighten a screw, or
change a bolt, or hammer a bar. The soil was, in fact, like a
sort of bank, managed by financiers. It was treated systematically, and cropped smooth and close to the very surface, yielding to impersonal and mechanical science ten times as much as
it offered to men's loving arms.

"And can you hope to carry on the struggle," he continued,
"with your twopenny-halfpenny tools?—you who are so
ignorant, so entirely without ambition, and who are quite contented to go grubbing on in the same old way as your forefathers? Ah! you are already sunk up to your bellies in the
corn from over the sea, and it is still rising about you, for the
ships are ever bringing larger quantities of it over. Wait a
little longer and you will find it up to your shoulders; then it
will reach your mouths, and then the flood will close over your
heads! A flood! aye, a torrent—a wild deluge that will
sweep you all away!"

The peasants opened their eyes widely, quite panic-stricken
by the thought of this inundation of foreign corn. They were
already suffering distress; were they really going to be altogether drowned and swept away, as the schoolmaster said?
They took his metaphors very literally. Would Rognes, their
fields, and the whole of La Beauce be swallowed up?

"No, never!" cried Delhomme, choking with emotion.
"The Government will protect us."

"A pretty protector, indeed, the Government will be!"
Lequeu resumed, contemptuously. "It will need all its time
to protect itself! You behaved most ridiculously in electing
Monsieur Rochefontaine. The master of La Borderie, at any
rate, behaved consistently in supporting Monsieur de Chédeville.
However, after all, whether you have the one or the other, it
is only putting the same plaster on a wooden leg. No Chamber
would ever dare to impose a duty high enough. Protection
cannot save you; you are doomed beyond all redemption!"

There was now a noisy outbreak, and all the peasants began
to speak at once. Couldn't something be done to stop the dis-

astrous influx of this foreign corn? They would sink the ships in the docks, and shoot the fellows who brought the corn over! Their voices quivered with emotion, and they almost seemed inclined to burst into tears, and stretch out their hands and pray that they might be saved from all this abundance—from this cheap bread which threatened to ruin the country. The schoolmaster grinned with malicious satisfaction, and told them that nobody had ever heard of such ideas as now possessed them. Their previous fears had always been of famine—that they would not have corn enough; and surely it must now be all u.p. with them since they felt afraid of having too much! He was growing quite intoxicated with his own eloquence, and he shouted above the furious cries of protest:

"You are a perishing and worn-out race. Your imbecile love of the soil has eaten you up. Yes, you are each the slave of a patch of ground, which has so narrowed your minds that, for the sake of it, you would murder your fellows! For centuries past you have been wedded to the soil, and it has always betrayed you! Look at America! There the agriculturist is master of the soil. He isn't bound to it by any family ties, any sentimental considerations; as soon as one plot is exhausted, he goes further on and takes another. If he hears that more fertile plains have been discovered some three hundred leagues away, he moves his tent and goes off there. Thanks to his machines, he has only to will and do. He is free, and he's growing rich; while you are slaves, and are dying of starvation!"

Buteau's face had grown pale, for Lequeu had looked at him when speaking of murder. He tried to appear quite unconcerned, however.

"Well, we are as we are," he said. "What is the good of our troubling ourselves, since you yourself say that it will be all to no purpose?"

Delhomme signified his approval of this, and every one began to laugh: Lengaigne, Clou, Fouan, even Delphin and the conscripts, who derived a certain amount of amusement from what was going on, as they hoped it would lead to blows. Canon and Hyacinthe, annoyed at seeing "inky fingers," as they called the schoolmaster, shout louder than themselves, also affected to snigger merrily. They were even inclined to side with the peasants.

"It's folly to quarrel," said Canon, shrugging his shoulders. "What is wanted is organisation."

Lequeu made a gesture of hot anger.

"I've no patience to hear such folly talked! I am for making a clean sweep of everything!"

His face was quite livid, and he flung these words in their faces as though he wished to knock them down with them.

"You pitiful cowards!" he cried. "Yes, you're all of you cowards, you peasants! To think you are more numerous and stronger, and yet that you let yourselves be devoured by the middle-class townsfolk and the workmen! I've but one regret, and that is that my father and mother were peasants. Perhaps that is the reason why you fill me with such disgust. There is nothing to prevent you becoming the masters. But you won't combine together. You keep yourselves isolated from each other, full of suspicion and ignorance, and you exhaust all your knavery in preying upon one another. What is it that you are concealing beneath the surface of your stagnant water? for you are like stagnant pools which men believe to be deep, though they would not drown a cat! To think that you should be such a mighty, undeveloped force, a force which might mould the future, and yet you lie about as inert as logs of wood! And what makes it all the more exasperating is that you have ceased to believe in what the priests tell you. If there be no God, what is it that holds you back? As long as you stood in fear of hell, one could understand that you continued to grovel on your bellies; but now, rush forward! pillage everything! burn everything! As a commencement, it will perhaps be simpler for you to go on strike. You have all got some savings, and you could hold out as long as would be necessary. Cultivate the ground for yourselves, don't carry anything to market, not a single sack of corn, not a single bushel of potatoes! Let Paris starve! That's the way to set to work."

A gust of cold air, wafted from the distant blackness of the night, had rushed in through the open window. The flames of the lamps were shooting up very high. No one now attempted to interrupt the excited speaker, despite the abuse that he lavished upon everybody.

He now banged his book down on a table, making the glasses jingle, and proceeded to finish his oration:

"I have told you all that; but still I am quite easy about the future. Cowards you may be now, but when the proper time comes I know that you will be the fellows to make a clean sweep of everything. It has been so more than once before, and it will be so once again. Wait till misery and hunger send you rushing down upon the towns like so many wolves! Very likely the occasion will arise anent this corn which is being brought from over the sea. When there has been too much of it there won't be enough of it, and then there will be scarcity and famine again. It is always for the sake of corn that men rise up in rebellion and slay each other! Yes, let the towns be burned down and razed to the ground, the villages deserted, the fields uncultivated, overrun with brambles, and watered with streams of blood; then perhaps they will hereafter bring forth bread for those who are born into the world when we are gone!"

Lequeu now violently tore the door open and disappeared. A yell from the stupefied peasants followed him. The scoundrel! He wanted bleeding! A man who had always been so pacific and quiet! Surely he must be going mad! Delhomme, who had quite lost his habitual placidity, declared his intention of writing to the prefect, and the others pressed him to do so. However, it was Hyacinthe, with his '89 and his humanitarian motto of "Liberty, equality, and fraternity," and Canon, with his schemes for the compulsory and scientific reorganisation of society, who appeared the most indignant. They sat there with pale faces, exasperated at not having been able to find a word to say in reply, and now expressing themselves in much stronger terms than the peasants did; bellowing out, in fact, that a fellow of that sort ought to be guillotined. Buteau, upon hearing the orator demand so much blood—flowing streams of blood to which he seemed to point with his finger— had risen from his seat in trembling alarm, his head wagging involuntarily from nervous excitement, just as though he were signifying approval of what was being said. Then he glided along the wall, casting furtive glances to make sure that he was not being followed, and on reaching the door, he, too, disappeared.

The conscripts now reverted to their uproarious merriment again. They were bellowing loudly, and insisting upon Flore cooking them some sausages, when Nénesse suddenly hustled them aside and sprang over a bench to reach Delphine, who had just fainted away, with his face lying on the table. The poor fellow was as white as a sheet. His handkerchief, which had slipped off his wounded hand, was covered with crimson stains. The conscripts yelled into Bécu's ear, for he was still hard asleep; but at last he awoke, and gazed at his son's mutilated hand. He knew what it meant, for, seizing hold of a bottle, he brandished it as if anxious to kill the lad. Then, as he led him, tottering, away, he could be heard indulging in noisy oaths, amid which he burst into tears.

Hourdequin, having heard of Françoise's accident while he was dining, repaired to Rognes that evening, prompted by his kindly feeling for Jean, to inquire how the young woman was getting on. Setting out on foot, he smoked his pipe as he walked along through the black darkness, brooding over his troubles and vexations amid the unbroken silence of the night. Feeling at last somewhat calmer, and wishing to prolong his walk, he went down the hill before calling at his old servant's house. When he reached the foot of the declivity, the sound of Lequeu's voice, which streamed forth from the open window of the tavern, penetrating the darkness of the surrounding country, made him halt, and he remained listening for a long time, standing motionless in the gloom. When he at length began to ascend the hill again, the schoolmaster's voice followed him, and even when he reached Jean's house, he could still hear it, sounding weaker, and seemingly shriller in the distance, but still as sharply incisive as the keen edge of a knife.

Jean was standing at his door, leaning against the wall. He had not been able to remain any longer at Françoise's bed-side. He felt suffocated there, and altogether too miserable.

" Well, my poor fellow," Hourdequin now asked, " how is your wife ? "

The unhappy man broke into a gesture of despair.

" Ah, sir, she's dying ! "

Then neither of them said another word ; and the deep silence around them was only broken by the distant sound of Lequeu's voice, which still persistently rang out.

The farmer could not help listening, despite himself, and presently he angrily exclaimed :

" Do you hear that fellow ranting ? How awful such talk as that sounds when one's in trouble ! "

The sound of the schoolmaster's fulminating voice, combined with the proximity of Françoise in her death-agony, again revived the farmer's anguish of heart. The soil which he loved so dearly, loved with a sentimental passion, nay, almost with an intellectual one, had well nigh completed his ruin this last harvest. His fortune had all been drained away, and soon La Borderie would not even provide him with bare sustenance. Nothing seemed to do any good there—neither hard work, nor new systems, nor manures, nor machines. He habitually ascribed his failure to insufficient capital ; but in his own mind he had some doubts about this, for ruin seemed to be general. The Robiquets had just been ejected by the bailiffs from La Chamade, and the Coquarts had been compelled to sell their

farm of Saint-Juste. He himself could see no way of breaking his bonds; he had never more completely felt himself the
prisoner of his land, and every day the money he spent and the
labour he bestowed seemed to chain him more tightly to it.
The final catastrophe, which would put an end to the antagonism
of centuries between the small landowners and the large ones
by annihilating them both, was now rapidly approaching. This
was the advent of the predicted time; corn had fallen below
fifty-six francs the quarter, so that it was being sold at a loss;
and social transformations, stronger than the will of men, were
bringing about the bankruptcy of the soil.

Stung with the consciousness of his ruin, Hourdequin now
suddenly expressed approval of what Lequeu was saying.

"Deuce take it all, he's right! Let everything go to smash
and all of us perish, and the whole soil be covered with
weeds and brambles, since our race is decayed and the land
exhausted!"

Then, referring to Jacqueline, he added:

"However, thank God, there is another complaint that will
make an end of me before all that comes off!"

Inside the house La Grande and La Frimat could be heard
walking about and muttering to each other. Jean, who was
still leaning against the wall, shivered as he heard them. Then
he returned into the house, and found that all was over. Françoise was dead; she had probably passed away some time
previously. She had never opened her eyes again; and had
kept her lips sealed, carrying away with her the secret she was
so anxious to conceal. La Grande had only just discovered
that she was dead by touching her. With her white shrunken
face, on which there rested a resolute expression, she looked as
though she were sleeping. Jean stood at the foot of the bed
and stared at her, dazed and stupefied with confused thoughts,
with the grief he felt at losing her, with the surprise caused him
by the fact that she had refused to make a will, and with a
vague sensation that a part of his existence was now shivered
to pieces, and gone for ever.

Just at that moment, as Hourdequin, still gloomy and down-
hearted, took his leave with a silent grasp of the hand, Jean
saw a shadowy form flit away from the window and dart
hastily along the road into the darkness. He fancied it was
some prowling dog; but in reality it was Buteau, who had
been spying through the window, to watch for Françoise's
death, and who was now hastening to announce the news
to Lise.

CHAPTER V.

EARLY the next day, as Françoise's body was being placed in the coffin, which was resting upon two chairs in the middle of the bedroom, Jean was overcome with surprise and indignation at seeing Lise and Buteau enter the house, one behind the other. His first impulse was to summarily eject these stony-hearted relatives, who had not come to give Françoise a last kiss ere she died, but who lost no time in coming as soon as the coffin-lid had been screwed down over her, as though they now felt free from all fear of finding themselves face to face with her. However, the other members of the family who were present, Fanny and La Grande, restrained him. It would bring bad luck, they said, to begin quarrelling round a corpse. Besides, what good would it do? Lise could not be prevented from atoning for her previous vindictiveness by keeping watch over her sister's remains.

The Buteaus had reckoned upon the respect due to the presence of a dead body in the house, and they took advantage of it to install themselves in their old home once more. They made no actual profession of taking possession of the place, but still they did take possession of it, in a quiet easy way, and as though it were quite a matter of course that, as Françoise was no longer there, they themselves should return. True, her body was there, but it was packed ready for its final departure, and was really of no more account than a piece of furniture. Lise, after sitting down for some time with the others, so far forgot all sense of decency as to get up and examine the drawers and cupboards to satisfy herself that their contents had not been removed during her absence. Buteau had gone off to look at the stable and cowhouse, as though he were already quite at home, and were just giving a glance round to see that everything was all right. By evening they both appeared quite settled again on the premises, and the only thing that caused them any inconvenience was the coffin, which still blocked up the bedroom. However, there was merely another night to wait; the room would be quite at their disposal early the next day.

Jean kept wandering restlessly up and down, looking dazed

and confused, and seemingly quite at a loss as to what to do
with himself.   At first the house, and the furniture, and
Françoise's body had seemed to belong to him ; but, as the
time glided by, they appeared to sever their connection with him
and to pass away to others.   By the time night closed in,
every one had ceased to speak to him, and his presence in the
place was merely just tolerated.   Never before had he felt so
painfully conscious of being a stranger in the village, of being
quite alone, of not having a single kindred fellow-creature
among all these folks, who were related to each other and
fully agreed on the question of his own expulsion.   Even his
poor dead wife no longer seemed to belong to him ; in fact,
Fanny sent him away from the bedroom, where he wished to
stay and watch over the body, saying that there were quite
sufficient people for that purpose already.   He had for some
time refused to go, and finally, annoyed at Fanny's persistence,
he had resolved to take possession of the money in the drawer—
the hundred and twenty-seven francs—so as to make sure that
they wouldn't fly away.   Lise had seen them on opening the
drawer, together with the sheet of stamped paper which had
never been used, and the sight of the latter had led to her holding a whispered conversation with La Grande.   The result of
this chat had been to make her feel quite easy in mind, for
she had definitely learnt that there was no will, and that the
house was really her own again.   Jean, however, had made up
his mind that, at any rate, she should not have the money ; amid
his vague apprehensions as regards the morrow, he determined
that he would at least keep that for himself ; and after taking
possession of it, he passed the night on a chair.

    The funeral took place on the following morning, at nine
o'clock.   The Abbé Madeline, who was leaving Rognes that
same evening, was just able to say the mass and accompany
the body to the grave ; but when he reached it he fainted, and
they were obliged to carry him away.   Monsieur and Madame
Charles were present, together with Delhomme and Nénesse.
It was a very respectable funeral, though nothing out of the
way.   Jean shed tears, and Buteau also wiped his eyes, but
they were quite dry.   At the last moment Lise had declared
that her legs felt as though they were giving way beneath her,
and that she was too weak to accompany her sister's body to
the grave.   She had consequently remained alone in the house,
while La Grande, Fanny, La Frimat, Madame Bécu, and other
female friends attended the funeral.   On returning from the
graveyard all the company lingered in the open square in

front of the church, in anticipation of a scene which they had
been expecting since the previous evening.

So far the two men, Jean and Buteau, had avoided even
glancing at each other, fearing lest some violent outbreak
might ensue in presence of the corpse ere it was barely cold.
They, however, now both directed their steps towards the
house with the same resolute gait; and they kept glancing aside
at each other. Jean had at once understood why Lise had not
come to the funeral. She had stayed away in order to get her
effects into the house again—in a rough sort of fashion, at any
rate. An hour had sufficed for the purpose, for she had been
hard at work tossing her bundles over La Frimat's wall, and
wheeling round anything that was breakable. Finally, she
had dragged Laure and Jules into the yard, administering a
cuff a-piece to them, and there they were already fighting,
while old Fouan, whom she had also hustled inside, sat panting
on the stone bench. The house was reconquered.

" Where are you going?" Buteau suddenly asked, stopping
Jean in front of the gate.

" I'm going home."

" Home! home, indeed! Where is your home? It certainly
isn't here! This is my house."

Lise had rushed up, and resting her hands upon her hips,
she now began to yell, exhibiting even more offensive insolence
than her husband.

" Eh? what? What does he want, the rotten blackguard?
He's been poisoning my poor sister long enough; that's quite
clear, or she would never have died of her accident. And she
showed pretty plainly what she thought of him by not leaving
him anything. Knock him over, Buteau! Don't let him come
inside, or he'll give us all some beastly illness!"

Jean, although he was boiling over with indignation at this
virulent attack, still attempted to reason with her.

" I know very well," he said, " that the house and land
revert to you; but half of the furniture and live stock belong
to me."

" Half, indeed! You've got a lot of cheek, you have!"
cried Lise, interrupting him. " You foul stink-pot, how dare
you claim half of anything, you who didn't even bring a broken
comb into the place? You merely came here with the shirt on
your back! So you want to fatten yourself and get rich by
preying on women, eh? That's a dirty, swinish game."

Buteau backed her up, and, with a sweeping gesture across
the threshold, he cried out:

"She's telling the truth! Look sharp! You came with your jacket and breeches, and you've got them on, so take yourself off with 'em! Nobody wants to deprive you of them!"

The other members of the family, especially the women, Fanny and La Grande, who were standing in a group some thirty yards away, seemed by their silence to approve of Buteau's conduct. Jean, turning pale at the insults which were offered him, and stung to the quick by the accusation of mercenary scheming, now broke out into an angry retort:

"Very well, so you are bent upon making a disturbance, eh? I insist upon entering, for I have still the right of possession, as the formal partition has not yet been made. Then I shall at once go and fetch Monsieur Baillehache, who will put everything under seal, and appoint me guardian. The house is mine for the present, and it is for you to take yourselves off."

He now stepped up to Lise with such a threatening air that she retreated from the door-way. Buteau, however, rushed upon him, and a struggle ensued, the two men reeling into the middle of the kitchen. There another violent discussion followed as to which of the two parties should be ejected—the husband, or the sister and brother-in-law.

"Show me the document which makes the house yours!" cried Jean.

"Documents, indeed! It's quite sufficient that we have the right to it!"

"Very well, then, if you've the right to it, why don't you come and enforce your right with the bailiff and the gendarmes, as we did?"

"We want no bailiffs and gendarmes! It's only swindling scoundrels who have to go to them for help. An honest man can manage his affairs for himself."

Jean was bending over the table and clinging to it. He had resolved not to leave, bent on proving that he was the stronger of the two, and determined not to part with the house where his wife had just died, and where, it seemed to him, the only happy part of his life had been spent. Buteau, at the other side of the table, was also determined not to give up the house which he had just reconquered, and he resolved to bring the matter to a speedy issue.

"The long and the short of it," he cried, "is that we've had enough of you."

Then he rushed round the table at Jean, but the latter, catching hold of a chair and hurling it at his adversary's legs,

tripped him up; then, as he was about to take refuge in the
adjoining room, meaning to barricade himself inside it, Lise
suddenly bethought herself of the money, the hundred and
twenty-seven francs which she had observed in the drawer.
Fancying that Jean was hastening to secure them, she rushed
on before him and pulled the drawer open.   At once she burst
into a howl of angry disappointment.

"The money's gone! The cursed scamp has stolen the
money during the night!"

It was all over with Jean now that the onslaught was
directed against his pockets.   He cried out that the money belonged to him, and that he would go into a full account of everything, and that they would owe him money in addition to this
cash. But the Buteaus would not listen to him, and Lise rushed
upon him, pummelling him even more violently than her husband.
He was dislodged from the room by a furious onset, and
hustled back into the kitchen, round which the three of them
wildly revolved, writhing and struggling together in confusion,
and dashing against the furniture in their gyrations.   By dint of
kicking, Jean managed to rid himself of Lise.   She soon fell
upon him again, however, and dug her nails into his neck,
while Buteau, making a vigorous spring, threw him flat on the
road outside.   Then blocking up the door, the husband and
wife bellowed out:

"You thief! you've stolen our money! You thief! you
thief!

Jean picked himself up, and stammering from pain and
anger replied:

"All right, I shall go to the magistrate at Châteaudun, and
he will see that I am reinstated in my home.   And I shall bring
an action against you for damages.   You'll see me again
soon!"

With a parting gesture of menace, he then took himself off,
mounting the hill towards the plain.   When the other members
of the family had seen that matters were coming to blows, they
had prudently retired, feeling a wholesome fear of possible legal
proceedings.

The Buteaus now broke out into a wild yell of victory.   At
last they had succeeded in flinging the usurping alien into the
street!   And they had regained possession of the house!   Ah,
they had often said that they would have it back, and now they
had got it again!   The thought that they were once more in
possession of the old patrimonial dwelling-place, built so long
ago by an ancestor, filled them with such mad delight that they

rushed wildly through the rooms, yelling for the mere pleasure
of doing so.   The children, Laure and Jules, rushed up, and
began tapping an old frying-pan.   Old Fouan alone remained
quiet ; he was still sitting on the stone bench, whence he
gravely watched the others, with troubled, mournful eyes.

However, Buteau suddenly checked his display of delight
and exclaimed :

" God in heaven ! he's sloped off up the hill !   He may have
gone to wreak his spite on the land ! "

It was an idiotic fear, but it quite upset him.   The thought
of the soil returned to him ; a sensation of uneasiness mingling
with the consciousness of ownership.   The soil !   Ah, his love
for it was more deeply rooted in his vitals even than his love of
the house !   That strip of land on the hill would fill up the
gap between his two mutilated plots ; and he would again
have his field of seven acres, that fine stretch of land, of
which even Delhomme did not possess the equal !   Buteau
trembled with emotion from head to foot.   It was as though
he had just regained some dearly beloved mistress whom he
had thought lost for ever.   With a mad fear that Jean might
somehow have carried the land off, wondering whether it might
not have already disappeared, seized, too, with an eager desire
to view it again, he lost his head and set off running, muttering
that he could never feel easy till he knew for certain.

Jean had indeed gone up the hill in order to avoid passing
through the village, and on reaching the plateau he had instinctively followed the road towards La Borderie.   When Buteau
caught sight of him, he was just passing the plot of plough-
land, but he did not stop, he merely gave it a glance of mingled
sadness and distrust, as though he were mentally accusing it of
having brought him into misfortune ; for a memory of the past,
of the day when he had first spoken to Françoise, had just
brought the tears to his eyes.   Was it not here, while she was
still a romping girl, that La Coliche had dragged her into the
lucern ?   He strode on with downcast head and slackened
steps, and Buteau, who was anxiously watching him, suspecting that he was bent upon some malicious piece of revenge,
now walked up to the field.   For a long time he stood gazing
at it.   Yes, it was still there, and it seemed just the same as
usual, quite unharmed.   His heart heaved wildly, and yearned
towards it in the delight he felt at again possessing it—
this time for ever.   He squatted down on his knees, and took
up a clod in his hands, crushing it, sniffing it, and then letting
it filter through his fingers.   Yes, it was his own now !   Then

he turned homewards again, singing, as though the scent of the soil had intoxicated him.

Jean still tramped on with downcast eyes, without being conscious as to whether his feet were carrying him. His first impulse had been to run to Cloyes to see Monsieur Baillehache, and take steps for getting reinstated in the house. Then his feeling of anger had calmed down. Even if he went back to-day, he would have to leave again to-morrow; so why shouldn't he make up his mind to swallow his wrathful grief and acquiesce in the inevitable? Those wretches, too, had really spoken the truth. He had gone to the house as a poor man, and as a poor man he was leaving it. But what sent a pang through his heart more than aught else, and finally decided him to submit, was the reflection that Françoise's last wish must have been to let things follow this course, since she had not bequeathed her property to him. So he abandoned the idea of taking immediate steps; and by-and-bye as he walked on, whenever his anger rekindled afresh, he merely swore to himself that he would drag the Buteaus into court to recover his half-share of the personal property to which he was entitled as the dead woman's husband. They should see that he wouldn't let himself be fleeced like a sheep!

As he raised his eyes, he was surprised to find himself opposite La Borderie. Prompted by an instinct of which he had been scarcely conscious in his grief, he had made his way to the farm as to a place of refuge. Indeed, if he remained in the neighbourhood, this was the place to find work and food and lodging. Hourdequin had always held him in esteem, and he was sure of being well received.

However, the sight of La Cognette in the distance, flying wildly across the yard, thrilled him with an uneasy feeling of disquietude. Eleven o'clock was striking as he arrived, and some hours earlier a frightful catastrophe had happened. That morning, on coming down before the servant-girl, La Cognette had found the cellar trap-door—that trap-door situated so dangerously near the staircase—open, and Hourdequin lying below quite dead, with his back broken against the edge of a step. The young woman shrieked, the servants rushed up, and the whole place was overwhelmed with panic. The farmer's body was now lying on a mattress in the dining-room, while Jacqueline was in the kitchen fairly off her nut, with her face distorted but tearless.

As soon as Jean entered, she broke out, relieving herself in a choking voice:

" I said it would be so! and I tried to get the trap altered!
But who could it be that left it open? I'm positive it was
closed last night when I went upstairs to bed. I've been
racking **my** head all the morning in trying to make it out."

"The master came down before you did, then?" asked
Jean, quite stupefied by the accident.

" Yes, it was scarcely light, and I was asleep; I fancied I
heard some one calling from downstairs, but I may have
dreamt it. He frequently **got up in this way and went** down-
stairs without a light to see **the servants as soon** as they turned
out. **He could** not see that **the** trap was open, and **he** fell.
But who can have left it open? Oh, this will be the **death of**
me, it will!"

Jean had felt a passing suspicion, **but he at once thrust** it
away from him. Jacqueline could have no possible interest in
Hourdequin's death, and her grief was evidently sincere.

" It is a terrible misfortune," he murmured.

" **Yes,** indeed; **a terrible** misfortune for me, a terrible
one!"

Then she fell down on a chair, completely overcome, as
though the very walls were toppling over upon her. The
master, whose legitimate wife she had so confidently reckoned
on becoming! The master, who had sworn to leave her **every-**
thing **in** his will! And now he was dead, dead before **he had**
had time to sign a single paper! She would not even get any
wages; the son would come back and **kick her** out of the house
as he had threatened to **do!** She would **have nothing but** the
few ornaments and **the clothes she wore! It was** ruin, disastrous **and complete!**

But what Jacqueline omitted to **mention,** the matter,
indeed, having entirely slipped from her mind in her present
trouble, was the dismissal of Soulas, the shepherd, which she
had succeeded in effecting on the previous evening. Exasperated at finding him always at her elbow, playing the spy
upon her, she accused him of being too old, and no longer
competent to perform his duties. The farmer, although he did
not agree with **this** statement, yielded to her wishes; for he
was now completely under her domination, content to purchase
her goodwill by **slave-like** submission. Soulas looked his
master keenly in the face with his pale eyes as he was dismissed with kindly words and promises for the future, and then
he slowly began to relieve **his** mind anent the hussy who had
brought about his discharge. He accused her of dissolute
behaviour with Tron **and a score of** others. He gave full

particulars, mentioning the places where she and Tron had met, and declaring that their shameless amours were matter of common notoriety—to such a degree, indeed, that folks said that the master was content to take the servant's leavings, as it was impossible **he** could be so blind as **not to** see what was going on. The farmer, overwhelmed with **distress** and consternation at what he heard, vainly attempted **to stop** the old man, preferring **to remain in** ignorance, and fearful of being compelled to turn **the young** woman **out of the house**; but Soulas persisted in **finishing** his indictment, and did not stop until he had specified each **separate occasion upon** which he had found **the two together.** Then he felt somewhat soothed and easier in his mind, having at last unburdened himself of his long pent up wrath and spite. Jacqueline knew nothing of this, for Hourdequin had at once rushed into **the fields, fearing lest he** should strangle her if he came across her **in his present mood.** When he returned **to the** house he **quietly dismissed** Tron, upon the pretext that **the** young fellow **left the** yard **in a** filthily dirty **condition.** Upon hearing of this, Jacqueline certainly had some suspicions; but she did not **venture to** plead in the cowherd's favour, contenting herself **by obtaining** permission that he should remain another **night on** the premises, and trusting that **she would be** able **to arrange** matters **in** the morning, so that he **might stay on.** At present the thought of all this had faded away **in the** presence **of that stroke** of fate which had shattered the castle in the air so **laboriously** erected during the last ten years.

Jean was quite alone with her in **the kitchen when** Tron **came in. She** had not seen the latter since **the previous** evening. The other servants, unoccupied and anxious, were wandering about the farm. When she now perceived **the** big, strapping **fellow, with his pinky face, she** broke **out into** a cry—occasioned by the suspicious sort of way in which he came in.

"**It is you who opened the trap!**" she screamed, and then she suddenly **understood the whole matter;** Tron meanwhile standing by, with **pale face, staring eyes, and open,** trembling lips.

" It was **you who opened** the trap, **and** then called to him to **come down, so that he might** break his neck ! "

Jean started back, quite overcome by what he had just **heard. In the** violence **of their** passionate agitation neither of **the** others seemed to **notice** his presence. With his head lowered Tron sullenly confessed the crime.

" Yes," he said, " I did **it.** He had dismissed me, and I should never have seen **you** again, and that was more than I

could bear.   And then I thought that if he were to die we
should be free."

Jacqueline listened to him, erect and rigid, her whole body
in a state of acute nervous tension. He went on complacently,
revealing the thoughts that had sprung up in his savage breast,
the fierce jealousy of a servant against his master, and the
treacherous plan which he had formed to secure unshared possession of the woman he loved.

"I felt sure that you would be pleased when it was over,"
said he ; "I didn't mention it to you beforehand, because I
didn't want to cause you any worry.   But now that he's out of
the way, I've come to take you off.   We'll go away together
and get married."

Jacqueline, wild with anger, now broke out in a harsh voice :
"Marry you !   But I don't love you !   I won't have you !
Ah ! so you killed him to get me ?   You must be even a
greater fool than I thought you were !   To act so stupidly before
he had married me, before he had made his will !   You have
ruined me !   You have taken the bread out of my mouth.   It
is my back, mine, that you have broken !   Can you understand
that much, now, you idiotic brute ?   And you imagine that I
will go away with you?   Why, you must take me for an
arrant fool ! "

Tron heard her in gaping amazement, quite stupefied by this
unexpected reception.

"Just because I've joked with you," she continued, "and
we've had a little amusement, you imagine that I'm going to
let myself be bored by you all the days of my life ?   Marry
you, indeed !   No, no, if ever I take a husband, I'll choose a
sharper fellow than you are !   Come, get out of my sight !   It
makes me ill to look at you !   I detest you, and I won't have
you !   Be off ! "

Tron quivered with rage.   What !   So he had committed
murder for nothing ?   No, no, she belonged to him, and he
would seize her by the throat and carry her off.

"You are a stuck-up, conceited drab ! " he growled ; "but
you'll come with me all the same.   If you don't, I shall settle
your hash as I settled his ! "

La Cognette stepped towards him, clenching her fists.

"Try it on, you murderer ! "

Tron was very strong and broad and tall, while Jacqueline
was weak and slight and delicately made.   However, it was he
who started back, so threatening did she look, with her teeth
ready to bite and her eyes gleaming like daggers.

" It's all over," she resumed ; " take yourself off ! I would rather never see a man again than allow you to touch me now. Be off—be off—be off ! "

Then Tron went out, stepping backwards like some wild beast giving way to fear, and deferring vengeance.

" Dead or alive, I'll have you ! " he blurted out threateningly.

Jacqueline watched him leave the farm, heaving a sigh of relief. Then as she turned round, quivering all over, she did not seem at all surprised to see Jean; but, in an outburst of frankness, exclaimed :

" Ah, the villain ! I would have him marched off by the gendarmes, if I weren't afraid that they would lock me up with him."

Jean was frozen with horror by what he had just heard, and could not find a word to say. The young woman, too, now underwent a nervous reaction. She seemed to be suffocating, and fell into Jean's arms, sobbing and wailing that she was very wretched—oh, so very wretched and miserable ! Her tears continued to flow in streams down her face ; she seemed craving for sympathy and love, and clung to Jean as though she were yearning for him to take her away and protect her. The young man was beginning to feel very uncomfortable, when the dead farmer's brother-in-law, Monsieur Baillehache, who had been fetched by one of the farm-servants, sprang out of his gig in the yard. Jacqueline at once rushed off to him and paraded her despair.

Jean, making his escape from the kitchen, presently found himself again on the bare plain beneath a rainy March sky. But he scarcely knew where he was, being completely upset by the tragedy of Hourdequin's death, which added another pang to all his troubles. However, he had his own load of worry to bear, and, despite his sorrow for his old master's fate, he quickened his steps, thinking of his own interests. It was no business of his to hand La Cognette and her lover over to justice. The authorities ought to open their eyes. Twice he turned round, fancying he heard some one shouting after him, and vaguely feeling as though he were an accomplice in the murder. It was only when he reached the outskirts of Rognes that he again breathed freely ; he said to himself that the farmer's death was the result of his own sin ; and he pondered anent that great truth that men would be much happier if there were no women in the world. His mind reverted to Françoise, and a big lump seemed to rise in his throat and nearly choke him.

When he found himself in the village again he recollected that he had gone to the farm to seek work. He now began to feel very uneasy, and racked his brains as to whom he could next apply to. Then it struck him that Monsieur Charles had been looking out for a gardener recently. Why should he not go and offer his services? He was still, in a way, somewhat of the family, and perhaps that might be a recommendation. So he hastened off in the direction of Roseblanche.

It was one o'clock, and Monsieur and Madame Charles were just finishing their late breakfast as the servant introduced him. Elodie was pouring out the black coffee, and Monsieur Charles, making his cousin sit down, asked him to take a cup. Jean accepted it; he had eaten nothing since the previous evening, and his stomach felt very drawn. The coffee would do him good. Now that he found himself sitting at table with this well-to-do family, he could not bring himself to ask point-blank for the gardener's place. He must wait for an opportunity. As Madame Charles began to sympathise with him and to bewail poor Françoise's death, he felt very melancholy and depressed again. The family evidently believed that he had come to say good-bye to them.

The servant soon came into the room again to say that the Delhommes, father and son, had called; and Jean was quite forgotten.

"Show them in here, and bring two more cups," said Monsieur Charles.

It had been a somewhat exciting morning altogether for the Charleses. Nénesse had accompanied them to Roseblanche after the funeral, and, while Madame Charles and Elodie went into the house, he had detained the husband and openly proposed to purchase Number 19, providing they could agree as to terms. According to his account, the house, which he knew very well, would only fetch a miserable price if it went into the market. Vaucogne, he said, would not get five thousand francs for it, so greatly had it depreciated in value under his management. A complete change would have to be made in every particular. The furniture was shabby and ricketty, and the staff had been so badly chosen and was so unsatisfactory that even the soldiers were deserting the place. He went on for a whole hour running down the house in this fashion, quite bewildering his uncle, and amazing him by his acute shrewdness and bargaining powers, and by the extraordinary business talent he showed for one so young. Ah, here was a capital young fellow! thought Monsieur Charles; one with a sharp eye and a

ready hand. Nénesse concluded by saying that he would come
again after breakfast with his father, so that they might talk
the matter over seriously.

On getting indoors, Monsieur Charles informed his wife of
what had occurred, and she expressed great astonishment at
the young man's ability. If only their son-in-law, Vaucogne,
had had but half his capacity! They would have to be
careful as **to** what they were about, if they wished to avoid
getting the worst of the bargain with this young fellow. It
was Elodie's dowry that was at stake. Mingled, however,
with the fear they felt, there was a strong sympathy
with Nénesse, and a keen desire to see Number 19 in the
hands **of** a clever, energetic master, who would restore **it to**
its **old** position, even although this entailed a loss upon themselves. And so, when the Delhommes made their appearance,
both Monsieur and Madame Charles greeted them in the most
cordial fashion.

" You'll have some coffee won't you ? Elodie, pass the
sugar."

Jean had pushed his chair back, and they were now all
seated round the table. Delhomme, with his expressionless,
freshly-shaven, tanned face, sat perfectly silent, maintaining a
diplomatic reserve ; while Nénesse in his smartest clothes,
his patent leather boots, gold-flowered waistcoat and mauve
neckerchief, seemed quite at his ease, and smiled in his most
winning way. As the blushing Elodie handed him the sugar-
basin, he looked into her eyes and sought **for some** pretty
compliment to pay her.

" Your lumps of sugar are very large, cousin," he said.

The girl's blushes deepened, and she could not find anything
to reply, **being utterly** confused by the amiable young fellow's
words.

Nénesse, like the artful scamp he was, had only disclosed
one half of his scheme in the morning. Since he had seen
Elodie at the funeral, he had suddenly widened his plans. He
would not only obtain Number 19, he wanted the girl as well ;
that would simplify matters. In the first place, he would get
the **business** for nothing, for he would only take Elodie with
the house as her dowry ; and, then, even allowing that this
declining business was the only dowry he got with her in the
immediate present, she **would** later **on** inherit all Monsieur and
Madame Charles's property, a fortune in itself. It was for
these reasons that he had brought his father with him, resolved
to make his proposal without delay.

For a moment or two they talked about the weather, which was very mild **for** that time of year. The pear-trees were looking well, **but would** the **bloom set** ? As they finished their coffee, **the** conversation began to flag.

" **My** dear," Monsieur Charles **now said** abruptly to Elodie, " suppose you go and take a **turn** in the garden."

He was anxious to get her out of the room, so that he might make his bargain with the Delhommes.

However Nénesse interposed : " Excuse me, uncle," **said he,** " **but** I should be much obliged if you would kindly allow my **cousin to remain.** There is a matter which **interests me deeply that I want to speak to** you about ; and it's always **better—don't you think so ?—to settle matters at once than to return** to them two or three times."

Then rising from his seat, he **proceeded to make his pro**posal like a well-mannered **young man.**

" I wish **to tell you that it would** make me very happy to have my **cousin** for my **wife,** if you would consent to it, and **if** she would **also.**"

This declaration caused great surprise. Elodie was so overwhelmed with confusion that she sprang up **from** her seat **and** threw herself on Madame Charles's breast, in such a thrill **of** speechless bashfulness that she blushed to her **very ears.** Her grandmother exerted herself to calm her.

" Come, come, my little puss, this is really **foolish of you !"** said she. " Be reasonable, my dear. **Your cousin won't eat** you because he wants to marry **you. I'm sure he said nothing** that wasn't very **nice and proper. Come, look at him, and** don't be foolish."

Nothing, however, that her **grandmother said could induce** Elodie to show her face again.

" Upon **my word, my lad,"** Monsieur **Charles** now said, " your proposal has taken me altogether by surprise. Perhaps it would have **been** better **if you** had spoken to me privately **about it,** for you see how very sensitive our darling is. But, whatever happens, you may satisfy yourself that you possess my esteem and respect, for you seem to me a good and industrious young fellow."

Delhomme, whose face had hitherto remained **a perfect** blank, now allowed three words to escape him :

" That he is ! "

Then Jean felt called upon to say something polite, and so **he** added :

" Ah! yes, indeed ! "

Monsieur Charles was recovering his composure, and he had already come to the conclusion that Nénesse would be no bad match for his grand-daughter. He was young, well mannered, active, and the only son of comfortably-situated parents. Thus Elodie could hardly do better. And so, after exchanging a glance with Madame Charles, he continued:

"You will understand, of course, that my wife and I say neither yes nor no. We shall leave it entirely with Elodie. We shall not in any way constrain her. We shall leave her perfectly at liberty to please herself."

Then Nénesse gallantly renewed his proposal to his cousin.

"My dear cousin," he began, "will you confer upon me the happiness and the honour——"

The girl's face was still buried in her grandmother's bosom, but she did not allow her cousin to complete his sentence; she accepted him at once by an energetic nod of her head, which she repeated three times, burying her face still more deeply out of sight. She seemed to gain courage by not looking at anything. The company sat in silence, quite astonished by the girl's hurry to consent. Could she be in love with this young man whom she had so seldom seen? Or was it that she was anxious for a husband, no matter whom, so long as he was a good-looking fellow?

Madame Charles smiled, and kissed the girl's hair.

"My poor little darling!" she said; "my poor little darling!"

"Very well," exclaimed Monsieur Charles, "since she is satisfied, we are."

Then a sudden reflection saddened him. His heavy eyelids drooped, and an expression of regret passed over his countenance.

"Of course, my good lad," he said, "we shall now abandon the other scheme which you proposed to me this morning."

Nénesse seemed overcome with astonishment.

"Why?" said he.

"What? Why? Why, because—because—well, you surely know why! You may be sure that we didn't leave the child with the Sisters of the Visitation till twenty years of age to—well, in short, it is quite impossible!"

He winked his eyes and twisted his mouth in his attempts to make himself understood without saying too much. To think of the girl being in the Rue aux Juifs! a young lady who had received such an education! a maiden of such absolute purity, brought up in complete ignorance of evil, and carefully screened from its slightest breath!

" Excuse me," exclaimed Nénesse, bluntly, " but that won't
suit me at all. I am taking a wife because I wish to settle
down **to work, and** I want both my cousin and **the** business——"

" The confectionery business!" exclaimed Madame Charles.
She then began to discuss the question more openly, though
they continued to call the establishment the confectionery shop.
For instance, was it reasonable that the confectionery business
should be given **up?** The young man and his father persisted
in claiming **it as Élodie's** dowry. They could not allow it to
be relinquished, they said; it would certainly prove **a hand-**
some fortune in the future; and they called upon Jean **to**
support **them in their** assertions, **which he did by** wagging his
chin. At last they all spoke at once, and they **were** quickly
forgetting all their previous caution, going into details and
calling things by their **real names,** then suddenly **an unex-**
pected incident **reduced them to silence.**

Élodie had at last gradually raised her head from her
grandmother's **bosom;** and she was now standing up, looking
like some tall lily that had grown in a shady corner, with her
chlorotic white face, her pale eyes and colourless hair. She
gazed at the others for a moment, and then said very quietly:

"**My cousin is right; the business** ought not to be given
up."

" Oh ! my darling, if you only knew——" **Madame Charles**
began to stammer in confusion.

" I do know," **Élodie** interrupted. "Victorine, the maid
whom you sent away on account of the men, told me all about
it long ago. Yes, I know all about it, and I have thought it
well over, and I am quite convinced that it must **not be given
up.**"

Monsieur and Madame Charles **were** perfectly stupefied
They opened their eyes, and sat staring at the girl in a state
of amazement. What! She knew all about Number 19, what
was done there, and what was sold there ; she knew all about
it, and yet spoke of it in this calm, placid fashion ! Ah, blessed
innocence! it is too pure to see harm in anything !

"**It** must certainly not be given up," she repeated with
increasing decision. " It is too good and profitable a business
for that. And then, too, a house which you established yourselves, and where you worked so hard, could you think of
allowing it to go out of the family ? "

Monsieur Charles was completely bewildered. An inde-
scribable thrill shot up from his heart and seemed to choke him.

He rose up from his seat, reeled and tottered, and then supported himself upon Madame Charles, who was also standing trembling and feeling suffocated. They both of them seemed to look upon the girl's offer as a sacrifice, and called out in distracted tones:

"Oh darling, darling, it cannot be; it really cannot be."

Elodie's eyes were growing moist, and she kissed her mother's old wedding-ring which **she wore** upon her finger, that wedding-ring which had grown so thin owing to hard work.

"Yes, yes," she resumed, "let me follow my own inclination. I **want** to follow in my mother's steps. What she did, I can do. There is no dishonour in it, for you did it yourselves. The **idea** affords **me** great pleasure, I assure you. And you will see how I'll help my cousin, and how we will raise **the** house between us. Ah! you don't know me, but I will **show** you what I can do!"

This outburst carried the day. Monsieur and Madame Charles, overwhelmed with deep emotion, burst into tears, and sobbed like a couple of children. Although they had certainly brought Elodie up with very different intentions, still what was to be done when the instinct of her blood spoke out like that? They recognised in it the accents of a genuine vocation. It had been the same with Estelle. She, too, had led a secluded life with the Sisters of the Visitation, had been kept in perfect ignorance of the world, and instructed in the principles of the most rigid morality; but in spite of everything she had become an excellent woman of business. It was clear that education went for naught; it was natural sentiment which settled everything. However, the Charles's emotion deepened, **and** the tears which fell from their eyes streamed yet more copiously at the glorious thought that Number 19, their own creation, their very flesh, so to say, was about to be saved from ruin. Their work would still be continued there by Elodie and Nénesse with all the fresh energy of youth. They already saw the house restored to its former glory, established once more in public favour, with the same brilliant reputation as it had possessed in the palmiest days of their own reign.

As soon as Monsieur Charles was able to speak, he clasped his grand-daughter in his arms. "Your father has been the cause of much anxiety to us," he said," but you, my angel, will console us for everything!"

Madame Charles also strained the girl to her breast, and they all three of them stood in one another's arms, mingling their tears.

"Then we may consider everything settled now?" asked
Nénesse, who was anxious to have matters definitely decided.

"Yes, quite settled."

Delhomme was now radiant, like a father delighted at having set his son up in life in an unhoped-for manner. He began
to shuffle about as though he felt called upon to make some
observation, and, indeed, at last he delivered himself in these
words:

"Well, if there's never any regret on your side, I'm sure
there'll never be any on ours. There's no need to wish the
young people good luck. That always attends honest hard
work."

Then they all sat down again in view of quietly talking
over details.

Jean now felt conscious that he was in the way. He had
been greatly embarrassed at finding himself amid the previous
emotional, tearful outbursts, and he would have made his escape
much sooner had he known how to do so. He now summoned
up his courage to take Monsieur Charles aside, and speak to
him about the gardener's place. But Monsieur Charles's
dignified face assumed a severe expression. A relation of his
own holding a situation in his service! No, no, that would
never do! A relation was never a profitable servant; it was
impossible to treat him with necessary severity. Besides, the
situation had been promised to another person on the previous
day. Jean, therefore, took his leave, while Elodie was saying,
in her soft voice, that if her father made himself disagreeable
she would undertake to bring him to reason.

When Jean got outside the house he walked on slowly,
quite at a loss as to where he should now turn in search of
work. Out of the hundred and twenty-seven francs he had
already paid for his wife's funeral, for the cross at the head of
the grave, and for the railings round it, barely half of the money
was left, but this would still keep him some time, and then he
would see what happened. He was not afraid of poverty and
hard work; his only anxiety arose from his unwillingness to
leave Rognes on account of the legal proceedings he was contemplating. Three o'clock struck, then four, and then five.
For a long time he continued wandering about the country, his
brain full of confused ideas, his thoughts now dwelling upon
La Borderie, and now upon the Charles family. Everywhere
it was the same story, money and women; they seemed to
over-ride everything else. Consequently there was little to
wonder at in the fact that his own misfortunes arose from the

same sources. At last he began to feel weak and faint, **and** bethought himself that as yet he had not had anything to eat; so he set off in the direction of the village, resolving to take up his quarters with the Lengaignes, who let lodgings. However, as he crossed the open square in front of the church, **the** sight of the house from which he had been expelled in the morning rekindled an angry glow in his veins. Why should he let those knavish wretches keep his frock-coat and two pairs of trousers? They were **his own, and he** would **have** them, even at the risk of coming to **blows again.**

It was growing **dark when Jean entered** the yard, and he was scarcely able to **distinguish old Fouan, who** was sitting **on** the stone bench. However, as he reached the door leading to the kitchen, in which a candle was burning, Buteau caught sight of him and sprang forward to bar his passage.

" God in heaven ! you here again ! What do you want ? "

" I want my two pairs of trousers and my frock-coat."

A frightful quarrel now ensued. Jean doggedly insisted on getting his things out of the drawer; while Buteau, who had seized a bill-hook, swore that he would cut his throat if he crossed the threshold. **At** last Lise's voice sounded from inside.

" Let him have his rags !" **she cried. " You'd** never think of touching the rotten fellow's clothes **yourself."**

The two men now relapsed **into silence, and Jean was** standing waiting, when **all at once old Fouan, who was still** sitting on the stone bench behind his back, **gave utterance to the** alarm which was troubling his dazed brain.

" Make your escape," he stammered **in** his husky voice, " or they'll bleed you as they bled the little one."

This was a terrible revelation. Jean understood everything now—both the cause **of** Françoise's death and that of her obstinate silence. He had had his suspicions before, but now **he no longer** doubted but what she had remained silent in order **to save her relatives from** the guillotine. An icy chill froze him ; he felt terrified, and he was incapable of either speech or motion when Lise, through the open doorway, hurled his trousers and coat in his face.

" There, **take** your filthy things ! They stink so vilely that they'd have given us all some disease if they'd stayed any longer in the house!"

Jean picked them up and went off. However, when he got out of the yard, and once more found himself on the high-road, he turned round and shook his fists at the house, shouting

out a single word which reverberated in the surrounding
silence: " Murderers!"

Then he disappeared in the black darkness.

Buteau was standing in a state of terrified consternation,
for he had heard what old Fouan had growled out, and Jean's
word had penetrated his heart like a bullet. What was in
store for him? Would the gendarmes be down upon him,
now when he had just fancied that the secret of Françoise's
death would be buried for ever with her in her coffin? When
he had seen her lowered into her grave in the morning he had
begun to breathe freely again, and yet now it was evident that
the old fellow knew everything! Was it possible that he had
been shamming idiocy for the sake of playing the spy upon
them? This last thought completed Buteau's terrified alarm,
and he was so completely upset when he went back into the
house that he left half of his plateful of soup untouched. Lise,
to whom he had told what had happened, shivered and trembled,
and could eat no more than he did.

They had looked forward to keeping high festival upon this
their first night in the reconquered house, but it was a night of
abominable unhappiness. They had put Laure and Jules to
bed on a mattress in front of the chest of drawers, pending an
opportunity to arrange other accommodation ; and the children
were still wide awake when they themselves got into bed,
after blowing out the candle. But they could not sleep, they
tossed about as though they were on a red-hot gridiron. At
last they began to talk to each other in muttered tones. Oh,
what a burden the old man had become, now that he had fallen
into his dotage! It was really more than they could bear,
such an expense he was! No one could believe the quantity
of bread he swallowed! And then, too, he was so greedy,
seizing the meat in his fingers, and spilling the wine on his
beard, and making such a dirty mess of himself that one felt
ill merely on looking at him. Besides all that, he was constantly going about with his trousers disarranged ; a sad ending for a man who had once been as cleanly and as respectable
as any of his fellows. Really, since he seemed determined not
to go off of his own accord, it made one feel inclined to make
an end of him with a pick-axe.

" When one thinks that a breath would blow him over ! "
muttered Buteau. " Ah ! I really believe that he sticks on just
for the sake of annoying us! Those gibbering old idiots, the
less good they are the more closely they hug on to life! I
don't believe he will ever die, ever ! "

Then Lise, lying on her back, replied :

"It's a pity he came here. He'll feel too comfortable, **and** be inclined to take a fresh lease of life. If I had been a praying woman I should have prayed that he might not be allowed to pass a single night in the house."

Neither of them spoke of the real source of their anxiety, of the old man's knowledge of their secret, and the possibility of his betraying them, even without meaning to do so. That was the bother. Although he was an expense **and** a nuisance, and prevented them from enjoying the dividends of the stolen scrip at their ease, they had still put **up with** his presence for a long time. **But now** that a **word from him** might endanger their necks, all **limits of toleration were past.** Something definite would have to de done.

" I'll go and see if he's asleep," **said Lise** abruptly.

She lighted the candle, and then, making sure that Laure and Jules were soundly slumbering, she glided in her night-dress into **the** room where the beet-root was stored, and where the old man's iron **bed had** again been placed. When she came back she was shivering with cold, her feet half frozen by passing over the tiled floor. **She** buried herself beneath the bed-clothes, and pressed closely against **her** husband, who clasped her in his arms to warm **her.**

" Well ? "

" Yes, he's asleep; but **his breath's very** faint, **and his** mouth is gaping open like a fish's."

They now both remained quiet **for a** time, but, in spite of their silence, they could read each **other's thoughts.** The old **man** seemed constantly on the point of choking, **so** it would be an easy matter to suffocate him altogether. A handkerchief, or even a hand, held over his mouth, and then they would be freed **from** him. And really it would **be** a kindness to the old man him-**self.** He would **be** better off quietly asleep in **the** graveyard, than living on, **a source** of pain and discomfort to himself **as** well as others.

Buteau's and **Lise's blood** was flowing hotly, as though some burning desire had just thrilled them. Suddenly the former sprang **out of** the bed on to the tiled floor.

" I'll go and have a look at him, too," he said.

He then went off with the candle, which had been left standing on the edge of the chest of drawers, while Lise held her breath and listened, her eyes staring widely open in the dark. The minutes glided by, and no sound came from the adjoining **room.** After a time, however, she heard Buteau's

feet pattering gently back again; he had left the light in the
old man's room, and was so overcome with excitement that he
could not prevent himself from panting. He stepped up to the
bed, felt about in the dark for his wife, and then whispered in
her ear :

"You come too! I daren't do it alone!"

Lise got up and followed her husband; both of them groping their way forwards with their hands to avoid coming into
collision with anything. They no longer felt cold; even their
night-dresses were too hot for them. The candle was standing
on the floor, in a corner of the old man's room, but it afforded
sufficient light for them to see him lying on his back. His
head had fallen off the pillow, and he was lying there so rigidly,
and looked so emaciated with age, that one might have
thought he was already dead, had it not been for the
struggling, painful breathing from his gaping mouth. His
teeth had all gone, and his lips were turned inwards, round
what merely looked like a black hole, a hole over which the
husband and wife now stooped, as though they were trying to
ascertain how much life still remained at the bottom of it. For
a long time they stood looking at it, side by side, with their
hips touching one another. Their arms felt limp and nerveless.
It was such an easy and yet such a perilous matter to take
something and stop up that black hole with it. They went
away, and then came back again. Their parched tongues could
not have pronounced a single word; it was only their eyes that
spoke. Lise pointed out the pillow to her husband with a
glance. That would do. What was he waiting for? But
Buteau's eyes blinked nervously, and he thrust his wife into
his place. Then Lise, in her impatient irritation, suddenly
seized the pillow, and clapped it down on the old man's face.

"You miserable coward! Must you always leave everything for your wife to do?" she gasped.

Buteau now sprang forward and pressed upon the pillow
with the whole weight of his body, while Lise, mounting on to
the bed, sat on it, forcing down her huge swollen buttocks.
They were both pressing and sprawling over Fouan's body,
crushing it beneath their fists and shoulders and legs. At first
the old man had started violently, and when his legs were
flattened down there came a sound like that of the snapping of
springs. Now he was wriggling about like a fish on dry land;
but all this was soon over. As they pressed him down they
could feel his struggles ceasing and his life ebbing away.
Eventually there came a prolonged quiver, then the last spasm,

and finally it was all over; he lay there as inert as a log, as
limp as an old rag.

"There, I think we've done it now," muttered Buteau,
quite out of breath.

Lise, who was still squatting all of a heap on the bed, ceased
pressing, and remained quite still to ascertain if the old man
stirred.

"Yes, it's done," she soon said. "There isn't a sign of life
about him."

Then she slipped off the bed and removed the pillow. But
at the sight presented to their view they both broke out into a
groan of terror.

"God in heaven! he's quite black! We shall be found
out!"

It would, indeed, be impossible to assert that the old man
had put himself into such a condition. In their impetuosity the
Buteaus had pressed so violently that his nose was jammed
into his mouth, and his face was as black as a negro's. At this
sight it seemed to them as if the ground were giving way
beneath them, and they already fancied they could hear the
foot-falls of the gendarmes, the clanking of manacles, and the
descent of the blade of the guillotine. They were filled with
terrible regret as they gazed upon their clumsy piece of work.
What could be done? It was of no use washing the old man's
face; that would not whiten it. Presently the terror with
which his sooty appearance inspired them gave them an idea.

"Suppose we set him alight," murmured Lise.

Buteau felt relieved at this suggestion, and drew a heavy
breath.

"Capital! and we'll say he did it himself."

Then, as the thought of the scrip flashed through his mind,
he clapped his hands, and his face brightened up with a
triumphant smile.

"God in heaven!" he cried, "we'll make them believe
that he burnt the papers as well as himself, and then we shan't
have to give any account of them."

He now turned to take up the candle; but Lise, who was
afraid of incurring too much danger, would not let him set the
bed on fire with it. There were some straw-bands behind
some beet-root in a corner of the room, and she took one of
these, lighted it, and then applied it to the old man's long white
hair and beard. There was a strong smell and sputtering
like that of burning grease. Suddenly Lise and Buteau recoiled in terrified stupefaction, as though some cold, ghostly

hand had seized them by the hair. Tortured into life by the frightful agony of burning, the old man, who had not been effectually suffocated, had just opened his eyes ; and now, as he lay there with **his hideous** blackened face, his **great nose** battered and broken, and his hair and beard burnt away, **he** gazed at them with a fearful look of mingled pain and hatred. Then **all his** face seemed to fall **into utter** blankness, and he died.

Quite wild with terror, Buteau had just burst out into an awful groan when he heard some screams at the **door.** They came from the two children, Laure and Jules, who had been awakened by the noise. Attracted by the light of the burning straw, they had hurried along in their night-dresses to the open door, whence **they had seen all. They** shrieked with terror.

"You cursed little vermin!" roared Buteau, dashing at them ; " if **you** say a word to anybody, I'll murder you! Take that to remind you of what I say."

With these words he gave them each such a violent cuff that they rolled over **on** the floor. They picked themselves up, however, without shedding a tear, and rushed off to their mattress, where they remained without daring to move.

Buteau, who was determined to make an end of the matter, now set fire to the palliasse in spite of his wife's protes**tations.** Fortunately the room **was so** damp that the straw burnt very slowly, giving **out, however,** such **a dense** and copious smoke, that they **were nearly suffocated, and had** to open the window. Then **the flames shot up** higher and licked the **ceiling. The** old **man's body began to** crackle amid the blaze, **and** the room was **filled with an** intolerable stench of burning flesh. The old house would certainly have taken fire, and burnt away like a **stack, if the straw had not** begun to smoke again owing to **the melting of the body.** Nothing now remained on the cross-ribs of the iron bedstead save the half-calcined, disfigured, unrecognisable corpse. Only a small corner of the palliasse had remained unburnt, and a mere scrap of sheeting **hung** over the edge of the bed.

"Let **us be** off!" said Lise, who **had** begun **to** shiver again, despite **the** excessive **heat.**

"Wait a moment," **replied Buteau; "we must arrange** things properly."

He then placed a chair by **the bedside, and** upset the old man's candlestick at the foot of **it, to make it** appear as though it had fallen **upon** the palliasse. **Then he** was crafty enough to throw some scraps of lighted paper on the floor. When the ashes were discovered, he intended to say that the old **man** had found his papers **again on the** previous evening, and **had secured** possession of **them.**

"There, that **will do!**" repeated Lise. " Now let us go to bed."

They then hurried away, jostling **each other in their haste,** and **plunged into their** bed, which was **now quite cold.** Daylight began to dawn, but still they **lay awake, unable to get** to sleep. They did not speak to each other, but kept starting and quivering, and could hear their hearts beating wildly. They had left the door of the adjoining room open, and the thought of it disturbed them greatly; however, the idea of getting up and shutting it was still more distasteful and disquieting. **At last they** dozed off, still clinging closely to each other.

A few hours later the neighbours rushed up on hearing Buteau's wild calls. La Frimat and the other woman noticed the fallen candle, the charred remains of the palliasse, and the ashes of the scraps of paper. **Then** they all exclaimed that they had always felt sure that this would happen some day or **other.** They declared they had prophesied a score of times that the old man would **do** it in his dotage! The Buteaus might be very thankful that the whole house hadn't been burnt down at the same time!

CHAPTER VI.

Two days afterwards, on the very morning on which old Fouan was to be buried, Jean, tired from having remained in bed for hours without being able to sleep, woke up very late in the little room which he occupied at Lengaigne's. He had not yet been to Châteaudun to initiate proceedings against the Buteaus, though his intention to do so was the only thing that still kept him at Rognes. Each evening, however, he deferred the matter till the next day, feeling increasing hesitation about it, as his anger gradually calmed down. It was a prolonged mental struggle which had just kept him awake half the night, tossing feverishly about in his bed, and full of doubt as to what course he had best take.

Oh! those Buteaus, he thought, what murderous brutes, what abominable assassins they were! Some honest man ought to have their heads lopped off. As soon as he heard of old Fouan's death, he guessed how it had been brought about. The villains, he felt sure of it, had burnt the old man alive to prevent him from blabbing. Françoise! Fouan! the murder of the one had forced them to murder the other. Whose turn would it be next? Most likely his own, he thought; for they knew that he possessed their secret, and they would certainly send a bullet into him from some quiet corner of the road if he persisted in remaining in the neighbourhood. Had he not better denounce them at once? He made up his mind that he would. He would lay an information against them as soon as he got up. Then he began to hesitate again, feeling considerable timidity as to embarking upon a serious proceeding like this. He would be called as a witness, and he felt afraid lest he might be made to suffer as much as the very criminals themselves. Why should he create fresh troubles and anxieties for himself? This, as he acknowledged, was a cowardly way of looking at matters, but he found an excuse for his silence in the reflection that by holding his tongue he would be obeying Françoise's last wishes. A score of times that night he came to a decision, and then a

score of times he cast that decision aside, till he **felt quite ill**
from thinking of this duty from which he recoiled.

It was nearly nine o'clock when he sprang out of bed, **and**
plunged his head into a basin of cold water. He now suddenly
came to a resolution. He would **neither** lay an information,
nor would he take any steps to initiate proceedings for the
recovery of his share of the furniture. The game was not
worth the candle. A feeling of proud **independence** had restored his mind to perfect calmness ; **he would claim** nothing
from those swindling wretches ; **henceforth** he would have
nothing to do **with** them. He had no further **concern** in them,
and he would **leave them to** prey **upon themselves.** If they
would only contrive **to** make **an end of one** another all
round, it would **be a** good **riddance for** everybody. He
flushed with anger **as** he **thought of what he** had suffered
and endured during the **ten years he had spent in** Rognes ;
and yet he had been so happy **in the thought of** leaving **the
army,** after the **Italian** war; so **happy in** ceasing to handle
the sabre and **slay** his fellow-men ! **Still,** ever since his **dis-**
charge, he had been living amid filth, surrounded by savages.
At the period **of his** marriage **he** had **had** troubles enough,
but he had fallen upon even worse times **now ;** the villains had
taken **to robbery and** murder. **Ah,** they **were** savage wolves,
let loose over that peaceful, far-reaching plain. For his own
part, he had had quite enough **of it!** These devouring wild
beasts had spoilt the country **for** him ! **What would** be the
good of hunting down just a couple **of them—a male** and his
female—when the whole pack ought **to be destroyed?** No ;
he preferred to go away.

At that moment his eyes happened **to light upon a** newspaper which **he had** brought up **with** him **from** the public
room **on the** previous evening. **He** had **been** interested
in an **article on** the approaching war, **for** alarming rumours
had been **in** circulation for several **days** past, and the
martial **feeling, which he** thought **extinct** within **him, had**
suddenly sprung **up into** fresh **glowing** life at the **report
of a** coming call **to arms.** His **last** lingering hesitation **to
leave** Rognes, his doubts **as to** where he should go, **were
all utterly** and entirely swept away as by **a** rushing blast
of **wind.** Yes, he would **go** and fight; he would enlist!
He **had** certainly paid the debt he owed **his** country; but
when a man has no occupation left, when life is full of weari-
some cares, and when one is angered by the persecution of
one's enemies, the best plan is still to fall upon them boldly.

This determination eased his feelings and thrilled him with stern joy. As he dressed himself, he whistled the bugle-march that had resounded when they advanced to battle in Italy. Mankind was really too hateful and abominable, and he found a great consolation in **the** thought of demolishing some of the Prussians. Since he had not found peace in this country nook, where the peasant folk drank each other's blood, he might just **as well return** to the carnage of the battlefield. **The** more of the foe he slew, the redder would the **soil be, and** the more would he feel avenged **for** all the hardship and trouble with which men had visited him.

When **he came** downstairs he ate **the two eggs and the** rasher of bacon which Flore served him. **Then he** called Lengaigne and paid his score.

" Are you **going** to **leave us, Corporal ? "** asked the landlord.

" **Yes.**"

" But you'll **be** coming back again, **won't you ? "**

" No."

Lengaigne looked at **him** in amazement, but he kept his reflections to himself. **So the great booby was** going to give **up** all his rights!

" **What are** you thinking of doing now ? **Do you mean to turn** carpenter again ? "

" No ; soldier."

Upon hearing this, Lengaigne opened **his** eyes in still greater amazement, and could no longer restrain a smile of contempt. **What a fool the** man must be !

Jean **had already started on his** way to Cloyes, when a last **thrill of feeling made** him check his steps and turn up the hill. **He felt that he could not** leave Rognes without saying good-**bye to Françoise's** grave. There was also another desire **which he wished** to satisfy: **to** gaze once more upon the mighty plain, that **mournful La** Beauce, which he had learned to love during **his long** solitary hours of toil.

The **gra**veyard stretched behind the church, enclosed **by a** crumbling wall so low that, when one stood amid the tombs, a clear view could be obtained from horizon to horizon. A pale March sun was shining coldly in the sky, which was veiled by a **soft,** white, fleecy haze, scarcely showing a patch of blue. Beneath the softly smiling heavens, La Beauce, still torpid from the winter frosts, seemed to lie half-dozing and half-awake, basking in sweet indolence. The distant fields, bathed in a suffused light, were already green with the wheat, oats, and rye sown during the autumn. In those plough-lands that remained bare, the spring sowing had recently been commenced. All around men could be seen striding over the rich soil scattering their seed with the same uniform gesture. The grains could be distinctly perceived falling like a flashing gilded stream from the hands of the nearer **sowers.** Then with the increasing distance the figures of the **sowers** seemed to dwindle in size till they were altogether **lost** to sight, and as the seed streamed around them it looked like some mere vibration of light. For leagues around, in every direction, the life-germs of the coming summer were raining down amid the sunshine.

Jean stood in **front of** Françoise's grave. It was **half-way** along a row of other graves, and an open one beside **it was** waiting to receive old Fouan's body. The graveyard **was** over-run with **a** rank growth of weeds, for the municipal council had never consented to grant the rural constable fifty francs to make it neat and trim. Wooden crosses and railings **were** rotting away, **and** only a few mouldering stones still stood in position. The charm of this lonely nook, however, lay in its very condition of neglect, in its profound tranquillity, which was only broken by the croaking of the ancient crows which wheeled around the church steeple. Here the villagers slept their last sleep in perfect peace and **oblivion.** Jean, amid the death-like stillness, dropped **into a** reverie, gazing at the vast expanse of La Beauce and the seed grains which permeated it as with a thrill of life. But at last he was aroused, hearing **the** bell toll slowly, first three times, then twice more, and finally break into a continuous clanging. The bearers **were** lifting Fouan's coffin, and were bringing it towards **the grave-**yard.

The bandy-legged gravedigger **came** limping along to see that the grave was all right.

"Isn't it too small?" asked **Jean, who** still tarried, his **heart softening** with a desire to see the last of the old man.

" **Not it,**" replied **the** bandy-legged sexton. "They **could** get four like him into it. That roasting has brought down his size."

On the evening following **upon** Fouan's death, the Buteaus had awaited the arrival of Doctor Finet with great trepidation. But the surgeon had signed the burial certificate at once, his only thought being to get away again as soon as possible. He came, looked at the body, and then angrily railed at the stupidity of country-folks in leaving an addle-pated old man

with a lighted candle. If he felt any suspicions, he wisely
kept them to himself. This father had been so obstinate in
living on, that maybe he had deserved to be roasted a bit.
Besides, he (Finet) had seen so many strange things that a
matter like this seemed of no great account. In his callous
indifference, born of mingled contempt and bitterness, he
merely shrugged his shoulders—a scampish, bad lot those
peasants! thought he.

Relieved upon this point, the Buteaus then had to prepare
themselves to meet their relatives and allay any possible suspicions. As soon as La Grande presented herself they burst into
tears, thinking that this would have a good effect. The old woman
looked at them with surprise, and thought to herself that they
were really over-acting their part in crying so much. However,
she had merely come for the sake of something to do, for she
had no claim upon any of the old man's property. The real
danger began when Fanny and Delhomme arrived. The latter
had just been nominated mayor in place of Macqueron, and his
wife was almost bursting with pride. She had kept her oath,
and her father had died without any reconciliation on her part.
Indeed, with her extreme susceptibility, she even yet felt hurt
by his conduct, and she showed this by standing with dry eyes
in front of the corpse. However, if she shed no tears, there
was withal a sound of loud sobbing. This arose when
Hyacinthe arrived, very drunk, and overflowing with the tender
emotion which he found at the bottom of his bottle. He quite
saturated the corpse with his tears, and bellowed out that he
had received a blow from which he would never recover.

In the kitchen Lise had set out a row of glasses and bottles
of wine; and a general discussion ensued. It was at once
agreed that the hundred and fifty francs a year arising
from the sale of the house were outside the debate, for it had
always been understood that this sum should be retained by
those who looked after the old man during his last days.
But then there was the secret hoard, the three hundred francs
a year that were derived from the scrip of which they had
all now heard. Buteau thereupon related his story, stating
how his father had discovered the papers underneath the
marble slab on the top of the chest of drawers, and how,
while examining them at night, he must have set his hair on
fire. The ashes of the papers had been found lying on the
floor, as La Frimat and La Bécu could testify. As he told
his story the others scrutinised him keenly, but this in no way
confused him, and he smote his breast with his hands and

swore by the light of day that he was speaking the truth.
He could see that the family had their suspicions, but he
cared nothing about that so long as they did not worry him,
and he kept the money. Fanny, however, with her impetuous
outspokenness, unbosomed herself of her surmises, and angrily
assailed Buteau and Lise as thieves and murderers. Yes, they
had burned her father and robbed him! That was plain to
everybody's eyes! The Buteaus replied with a flood of abuse
and equally abominable accusations against herself. She and
her husband, they cried, had plotted to destroy the old man,
who had nearly perished from taking some poisoned soup that
had been given him in his daughter's house. They, the Buteaus,
would be able to tell a great deal if anything was said about
them!

Hyacinthe had again begun to cry and bellow lugubriously
on hearing that such awful crimes were possible. God in
heaven! his poor father! Could it be possible that there
were sons wicked enough to roast their father? La Grande,
whose eyes were glistening brightly, let a few words drop
whenever the contending parties seemed getting out of
breath, and her remarks at once set them going at each other
again. Delhomme, feeling uneasy at the aspect of affairs, at
last went and closed the doors and windows. He had his
official position to think of; and, besides, he was always in
favour of settling matters quietly. He now protested that
such accusations were most unseemly. A pretty reputation
the family would get if the neighbours should hear what was
going on! The law would poke its nose into the matter, and
possibly the good ones would lose more than the bad ones.
No, when there were scamps in a family, the best plan was
to leave them to their villany, in the hope that it would end
by destroying them. All the others sat in silence. Delhomme
was right. There was nothing to be got by washing their
dirty linen before the magistrates. Moreover, Buteau terrified
the others. This scoundrel was quite capable of ruining them.
At the bottom of their silent acquiescence in the murder and
robbery there lay that feeling which makes the peasantry the
accomplices of poachers, of the men who kill gamekeepers;
in fact, of all that class of lawless rustics who are saved
from being given up to justice by the fear they inspire in
those who are fully cognisant of their crimes.

La Grande remained to have some coffee and to spend the
evening with the Buteaus, while the others trooped off in a
blunt, unceremonious fashion, expressive of their contempt.

The Buteaus, however, did not care a straw about that, so long
as they kept the money and had the certainty of not being
worried any further. Lise raised her voice again to its wonted
pitch, and Buteau, resolving to do things properly, ordered the
coffin, and went to the churchyard to examine the place where
the grave was to be dug.

The peasants of Rognes felt a great dislike to resting after
their death by the side of those whom they had hated while
alive; but, as the graves were dug in regular rows, it was
altogether a matter of luck where each one was buried; and
whenever, as chance had it, two enemies died immediately one
after the other, the authorities experienced great embarrassment,
for the family of the one who had died the latest often talked
quite seriously of keeping his **body** above ground rather than
let it lie by the side of a person whom he had detested. Now, it
happened that when Macqueron was mayor he had abused his
official position to purchase for his grave a plot of ground
which would certainly not have been assigned to him in the
regular course of affairs. Unfortunately, too, this strip of
ground adjoined the grave in which Lengaigne's father was
buried, and in which Lengaigne had reserved room for himself.
Ever since Macqueron had purchased his plot, his **rival's**
indignation had known no end, his long-standing enmity
becoming more rancorous than ever. The thought that his
body would lie rotting beside that scoundrel's would embitter
the rest of his existence.

Buteau was filled with the same angry **feeling** when he
went to inspect the grave which chance had allotted to his
father. Françoise would lie on old Fouan's left-hand, which
was right and proper enough; but, as ill-luck would have it,
in the adjoining row of graves, and **just in front of** the one
where Fouan was to be buried, **there was the** grave of old
Saucisse's deceased wife, in which Saucisse had reserved room
for himself also. The result was that, whenever the old scamp
died, he would lie with his feet close to Fouan's skull. Could
this idea be tolerated for a moment? Here were two old men,
who had detested each other ever since that dishonourable
business about the daily payments of fifteen sous for the reversion of an acre of ground. and the greater rascal of the two—
the one who had tricked the other—was to go dancing on his
head through all eternity! Why, if the family were so unfeeling as to submit to such an arrangement, old Fouan's bones
would turn in their coffin and struggle with those of old
Saucisse! Boiling over with rebellious indignation, Buteau

how angrily rushed off to the municipal offices and attacked
Delhomme, trying to force him to take advantage of his official
position to assign another grave to old Fouan. But his brother-
in-law refused to depart from the established usage, dwelling
upon the deplorable example of Macqueron and Lengaigne.
Buteau then called him a coward, accused him of being bribed,
and finally roared out in the middle of the road that he himself
was the only dutiful and affectionate son, since the rest of the
family didn't care a straw whether the old man rested peacefully
in his grave or not. Drawing the whole village to the door-steps
in his **progress,** he went off home in a state of furious indignation.

Another **matter, and** one of more importance than this
question of the grave, had just been causing Delhomme great
embarrassment. The Abbé Madeline had gone away a couple
of days previously, and Rognes was once more without a
priest. The experiment of keeping one of their own within the
village had, on the whole, turned out so unsatisfactorily that the
municipal council had voted in favour of withdrawing the
grant, and returning to the previous state of affairs, the services being performed by the priest of Bazoches-le-Doyen. The
Abbé Godard, however, despite the bishop's remonstrances,
had sworn that he would never celebrate the blessed sacrament
in the place, and, in his exasperation at the departure of his
colleague, he accused the villagers of having half-murdered
the poor fellow for the sole purpose of forcing him—Godard—
to return among them. He had already declared that,
although Bécu might ring the bell for mass from morning till
night, he would not come, when Fouan's sudden death complicated matters, and brought the situation to a crisis. **A** funeral
is not like a mass, **and** cannot be indefinitely postponed. With
some little mischievous satisfaction at the turn affairs had
taken, Delhomme **now** went to see the priest at Bazoches. As
soon as the **Abbé** Godard perceived him his face assumed a
wrathful expression, and, without giving the mayor time to
open his mouth, he cried out that nothing would make him
come, he would rather lose his place! When he learnt that his
presence was required for a funeral, he lost the power of arti-
culation through very rage. Those pagans died on purpose.
They fancied that by doing so they would force him to come to
them! Well, they might bury themselves, for he didn't mean
to help them up to heaven!

Delhomme quietly waited till the priest's first ebullition of
anger was exhausted, and then began to argue with him. The
Church, he said, did not refuse the last sprinkling of holy water

to any one; and a corpse could not be kept indefinitely in the
house. Then he tried more personal arguments; the dead
man was his father-in-law, the father-in-law of the mayor of
Rognes. Come, now, shouldn't they say to-morrow at ten
o'clock? No! no! no! cried **the** Abbé Godard, blustering
and almost choking in his wrath, and Delhomme had to go
away without being able to make **him** yield, **though he hoped
that** he would think better of it before morning.

"**I tell** you that I won't come," the priest shouted at him
for the last time from his door. "Don't ring **the bell, for** I tell
you I won't come; **no, a** thousand times no!"

The next morning, however, Bécu received the mayor's
orders to ring the bell at ten o'clock. **They would see what**
would happen. Everything **was ready at the Buteaus'** for the
funeral; the body had been **placed in the coffin on the previous**
evening under the experienced eyes of **La Grande. The room,**
too, had been washed, and **the** only trace **left of the fire was**
the old man's corpse screwed **down ready** for interment.

The bell was tolling, and **the family had** met together in
front of the house, waiting **for the removal of** the body, when
the Abbé Godard was seen hurrying along up the street, quite
out of breath from running, and so flushed and furious that he
held his hat in his hand, half afraid lest he should fall **down in
a fit.** Without looking at any one he dashed into the **church,**
immediately reappearing again in his surplice, followed by two
choir-boys, one of whom carried the **cross,** and the other the
vessel of holy water. Then he rapidly proceeded to mutter over
the corpse, and, without troubling himself as **to whether the**
bearers were following **him** with the coffin, he returned **to the**
church, **where he** began to say mass at a furious pace. Clou
and his trombone and the two choristers quite lost their breath
in their attempts to keep up with **him.** In the front row were
the members of **the** family, Buteau and Lise, Fanny and
Delhomme, Hyacinthe and La Grande. Monsieur Charles also
honoured the funeral with **his** presence, but Madame Charles
had been at Chartres for the last two days with Elodie and
Nénesse. **As for** La Trouille, just as she was on the point of
starting for the ceremony, she discovered that three of her
geese were missing, and she rushed off to search for **them.**
Behind Lise stood the two children, Laure and Jules, comporting themselves very decorously, with their arms crossed,
and an expression of deep gravity on their widely-opened eyes.
The other seats were crowded with acquaintances, women for
the most part, including La Frimat, La Bécu, Coelina, Flore,

and many others, making up such a gathering as the family might well be proud of. As the priest turned to the congregation, he threw his arms open with such a terribly threatening expression that it looked as though he were going to cuff them all. Bécu, who was very drunk, was still tugging at the bell.

Altogether it was a very satisfactory mass, though solemnised somewhat hurriedly. The congregation, however, showed no signs of vexation, and they even smiled secretly at the Abbé's anger, which they quite excused, for it was only natural that he should be a little sulky over his defeat, just as they themselves felt elated at the victory of their village. An expression of sly satisfaction beamed on all their countenances. They had forced him to celebrate the blessed sacrament amongst them, though in reality they cared nothing at all about it.

When the mass was over, the aspersorium was passed from hand to hand, and then the procession reformed. First came the cross and the chanters, then Clou and his trombone, then the priest, choking from his breathless haste, next the body carried by four peasants, then the family, and finally the crowd of acquaintances. Bécu had now commenced to tug so energetically at the bell that the crows flew off from the steeple, croaking in distress. The funeral party reached the graveyard at once ; they had only to turn the corner of the church. The chants and music broke out into fuller sound amid the hushed silence, beneath the vapoury sun which imparted warmth to the quivering peacefulness of the weeds and grass. When the coffin appeared in the open air, it seemed so small that every one looked at it in surprise. Jean, who was still standing by the grave, was painfully affected by the sight. Ah, poor old man! to be so emaciated by age, so shrunken owing to the wretchedness of his life, that he had room enough to lie completely in that mere toy-box! that mere pretence of a coffin! But little room would he want for his grave, and but a very slight incumbrance would he be to the soil, that mighty mother earth, whom he had so passionately loved.

As the coffin was laid down by the edge of the yawning grave, Jean's eyes followed it, and then strayed further away, over the little wall, sweeping La Beauce from end to end. Again he beheld the sowers stretching away into the far distance ceaselessly swinging their arms, while the seed streamed over the gaping furrows.

When the Buteaus caught sight of Jean, they exchanged an uneasy glance. Could the scoundrel be waiting there with the intention of creating some disturbance? They would never be able to sleep at ease as long as he remained in Rognes! The boy who carried the cross had just planted it at the foot of the grave, and now the Abbé Godard, standing in front of the coffin which was lying on the grass, hurriedly repeated the last prayers. The spectators' attention was, however, diverted on noticing that Macqueron and Lengaigne, who had arrived late, were gazing intently towards the plain. Every one now turned to look in the same direction, and noticed a thick cloud of smoke rolling up into the sky. It seemed to come from La Borderie; probably some stacks behind the farm had caught fire.

" *Ego sum*—" exclaimed the priest in a tone of fury: and then the funeral-party again turned towards him, fixing their eyes once more upon the coffin; Monsieur Charles alone was inattentive, continuing a whispered conversation with Delhomme. He had that morning received from Madame Charles a letter which filled him with delight. During the four-and-twenty hours she had been in Chartres, Elodie had shown herself in the most surprising light, displaying as much energy and shrewdness as even Nénesse himself. She had got the better of her father, and was already in possession of the house. Ah, she had the proper gifts, a ready hand and a sharp eye! Monsieur Charles was quite overcome with emotion as he thought of the happy old age that was now in store for him at Roseblanche, where his rose-trees and his carnations had never looked better than they were doing now; and it seemed to him, too, that his birds had quite recovered their health during the last few days, for they sang again so sweetly as to stir his very soul.

" *Amen!* " now cried the boy who was carrying the vessel of holy water.

Then the Abbé Godard, in his angry voice, immediately commenced the psalm:

" *De profundis clamavi ad te, Domine*——"

And as he continued, Hyacinthe, who had taken Fanny aside, began to abuse the Buteaus again.

"If only I hadn't been so drunk the other day," he began. " But really it isn't possible, you know; we can't submit to be robbed in this way."

" Yes, there's no doubt but what we are being robbed," murmured Fanny.

" Those two wretches have got the scrip, that's quite certain," her brother continued. " They've been enjoying the dividends for a long time past; they settled it all with old Saucisse, I know that for a fact. God in heaven! aren't we going to take proceedings against them?"

On hearing this Fanny started back, and shook her head energetically.

" No, no," she said; " I certainly sha'n't. I've got quite enough on my hands as it is. But you can, if you like."

Hyacinthe, in his turn, now made a gesture of alarm and refusal. As he couldn't get his sister to interfere, he didn't care to come into close contact with the law; his own antecedents worried him.

" Oh, no, no! I can't do anything," said he. " People have a spite against me. Never mind, even if we don't send them to gaol, we at least have the satisfaction of knowing that we can carry our heads erect."

La Grande, who was listening, watched him as he drew himself up with an air of unsullied integrity. She had always considered him a simpleton, blackguard though he was, and she felt quite vexed that such a great big fellow didn't go and smash everything in his brother's house to compel him to give him his share. Then, with a desire to make game of the brother and sister, she abruptly launched out into her customary statement, without any preliminaries.

" Ah, well, you'll never find me wronging any one. My will's been made a long time past, and every one will get a fair share. I couldn't die with an easy mind if I had shown an unfair preference for any one. Hyacinthe is down in it, and you, too, Fanny. I'm ninety years old now, and the day will soon come. Yes, it will come indeed."

However, she did not believe a word of it; she had made up her mind that she would never die, such was her obstinate determination to stick to her property. She would see all her relations buried. Here was another one, her brother, whom she was seeing being put away. The whole affair, the carrying of the corpse, the open grave, the final ceremony, all seemed matters which concerned her neighbours, and not herself. Tall and fleshless, with her stick under her arm, she stood firmly erect amid the graves, without showing the slightest sign of emotion, merely exhibiting a feeling of curiosity in her neighbours' shrinking from death.

The priest was now sputtering out the last verse of the psalm.

" *Et ipse redimet Israel ex omnibus iniquitatibus ejus.*"

Then he took the sprinkler out of the holy water vessel and shook it over the coffin, exclaiming in a louder tone:

" *Requiescat in pace.*"

" *Amen*," responded the two boys.

Then the coffin was let down into the grave. The grave-digger had already slipped the ropes under it, and a couple of men amply sufficed to lower it, for the old man's corpse didn't weigh more that that of a little child. The funeral party now passed in procession in front of the grave, and the sprinkler again passed from hand to hand, every one shaking it crossways over the coffin.

Jean, who now stepped up, received the aspersorium from the hands of Monsieur Charles, and his eyes sought the bottom of the grave. He was rather dazzled, as he had gazed so long upon the far-stretching plain of La Beauce, watching the sowers as they sowed the bread of the future, from one end of the expanse to the other, and dwindled away in the suffused light of the vaporous horizon. However, down in the depths of the soil Jean could distinguish the coffin, looking still smaller than before, with its narrow lid of pale corn-yellow pinewood. The clods of rich earth were falling over it and gradually concealing it from view; and now there was only a pale glimmering patch to be seen, looking like a handful of the corn which the sowers were scattering in the furrows over yonder. He shook the sprinkler, and then handed it to Hyacinthe.

" Your reverence ! your reverence !" Delhomme now called, running after the priest, who, as the service was over, was striding off with a furious gait, forgetting all about the boys.

" Well, what is it now ?" asked the priest.

" I only wanted to thank you for your kindness in coming. I suppose we may have the bell rung for mass at ten o'clock on Sunday, as usual, eh ? "

The priest looked at him keenly without making any reply, and Delhomme hastily added :

" By the way, there's a poor old woman who is very ill, and absolutely alone, and she hasn't got a farthing either—Rosalie, the chair-mender ; you know her, don't you ? I have sent her some food, but I can't do everything."

The Abbé Godard's features lost their stern expression, and a thrill of charity swept away his wrath. He began fumbling in his pockets, but could only find seven coppers.

" Lend me ten francs," said he. " I'll give you them back on Sunday. Good-bye till Sunday, then."

Then he rushed on again, in a fresh burst of haste. Although it was quite certain that the good God whom they had forced

him to bring amongst them would send all these cursed villagers to roast in hell, still, that was no reason why they should **be** left in too great suffering and tribulation in this life.

When Delhomme joined the others, he found himself in the midst of a violent quarrel. For some time the funeral party had stood quietly watching the sexton shovelling the soil on to the coffin. Presently, however, chance having brought Macqueron and **Lengaigne** close together beside the grave, the **latter** began **to abuse the former** on the subject of the plots. **The** family group, **which had** just been going away, thereupon remained to listen, **and** soon took an excited interest in the war of words, to which **the** sound of the falling soil furnished a muffled, regular accompaniment.

" **Y**ou had no right to **do it !**" cried Lengaigne. " Your being mayor made **no** difference at all ! You ought to have followed the row ! **You** only shove yourself close up to my **father to** annoy me. Confound it all ! You haven't gained **your ends** yet, I can tell you ! "

" Aren't you going to shut up !" replied Macqueron. " I have **paid** for the plot, and it's my own property. And when my **time** comes, it won't be a foul swine like you who will prevent me from being laid there."

The two **men** had stepped **apart, and** each was now standing by **his** own plot, the few **feet** of earth where they would some day sleep their long sleep.

" But, **you** confounded villain, can you stomach the thought that **we shall** be lying there, shoulder to shoulder, like a couple of bosom friends ? As for me, it makes my blood boil to think of it ! **To** think that, after being enemies all our lives, we shall **patch up a peace** down there, and lie quietly side by side ! No, no, **indeed ! No patching** up, no forgetting for me ! "

" Ah, **well, I don't care a** curse ! You can blow yourself out with **rage till you burst,** if you like, but I've too much contempt for **you to trouble** myself about knowing whether your carcass **will rot near mine** or not ! "

This **scornful reply** capped Lengaigne's exasperation ; and he **blurted** out that **if he** lived the longer, he'd come in the night **and** dig up Macqueron's bones and toss them outside the graveyard, rather than submit to lie beside them. Macqueron sniggered, and said he should like to see him do it ; and then the women joined in the fray, that dark, skinny wench, Coelina, making an angry attack upon her husband.

" You are acting shamefully !" she cried. " I told you so before. You don't seem **to have any** feelings! However, I can

tell you this, unless you make a change, you may lie in your
hole by yourself. I shall have myself taken somewhere else,
for I'll never consent to let my bones be poisoned by that drab
there !"

As she spoke she jerked her chin in the direction of Flore ;
but the latter was not going to submit to this abuse.

" You'd be no very pleasant neighbour yourself ! " she
retorted, in a drawling, whining tone. " Make yourself quite
easy, my dear; I don't intend to let your bones give the
disease to mine."

" Eh, what ? What disease ? "

" Oh, you know what disease very well ! "

La Bécu and La Frimat were now obliged to interpose and
separate the two women.

" Come, come," urged the former, " you won't lie together
since you are both of the same way of thinking. Every one is
at liberty to choose her own company."

La Frimat expressed her acquiescence in this.

" It's only natural," she said. " I'm sure that when my
old man's time comes I'd rather keep him in the house with
me than let him lie alongside of old Couillot, with whom he
had differences once on a time."

The tears welled to her eyes as she thought that her paralytic
husband would probably pass away before the week was over.
She had fallen with him on the previous evening as she was
trying to put him to bed, and whenever he departed she
wouldn't be long in following him.

It was at this moment that Delhomme came up, and Lengaigne
at once appealed to him.

" Now, then," said he, " folks say you are a just man; well,
will you allow such injustice ? Now that you are mayor, you
can make this scamp turn out of here and take his place in the
regular order."

Macqueron shrugged his shoulders, and Delhomme proceeded to explain that as he had paid his money the plot belonged to him. The matter was settled now, and there was
an end of it. Buteau, who had hitherto quieted himself by
force, then lost his head and rushed into the fray. All the
members of the family should have maintained a decorous bearing as the clods of soil were still falling with heavy thuds upon
the old man's coffin ; however, Buteau's indignation was too
great to be restrained.

" Ah ! curse it, you're mightily mistaken if you expect to
find any proper feeling in that fellow ! " he cried to Lengaigne,

as he pointed to Delhomme. "He let his own father be buried by the side of a thief!"

This remark caused a general explosion, the different members of the family taking part in the row. Fanny supported her husband, saying that the real mistake lay in not having purchased a plot for their father at the time when their mother Rose died; he might have laid close to her. Thereupon Hyacinthe and La Grande assailed Delhomme with abuse, also expressing their disgust at old Fouan's proximity to Saucisse, a most inhuman proceeding admitting of no excuse whatever. Monsieur Charles was of the same opinion, but expressed himself more moderately.

They were now all wrangling and shouting at once. Buteau, however, managed to make himself heard above the others, as he roared out: "Yes, their very bones will struggle under the ground to attack each other again!"

The whole company, relatives, friends, and acquaintances, eagerly seized hold of this phrase. Yes, that was the truth! Their very bones would continue the fight underground. When they were buried, the Fouans would still pursue each other with that savage animosity which they had mutually manifested during life. Lengaigne and Macqueron would go on bickering and quarrelling till they had quite rotted; and the women, Cœlina, Flore, and La Bécu, would still attack each other with their tongues and claws. It was the universal opinion in Rognes that foes in life could never rest peacefully together when they were buried. The hatred between them never perished; it lasted beyond life right away to the end of time. In this sunny graveyard, beneath the rank growth of grass and weeds, a savage, timeless warfare was waging between coffin and coffin, just such a warfare as was now being waged by these living mortals who were grouped together amid the graves, clenching their fists and reviling one another. However, a shout from Jean separated the adversaries, and made them turn their heads: "La Borderie is on fire!"

Doubt was no longer possible. The flames were leaping up from the roof, quivering and paling in the light of day. A dense cloud of ruddy smoke was gently rolling away towards the north. Then La Trouille came into sight, running hastily from the direction of the farm. While hunting for her geese she had noticed the first sparks, and she had stood gloating over the spectacle till the idea of telling the others of the sight occurred to her, whereupon she set off at a run. Jumping astride the low wall, she cried out in her childish voice:

"Oh, isn't it just blazing? That big beast Tron came back and set it on fire in three different places—in the barn, in the stables, and in the kitchen. **They caught** him just as he **was** setting the straw alight, **and the waggoners nearly** killed him. The horses and the cows **and the sheep are all roasting!** Oh, you should hear the noise **they're making! You** never heard **such a row!**"

Her green eyes glistened, **and she laughed as she continued:** "Oh, and there's La Cognette! She's been ill, you know, ever since the master died, and they had forgotten her in her bed. She was already getting singed, and she'd only just time to cut and run in her shift. Oh, it was a rare sight to see her prancing about in **the open fields with her bare legs.** She hopped and skipped along, **and the folks shouted out, 'hou!** hou!' as she passed **them.** They're **not very fond of her,** you know, and one **old man said: 'She's come out just as she** went in, **with only a shift on her back!'**"

At this **point a fresh thrill of merriment made the girl** wriggle **with laughter.**

"Do **come! it's such a lark! I'm off back again.**"

Then **she sprang down from the wall, and ran as fast as** her legs could carry **her in the direction of the blazing farm.**

Monsieur Charles, **Delhomme, Macqueron, and nearly all the** peasants followed **her;** while **the women, with La Grande** at their head, **also** left **the** graveyard **for the road, so as to** get a better view. Buteau and Lise **had stayed behind, and** the latter detained Lengaigne, **being anxious to question him** about Jean, without appearing **to show too much interest in** him. Had he found **some work, she asked, as he was lodging** in the **neighbourhood? When the innkeeper replied that he** was going away **to re-enlist, both** Buteau and **Lise, feeling** vastly relieved, broke out into the same exclamation:

"What a fool he must be!"

So this **troublesome bother was at an** end, and they would be able **to live happily again! They** cast a last glance at Fouan's **grave, which** the sexton **had now** almost filled up; and as the **two children** lingered behind **to** watch, their mother called them.

"Come along, **Jules and Laure, come along!** Mind you're **good** children, now, and **do what you're told, or the** man will **come** and put you in the **earth too.**"

The Buteaus then **went off, pushing Laure and** Jules in front of them. The children, **who knew** the truth, looked very grave **and** earnest **with** their big **solemn** black eyes.

Jean and Hyacinthe were now the only ones left in the graveyard. The latter just watched the fire from a distance, disdaining to hurry off like the others. As he stood, quite motionless between two graves, he seemed to be absorbed in some visionary dream, and his sad, dissipated face expressed the mournful melancholy that lies at the end of every system of philosophy. Perhaps he was thinking that existence glides away and vanishes like smoke! And as serious meditation always had an exciting effect on him, he ended by giving vent to three detonations.

"God in heaven!" exclaimed the drunken Bécu, as he passed through the graveyard on his way to the fire, "if this wind continues, we may expect a downfall of dung!"

"Yes, indeed," replied Hyacinthe; and hurrying off he disappeared round the wall.

Jean was now alone. Away in the distance some huge whirling clouds of black smoke were rising from the ruins of La Borderie, casting shadows over the fields and the scattered sowers, who were still plodding backwards and forwards, making the same monotonous gestures. Then Jean's eyes slowly wandered back to the ground at his feet, and he gazed at the mounds of fresh soil beneath which Françoise and old Fouan were sleeping. His anger of the morning and his disgust for people and circumstances had vanished in a feeling of profound calm. In spite of himself he felt full of restfulness and hope; maybe it was owing to the warm sunshine.

Ah, yes, his master Hourdequin had had any amount of worry with all those new inventions; he had never reaped much advantage from his machines and artificial manures, and other scientific devices. And then La Cognette had come to finish him off; he was now asleep in the graveyard, and nothing remained of the farm, the very ashes of which the wind was now sweeping away. But what did it matter after all? Walls might be burned down, but the soil could not be burned. Earth, Mother earth, would always be there ready to nourish all who cast their seed upon her bosom. She had time enough before her, and space in plenty, and even now she yielded corn, and would yield still more when men knew how to treat her.

It was the same with the stories of the revolutionists—those political cataclysms which were predicted. The soil, it was said, would pass into other hands, and the harvests of other countries would swamp our own, till our land was over-run with brambles. Well, and what then? Is it within any one's

power to harm the soil? It will always be there for any one
who may be obliged to till it to escape dying from hunger.
And even if weeds were to cover its surface for years together,
that would be a rest for it, and it would grow young and fertile again. The soil cares nothing about our quarrels; this
mighty toiler, ever absorbed in her workings, troubles herself
no more about man than about a swarm of ants.

Jean had had his share of grief and trouble, pain and
rebellion. And now Françoise was slain, Fouan was slain, the
wicked seemed triumphant, the foul and sanguinary vermin of
the villages were able to pollute and prey upon the soil. Ah,
but who can tell? The frost which sears the crops, the hail
which breaks them, the deluge which beats them down, are all
perhaps necessary, and so it may be that blood and tears are
equally essential to the world's progress. What does our unhappiness weigh in the great system of the stars and the sun?
We only gain our bread by dint of a terrible daily struggle
The soil alone remains fixed and imperishable, the mother from
whom we all spring, and to whom we must all return; she
whom her children love so keenly that they sin for her sake;
she who utilises everything, even our crimes and our
wretchedness, for purposes of creation, in view of attaining
her own secret, mysterious ends.

For a long time some such confused, ill-formulated reverie
as this rolled vaguely through Jean's mind as he lingered in
the graveyard; but suddenly a trumpet sounded in the
distance, the trumpet of the firemen of Bazoches-le-Doyen, who
were arriving too late at the double-quick. Then, hearing the
clarion-call, Jean drew himself up. It was like warfare passing
by amid smoke; warfare with its horses, its cannons, and its
clamorous carnage! Ah! confound it, since he no longer had
the heart to till the old soil of France, he would defend it from
invaders!

He was going off, when for a last time he turned his eyes
from the two grassless graves to the endless plough-lands of
La Beauce filled with sowers, all making the same ceaseless
gesture. Mid corpses and seeds, sustenance was springing
from the soil.

THE END.